# The Speciality
## of the House

Stanley Ellin was born in Brooklyn, New York, in 1916, and educated at Brooklyn College. He worked as a teacher, a steelworker and a dairy farmer, and served in the US Army in World War 2, before becoming a full-time writer in 1946. His longer fiction includes *House of Cards*, *The Eighth Circle*, which won him an Edgar in 1958, *Mirror, Mirror on the Wall*, awarded *Le Grand Prix de la Littérature Policière* in 1975 and selected by H. R. F. Keating for his list of the hundred best crime novels in 1987. Stanley Ellin died in 1986.

## Also by Stanley Ellin

### Novels

DREADFUL SUMMIT
THE KEY TO NICHOLAS STREET
THE EIGHTH CIRCLE
THE WINTER AFTER THIS SUMMER
THE PANAMA PORTRAIT
HOUSE OF CARDS
THE VALENTINE ESTATE
THE BIND
MIRROR, MIRROR ON THE WALL
STRONGHOLD
THE LUXEMBOURG RUN
STAR LIGHT, STAR BRIGHT
THE DARK FANTASTIC
VERY OLD MONEY

### Short Story Collections

MYSTERY STORIES
THE BLESSINGTON METHOD
KINDLY DIG YOUR GRAVE

**crime**masterworks

Stanley Ellin

# The Speciality of the House

## The Complete Mystery Tales, 1948–1978

**ORION**

First published in the United States of America 1979

This edition published in Great Britain in 2002
by Orion Books
an imprint of The Orion Publishing Group
Orion House, 5 Upper St Martin's Lane,
London WC2H 9EA

A CIP catalogue record for this book is available from
the British Library

ISBN 0 75285 140 3 (cased)
ISBN 0 75285 141 1 (paperback)

Typeset by SetSystems Ltd
Saffron Walden, Essex
Printed and bound in Great Britain by
Clays Ltd, St Ives plc

Grateful acknowledgement is made to *Ellery Queen's Mystery Magazine* for permission to reprint the following stories:

'The Speciality of the House', May 1948
'The Cat's-Paw', June 1949
'Death on Christmas Eve', January 1950
'The Orderly World of Mr Appleby', May 1950
'Fool's Mate', November 1951
'The Best of Everything', September 1952
'The Betrayers', June 1953
'The House Party', May 1954
'The Moment of Decision', March 1955
'Broker's Special', January 1956
'The Blessington Method', June 1956
'The Faith of Aaron Menefee', September 1957
'You Can't Be a Little Girl All Your Life', May 1958
'Unreasonable Doubt', September 1958
'The Day of the Bullet', October 1959
'Beidenbauer's Flea', February 1960
'The Seven Deadly Virtues', June 1960
'The Nine-to-Five Man', November 1961
'The Question' (originally published as 'The Question My Son Asked'), November 1962
'The Crime of Ezechiele Coen', November 1963
'The Great Persuader', March 1964
'The Day the Thaw Came to 127', March 1965
'Death of an Old-Fashioned Girl', June 1966
'The Twelth Statue', February 1967
'The Last Bottle in the World', February 1968
'Coin of the Realm', February 1969
'Kindly Dig Your Grave', November 1970
'The Payoff', November 1971
'The Other Side of the Wall,' August 1972
'The Corruption of Officer Avakadian', December 1973
'A Corner of Paradise', October 1975
'Generation Gap', September 1976
'The Family Circle', December 1977
'Reasons Unknown', December 1978

And to *Sleuth Mystery Magazine*, which published 'Robert' in October 1958

To Otto Penzler,
partner in crime

# Contents

# Introduction

Dear Reader,
  I must open with an introduction to the Introduction. It is rumored that the editor of this volume, a young man with innocent eyes and a mouth in which butter would never melt, once worked at the Bronx Zoo's Reptile House where he had the most venomous inmates contentedly eating out of his bare hand.

My doubts about that were resolved the day he and I were engaged in discussing the publication of this collection.

'Of course,' he said, 'you'll do an introduction for it.'

'Of course,' said I, nonchalant as could be.

After a few sleepless hours in bed that night, I clearly saw what I had gotten myself into. First thing next morning I reported back to headquarters and informed the editor that I had changed my mind about doing an introduction.

'You can't change your mind,' he said in the mildest of tones. 'You gave me your promise.'

'Yes, but consider the problem. A proper introduction should be a rousing panegyric to the author's dazzling talent. I can't write anything like that about myself. I mean, I probably could, but I don't think the reader would take it kindly.'

'You've got a point there,' said the editor. 'All right, no panegyric.'

'You see?' I said, pleased that he was being reasonable about it. 'And what does that leave? A solemn analysis of the stories themselves? A weighty explication of their subtleties?'

'Why not?'

'Because these are short stories, for God's sake, not some great overblown kapok-stuffed novel. Look at them. Each one is a story and it's short. It tells all without being laid out on the literary rack.'

The editor nodded. 'True,' he said.

'In that case—'

'Nevertheless,' said the editor, sliding a Florentine dagger from his sleeve and holding it up so that I could observe the play of light on its blade, 'within one week you will have ready an introduction as promised.'

Herewith, the Introduction.

Facts are good to start with. Let us start with facts.

All the stories in this collection except one deal with that streak of wickedness in human nature which makes human nature so deplorably fascinating. The one exception deals with a certain flea (*Ctenocephalides canis*) who is only too human in nature and disposition, and it stemmed from visits made in my youth to Hubert's Flea Circus just off Times Square. Hubert's is long gone now, which is too bad. Fleas of even low character would be a great improvement over much of the human traffic in the area nowadays.

The public appearance of the stories in the collection encompassed thirty years, and the works themselves are presented in chronological order. The extent of the evolution our society has undergone in these thirty years will occasionally make itself felt in the earlier stories by references that, depending on your age, may strike you as either achingly nostalgic or grotesquely unbelievable. For example, along the way you will encounter a man who is ready to sell his soul for an assured income of fifty dollars a week, a comfortable amount in those days. I should also like to remark that in the early stories all male characters wear their hair short and all female characters wear their hair long, thus making it fairly easy to differentiate between the sexes even while observing them from the rear.

The stories are not of equal merit. In view of this, it would seem convenient that I use some device like the clichéd Scale Of One To Ten to set down exact ratings for each piece so that you could, before reading it, adjust your own response to the proper wave length. However, I have learned over three rough decades that this would be folly. As its author, I tend to judge the merits of any piece by the degree to which it meets the expectations I have for it while it is yet barely conceived. Where expectations are met by the finished work I rejoice. Where expectations are not met I am downcast and hard to live with. But of course the reader, never having shared with me the process of conception and parturition, shares none of my expectations and time and again will frown at my triumphs and smile upon my failures. Eventually, like all writers when they enter their dotage, I came to the conclusion that there is no way of telling what the reader will be up to, and that the best way of dealing with him is to just hand him the goods and then quickly step back out of range.

Now to broaden the canvas.

Underlying this confessional is the assumption that you are a devotee of that peculiar narrative form, the short story, and here we are surely in the same happy company. I became a member of it very young. At age three, I was shipped off in my mother's care to a boarding house in Lakewood, New Jersey, to recuperate from some lingering ailment. In my earliest days I was always recuperating from some lingering ailment or other, and this one must have been particularly interesting to have led to that hegira from Brooklyn to the remote wilderness of New Jersey where, as everyone in my family knew, the fresh air alone was life-restoring.

I have some vivid memories of that bucolic episode, but most vivid is the memory of my father, on a weekend visit, sitting by my bed filling me with bliss as he read *Peter Rabbit* to me, patiently read it over and over on demand until I was letter perfect in it. He must have read other stories to me as well, but of them I have no recollection because they lacked the true magic. The true magic is what sticks in the mind.

Then in my first or second year at school I met *The Gingerbread Man* and reeled under the encounter. Plainly, the ultimate in literature had been achieved. Homeric in theme, penetrating in characterization, *The Gingerbread Man* raised me to the heavens and drove my fond parents to distraction as, making a sort of Vedic chant of it, I would deliver it to them between mouthfuls at the dinner table. It may have been out of their desperation that I suddenly found myself the recipient of a subscription to the late-lamented, ever memorable *St Nicholas Magazine* for children.

Here was my introduction to the wonderful world of magazines, and it didn't take me long to realize that this was not the only subscription being delivered to my address. My father, it seemed, was hopelessly addicted to magazine fiction. That was a long time ago, the 1920's, and it was indeed a Golden Age of the short story. Most Golden Ages, when you scratch them hard enough, turn out to have been largely brass, but this one was authentic: an era before long-distance automobile travel and television when a fast expanding and increasingly prosperous middle class put a good deal of its loose change into magazines principally devoted to fiction.

Even so, I suspect that the variety of publications arriving on my doorestep was out of the ordinary, extending from the glittering weekly *Saturday Evening Post, Collier's*, and *Liberty* to the sobersided *Atlantic Monthly* and *Harper's*. Following Lewis Carroll's sagacious observation: 'After all, what is the good of a book without pictures or conversation?' I soon learned to sort out the fiction from the rest of the contents in any magazine and, however hard the struggle and small the reward ofttimes, wound my mesmerized way through it.

So it was that even before adolescence I was deep into popular magazine writers who, forgiven their early indiscretions, now stand propped up as literary monuments on academia's lawns. I read Hemingway, Faulkner, and Scott Fitzgerald hot off the press. Ring Lardner, who still eludes the monument-makers, I worshipped. Simultaneously, there was the exploration of the volumes in the family bookcase, among them collections of Mark Twain, Kipling, Poe, Stevenson, and de Maupassant. I must note that there was no precocity in this and that I was but one of many among my peers. Remember that this was before the simple-minded Dick and Jane had been invented. Those years, when one entered high school he was expected to read with a certain fluency, and it was just a case of applying the fluency to suitable love objects. And of course I always read for pleasure alone, never having been misled into believing that one should read any fiction for the self-conscious improvement of his character or intellect.

But I did find that pleasure has considerable shadings. Poe bred the blackest fancies in me. De Maupassant's stories made me uneasy. I knew that something highly interesting was going on between the lines but couldn't quite fathom what it was. I also knew intuitively, even in my extreme youth, that here was a writer who reduced stories to their absolute essence. And that the ending of each story, however unpredictable, was, when I thought of it, as inevitable as doom.

The true magic again.

In high school I expanded horizons considerably, discovering in the process the recently founded *New Yorker* and a wide range of detective story magazines, most notably *Black Mask*. *The New Yorker* became a pervasive influence, generally enlightening and brightening, although it sometimes bothered me that so many of its stories seemed to fix on nothing more than terribly sensitive people bound and determined to give themselves a hard time.

There was no such problem with the more insensitive characters who inhabited *Black Mask* and its imitators, even when I began to take notice that their adventures were usually more of the same. What these pulps communicated to me was an exciting sense of immediacy. The clipped, flat, declarative style colored by dialogue with a frequently sardonic edge had the texture of the neighborhood I lived in. Today, with the absorption of that style into respected literature, one realizes the huge debt owed its creators and early masters, writers like James M. Cain and Dashiell Hammett. Indeed, Hemingway's most effective story, 'The Killers,' is pure pulp in style. What raises it to the heights is an extraordinary narrowness of focus which makes the reader contribute as much to the narrative as the writer. The more things change, the more they remain the same. Pulp readers in my palmy days would never go for that degree of subtlety any more than television crime-show viewers would today, these crime-shows, some of which I dote on, being no more than gussied-up electronic pulp.

It was late in my college years that I started to write stories,

5

having been struck by the fancy that my vocation lay that way. Certainly in my childhood I had borne all the characteristics of the author-to-be. I had been an incorrigible daydreamer and prevaricator with an unbounded imagination and a handsomely contrived excuse for every occasion. Now I felt it was time to put the imagination to work for fun and profit, and so for the next ten years, between and around jobs as farmer, school-teacher, ship-builder, ironworker, and infantryman, urged on by an insanely devoted and endlessly patient wife – the very same one who will be copy-reading these pages – I made sporadic attempts to join the ranks of the illustrious published.

I wish at this point, since every fiction writer likes to draw on his reader's tear ducts now and then, that I could describe my veritable martyrdom to the craft of writing during those ten years. A wholesome respect for hellfire forbids this, because, in fact, as the years rolled on my urge to write became fitful at best. Persistent failure did not kindle ever brighter in me the flame. Rather it led to the sensible conclusion that there were better ways of spending time away from my paid employment than in the harvesting of rejection slips.

However, there was a rekindling when, an overripe thirty and just home from military service, I was urged by my helpmeet to give the game one glorious, full-time try before returning to gainful employment. It was during that period that I was struck by an idea for a story so outrageous that even as I was putting it down on paper I knew it was destined for oblivion. As if to confirm this foreboding it then bounced like a pinball from one editorial office to another until – the helpmeet stepping in again – it was directed to an editor who apparently had a taste for the outrageous, that half of Ellery Queen known as Frederic Dannay. And now, some thirty years after its maiden publication, it serves as the title piece of this collection.

So here we are, and if this sketchy, lopsided, and self-serving autobiography demonstrates nothing else, it does show that I go back a long way into antiquity. Indeed, back to a time when horse-drawn fire engines still dramatically clattered through the streets in my part of Brooklyn, the lamplighter man mysteriously appeared at dusk each evening to bring a glow to the gas lamps along the block, and, thanks to the Volstead Act, your friendly neighborhood bootlegger did a thriving business in Scotch aged at least two hours in the bottle.

I have pleasant memories of that era, but I can't say that I'm moved by any profound nostalgia for it. We born and bred New Yorkers are like that. The action is so damn fast around these parts that if we feel any nostalgia at all, it is likely to be for the way things were last year. Or even last month.

But I do mourn all those wondrous publications devoted in large part to fiction which have disappeared along the way or have now been converted into picture books or journals of alleged information or anything else that doesn't make demands on a reader's imagination. Because that is what all storytelling comes down to: the writer's imagination beckoning to the reader's. A joint venture, and as I've come to learn whichever half of it I am, one of the most intriguing of all.

Here, too, having seen to the making of both short stories and novels, I am moved to confide that the short story is certainly the less self-indulgent and the one more likely to provide an immediate and interesting aftertaste, acid or alkali.

*Multum in parvo*, sayeth the sage.

I can only hope that you will find *multum* in all the *parvo* to follow.

*Stanley Ellin*

*Brooklyn, New York*
*August, 1979*

# The Speciality
## of the House

The Complete
Mystery Tales, 1948–1978

# The Speciality
## of the House

**A**nd this,' said Laffler, 'is Sbirro's.' Costain saw a square brownstone facade identical with the others that extended from either side into the clammy darkness of the deserted street. From the barred windows of the basement at his feet, a glimmer of light showed behind heavy curtains.

'Lord,' he observed, 'it's a dismal hole, isn't it?'

'I beg you to understand,' said Laffler stiffly, 'that Sbirro's is the restaurant without pretensions. Besieged by these ghastly, neurotic times, it has refused to compromise. It is perhaps the last important establishment in this city lit by gas jets. Here you will find the same honest furnishings, the same magnificent Sheffield service, and possibly, in a far corner, the very same spider webs that were remarked by the patrons of a half century ago!'

'A doubtful recommendation,' said Costain, 'and hardly sanitary.'

'When you enter,' Laffler continued, 'you leave the insanity of this year, this day, and this hour, and you find yourself for a brief span restored in spirit, not by opulence, but by dignity, which is the lost quality of our time.'

Costain laughed uncomfortably. 'You make it sound more like a cathedral than a restaurant,' he said.

In the pale reflection of the street lamp overhead, Laffler peered at his companion's face. 'I wonder,' he said abruptly, 'whether I have not made a mistake in extending this invitation to you.'

Costain was hurt. Despite an impressive title and large salary, he was no more than a clerk to this pompous little man, but he was impelled to make some display of his feelings. 'If you wish,' he said coldly, 'I can make other plans for my evening with no trouble.'

With his large, cowlike eyes turned up to Costain, the mist drifting into the ruddy, full moon of his face, Laffler seemed strangely ill at ease. Then 'No, no,' he said at last, 'absolutely not. It's important that you dine at Sbirro's with me.' He grasped Costain's arm firmly and led the way to the wrought-iron gate of the basement. 'You see, you're the sole person in my office who seems to know anything at all about good food. And on my part, knowing about Sbirro's but not having some appreciative friend to share it is like having a unique piece of art locked in a room where no one else can enjoy it.'

Costain was considerably mollified by this. 'I understand there are a great many people who relish that situation.'

'I'm not one of that kind!' Laffler said sharply. 'And having the secret of Sbirro's locked in myself for years has finally become unendurable.' He fumbled at the side of the gate and from within could be heard the small, discordant jangle of an ancient pull-bell. An interior door opened with a groan, and Costain found himself peering into a dark face whose only discernible feature was a row of gleaming teeth.

'Sair?' said the face.

'Mr Laffler and a guest.'

'Sair,' the face said again, this time in what was clearly an invitation. It moved aside and Costain stumbled down a single step behind his host. The door and gate creaked behind him, and he stood blinking in a small foyer. It took him a moment to realize that the figure he now stared at was his own reflection in a gigantic pier glass that extended from floor to ceiling. 'Atmosphere,' he said under his breath and chuckled as he followed his guide to a seat.

He faced Laffler across a small table for two and peered curiously around the dining room. It was no size at all, but the half-dozen guttering gas jets which provided the only illumination threw such a deceptive light that the walls flickered and faded into uncertain distance.

There were no more than eight or ten tables about, arranged to insure the maximum privacy. All were occupied, and the few waiters serving them moved with quiet efficiency. In the air were a soft clash and scrape of cutlery and a soothing murmur of talk. Costain nodded appreciatively.

Laffler breathed an audible sigh of gratification. 'I knew you would share my enthusiasm,' he said. 'Have you noticed, by the way, that there are no women present?'

Costain raised inquiring eyebrows.

'Sbirro,' said Laffler, 'does not encourage members of the fair sex to enter the premises. And, I can tell you, his method is decidedly effective. I had the experience of seeing a woman get a taste of it not long ago. She sat at a table for not less than an hour waiting for service which was never forthcoming.'

'Didn't she make a scene?'

'She did.' Laffler smiled at the recollection. 'She succeeded in annoying the customers, embarrassing her partner, and nothing more.'

'And what about Mr Sbirro?'

'He did not make an appearance. Whether he directed affairs from behind the scenes, or was not even present during the episode, I don't know. Whichever it was, he won a complete victory. The woman never reappeared nor, for that matter, did the witless gentleman who by bringing her was really the cause of the entire contretemps.'

'A fair warning to all present,' laughed Costain.

A waiter now appeared at the table. The chocolate dark skin, the thin, beautifully molded nose and lips, the large liquid eyes, heavily lashed, and the silver white hair so heavy and silken that it lay on the skull like a cap, all marked him definitely as an East Indian of some sort, Costain decided. The man arranged the stiff table linen, filled two tumblers from a huge, cut-glass pitcher, and set them in their proper places.

'Tell me,' Laffler said eagerly, 'is the special being served this evening?'

The waiter smiled regretfully and showed teeth as spectacular as those of the majordomo. 'I am so sorry, sair. There is no special this evening.'

Laffler's face fell into lines of heavy disappointment. 'After waiting so long. It's been a month already, and I hoped to show my friend here . . .'

'You understand the difficulties, sair.'

'Of course, of course.' Laffler looked at Costain sadly and shrugged. 'You see, I had in mind to introduce you to the greatest treat that Sbirro's offers, but unfortunately it isn't on the menu this evening.'

The waiter said, 'Do you wish to be served now, sair?' and Laffler nodded. To Costain's surprise the waiter made his way off without waiting for any instructions.

'Have you ordered in advance?' he asked.

'Ah,' said Laffler, 'I really should have explained. Sbirro's offers no choice whatsoever. You will eat the same meal as everyone else in this room. Tomorrow evening you would eat an entirely different meal, but again without designating a single preference.'

'Very unusual,' said Costain, 'and certainly unsatisfactory at times. What if one doesn't have a taste for the particular dish set before him?'

'On that score,' said Laffler solemnly, 'you need have no fears. I give you my word that no matter how exacting your tastes, you will relish every mouthful you eat in Sbirro's.'

Costain looked doubtful, and Laffler smiled. 'And consider the subtle advantages of the system,' he said. 'When you pick up the menu of a popular restaurant, you find yourself confronted with innumerable choices. You are forced to weigh, to evaluate, to make uneasy decisions which you may instantly regret. The effect of all this is a tension which, however slight, must make for discomfort.

'And consider the mechanics of the process. Instead of a hurly-burly of sweating cooks rushing about a kitchen in a frenzy to prepare a hundred varying items, we have a chef who stands serenely alone, bringing all his talents to bear on one task, with all assurance of a complete triumph!'

'Then you have seen the kitchen?'

'Unfortunately, no,' said Laffler sadly. 'The picture I offer is hypothetical, made of conversational fragments I have pieced together over the years. I must admit, though, that my desire to see the functioning of the kitchen here comes very close to being my sole obsession nowadays.'

'But have you mentioned this to Sbirro?'

'A dozen times. He shrugs the suggestion away.'

'Isn't that a rather curious foible on his part?'

'No, no,' Laffler said hastily, 'a master artist is never under the compulsion of petty courtesies. Still,' he sighed, 'I have never given up hope.'

The waiter now reappeared bearing two soup bowls which he set in place with mathematical exactitude and a small tureen from which he slowly ladled a measure of clear, thin broth. Costain dipped his spoon into the broth and tasted it with some curiosity. It was delicately flavored, bland to the verge of tastelessness. Costain frowned, tentatively reached for the salt and pepper cellars, and discovered there were none on the table. He looked up, saw Laffler's eyes on him, and although unwilling to compromise with his own tastes, he hesitated to act as a damper on Laffler's enthusiasm. Therefore he smiled and indicated the broth.

'Excellent,' he said.

Laffler returned his smile. 'You do not find it excellent at all,' he said coolly. 'You find it flat and badly in need of condiments. I know this,' he continued as Costain's eyebrows shot upward, 'because it was my own reaction many years ago, and because like yourself I found myself reaching for salt and pepper after the first mouthful. I also learned with surprise that condiments are not available in Sbirro's.'

Costain was shocked. 'Not even salt!' he exclaimed.

'Not even salt. The very fact that you require it for your soup stands as evidence that your taste is unduly jaded. I am confident that you will now make the same discovery that I did: by the time you have nearly finished your soup, your desire for salt will be nonexistent.'

Laffler was right; before Costain had reached the bottom of his plate, he was relishing the nuances of the broth with steadily increasing delight. Laffler thrust aside his own empty bowl and rested his elbows on the table. 'Do you agree with me now?'

'To my surprise,' said Costain, 'I do.'

As the waiter busied himself clearing the table, Laffler lowered his voice significantly. 'You will find,' he said, 'that the absence of condiments is but one of several noteworthy characteristics which mark Sbirro's. I may as well prepare you for these. For example, no alcoholic beverages of any sort are served here, nor for that matter any beverage except clear, cold water, the first and only drink necessary for a human being.'

'Outside of mother's milk,' suggested Costain dryly.

'I can answer that in like vein by pointing out that the average patron of Sbirro's has passed that primal stage of his development.'

Costain laughed. 'Granted,' he said.

'Very well. There is also a ban on the use of tobacco in any form.'

'But, good heavens,' said Costain, 'doesn't that make Sbirro's more a teetotaler's retreat than a gourmet's sanctuary?'

'I fear,' said Laffler solemnly, 'that you confuse the words, *gourmet* and *gourmand*. The gourmand, through glutting himself, requires a wider and wider latitude of experience to stir his surfeited senses, but the very nature of the gourmet is simplicity. The ancient Greek in his coarse chiton savoring the ripe olive; the Japanese in his bare room contemplating the curves of a single flower stem – these are the true gourmets.'

'But an occasional drop of brandy or pipeful of tobacco,' said Costain dubiously, 'are hardly overindulgence.'

'By alternating stimulant and narcotic,' said Laffler, 'you seesaw the delicate balance of your taste so violently that it loses its most precious quality: the appreciation of fine food. During my years as a patron of Sbirro's, I have proved this to my satisfaction.'

'May I ask,' said Costain, 'why you regard the ban on these things as having such deep esthetic motives? What about such mundane reasons as the high cost of a liquor license, or the possibility that patrons would object to the smell of tobacco in such confined quarters?'

Laffler shook his head violently. 'If and when you meet Sbirro,' he said, 'you will understand at once that he is not the man to make decisions on a mundane basis. As a matter of fact, it was Sbirro himself who first made me cognizant of what you call "esthetic" motives.'

'An amazing man,' said Costain as the waiter prepared to serve the entree.

Laffler's next words were not spoken until he had savored and swallowed a large portion of meat. 'I hesitate to use superlatives,' he said, 'but to my way of thinking, Sbirro represents man at the apex of his civilization!'

Costain cocked an eyebrow and applied himself to his roast which rested in a pool of stiff gravy ungarnished by green or vegetable. The thin steam rising from it carried to his nostrils a subtle, tantalizing odor which made his mouth water. He chewed a piece as slowly and thoughtfully as if he were analyzing the intricacies of a Mozart symphony. The range of taste he discovered was really extraordinary, from the pungent nip of the crisp outer edge to the peculiarly flat, yet soul-satisfying ooze of blood which the pressure of his jaws forced from the half-raw interior.

Upon swallowing he found himself ferociously hungry for another piece, and then another, and it was only with an effort that he prevented himself from wolfing down all his share of the meat and gravy without waiting to get the full voluptuous satisfaction from each mouthful. When he had scraped his platter clean, he realized that both he and Laffler had completed the entire course without exchanging a single word. He commented on this, and Laffler said, 'Can you see any need for words in the presence of such food?'

Costain looked around at the shabby, dimly lit room, the quiet diners, with a new perception. 'No,' he said humbly, 'I cannot. For any doubts I had I apologize unreservedly. In all your praise of Sbirro's there was not a single word of exaggeration.'

'Ah,' said Laffler delightedly. 'And that is only part of the story. You heard me mention the special which unfortunately was not on the menu tonight. What you have just eaten is as nothing when compared to the absolute delights of that special!'

'Good Lord!' cried Costain. 'What is it? Nightingale's tongues? Filet of unicorn?'

'Neither,' said Laffler. 'It is lamb.'

'Lamb?'

Laffler remained lost in thought for a minute. 'If,' he said at last, 'I were to give you in my own unstinted words my opinion of this dish, you would judge me completely insane. That is how deeply the mere thought of it affects me. It is neither the fatty chop, nor the too solid leg; it is, instead, a select portion of the rarest sheep in existence and is named after the species – lamb Amirstan.'

Costain knit his brow. 'Amirstan?'

'A fragment of desolation almost lost on the border which separates Afghanistan and Russia. From chance remarks dropped by Sbirro, I gather it is no more than a plateau which grazes the pitiful remnants of a flock of superb sheep. Sbirro, through some means or other, obtained rights to the traffic in this flock and is, therefore, the sole restaurateur ever to have lamb Amirstan on his bill of fare. I can tell you that the appearance of this dish is a rare occurrence indeed, and luck is the only guide in determining for the clientele the exact date when it will be served.'

'But surely,' said Costain, 'Sbirro could provide some advance knowledge of this event.'

'The objection to that is simply stated,' said Laffler. 'There exists in this city a huge number of professional gluttons. Should advance information slip out, it is quite likely that they will, out of curiosity, become familiar with the dish and thenceforth supplant the regular patrons at these tables.'

'But you don't mean to say,' objected Costain, 'that these few people present are the only ones in the entire city, or for that matter, in the whole wide world, who know of the existence of Sbirro's!'

'Very nearly. There may be one or two regular patrons who, for some reason, are not present at the moment.'

'That's incredible.'

'It is done,' said Laffler, the slightest shade of menace in his voice, 'by every patron making it his solemn obligation to keep the secret. By accepting my invitation this evening you automatically assume that obligation. I hope you can be trusted with it.'

Costain flushed. 'My position in your employ should vouch for me. I only question the wisdom of a policy which keeps such magnificent food away from so many who would enjoy it.'

'Do you know the inevitable result of the policy *you* favor?' asked Laffler bitterly. 'An influx of idiots who would nightly complain that they are never served roast duck with chocolate sauce. Is that picture tolerable to you?'

'No,' admitted Costain, 'I am forced to agree with you.'

Laffler leaned back in his chair wearily and passed his hand over his eyes in an uncertain gesture. 'I am a solitary man,' he said quietly, 'and not by choice alone. It may sound strange to you, it may border on eccentricity, but I feel to my depths that this restaurant, this warm haven in a coldly insane world, is both family and friend to me.'

And Costain, who to this moment had never viewed his companion as other than tyrannical employer or officious host, now felt an overwhelming pity twist inside his comfortably expanded stomach.

By the end of two weeks the invitations to join Laffler at Sbirro's had become something of a ritual. Every day, at a few minutes after five, Costain would step out into the office corridor and lock his cubicle behind him; he would drape his overcoat neatly over his left arm, and peer into the glass of the door to make sure his Homburg was set at the proper angle. At one time he would have followed this by lighting a cigarette, but under Laffler's prodding he had decided to give abstinence a fair trial. Then he would start down the corridor, and Laffler would fall in step at his elbow, clearing his throat. 'Ah, Costain. No plans for this evening, I hope.'

'No,' Costain would say, 'I'm footloose and fancy-free,' or 'At your service,' or something equally inane. He wondered at times whether it would not be more tactful to vary the ritual with an occasional refusal, but the glow with which Laffler received his answer, and the rough friendliness of Laffler's grip on his arm, forestalled him.

Among the treacherous crags of the business world, reflected Costain, what better way to secure your footing than friendship with one's employer. Already, a secretary close to the workings of the inner office had commented publicly on Laffler's highly favorable opinion of Costain. That was all to the good.

And the food! The incomparable food at Sbirro's! For the first time in his life, Costain, ordinarily a lean and bony man, noted with gratification that he was certainly gaining weight; within two weeks his bones had disappeared under a layer of sleek, firm flesh, and here and there were even signs of incipient plumpness.

It struck Costain one night, while surveying himself in his bath, that the rotund Laffler, himself, might have been a spare and bony man before discovering Sbirro's.

So there was obviously everything to be gained and nothing to be lost by accepting Laffler's invitations. Perhaps after testing the heralded wonders of lamb Amirstan and meeting Sbirro, who thus far had not made an appearance, a refusal or two might be in order. But certainly not until then.

That evening, two weeks to a day after his first visit to Sbirro's, Costain had both desires fulfilled: he dined on lamb Amirstan, and he met Sbirro. Both exceeded all his expectations.

When the waiter leaned over their table immediately after seating them and gravely announced: 'Tonight is special, sair,' Costain was shocked to find his heart pounding with expectation. On the table before him he saw Laffler's hands trembling violently. But it isn't natural, he thought suddenly. Two full grown men, presumably intelligent and in the full possession of their senses, as jumpy as a pair of cats waiting to have their meat flung at them!

'This is it!' Laffler's voice startled him so that he almost leaped from his seat. 'The culinary triumph of all times! And faced by it you are embarrassed by the very emotions it distills.'

'How did you know that?' Costain asked faintly.

'How? Because a decade ago I underwent your embarrassment. Add to that your air of revulsion and it's easy to see how affronted you are by the knowledge that man has not yet forgotten how to slaver over his meat.'

'And these others,' whispered Costain, 'do they all feel the same thing?'

'Judge for yourself.'

Costain looked furtively around at the nearby tables. 'You are right,' he finally said. 'At any rate, there's comfort in numbers.'

Laffler inclined his head slightly to the side. 'One of the numbers,' he remarked, 'appears to be in for a disappointment.'

Costain followed the gesture. At the table indicated a gray-haired man sat conspicuously alone, and Costain frowned at the empty chair opposite him.

'Why, yes,' he recalled, 'that very stout, bald man, isn't it? I believe it's the first dinner he's missed here in two weeks.'

'The entire decade more likely,' said Laffler sympathetically. 'Rain or shine, crisis or calamity, I don't think he's missed an evening at Sbirro's since the first time I dined here. Imagine his expression when he's told that, on his very first defection, lamb Amirstan was the *plat de jour*.'

Costain looked at the empty chair again with a dim discomfort. 'His very first?' he murmured.

'Mr Laffler! And friend! I am so pleased. So very, very pleased. No, do not stand; I will have a place made.' Miraculously a seat appeared under the figure standing there at the table. 'The lamb Amirstan will be an unqualified success, hurr? I myself have been stewing in the miserable kitchen all the day, prodding the foolish chef to do everything just so. The just so is the important part, hurr? But I see your friend does not know me. An introduction, perhaps?'

The words ran in a smooth, fluid eddy. They rippled, they purred, they hypnotized Costain so that he could do no more than stare. The mouth that uncoiled this sinuous monologue was alarmingly wide, with thin mobile lips that curled and twisted with every syllable. There was a flat nose with a straggling line of hair under it; wide-set eyes, almost oriental in appearance, that glittered in the unsteady flare of gaslight; and the long, sleek hair that swept back from high on the unwrinkled forehead – hair so pale that it might have been bleached of all color. An amazing face surely, and the sight of it tortured Costain with the conviction that it was somehow familiar. His brain twitched and prodded but could not stir up any solid recollection.

Laffler's voice jerked Costain out of his study. 'Mr Sbirro. Mr Costain, a good friend and associate.' Costain rose and shook the proffered hand. It was warm and dry, flint-hard against his palm.

'I am so very pleased, Mr Costain. So very, very pleased,' purred the voice. 'You like my little establishment, hurr? You have a great treat in store, I assure you.'

Laffler chuckled. 'Oh, Costain's been dining here regularly for two weeks,' he said. 'He's by way of becoming a great admirer of yours, Sbirro.'

The eyes were turned on Costain. 'A very great compliment.

You compliment me with your presence and I return same with my food, hurr? But the lamb Amirstan is far superior to anything of your past experience, I assure you. All the trouble of obtaining it, all the difficulty of preparation, is truly merited.'

Costain strove to put aside the exasperating problem of that face. 'I have wondered,' he said, 'why with all these difficulties you mention, you even bother to present lamb Amirstan to the public. Surely your other dishes are excellent enough to uphold your reputation.'

Sbirro smiled so broadly that his face became perfectly round. 'Perhaps it is a matter of the psychology, hurr? Someone discovers a wonder and must share it with others. He must fill his cup to the brim, perhaps, by observing the so evident pleasure of those who explore it with him. Or,' he shrugged, 'perhaps it is just a matter of good business.'

'Then in the light of all this,' Costain persisted, 'and considering all the conventions you have imposed on your customers, why do you open the restaurant to the public instead of operating it as a private club?'

The eyes abruptly glinted into Costain's, then turned away. 'So perspicacious, hurr? Then I will tell you. Because there is more privacy in a public eating place than in the most exclusive club in existence! Here no one inquires of your affairs; no one desires to know the intimacies of your life. Here the business is eating. We are not curious about names and addresses or the reasons for the coming and going of our guests. We welcome you when you are here; we have no regrets when you are here no longer. That is the answer, hurr?'

Costain was startled by this vehemence. 'I had no intention of prying,' he stammered.

Sbirro ran the tip of his tongue over his thin lips. 'No, no,' he reassured, 'you are not prying. Do not let me give you that impression. On the contrary, I invite your questions.'

'Oh, come, Costain,' said Laffler. 'Don't let Sbirro intimidate you. I've known him for years and I guarantee that his bark is worse than his bite. Before you know it, he'll be showing you all the privileges of the house – outside of inviting you to visit his precious kitchen, of course.'

'Ah,' smiled Sbirro, 'for that, Mr Costain may have to wait a little while. For everything else I am at his beck and call.'

Laffler slapped his hand jovially on the table. 'What did I tell you!' he said. 'Now let's have the truth, Sbirro. Has anyone, outside of your staff, ever stepped into the sanctum sanctorum?'

Sbirro looked up. 'You see on the wall above you,' he said earnestly, 'the portrait of one to whom I did the honor. A very dear friend and a patron of most long standing, he is evidence that my kitchen is not inviolate.'

Costain studied the picture and started with recognition. 'Why,' he said excitedly, 'that's the famous writer – you know the one, Laffler – he used to do such wonderful short stories and cynical bits and then suddenly took himself off and disappeared in Mexico!'

'Of course!' cried Laffler, 'and to think I've been sitting under his portrait for years without even realizing it!' He turned to Sbirro. 'A dear friend, you say? His disappearance must have been a blow to you.'

Sbirro's face lengthened. 'It was, it was, I assure you. But think of it this way, gentlemen: he was probably greater in his death than in his life, hurr? A most tragic man, he often told me that his only happy hours were spent here at this very table. Pathetic, is it not? And to think the only favor I could ever show him was to let him witness the mysteries of my kitchen, which is, when all is said and done, no more than a plain, ordinary kitchen.'

'You seem very certain of his death,' commented Costain. 'After all, no evidence has ever turned up to substantiate it.'

Sbirro contemplated the picture. 'None at all,' he said softly. 'Remarkable, hurr?'

With the arrival of the entree Sbirro leaped to his feet and set about serving them himself. With his eyes alight he lifted the casserole from the tray and sniffed at the fragrance from within with sensual relish. Then, taking great care not to lose a single drop of gravy, he filled two platters with chunks of dripping meat. As if exhausted by this task, he sat back in his chair, breathing heavily. 'Gentlemen,' he said, 'to your good appetite.'

Costain chewed his first mouthful with great deliberation and swallowed it. Then he looked at the empty tines of his fork with glazed eyes.

'Good God!' he breathed.

'It is good, hurr? Better than you imagined?'

Costain shook his head dazedly. 'It is as impossible,' he said slowly, 'for the uninitiated to conceive the delights of lamb Amirstan as for mortal man to look into his own soul.'

'Perhaps—' Sbirro thrust his head so close that Costain could feel the warm, fetid breath tickle his nostrils – 'perhaps you have just had a glimpse into your soul, hurr?'

Costain tried to draw back slightly without giving offence. 'Perhaps.' He laughed. 'And a gratifying picture it made: all fang and claw. But without intending any disrespect, I should hardly like to build my church on *lamb en casserole*.'

Sbirro rose and laid a hand gently on his shoulder. 'So perspicacious,' he said. 'Sometimes when you have nothing to do, nothing, perhaps, but sit for a very little while in a dark room and think of this world – what it is and what it is going to be – then you must turn your thoughts a little to the significance of the Lamb in religion. It will be so interesting. And now—' he bowed deeply to both men – 'I have held you long enough from your dinner. I was most happy,' he said, nodding to Costain, 'and I am sure we will meet again.' The teeth gleamed, the eyes glittered, and Sbirro was gone down the aisle of tables.

Costain twisted around to stare after the retreating figure. 'Have I offended him in some way?' he asked.

Laffler looked up from his plate. 'Offended him? He loves that kind of talk. Lamb Amirstan is a ritual with him; get him started and he'll be back at you a dozen times worse than a priest making a conversion.'

Costain turned to his meal with the face still hovering before him. 'Interesting man,' he reflected. 'Very.'

It took him a month to discover the tantalizing familiarity of that face, and when he did, he laughed aloud in his bed. Why, of course! Sbirro might have sat as the model for the Cheshire cat in *Alice*!

\*

He passed this thought on to Laffler the very next evening as they pushed their way down the street to the restaurant against a chill, blustering wind. Laffler only looked blank.

'You may be right,' he said, 'but I'm not a fit judge. It's a far cry back to the days when I read the book. A far cry, indeed.'

As if taking up his words, a piercing howl came ringing down the street and stopped both men short in their tracks. 'Someone's in trouble there,' said Laffler. 'Look!'

Not far from the entrance to Sbirro's two figures could be seen struggling in the near darkness. They swayed back and forth and suddenly tumbled into a writhing heap on the sidewalk. The piteous howl went up again, and Laffler, despite his girth, ran toward it at a fair speed with Costain tagging cautiously behind.

Stretched out full-length on the pavement was a slender figure with the dusky complexion and white hair of one of Sbirro's servitors. His fingers were futilely plucking at the huge hands which encircled his throat, and his knees pushed weakly up at the gigantic bulk of a man who brutally bore down with his full weight.

Laffler came up panting. 'Stop this!' he shouted. 'What's going on here?'

The pleading eyes almost bulging from their sockets turned toward Laffler. 'Help, sair. This man – drunk—'

'Drunk am I, ya dirty—' Costain saw now that the man was a sailor in a badly soiled uniform. The air around him reeked with the stench of liquor. 'Pick me pocket and then call me drunk, will ya!' He dug his fingers in harder, and his victim groaned.

Laffler seized the sailor's shoulder. 'Let go of him, do you hear! Let go of him at once!' he cried, and the next instant was sent careening into Costain, who staggered back under the force of the blow.

The attack on his own person sent Laffler into immediate and berserk action. Without a sound he leaped at the sailor, striking and kicking furiously at the unprotected face and flanks. Stunned at first, the man came to his feet with a rush and turned on Laffler. For a moment they stood locked together, and then as Costain joined the attack, all three went sprawling to the ground. Slowly Laffler and Costain got to their feet and looked down at the body before them.

'He's either out cold from liquor,' said Costain, 'or he struck his head going down. In any case, it's a job for the police.'

'No, no, sair!' The waiter crawled weakly to his feet, and stood swaying. 'No police, sair. Mr Sbirro do not want such. You understand, sair.' He caught hold of Costain with a pleading hand, and Costain looked at Laffler.

'Of course not,' said Laffler. 'We won't have to bother with the police. They'll pick him up soon enough, the murderous sot. But what in the world started all this?'

'That man, sair. He make most erratic way while walking, and with no meaning I push against him. Then he attack me, accusing me to rob him.'

'As I thought.' Laffler pushed the waiter gently along. 'Now go in and get yourself attended to.'

The man seemed ready to burst into tears. 'To you, sair, I owe my life. If there is anything I can do—'

Laffler turned into the areaway that led to Sbirro's door. 'No, no, it was nothing. You go along, and if Sbirro has any questions send him to me. I'll straighten it out.'

'My life, sair,' were the last words they heard as the inner door closed behind them.

'There you are, Costain,' said Laffler, as a few minutes later he drew his chair under the table, 'civilized man in all his glory. Reeking with alcohol, strangling to death some miserable innocent who came too close.'

Costain made an effort to gloss over the nerve-shattering memory of the episode. 'It's the neurotic cat that takes to alcohol,' he said. 'Surely there's a reason for that sailor's condition.'

'Reason? Of course there is. Plain atavistic savagery!' Laffler swept his arm in an all-embracing gesture. 'Why do we all sit here at our meat? Not only to appease physical demands, but because our atavistic selves cry for release. Think back, Costain. Do you remember that I once described Sbirro as the epitome of civilization? Can you now see why? A brilliant man, he fully understands the nature of human beings. But unlike lesser men he bends all his efforts to the satisfaction of our innate nature without resultant harm to some innocent bystander.'

'When I think back on the wonders of lamb Amirstan,' said Costain, 'I quite understand what you're driving at. And, by the way, isn't it nearly due to appear on the bill of fare? It must have been over a month ago that it was last served.'

The waiter, filling the tumblers, hesitated. 'I am so sorry, sair. No special this evening.'

'There's your answer,' Laffler grunted, 'and probably just my luck to miss out on it altogether the next time.'

Costain stared at him. 'Oh, come, that's impossible.'

'No, blast it.' Laffler drank off half his water at a gulp and the waiter immediately refilled the glass. 'I'm off to South America for a surprise tour of inspection. One month, two months, Lord knows how long.'

'Are things that bad down there?'

'They could be better.' Laffler suddenly grinned. 'Mustn't forget it takes very mundane dollars and cents to pay the tariff at Sbirro's.'

'I haven't heard a word of this around the office.'

'Wouldn't be a surprise tour if you had. Nobody knows about this except myself – and now you. I want to walk in on them completely unexpected. Find out what flimflammery they're up to down there. As far as the office is concerned, I'm off on a jaunt somewhere. Maybe recuperating in some sanatorium from my hard work. Anyhow, the business will be in good hands. Yours, among them.'

'Mine?' said Costain, surprised.

'When you go in tomorrow you'll find yourself in receipt of a promotion, even if I'm not there to hand it to you personally. Mind you, it has nothing to do with our friendship either; you've done fine work, and I'm immensely grateful for it.'

Costain reddened under the praise. 'You don't expect to be in tomorrow. Then you're leaving tonight?'

Laffler nodded. 'I've been trying to wangle some reservations. If they come through, well, this will be in the nature of a farewell celebration.'

'You know,' said Costain slowly, 'I devoutly hope that your reservations don't come through. I believe our dinners here have come to mean more to me than I ever dared imagine.'

The waiter's voice broke in. 'Do you wish to be served now, sair?' and they both started.

'Of course, of course,' said Laffler sharply, 'I didn't realize you were waiting.'

'What bothers me,' he told Costain as the waiter turned away, 'is the thought of the lamb Amirstan I'm bound to miss. To tell you the truth, I've already put off my departure a week, hoping to hit a lucky night, and now I simply can't delay any more. I do hope that when you're sitting over your share of lamb Amirstan, you'll think of me with suitable regrets.'

Costain laughed. 'I will indeed,' he said as he turned to his dinner.

Hardly had he cleared the plate when a waiter silently reached for it. It was not their usual waiter, he observed; it was none other than the victim of the assault.

'Well,' Costain said, 'how do you feel now? Still under the weather?'

The waiter paid no attention to him. Instead, with the air of a man under great strain, he turned to Laffler. 'Sair,' he whispered. 'My life. I owe it to you. I can repay you!'

Laffler looked up in amazement, then shook his head firmly. 'No,' he said. 'I want nothing from you, understand? You have repaid me sufficently with your thanks. Now get on with your work and let's hear no more about it.'

The waiter did not stir an inch, but his voice rose slightly. 'By the body and blood of your God, sair, I will help you even if you do not want! *Do not go into the kitchen, sair*. I trade you my life for yours, sair, when I speak this. Tonight or any night of your life, do not go into the kitchen at Sbirro's!'

Laffler sat back, completely dumbfounded. 'Not go into the kitchen? Why shouldn't I go into the kitchen if Mr Sbirro ever took it into his head to invite me there? What's all this about?'

A hard hand was laid on Costain's back, and another gripped the waiter's arm. The waiter remained frozen to the spot, his lips compressed, his eyes downcast.

'What is all *what* about, gentlemen?' purred the voice. 'So opportune an arrival. In time as ever, I see, to answer all the questions, hurr?'

Laffler breathed a sigh of relief. 'Ah, Sbirro, thank heaven you're here. This man is saying something about my not going into your kitchen. Do you know what he means?'

The teeth showed in a broad grin. 'But of course. This good man was giving you advice in all amiability. It so happens that my too emotional chef heard some rumor that I might have a guest into his precious kitchen, and he flew into a fearful rage. Such a rage, gentlemen! He even threatened to give notice on the spot, and you can understand what that would mean to Sbirro's, hurr? Fortunately, I succeeded in showing him what a signal honor it is to have an esteemed patron and true connoisseur observe him at his work firsthand, and now he is quite amenable. Quite, hurr?'

He released the waiter's arm. 'You are at the wrong table,' he said softly. 'See that it does not happen again.'

The waiter slipped off without daring to raise his eyes and Sbirro drew a chair to the table. He seated himself and brushed his hand lightly over his hair. 'Now I am afraid that the cat is out of the bag, hurr? This invitation to you, Mr Laffler, was to be a surprise; but the surprise is gone, and all that is left is the invitation.'

Laffler mopped beads of perspiration from his forehead. 'Are you serious?' he said huskily. 'Do you mean that we are really to witness the preparation of your food tonight?'

Sbirro drew a sharp fingernail along the tablecloth, leaving a thin, straight line printed in the linen. 'Ah,' he said, 'I am faced with a dilemma of great proportions.' He studied the line soberly. 'You, Mr Laffler, have been my guest for ten long years. But our friend here—'

Costain raised his hand in protest. 'I understand perfectly. This invitation is solely to Mr Laffler, and naturally my presence is embarrassing. As it happens, I have an early engagement for this evening and must be on my way anyhow. So you see there's no dilemma at all, really.'

'No,' said Laffler, 'absolutely not. That wouldn't be fair at all.

We've been sharing this until now, Costain, and I won't enjoy the experience half as much if you're not along. Surely Sbirro can make his conditions flexible, this one occasion.'

They both looked at Sbirro who shrugged his shoulders regretfully.

Costain rose abruptly. 'I'm not going to sit here, Laffler, and spoil your great adventure. And then, too,' he bantered, 'think of that ferocious chef waiting to get his cleaver on you. I prefer not to be at the scene. I'll just say goodbye,' he went on, to cover Laffler's guilty silence, 'and leave you to Sbirro. I'm sure he'll take pains to give you a good show.' He held out his hand and Laffler squeezed it painfully hard.

'You're being very decent, Costain,' he said. 'I hope you'll continue to dine here until we meet again. It shouldn't be too long.'

Sbirro made way for Costain to pass. 'I will expect you,' he said. '*Au 'voir.*'

Costain stopped briefly in the dim foyer to adjust his scarf and fix his Homburg at the proper angle. When he turned away from the mirror, satisfied at last, he saw with a final glance that Laffler and Sbirro were already at the kitchen door, Sbirro holding the door invitingly wide with one hand, while the other rested, almost tenderly, on Laffler's meaty shoulders.

# The Cat's-Paw

There was little to choose among any of the rooms in the boarding house in their dingy, linoleum-floored, brass-bedsteaded uniformity, but the day he answered the advertisement on the *Help Wanted* page, Mr Crabtree realized that one small advantage accrued to his room: the public telephone in the hallway was opposite his door, and simply by keeping an ear cocked he could be at the instrument a moment after the first shrill warning ring had sounded.

In view of this he closed his application for employment not only with his signature but with the number of the telephone as well. His hand shook a little as he did so; he felt party to a gross deception in implying that the telephone was his personal property, but the prestige to be gained this way, so he thought, might somehow weight the balance in his favor. To that end he tremorously sacrificed the unblemished principles of a lifetime.

The advertisement itself had been nothing less than a miracle. *Man wanted,* it said, *for hard work at moderate pay. Sober, honest, industrious former clerk, age 45–50 preferred. Write all details. Box 111*; and Mr Crabtree, peering incredulously through his spectacles, had read it with a shuddering dismay at the thought of all his fellows, age 45–50, who might have read the same notice minutes, or perhaps, hours, before.

His answer could have served as a model Letter of Application for Employment His age was forty-eight, his health excellent. He was unmarried. He had served one single firm for thirty years; had served it faithfully and well; had an admirable record for attendance and punctuality. Unfortunately, the firm had merged with another and larger; regrettably, many capable employees had to be released. Hours? Unimportant. His only interest was in doing a good job no matter the time involved. Salary? A matter entirely in the hands of his prospective employer. His previous salary had been fifty dollars per week, but naturally that had come after years of proved worth. Available for an interview at any time. References from the following. The signature. And then, the telephone number.

All this had been written and rewritten a dozen times until Mr Crabtree had been satisfied that every necessary word was there, each word in its proper place. Then, in the copperplate hand that had made his ledgers a thing of beauty, the final draft had been transferred to fine bond paper purchased toward this very contingency, and posted.

After that, alone with his speculations on whether a reply would come by mail, by telephone, or not at all, Mr Crabtree spent two endless and heart-fluttering weeks until the moment when he answered a call and heard his name come over the wire like the crack of doom.

'Yes,' he said shrilly, 'I'm Crabtree! I sent a letter!'

'Calmly, Mr Crabtree, calmly,' said the voice. It was a clear, thin voice, which seemed to pick up and savor each syllable before delivering it, and it had an instant and chilling effect on Mr Crabtree who was clutching the telephone as if pity could be squeezed from it.

'I have been considering your application,' the voice went on with the same painful deliberation, 'and I am most gratified by it. Most gratified. But before calling the matter settled, I should like to make clear the terms of employment I am offering. You would not object to my discussing it now?'

The word *employment* rang dizzily through Mr Crabtree's head. 'No,' he said, 'please do.'

'Very well. First of all, do you feel capable of operating your own establishment?'

'My own establishment?'

'Oh, have no fears about the size of the establishment or the responsibilities involved. It is a matter of some confidential reports which must be drawn up regularly. You would have your own office, your name on the door, and, of course, no supervision directly over you. That should explain the need for an exceptionally reliable man.'

'Yes,' said Mr Crabtree, 'but those confidential reports . . .'

'Your office will be supplied with a list of several important corporations. It will also receive subscriptions to a number of financial journals which frequently make mention of those same corporations. You will note all such references as they appear, and, at the end of each day, consolidate them into a report which will be mailed to me. I must add that none of this calls for any theoretical work or literary treatment. Accuracy, brevity, clarity: those are the three measures to go by. You understand that, of course?'

'Yes, indeed,' said Mr Crabtree fervently.

'Excellent,' said the voice. 'Now your hours will be from nine to five, six days a week, with an hour off at noon for lunch. I must stress this: I am insistent on punctuality and attendance, and I expect you to be as conscientious about these things as if you were under my personal supervision every moment of the day. I hope I do not offend you when I emphasize this?'

'Oh, no, sir!' said Mr Crabtree. 'I . . .'

'Let me continue,' the voice said. 'Here is the address where you will appear one week from today, and the number of your room' – Mr Crabtree without pencil or paper at hand pressed the numbers frantically into his memory – 'and the office will be completely prepared for you. The door will be open, and you will find two keys in a drawer of the desk: one for the door and one for the cabinet in the office. In the desk you will also find the list I mentioned, as well as the materials needed in making out your reports. In the cabinet you will find a stock of periodicals to start work on.'

'I beg your pardon,' said Mr Crabtree, 'but those reports . . .'

'They should contain every single item of interest about the corporations on your list, from business transactions to changes in personnel. And they must be mailed to me immediately upon your leaving the office each day. Is that clear?'

'Only one thing,' said Mr Crabtree. 'To whom – where do I mail them?'

'A pointless question,' said the voice sharply, much to Mr Crabtree's alarm. 'To the box number with which you are already familiar, of course.'

'Of course,' said Mr Crabtree.

'Now,' said the voice with a gratifying return to its original deliberate tones, 'the question of salary. I have given it a good deal of thought, since as you must realize, there are a number of factors involved. In the end, I let myself be guided by the ancient maxim: a good workman is worthy of his hire – you recall those words?'

'Yes,' said Mr Crabtree.

'And,' the voice said, 'a poor workman can be easily dispensed with. On that basis, I am prepared to offer you fifty-two dollars a week. Is that satisfactory?'

Mr Crabtree stared at the telephone dumbly and then recovered his voice. 'Very,' he gasped. 'Oh, very much so. I must confess I never . . .'

The voice brought him up sharply. 'But that is conditional, you understand. You will be – to use a rather clumsy term – on probation until you have proved yourself. Either the job is handled to perfection, or there is no job.'

Mr Crabtree felt his knees turn to water at the grim suggestion. 'I'll do my best,' he said. 'I most certainly will do my absolute best.'

'And,' the voice went on relentlessly, 'I attach great significance to the way you observe the confidential nature of your work. It is not to be discussed with anyone, and since the maintenance of your office and supplies lies entirely in my hands there can be no excuse for a defection. I have also removed temptation in the form of a telephone which you will *not* find on your desk. I hope I do not seem unjust in my abhorrence of the common practice where employees waste their time in idle conversation during working hours.'

Since the death of an only sister twenty years before, there was not a soul in the world who would have dreamed of calling Mr Crabtree to make any sort of conversation whatsoever; but he only said, 'No, sir. Absolutely not.'

'Then you are in agreement with all the terms we have discussed?'

'Yes, sir,' said Mr Crabtree.

'Any further questions?'

'One thing,' said Mr Crabtree. 'My salary. How . . .'

'It will reach you at the end of each week,' said the voice, 'in cash. Anything else?'

Mr Crabtree's mind was now a veritable logjam of questions, but he found it impossible to fix on any particular one. Before he could do so, the voice said crisply, 'Good luck, then,' and there was the click which told him his caller had hung up. It was only when he attempted to do the same that he discovered his hand had been clenched so tightly around the receiver that it cost him momentary anguish to disengage it.

It must be admitted that the first time Mr Crabtree approached the address given him, it would not have surprised him greatly to find no building there at all. But the building was there, reassuring in its immensity, teeming with occupants who packed the banks of elevators solidly, and, in the hallways, looked through him and scurried around him with efficient disinterest.

The office was there too, hidden away at the end of a devious corridor of its own on the very top floor, a fact called to Mr Crabtree's attention by a stairway across the corridor, which led up to an open door through which the flat grey of the sky could be seen.

The most impressive thing about the office was the CRABTREE'S AFFILIATED REPORTS boldly stenciled on the door. Opening the door, one entered an incredibly small and narrow room made even smaller by the massive dimensions of the furniture that crowded it. To the right, immediately inside the door, was a gigantic filing cabinet. Thrust tightly against it, but still so large that it utilized the remainder of the wall space on that side, was a huge, old-fashioned desk with a swivel chair before it.

The window set in the opposite wall was in keeping with the furniture. It was an immense window, broad and high, and its sill came barely above Mr Crabtree's knees. He felt a momentary qualm when he first glanced through it and saw the sheer dizzying drop below, the terrifying quality of which was heightened by the blind, windowless walls of the building directly across from him.

One look was enough; henceforth, Mr Crabtree kept the

bottom section of the window securely fastened and adjusted only the top section to his convenience.

The keys were in a desk drawer; pen, ink, a box of nibs, a deck of blotters, and a half-dozen other accessories more impressive than useful were in another drawer; a supply of stamps was at hand; and, most pleasant, there was a plentiful supply of stationery, each piece bearing the letterhead, *Crabtree's Affiliated Reports*, the number of the office, and the address of the building. In his delight at this discovery Mr Crabtree dashed off a few practice lines with some bold flourishes of the pen, and then, a bit alarmed at his own prodigality, carefully tore the sheet to minute shreds and dropped it into the wastebasket at his feet.

After that, his efforts were devoted wholly to the business at hand. The filing cabinet disgorged a dismayingly large file of publications which had to be pored over, line by line, and Mr Crabtree never finished studying a page without the harrowing sensation that he had somehow bypassed the mention of a name which corresponded to one on the typed list he had found, as promised, in the desk. Then he would retrace the entire page with an awful sense of dallying at his work, and groan when he came to the end of it without finding what he had not wanted to find in the first place.

It seemed to him at times that he could never possibly deplete the monstrous pile of periodicals before him. Whenever he sighed with pleasure at having made some headway, he would be struck with the gloomy foreknowledge that the next morning would find a fresh delivery of mail at his door and, consequently, more material to add to the pile.

There were, however, breaks in this depressing routine. One was the preparation of the daily report, a task which, somewhat to Mr Crabtree's surprise, he found himself learning to enjoy; the other was the prompt arrival each week of the sturdy envelope containing his salary down to the last dollar bill, although this was never quite the occasion for unalloyed pleasure it might have been.

Mr Crabtree would carefully slit open one end of the envelope, remove the money, count it, and place it neatly in his ancient wallet. Then he would poke trembling exploratory fingers into the envelope, driven by the fearful recollection of his past experience to look for the notice that would tell him his services were no longer required. That was always a bad moment, and it had the unfailing effect of leaving him ill and shaken until he could bury himself in his work again.

The work was soon part of him. He had ceased bothering with the typed list; every name on it was firmly imprinted in his mind, and there were restless nights when he could send himself off to sleep merely by repeating the list a few times. One name in particular had come to intrigue him, merited special attention. *Efficiency Instruments, Ltd* was unquestionably facing stormy weather. There had been drastic changes in personnel, talks of a merger, sharp fluctuations on the market.

It rather pleased Mr Crabtree to discover that with the passage of weeks into months each of the names on his list had taken on a vivid personality for him. *Amalgamated* was steady as a rock, stolid in its comfortable success. *Universal* was high-pitched, fidgety in its exploration of new techniques; and so on down the line. But *Efficiency Instruments, Ltd* was Mr Crabtree's pet project, and he had, more than once, nervously caught himself giving it perhaps a shade more attention than it warranted. He brought himself up sharply at such times; impartiality must be maintained, otherwise . . .

It came without any warning at all. He returned from lunch, punctual as ever, opened the door of the office, and knew he was standing face to face with his employer.

'Come in, Mr Crabtree,' said the clear, thin voice, 'and shut the door.'

Mr Crabtree closed the door and stood speechless.

'I must be a prepossessing figure,' said the visitor with a certain relish, 'to have such a potent effect on you. You know who I am, of course?'

To Mr Crabtree's numbed mind, the large, bulbous eyes fixed unwinkingly on him, the wide, flexible mouth, the body, short and round as a barrel, bore a horrifying resemblance to a frog sitting comfortably at the edge of a pond, with himself in the unhappy role of a fly hovering close by.

'I believe,' said Mr Crabtree shakily, 'that you are my employer, Mr . . . Mr . . .'

A stout forefinger nudged Mr Crabtree's ribs playfully. 'As long as the bills are paid, the name is unimportant, eh, Mr Crabtree? However, for the sake of expedience, let me be known to you as – say – George Spelvin. Have you ever encountered the ubiquitous Mr Spelvin in your journeyings, Mr Crabtree?'

'I'm afraid not,' said Mr Crabtree miserably.

'Then you are not a playgoer, and that is all to the good. And if I may hazard a guess, you are not one to indulge yourself in literature or the cinema either?'

'I do try to keep up with the daily newspaper,' said Mr Crabtree stoutly. 'There's a good deal to read in it, you know, Mr Spelvin, and it's not always easy, considering my work here, to find time for other diversions. That is, if a man wants to keep up with the newspapers.'

The corners of the wide mouth lifted in what Mr Crabtree hoped was a smile. 'That is precisely what I hoped to hear you say. Facts, Mr Crabtree, facts! I wanted a man with a single-minded interest in facts, and your words now as well as your application to your work tell me I have found him in you. I am very gratified, Mr Crabtree.'

Mr Crabtree found that the blood was thumping pleasantly through his veins. 'Thank you. Thank you again, Mr Spelvin. I know I've been trying very hard, but I didn't know whether . . . Won't you sit down?' Mr Crabtree tried to get his arm around the barrel before him in order to swing the chair into position, and failed. 'The office is a bit small. But very comfortable,' he stammered hastily.

'I am sure it is suitable,' said Mr Spelvin. He stepped back until he was almost fixed against the window and indicated the chair. 'Now I should like you to be seated, Mr Crabtree, while I discuss the matter I came on.'

Under the spell of that commanding hand Mr Crabtree sank into the chair and pivoted it until he faced the window and the squat figure outlined against it. 'If there is any question about today's report,' he said, 'I am afraid it isn't complete yet. There were some notes on *Efficiency Instruments* . . .'

Mr Spelvin waved the matter aside indifferently. 'I am not here to discuss that,' he said slowly. 'I am here to find the answer to a problem which confronts me. And I rely on you, Mr Crabtree, to help me find that answer.'

'A problem?' Mr Crabtree found himself warm with a sense of well-being. 'I'll do everything I can to help, Mr Spelvin. Everything I possibly can.'

The bulging eyes probed his worriedly. 'Then tell me this, Mr Crabtree: how would you go about killing a man?'

'I?' said Mr Crabtree. 'How would I go . . . I'm afraid I don't understand, Mr Spelvin.'

'I said,' Mr Spelvin repeated, carefully stressing each word, 'how would you go about killing a man?'

Mr Crabtree's jaw dropped. 'But I couldn't. I wouldn't. That,' he said, 'that would be murder!'

'Exactly,' said Mr Spelvin.

'But you're joking,' said Mr Crabtree, and tried to laugh, without managing to get more than a thin, breathless wheeze through his constricted throat. Even that pitiful effort was cut short by the sight of the stony face before him. 'I'm terribly sorry, Mr Spelvin, terribly sorry. You can see it's not the customary . . . it's not the kind of thing . . .'

'Mr Crabtree. In the financial journals you study so assiduously you will find my name – my own name – repeated endlessly. I have a finger in many pies, Mr Crabtree, and it always prods the plum. To use the more blatant adjectives, I am wealthy and powerful far beyond your wildest dreams – granting that you are capable of wild dreams – and a man does not attain that position by idling his time away on pointless jokes, or in passing the time of day with hirelings. My time is limited, Mr Crabtree. If you cannot answer my question, say so, and let it go at that!'

'I don't believe I can,' said Mr Crabtree piteously.

'You should have said that at once,' Mr Spelvin replied, 'and spared me my moment of choler. Frankly, I did not believe you could answer my question, and if you had, it would have been a most disillusioning experience. You see, Mr Crabtree, I envy, I deeply envy, your serenity of existence where such questions never even enter. Unfortunately, I am not in that position. At one point in my career, I made a mistake, the only mistake that has ever marked my rise to fortune. This, in time, came to the attention of a man who combines ruthlessness and cleverness to a dangerous degree, and I have been in the power of that man ever since. He is, in fact, a blackmailer, a common blackmailer who has come to set too high a price on his wares, and so, must now pay for them himself.'

'You intend,' said Mr Crabtree hoarsely, 'to kill him?'

Mr Spelvin threw out a plump hand in protest. 'If a fly rested on the palm of that hand,' he said sharply, 'I could not find the power to close my fingers and crush the life from it. To be blunt, Mr Crabtree, I am totally incapable of committing an act of violence, and while that may be an admirable quality in many ways, it is merely an embarrassment now, since the man must certainly be killed.' Mr Spelvin paused. 'Nor is this a task for a paid assassin. If I resorted to one, I would most assuredly be exchanging one blackmailer for another, and that is altogether impractical.' Mr Spelvin paused again. 'So, Mr Crabtree, you can see there is only one conclusion to be drawn: the responsibility for destroying my tormentor rests entirely on you.'

'Me!' cried Mr Crabtree. 'Why, I could never – no, never!'

'Oh, come,' said Mr Spelvin brusquely. 'You are working yourself into a dangerous state. Before you carry it any further, Mr Crabtree, I should like to make clear that your failure to carry out my request means that when you leave this office today, you leave it permanently. I cannot tolerate an employee who does not understand his position.'

'Not tolerate!' said Mr Crabtree. 'But that is not right, that is not right at all, Mr Spelvin. I've been working hard.' His spectacles blurred. He fumbled with them, cleaned them carefully, replaced them on his nose. 'And to leave me with such a secret. I don't see it; I don't see it at all. Why,' he said in alarm, 'it's a matter for the police!'

To his horror Mr Spelvin's face turned alarmingly red, and the huge body started to shake in a convulsion of mirth that rang deafeningly through the room.

'Forgive me,' he managed to gasp at last. 'Forgive me, my dear fellow. I was merely visualizing the scene in which you go to the authorities and tell them of the incredible demands put upon you by your employer.'

'You must understand,' said Mr Crabtree, 'I am not threat-ening you, Mr Spelvin. It is only . . .'

'Threatening me? Mr Crabtree, tell me, what connection do you think there is between us in the eyes of the world?'

'Connection? I work for you, Mr Spelvin. I'm an employee here. I . . .'

Mr Spelvin smiled blandly. 'What a curious delusion,' he said, 'when one can see that you are merely a shabby little man engaged in some pitiful little enterprise that could not possibly be of interest to me.'

'But you employed me yourself, Mr Spelvin! I wrote a letter of application!'

'You did,' said Mr Spelvin, 'but unfortunately the position was already filled, as I informed you in my very polite letter of explanation. You look incredulous, Mr Crabtree, so let me inform you that your letter and a copy of my reply rest securely in my files should the matter ever be called to question.'

'But this office! These furnishings! My subscriptions!'

'Mr Crabtree, Mr Crabtree,' said Mr Spelvin, shaking his head heavily, 'did *you* ever question the source of your weekly income? The manager of this building, the dealers in supplies, the publishers who deliver their journals to you were no more interested in my identity than you were. It is, I grant, a bit irregular for me to deal exclusively in currency sent through the mails in your name, but have no fears for me, Mr Crabtree. Prompt payments are the opiate of the businessman.'

'But my reports!' said Mr Crabtree, who was seriously starting to doubt his own existence.

'To be sure, the reports. I daresay that the ingenious Mr Crabtree, after receiving my unfavorable reply to his application, decided to go into business for himself. He thereupon instituted a service of financial reports and even attempted to make *me* one of his clients! I rebuffed him sharply, I can tell you (I have his first report *and* a copy of my reply to it), but he foolishly persists in his efforts. Foolishly, I say, because his reports are absolutely useless to me; I have no interest in any of the corporations he discusses, and why he should imagine I would have is beyond my reckoning. Frankly, I suspect the man is an eccentric of the worst type, but since I have had dealings with many of that type

I merely disregard him, and destroy his daily reports on their arrival.'

'Destroy them?' said Mr Crabtree, stupefied.

'You have no cause for complaint, I hope,' said Mr Spelvin with some annoyance. 'To find a man of your character, Mr Crabtree, it was necessary for me to specify *hard work* in my advertisement. I am only living up to my part of the bargain in providing it, and I fail to see where the final disposition of it is any of your concern.'

'A man of my character,' echoed Mr Crabtree helplessly, 'to commit murder?'

'And why not?' The wide mouth tightened ominously. 'Let me enlighten you, Mr Crabtree. I have spent a pleasant and profitable share of my life in observing the human species, as a scientist might study insects under glass. And I have come to one conclusion, Mr Crabtree, one above all others which has contributed to the making of my own success. I have come to the conclusion that to the majority of our species it is the function that is important, not the motives, nor the consequences.

'My advertisement, Mr Crabtree, was calculated to enlist the services of one like that; a perfect representative of the type, in fact. From the moment you answered that advertisement to the present, you have been living up to all my expectations: you have been functioning flawlessly with no thought of either motive or consequence.

'Now murder has been made part of your function. I have honored you with an explanation of its motives; the consequences are clearly defined. Either you continue to function as you always have, or, to put it in a nutshell, you are out of a job.'

'A job!' said Mr Crabtree wildly. 'What does a job matter to a man in prison! Or to a man being hanged!'

'Oh, come,' remarked Mr Spelvin placidly. 'Do you think I'd lead you into a trap which might snare me as well? I am afraid you are being obtuse, my dear man. If you are not, you must realize clearly that my own security is tied in the same package as yours. And nothing less than your permanent presence in this office and your steadfast application to your work is the guarantee of that security.'

'That may be easy to say when you're hiding under an assumed name,' said Mr Crabtree hollowly.

'I assure you, Mr Crabtree, my position in the world is such that my identity can be unearthed with small effort. But I must also remind you that should you carry out my request you will then be a criminal and, consequently, very discreet.

'On the other hand, if you do not carry out my request – and you have complete freedom of choice in that – any charges you may bring against me will be dangerous only to you. The world, Mr Crabtree, knows nothing about our relationship, and nothing about my affair with the gentleman who has been victimizing me and must now become my victim. Neither his demise nor your charges could ever touch me, Mr Crabtree.

'Discovering my identity, as I said, would not be difficult. But using that information, Mr Crabtree, can only lead you to a prison or an institution for the deranged.'

Mr Crabtree felt the last dregs of his strength seeping from him. 'You have thought of everything,' he said.

'Everything, Mr Crabtree. When you entered my scheme of things, it was only to put my plan into operation; but long before that I was hard at work weighing, measuring, evaluating every step of that plan. For example, this room, this very room, has been chosen only after a long and weary search as perfect for my purpose. Its furnishings have been selected and arranged to further that purpose. How? Let me explain that.

'When you are seated at your desk, a visitor is confined to the space I now occupy at the window. The visitor is, of course, the gentleman in question. He will enter and stand here with the window *entirely open* behind him. He will ask you for an envelope a friend has left. This envelope,' said Mr Spelvin, tossing one to the desk. 'You will have the envelope in your desk, will find it, and hand it to him. Then, since he is a very methodical man (I have learned that well), he will place the envelope in the inside pocket of his jacket – and at that moment one good thrust will send him out the window. The entire operation should take less than a minute. Immediately after that,' Mr Spelvin said calmly, 'you will close the window to the bottom and return to your work.'

'Someone,' whispered Mr Crabtree, 'the police . . .'

'Will find,' said Mr Spelvin, 'the body of some poor unfortunate who climbed the stairs across the hallway and hurled himself from the roof above. And they will know this because inside that envelope secured in his pocket is not what the gentleman in question expects to find there, but a neatly typewritten note explaining the sad affair and its motives, an apology for any inconvenience caused (suicides are great ones for apologies, Mr Crabtree), and a most pathetic plea for a quick and peaceful burial. And,' said Mr Spelvin, gently touching his fingertips together, 'I do not doubt he will get it.'

'What,' Mr Crabtree said, 'what if something went wrong? If the man opened the letter when it was given to him. Or . . . if something like that happened?'

Mr Spelvin shrugged. 'In that case the gentleman in question would merely make his way off quietly and approach me directly about the matter. Realize, Mr Crabtree, that anyone in my friend's line of work expects occasional little attempts like this, and, while he may not be inclined to think them amusing, he would hardly venture into some precipitous action that might kill the goose who lays the golden eggs. No, Mr Crabtree, if such a possibility as you suggest comes to pass, it means only that I must reset my trap, and even more ingeniously.'

Mr Spelvin drew a heavy watch from his pocket, studied it, then replaced it carefully. 'My time is growing short, Mr Crabtree. It is not that I find your company wearing, but my man will be making his appearance shortly, and matters must be entirely in your hands at that time. All I require of you is this: when he arrives, the window will be open.' Mr Spelvin thrust it up hard and stood for a moment looking appreciatively at the drop below. 'The envelope will be in your desk.' He opened the drawer and dropped it in, then closed the drawer firmly. 'And at the moment of decision, you are free to act one way or the other.'

'Free?' said Mr Crabtree. 'You said he would ask for the envelope!'

'He will. He will, indeed. But if you indicate that you know nothing about it, he will quietly make his departure, and later communicate with me. And that will be, in effect, a notice of your resignation from my employ.'

Mr Spelvin went to the door and rested one hand on the knob. 'However,' he said, 'if I do *not* hear from him, that will assure me that you have successfully completed your term of probation and are to be henceforth regarded as a capable and faithful employee.'

'But the reports!' said Mr Crabtree. 'You destroy them . . .'

'Of course,' said Mr Spelvin, a little surprised. 'But you will continue with your work and send the reports to me as you have always done. I assure you, it does not matter to me that they are meaningless, Mr Crabtree. They are part of a pattern, and your adherence to that pattern, as I have already told you, is the best assurance of my own security.'

The door opened, closed quietly, and Mr Crabtree found himself alone in the room.

The shadow of the building opposite lay heavily on his desk. Mr Crabtree looked at his watch, found himself unable to read it in the growing dimness of the room, and stood up to pull the cord of the light over his head. At that moment a peremptory knock sounded on the door.

'Come in,' said Mr Crabtree.

The door opened on two figures. One was a small, dapper man, the other a bulky police officer who loomed imposingly over his companion. The small man stepped into the office and, with the gesture of a magician pulling a rabbit from a hat, withdrew a large wallet from his pocket, snapped it open to show the gleam of a badge, closed it, and slid it back into his pocket.

'Police,' said the man succinctly. 'Name's Sharpe.'

Mr Crabtree nodded politely. 'Yes?' he said.

'Hope you don't mind,' said Sharpe briskly. 'Just a few questions.'

As if this were a cue, the large policeman came up with an efficient-looking notebook and the stub of a pencil, and stood there poised for action. Mr Crabtree peered over his spectacles at the notebook, and through them at the diminutive Sharpe. 'No,' said Mr Crabtree, 'not at all.'

'You're Crabtree?' said Sharpe, and Mr Crabtree started, then remembered the name on the door.

'Yes,' he said.

Sharpe's cold eyes flickered over him and then took in the room with a contemptuous glance. 'This your office?'

'Yes,' said Mr Crabtree.

'You in it all afternoon?'

'Since one o'clock,' said Mr Crabtree. 'I go to lunch at twelve and return at one promptly.'

'I'll bet,' said Sharpe, then nodded over his shoulder. 'That door open any time this afternoon?'

'It's always closed while I am working,' said Mr Crabtree.

'Then you wouldn't be able to see anybody going up that stairs across the hall there.'

'No,' replied Mr Crabtree, 'I wouldn't.'

Sharpe looked at the desk, then ran a reflective thumb along his jaw. 'I guess you wouldn't be in a position to see anything happening outside the window either.'

'No, indeed,' said Mr Crabtree. 'Not while I'm at work.'

'Now,' said Sharpe, 'did you *hear* something outside of that window this afternoon? Something out of the ordinary, I mean?'

'Out of the ordinary?' repeated Mr Crabtree vaguely.

'A yell. Somebody yelling. Anything like that?'

Mr Crabtree puckered his brow. 'Why, yes,' he said, 'yes, I did. And not long ago either. It sounded as if someone had been startled – or frightened. Quite loud, too. It's always so quiet here I couldn't help hearing it.'

Sharpe looked over his shoulder and nodded at the policeman who closed his notebook slowly. 'That ties it up,' said Sharpe. 'The guy made the jump, and the second he did it he changed his mind, so he came down hollering all the way. Well,' he said, turning to Mr Crabtree in a burst of confidence, 'I guess you've got a right to know what's going on here. About an hour ago some character jumped off that roof right over your head. Clear case of suicide, note in his pocket and everything, but we like to get all the facts we can.'

'Do you know,' said Mr Crabtree, 'who he was?'

Sharpe shrugged. 'Another guy with too many troubles. Young, good-looking, pretty snappy dresser. Only thing beats me is why a guy who could afford to dress like that would figure he has more troubles than he can handle.'

The policeman in uniform spoke for the first time. 'That letter he left,' he said deferentially, 'sounds like he was a little crazy.'

'You have to be a little crazy to take that way out,' said Sharpe.

'You're a long time dead,' said the policeman heavily.

Sharpe held the doorknob momentarily. 'Sorry to bother you,' he said to Mr Crabtree, 'but you know how it is. Anyhow, you're lucky in a way. Couple of girls downstairs saw him go by and passed right out.' He winked as he closed the door behind him.

Mr Crabtree stood looking at the closed door until the sound of heavy footsteps passed out of hearing. Then he seated himself in the chair and pulled himself closer to the desk. Some magazines and sheets of stationery lay there in mild disarray, and he arranged the magazines in a neat pile, stacking them so that all corners met precisely. Mr Crabtree picked up his pen, dipped it into the ink bottle, and steadied the paper before him with his other hand.

*Efficiency Instruments, Ltd*, he wrote carefully, *shows increased activity* . . .

# Death on
# Christmas Eve

As a child I had been vastly impressed by the Boerum house. It was fairly new then, and glossy; a gigantic pile of Victorian rickrack, fretwork, and stained glass, flung together in such chaotic profusion that it was hard to encompass in one glance. Standing before it this early Christmas Eve, however, I could find no echo of that youthful impression. The gloss was long since gone; woodwork, glass, metal, all were merged to a dreary gray, and the shades behind the windows were drawn completely so that the house seemed to present a dozen blindly staring eyes to the passerby.

When I rapped my stick sharply on the door, Celia opened it.

'There is a doorbell right at hand,' she said. She was still wearing the long outmoded and badly wrinkled black dress she must have dragged from her mother's trunk, and she looked, more than ever, the image of old Katrin in her later years: the scrawny body, the tightly compressed lips, the colorless hair drawn back hard enough to pull every wrinkle out of her forehead. She reminded me of a steel trap ready to snap down on anyone who touched her incautiously.

I said, 'I am aware that the doorbell has been disconnected, Celia,' and walked past her into the hallway. Without turning my head, I knew that she was glaring at me; then she sniffed once, hard and dry, and flung the door shut. Instantly we were in a murky dimness that made the smell of dry rot about me stick in my throat. I fumbled for the wall switch, but Celia said sharply, 'No! This is not the time for lights.'

I turned to the white blur of her face, which was all I could see of her. 'Celia,' I said, 'spare me the dramatics.'

'There has been a death in this house. You know that.'

'I have good reason to,' I said, 'but your performance now does not impress me.'

'She was my own brother's wife. She was very dear to me.'

I took a step toward her in the murk and rested my stick on her shoulder. 'Celia,' I said, 'as your family's lawyer, let me give you a word of advice. The inquest is over and done with, and you've been cleared. But nobody believed a word of your precious sentiments then, and nobody ever will. Keep that in mind, Celia.'

She jerked away so sharply that the stick almost fell from my hand. 'Is that what you have come to tell me?' she said.

I said, 'I came because I knew your brother would want to see me today. And if you don't mind my saying so, I suggest that you keep to yourself while I talk to him. I don't want any scenes.'

'Then keep away from him yourself!' she cried. 'He was at the inquest. He saw them clear my name. In a little while he will forget the evil he thinks of me. Keep away from him so that he can forget.'

She was at her infuriating worst, and to break the spell I started up the dark stairway, one hand warily on the balustrade. But I heard her follow eagerly behind, and in some eerie way it seemed as if she were not addressing me, but answering the groaning of the stairs under our feet.

'When he comes to me,' she said, 'I will forgive him. At first I was not sure, but now I know. I prayed for guidance, and I was told that life is too short for hatred. So when he comes to me I will forgive him.'

I reached the head of the stairway and almost went sprawling. I swore in annoyance as I righted myself. 'If you're not going to use lights, Celia, you should, at least, keep the way clear. Why don't you get that stuff out of here?'

'Ah,' she said, 'those are all poor Jessie's belongings. It hurts Charlie so to see anything of hers, I knew this would be the best thing to do – to throw all her things out.'

Then a note of alarm entered her voice. 'But you won't tell Charlie, will you? You won't tell him?' she said, and kept repeating it on a higher and higher note as I moved away from her, so that when I entered Charlie's room and closed the door behind me it almost sounded as if I had left a bat chittering behind me.

As in the rest of the house, the shades in Charlie's room were drawn to their full length. But a single bulb in the chandelier overhead dazzled me momentarily, and I had to look twice before I saw Charlie sprawled out on his bed with an arm flung over his eyes. Then he slowly came to his feet and peered at me.

'Well,' he said at last, nodding toward the door, 'she didn't give you any light to come up, did she?'

'No,' I said, 'but I know the way.'

'She's like a mole,' he said. 'Gets around better in the dark than I do in the light. She'd rather have it that way too. Otherwise she might look into a mirror and be scared of what she sees there.'

'Yes,' I said, 'she seems to be taking it very hard.'

He laughed short and sharp as a sea-lion barking. 'That's because she's still got the fear in her. All you get out of her now is how she loved Jessie, and how sorry she is. Maybe she figures if she says it enough, people might get to believe it. But give her a little time and she'll be the same old Celia again.'

I dropped my hat and stick on the bed and laid my overcoat beside them. Then I drew out a cigar and waited until he fumbled for a match and helped me to a light. His hand shook so violently that he had hard going for a moment and muttered angrily at himself. Then I slowly exhaled a cloud of smoke toward the ceiling, and waited.

Charlie was Celia's junior by five years, but seeing him then it struck me that he looked a dozen years older. His hair was the same pale blond, almost colorless so that it was hard to tell if it was graying or not. But his cheeks wore a fine, silvery stubble, and there were huge blue-black pouches under his eyes. And where Celia was braced against a rigid and uncompromising backbone, Charlie sagged, standing or sitting, as if he were on the verge of falling forward. He stared at me and tugged uncertainly at the limp mustache that drooped past the corners of his mouth.

'You know what I wanted to see you about, don't you?' he said.

'I can imagine,' I said, 'but I'd rather have you tell me.'

'I'll put it to you straight,' he said. 'It's Celia. I want to see her get what's coming to her. Not jail. I want the law to take her and kill her, and I want to be there to watch it.'

A large ash dropped to the floor, and I ground it carefully into the rug with my foot. I said, 'You were at the inquest, Charlie; you saw what happened. Celia's cleared, and unless additional evidence can be produced, she stays cleared.'

'Evidence! My God, what more evidence does anyone need! They were arguing hammer and tongs at the top of the stairs. Celia just grabbed Jessie and threw her down to the bottom and killed her. That's murder, isn't it? Just the same as if she used a gun or poison or whatever she would have used if the stairs weren't handy?'

I sat down wearily in the old leather-bound armchair there and studied the new ash that was forming on my cigar. 'Let me show it to you from the legal angle,' I said, and the monotone of my voice must have made it sound like a well-memorized formula. 'First, there were no witnesses.'

'I heard Jessie scream and I heard her fall,' he said doggedly, 'and when I ran out and found her there, I heard Celia slam her door shut right then. She pushed Jessie and then scuttered like a rat to be out of the way.'

'But you didn't *see* anything. And since Celia claims that she wasn't on the scene, there were no witnesses. In other words, Celia's story cancels out your story, and since you weren't an eyewitness you can't very well make a murder out of what might have been an accident.'

He slowly shook his head.

'You don't believe that,' he said. 'You don't really believe that. Because if you do, you can get out now and never come near me again.'

'It doesn't matter what I believe; I'm showing you the legal aspects of the case. What about motivation? What did Celia have to gain from Jessie's death? Certainly there's no money or property involved; she's as financially independent as you are.'

Charlie sat down on the edge of his bed and leaned toward me with his hands resting on his knees. 'No,' he whispered, 'there's no money or property in it.'

I spread my arms helplessly. 'You see?'

'But you know what it is,' he said. 'It's me. First, it was the old lady with her heart trouble any time I tried to call my soul my own. Then when she died and I thought I was free, it was Celia. From the time I got up in the morning until I went to bed at night, it was Celia every step of the way. She never had a husband or a baby – but she had me!'

I said quietly, 'She's your sister, Charlie. She loves you,' and he laughed that same unpleasant, short laugh.

'She loves me like ivy loves a tree. When I think back now, I still can't see how she did it, but she would just look at me a certain way and all the strength would go out of me. And it was like that until I met Jessie ... I remember the day I brought Jessie home, and told Celia we were married. She swallowed it, but that look was in her eyes the same as it must have been when she pushed Jessie down those stairs.'

I said, 'But you admitted at the inquest that you never saw her threaten Jessie or do anything to hurt her.'

'Of course I never *saw*! But when Jessie would go around sick to her heart every day and not say a word, or cry in bed every night and not tell me why, I knew damn well what was going on. You know what Jessie was like. She wasn't so smart or pretty, but she was good-hearted as the day was long, and she was crazy about me. And when she started losing all that sparkle in her after only a month, I knew why. I talked to her and I talked to Celia, and both of them just shook their heads. All I could do was go around in circles, but when it happened, when I saw Jessie lying there, it didn't surprise me. Maybe that sounds queer, but it didn't surprise me at all.'

'I don't think it surprised anyone who knows Celia,' I said, 'but you can't make a case out of that.'

He beat his fist against his knee and rocked from side to side. 'What can I do?' he said. 'That's what I need you for – to tell me what to do. All my life I never got around to doing anything because of her. That's what she's banking on now – that I won't do anything, and that she'll get away with it. Then after a while, things'll settle down, and we'll be right back where we started from.'

I said, 'Charlie, you're getting yourself all worked up to no end.' He stood up and stared at the door, and then at me. 'But I can do something,' he whispered. 'Do you know what?'

He waited with the bright expectancy of one who has asked a clever riddle that he knows will stump the listener. I stood up facing him, and shook my head slowly. 'No,' I said. 'Whatever you're thinking, put it out of your mind.'

'Don't mix me up,' he said. 'You know you can get away with murder if you're as smart as Celia. Don't you think I'm as smart as Celia?'

I caught his shoulders tightly. 'For God's sake, Charlie,' I said, 'don't start talking like that.'

He pulled out of my hands and went staggering back against the wall. His eyes were bright, and his teeth showed behind his drawn lips. 'What should I do?' he cried. 'Forget everything now that Jessie is dead and buried? Sit here until Celia gets tired of being afraid of me and kills me too?'

My years and girth had betrayed me in that little tussle with him, and I found myself short of dignity and breath. 'I'll tell you one thing,' I said. 'You haven't been out of this house since the inquest. It's about time you got out, if only to walk the streets and look around you.'

'And have everybody laugh at me as I go!'

'Try it,' I said, 'and see. Al Sharp said that some of your friends would be at his bar and grill tonight, and he'd like to see you there. That's my advice – for whatever it's worth.'

'It's not worth anything,' said Celia. The door had been opened, and she stood there rigid, her eyes narrowed against the light in the room. Charlie turned toward her, the muscles of his jaw knotting and unknotting.

'Celia,' he said, 'I told you never to come into this room!'

Her face remained impassive. 'I'm not in it. I came to tell you that your dinner is ready.'

He took a menacing step toward her. 'Did you have your ear at that door long enough to hear everything I said? Or should I repeat it for you?'

'I heard an ungodly and filthy thing,' she said quietly, 'an invitation to drink and roister while this house is in mourning. I think I have every right to object to that.'

He looked at her incredulously and had to struggle for words.

'Celia,' he said, 'tell me you don't mean that! Only the blackest hypocrite alive or someone insane could say what you've just said and mean it.'

That struck a spark in her. 'Insane!' she cried. '*You* dare use that word? Locked in your room, talking to yourself, thinking heaven knows what!' She turned to me suddenly. 'You've talked to him. You ought to know. Is it possible that—'

'He is as sane as you, Celia,' I said heavily.

'Then he should know that one doesn't drink in saloons at a time like this. How could you ask him to do it?'

She flung the question at me with such an air of malicious triumph that I completely forgot myself. 'If you weren't preparing to throw out Jessie's belongings, Celia, I would take that question seriously!'

It was a reckless thing to say, and I had instant cause to regret it. Before I could move, Charlie was past me and had Celia's arms pinned in a paralyzing grip.

'Did you dare to go into her room?' he raged, shaking her savagely. 'Tell me!' And then, getting an immediate answer from the panic in her face, he dropped her arms as if they were red hot, and stood there sagging with his head bowed.

Celia reached out a placating hand toward him. 'Charlie,' she whimpered, 'don't you see? Having her things around bothers you. I only wanted to help you.'

'Where are her things?'

'By the stairs, Charlie. Everything is there.'

He started down the hallway, and with the sound of his uncertain footsteps moving away I could feel my heartbeat slowing down to its normal tempo. Celia turned to look at me, and there was such a raging hatred in her face that I knew only a desperate need to get out of that house at once. I took my things from the bed and started past her, but she barred the door.

'Do you see what you've done?' she whispered hoarsely. 'Now I will have to pack them all over again. It tires me, but I will have to pack them all over again just because of you.'

'That is entirely up to you, Celia,' I said coldly.

'You,' she said. 'You old fool. It should have been you along with her when I—'

I dropped my stick sharply on her shoulder and could feel her wince under it. 'As your lawyer, Celia,' I said, 'I advise you to exercise your tongue only during your sleep, when you can't be held accountable for what you say.'

She said no more, but I made sure she stayed safely in front of me until I was out in the street again.

From the Boerum house to Al Sharp's Bar and Grill was only a few minutes' walk, and I made it in good time, grateful for the sting of the clear winter air in my face. Al was alone behind the bar, busily polishing glasses, and when he saw me enter he greeted me cheerfully. 'Merry Christmas, counselor,' he said.

'Same to you,' I said, and watched him place a comfortable-looking bottle and a pair of glasses on the bar.

'You're regular as the seasons, counselor,' said Al, pouring out two stiff ones. 'I was expecting you along right about now.'

We drank to each other and Al leaned confidingly on the bar. 'Just come from there?'

'Yes,' I said.

'See Charlie?'

'And Celia,' I said.

'Well,' said Al, 'that's nothing exceptional. I've seen her too when she comes by to do some shopping. Runs along with her head down and that black shawl over it like she was being chased by something. I guess she is at that.'

'I guess she is,' I said.

'But Charlie, he's the one. Never see him around at all. Did you tell him I'd like to see him some time?'

'Yes,' I said. 'I told him.'

'What did he say?'

'Nothing. Celia said it was wrong for him to come here while he was in mourning.'

Al whistled softly and expressively, and twirled a forefinger at his forehead. 'Tell me,' he said, 'do you think it's safe for them to be alone together like they are? I mean, the way things stand, and the way Charlie feels, there could be another case of trouble there.'

'It looked like it for a while tonight,' I said. 'But it blew over.'

'Until next time.' said Al.

'I'll be there,' I said.

Al looked at me and shook his head. 'Nothing changes in that house,' he said. 'Nothing at all. That's why you can figure out all the answers in advance. That's how I knew you'd be standing here right about now talking to me about it.'

I could still smell the dry rot of the house in my nostrils, and I knew it would take days before I could get it out of my clothes.

'This is one day I'd like to cut out of the calendar permanently,' I said.

'And leave them alone to their troubles. It would serve them right.'

'They're not alone,' I said. 'Jessie is with them. Jessie will always be with them until that house and everything in it is gone.'

Al frowned. 'It's the queerest thing that ever happened in this town, all right. The house all black, her running through the streets like something hunted, him lying there in that room with only the walls to look at, for – when was it Jessie took that fall, counselor?'

By shifting my eyes a little I could see in the mirror behind Al the reflection of my own face: ruddy, deep jowled, a little incredulous.

'Twenty years ago,' I heard myself saying. 'Just twenty years ago tonight.'

# The Orderly World
## of Mr Appleby

M r Appleby was a small, prim man who wore rimless spectacles, parted his graying hair in the middle, and took sober pleasure in pointing out that there was no room in the properly organized life for the operations of Chance. Consequently, when he decided that the time had come to investigate the most efficient methods for disposing of his wife he knew where to look.

He found the book, a text on forensic medicine, on the shelf of a second-hand bookshop among several volumes of like topic, and since all but one were in a distressingly shabby and dog-eared state which offended him to his very core, he chose the only one in reasonably good condition. Most of the cases it presented, he discovered on closer examination, were horrid studies of the results (vividly illustrated) of madness and lust – enough to set any decent man wondering at the number of monsters inhabiting the earth. One case, however, seemed to be exactly what he was looking for, and this he made the object of his most intensive study.

It was the case of Mrs X (the book was replete with Mrs X's, and Mr Y's, and Miss Z's) who died after what was presumably an accidental fall on a scatter rug in her home. However, a lawyer representing the interests of the late lamented charged her husband with murder, and at a coroner's investigation was attempting to prove his charge when the accused abruptly settled matters by dropping dead of a heart attack.

All this was of moderate interest to Mr Appleby whose motive, a desire to come into the immediate possession of his wife's estate, was strikingly similar to the alleged motive of Mrs X's husband. But more important were the actual details of the case. Mrs X had been in the act of bringing him a glass of water, said her husband, when the scatter rug, as scatter rugs will, had suddenly slipped from under her feet.

In rebuttal the indefatigable lawyer had produced a medical authority who made clear through a number of charts (all of which were handsomely reproduced in the book) that in the act of receiving the glass of water it would have been child's play for the husband to lay one hand behind his wife's shoulder, another hand along her jaw, and with a sudden thrust produce the same drastic results as the fall on the scatter rug, without leaving any clues as to the nature of his crime.

It should be made clear now that in studying these charts and explanations relentlessly Mr Appleby was not acting the part of the greedy man going to any lengths to appease that greed. True, it was money he wanted, but it was money for the maintenance of what he regarded as a holy cause. And that was the Shop: *Appleby, Antiques and Curios.*

The Shop was the sun of Mr Appleby's universe. He had bought it twenty years before with the pittance left by his father, and at best it provided him with a poor living. At worst – and it was usually at worst – it had forced him to draw on his mother's meager store of good will and capital. Since his mother was not one to give up a penny lightly, the Shop brought about a series of pitched battles which, however, always saw it the victor – since in the last analysis the Shop was to Mr Appleby what Mr Appleby was to his mother.

This unhappy triangle was finally shattered by his mother's death, at which time Mr Appleby discovered that she had played a far greater role in maintaining his orderly little world than he had hitherto realized. This concerned not only the money she occasionally gave him, but also his personal habits.

He ate lightly and warily. His mother had been adept at toasting and boiling his meals to perfection. His nerves were violently shaken if anything in the house was out of place, and she had been a living assurance he would be spared this. Her death, therefore, left a vast and uncomfortable gap in his life, and in studying methods to fill it he was led to contemplate marriage, and then to the act itself.

His wife was a pale, thin-lipped woman so much like his

mother in appearance and gesture that sometimes on her entrance into a room he was taken aback by the resemblance. In only one respect did she fail him: she could not understand the significance of the Shop, nor his feelings about it. That was disclosed the first time he broached the subject of a small loan that would enable him to meet some business expenses.

Mrs Appleby had been well in the process of withering on the vine when her husband-to-be had proposed to her, but to give her full due she was not won by the mere prospect of finally making a marriage. Actually, though she would have blushed at such a blunt statement of her secret thought, it was the large, mournful eyes behind his rimless spectacles that turned the trick, promising, as they did, hidden depths of emotion neatly garbed in utter respectability. When she learned very soon after her wedding that the hidden depths were evidently too well hidden ever to be explored by her, she shrugged the matter off and turned to boiling and toasting his meals with good enough grace. The knowledge that the impressive *Appleby, Antiques and Curios* was a hollow shell she took in a different spirit.

She made some brisk investigations and then announced her findings to Mr Appleby with some heat.

'Antiques and curios!' she said shrilly. 'Why, that whole collection of stuff is nothing but a pile of junk. Just a bunch of worthless dust-catchers, that's all it is!'

What she did not understand was that these objects, which to the crass and commercial eye might seem worthless, were to Mr Appleby the stuff of life itself. The Shop had grown directly from his childhood mania for collecting, assorting, labeling, and preserving anything he could lay his hands on. And the value of any item in the Shop increased proportionately with the length of time he possessed it; whether a cracked imitation of Sévres, or clumsily faked Chippendale, or rusty saber made no difference. Each piece had won a place for itself; a permanent, immutable place, as far as Mr Appleby was concerned; and strangely enough it was the sincere agony he suffered in giving up a piece that led to the few sales he made. The customer who was uncertain of values had only to get a glimpse of this agony to be convinced that he was getting a rare bargain. Fortunately, no customer could have imagined for a moment that it was the thought of the empty space left by the object's departure – the brief disorder which the emptiness made – and not a passion for the object itself that drew Mr Appleby's pinched features into a mask of pain.

So, not understanding, Mrs Appleby took an unsympathetic tack. 'You'll get my mite when I'm dead and gone,' she said, 'and only when I'm dead and gone.'

Thus unwittingly she tried herself, was found wanting, and it only remained for sentence to be executed. When the time came Mr Appleby applied the lessons he had gleaned from his invaluable textbook, and found them accurate in every detail. It was over quickly, quietly, and, outside of a splash of water on his trousers, neatly. The Medical Examiner growled something about those indescribable scatter rugs costing more lives than drunken motorists; the policeman in charge kindly offered to do whatever he could in the way of making funeral arrangements; and that was all there was to it.

It had been so easy – so undramatic, in fact – that it was not until a week later when a properly sympathetic lawyer was making him an accounting of his wife's estate that Mr Appleby suddenly understood the whole, magnificent new world that had been opened up to him.

Discretion must sometimes outweigh sentiment, and Mr Appleby was, if anything, a discreet man. After his wife's estate had been cleared, the Shop was moved to another location far from its original setting. It was moved again after the sudden demise of the second Mrs Appleby, and by the time the sixth Mrs Appleby had been disposed of, the removals were merely part of a fruitful pattern.

Because of their similarities – they were all pale, thin-featured women with pinched lips, adept at toasting and boiling, and adamant on the subjects of regularity and order – Mr Appleby was inclined to remember his departed wives rather vaguely *en masse*. Only in one regard did he qualify them: the number of digits their bank accounts totaled up to. For that reason he thought of the first two Mrs Applebys as Fours; the third as a Three (an unpleasant surprise); and the last three as Fives. The sum would have been a pretty penny by anyone else's standards, but since each succeeding portion of it had been snapped up by the insatiable *Appleby, Antiques and Curios* – in much the way a fly is snapped up by a hungry lizard – Mr Appleby found himself soon after the burial of the sixth Mrs Appleby in deeper and warmer financial waters than ever. So desperate were his circumstances that although he dreamed of another Five he would have settled for a Four on the spot. It was at this opportune moment that Martha Sturgis entered his life, and after fifteen minutes' conversation with her he brushed all thoughts of Fours and Fives from his mind.

Martha Sturgis, it seemed, was a Six.

It was not only in the extent of her fortune that she broke the pattern established by the women of Mr Appleby's previous experience. Unlike them, Martha Sturgis was a large, rather shapeless woman who in person, dress, and manner might almost be called (Mr Appleby shuddered a little at the word) blowsy.

It was remotely possible that properly veneered, harnessed, coiffured, and appareled she might have been made into something presentable, but from all indications Martha Sturgis was a woman who went out of her way to defy such conventions. Her hair, dyed a shocking orange-red, was piled carelessly on her head; her blobby features were recklessly powdered and painted entirely to their disadvantage; her clothes, obviously worn for comfort, were, at the same time, painfully garish; and her shoes gave evidence of long and pleasurable wear without corresponding care being given their upkeep.

Of all this and its effect on the beholder Martha Sturgis seemed totally unaware. She strode through *Appleby, Antiques and Curios* with an energy that set movable objects dancing in their places; she smoked incessantly, lighting one cigarette from another, while Mr Appleby fanned the air before his face and coughed suggestively; and she talked without pause, loudly and in a deep, hoarse voice that dinned strangely in a Shop so accustomed to the higher, thinner note.

In the first fourteen minutes of their acquaintance, the one quality she displayed that led Mr Appleby to modify some of his immediate revulsion even a trifle was the care with which she priced each article. She examined, evaluated, and cross-examined in detail before moving on with obvious disapproval, and he moved along with her with mounting assurance that he could get her out of the Shop before any damage was done to the stock or his patience. And then in the fifteenth minute she spoke the Word.

'I've got a half million dollars in the bank,' Martha Sturgis remarked with cheerful contempt, 'but I never thought I'd get around to spending a nickel of it on this kind of stuff.'

Mr Appleby had his hand before his face preparatory to waving aside some of the tobacco smoke that eddied about him. In the time it took the hand to drop nervelessly to his side his mind attacked an astonishing number of problems. One concerned the important finger on her left hand which was ringless; the others concerned certain mathematical problems largely dealing with short-term notes, long-term notes, and rates of interest. By the time the hand touched his side, the problems, as far as Mr Appleby was concerned, were well on the way to solution.

And it may be noted there was an added fillip given the matter by the very nature of Martha Sturgis' slovenly and strident being. Looking at her after she had spoken the Word, another man might perhaps have seen her through the sort of veil that a wise photographer casts over the lens of his camera in taking the picture of a prosperous, but unprepossessing, subject. Mr Appleby, incapable of such self-deceit, girded himself instead with the example of the man who carried a heavy weight on his back for the pleasure it gave him in laying it down. Not only would the final act of a marriage to Martha Sturgis solve important mathematical problems, but it was an act he could play out with the gusto of a man ridding the world of an unpleasant object.

Therefore he turned his eyes, more melancholy and luminous than ever, on her and said, 'It's a great pity, Mrs . . .'

She told him her name, emphasizing the *Miss* before it, and Mr Appleby smiled apologetically.

'Of course. As I was saying, it's a great pity when someone of refinement and culture—' (the *like yourself* floated delicately unsaid on the air) '—should never have known the joy in possession of fine works of art. But, as we all learn, it is never too late to begin, is it?'

Martha Sturgis looked at him sharply and then laughed a hearty bellow of laughter that stabbed his eardrums painfully. For a moment Mr Appleby, a man not much given to humor, wondered darkly if he had unwittingly uttered something so excruciatingly epigrammatic that it was bound to have this alarming effect.

'My dear man,' said Martha Sturgis, 'if it is your idea that I am here to start cluttering up my life with your monstrosities, perish the thought. What I'm here for is to buy a gift for a friend, a thoroughly infuriating and loathsome person who happens to have the nature and disposition of a bar of stainless steel. I can't think of a better way of showing my feelings toward her than by presenting her with almost anything displayed in your shop. If possible, I should also like delivery arranged so that I can be on the scene when she receives the package,'

Mr Appleby staggered under this, then rallied valiantly. 'In that case,' he said, and shook his head firmly, 'it is out of the question. Completely out of the question.'

'Nonsense,' Martha Sturgis said. 'I'll arrange for delivery myself if you can't handle it. Really, you ought to understand that there's no point in doing this sort of thing unless you're on hand to watch the results.'

Mr Appleby kept tight rein on his temper. 'I am not alluding to the matter of delivery,' he said. 'What I am trying to make clear is that I cannot possibly permit anything in my Shop to be bought in such a spirit. Not for any price you could name.'

Martha Sturgis's heavy jaw dropped. 'What was that you said?' she asked blankly.

It was a perilous moment, and Mr Appleby knew it. His next words could set her off into another spasm of that awful laughter that would devastate him completely; or, worse, could send her right out of the Shop forever; or could decide the issue in his favor then and there. But it was a moment that had to be met, and, thought Mr Appleby desperately, whatever else Martha Sturgis might be, she was a Woman.

He took a deep breath. 'It is the policy of this Shop,' he said quietly, 'never to sell anything unless the prospective purchaser shows full appreciation for the article to be bought and can assure it the care and devotion to which it is entitled. That has always been the policy, and always will be as long as I am here. Anything other than that I would regard as desecration.'

He watched Martha Sturgis with bated breath. There was a chair nearby, and she dropped into it heavily so that her skirts were drawn tight by her widespread thighs, and the obscene shoes were displayed mercilessly. She lit another cigarette, regarding him meanwhile with narrowed eyes through the flame of the match, and then fanned the air a little to dispel the cloud of smoke.

'You know,' she said, 'this is very interesting. I'd like to hear more about it.'

To the inexperienced the problem of drawing information of the most personal nature from a total stranger would seem a perplexing one. To Mr Appleby, whose interests had so often been dependent on such information, it was no problem at all. In very shoft time he had evidence that Martha Sturgis's estimate of her fortune was quite accurate, that she was apparently alone in the world without relatives or intimate friends, and – that she was not averse to the idea of marriage.

This last he drew from her during her now regular visits to the Shop where she would spread herself comfortably on a chair and talk to him endlessly. Much of her talk was about her father to whom Mr Appleby evidently bore a striking resemblance.

'He even dressed like you,' Martha Sturgis said reflectively. 'Neat as a pin, and not only about himself either. He used to make an inspection of the house every day – march through and make sure everything was exactly where it had to be. And he kept it up right to the end. I remember an hour before he died how he went about straightening pictures on the wall.'

Mr Appleby, who had been peering with some irritation at a picture that hung slightly awry on the Shop wall, turned his attentions reluctantly from it.

'And you were with him to the end?' he asked sympathetically.

'Indeed I was.'

'Well,' Mr Appleby said brightly, 'one does deserve some

reward for such sacrifice, doesn't one? Especially – and I hope this will not embarrass you, Miss Sturgis – when one considers that such a woman as yourself could undoubtedly have left the care of an aged father to enter matrimony almost at will. Isn't that so?'

Martha Sturgis sighed. 'Maybe it is, and maybe it isn't,' she said, 'and I won't deny that I've had my dreams. But that's all they are, and I suppose that's all they ever will be.'

'Why?' asked Mr Appleby encouragingly.

'Because,' said Martha Sturgis somberly, 'I have never yet met the man who could fit those dreams. I am not a simpering schoolgirl, Mr Appleby; I don't have to balance myself against my bank account to know why any man would devote himself to me, and, frankly, his motives would be of no interest. But he must be a decent, respectable man who would spend every moment of his life worrying about me and caring for me; and he must be a man who would make the memory of my father a living thing.'

Mr Appleby rested a hand lightly on her shoulder.

'Miss Sturgis,' he said gravely, 'you may yet meet such a man.'

She looked at him with features that were made even more blobby and unattractive by her emotion.

'Do you mean that, Mr Appleby?' she asked. 'Do you really believe that?'

Faith glowed in Mr Appleby's eyes as he smiled down at her. 'He may be closer than you dare realize,' he said warmly.

Experience had proved to Mr Appleby that once the ice is broken the best thing to do is take a deep breath and plunge in. Accordingly, he let very few days elapse before he made his proposal.

'Miss Sturgis,' he said, 'there comes a time to every lonely man when he can no longer bear his loneliness. If at such a time he is fortunate enough to meet the one woman to whom he could give unreservedly all his respect and tender feelings, he is a fortunate man indeed. Miss Sturgis – I am that man.'

'Why, Mr Appleby!' said Martha Sturgis, coloring a trifle. 'That's really very good of you, but . . .'

At this note of indecision his heart sank. 'Wait!' he interposed hastily. 'If you have any doubts, Miss Sturgis, please speak them now so that I may answer them. Considering the state of my emotions, that would only be fair, wouldn't it?'

'Well, I suppose so,' said Martha Sturgis. 'You see, Mr Appleby, I'd rather not get married at all than take the chance of getting someone who wasn't prepared to give me exactly what I'm looking for in marriage: absolute, single-minded devotion all the rest of my days.'

'Miss Sturgis,' said Mr Appleby solemnly, 'I am prepared to give you no less.'

'Men say these things so easily,' she sighed. 'But – I shall certainly think about it, Mr Appleby.'

The dismal prospect of waiting an indefinite time for a woman of such careless habits to render a decision was not made any lighter by the sudden receipt a few days later of a note peremptorily requesting Mr Appleby's presence at the offices of Gainsborough, Gainsborough, and Golding, attorneys-at-law. With his creditors closing in like a wolf pack, Mr Appleby could only surmise the worst, and he was pleasantly surprised upon his arrival at Gainsborough, Gainsborough, and Golding to find that they represented, not his creditors, but Martha Sturgis herself.

The elder Gainsborough, obviously very much the guiding spirit of the firm, was a short, immensely fat man with pendulous dewlaps that almost concealed his collar, and large fishy eyes that goggled at Mr Appleby. The younger Gainsborough was a duplicate of his brother, with jowls not quite so impressive, while Golding was an impassive young man with a hatchet face.

'This,' said the elder Gainsborough, his eyes fixed glassily on Mr Appleby, 'is a delicate matter. Miss Sturgis, an esteemed client' – the younger Gainsborough nodded at this – 'has mentioned entering matrimony with you, sir.'

Mr Appleby sitting primly on his chair was stirred by a pleased excitement. 'Yes?' he said.

'And,' continued the elder Gainsborough, 'while Miss Sturgis is perfectly willing to concede that her fortune may be the object of attraction in any suitor's eyes—' he held up a pudgy hand to cut short Mr Appleby's shocked protest – 'she is also willing to dismiss that issue—'

'To ignore it, set it aside,' said the younger Gainsborough sternly.

'—if the suitor is prepared to meet all other expectations in the marriage.'

'I am,' said Mr Appleby fervently.

'Mr Appleby,' said the elder Gainsborough abruptly, 'have you been married before?'

Mr Appleby thought swiftly. Denial would make any chance word about his past a deadly trap; admission, on the other hand, was a safeguard against that, and a thoroughly respectable one.

'Yes,' he said.

'Divorced?'

'Good heavens, no!' said Mr Appleby, genuinely shocked.

The Gainsboroughs looked at each other in approval. 'Good,' said the elder, 'very good. Perhaps, Mr Appleby, the question seemed impertinent, but in these days of moral laxity—'

'I should like it known in that case,' said Mr Appleby sturdily, 'that I am as far from moral laxity as any human being can be. Tobacco, strong drink, and – ah—'

'Loose women,' said the younger Gainsborough briskly.

'Yes,' said Mr Appleby reddening, '—are unknown to me.'

The elder Gainsborough nodded. 'Under any conditions,' he said, 'Miss Sturgis will not make any precipitate decision. She should have her answer for you within a month, however, and during that time, if you don't mind taking the advice of an old man, I suggest that you court her assiduously. She is a woman, Mr Appleby, and I imagine that all women are much alike.'

'I imagine they are,' said Mr Appleby.

'Devotion,' said the younger Gainsborough, 'Constancy. That's the ticket.'

What he was being asked to do, Mr Appleby reflected in one of his solitary moments, was to put aside the Shop and the orderly world it represented and to set the unappealing figure of Martha Sturgis in its place. It was a temporary measure, of course; it was one that would prove richly rewarding when Martha Sturgis had been properly wed and sent the way of the preceding Mrs Applebys; but it was not made any easier by enforced familiarity with the woman. It was inevitable that since

Mr Appleby viewed matters not only as a prospective bride-groom, but also as a prospective widower, so to speak, he found his teeth constantly set on edge by the unwitting irony which crept into so many of her tedious discussions on marriage.

'The way I see it,' Martha Sturgis once remarked, 'is that a man who would divorce his wife would divorce any other woman he ever married. You take a look at all these broken marriages today, and I'll bet that in practically every case you'll find a man who's always shopping around and never finding what he wants. Now, the man *I* marry,' she said pointedly, 'must be willing to settle down and stay settled.'

'Of course,' said Mr Appleby.

'I have heard,' Martha Sturgis told him on another, and particularly trying, occasion, 'that a satisfactory marriage increases a woman's span of years. That's an excellent argument for marriage, don't you think?'

'Of course,' said Mr Appleby.

It seemed to him that during that month of trial most of his conversation was restricted to the single phrase 'of course,' delievered with varying inflections; but the tactic must have been the proper one since at the end of the month he was able to change the formula to 'I do,' in a wedding ceremony at which Gainsborough, Gainsborough, and Golding were the sole guests.

Immediately afterward, Mr Appleby (to his discomfort) was borne off with his bride to a photographer's shop where innumerable pictures were made under the supervision of the dour Golding, following which, Mr Appleby (to his delight) exchanged documents with his wife which made them each other's heirs to all properties, possessions, *et cetera*, whatsoever.

If Mr Appleby had occasionally appeared rather abstracted during these festivities, it was only because his mind was neatly arranging the program of impending events. The rug (the very same one that had served so well in six previous episodes) had to be placed; and then there would come the moment when he would ask for a glass of water, when he would place one hand on her shoulder, and with the other ... It could not be a moment that took place without due time passing; yet it could not be forestalled too long in view of the pressure exercised by the Shop's various creditors. Watching the pen in his wife's hand as she signed her will, he decided there would be time within a few weeks. With the will in his possession there would be no point in waiting longer than that.

Before the first of those weeks was up, however, Mr Appleby knew that even this estimate would have to undergo drastic revision. There was no question about it; he was simply not equipped to cope with his marriage.

For one thing, her home (and now his), a brownstone cavern inherited from her mother, was a nightmare of disorder. On the principle, perhaps, that anything flung casually aside was not worth picking up since it would only be flung aside again, an amazing litter had accumulated in every room. The contents of brimming closets and drawers were recklessly exchanged, mislaid, or added to the general litter, and over all lay a thin film of dust. On Mr Appleby's quivering nervous system all this had the effect of a fingernail dragging along an endless blackboard.

The one task to which Mrs Appleby devoted herself, as it happened, was the one which her husband prayerfully wished she would spare herself. She doted on cookery, and during mealtimes would trudge back and forth endlessly between kitchen and dining room laden with dishes outside any of Mr Appleby's experience.

At his first feeble protests his wife had taken pains to explain in precise terms that she was sensitive to any criticism of her cooking, even the implied criticism of a partly emptied plate; and thereafter, Mr Appleby, plunging hopelessly through rare meats, rich sauces, and heavy pastries, found added to his tribulations the incessant pangs of dyspepsia. Nor were his pains eased by his wife's insistence that he prove himself a trencherman of her mettle. She would thrust plates heaped high with indigestibles under his quivering nose, and, bracing himself like a martyr facing the lions, Mr Appleby would empty his portion into a digestive tract that cried for simple fare properly boiled or toasted.

It became one of his fondest waking dreams, that scene where he returned from his wife's burial to dine on hot tea and toast and, perhaps, a medium-boiled egg. But even that dream and its sequel – where he proceeded to set the house in order – were not sufficient to buoy him up each day when he awoke and reflected on what lay ahead of him.

Each day found his wife more insistent in her demands for his attentions. And on that day when she openly reproved him for devoting more of those attentions to the Shop than to herself, Mr Appleby knew the time had come to prepare for the final act. He brought home the rug that evening and carefully laid it in place between the living room and the hallway that led to the kitchen. Martha Appleby watched him without any great enthusiasm.

'That's a shabby-looking thing, all right,' she said. 'What is it, Appie, an antique or something?'

She had taken to calling him by that atrocious name and seemed cheerfully oblivious to the way he winced under it. He winced now.

'It is not an antique,' Mr Appleby admitted, 'but I hold it dear for many reasons. It has a great deal of sentimental value to me.'

Mrs Appleby smiled fondly at him. 'And you brought it for me, didn't you?'

'Yes,' said Mr Appleby, 'I did.'

'You're a dear,' said Mrs Appleby. 'You really are.'

Watching her cross the rug on slipshod feet to use the telephone, which stood on a small table the other side of the hallway, Mr Appleby toyed with the idea that since she used the telephone at about the same time every evening he could schedule the accident for that time. The advantages were obvious: since those calls seemed to be the only routine she observed with any fidelity, she would cross the rug at a certain time, and he would be in a position to settle matters then and there.

However, thought Mr Appleby as he polished his spectacles, that brought up the problem of how best to approach her under such cirumstances. Clearly the tried and tested methods were best, but if the telephone call and the glass of water could be synchronized . . .

'A penny for your thoughts, Appie,' said Mrs Appleby brightly. She had laid down the telephone and crossed the hallway so that she stood squarely on the rug. Mr Appleby replaced his spectacles and peered at her through them.

'I wish,' he said querulously, 'you would not address me by that horrid name. You know I detest it.'

'Nonsense,' his wife said briefly. 'I think it's cute.'

'I do not.'

'Well, I like it,' said Mrs Appleby with the air of one who has settled a matter once and for all. 'Anyhow,' she pouted, 'that couldn't have been what you were thinking about before I started talking to you, could it?'

It struck Mr Appleby that when this stout, unkempt woman pouted, she resembled nothing so much as a wax doll badly worn by time and handling. He pushed away the thought to frame some suitable answer.

'As it happens,' he said, 'my mind was on the disgraceful state of my clothes. Need I remind you again that there are buttons missing from practically every garment I own?'

Mrs Appleby yawned broadly. 'I'll get to it sooner or later.'

'Tomorrow perhaps?'

'I doubt it,' said Mrs Appleby. She turned toward the stairs. 'Come to sleep, Appie. I'm dead tired.'

Mr Appleby followed her thoughtfully. Tomorrow, he knew, he would have to get one of his suits to the tailor if he wanted to have anything fit to wear at the funeral.

He had brought home the suit and hung it neatly away; he had eaten his dinner; and he had sat in the living room listening to his wife's hoarse voice go on for what seemed interminable hours, although the clock was not yet at nine.

Now with rising excitement he saw her lift herself slowly from her chair and cross the room to the hallway. As she reached for the telephone Mr Appleby cleared his throat sharply. 'If you don't mind,' he said, 'I'd like a glass of water.'

Mrs Appleby turned to look at him. 'A glass of water?'

'If you don't mind,' said Mr Appleby, and waited as she hesitated, then set down the telephone, and turned toward the kitchen. There was the sound of a glass being rinsed in the kitchen, and then Mrs Appleby came up to him holding it out.

He laid one hand appreciatively on her plump shoulder, and then lifted the other as if to brush back a strand of untidy hair at her cheek. 'Is that what happened to all the others?' said Mrs Appleby quietly.

Mr Appleby felt his hand freeze in midair and the chill from it run down into his marrow. 'Others?' he managed to say. 'What others?'

His wife smiled grimly at him, and he saw that the glass of water in her hand was perfectly steady. 'Six others,' she said. 'That is, six by my count. Why? Were there any more?'

'No,' he said, then caught wildly at himself. 'I don't understand what you're talking about!'

'Dear Appie. Surely you couldn't forget six wives just like that. Unless, of course, I've come to mean so much to you that you can't bear to think of the others. That would be a lovely thing to happen, wouldn't it?'

'I *was* married before,' Mr Appleby said loudly. 'I made that quite clear myself. But this talk about six wives!'

'Of course you were married before, Appie. And it was quite easy to find out to whom – and it was just as easy to find out about the one before that – and all the others. Or even about your mother, or where you went to school, or where you were born. You see, Appie, Mr Gainsborough is really a very clever man.'

'Then it was Gainsborough who put you up to this!'

'Not at all, you foolish little man,' his wife said contemptuously. 'All the time you were making your plans I was unmaking them. From the moment I laid eyes on you I knew you for what you are. Does that surprise you?'

Mr Appleby struggled with the emotions of a man who has picked up a twig to find a viper in his hand. 'How could you know?' he gasped.

'Because you were the image of my father. Because in everything – the way you dress, your insufferable neatness, your priggish arrogance, the little moral lectures you dote on – you are what he was. And all my life I hated him for what he was, and what it did to my mother. He married her for her money, made her every day a nightmare, and then killed her for what was left of her fortune.'

'Killed her?' said Mr Appleby, stupefied.

'Oh, come,' his wife said sharply. 'Do you think you're the only man who was ever capable of that? Yes, he killed her – murdered her, if you prefer – by asking for a glass of water, and then breaking her neck when she offered it to him. A method strangely similar to yours, isn't it?'

Mr Appleby found the incredible answer rising to his mind, but refused to accept it. 'What happened to him?' he demanded. 'Tell me what happened! Was he caught?'

'No, he was never caught. There were no witnesses to what he did, but Mr Gainsborough had been my mother's lawyer, a dear friend of hers. He had suspicions and demanded a hearing. He brought a doctor to the hearing who made it plain how my father could have killed her and made it look as if she had slipped on a rug, but before there was any decision my father died of a heart attack.'

'That was the case – the case I read!' Mr Appleby groaned, and then was silent under his wife's sardonic regard.

'When he was gone,' she went on inexorably, 'I swore I would someday find a man exactly like him, and I would make that man live the life my father should have. I would know his every habit and every taste, and none of them should go satisfied. I would know he married me for my money, and he would never get a penny of it until I was dead and gone. And that would be a long, long time, because he would spend his life taking care that I should live out my life to the last possible breath.'

Mr Appleby pulled his wits together, and saw that despite her emotion she had remained in the same position. 'How can you make him do that?' he asked softly, and moved an inch closer.

'It does sound strange, doesn't it, Appie?' she observed. 'But hardly as strange as the fact that your six wives died by slipping on a rug – very much like this one – while bringing you a glass of water – very much like this one. So strange, that Mr Gainsborough was led to remark that too many coincidences will certainly hang a man. Especially if there is reason to bring them to light in a trial for murder.'

Mr Appleby suddenly found the constriction of his collar unbearable. 'That doesn't answer my question,' he said craftily.

'How can you make sure that I would devote my life to prolonging yours?'

'A man whose wife is in a posittition to have him hanged should be able to see that clearly.'

'No,' said Mr Appleby in a stifled voice, 'I only see that such a man is forced to rid himself of his wife as quickly as possible.'

'Ah, but that's where the arrangements come in.'

'Arrangements? What arrangements?' demanded Mr Appleby.

'I'd like very much to explain them,' his wife said. 'In fact, I see the time has come when it's imperative to do so. But I do find it uncomfortable standing here like this.'

'Never mind that,' said Mr Appleby impatiently, and his wife shrugged.

'Well, then,' she said coolly, 'Mr Gainsborough now has all the documents about your marriages – the way the previous deaths took place, the way you always happened to get the bequests at just the right moment to pay your shop's debts.

'Besides this, he has a letter from me, explaining that in the event of my death an investigation be made immediately and all necessary action be taken. Mr Gainsborough is really very efficient. The fingerprints and photographs . . .'

'Fingerprints and photographs!' cried Mr Appleby.

'Of course. After my father's death it was found that he had made all preparations for a quick trip abroad. Mr Gainsborough has assured me that in case you had such ideas in mind you should get rid of them. No matter where you are, he said, it will be quite easy to bring you back again.'

'What do you want of me?' asked Mr Appleby numbly. 'Surely you don't expect me to stay now, and—'

'Oh, yes, I do. And since we've come to this point I may as well tell you I expect you to give up your useless shop once and for all, and make it a point to be at home with me the entire day.'

'Give up the Shop!' he exclaimed.

'You must remember, Appie, that in my letter asking for a full investigation at my death, I did not specify death by any particular means. I look forward to a long and pleasant life with you always at my side, and perhaps – mind you, I only say *perhaps* – someday I shall turn over that letter and all the evidence to you. You can see how much it is to your interest, therefore, to watch over me very carefully.'

The telephone rang with abrupt violence, and Mrs Appleby nodded toward it. 'Almost as carefully,' she said softly, 'as Mr Gainsborough. Unless I call him every evening at nine to report I am well and happy, it seems he will jump to the most shocking conclusions.'

'Wait,' said Mr Appleby. He lifted the telephone, and there was no mistaking the voice that spoke.

'Hello,' said the elder Gainsborough. 'Hello, Mrs Appleby?'

Mr Appleby essayed a cunning move. 'No,' he said, 'I'm afraid she can't speak to you now. What is it?'

The voice in his ear took on an unmistakable cold menace. 'This is Gainsborough, Mr Appleby, and I wish to speak to your wife immediately. I will give you ten seconds to have her at this telephone, Mr Appleby. Do you understand?'

Mr Appleby turned dully toward his wife and held out the telephone. 'It's for you,' he said, and then saw with a start of terror that as she turned to set down the glass of water the rug skidded slightly under her feet. Her arms flailed the air as she fought for balance, the glass smashed at his feet drenching his neat trousers, and her face twisted into a silent scream. Then her body struck the floor and lay inertly in the position with which he was so familiar.

Watching her, he was barely conscious of the voice emerging tinnily from the telephone in his hand.

'The ten seconds are up, Mr Appleby,' it said shrilly. 'Do you understand? *Your time is up!*'

# Fool's Mate

When George Huneker came home from the office that evening he was obviously fired by a strange excitement. His ordinarily sallow cheeks were flushed, his eyes shone behind his rimless spectacles, and instead of carefully removing his rubbers and neatly placing them on the strip of mat laid for that purpose in a corner of the hallway, he pulled them off with reckless haste and tossed them aside. Then, still wearing his hat and overcoat, he undid the wrappings of the package he had brought with him and displayed a small, flat, leather case. When he opened the case Louise saw a bed of shabby green velvet in which rested the austere black and white forms of a set of chessmen.

'Aren't they beautiful?' George said. He ran a finger lovingly over one of the pieces. 'Look at the work on this: nothing fancy to stick away in a glass case, you understand, but everything neat and clean and ready for action the way it ought to be. All genuine ivory and ebony, and all handmade, every one of them.'

Louise's eyes narrowed. 'And just how much did you pay out for this stuff?'

'I didn't,' George said. 'That is, I didn't buy it. Mr Oelrichs gave it to me.'

'Oelrichs?' said Louise. 'You mean that old crank you brought home to dinner that time? The one who just sat and watched us like the cat that ate the canary, and wouldn't say a word unless you poked it out of him?'

'Oh, Louise!'

'Don't you "Oh, Louise" me! I thought I made my feelings about him mighty clear to you long before this. And, may I ask, why should our fine Mr Oelrichs suddenly decide to give you this thing?'

'Well,' George said uneasily, 'you know he's been pretty sick, and what with him needing only a few months more for retirement I was carrying most of his work for him. Today was his last day, and he gave me this as a kind of thank-you present. Said it was his favorite set, too, but he wanted to give me the best thing he could, and this was it.'

'How generous of Mr Oelrichs,' Louise remarked frigidly. 'Did it ever occur to him that if he wanted to pay you back for your time and trouble, something practical would be a lot more to the point?'

'Why, I was just doing him a favor, Louise. Even if he did offer me money or anything like that, I wouldn't take it.'

'The more fool you,' Louise sniffed. 'All right, take off your things, put them away right, and get ready for supper. It's just about ready.'

She moved toward the kitchen, and George trailed after her placatingly. 'You know, Louise, Mr Oelrichs said something that was very interesting.'

'I'm sure he did.'

'Well, he said there were some people in the world who *needed* chess – that when they learned to play it real well they'd see for themselves how much they needed it. And what I thought was that there's no reason why you and I . . .'

She stopped short and faced him with her hands on her hips. 'You mean that after I'm done taking care of the house, and shopping, and cooking your hot meals, and mending and darning, then I'm supposed to sit down and learn how to play games with you! For a man going on fifty, George Huneker, you get some peculiar ideas.'

Pulling off his overcoat in the hallway, he reflected that there was small chance of his losing track of his age, at least not as long as Louise doted so much on reminding him. He had first heard about it a few months after his marriage when he was going on thirty and had been offered a chance to go into business for himself. He had heard about it every year since, on some occasion or other, although as he learned more and more about Louise he had fallen into fewer traps.

The only trouble was that Louise always managed to stay one jump ahead of him, and while in time he came to understand that she would naturally put her foot down at such things as his leaving a good steady job, or at their having a baby when times were hard (and in Louise's opinion they always were), or at buying the house outright when they could rent it so cheap, it still came as a surprise that she so bitterly opposed the idea of having company to the house, or of reading some book he had just enjoyed, or of tuning in the radio to a symphony, or, as in this case, of taking up chess.

Company, she made it clear, was a bother and expense, small print hurt her eyes, symphonies gave her a splitting headache, and chess, it seemed, was something for which she could not possibly find time. Before they had been married, George thought unhappily, it had all been different somehow. They were always in the midst of a crowd of his friends, and when books or music or anything like that were the topics of discussion, she followed the talk with bright and vivacious interest. Now she just wanted to sit with her knitting every night while she listened to comedians bellowing over the radio.

Not being well, of course, could be one reason for this. She suffered from a host of aches and pains which she dwelt on in such vivid detail at times that George himself could feel sympathetic twinges go through him. Their medicine chest bulged with remedies, their diet had dwindled to a bland and tasteless series of concoctions, and it was a rare month which did not find Louise running up a sizable doctor's bill for the treatment of what George vaguely came to think of as 'women's troubles.'

Still, George would have been the first to point out that despite the handicaps she worked under, Louise had been as good a wife as a man could ask for. His salary over the years had hardly been luxurious, but penny by penny she had managed to put aside fifteen thousand dollars in their bank account. This was a fact known only to the two of them since Louise made it a point to dwell on their relative poverty in her conversations with anyone, and while George always felt some embarrassment when she did this, Louise pointed out that one of the best ways to save your money was not to let the world at large know you had any, and since a penny saved was a penny earned she was contributing as much to their income in her way as George was in his. This, while not reducing George's embarrassment, did succeed in glossing it with increased respect for Louise's wisdom and capability.

And when added to this was the knowledge that his home was always neat as a pin, his clothing carefully mended, and his health fanatically ministered to, it was easy to see why George chose to count his blessings rather than make an issue of anything so trivial as his wife's becoming his partner at chess. Which, as George himself might have admitted had you pinned him down to it, was a bit of a sacrifice, for in no time at all after receiving the set of chessmen he found himself a passionate devotee of the game. And chess, as he sometimes reflected while poring over his board of an evening with the radio booming in his ears and his wife's knitting needles flickering away contentedly, would seem to be a game greatly enhanced by the presence of an opponent. He did not reflect this ironically; there was no irony in George's nature.

Mr Oelrichs, in giving him the set, had said he would be available for instruction at any time. But since Louise had already indicated that the gentleman would hardly be a welcome guest in her home, and since she had often expressed decided opinions on any man who would leave his hearth and home to go traipsing about for no reason, George did not even think the matter worth broaching. Instead, he turned to a little text aptly entitled *Invitation to Chess*, was led by the invitation to essay other and more difficult texts, and was thence led to a whole world of literature on chess, staggering in its magnitude and complexity.

He ate chess, drank chess, and slept chess. He studied the masters and past masters until he could quote chapter and verse from even their minor triumphs. He learned the openings, the middle game, the end game. He learned to eschew the reckless foray which led nowhere in favor of the positional game where cunning strategy turned a side into a relentless force that inevitably broke and crushed the enemy before it. Strange names danced across his horizon: Alekhine, Capablanca, Lasker, Nimzovich, and he pursued them, drunk with the joy of discovery, through the ebony and ivory mazes of their universe.

But in all this there was still that one thing lacking: an opponent, a flesh-and-blood opponent against whom he could test himself. It was one thing, he sometimes thought disconsolately, to have a book at one's elbow while pondering a move; it would be quite another to ponder even the identical move with a man waiting across the board to turn it to his own advantage and destroy you with it. It became a growing hunger, that desire to make a move and see a hand reach across the table to answer it; it became a curious obsession so that at times, when Louise's shadow moved abruptly against the wall or a log settled in the fireplace, George would look up suddenly, half expecting to see the man seated in the empty chair opposite him.

He came to visualize the man quite clearly after a while. A quiet contemplative man much like himself, in fact, with graying hair and rimless spectacles that tended to slide a bit when he bent over the board. A man who played just a shade better than himself; not so well that he could not be beaten, but well enough to force George to his utmost to gain an occasional victory.

And there was one thing more he expected of this man: something a trifle unorthodox, perhaps, if one was a stickler for chess ritual. The man must prefer to play the white side all the time. It was the white side that moved first, that took the offensive until, perhaps, the tide could be turned against it. George himself infinitely preferred the black side, preferred to parry the thrusts and advances of white while he slowly built up a solid wall of defense against its climactic moves. *That* was the way to learn the game, George told himself: after a player learned how to make himself invulnerable on the defense, there was nothing he couldn't do on attack.

However, to practice one's defense still required a hand to set the offense into motion, and eventually George struck on a solution which, he felt with mild pride, was rather ingenious. He would set up the board, seat himself behind the black side, and then make the opening move for white. This he would counter with a black piece, after which he would move again for white, and so on until some decision was reached.

It was not long before the flaws in this system became distressingly obvious. Since he naturally favored the black side, and since he knew both plans of battle from their inception, black won game after game with ridiculous ease. And after the twentieth fiasco of this sort George sank back into his chair despairingly. If he could only put one side out of his mind completely while he was moving for the other, why, there would be no problem at all! Which, he realized cheerlessly, was a prospect about as logical as an ancient notion he had come across in his reading somewhere, the notion that if you cut a serpent in half, the separated halves would then turn on each other and fight themselves savagely to death.

He set up the board again after this glum reflection, and then walked around the table and seated himself in white's chair. Now, if he were playing the white side what would he do? A game depends not only on one's skill, he told himself, but also on one's knowledge of his opponent. And not only on the opponent's style of play, but also on his character, his personality, his whole nature. George solemnly looked across the table at black's now empty chair and brooded on this. Then slowly, deliberately, he made his opening move.

After that, he quickly walked around the table and sat down on black's side. The going, he found, was much easier here, and almost mechanically he answered white's move. With a thrill of excitement chasing inside him, he left his seat and moved around to the other side of the board again, already straining hard to put black and its affairs far out of his mind.

'For pity's sake, George, what *are* you doing!'

George started, and looked around dazedly. Louise was watching him, her lips compressed, her knitting dropped on her lap, and her manner charged with such disapproval that the whole room seemed to frown at him. He opened his mouth to explain, and hastily thought better of it.

'Why, nothing,' he said, 'nothing at all.'

'Nothing at all!' Louise declared tartly. 'The way you're tramping around, somebody would think you can't find a comfortable chair in the house. You know I . . .'

Then her voice trailed off, her eyes became glassy, her body straightened and became rigid with devouring attention. The comedian on the radio had answered an insult with another evidently so devastating that the audience in the studio could do no more than roar in helpless laughter. Even Louise's lips turned up ever so slightly at the corners as she reached for her knitting again, and George gratefully seized this opportunity to drop into the chair behind black's side.

He had been on the verge of a great discovery, he knew that; but what exactly had it been? Was it that changing places physically had allowed him to project himself into the forms of two players, each separate and distinct from the other? If so, he was at the end of the line, George knew, because he would never be able to explain all that getting up and moving around to Louise.

But suppose the board itself were turned around after each move? Or, and George found himself charged with a growing excitement, since chess was completely a business of the mind anyhow – since, when one had mastered the game sufficiently it wasn't even necessary to use a board at all – wasn't the secret simply a matter of *turning oneself into the other player* when his move came?

It was white's move now, and George bent to his task. He was playing white's side, he must do what white would do – more than that, he must feel white's very emotions – but the harder he struggled and strained in his concentration, the more elusive became his goal. Again and again, at the instant he was about to reach his hand out, the thought of what black intended to do, of what black was surely *going* to do, slipped through his mind like a dot of quicksilver and made him writhe inwardly with a maddening sense of defeat.

This now became the obsession, and evening after evening he exercised himself at it. He lost weight, his face drew into haggard lines so that Louise was always at his heels during mealtimes trying to make him take an interest in her wholly uninteresting recipes. His interest in his job dwindled until it was barely perfunctory, and his superior, who at first had evinced no more than a mild surprise and irritation, started to shake his head ominously.

But with every game, every move, every effort he made, George felt with exultation he was coming nearer that goal. There would come a moment, he told himself with furious certainty, when he could view the side across the board with objectivity, with disinterest, with no more knowledge of its intentions and plans than he would have of any flesh-and-blood player who sat there; and when that day came, he would have achieved a triumph no other player before him could ever claim!

He was so sure of himself, so confident that the triumph lay beyond the next move each time he made a move, that when it came at last his immediate feeling was no more than a comfortable gratification and an expansive easing of all his nerves. Something like the feeling, he thought pleasurably, that a man gets after a hard day's work when he sinks into bed at night. Exactly that sort of feeling, in fact.

He had left the black position on the board perilously exposed through a bit of carelessness, and then in an effort to recover himself had moved the king's bishop in a neat defensive gesture that could cost white dear. When he looked up to study white's possible answer he saw White sitting there in the chair across the table, his fingertips gently touching each other, an ironic smile on his lips. 'Good,' said White pleasantly. 'Surprisingly good for you, George.'

At this, George's sense of gratification vanished like a soap bubble flicked by a casual finger. It was not only the amiable insult conveyed by the words which nettled him; equally disturbing was the fact that White was utterly unlike the man that George had been prepared for. He had not expected White to resemble him as one twin resembles another, yet feature for feature the resemblance was so marked that White could have been the image that stared back at him from his shaving mirror each morning. An image, however, which, unlike George's, seemed invested with a power and arrogance that were quite overwhelming. Here, George felt with a touch of resentment, was no man to hunch over a desk computing dreary rows of figures, but one who with dash and brilliance made great decisions at the head of a long committee table. A man who thought a little of tomorrow, but much more of today and the good things it offered. And one who would always find the price for those good things.

That much was evident in the matchless cut of White's clothing, in the grace and strength of the lean, well-manicured hands, in the merciless yet merry glint in the eyes that looked back into George's. It was when he looked into those eyes that George found himself fumbling for some thought that seemed to lie just beyond him. The image of himself was reflected so clearly in those eyes; perhaps it was not an image. Perhaps . . .

He was jarred from his train of thought by White's moving a piece. 'Your move,' said White carelessly, 'that is, if you want to continue the game.'

George looked at the board and found his position still secure. 'Why shouldn't I want to continue the game? Our positions . . .'

'For the moment are equal,' White interposed promptly. 'What you fail to consider is the long view: I am playing to win; you are playing only to keep from losing.'

'It seems very much the same thing,' argued George.

'But it is not,' said White, 'and the proof of that lies in the fact that I shall win this game, and every other game we ever play.'

The effrontery of this staggered George. 'Maroczy was a master who relied a good deal on defensive strategy,' he protested, 'and if you are familiar with his games . . .'

'I am exactly as well acquainted with Maroczy's games as you are,' White observed, 'and I do not hesitate to say that had we ever played, I should have beaten him every game as well.'

George reddened. 'You think very well of yourself, don't you,' he said, and was surprised to see that instead of taking offense White was regarding him with a look of infinite pity.

'No,' White said at last, 'it is you who think well of me,' and then as if he had just managed to see and avoid a neatly baited trap, he shook his head and drew his lips into a faintly sardonic grimace. 'Your move,' he said.

With an effort George put aside the vaguely troubling thoughts that clustered in his mind, and made the move. He made only a few after that when he saw clearly that he was hopelessly and ignominiously beaten. He was beaten a second game, and then another after that, and then in the fourth game, he made a despairing effort to change his tactics. On his eleventh move he saw a devastating opportunity to go on the offensive, hesitated, refused it, and was lost again. At that George grimly set about placing the pieces back in their case.

'You'll be back tomorrow?' he said, thoroughly put out at White's obvious amusement.

'If nothing prevents me.'

George suddenly felt cold with fear. 'What could prevent you?' he managed to say.

White picked up the white queen and revolved it slowly between his fingers. 'Louise, perhaps. What if she decided not to let you indulge yourself in this fashion?'

'But why? Why should she? She's never minded up to now!'

'Louise, my good man, is an extremely stupid and petulant woman . . .'

'Now, that's uncalled for!' George said, stung to the quick.

'And,' White continued as if he had not been interrupted at all, 'she is the master here. Such people now and then like to affirm their mastery seemingly for no reason at all. Actually, such gestures are a sop to their vanity – as necessary to them as the air they breathe.'

George mustered up all the courage and indignation at his command. 'If those are your honest opinions,' he said bravely, 'I don't think you have the right to come to this house ever again.'

On the heels of his words Louise stirred in her armchair and turned toward him. 'George,' she said briskly, 'that's quite enough of that game for the evening. Don't you have anything better to do with your time?'

'I'm putting everything away now,' George answered hastily, but when he reached for the chessman still gripped between his opponent's fingers, he saw White studying Louise with a look that made him quail. White turned to him then, and his eyes were like pieces of dark glass through which one can see the almost unbearable light of a searing flame.

'Yes,' White said slowly. 'For what she is and what she has done to you I hate her with a consuming hate. Knowing that, do you wish me to return?'

The eyes were not unkind when they looked at him now, George saw, and the feel of the chessman which White thrust into his hand was warm and reassuring. He hesitated, cleared his throat, then, 'I'll see you tomorrow,' he said at last.

White's lips drew into that familiar sardonic grimace.

'Tomorrow, the next day, any time you want me,' he said. 'But it will always be the same. You will never beat me.'

Time proved that White had not underestimated himself. And time itself, as George learned, was something far better measured by an infinite series of chess games, by the moves within a chess game, than by any such device as a calendar or clock. The discovery was a delightful one; even more delightful was the realization that the world around him, when viewed clearly, had come to resemble nothing so much as an object seen through the wrong end of a binocular. All those people who pushed and prodded and poked and demanded countless explanations and apologies could be seen as sharp and clear as ever but nicely reduced in perspective, so that it was obvious that no matter how close they came, they could never really touch one.

There was a single exception to this: Louise. Every evening the world would close in around the chessboard and the figure of White lounging in the chair on the other side of it. But in a corner of the room sat Louise over her knitting, and the air around her was charged with a mounting resentment which would now and then eddy around George in the form of querulous complaints and demands from which there was no escape.

'How *can* you spend every minute at that idiotic game!' she demanded. 'Don't you have anything to talk to me about?' And, in fact, he did not, any more than he had since the very first years of his marriage when he had been taught that he had neither voice nor vote in running his home, that she did not care to hear about the people he worked with in his office, and that he could best keep to himself any reflections he had on some subject which was, by her own word, Highbrow.

'And how right she is,' White had once taken pains to explain derisively. 'If *you* had furnished your home it would be uncluttered and graceful, and Louise would feel awkward and out of place in it. If she comes to know the people you work with too well, she might have to befriend them, entertain them, set her blatant ignorance before them for judgment. No, far better under the circumstances that she dwells in her vacuum, away from unhappy judgments.'

As it always could, White's manner drove George to furious

resentment. 'For a set of opinions pulled out of a cocked hat that sounds very plausible,' he burst out. 'Tell me, how do you happen to know so much about Louise?'

White looked at him through veiled eyes. 'I know only what you know,' he said. 'No more and no less.'

Such passages left George sore and wounded, but for the sake of the game he endured them. When Louise was silent all the world retreated into unreality. Then the reality was the chessboard with White's hand hovering over it, mounting the attack, sweeping everything before it with a reckless brilliance that could only leave George admiring and dismayed.

In fact, if White had any weakness, George reflected mournfully, it was certainly not in his game, but rather in his deft and unpleasant way of turning each game into the occasion for a little discourse on the science of chess, a discourse which always wound up with some remarkably perverse and impudent reflections on George's personal affairs.

'You know that the way a man plays chess demonstrates that man's whole nature,' White once remarked. 'Knowing this, does it not strike you as significant that you always choose to play the defensive – and always lose?'

That sort of thing was bad enough, but White was at his most savage those times when Louise would intrude in a game: make some demand on George or openly insist that he put away the board. Then White's jaw would set, and his eyes would flare with that terrible hate that always seemed to be smoldering in them when he regarded the woman.

Once when Louise had gone so far as to actually pick up a piece from the board and bang it back into the case, White came to his feet so swiftly and menacingly that George leaped up to forestall some rash action. Louise glared at him for that.

'You don't have to jump like that,' she snapped. 'I didn't break anything. But I can tell you, George Huneker: if you don't stop this nonsense I'll do it for you. I'll break every one of these things to bits if that's what it takes to make you act like a human being again!'

'Answer her!' said White. 'Go ahead, why don't you answer her!' And caught between these two fires George could do no more than stand there and shake his head helplessly.

It was this episode, however, which marked a new turn in White's manner: the entrance of a sinister purposefulness thinly concealed in each word and phrase.

'If she knew how to play the game,' he said, 'she might respect it, and you would have nothing to fear.'

'It so happens,' George replied defensively, 'that Louise is too busy for chess.'

White turned in his chair to look at her and then turned back with a grim smile. 'She is knitting. And, it seems to me, she is always knitting. Would you call that being busy?'

'Wouldn't you?'

'No,' said White, 'I wouldn't. Penelope spent her years at the loom to keep off importunate suitors until her husband returned. Louise spends her years at knitting to keep off life until death comes. She takes no joy in what she does; one can see that with half an eye. But each stitch dropping off the end of those needles brings her one instant nearer death, and, although she does not know it, she rejoices in it.'

'And you make all that out of the mere fact that she won't play at chess?' cried George incredulously.

'Not alone chess,' said White. 'Life.'

'And what do you mean by that word *life*, the way you use it?'

'Many things,' said White. 'The hunger to learn, the desire to create, the ability to feel vast emotions. Oh, many things.'

'Many things, indeed,' George scoffed. 'Big words, that's all they are.' But White only drew his lips into that sardonic grimace and said, 'Very big. Far too big for Louise, I'm afraid,' and then by moving a piece forced George to redirect his attention to the board.

It was as if White had discovered George's weak spot, and took a sadistic pleasure in returning to probe it again and again. And he played his conversational gambits as he made his moves at chess: cruelly, unerringly, always moving forward to the inescapable conclusion with a sort of flashing audacity. There were times when George, writhing helplessly, thought of asking him to drop the subject of Louise once and for all, but he could never bring himself to do so. Something in the recesses of

George's mind warned him that these conversational fancies were as much a part of White as his capacity for chess, and that if George wanted him at all it would have to be on his own terms.

And George did want him, wanted him desperately, the more so on such an evening as that dreadful one when he came home to tell Louise that he would not be returning to his office for a while. He had not been discharged, of course, but there had been something about his taking a rest until he felt in shape again. Although, he hastily added in alarm as he saw Louise's face go slack and pale, he never felt better in his life.

In the scene that followed, with Louise standing before him and passionately telling him things about himself that left him sick and shaken, he found White's words pouring through his mind in a bitter torrent. It was only when Louise was sitting exhausted in her armchair, her eyes fixed blankly on the wall before her, her knitting in her lap to console her, and he was at his table setting up the pieces, that he could feel the brackish tide of his pain receding.

'And yet there is a solution for all this,' White said softly, and turned his eyes toward Louise. 'A remarkably simple solution when one comes to think of it.'

George felt a chill run through him. 'I don't care to hear about it,' he said hoarsely.

'Have you ever noticed, George,' White persisted, 'that that piddling, hackneyed picture on the wall, set in that baroque monstrosity of a frame that Louise admires so much, is exactly like a pathetic little fife trying to make itself heard over an orchestra that is playing its loudest?'

George indicated the chessboard. 'You have the first move,' he said.

'Oh, the game,' White said. 'The game can wait, George. For the moment I'd much prefer to think what this room – this whole fine house, in fact – could be if it were all yours, George. Yours alone.'

'I'd rather get on with the game,' George pleaded.

'There's another thing, George,' White said slowly, and when he leaned forward George saw his own image again staring at him strangely from those eyes, 'another fine thing to think of. If you were all alone in this room, in this house, why, there wouldn't be anyone to tell you when to stop playing chess. You could play morning, noon, and night, and all around to the next morning if you cared to!

'And that's not all, George. You can throw that picture out the window and hang something respectable on the wall: a few good prints, perhaps – nothing extravagant, mind you – but a few good ones that stir you a bit the first time you come into the room each day and see them.

'And recordings! I understand they're doing marvelous things with recordings today, George. Think of a whole room filled with them: opera, symphony, concerto, quartet – just take your pick and play them to your heart's content!'

The sight of his image in those eyes always coming nearer, the jubilant flow of words, the terrible meaning of those words set George's head reeling. He clapped his hands over his ears and shook his head frantically.

'You're mad!' he cried. 'Stop it!' And then he discovered to his horror that even with his hands covering his ears he could hear White's voice as clearly and distinctly as ever.

'Is it the loneliness you're afraid of, George? But that's foolish. There are so many people who would be glad to be your friends, to talk to you, and, what's better, to listen to you. There are some who would even love you, if you chose.'

'Loneliness?' George said unbelievingly. 'Do you think it's loneliness I'm afraid of?'

'Then what is it?'

'You know as well as I,' George said in a shaking voice, 'what you're trying to lead me to. How could you expect me, expect any decent man, to be that cruel!'

White bared his teeth disdainfully. 'Can you tell me anything more cruel than a weak and stupid woman whose only ambition in life was to marry a man infinitely superior to her and then cut him down to her level so that her weakness and stupidity could always be concealed?'

'You've got no right to talk about Louise like that!'

'I have every right,' said White grimly, and somehow George knew in his heart that this was the dreadful truth. With a rising panic he clutched the edge of the table.

'I won't do it!' he said distractedly. 'I'll never do it, do you understand!'

'But it will be done!' White said, and his voice was so naked with terrible decision that George looked up to see Louise coming toward the table with her sharp little footsteps. She stood over it, her mouth working angrily, and then through the confusion of his thoughts he heard her voice echoing the same words again and again. 'You fool!' she was saying wildly. 'It's this chess! I've had enough of it!' And suddenly she swept her hand over the board and dashed the pieces from it.

'No!' cried George, not at Louise's gesture, but at the sight of White standing before her, the heavy poker raised in his hand. 'No!' George shouted again, and started up to block the fall of the poker, but knew even as he did so that it was too late.

Louise might have been dismayed at the untidy way her remains were deposited in the official basket; she would certainly have cried aloud (had she been in a position to do so) at the unsightly scar on the polished woodwork made by the basket as it was dragged along the floor and borne out of the front door. Inspector Lund, however, merely closed the door casually behind the little cortege and turned back to the living room.

Obviously the Lieutenant had completed his interrogation of the quiet little man seated in the chair next to the chess table, and obviously the Lieutenant was not happy. He paced the center of the floor, studying his notes with a furrowed brow, while the little man watched him, silent and motionless.

'Well?' said Inspector Lund.

'Well,' said the Lieutenant, 'there's just one thing that doesn't tie in. From what I put together, here's a guy who's living his life all right, getting along fine, and all of a sudden he finds he's got another self, another personality. He's like a man split into two parts, you might say.'

'Schizoid,' remarked Inspector Lund. 'That's not unusual.'

'Maybe not,' said the Lieutenant. 'Anyhow, this other self is no good at all, and sure enough it winds up doing this killing.'

'That all seems to tie in.' said Inspector Lund. 'What's the hitch?'

'Just one thing,' the Lieutenant stated: 'a matter of identity.' He frowned at his notebook, and then turned to the little man in the chair next to the chess table. 'What did you say your name was?' he demanded.

The little man drew his lips into a faintly sardonic grimace of rebuke. 'Why, I've told you that so many times before, Lieutenant, surely you couldn't have forgotten it again.' The little man smiled pleasantly. 'My name is White.'

# The Best of
# Everything

In Arthur's eyes they were all seemingly cut from one pattern. They were uniformly tall and well-built. They had regular features set into nicely tanned faces and capped by crew cuts. Their clothing was expensively staid; their manners were impeccable. They came from impressive Families and impressive Schools; and they regarded all these things casually. Among the bees that swarmed through the midtown hive, through Gothic piles redolent with the pleasant scent of gilt-edged securities, through glass pinnacles like futuristic fish bowls, they were not the most obtrusive, yet they were not lost.

To their jobs they brought the qualifications of Family and School and the capacity for looking politely eager when a superior addressed them. Actually, they were as casual about their jobs as they were about everything else, because they were cushioned with money. And for all this Arthur hated them, and would have sold his soul to be one of them.

Physically he might have passed muster. He was a tall, extremely good-looking young man – when he walked by, few women could resist giving him that quick little sidelong glance which means they are interested, even if unavailable – and he had a sober poise which was largely the product of shrewd observation and good self-control. But he came from no impressive Family, no impressive School – and he had no money outside of his moderate salary. His parents were dead (their legacy had barely paid their funeral expenses), he had left high school before graduation to go to work, and uneasily shifted jobs until he had recently come to port in Horton & Son, and he could, at any moment he was asked, have stated his net worth to the penny: the total of bank account, wallet, and change pocket. Obviously, he could not afford to be casual, as a fine young man should.

That phrase, *fine young man*, crystallized his hatred of the type. He had been standing outside Mr Horton's door one morning when the two sons of a client had been ushered out. Their eyes flicked over Arthur in the fraction of a second, instantly marked that he was not one of them, and turned blankly indifferent. Nothing was said, nothing done, but he was put neatly in his place in that moment and left to stand there with the hate and anger boiling in him. And he couldn't hit back, that was the worst of it; there was no way of touching them. Their homes, their clubs, their lives were inaccessible.

When the elevator door closed behind them Mr Horton seemed to notice Arthur for the first time. 'Fine young men,' he observed, almost wistfully, gesturing toward the elevator door, and the phrase had been planted. Not only planted, but fertilized on the spot by Mr Horton's tone which, to Arthur's inflamed mind, appeared to add: *They belong to my world, but you do not.*

And to make it worse, of course, there was Ann. Ann Horton.

It is the traditional right of every enterprising young man to apply himself as diligently to romance as to business, and to combine the highest degree of success in both by marrying the boss's daughter. And if the daughter happened to be as beautiful and desirable, and, to use the admiring expression of those who knew her, unspoiled, as Ann Horton, so much the better.

But what Arthur knew instinctively was that there are different degrees of being unspoiled. Thus, if a girl who desperately yearns for a forty-foot cabin cruiser and finally settles for a twenty-foot speedboat is unspoiled, Ann Horton was unspoiled. It is not quite sufficient to approach someone like this bringing only a burning passion and an eagerness to slay dragons. It is also necessary to come riding in golden armor, mounted on a blooded horse, and bearing orchestra seats to the best musical comedy in town. And, if the suitor is to make his point explicit, not on rare occasions, but frequently.

All this and more Arthur brooded over as he lay on his bed in Mrs Marsh's rooming house night after night and studied the ceiling. His thoughts were maddening, whirling around on themselves like the apocryphal snake seizing its own tail and then devouring itself. Ann Horton had looked at him more than once the way all women looked at him. If he could only meet her, offer her the image of himself that she required, was marriage out of the question? But to meet her on her terms took money, and, ironically, the only chance he ever had of getting money was to marry her! Good Lord, he thought, if he ever could do that he'd have enough money to throw into the face of every fine young man he'd ever hated.

So the thoughts slowly reshaped themselves, and without his quite knowing it Ann Horton became the means, not the end. The end would be the glory that comes to those who, without counting their money, can afford the best of everything. *The best of everything*, Arthur would say dreamily to himself, and his eyes would see beautiful, expensive pictures like clouds moving across the ceiling.

Charlie Prince was a young man who obviously had known the best of everything. He made his entrance into Arthur's life one lunch hour as Arthur sat finishing his coffee, his eyes on a Horton & Son prospectus spread on the table before him, his thoughts in a twenty-foot speedboat with Ann Horton.

'Hope you don't mind my asking,' said Charlie Prince, 'but do you work for old Horton?'

The voice was the voice of someone from a Family and a School; even the use of the word 'old' was a natural part of it, since the word was now in vogue among *them*, and could be applied to anything, no matter what its age might be. Arthur looked up from shoes, to suit, to shirt, to necktie, to hat, his mind mechanically tabbing them *Oliver Moore, Brooks, Sulka, Bronzini, Cavanaugh*, and then stopped short at the face. True, it was tanned, marked by regular features, and capped by the inevitable crew haircut, but there was something else about it. Some small lines about the eyes, some twist of the lips . . .

'That's right,' Arthur said warily, 'I work for Horton's.'

'Is it all right if I sit down here? My name's Charlie Prince.'

It turned out that Charlie Prince had seen the prospectus on the table, had once worked for Horton's himself, and couldn't resist stopping to ask how the old place was coming along.

'All right, I guess,' said Arthur, and then remarked, 'I don't remember seeing you around.'

'Oh, that was before your time, I suppose, and I'm sure the office is hardly encouraged to talk about me. You see, I'm sort of a blot on its escutcheon. I left under rather a cloud, if you get what I mean.'

'Oh,' said Arthur, and felt a quick, bitter envy for anyone who could afford to be incompetent, insubordinate even, and could leave a firm like Horton's so casually.

Charlie Prince, it appeared, read his thoughts quite accurately. 'No,' he said, 'it doesn't have anything to do with my not being able to hold down the job, if that's what you're thinking. It was a bit of dishonesty, really. Some checks I forged – stuff like that.'

Arthur's jaw dropped.

'I know,' observed Charlie Prince cheerfully. 'You figure that when someone gets caught in a business like that he ought to be all tears and remorse, all sackcloth and ashes, and such. But I'm not. Oh, of course, I was all remorse at getting caught by that idiot, meddling accountant, but you can hardly blame me for that.'

'But why did you do it?'

Charlie Prince frowned. 'I don't look like one of those silly psychopaths who just steals to get a thrill from it, do I? It was for the money, of course. It's always for money.'

'Always?'

'Oh, I worked in other places besides Horton's, and I was always leaving under a cloud. Matter of fact, it wasn't until I was in Horton's that I learned the biggest lesson of my life.' He leaned forward and tapped his forefinger on the table significantly. 'That business of tracing someone's signature is the bunk. Absolute bunk. If you're going to forge a name you just have to practice writing it freehand, and keep on practicing until you can set it down slapdash, like that. It's the only way.'

'But you got caught there, too.'

'That was carelessness. I was cashing the checks, but I didn't bother to make entries about them in the books. And you know what an accountant can be if his books don't balance.'

Arthur found himself fascinated, but also found himself unable to frame the question he wanted to ask and yet remain within the bounds of politeness. 'Then what happened? Did they – did you . . .?'

'You mean, arrested, sent to jail, stuff like that?' Charlie Prince looked at Arthur pityingly. 'Of course not. You know how these companies are about publicity like that, and when my father made the money good that's all there was to it.'

'And nothing at all happened to you?' Arthur said, awestruck.

'Well,' Charlie Prince admitted, 'something *had* to happen, of course, especially after that last performance when my father boiled up like an old steam kettle about it. But it wasn't too bad, really. It was just that I became a sort of local remittance man.'

'A what?' said Arthur blankly.

'A sort of local remittance man. You know how those old families in England would ship their black-sheep offspring off to Australia or somewhere just to keep them off the scene, then send them an allowance and tell them it would show up regularly as long as sonny stayed out of sight? Well, that's what happened to me. At first the old man was just going to heave me out into the cold and darkness without even a penny, but the women in my family have soft hearts, and he was convinced otherwise. I would get a monthly allowance – about half of what I needed to live on, as it turned out – but for the rest of my life I had to steer clear of my family and its whole circle. And I can tell you, it's a mighty big circle.'

'Then you're not supposed to be in New York, are you?'

'I said I was a local remittance man. Meaning, I can be anywhere I please as long as I am not heard or seen by any of my family or its three million acquaintances. In which case I merely drop a note to the family lawyer stating my address, and on the first of each month I receive my allowance.'

'Well,' said Arthur, 'considering everything, I'd say your father was being very decent about it.'

Charlie Prince sighed. 'Truth to tell, he's not a bad old sort at all. But he's cursed by a morbid yearning toward a certain kind of holy young prig which I am not. You know what I mean. The sort of young squirt who's all bland exterior, bland interior, and not a spark anywhere. If I had turned out like that, everything would have been just dandy. But I didn't. So here I am, a veritable Ishmael, two weeks before allowance comes due, locked out of his hotel room . . .'

Arthur felt an inexplicable stirring of excitement. 'Locked out?'

'That's what happens when you can't pay your rent. It's a law or a code or something. Anyhow, it's damn thoughtless whatever it is, and what I'm leading up to is, in return for the story of my life, such as it is, you might see your way clear to making a loan. Not too small a one either; a sort of medium-sized loan. I'll guarantee to pay you back the first of the month and with fair interest.' Charlie Prince's voice now had an openly pleading note. 'I'll admit that I have my dishonest side, but I've never welshed on a debt in my whole life. Matter of fact,' he explained, 'the only reason I got myself into trouble was because I was so anxious to pay my debts.'

Arthur looked at Charlie Prince's perfect clothes; he saw Charlie Prince's easy poise; he heard Charlie Prince's well-modulated voice sounding pleasantly in his ears, and the stirring of excitement suddenly took meaning.

'Look,' he said, 'where do you live now?'

'Nowhere, of course, not as long as I'm locked out. But I'll meet you here the first of the month on the minute. I can swear you don't have to worry about getting the money back. The way I've been talking about things ought to prove I'm on the dead level with you.'

'I don't mean that,' said Arthur. 'I mean, would you want to share a room with me? If I lent you enough money to clear up your hotel bill and get your things out of there, would you move in with me? I've got a nice room; it's in an old house but very well kept. Mrs Marsh – that is, the landlady – is the talky kind and very fussy about things, but you can see she's the sort to keep a place nice. And it's very cheap; it would save you a lot of money.'

He stopped short then with the realization that this was turning into a vehement sales talk, and that Charlie Prince was regarding him quizzically.

'What is it?' said Charlie Prince. 'Are you broke, too?'

'No, it has nothing to do with money. I have the money to lend you, don't I?'

'Then why the fever to share the room? Especially with me, that is.'

Arthur took his courage in both hands. 'All right, I'll tell you. You have something I want.'

Charlie Prince blinked. 'I do?'

'Listen to me,' Arthur said. 'I never had any of the things you had, and it shows. Somehow, it shows. I know it does, because you wouldn't ever talk to any of those young men, the sort your father likes, the way you talk to me. But I don't care about that. What I care about is finding out exactly what makes you like that, what makes them all like that. It's some kind of polish that a good family and money can rub on you so that it never comes off. And that's what I want.'

Charlie Prince looked at him wonderingly. 'And you think that if we share a room some of this mysterious polish, this whatever-it-is, will rub off on you?'

'You let me worry about that,' said Arthur. He drew out his checkbook and a pen, and laid them on the table before him. 'Well?' he said.

Charlie Prince studied the checkbook thoughtfully. 'I'll admit I haven't any idea of what I'm selling,' he said, 'but it's a sale.'

As it turned out, they made excellent roommates. There is no greater compatability than that between a good talker and a good listener, and since Charlie Prince liked nothing better than to pump amiably from a bottomless well of anecdote and reminiscence, and Arthur made an almost feverishly interested audience, life in the second-floor front at Mrs Marsh's rooming house was idyllic.

There were some very small flies in the ointment, of course. At times, Charlie Prince might have had cause to reflect that he had found too good a listener in Arthur, considering Arthur's insatiable appetite for detail. It can be quite disconcerting for a raconteur embarked on the story of a yachting experience to find that he must describe the dimensions of the yacht, its structure, its method of operation, and then enter into a lecture on the comparative merits of various small boats, before he can get to the point of the story itself. Or to draw full value from the narrative of an intriguing little episode concerning a young woman met in a certain restaurant, when one is also required to add footnotes on the subject of what to say to a *maitre d'hotel*, how to order, how to tip, how to dress for every occasion, and so on, *ad infinitum*.

It might also have distressed Charlie Prince, who had commendable powers of observation, to note that Arthur was becoming subtly cast in his own image. The inflection of voice, the choice of words and their usage, the manner of sitting, walking, standing, the gestures of the hands, the very shades of expression which Arthur came to adopt, all had the rather uncomfortable quality of showing Charlie Prince to himself in a living mirror.

For Arthur's part the one thing that really shocked him in his relationship was the discovery of the childishness of Charlie Prince and his small world. From all he could gather, Arthur decided somberly, Charlie Prince and his like emerged from childhood into adolescence, and stopped short there. Physically, they might grow still larger and more impressive. but mentally and emotionally, they were all they would ever be. They would learn adult catchwords and mannerisms, but underneath? Of course, it was nothing that Arthur ever chose to mention aloud.

His feeling on the subject was heightened by the matter of Charlie Prince's allowance. On the first of each month Mrs Marsh would smilingly enter the room bearing an envelope addressed to Charlie Prince. It was an expensive-looking envelope, and if one held it up to the light reflectively, as Charlie Prince always did before opening it, it was possible to make out the outlines of an expensive-looking slip of paper. A check for five hundred dollars signed by James Llewellyn. 'The family's personal lawyer,' Charlie Prince had once explained, and added with some bitterness, 'It wasn't hard enough having one father like mine, so old Llewellyn's been playing second father since I was a kid.'

To Charlie Prince the amount was a pittance. To Arthur it was the Key. The Key to the enchanted garden just outside Arthur's reach; the Key to Bluebeard's chamber which you were forbidden to use; the Key to Ann Horton. It would not pay for what you wanted, but it would open the door.

Even more tantalizing to Arthur was the fact that for a few hours each month it was all his. Charlie Prince would endorse it, and then Arthur would obligingly stop in at the bank where he had his own small account and cash it there. On his return he would carefully deduct the amount of Charlie Prince's share of the rent, the amount that Charlie Prince had borrowed from him the last week or two of the preceding month, and then turn the rest over to his roommate. It was at Charlie Prince's insistence that he did this. 'If you want to make sure that I'm square with my rent and whatever I owe you,' he had explained, 'this is the best way. Besides, you can cash it easily, and I seem to have a lot of trouble that way.'

Thus, for a few hours each month Arthur was another man. Charlie Prince was generous about lending his wardrobe, and Arthur made it a point on check-cashing day especially to wear one of those wondrously cut and textured suits, which looked as if it had been tailored for him. And in the breast pocket of that suit was a wallet containing five hundred dollars in crisp new bills. It was no wonder that it happened to be one of those days on which he made the impression he had dreamed of making.

He entered his employer's office, and Ann Horton was seated on a corner of the desk there, talking to her father. She glanced at Arthur as he stood there, and then stopped short in what she was saying to look him up and down with open admiration.

'Well,' she said to her father, 'I've seen this young man here and there in the office several times. Don't you think it's about time you had the manners to introduce us?'

Her manner of address startled Arthur, who had somehow always visualized Mr Horton as a forbidding figure poised on a mountaintop fingering a thunderbolt. But it was even more startling when Mr Horton, after what seemed to be a moment of uncertain recognition, made the introduction in terms that sounded like music to Arthur's ears. Arthur, he said warmly, was a fine young man. It would be a pleasure to introduce him.

That was Arthur's golden opportunity – and he flubbed it. Flubbed it miserably. What he said was pointless; the way he said it made it sound even more mawkish and clumsy than seemed possible. And even while he was watching the glow fade from Ann Horton's face he knew what the trouble was, and cursed himself and the whole world for it.

The money wasn't *his*, that was the thing. If it were he could be seeing her that evening, and the next, and the next, and the one after that. But it wasn't. It was a meaningless bulge in his wallet that could take him this far, and no farther. And that knowledge made everything else meaningless: the clothes, the manner, everything he had made himself into. Without the money it was all nonsense. With it . . .

With it! He had been looking merely ill at ease; now he looked physically ill under the impact of the thought that struck him. An instant concern showed in Ann Horton's lovely eyes. Apparently she was a girl with strong maternal instinct.

'You're not well,' she said.

The idea, the glorious realization, was a flame roaring through him now. He rose from it like a phoenix.

'No, I don't feel very well,' he answered, and could hardly recognize his own voice as he spoke, 'but it's nothing serious. Really, it isn't.'

'Well, you ought to go home right now,' she said firmly. 'I have the car downstairs, and it won't be any trouble at all . . .'

Arthur mentally struck himself on the forehead with his fist. He had thrown away one opportunity; did he have to throw this one away as well? Yet, Mrs Marsh's rooming house had never appeared as wretched as it did just then; it was impossible to have her drive him there.

Inspiration put the words into his mouth, the proper words to impress the father and daughter. 'There's so much work to be done,' said Arthur, wistfully courageous, 'that I can't possibly leave it.' And then he added with as much ease as if he had practiced the lines for hours. 'But I do want to see you again. Do you think if I called tomorrow evening . . .?'

After that, he told himself grimly whenever the fire inside him threatened to flicker uncertainly, he had no choice. And Charlie Prince, of course, was not even offered a choice. At exactly seven minutes before midnight, after considerable choked protest and thrashing around, Charlie Prince lay dead on his bed. Entirely dead, although Arthur's fingers remained clasped around his throat for another long minute just to make sure.

It has been remarked that the man with the likeliest chance of getting away with murder is the man who faces his victim in a crowd, fires a bullet into him, and then walks off – which is a way of saying that it is the devious and overly ingenious method of murder that will hang the murderer. To that extent Arthur had committed his murder wisely, although not out of wisdom.

The fact is that from the moment he had left Ann Horton to the moment he finally released his fingers from Charlie Prince's throat he had lived in a sort of blind fever of knowing what had to be done without a thought of how it was to be done. And when at last he stood looking down at the body before him, with the full horror of what had happened bursting in his mind, he was at a complete loss. The soul had departed, no question about that. But the body remained, and what in the Lord's name was one to do with it?

He could bundle it into the closet, get it out of sight at least, but what would be the point of that? Mrs Marsh came in every morning to make up the room and empty the wastebaskets. Since there was no lock on the closet door there was no way of keeping her out of it.

Or take Charlie Prince's trunk standing there in the corner. He could deposit the body in it, and ship it somewhere. Ship it where? He put his mind to the question desperately, but was finally forced to the conclusion that there was no place in the world to which you could ship a trunk with a body in it, and rest assured that murder wouldn't out.

But he was on the right track with that trunk, and when the solution came at last, he recognized it instantly and eagerly. The storage room in Mrs Marsh's was a dank cavern in the depths of the house, barred by a heavy door, which, though never locked, made it a desolate and chilly place no matter what the season. Since there was no traffic in that room, a body could molder there for years without anyone being the wiser. Eventually, it could be disposed of with no difficulty; the object now was to get it into the trunk and down to the storage room.

To Arthur's annoyance he discovered that even though the

trunk was a large one it made a tight fit, and it was a messy business getting everything arranged neatly. But at last he had it bolted tightly, and out into the hallway. It was when he was midway down the stairs that the accident happened. He felt the trunk slipping down his back, gave it a violent heave to right it, and the next instant saw it go sliding over his head to crash down the rest of the distance to the floor with a thunder that shook the house. He was after it in an instant, saw that it remained firmly bolted, and then realized that he was standing eye to eye with Mrs Marsh.

She was poised there like a frightened apparition, clad in a white flannel nightgown that fell to her ankles, her fingers to her lips, her eyes wide.

'Dear me,' she said, 'dear me, you should be more careful!'

Arthur flung himself in front of the trunk as if she had vision that could penetrate its walls. 'I'm sorry,' he stammered. 'I'm terribly sorry. I didn't mean to make any noise, but somehow it slipped . . .'

She shook her head with gentle severity. 'You might have scratched the walls. Or hurt yourself.'

'No,' he assured her hastily, 'there's no damage done. None.'

She peered around him at the trunk. 'Why, that's that nice Mr Prince's trunk, isn't it? Wherever can you be taking it at this hour?'

Arthur felt the perspiration start on his forehead. 'Nowhere,' he said hoarsely, and then when she knit her brows in wonder at this he quickly added, 'That is, to the storage room. You see, Charlie – Mr Prince – was supposed to give me a hand with it, but when he didn't show up I decided to try it myself.'

'But it must be so heavy.'

Her warmly sympathetic tone served nicely to steady his nerves. His thoughts started to move now with the smooth precision of the second hand on a good watch.

'I suppose it is,' he said, and laughed deprecatingly, 'but it seemed better to do it myself than keep waiting for Mr Prince to help. He's very unreliable, you know. Just takes off when he wants to, and you never know how long he'll be gone.'

'I think it's a shame,' said Mrs Marsh firmly.

'No, no, he's a bit eccentric, that's all. But really very nice when you get to know him.' Arthur took a grip on the trunk. 'I'll get it down the rest of the way easily enough,' he said.

A thought struck Mrs Marsh. 'Oh, dear me,' she chirped, 'perhaps everything did happen for the best. I mean, your making a noise and bringing me out and all. You see, there's a lock on the storage room now, and you'd never have got in. I'll just slip on a robe and take care of that.'

She went ahead of him down the creaking cellar steps, and waited in the storage room until he trundled the trunk into it. A dim light burned there, and, as he had remembered, dust lay thick over everything in sight. Mrs Marsh shook her head over it.

'It's dreadful,' she said, 'but there's really no point in trying to do anything about it. Why, I don't believe anyone uses this room from one year to the next! The only reason I put the lock on the door was because the insurance company wanted it there.'

Arthur shifted from one foot to the other. His mission completed, he was willing, in fact, anxious, to leave, but Mrs Marsh seemed oblivious to this.

'I don't encourage transients,' she said. 'What I like is a nice steady gentleman boarder who's no fuss and bother. Now, take that trunk there,' she pointed a bony forefinger at what appeared to be a mound of ashes, but which proved on a second look to be a trunk buried under years of dust. 'When that gentleman moved in . . .'

Arthur felt himself swaying on his feet while the gentle chirping went on and on. In this fashion he learned about the gentleman in the first-floor rear, the gentleman in the second-floor rear, and the gentleman in the third-floor front. It was as though her conversational stream had been dammed up so long that now it was released there was no containing it. And through it all he sustained himself with one thought. He had got away with murder – really and literally got away with murder. When the door to the storage room closed behind him, Charlie Prince could rot away without a soul in the world being the wiser. The checks would come every month, five hundred dollars each and every month, and there was Ann Horton and the world of glory ahead. *The best of everything*, Arthur thought in and around Mrs

Marsh's unwearying voice, and he knew then what it felt like to be an emperor incognito.

The monologue had to come to an end sometime, the heavy door was locked and stayed locked, and Arthur entered his new station with the confidence that is supposed to be the lot of the righteous, but which may also come to those who have got away with murder and know it beyond the shadow of a doubt. And even the tiniest fragment of unease could not possibly remain after he met Mrs Marsh in the hallway one evening a few weeks later.

'You were right,' she said, pursing her lips sympathetically. 'Mr Prince *is* eccentric, isn't he?'

'He is?' said Arthur uncertainly.

'Oh, yes. Like practicing writing his name on every piece of paper he can get his hands on. Just one sheet of paper after another with nothing on it but his name!'

Arthur abruptly remembered his wastebasket, and then thought with a glow of undeserved self-admiration how everything, even unforgivable carelessness, worked for him.

'I'm sure,' observed Mrs Marsh, 'that a grown man can find better things to do with his time than that. It just goes to show you.'

'Yes,' said Arthur. 'it certainly does.'

So, serenity reigned over Mrs Marsh's. It reigned elsewhere, too, since Arthur had no difficulty at all in properly endorsing those precious checks, and even less trouble in spending the money. Using Charlie Prince's wardrobe as his starting point, he built his into a thing of quiet splendor. Drawing from Charlie Prince's narratives, he went to the places where one should be seen, and behaved as one should behave. His employer beamed on him with a kindly eye which became almost affectionate when Arthur mentioned the income a generous aunt had provided for him; his acquaintance with Ann Horton, who had seemed strangely drawn to him from the first evening they spent together, soon blossomed into romance.

He found Ann Horton everything he had ever imagined – passionate, charming, devoted. Of course, she had her queer little reticences, dark little places in her own background that she chose not to touch upon, but, as he reminded himself, who was he to cast stones? So he behaved himself flawlessly up to the point where they had to discuss the wedding, and then they had their first quarrel.

There was no question about the wedding itself. It was to take place in June, the month of brides; it was to be followed by a luxurious honeymoon; after which, Arthur would enter into a position of importance in the affairs of Horton & Son at a salary commensurate with that position, of course. No, there was no question about the wedding – the envy in the eyes of every fine young man who had ever courted Ann Horton attested to that – but there was a grave question about the ceremony.

'But *why* do you insist on a big ceremony?' she demanded. 'I think they're dreadful things. All those people and all that fuss. It's like a Roman circus.'

He couldn't explain to her, and that complicated matters. After all, there is no easy way of explaining to any girl that her wedding is not only to be a nuptial, but also a sweet measure of revenge. It would be all over the papers; the whole world of fine young men would be on hand to witness it. They had to be there, or it would be tasteless in the mouth.

'And why do you insist on a skimpy little private affair?' he asked in turn. 'I should think a girl's wedding would be the most important thing in the world to her. That she'd want to do it up proud. Standing there in the living-room with your father and aunt doesn't seem like any ceremony at all.'

'But you'll be there, too,' she said. 'That's what makes it a ceremony.'

He was not to be put off by any such feminine wit, however, and he let her know it. In the end, she burst into tears and fled, leaving him as firm in his convictions as ever. If it cost him his neck, he told himself angrily, he was not going to have any hit-and-run affair fobbed off on him as the real thing. He'd have the biggest cathedral in town, the most important people – the best of everything.

When they met again she was in a properly chastened mood, so he was properly magnanimous.

'Darling,' she said, 'did you think I was very foolish carrying on the way I did?'

'Of course not, Ann. Don't you think I understand how high-strung you are, and how seriously you take this?'

'You are a darling, Arthur,' she said, 'really you are. And perhaps, in a way, your insistence on a big ceremony has done more for us than you'll ever understand.'

'In what way?' he asked.

'I can't tell you that. But I can tell you that I haven't been as happy in years as I'm going to be if things work out.'

'What things?' he asked, completely at sea in the face of this feminine ambiguity.

'Before I can even talk about it there's one question you must answer, Arthur. And please, promise you'll answer truthfully.'

'Of course I will.'

'Then can you find it in your heart to forgive someone who's done a great wrong? Someone who's done wrong, but suffered for it?'

He grimaced inwardly. 'Of course I can. I don't care what wrong anyone's done. It's my nature to forgive him.'

He almost said *her* but caught himself in time. After all, if that was the way she wanted to build up to a maidenly confession, why spoil it? But there seemed to be no confession forthcoming. She said nothing more about the subject – instead, spent the rest of the evening in such a giddy discussion of plans and arrangements that by the time he left her the matter was entirely forgotten.

He was called into Mr Horton's office late the next afternoon, and when he entered the room he saw Ann there. From her expression and from her father's he could guess what they had been discussing, and he felt a pleasant triumph in that knowledge.

'Arthur,' said Mr Horton, 'please sit down.'

Arthur sat down, crossed his legs, and smiled at Ann.

'Arthur,' said Mr Horton, 'I have something serious to discuss with you.'

'Yes, sir,' said Arthur, and waited patiently for Mr Horton to finish arranging three pencils, a pen, a letter opener, a memorandum pad, and a telephone before him on the desk.

'Arthur,' Mr Horton said at last, 'what I'm going to tell you is something few people know, and I hope you will follow their example and never discuss it with anyone else.'

'Yes, sir,' said Arthur.

'Ann has told me that you insist on a big ceremony with all the trimmings, and that's what makes the problem. A private ceremony would have left things as they were, and no harm done. Do you follow me?'

'Yes, sir,' said Arthur, lying valiantly. He looked furtively at Ann, but no clue was to be found there. 'Of course, sir,' he said.

'Then, since I'm a man who likes to get to the point quickly I will tell you that I have a son. You're very much like him – in fact, Ann and I were both struck by that resemblance some time ago – but unfortunately, my son happens to be a thoroughgoing scoundrel. And after one trick too many he was simply bundled off to fend for himself on an allowance I provided. I haven't heard from him since – my lawyer takes care of the details – but if there is to be a big ceremony with everyone on hand to ask questions he must be there. You understand that, of course.'

The room seemed to be closing in around Arthur, and Mr Horton's face was suddenly a diabolic mask floating against the wall.

'Yes, sir,' Arthur whispered.

'That means I must do something now that Ann's been after me to do for years. I have the boy's address; we're all going over right now to meet him, to talk to him, and see if he can't get off to a fresh start with your example before him.'

'Prince Charlie,' said Ann fondly. 'That's what we all used to call him, he was so charming.'

The walls were very close now, the walls of a black chamber, and Ann's face floating alongside her father's. And, strangely enough, there was the face of Mrs Marsh. The kindly, garrulous face of Mrs Marsh growing so much bigger than the others.

And a trunk, waiting.

# The Betrayers

Between them was a wall. And since it was only a flimsy,
jerry-built partition, a sounding board between apartments, Robert came to know the girl that way.

At first she was the sound of footsteps, the small firm rap of
high heels moving in a pattern of activity around her room. She
must be very young, he thought idly, because at the time he was
deep in *Green Mansions*, pursuing the lustrous Rima through a
labyrinth of Amazonian jungle. Later he came to know her
voice, light and breathless when she spoke, warm and gay when
she raised it in chorus to some popular song dinning from her
radio. She must be very lovely, he thought then, and after that
found himself listening deliberately, and falling more and more
in love with her as he listened.

Her name was Amy, and there was a husband, too, a man
called Vince who had a flat, unpleasant voice, and a sullen way
about him. Occasionally there were quarrels which the man
invariably ended by slamming the door of their room and
thundering down the stairs as loud as he could. Then she would
cry, a smothered whimpering, and Robert, standing close to the
wall between them, would feel as if a hand had been thrust
inside his chest and was twisting his heart. He would think
wildly of the few steps that would take him to her door, the few
words that would let her know he was her friend, was willing to
do something – anything – to help her. Perhaps, meeting face
to face, she would recognize his love. Perhaps–

So the thoughts whirled around and around, but Robert only
stood there, taut with helplessness.

And there was no one to confide in, which made it that much
harder. The only acquaintances he numbered in the world were

the other men in his office, and they would never have understood. He worked, prosaically enough, in the credit department of one of the city's largest department stores, and too many years there had ground the men around him to a fine edge of cynicism. The business of digging into people's records, of searching for the tax difficulties, the clandestine affairs with expensive women, the touch of larceny in every human being – all that was bound to have an effect, they told Robert, and if he stayed on the job much longer he'd find it out for himself.

What would they tell him now? *A pretty girl next door? Husband's away most of the time? Go on, make yourself at home!*

How could he make them understand that that wasn't what he was looking for? That what he wanted was someone to meet his love halfway, someone to put an end to the cold loneliness that settled in on him like a stone during the dark hours of each night.

So he said nothing about it to anyone, but stayed close to the wall, drawing from it what he could. And knowing the girl as he had come to, he was not surprised when he finally saw her. The mail for all the apartments was left on a table in the downstairs hallway, and as he walked down the stairs to go to work that morning, he saw her take a letter from the table and start up the stairway toward him.

There was never any question in his mind that this was the girl. She was small and fragile and dark-haired, and all the loveliness he had imagined in her from the other side of the wall was there in her face. She was wearing a loose robe, and as she passed him on the stairway she pulled the robe closer to her breast and slipped by almost as if she were afraid of him. He realized with a start that he had been staring unashamedly, and with his face red he turned down the stairs to the street. But he walked the rest of his way in a haze of wonderment.

He saw her a few times after that, always under the same conditions, but it took weeks before he mustered enough courage to stop at the foot of the stairs and turn to watch her retreating form above: the lovely fine line of ankle, the roundness of calf, the curve of body pressing against the robe. And then as she reached the head of the stairs, as if aware he was watching her, she looked down at him and their eyes met.

For a heart-stopping moment Robert tried to understand what he read in her face, and then her husband's voice came flat and belligerent from the room. 'Amy,' it said, 'what's holdin' you up!' – and she was gone, and the moment with her.

When he saw the husband he marveled that she had chosen someone like that. A small, dapper gamecock of a man, he was good-looking in a hard way, but with the skin drawn so tight over his face that the cheekbones jutted sharply and the lips were drawn into a thin menacing line. He glanced at Robert up and down out of the corners of blank eyes as they passed, and in that instant Robert understood part of what he had seen in the girl's face. This man was as dangerous as some half-tamed animal that would snap at any hand laid on him, no matter what its intent. Just being near him you could smell danger, as surely the girl did her every waking hour.

The violence in the man exploded one night with force enough to waken Robert from a deep sleep. It was not the pitch of the voice, Robert realized, sitting up half-dazed in bed, because the words were almost inaudible through the wall; it was the vicious intensity that was so frightening.

He slipped out of bed and laid his ear against the wall. Standing like that, his eyes closed while he strained to follow the choppy phrases, he could picture the couple facing each other as vividly as if the wall had dissolved before him.

'*So you know*,' the man said. '*So what?*'

'*. . . getting out!*' the girl said.

'*And then tell everybody? Tell the whole world?*'

'*I won't!*' The girl was crying now. '*I swear I won't!*'

'*Think I'd take a chance?*' the man said, and then his voice turned soft and derisive. '*Ten thousand dollars*,' he said. '*Where else could I get it? Digging ditches?*'

'*Better that way! This way . . . I'm getting out!*'

His answer was not delivered in words. It came in the form of a blow so hard that when she reeled back and struck the wall, the impact stung Robert's face. '*Vince!*' she screamed; the sound high and quavering with terror. '*Don't, Vince!*'

Every nerve in Robert was alive now with her pain as the next blow was struck. His fingernails dug into the wall at the hard-breathing noises of scuffling behind it as she was pulled away.

'*Ahh, no!*' she cried out, and then there was the sound of a breath being drawn hoarsely and agonizingly into lungs no longer responsive to it, the thud of a flaccid weight striking the floor, and suddenly silence. A terrible silence.

As if the wall itself were her cold, dead flesh Robert recoiled from it, then stood staring at it in horror. His thoughts twisted and turned on themselves insanely, but out of them loomed one larger and larger so that he had to face it and recognize it.

She had been murdered, and as surely as though he had been standing there beside her he was a witness to it! He had been so close that if the wall were not there he could have reached out his hand and touched her. Done something to help her. Instead, he had waited like a fool until it was too late.

But there was still something to be done, he told himself wildly. And as long as this madman in the next room had no idea there was a witness he could still be taken red-handed. A call to the police, and in five minutes . . .

But before he could take the first nerveless step Robert heard the room next door stealthily come to life again. There was a sound of surreptitious motion, of things being shifted from their place; then, clearly defined, a lifeless weight being pulled along the floor, and the cautious creaking of a door opened wide. It was that last sound which struck Robert with a sick comprehension of what was happening.

The murderer was a monster, but he was no fool. If he could safely dispose of the body now during these silent hours of the night he was, to all intents and purposes, a man who had committed no crime at all!

At his door Robert stopped short. From the hallway came the deliberate thump of feet finding their way down the stairs with the weight dragging behind them. The man had killed once. He was reckless enough in this crisis to risk being seen with his victim. What would such a man do to anyone who confronted him at such a time?

Robert leaned back against his door, his eyes closed tight, a choking constriction in his throat as if the man's hands were already around it. He was a coward, there was no way around it. Faced with the need to show some courage he had discovered he was a rank coward, and he saw the girl's face before him now, not with fear in it, but contempt.

But – and the thought gave him a quick sense of triumph – he could still go to the police. He saw himself doing it, and the sense of triumph faded away. He had heard some noises, and from that had constructed a murder. The body? There would be none. The murderer? None. Only a man whose wife had left him because he had quarreled with her. The accuser? A young man who had wild dreams. A perfect fool. In short, Robert himself.

It was only when he heard the click of the door downstairs that he stepped out into the hallway and started down, step by careful step. Halfway down he saw it, a handkerchief, small and crumpled and blotched with an ugly stain. He picked it up gingerly, and holding it up toward the dim light overhead let it fall open. The stain was bright sticky red almost obscuring in one corner the word *Amy* carefully embroidered there. Blood. *Her* blood. Wouldn't that be evidence enough for anyone?

*Sure*, he could hear the policeman answer him jeeringly, *evidence of a nosebleed, all right*, and he could feel the despair churn in him.

It was the noise of the car that roused him, and then he flew down the rest of the stairs, but too late. As he pressed his face to the curtain of the front door the car roared away from the curb, its taillights gleaming like malevolent eyes, its license plate impossible to read in the dark. If he had only been an instant quicker, he raged at himself, only had sense enough to understand that the killer must use a car for his purpose, he could easily have identified it. Now, even that chance was gone. Every chance was gone.

He was in his room pacing the floor feverishly when within a half hour he heard the furtive sounds of the murderer's return. *And why not*, Robert thought; *he's gotten rid of her, he's safe now, he can go on as if nothing at all had happened.*

*If I were only someone who could go into that room and beat the truth out of him*, the thought boiled on, *or someone with such wealth or position that I would be listened to . . .*

But all that was as unreal and vaporous as his passion for the girl had been. What weapon of vengeance could he possibly have at his command, a nobody working in a . . .

Robert felt the sudden realization wash over him in a cold wave. His eyes narrowed on the wall as if, word by word, the idea was being written on it in a minute hand.

Everyone has a touch of larceny in him – wasn't that what the old hands in his department were always saying? Everyone was suspect. Certainly the man next door, with his bent for violence, his talk of ten thousand dollars come by in some unlikely way, must have black marks on his record that the authorities, blind as they might be, could recognize and act on. If someone skilled in investigation were to strip the man's past down, layer by layer, justice would have to be done. That was the weapon: the dark past itself stored away in the man, waiting only to be ignited!

Slowly and thoughtfully Robert slipped the girl's crumpled handkerchief into an envelope and sealed it. Then, straining to remember the exact words, he wrote down on paper the last violent duologue between murderer and victim. Paper and envelope both went into a drawer of his dresser, and the first step had been taken.

But then, Robert asked himself, what did he know about the man? His name was Vince, and that was all. Hardly information which could serve as the starting point of a search through the dark corridors of someone's past. There must be something more than that, something to serve as a lead.

It took Robert the rest of a sleepless night to hit on the idea of the landlady. A stout and sleepy-eyed woman whose only interest in life seemed to lie in the prompt collection of her rent, she still must have some information about the man. She occupied the rear apartment on the ground floor, and as early in the morning as he dared Robert knocked on her door.

She looked more sleepy-eyed than ever as she pondered his question. 'Them?' she said at last. 'That's the Sniders. Nice people, all right.' She blinked at Robert. 'Not having any trouble with them, are you?'

'No. Not at all. But is that all you can tell me about them? I mean, don't you know where they're from, or anything like that?'

The landlady shrugged. 'I'm sure it's none of my business,' she said loftily. 'All I know is they pay on the first of the month right on the dot, and they're nice respectable people.'

He turned away from her heavily, and as he did so he saw the street door close behind the postman. It was as if a miracle had been passed for him. The landlady was gone, he was all alone with that little heap of mail on the table, and there staring up at him was an envelope neatly addressed to Mrs Vincent Snider.

All the way to his office he kept that envelope hidden away in an inside pocket, and it was only when he was locked in the seclusion of his cubicle that he carefully slit it open and studied its contents. A single page with only a few lines on it, a noncommittal message about the family's well-being, and the signature: *Your sister, Celia*. Not much to go on – but wait, there was a return address on the stationery, an address in a small upstate town.

Robert hesitated only a moment, then thrust letter and envelope into his pocket, straightened his jacket, and walked into the office of his superior. Mr Sprague, in charge of the department and consequently the most ulcerated and cynical member of it, regarded him sourly.

'Yes?' he said.

'I'm sorry, sir,' said Robert, 'but I'll need a few days off. You see, there's been a sudden death.'

Mr Sprague sighed at this pebble cast into the smooth pool of his department's routine, but his face fell into the proper sympathetic lines.

'Somebody close?'

'Very close,' said Robert.

The walk from the railroad station to the house was a short one. The house itself had a severe and forbidding air about it, as did the young woman who opened the door in answer to Robert's knock.

'Yes,' she said, 'my sister's name is Amy Snider. Her married name, that is. I'm Celia Thompson.'

'What I'm looking for,' Robert said, 'is some information about her. About your sister.'

The woman looked stricken. 'Something's happened to her?'

'In a way,' Robert said. He cleared his throat hard. 'You see, she's disappeared from her apartment, and I'm looking into it. Now, if you . . .'

'You're from the police?'

'I'm acting for them,' Robert said, and prayed that this ambiguity would serve in place of identification. The prayer was answered, the woman gestured him into the house, and sat down facing him in the bare and uninviting living room.

'I knew,' the woman said, 'I knew something would happen,' and she rocked piteously from side to side in her chair.

Robert reached forward and touched her hand gently. 'How did you know?'

'How? What else could you expect when you drive a child out of her home and slam the door in her face! When you throw her out into the world not even knowing how to take care of herself!'

Robert withdrew his hand abruptly. 'You did *that*?'

'My father did it. *Her* father.'

'But why?'

'If you knew him,' the woman said. 'A man who thinks anything pretty is sinful. A man who's so scared of hellfire and brimstone that he's kept us in it all our lives!

'When she started to get so pretty, and the boys pestering her all the time, he turned against her just like that. And when she had her trouble with that man he threw her out of the house, bag and baggage. And if he knew I was writing letters to her,' the woman said fearfully, 'he'd throw me out, too. I can't even say her name in front of him, the way he is.'

'Look,' Robert said eagerly, 'that man she had trouble with. Was that the one she married? That Vincent Snider?'

'I don't know,' the woman said vaguely. 'I just don't know. Nobody knows except Amy and my father, the way it was kept such a secret. I didn't even know she was married until all of a sudden she wrote me a letter about it from the city.'

'But if your father knows, I can talk to him about it.'

'No! You can't! If he even knew I told you as much as I did . . .'

'But I can't let it go at that,' he pleaded. 'I have to find out about this man, and then maybe we can straighten everything out.'

'All right,' the woman said wearily, 'there is somebody. But not my father, you've got to keep away from him for my sake. There's this teacher over at the high school, this Miss Benson. She's the one to see. And she liked Amy; she's the one Amy mails my letters to, so my father won't know. Maybe she'll tell you, even if she won't tell anybody else. I'll write you a note to her, and you go see her.'

At the door he thanked her, and she regarded him with a hard, straight look. 'You have to be pretty to get yourself in trouble,' she said, 'so it's something that'll never bother me. But you find Amy, and you make sure she's all right.'

'Yes,' Robert said. 'I'll try.'

At the school he was told that Miss Benson was the typewriting teacher, that she had classes until three, and that if he wished to speak to her alone he would have to wait until then. So for hours he fretfully walked the few main streets of the town, oblivious of the curious glances of passers-by, and thinking of Amy. These were the streets she had known. These shop windows had mirrored her image. And, he thought with a sharp jealousy, not always alone. There had been boys. Attracted to her, as boys would be, but careless of her, never realizing the prize they had. But if he had known her then, if he could have been one of them . . .

At three o'clock he waited outside the school building until it had emptied, and then went in eagerly. Miss Benson was a small woman, gray-haired and fluttering, almost lost among the grim ranks of hooded typewriters in the room. After Robert had explained himself and she had read Celia Thompson's note she seemed ready to burst into tears.

'It's wrong of her!' she said. 'It's dreadfully wrong of her to send you to me. She must have known that.'

'But why is it wrong?'

'Why? Because she knows I don't want to talk about it to anyone. She knows what it would cost me if I did, that's why!'

'Look,' Robert said patiently, 'I'm not trying to find out what happened. I'm only trying to find out about this man Amy had trouble with, what his name is, where he comes from, where I can get more information about him.'

'No,' Miss Benson quavered, 'I'm sorry.'

'Sorry,' Robert said angrily. 'A girl disappears, this man may be at the bottom of it, and all you can do is say you're sorry!'

Miss Benson's jaw went slack. 'You mean that he – that he *did* something to her?'

'Yes,' Robert said, 'he did,' and had to quickly catch her arm as she swayed unsteadily, apparently on the verge of fainting.

'I should have known,' she said lifelessly. 'I should have known when it happened that it might come to this. But at the time . . .'

At the time the girl had been one of her students. A good student – not brilliant, mind you – but a nice girl always trying to do her best. And well brought up, too, not like so many of the young snips you get nowadays.

That very afternoon when it all happened the girl herself had told Miss Benson she was going to the Principal's office after school hours to get her program straightened out. Certainly if she meant to do anything wicked she wouldn't have mentioned that, would she? Wasn't that all the evidence anyone needed?

'Evidence?' Robert said in bewilderment.

Yes, evidence. There had been that screaming in the Principal's office, and Miss Benson had been the only one left in the whole school. She had run to the office, flung open the door, and that was how she found them. The girl sobbing hysterically, her dress torn halfway down; Mr Price standing behind her, glaring at the open door, at the incredulous Miss Benson.

'Mr Price?' Robert said. He had the sense of swimming numbly through some gelatinous depths, unable to see anything clearly.

Mr Price, the Principal, of course. He stood glaring at her, his face ashen. Then the girl had fled through the door and Mr Price had taken one step after her, but had stopped short. He had pulled Miss Benson into the office, and closed the door, and then he had talked to her.

The long and the short of what he told her was that the girl was a wanton. She had waltzed into his office, threatened him with blackmail, and when he had put her into her place she had artfully acted out her little scene. But he would be merciful, very merciful. Rather than call in the authorities and blacken the name of the school and of her decent, respectable father he would simply expel her and advise her father to get her out of town promptly.

And, Mr Price had remarked meaningfully, it was a lucky thing indeed that Miss Benson had walked in just in time to be his witness. Although if Miss Benson failed him as a witness it could be highly unlucky for her.

'And he meant it,' Miss Benson said bitterly. 'It's his family runs the town and everything in it. If I said anything of what I really thought, if I dared open my mouth, I'd never get another job anywhere. But I should have talked up, I know I should have, especially after what happened next!'

She had managed to get back to her room at the far end of the corridor although she had no idea of where she got the strength. And as soon as she had entered the room she saw the girl there, lying on the floor beneath the bulletin board from which usually hung the sharp, cutting scissors. But the scissors were in the girl's clenched fist as she lay there, and blood over everything. All that blood over everything.

'She was like that,' Miss Benson said dully. 'If you reprimanded her for even the littlest thing she looked like she wanted to sink through the floor, to die on the spot. And after what she went through it must have been the first thing in her head: just to get rid of herself. It was a mercy of God that she didn't succeed then and there.'

It was Miss Benson who got the doctor, a discreet man who asked no questions, and it was she who tended the girl after her father barred his door to her.

'And when she could get around,' Miss Benson said, 'I placed her with this office over at the county seat. She wasn't graduated, of course, or really expert, but I gave her a letter explaining she had been in some trouble and needed a helping hand, and they gave her a job.'

Miss Benson dug her fingers into her forehead. 'If I had only talked up when I should have. I should have known he'd never feel safe, that he'd hound her and hound her until he . . .'

'But he isn't the one!' Robert said hoarsely. 'He isn't the right man at all!'

She looked at him wonderingly. 'But you said . . .'

'No,' Robert said helplessly, 'I'm looking for someone else. A different man altogether.'

She shrank back. 'You've been trying to fool me!'

'I swear I haven't.'

'But it doesn't matter,' she whispered. 'If you say a word about this nobody'll believe you. I'll tell them you were lying, you made the whole thing up!'

'You won't have to,' Robert said. 'All you have to do is tell me where you sent her for that job. If you do that you can forget everything else.'

She hesitated, studying his face with bright, frightened eyes. 'All right,' she said at last. 'All right.'

He was about to go when she placed her hand anxiously on his arm. 'Please,' she said. 'You don't think unkindly of me because of all this, do you?'

'No,' Robert said, 'I don't have the right to.'

The bus trip which filled the remainder of the day was a wearing one, the hotel bed that night was no great improvement over the bus seat, and Mr Pardee of *Grace, Grace, & Pardee* seemed to Robert the hardest of all to take. He was a cheery man, too loud and florid to be properly contained by his small office.

He studied Robert's business card with interest. 'Credit research, eh?' he said admiringly. 'Wonderful how you fellows track 'em down wherever they are. Sort of a Northwest Mounted Police just working to keep business healthy, that's what it comes to, doesn't it? And anything I can do to help . . .'

Yes, he remembered the girl very well.

'Just about the prettiest little thing we ever had around here,' he said pensively. 'Didn't know much about her job, of course, but you got your money's worth just watching her walk around the office.'

Robert managed to keep his teeth clenched. 'Was there any man she seemed interested in? Someone around the office, maybe, who wouldn't be working here any more? Or even someone outside you could tell me about?'

Mr Pardee studied the ceiling with narrowed eyes. 'No,' he said, 'nobody I can think of. Must have been plenty of men after her, but you'd never get anything out of her about it. Not with the way she was so secretive and all. Matter of fact, her being that way was one of the things that made all the trouble.'

'Trouble?'

'Oh, nothing serious. Somebody was picking the petty cash box every so often, and what with all the rest of the office being so friendly except her it looked like she might be the one. And then that letter she brought saying she had already been in some trouble – well, we just had to let her go.

'Later on,' continued Mr Pardee pleasantly, 'when we found out it wasn't her after all, it was too late. We didn't know where to get in touch with her.' He snapped his fingers loudly. 'Gone, just like that.'

Robert drew a deep breath to steady himself. 'But there must be somebody in the office who knew her,' he pleaded. 'Maybe some girl she talked to.'

'Oh, that,' said Mr Pardee. 'Well, as I said, she wasn't friendly, but now and then she did have her head together with Jenny Rizzo over at the switchboard. If you want to talk to Jenny go right ahead. Anything I can do to help . . .'

But it was Jenny who helped him. A plain girl dressed in defiant bad taste, she studied him with impersonal interest and told him coolly that she had nothing to say about Amy. The kid had taken enough kicking around. It was about time they let her alone.

'I'm not interested in her,' Robert said. 'I'm trying to find out about the man she married. Someone named Vincent Snider. Did you know about him?'

From the stricken look on her face Robert realized exultantly that she did.

'Him!' she said. 'So she went and married him, anyhow!'

'What about it?'

'What about it? I told her a hundred times he was no good. I told her just stay away from him.'

'Why?'

'Because I knew his kind. Sharp stuff hanging around with money in his pocket, you never knew where it came from. The kind of guy's always pulling fast deals, but he's too smart to get caught, that's why!'

'How well did you know him?'

'How well? I knew him from the time he was a kid around my neighborhood here. Look,' Jenny dug into a desk drawer deep laden with personal possessions. She came out with a handful of snapshots which she thrust at Robert. 'We even used to double-date together, Vince and Amy, and me and my boyfriend. Plenty of times I told her right in front of Vince that he was no good, but he gave her such a line she wouldn't even listen. She was like a baby that way; anybody was nice to her she'd go overboard.'

They were not good photographs, but there were Vince and Amy clearly recognizable.

'Could I have one of these?' Robert asked, his voice elaborately casual.

Jenny shrugged. 'Just go ahead and help yourself,' she said, and Robert did.

'Then what happened?' he said. 'I mean, to Vince and Amy?'

'You got me there. After she got fired they both took off. She said something about Vince getting a job downstate a-ways, in Sutton, and that was the last I saw of them. I could just see him working at anything honest, but the way she said it she must have believed him. Anyhow, I never heard from her after that.'

'Could you remember exactly when you saw her last? That time she told you they were going to Sutton?'

Jenny could and did. She might have remembered more, but Robert was out of the door by then, leaving her gaping after him, her mouth wide open in surprise.

The trip to Sutton was barely an hour by bus, but it took another hour before Robert was seated at a large table with the Sutton newspaper files laid out before him. The town's newspaper was a large and respectable one, its files orderly and well-kept. And two days after the date Jenny Rizzo had given him there was the news Robert had hoped to find. Headline news emblazoned all across the top of the first page.

Ten thousand dollars stolen, the news report said. A daring, lone bandit had walked into the Sutton Bank and Trust, had bearded the manager without a soul around knowing it, and had calmly walked out with a small valise containing ten thousand dollars in currency. The police were on the trail. An arrest was expected momentarily . . .

Robert traced through later dates with his hands shaking. The police had given up in their efforts. No arrest was ever made . . .

Robert had carefully scissored the photograph so that Vince now stood alone in the picture. The bank manager irritably looked at the picture, and then swallowed hard.

'It's him!' he told Robert incredulously. 'That's the man! I'd know him anywhere. If I can get my hands on him . . .'

'There's something you'll have to do first,' said Robert.

'I'm not making any deals,' the manager protested. 'I want him, and I want every penny of the money he's got left.'

'I'm not talking about deals,' Robert said. 'All you have to do is put down on paper that you positively identify this man as the one who robbed the bank. If you do that the police'll have him for you tomorrow.'

'That's all?' the man said suspiciously.

'That's all,' Robert said.

He sat again in the familiar room, the papers, the evidence arranged before him. His one remaining fear had been that in his absence the murderer had somehow taken alarm and fled. He had not breathed easy until the first small, surreptitious noises from next door made clear that things were as he had left them.

Now he carefully studied all the notes he had painstakingly prepared, all the reports of conversations held. It was all here, enough to see justice done, but it was more than that, he told himself bitterly. It was the portrait of a girl who, step by step, had been driven through a pattern of betrayal.

Every man she had dealt with had been an agent of betrayal. Father, school principal, employer, and finally her husband, each was guilty in his turn. Jenny Rizzo's words rang loud in Robert's ears.

*Anybody was nice to her she'd go overboard.* If he had spoken, if he had moved, he could have been the one. When she turned at the top of the stairs to look at him she might have been waiting for him to speak or move. Now it was too late, and there was no way of letting her know what these papers meant, what he had done for her . . .

The police were everything Robert had expected until they read the bank manager's statement. Then they read and reread the statement, they looked at the photograph, and they courteously passed Robert from hand to hand until finally there was a door marked *Lieutenant Kyserling*, and behind it a slender, soft-spoken man.

It was a long story – Robert had not realized until then how long it was or how many details there were to explain – but it was told from start to finish without interruption. At its conclusion Kyserling took the papers, the handkerchief, and the photographs, and pored over them. Then he looked at Robert curiously.

'It's all here,' he said. 'The only thing you left out is why you did it, why you went to all this trouble. What's your stake in this?'

It was not easy to have your most private dream exposed to a complete stranger. Robert choked on the words. 'It's because of her. The way I felt about her.'

'Oh.' Kyserling nodded understandingly. 'Making time with her?'

'No,' Robert said angrily. 'We never even spoke to each other!'

Kyserling tapped his fingers gently on the papers before him.

'Well,' he said, 'it's none of my business anyhow. But you've done a pretty job for us. Very pretty. Matter of fact, yesterday we turned up the body in a car parked a few blocks away from your place. The car was stolen a month ago, there wasn't a stitch of identification on the clothing or anything; all we got is a body with a big wound in it. This business could have stayed up in the air for a hundred years if it wasn't for you walking in with a perfect case made out from A to Z.'

'I'm glad,' Robert said. 'That's the way I wanted it.'

'Yeah,' Kyserling said. 'Any time you want a job on the force you just come and see me.'

Then he was gone from the office for a long while, and when he returned it was in the company of a big, stolid plainclothesman who smiled grimly.

'We're going to wrap it up now,' Kyserling told Robert, and gestured at the man.

They went softly up the stairs of the house and stood to the side of the door while Kyserling laid his ear against it for some assurance of sound. Then he briskly nodded to the plainclothesman and rapped hard.

'Open up!' he called. 'It's the police.'

There was an ear-ringing silence, and Robert's mouth went dry as he saw Kyserling and the plainclothesman slip the chill blue steel of revolvers from their shoulder holsters.

'I got no use for these cute little games,' growled Kyserling, and suddenly raised his foot and smashed the heel of his shoe hard against the lock of the door. The door burst open, Robert cowered back against the balustrade of the staircase– And then saw her.

She stood in the middle of the room facing him wildly, the same look on her face, he knew in that fantastic moment, that she must have worn each time she came face to face with a betrayer exposed. Then she took one backward step, and suddenly whirled toward the window.

'*Ahh, no!*' she cried, as Robert had heard her cry it out once before, and then was gone through the window in a sheet of broken glass. Her voice rose in a single despairing shriek, and then was suddenly and mercifully silent.

Robert stood there, the salt of sweat suddenly in his eyes, the salt of blood on his lips. It was an infinity of distance to the window, but he finally got there, and had to thrust Kyserling aside to look down.

She lay crumpled on the sidewalk, and the thick black hair in loose disorder around her face shrouded her from the eyes of the curious.

The plainclothesman was gone, but Kyserling was still there watching Robert with sympathetic eyes.

'I thought he had killed her,' Robert whispered. 'I could swear he had killed her!'

'It was his body we found,' said Kyserling. 'She was the one who did it.'

'But why didn't you tell me then!' Robert begged. 'Why didn't you let me know!'

Kyserling looked at him wisely. 'Yeah?' he said. 'And then what? You tip her off so that she gets away; then we really got troubles.'

There could be no answer to that. None at all.

'She just cracked up,' Kyserling said reasonably. 'Holed up here like she was, not knowing which way to turn, nobody she could trust . . . It was in the cards. You had nothing to do with it.'

He went downstairs then, and Robert was alone in her room. He looked around it slowly, at all the things that were left of her, and then very deliberately picked up a chair, held it high over his head, and with all his strength smashed it against the wall . . .

# The House Party

*He's coming around,'* said the voice.

He was falling. His hands were outflung against the stone-cold blackness of space, and his body tilted head over heels, heels over head, as he fell. If there were only a way of knowing what was below, of bracing himself against the moment of impact, the terror might not have been so great. This way he was no more than a lump of terror flung into a pit, his mind cowering away from the inevitable while his helpless body descended toward it.

'Good,' the voice said from far away, and it sounded to him as if someone were speaking to him quite calmly and cheerfully from the bottom of the pit. 'Very good.'

He opened his eyes. A glare of light washed in on him suddenly and painfully, and he squinted against it at the figures standing around him, at the faces, partly obscured by a sort of milky haze, looking down at him. He was lying on his back, and from the thrust of the cushions under him he knew he was on the familiar sofa. The milky haze was fading away now, and with it the panic. This was the old house at Nyack, the same living room, the same Utrillo on the wall, the same chandelier glittering over his head. *The same everything*, he thought bitterly, even to the faces around him.

That was Hannah, her eyes bright with tears – she could turn on tears like a faucet – and her hand was gripping his so hard that his fingers were numb under the pressure. Hannah with the over-developed maternal instinct, and only a husband to exercise it on ... That was Abel Roth chewing on a cigar – even at a time like this, that reeking cigar! – and watching him worriedly. Abel with his first successful production in five years, worrying about his investment . . . And that was Ben Thayer and Harriet, the eternal bumpkins . . . And Jake Hall . . . And Tommy McGowan . . . All the old familiar faces, the sickening familiar faces.

But there was a stranger, too. A short, stout man with a look of amiable interest on his face, and splendidly bald, with only a tonsure of graying hair to frame his gleaming scalp. He ran his fingers reflectively over his scalp and nodded at Miles.

'How do you feel now?' he asked.

'I don't know,' Miles said. He pulled his hand free of Hannah's and gingerly tried to raise himself to a sitting position. Halfway there he was transfixed by a shocking pain that was driven like a white-hot needle between his ribs. He heard Hannah gasp, and then the stranger's blunt fingers were probing deep into the pain, turning it to liquid, melting it away.

'See?' the man said. 'It's nothing. Nothing at all.'

Miles swung his legs around so that he sat erect on the sofa. He took a deep breath, then another. 'For a second I thought it was my heart,' he said. 'The way it hit me—'

'No, no,' the man said. 'I know what you thought. You can believe me when I say it is of no concern.' And then, as if it explained everything, he said, 'I am Dr Maas. Dr Victor Maas.'

'It was a miracle, darling,' Hannah said breathlessly. 'Dr Maas was the one who found you outside and brought you in. And he's been an absolute angel. If it weren't for him—'

Miles looked at her, and then looked at all the others standing there and watching him with concern. 'Well,' he demanded, 'what *did* happen? What was it? Heart? Stroke? Amnesia? I'm not a child, for God's sake. You don't have to play games with me.'

Abel Roth rolled his cigar from the left-hand corner of his mouth to the right-hand corner. 'You can't blame him for feeling that way, can you, doc? After all, the man is out cold for fifteen minutes, he wants to know where he stands. Maybe there's some kind of checkup you could give him, like blood pressure and stuff like that. Maybe we'd all feel better for it.'

Miles relished that, and relished even more the thought of what he had in store for Abel Roth. 'Maybe we would, Abel,' he said. 'Maybe we've got a theater sold out sixteen weeks in advance, and the SRO sign up every night. Maybe we've got a real little gold mine to dig so long as I can keep swinging the shovel eight performances a week.'

Abel's face turned red. 'Ah, now, Miles,' he said. 'The way you talk—'

'Yes?' Miles said. 'What about the way I talk?'

Ben Thayer shook his head slowly and solemnly. 'If you'd only take the chip off your shoulder for one minute, Miles,' he drawled. 'If you'd try to understand—'

'Please!' Dr Maas said sharply. 'Gentlemen, please!' He frowned at them. 'There is one thing I must make clear. Actually, I am not a medical physician. My interests, so to speak, lie more in the field of psychiatrics, and while I am, perhaps, qualified to make the examination of Mr Owen that you suggest, I have no intention of doing so. For Mr Owen's benefit I will also say that there is no need for me or anyone else to do so. He has my word on that.'

'And Dr Maas, I am sure,' said Miles, 'is an honorable man.' He stood up flexing his knees gingerly, and noting the relief on the faces around him. 'If you want to make yourself at home, doctor, go right ahead. There seems to be some kind of buffet over there, and while I can't vouch for the food I can promise that the liquor is very, very good.'

The doctor's grin gave him a surprising resemblance to a plump and mischievous boy. 'A delightful suggestion,' he said, and immediately made his way toward the buffet. Abel followed, and, Miles observed, before the doctor had even reached the buffet, the cigar was perilously close to his ear. Abel spent three hours a week on a psychoanalyst's couch, and at least as much time pouring out lists of frightening and inconsequential symptoms to a sleek and well-fed Park Avenue practitioner. Dr Maas, Miles thought with a wry sympathy, was in for some heavy going, whether he knew it or not.

The rest of the circle around the sofa broke up and eddied off, until only Hannah was left. She caught his arm in a panicky grip.

'Are you *sure* you're all right?' she demanded. 'You know you can tell me if there's anything wrong.'

There was something wrong. Every time she caught hold of him like that, tried to draw him close, he had the feeling of a web ensnaring him, closing over him so that he had to fight it savagely.

It had not been like that at the start. She had been so beautiful that he thought in her case it might be different. The rising together, the eating together, the talking together, the endless routine of marriage looked as if it might somehow be bearable as long as it was shared with that loveliness. But then after a year the loveliness had become too familiar, the affection too cloying, the routine too much of a crushing burden.

He had been unconscious for fifteen minutes. He wondered if he had babbled during that time, said something about Lily that could be seized on as a clue. It wasn't of much concern if he had; in fact, it might have been a good way of preparing Hannah for the blow. It was going to be quite a blow, too. He could picture it falling, and it wasn't a pleasant picture.

He shrugged off Hannah's hand. 'There's nothing wrong,' he said, and then could not resist adding, 'unless it's this business of your throwing a house party the one time of the week when I might expect a little peace and quiet.'

'I?' Hannah said uncertainly. 'What did *I* have to do with it?'

'Everything, as long as you've got that damn yen to be the perfect hostess and everybody's friend.'

'They're *your* friends,' she said.

'You ought to know by now that they're not my friends either. I thought I made it clear a hundred different ways that I hate them all, individually and collectively. They're nobody's friends. Why is it my obligation to feed them and entertain them the one time of the week I can get rid of them?'

'I don't understand you,' Hannah said. She looked as if she were about to break into tears. 'I know you bought the house up here so you could get away from everybody, but you were the one—'

The web was closing in again. 'All *right*,' he said. 'All *right!*'

The whole thing didn't matter, anyhow. After he cleared out she could throw a house party every night of the week if she wanted to. She could burn the damn house down if that suited her. It wasn't of any concern to him. He'd had enough of this country-squire life between every Saturday and Monday performance to last him the rest of his life, and, as Lily had once remarked, Central Park had all the trees she wanted to see. Just the realization that he would soon be packed and out of here made any arguments pointless.

He shouldered his way to the buffet past Bob and Liz Gregory who were mooning at each other as if doing it on the radio six mornings a week wasn't enough; past Ben Thayer who was explaining to Jake Hall the trouble he was having with the final act of his new play; past Abel who was saying something to Dr Maas about psychosomatic factors. The doctor had a tall glass in one hand, a sandwich in the other. 'Interesting,' he was saying. 'Very interesting.'

Miles tried to close his ears to all of them as he poured down two fingers of bourbon. Then he looked at his glass with distaste. The stuff was as flat as warm water, and as unpleasant to the palate. Obviously, one of the local help who took turns cleaning up the house had found the key to the liquor cabinet, and, after nearly emptying the bottle, had done a job on it at the kitchen tap. Damn fool. If you're going to sneak a drink, do it and forget it. But to ruin the rest of the bottle this way . . .

Abel poked him in the ribs. 'I was just telling the doctor here,' Abel said, 'if he gets an evening off I'll fix him up with a house seat for *Ambuscade*. I was telling him, if he hasn't seen Miles Owen in *Ambuscade* he hasn't seen the performance of all time. How does that sound to you, Miles?'

Miles was lifting another bottle after making sure its seal was unbroken. He looked at Abel, and then set the bottle down with great care.

'As a matter of fact,' he said, 'I don't know how it sounds to me, Abel. It's something I've wanted to talk to you about, and maybe this is as good a time as any.'

'Talk about what?' said Abel cheerfully, but there was a sudden worry in his eyes, a flickering of premonition on his face.

'It's private business, Abel,' Miles said, and nodded to Dr Maas who stood by interestedly. 'That is, if the doctor will excuse us.'

'Of course, of course,' the doctor said quickly. He waved his glass enthusiastically toward Miles. 'And you were altogether right about the liquor, Mr Owen. It is superb.'

'Fine,' Miles said. 'This way, Abel.'

He pushed his way through the crowd and crossed the room to the library, Abel trailing after him. When he closed the door of the library and switched on a lamp, the chill dampness of the room seemed to soak right into him, and he shivered. Logs and kindling had been laid on the fireplace, and he held a match to it until the wood crackled and caught. Then he lit a cigarette and drew deeply on it. He looked at the cigarette in surprise. There was a flatness about it, a lack of sensation which made him run his tongue over his lips questioningly. He drew again on the cigarette, and then flung it into the fire. First the liquor, he thought, and now this. Dr Maas might be a handy man with Freudian complexes, but the first thing Monday an honest-to-God MD would be checking up on this little problem. It is discomforting to find out suddenly that you've lost your capacity to taste anything. Ridiculous maybe, but still discomforting.

Abel was standing at the window. 'Look at the fog, will you. When I brought *Coxcomb* over to London I thought I saw the real thing there, but this makes it look like nothing. You could cut your way through this with a shovel.'

The fog was banked solidly outside the window, stirring in slow waves, sending threads of damp smoke against the glass. Where the threads clung, little beads of water trickled down the pane.

'You get that around here a couple of times a year,' Miles said impatiently. 'And I didn't come in here to talk about the weather.'

Abel turned away from the window and sat down reluctantly in an armchair. 'No, I guess you didn't. All right, Miles, what's bothering you?'

'*Ambuscade*,' Miles said. '*Ambuscade* is what's bothering me.'

Abel nodded wearily. 'It figured. It figured. Well, what particular thing? Your billing? We're using the biggest letters they make. Your publicity? All you have to do is name the time and you have your pick of any TV or radio guest spot in town. Remember what I told you after opening night, Miles? You name it, and if I can get it for you, I will.'

Miles found himself suddenly enjoying the scene. Ordinarily, he had a genuine horror of such scenes. 'Funny,' he said. 'I didn't hear you say anything about money just now, did I? I mean, in all that pretty speech it couldn't have slipped past me, could it?'

Abel sank down in his chair and sighed like a man deeply stricken. 'I thought it would come down to this. Even if I'm paying you twice as much as the biggest star I ever had, I could see it coming, Miles. All right, what's the beef?'

'As a matter of fact,' Miles said, 'there's no beef.'

'No?'

'None at all.'

'What are you getting at?' Abel demanded. 'What's all this about?'

Miles smiled. 'I'm not getting *at* anything, Abel. I'm getting *out*. I'm leaving the show.'

Miles had seen Abel meet more than one crisis before; he could have predicted every action before it took place. The face becoming an impassive mask, the hand searching for a match, the thumbnail flicking the match into a light, the elaborate drawing on the cigar stump, the neat flick of the match across the room. Abel fooled him. The match was snapped with sudden violence between the fingers, and then slowly rolled back and forth, back and forth.

'You're a cute boy, Miles,' Abel said. 'This wouldn't be your idea of a joke, would it?'

'I'm getting out, Abel. Tonight was positively the last appearance. That gives you all day tomorrow to line up another boy for the Monday-night curtain.'

'What other boy?'

'Well, you've got Jay Welker on tap, haven't you? He's been understudying me for five months, and hoping I'd break a leg every night of it.'

'Jay Welker couldn't carry *Ambuscade* one week, and you know it, Miles. Nobody can carry that show but you, and you know that, too.'

Abel leaned forward in his chair and shook his head from side to side unbelievingly. 'And knowing that, you don't give a damn. You'd close the biggest thing on Broadway just like that, and to hell with the whole world, is that it?'

Miles felt his heart starting to pound heavily, his throat tightening. 'Wait a second, Abel, before you start on the dirty words. One thing has already come through pretty well. In all this, you haven't yet asked me why I'm leaving. For all you know I might have some condition that's going to kill me an hour from now, but that would bother you less than keeping your show running! Have you thought about that side of it?'

'What side of it? I was standing right there when the doctor said you were in good shape. What am I supposed to do now? Get affidavits from the American Medical Association?'

'Then it's your idea that I'm pulling out because of a whim?'

'Let's not kid each other, Miles. You did this to Barrow five years ago, you did it to Goldschmidt after that, you did it to Howie Freeman last year, and I know, because that's how I got my chance to grab you for *Ambuscade*. But all the time I figured these others didn't know how to handle you, they didn't see just how much you meant to a show. Now I tell you they were right all along, and I was a prize sucker. They told me you would be going along fine, and then all of a sudden you would get a bug in your ear, and that was it. Bug in your ear, Miles. That's my low, ignorant way of saying whim, which is what it adds up to.'

Abel paused. 'The difference between me and them, Miles, is that I didn't take chances, and that's why you signed the first run-of-the-play contract you ever got since you were a nobody. You think you're walking out on that contract? Think again, my friend.'

Miles nodded. 'All right,' he said thickly, 'I'm thinking. Do you want to know about what?'

'They're your dice, my friend.'

'I'm thinking about eight performances a week, Abel. Eight times a week I say the same lines, walk the same steps, make the same faces. I've done it for five months, which is the biggest break you ever got in your life, but if you had your way I'd be doing it for five years! Right now it's turned into one of those nightmares where you do the same thing over and over without being able to stop, but you wouldn't know about that because

135

*you're* a guy in love with routine! But *I'm* not! After a while it's like being in jail with the key thrown away. What do you tell a man when he can walk out of jail? To stay there and like it?'

'Jail!' Abel cried. 'Tell me somebody in this country who wouldn't give his right eye to be in the kind of jail you're in!'

'Listen,' Miles said. He leaned forward urgently. 'Do you remember before the show opened when we were rehearsing that kitchen scene? Do you remember when we ran through it that night ten times, fifteen times, twenty times? Do you know how I felt then? I felt as if I was plunked right down in hell, and all I would do for eternity was just play that scene over and over again. That's my idea of hell, Abel: a sweet little place where you do the same thing over and over, and they won't even let you go nuts at it, because that would spoil the fun for them. Do you get that? Because if you do, you can see just how I feel about *Ambuscade*!'

'I get it,' Abel said. 'I also get a certain little run-of-the-play contract tucked away in my safe deposit box. If you think rehearsing a scene a few times is hell you'll find out different when Equity lands on you. They look at this a little different from you.'

'Don't try to scare me, Abel.'

'Scare you, hell. I'm going to sue you black and blue, and I'm going to make it stick. I'm dead serious about that, Miles.'

'Maybe. But isn't it hard to sue a man who's too sick to work?'

Abel nodded with grim understanding. 'I figured you'd get around to that angle. I'm the patsy, because to the rest of the world you're sick.' His eyes narrowed. 'And that explains something else, too. That little business of your little blackout on the front doorstep, with a doctor handy, and twenty witnesses to swear to it. I have to hand it to you, Miles, you don't miss a trick. Only it'll take more than a smart trick and a quack doctor to work things your way.'

Miles choked down the rage rising in him. 'If you think that was a trick—'

'What was a trick?' Harriet Thayer's voice said gaily behind him. Harriet and Ben were standing in the doorway, regarding him with a sort of cheerful curiosity. They made an incongruous couple, Ben's gauntness towering high over Harriet's little-girl fragility, and they had an eager, small-town friendliness that grated on Miles's nerves like a fingernail drawn down a slate. 'It sounds terribly exciting and interesting,' Harriet said. 'Don't let us stop you.'

Abel pointed at Miles with a shaking forefinger. 'This'll stop you all right,' he said, 'and I'll give it to you in one line. Our friend here is walking out on *Ambuscade*. Maybe *you* can do something to change his mind!'

Ben stared with slow incredulity, and Miles had to marvel, as he had done so many times before, that any man who could write even the few good lines to be found in *Ambuscade* could be so slow on his feet.

'But you can't,' Ben said. 'Your contract runs as long as the play does.'

'Sure,' Abel jeered, 'but he's a sick man. He falls down and has fits. You saw him, didn't you?'

Harriet nodded dumbly. 'Yes, but I never thought—'

'And you were right,' Abel said. 'He's faking it. He's just fed up with making all that money and having all those nice things printed about him, so he's going to close the show. That's all. Just fold it up tight.'

Miles slammed his hand down hard on the arm of Abel's chair. 'All right,' he said, 'now that you've made everything so clear I'll ask you something. Do you think if *Ambuscade* was really a good play that any one person could close it up? Did it ever strike you that no one comes to see your crummy play; they come to see me walk through it? If you gave me *Jabberwocky* to read up there they'd come to see me! Who's to tell a one-man show that he has to keep playing when he doesn't want to!'

'It *is* a good play!' Harriet shouted at him. 'It's the best play you ever acted in, and if you don't know that—'

Miles was shouting himself now. 'Then get someone else to play it! It might be even better that way!'

Ben held his hands out, palms up, in a pleading gesture. 'Now, Miles, you know you've been identified with that part so no one else could take it over,' he said. 'And try to see it my way, Miles. I've been writing fifteen years, and this is the first real break—'

Miles walked up to him slowly. 'You clown,' he said softly. 'Don't you have any self-respect at all?'

When he walked out of the library he quickly slammed the door behind him to forestall any belated answer to that.

The party had broken into several small knots of people scattered around the room, a deafening rise and fall of voices, a haze of blue smoke which lay like a transparent blanket midway between floor and ceiling. Someone, Miles observed, had overturned a drink on the piano; the puddle ran down in a glittering string along the side of the mahogany and was leaving a damp stain on the Wilton rug beneath. Tommy McGowan and his latest, an overripe blonde – Norma or Alma or something – sat on the floor shuffling through piles of phonograph records, arranging some into a dangerously high stack and carelessly tossing the others aside. The buffet looked as if a cyclone had hit it; only some empty platters and broken pieces of bread remained amidst the wreckage. From the evidence, Miles thought sardonically, the party would have to be rated a roaring success.

But even the sense of heat and excitement in the room could not erase the chill that he seemed to have brought with him from the library. He rubbed his hands together hard, but this didn't help any, and he felt a small pang of fright at the realization. What if there really were something wrong with him? Lily was not the kind of woman to take gracefully to the role of nursemaid to an invalid. Not that she was wrong about that, as far as he was concerned; if the shoe were on the other foot he couldn't see himself playing any Robert Browning to her Elizabeth Barrett either. Not for Lily or anyone else in the world. In that case it was better not to even bother about a checkup. If there was something, he didn't even want to know about it!

'You are disturbed about something, I think.'

It was Dr Maas. He was leaning casually against the wall, not an arm's length away, his hands thrust into his pockets, his eyes fixed reflectively on Miles. Taking in everything, Miles thought angrily, like some damn scientist looking at a bug under a microscope.

'No,' Miles snapped. Then he thought better of it. 'Yes,' he said. 'As a matter of fact, I am.'

'Ah?'

'I don't feel right. I know you told me I was fine, but I don't feel fine.'

'Physically?'

'Of course, physically! What are you trying to tell me? That it's all in my mind, or some claptrap like that?'

'I am not trying to tell you anything, Mr Owen. You are telling me.'

'All right. Then I want to know what makes you so sure of yourself. No examination, no X-ray, no anything, and you come up with your answer just like that. What's the angle here? Do we somehow get around to the idea that there's nothing wrong physically, but if I put myself in your hands for a nice long expensive psychoanalysis—'

'Stop right there, Mr Owen,' Dr Maas said coldly. 'I will take for granted that your manners are abominable because you are clearly under some pressure. But you should rein in your imagination. I do not practice psychoanalysis, and I never said I did. I am not a healer of any sort. The people I deal with are, unfortunately, always past the point of any cure, and my interest in them, as you can see, must be wholly academic. To be taken for some kind of sharper seeking a victim—'

'Look,' Miles said abruptly, 'I'm sorry. I'm terribly sorry. I don't know what made me go off like that. Maybe it's this party. I hate these damn parties; they always do things to me. Whatever it is, I'm honestly sorry for taking it out on you.'

The doctor nodded gravely. 'Of course,' he said. 'Of course.' Then he nervously ran his fingers over his shining scalp. 'There is something else I should like to say. I am afraid, however, I would risk offending you.'

Miles laughed. 'I think you owe it to me.'

The doctor hesitated, and then gestured toward the library. 'As it happens, Mr Owen, I heard much of what went on in there. I am not an eavesdropper, but the discussion got a little – well, heated, shall we say? – and it was impossible not to overhear it from outside the door here.'

'Yes?' Miles said warily.

'The clue to your condition, Mr Owen, lies in that discussion. To put it bluntly, you are running away. You find what you call routine unbearable, and so you are fleeing from it.'

Miles forced himself to smile. 'What do you mean, what *I* call routine? Is there another word for it in your language?'

'I think there is. I think I would call it responsibility. And since your life, Mr Owen – both your professional and your private life – is very much an open book to the world, I will draw on it and say that most of this life has also been spent fleeing from responsibility of one sort or another. Does it strike you as strange, Mr Owen, that no matter how far and fast you run you always find yourself facing the same problem over and over again?'

Miles clenched and unclenched his fist. 'After all,' he said, 'it's my problem.'

'That is where you're wrong, Mr Owen. When you suddenly leave your role in a play, it affects everyone concerned with that play, and, in turn, everyone concerned with those people. In your relations with women you may move on, but they do not stay motionless either. They move on, too, dangerous to themselves and perhaps to others. Forgive me if I seem sententious, Mr Owen, but you cannot cast pebbles in the water without sending ripples to the far shore.

'That is why when you say *routine*, it is because you are thinking only of yourself caught in a situation. And when I say *responsibility*, I am thinking of everything else concerned with it.'

'And what's the prescription, Doctor?' Miles demanded. 'To stay sunk in a private little hell because if you try to get away you might step on somebody's toes in the process?'

'Get away?' the doctor said in surprise. 'Do you really think you can get away?'

'You've got a lot to learn, Doctor. Watch me and see.'

'I am watching you, Mr Owen, and I do see. In a wholly academic way, as I said. It is both fascinating and bewildering to see a man trying to flee, as he calls it, his private little hell, while all the time he is carrying it with him.'

Miles's hand was half raised, and then it dropped limp at his side. 'In other words, Doctor,' he said mockingly, 'you're replacing good old-fashioned sulphur-and-brimstone with something even bigger and better.'

The doctor shrugged. 'Of course, you don't believe that.'

'No,' Miles said. 'I don't.'

'I have a confession to make, Mr Owen.' The doctor smiled, and suddenly he was the plump and mischievous boy again. 'I knew you wouldn't. In fact, that is why I felt free to discuss the matter with you.'

'In an academic way, of course.'

'Of course.'

Miles laughed. 'You're quite a man, Doctor. I think I'd like to see more of you.'

'I am sure you will, Mr Owen. But right now I believe that someone is trying to attract your notice. There, by the door.'

Miles followed the doctor's gesturing finger, and his heart stopped. All he could do was pray that no one else had noticed, as he swiftly crossed the room and blocked off the woman who was entering it from the hallway that led to the front door. He thrust her back against the door, and catching hold of her shoulders he shook her once, sharply and angrily.

'Are you crazy?' he demanded. 'Don't you have any more sense than to show up here like this?'

She twisted her shoulders away from his grasp, and carefully brushed at the collar of her coat with her fingertips. The coat had cost Miles a month's pay.

'Aren't you sweet, Miles? Do you invite all your guests in this way?'

Even in the dimness of the hallway she was startling to look at. The sulky lips against the gardenia pallor of the face, the high cheekbones, the slanted eyes darting fire at him. He quailed.

'All right, I'm sorry. I'm sorry. But, my God, Lily, there are two dozen of the biggest mouths on Broadway in that room. If you want the whole world to know about this, why don't you just tip off Winchell?'

She knew when she had him beaten. 'I don't like that, darling.

I don't like that at all. I mean, to make it sound as obscene and disgusting as all that. It really isn't supposed to be like that, is it?'

'You know damn well it isn't like that, Lily. But use your head, will you? There is such a thing as discretion.'

'There's also such a thing as working a word to death, darling. And I don't mind telling you that in the last two months you've filled me up to here with that one.'

Miles said angrily, 'I've been trying to make it clear that we'd work this thing out in the right way at the right time. I've already told old Abel I was leaving the show. I was going to talk to Hannah, too, but this party has fouled everything up. Tomorrow, when I can be alone with her—'

'Ah, but tomorrow may be a long time away, darling. Much longer than you realize.'

'What exactly does that mean?'

She fumbled through her purse and drew an envelope from it. She waved the envelope back and forth under his nose with a fine air of triumph.

'It means this, Miles. Two pretty little reservations, outward bound, for tomorrow's sailing. You see, you don't have nearly as much time as you thought, do you, darling?'

'Tomorrow! The agent said he couldn't possibly have anything for us within a month!'

'He didn't count on cancellations. This one came through just two hours ago, which is exactly how long it took me to get here. And if it wasn't for that awful fog on the road I would have been here that much sooner. I have the car outside, Miles. You can pack whatever is handy, and get the rest of what you need on the boat. When I go back I expect you to be with me, Miles, because whether you are or not I'll be sailing tomorrow. You can't really blame me for that, can you, darling? After all, none of us are getting any younger.'

He tried to straighten out the aching confusion of his thoughts. He wanted to escape Hannah's web, and now it seemed, somehow or other, there was another waiting to be dropped around him. Running, the doctor had said. Always running and never getting anywhere. There was a great weight of weariness in his arms, his legs, his whole body. Running did that to you.

'Well,' Lily said, 'make up your mind, darling.'

He rubbed his hand over his forehead. 'Where's the car?'

'Right across the road.'

'All right,' Miles said, 'you wait in it. Just stay there, and don't blow the horn for me, or anything like that. I'll be down in ten minutes. Fifteen minutes at the most. Most of my stuff is in town, anyhow. We'll pick it up on the way to the boat.'

He opened the door and gently pushed her toward it.

'You'll have to feel your way to the car, Miles. I've never seen anything like what's outside.'

'I'll find it,' he said. 'You just wait there.'

He closed the door, then leaned against it fighting the sickness that kept rising in his throat. The loud voices in the next room, the shrieks of idiot laughter that now and then cut through it, the roar of music from the phonograph tuned at its greatest volume – everything seemed conspiring against him, not allowing him to be alone, not allowing him to think things out.

He went up the stairs almost drunkenly, and into the bedroom. He pulled out his valise, and then at random started cramming it full. Shirts, socks, the contents of the jewel case on his dresser. He thrust down hard with all his weight, making room for more.

'What are you doing, Miles?'

He didn't look up. He knew exactly what the expression on her face would be, and he didn't want to meet it then. It would have been too much.

'I'm leaving, Hannah.'

'With that woman?' Her voice was a vague, uncomprehending whisper.

He had to look at her then. Her eyes stared at him, enormous against the whiteness of her skin. Her hand fumbled with the ornament at her breast. It was the silver mask of comedy he had picked up for her on Fifth Avenue a week before their marriage.

She said wonderingly, 'I saw you with her in the hallway. I wasn't prying or anything like that, Miles, but when I asked the doctor where you were—'

'Stop it!' Miles shouted. 'What do you have to apologize for!'

'But she's the one, isn't she?'

'Yes, she's the one.'

'And you want to go away with her?'

His hands were on the lid of the valise. He rested his weight on them, head down, eyes closed.

'Yes,' he said at last. 'That's what it comes to.'

'No!' she cried with a sudden fervor. 'You don't really want to. You know she's not good for you. You know there's nobody in the whole world as good for you as I am!'

He pressed the lid of the valise down. The lock caught with a tiny click.

'Hannah, it would have been better for you not to have come up just now. I would have written to you, explained it somehow—'

'Explained it? When it would be too late? When you'd know what a mistake you made? Miles, listen to me. Listen to me, Miles. I'm talking to you out of all my love. It would be a terrible mistake.'

'I'll have to be the judge of that, Hannah.'

He stood up, and she came toward him, her fingers digging into his arms frantically. 'Look at me, Miles,' she whispered. 'Can't you see how I feel? Can't you understand that I'd rather have the both of us dead than to have you go away like this and leave the whole world empty for me?'

It was horrible. It was the web constricting around him so hard that it was taking all his strength to pull himself free. But he did, with a brutal effort, and saw her fall back against the dresser. Then she suddenly wheeled toward it, and when she faced him again he saw the pistol leveled at him. It shone a cold, deadly blue in her hand, and then he realized her hand was trembling so violently that the gun must be frightening her as much as it did him. The whole grotesquerie of the scene struck him full force, melting away the fear, filling him with a sense of outrage.

'Put that thing down,' he said.

'No.' He could hardly hear her. 'Not unless you tell me that you're not going.'

He took a step toward her, and she shrank farther back

against the dresser, but the gun remained leveled at him. She was like a child afraid someone was going to trick her out of a toy. He stopped short, and then shrugged with exaggerated indifference.

'You're making a fool of yourself, Hannah. People are paid for acting like this on the stage. They're not supposed to make private shows of themselves.'

Her head moved from side to side in a slow, aimless motion. 'You still don't believe me, do you, Miles?'

'No,' he said. 'I don't.'

He turned his back on her, half expecting to hear the sudden explosion, feel the impact between his shoulder blades, but there was nothing. He picked up the valise and walked to the door. 'Good-by, Hannah,' he said. He didn't turn his head to look at her.

The weakness in his knees made each step a trial. He stopped at the foot of the staircase to shift the valise from one hand to the other, and saw Dr Maas standing there, hat in hand, a topcoat thrown over his arm.

'Ah?' said the doctor inquiringly. 'So you, too, are leaving the party, Mr Owen?'

'Party?' Miles said, and then laughed short and sharp. 'Leaving the nightmare, if you don't mind, Doctor. I hate to tell this to a guest, but I think you'll understand me when I say that this past hour has been a nightmare that gets thicker and thicker. That's what I'm leaving, Doctor, and you can't blame me for being happy about it.'

'No, no,' said the doctor. 'I quite understand.'

'The car is waiting for me outside. If I can give you a lift anywhere—?'

'Not at all,' the doctor said. 'I really do not have far to go.' They went to the doorway together and stepped outside. The fog moved in on them, cold and wet, and Miles turned up his jacket collar against it.

'Rotten weather,' he said.

'Terrible,' the doctor agreed. He glanced at his watch, and then lumbered down the steps to the walk like a walrus disappearing into a snowbank. 'I'll be seeing you, Mr Owen,' he called.

Miles watched him go, then lifted the valise and went down the steps himself, burying his nose in his collar against the smothering dampness all around him. He was at the bottom step when he heard the sibilance of the door opening behind him, the faraway whisper of danger in his bones.

He turned, and, as he knew it would be, there was Hannah standing at the open door, still holding the gun. But the gun was gripped tightly in both hands now, and the menace of it was real and overwhelming.

'I tried to make you understand, Miles,' she said, like a child saying the words. 'I tried to make you understand.'

He flung his arms out despairingly.

'No!' he cried wildly. 'No!'

And then there was the roar of the explosion in his ears, the gout of flame leaping out toward him, the crushing impact against his chest, and the whole world dissolving. In it, only one thing stood sharp and definable: the figure of the doctor bending over him, the face strangely Satanic in its cruel indifference.

For that single moment Miles understood everything. He had been here before. He had lived this hour a thousand times before, and would live it again and again for all eternity. The curtain was falling now, but when it rose again the stage would be set once more for the house party. Because he was in Hell, and the most terrible thing of all, the terror which submerged all others, was this moment of understanding given him so that he could know this, and could see himself crawling the infinite treadmill of his doom. Then the darkness closed in with a rush, blotting out all understanding – until next time . . .

*'He's coming around,' said the voice.*

He was falling. His hands were outflung . . .

# The Moment
of Decision

Hugh Lozier was the exception to the rule that people who are completely sure of themselves cannot be likeable. We have all met the sure ones, of course – those controlled but penetrating voices which cut through all others in a discussion, those hard forefingers jabbing home opinions on your chest, those living Final Words on all issues – and I imagine we all share the same amalgam of dislike and envy for them. Dislike, because no one likes to be shouted down or prodded in the chest, and envy, because everyone wishes he himself were so rich in self-assurance that he could do the shouting down and the prodding.

For myself, since my work took me regularly to certain places in this atomic world where the only state was confusion and the only steady employment that of splitting political hairs, I found absolute judgments harder and harder to come by. Hugh once observed of this that it was a good thing my superiors in the Department were not cut of the same cloth, because God knows what would happen to the country then. I didn't relish that, but – and there was my curse again – I had to grant him his right to say it.

Despite this, and despite the fact that Hugh was my brother-in-law – a curious relationship, when you come to think of it – I liked him immensely, just as everyone else did who knew him. He was a big, good-looking man, with clear blue eyes in a ruddy face, and with a quick, outgoing nature eager to appreciate whatever you had to offer. He was overwhelmingly generous, and his generosity was of that rare and excellent kind which makes you feel as if you are doing the donor a favor by accepting it.

I wouldn't say he had any great sense of humor, but plain good humor can sometimes be an adequate substitute for that, and in Hugh's case it was. His stormy side was largely reserved for those times when he thought you might have needed his help in something and failed to call on him for it. Which meant that ten minutes after Hugh had met you and liked you, you were expected to ask him for anything he might be able to offer. A month or so after he married my sister Elizabeth she mentioned to him my avid interest in a fine Copley he had hanging in his gallery at Hilltop, and I can still vividly recall my horror when it suddenly arrived, heavily crated and with his gift card attached, at my barren room-and-a-half. It took considerable effort, but I finally managed to return it to him by forgoing the argument that the picture was undoubtedly worth more than the entire building in which I lived and by complaining that it simply didn't show to advantage on my wall. I think he suspected I was lying, but being Hugh he would never dream of charging me with that in so many words.

Of course, Hilltop and the two hundred years of Lozier tradition that went into it did much to shape Hugh this way. The first Loziers had carved the estate from the heights overlooking the river, had worked hard and flourished exceedingly; its successive generations had invested their income so wisely that money and position eventually erected a towering wall between Hilltop and the world outside. Truth to tell, Hugh was very much a man of the eighteenth century who somehow found himself in the twentieth, and simply made the best of it.

Hilltop itself was almost a replica of the celebrated, but long untenanted, Dane house nearby, and was striking enough to open anybody's eyes at a glance. The house was weathered stone, graceful despite its bulk, and the vast lawns reaching to the river's edge were tended with such fanatic devotion over the years that they had become carpets of purest green which magically changed luster under any breeze. Gardens ranged from the other side of the house down to the groves which half hid the stables and outbuildings, and past the far side of the groves ran the narrow road which led to town. The road was a courtesy road, each estate holder along it maintaining his share, and I think it safe to say that for all the crushed rock he laid in it Hugh made less use of it by far than any of his neighbors.

Hugh's life was bound up in Hilltop; he could be made to leave it only by dire necessity; and if you did meet him away from it you were made acutely aware that he was counting off the minutes until he could return. And if you weren't wary you would more than likely find yourself going along with him when he did return, and totally unable to tear yourself away from the place while the precious weeks rolled by. I know. I believe I spent more time at Hilltop than at my own apartment after my sister brought Hugh into the family.

At one time I wondered how Elizabeth took to this marriage, considering that before she met Hugh she had been as restless and flighty as she was pretty. When I put the question to her directly, she said, 'It's wonderful, darling. Just as wonderful as I knew it would be when I first met him.'

It turned out that their first meeting had taken place at an art exhibition, a showing of some ultramodern stuff, and she had been intently studying one of the more bewildering concoctions on display when she became aware of this tall, good-looking man staring at her. And, as she put it, she had been about to set him properly in his place when he said abruptly, 'Are you admiring that?'

This was so unlike what she had expected that she was taken completely aback. 'I don't know,' she said weakly. 'Am I supposed to?'

'No,' said the stranger, 'it's damned nonsense. Come along now, and I'll show you something which isn't a waste of time.'

'And,' Elizabeth said to me, 'I came along like a pup at his heels, while he marched up and down and told me what was good and what was bad, and in a good loud voice, so that we collected quite a crowd along the way. Can you picture it, darling?'

'Yes,' I said, 'I can.' By now I had shared similar occasions with Hugh, and learned at firsthand that nothing could dent his cast-iron assurance.

'Well,' Elizabeth went on, 'I must admit that at first I was a little put off, but then I began to see that he knew exactly what he was talking about, and that he was terribly sincere. Not a bit self-conscious about anything, but just eager for me to understand things the way he did. It's the same way with everything. Everybody else in the world is always fumbling and bumbling over deciding anything – what to order for dinner, or how to manage his job, or whom to vote for – but Hugh always *knows*. It's *not* knowing that makes for all those nerves and complexes and things you hear about it, isn't that so? Well, I'll take Hugh, thank you, and leave everyone else to the psychiatrists.'

So there it was. An Eden with flawless lawns and no awful nerves and complexes, and not even the glimmer of a serpent in the offing. That is, not a glimmer until the day Raymond made his entrance on the scene.

We were out on the terrace that day, Hugh and Elizabeth and I, slowly being melted into a sort of liquid torpor by the August sunshine, and all of us too far gone to make even a pretence at talk. I lay there with a linen cap over my face, listening to the summer noises around me and being perfectly happy.

There was the low, steady hiss of the breeze through the aspens nearby, the plash and drip of oars on the river below, and now and then the melancholy *tink-tunk* of a sheep bell from one of the flock on the lawn. The flock was a fancy of Hugh's. He swore that nothing was better for a lawn than a few sheep grazing on it, and every summer five or six fat and sleepy ewes were turned out on the grass to serve this purpose and to add a pleasantly pastoral note to the view.

My first warning of something amiss came from the sheep – from the sudden sound of their bells clanging wildly and then a baa-ing which suggested an assault by a whole pack of wolves. I heard Hugh say, 'Damn!' loudly and angrily, and I opened my eyes to see something more incongruous than wolves. It was a large black poodle in the full glory of a clownish haircut, a bright red collar, and an ecstasy of high spirits as he chased the frightened sheep around the lawn. It was clear the poodle had no intention of hurting them – he probably found them the most wonderful playmates imaginable – but it was just as clear that the panicky ewes didn't understand this, and would very likely end up in the river before the fun was over.

In the bare second it took me to see all this, Hugh had

already leaped the low terrace wall and was among the sheep, herding them away from the water's edge, and shouting commands at the dog who had different ideas.

'Down, boy!' he yelled. 'Down!' And then as he would to one of his own hounds, he sternly commanded, 'Heel!'

He would have done better, I thought, to have picked up a stick or stone and made a threatening gesture, since the poodle paid no attention to Hugh's words. Instead, continuing to bark happily, the poodle made for the sheep again, this time with Hugh in futile pursuit. An instant later the dog was frozen into immobility by a voice from among the aspens near the edge of the lawn.

'*Assieds!*' the voice called breathlessly. '*Assieds-toi!*'

Then the man appeared, a small, dapper figure trotting across the grass. Hugh stood waiting, his face darkening as we watched.

Elizabeth squeezed my arm. 'Let's get down there,' she whispered. 'Hugh doesn't like being made a fool of.'

We got there in time to hear Hugh open his big guns. 'Any man,' he was saying, 'who doesn't know how to train an animal to its place shouldn't own one.'

The man's face was all polite attention. It was a good face, thin and intelligent, and webbed with tiny lines at the corners of the eyes. There was also something behind those eyes that couldn't quite be masked. A gentle mockery. A glint of wry perception turned on the world like a camera lens. It was nothing anyone like Hugh would have noticed, but it was there all the same, and I found myself warming to it on the spot. There was also something tantalizingly familiar about the newcomer's face, his high forehead, and his thinning grey hair, but much as I dug into my memory during Hugh's long and solemn lecture I couldn't come up with an answer. The lecture ended with a few remarks on the best methods of dog training, and by then it was clear that Hugh was working himself into a mood of forgiveness.

'As long as there's no harm done—' he said.

The man nodded soberly. 'Still, to get off on the wrong foot with one's new neighbors—'

Hugh looked startled. 'Neighbors?' he said almost rudely. 'You mean that you live around here?'

The man waved toward the aspens. 'On the other side of those woods.'

'The *Dane* house?' The Dane house was almost as sacred to Hugh as Hilltop, and he had once explained to me that if he were ever offered a chance to buy the place he would snap it up. His tone now was not so much wounded as incredulous. 'I don't believe it!' he exclaimed.

'Oh, yes,' the man assured him, 'the Dane house. I performed there at a party many years ago, and always hoped that some day I might own it.'

It was the word *performed* which gave me my clue – that and the accent barely perceptible under the precise English. He had been born and raised in Marseilles – that would explain the accent – and long before my time he had already become a legend.

'You're Raymond, aren't you?' I said. 'Charles Raymond.'

'I prefer Raymond alone.' He smiled in deprecation of his own small vanity. 'And I am flattered that you recognize me.'

I don't believe he really was. Raymond the Magician, Raymond the Great, would, if anything, expect to be recognized wherever he went. As the master of sleight of hand who had paled Thurston's star, as the escape artist who had almost outshone Houdini, Raymond would not be inclined to underestimate himself.

He had started with the standard box of tricks which makes up the repertoire of most professional magicians; he had gone far beyond that to those feats of escape which, I suppose, are known to us all by now. The lead casket sealed under a foot of lake ice, the welded-steel strait jackets, the vaults of the Bank of England, the exquisite suicide knot which nooses throat and doubles legs together so that the motion of a leg draws the noose tighter and tighter around the throat – all these Raymond had known and escaped from. And then at the pinnacle of fame he had dropped from sight and his name had become relegated to the past.

When I asked him why, he shrugged.

'A man works for money or for the love of his work. If he has all the wealth he needs and has no more love for his work, why go on?'

'But to give up a great career—' I protested.

'It was enough to know that the house was waiting here.'

'You mean,' Elizabeth said, 'that you never intended to live any place but here?'

'Never – not once in all these years.' He laid a finger along his nose and winked broadly at us. 'Of course, I made no secret of this to the Dane estate, and when the time came to sell I was the first and only one approached.'

'You don't give up an idea easily,' Hugh said in an edged voice.

Raymond laughed. 'Idea? It became an obsession really. Over the years I traveled to many parts of the world, but no matter how fine the place, I knew it could not be as fine as that house on the edge of the woods there, with the river at its feet and the hills beyond. Someday, I would tell myself, when my travels are done I will come here, and, like Candide, cultivate my garden.'

He ran his hand abstractedly over the poodle's head and looked around with an air of great satisfaction. 'And now,' he said, 'here I am.'

Here he was, indeed, and it quickly became clear that his arrival was working a change on Hilltop. Or, since Hilltop was so completely a reflection of Hugh, it was clear that a change was being worked on Hugh. He became irritable and restless, and more aggressively sure of himself than ever. The warmth and good nature were still there – they were as much part of him as his arrogance – but he now had to work a little harder at them. He reminded me of a man who is bothered by a speck in the eye, but can't find it, and must get along with it as best he can.

Raymond, of course, was the speck, and I got the impression at times that he rather enjoyed the role. It would have been easy enough for him to stay close to his own house and cultivate his garden, or paste up his album, or whatever retired performers do, but he evidently found that impossible. He had a way of drifting over to Hilltop at odd times, just as Hugh was led to find his way to the Dane house and spend long and troublesome sessions there.

Both of them must have known that they were so badly suited to each other that the easy and logical solution would have been to stay apart. But they had the affinity of negative and positive forces, and when they were in a room together the crackling of the antagonistic current between them was so strong you could almost see it in the air.

Any subject became a point of contention for them, and they would duel over it bitterly: Hugh armored and weaponed with his massive assurance, Raymond flicking away with a rapier, trying to find a chink in the armor. I think that what annoyed Raymond most was the discovery that there was no chink in the armor. As someone with an obvious passion for searching out all sides to all questions and for going deep into motives and causes, he was continually being outraged by Hugh's single-minded way of laying down the law.

He didn't hesitate to let Hugh know that. 'You are positively medieval,' he said. 'And of all things men should have learned since that time, the biggest is that there are no easy answers, no solutions one can give with a snap of the fingers. I can only hope for you that some day you may be faced with the perfect dilemma, the unanswerable question. You would find that a revelation. You would learn more in that minute than you dreamed possible.'

And Hugh did not make matters any better when he coldly answered: 'And *I* say, that for any man with a brain and the courage to use it there is no such thing as a perfect dilemma.'

It may be that this was the sort of episode that led to the trouble that followed, or it may be that Raymond acted out of the most innocent and esthetic motives possible. But, whatever the motives, the results were inevitable and dangerous.

They grew from the project Raymond outlined for us in great detail one afternoon. Now that he was living in the Dane house he had discovered that it was too big, too overwhelming. 'Like a museum,' he explained. 'I find myself wandering through it like a lost soul through endless galleries.'

The grounds also needed landscaping. The ancient trees were handsome, but, as Raymond put it, there were just too many of them. 'Literally,' he said, 'I cannot see the river for the trees, and I am one devoted to the sight of running water.'

Altogether there would be drastic changes. Two wings of the house would come down, the trees would be cleared away to make a broad aisle to the water, the whole place would be enlivened. It would no longer be a museum, but the perfect home he had envisioned over the years.

At the start of the recitative Hugh was slouched comfortably in his chair. Then as Raymond drew the vivid picture of what was to be, Hugh sat up straighter and straighter until he was as rigid as a trooper in the saddle. His lips compressed. His face became blood-red. His hands clenched and unclenched in a slow, deadly rhythm. Only a miracle was restraining him from an open outburst, but it was not the kind of miracle to last. I saw from Elizabeth's expression that she understood this, too, but was as helpless as I to do anything about it. And when Raymond, after painting the last glowing strokes of his description, said complacently, 'Well, now, what do you think?' there was no holding Hugh.

He leaned forward with deliberation and said, 'Do you really want to know what I think?'

'Now, Hugh,' Elizabeth said in alarm. 'Please, Hugh—'

He brushed that aside.

'Do you really want to know?' he demanded of Raymond.

Raymond frowned. 'Of course.'

'Then I'll tell you,' Hugh said. He took a deep breath. 'I think that nobody but a damned iconoclast could even conceive the atrocity you're proposing. I think you're one of those people who take pleasure in smashing apart anything that's stamped with tradition or stability. You'd kick the props from under the whole world if you could!'

'I beg your pardon,' Raymond said. He was very pale and angry. 'But I think you are confusing change with destruction. Surely, you must comprehend that I do not intend to destroy anything, but only wish to make some necessary changes.'

'Necessary?' Hugh gibed. 'Rooting up a fine stand of trees that's been there for centuries? Ripping apart a house that's as solid as a rock? *I* call it wanton destruction.'

'I'm afraid I do not understand. To refresh a scene, to reshape it—'

'I have no intention of arguing,' Hugh cut in. 'I'm telling you straight out that you don't have the right to tamper with that property!'

They were on their feet now, facing each other truculently, and the only thing that kept me from being really frightened was the conviction that Hugh would not become violent, and that Raymond was far too level-headed to lose his temper. Then the threatening moment was magically past. Raymond's lips suddenly quirked in amusement, and he studied Hugh with courteous interest.

'I see,' he said. 'I was quite stupid not to have understood at once. This property, which, I remarked, was a little too much like a museum, is to remain that way, and I am to be its custodian. A caretaker of the past, one might say, a curator of its relics.'

He shook his head smilingly. 'But I am afraid I am not quite suited to that role. I lift my hat to the past, it is true, but I prefer to court the present. For that reason I will go ahead with my plans, and hope they do not make an obstacle to our friendship.'

I remember thinking, when I left next day for the city and a long, hot week, at my desk, that Raymond had carried off the affair very nicely, and that, thank God, it had gone no further than it did. So I was completely unprepared for Elizabeth's call at the end of the week.

It was awful, she said. It was the business of Hugh and Raymond and the Dane house, but worse than ever. She was counting on my coming down to Hilltop the next day; there couldn't be any question about that. She had planned a way of clearing up the whole thing, but I simply had to be there to back her up. After all, I was one of the few people Hugh would listen to, and she was depending on me.

'Depending on me for what?' I said. I didn't like the sound of it. 'And as for Hugh's listening to me, Elizabeth, isn't that stretching it a good deal? I can't see him wanting my advice on his personal affairs.'

'If you're going to be touchy about it—'

'I'm *not* touchy about it,' I retorted. 'I just don't like getting mixed up in this thing. Hugh's quite capable of taking care of himself.'

'Maybe too capable.'

'And what does that mean?'

'Oh, I can't explain now,' she wailed. 'I'll tell you everything tomorrow. And, darling, if you have any brotherly feelings you'll be here on the morning train. Believe me, it's serious.'

I arrived on the morning train in a bad state. My imagination is one of the overactive kind that can build a cosmic disaster out of very little material, and by the time I arrived at the house I was prepared for almost anything.

But, on the surface, at least, all was serene. Hugh greeted me warmly, Elizabeth was her cheerful self, and we had an amiable lunch and a long talk which never came near the subject of Raymond or the Dane house. I said nothing about Elizabeth's phone call, but thought of it with a steadily growing sense of outrage until I was alone with her.

'Now,' I said, 'I'd like an explanation of all this mystery. The Lord knows what I expected to find out here, but it certainly wasn't anything I've seen so far. And I'd like some accounting for the bad time you've given me since that call.'

'All right,' she said grimly, 'and that's what you'll get. Come along.'

She led the way on a long walk through the gardens and past the stables and outbuildings. Near the private road which lay beyond the last grove of trees she suddenly said, 'When the car drove you up to the house didn't you notice anything strange about this road?'

'No, I didn't.'

'I suppose not. The driveway to the house turns off too far away from here. But now you'll have a chance to see for yourself.'

I did see for myself. A chair was set squarely in the middle of the road and on the chair sat a stout man placidly reading a magazine. I recognized the man at once: he was one of Hugh's stable hands, and he had the patient look of someone who has been sitting for a long time and expects to sit a good deal longer. It took me only a second to realize what he was there for, but Elizabeth wasn't leaving anything to my deductive powers. When we walked over to him, the man stood up and grinned at us.

'William,' Elizabeth said, 'would you mind telling my brother what instructions Mr Lozier gave you?'

'Sure,' the man said cheerfully. 'Mr Lozier told us there was always to be one of us sitting right here, and any truck we saw that might be carrying construction stuff or suchlike for the Dane house was to be stopped and turned back. All we had to do is tell them it's private property and they were trespassing. If they laid a finger on us we just call in the police. That's the whole thing.'

'Have you turned back any trucks?' Elizabeth asked for my benefit.

The man looked surprised. 'Why, you know that, Mrs Lozier,' he said. 'There was a couple of them the first day we were out here, and that was all. There wasn't any fuss either,' he explained to me. 'None of those drivers wants to monkey with trespass.'

When we were away from the road again I clapped my hand to my forehead. 'It's incredible!' I said. 'Hugh must know he can't get away with this. That road is the only one to the Dane place, and it's been in public use so long that it isn't even a private thoroughfare any more!'

Elizabeth nodded. 'And that's exactly what Raymond told Hugh a few days back. He came over here in a fury, and they had quite an argument about it. And when Raymond said something about hauling Hugh off to court, Hugh answered that he'd be glad to spend the rest of his life in litigation over this business. But that wasn't the worst of it. The last thing Raymond said was that Hugh ought to know that force only invited force, and ever since then I've been expecting a war to break out here any minute. Don't you see? That man blocking the road is a constant provocation, and it scares me.'

I could understand that. And the more I considered the matter, the more dangerous it looked.

'But I have a plan,' Elizabeth said eagerly, 'and that's why I wanted you here. I'm having a dinner party tonight, a very small, informal dinner party. It's to be a sort of peace conference. You'll be there, and Dr Wynant – Hugh likes you both a great deal – and,' she hesitated, 'Raymond.'

'No!' I said. 'You mean he's actually coming?'

'I went over to see him yesterday and we had a long talk. I explained everything to him – about neighbors being able to sit down and come to an understanding, and about brotherly love and – oh, it must have sounded dreadfully inspirational and sticky, but it worked. He said he would be there.'

I had a foreboding. 'Does Hugh know about this?'

'About the dinner? Yes.'

'I mean, about Raymond's being there.'

'No, he doesn't.' And then when she saw me looking hard at her, she burst out defiantly with, 'Well, *something* had to be done, and I did it, that's all! Isn't it better than just sitting and waiting for God knows what?'

Until we were all seated around the dining-room table that evening I might have conceded the point. Hugh had been visibly shocked by Raymond's arrival, but then, apart from a sidelong glance at Elizabeth which had volumes written in it, he managed to conceal his feelings well enough. He had made the introductions gracefully, kept up his end of the conversation, and, all in all, did a creditable job of playing host.

Ironically, it was the presence of Dr Wynant which made even this much of a triumph possible for Elizabeth, and which then turned it into a disaster. The doctor was an eminent surgeon, stocky and gray-haired, with an abrupt, positive way about him. Despite his own position in the world he seemed pleased as a schoolboy to meet Raymond, and in no time at all they were as thick as thieves.

It was when Hugh discovered during dinner that nearly all attention was fixed on Raymond and very little on himself that the mantle of good host started to slip, and the fatal flaws in Elizabeth's plan showed through. There are people who enjoy entertaining lions and who take pleasure in reflected glory, but Hugh was not one of them. Besides, he regarded the doctor as one of his closest friends, and I have noticed that it is the most assured of men who can be the most jealous of their friendships. And when a prized friendship is being impinged on by the man one loathes more than anything else in the world–! All in all, by simply imagining myself in Hugh's place and looking across the table at Raymond who was gaily and unconcernedly holding forth, I was prepared for the worst.

The opportunity for it came to Hugh when Raymond was deep in a discussion of the devices used in effecting escapes. They were innumerable, he said. Almost anything one could seize on would serve as such a device. A wire, a scrap of metal, even a bit of paper – at one time or another he had used them all.

'But of them all,' he said with a sudden solemnity, 'there is only one I would stake my life on. Strange, it is one you cannot see, cannot hold in your hand – in fact, for many people it does not even exist. Yet, it is the one I have used most often and which has never failed me.'

The doctor leaned forward, his eyes bright with interest. 'And it is—?'

'It is a knowledge of people, my friend. Or, as it may be put, a knowledge of human nature. To me it is as vital an instrument as the scalpel is to you.'

'Oh?' said Hugh, and his voice was so sharp that all eyes were instantly turned on him. 'You make sleight of hand sound like a department of psychology.'

'Perhaps,' Raymond said, and I saw he was watching Hugh now, gauging him. 'You see there is no great mystery in the matter. My profession – my art, as I like to think of it – is no more than the art of misdirection, and I am but one of its many practitioners.'

'I wouldn't say there were many escape artists around nowadays,' the doctor remarked.

'True,' Raymond said, 'but you will observe I referred to the art of misdirection. The escape artist, the master of legerdemain, these are a handful who practice the most exotic form of that art. But what of those who engage in the work of politics, of advertising, of salesmanship?' He laid his finger along his nose in the familiar gesture, and winked. 'I am afraid they have all made my art their business.'

The doctor smiled. 'Since you haven't dragged medicine into it I'm willing to go along with you,' he said. 'But what I want to know is, exactly how does this knowledge of human nature work in your profession?'

'In this way,' Raymond said. 'One must judge a person carefully. Then, if he finds in that person certain weaknesses, he can state a false premise and it will be accepted without question. Once the false premise is swallowed, the rest is easy. The victim will then see only what the magician wants him to see, or will give his vote to that politician, or will buy merchandise because of that advertising.' He shrugged. 'And that is all there is to it.'

'Is it?' Hugh said. 'But what happens when you're with people who have some intelligence and won't swallow your false premise? How do you do your tricks then? Or do you keep them on the same level as selling beads to the savage?'

'Now that's uncalled for, Hugh,' the doctor said. 'The man's expressing his ideas. No reason to make an issue of them.'

'Maybe there is,' Hugh said, his eyes fixed on Raymond. 'I have found he's full of interesting ideas. I was wondering how far he'd want to go in backing them up.'

Raymond touched the napkin to his lips with a precise little flick, and then laid it carefully on the table before him. 'In short,' he said, addressing himself to Hugh, 'you want a small demonstration of my art.'

'It depends,' Hugh said. 'I don't want any trick cigarette cases or rabbits out of hats or any damn nonsense like that. I'd like to see something good.'

'Something good,' echoed Raymond reflectively. He looked around the room, studied it, and then turned to Hugh, pointing toward the huge oak door which was closed between the dining room and the living room, where we had gathered before dinner.

'That door is not locked, is it?'

'No,' Hugh said, 'it isn't. It hasn't been locked for years.'

'But there is a key to it?'

Hugh pulled out his key chain, and with an effort detached a heavy, old-fashioned key. 'Yes, it's the same one we use for the butler's pantry.' He was becoming interested despite himself.

'Good. No, do not give it to me. Give it to the doctor. You have faith in the doctor's honor, I am sure?'

'Yes,' said Hugh drily, 'I have.'

'Very well. Now, Doctor, will you please go to that door and lock it.'

The doctor marched to the door, with his firm, decisive tread, thrust the key into the lock, and turned it. The click of the bolt snapping into place was loud in the silence of the room. The doctor returned to the table holding the key, but Raymond motioned it away. 'It must not leave your hand or everything is lost,' he warned.

'Now,' Raymond said, 'for the finale I approach the door. I flick my handkerchief at it—' the handkerchief barely brushed the keyhole '—and presto, the door is unlocked!'

The doctor went to it. He seized the doorknob, twisted it dubiously, and then watched with genuine astonishment as the door swung silently open.

'Well, I'll be damned,' he said.

'Somehow,' Elizabeth laughed, 'a false premise went down easy as an oyster.'

Only Hugh reflected a sense of personal outrage. 'All right,' he demanded, 'how was it done? How did you work it?'

'I?' Raymond said reproachfully, and smiled at all of us with obvious enjoyment. 'It was you who did it all. I used only my little knowledge of human nature to help you along the way.'

I said, 'I can guess part of it. That door was set in advance, and when the doctor thought he was locking it, he wasn't. He was really unlocking it. Isn't that the answer?'

Raymond nodded. 'Very much the answer. The door *was* locked in advance. I made sure of that, because with a little forethought I suspected there would be such a challenge during the evening. I merely made certain that I was the last one to enter this room, and when I did I used this.' He held up his hand so that we could see the sliver of metal in it. 'An ordinary skeleton key, of course, but sufficient for an old and primitive lock.'

For a moment Raymond looked grave, then he continued brightly. 'It was our host himself who stated the false premise when he said the door was unlocked. He was a man so sure of himself that he would not think to test anything so obvious. The doctor is also a man who is sure, and he fell into the same trap. It is, as you now see, a little dangerous always to be so sure.'

'I'll go along with that,' the doctor said ruefully, 'even though it's heresy to admit it in my line of work.' He playfully tossed the key he had been holding across the table to Hugh who let it fall in front of him and made no gesture toward it. 'Well, Hugh, like it or not, you must admit the man has proved his point.'

'Do I?' said Hugh softly. He sat there smiling a little now, and it was easy to see he was turning some thought over and over in his head.

'Oh, come on, man,' the doctor said with some impatience. 'You were taken in as much as we were. You know that.'

'Of course you were, darling,' Elizabeth agreed.

I think that she suddenly saw her opportunity to turn the proceedings into the peace conference she had aimed at, but I could have told her she was choosing her time badly. There was a look in Hugh's eye I didn't like – a veiled look which wasn't natural to him. Ordinarily, when he was really angered, he would blow up a violent storm, and once the thunder and lightning had passed he would be honestly apologetic. But this present mood of his was different. There was a slumberous quality in it which alarmed me.

He hooked one arm over the back of his chair and rested the other one on the table, sitting halfway around to fix his eyes on Raymond. 'I seem to be a minority of one,' he remarked, 'but I'm sorry to say I found your little trick disappointing. Not that it wasn't cleverly done – I'll grant that, all right – but because it wasn't any more than you'd expect from a competent locksmith.'

'Now there's a large helping of sour grapes,' the doctor jeered.

Hugh shook his head. 'No, I'm simply saying that where there's a lock on a door and the key to it in your hand, it's no great trick to open it. Considering our friend's reputation, I thought we'd see more from him than that.'

Raymond grimaced. 'Since I had hoped to entertain,' he said, 'I must apologize for disappointing.'

'Oh, as far as entertainment goes I have no complaints. But for a real test—'

'A real test?'

'Yes, something a little different. Let's say, a door without any locks or keys to tamper with. A closed door which can be opened with a fingertip, but which is nevertheless impossible to open. How does that sound to you?'

Raymond narrowed his eyes thoughtfully, as if he were considering the picture being presented to him. 'It sounds most interesting,' he said at last. 'Tell me more about it.'

'No,' Hugh said, and from the sudden eagerness in his voice

I felt that this was the exact moment he had been looking for. 'I'll do better than that. I'll *show* it to you.'

He stood up brusquely and the rest of us followed suit – except Elizabeth, who remained in her seat. When I asked her if she wanted to come along, she only shook her head and sat there watching us hopelessly as we left the room.

We were bound for the cellars, I realized when Hugh picked up a flashlight along the way, but for a part of the cellars I had never seen before. On a few occasions I had gone downstairs to help select a bottle of wine from the racks there, but now we walked past the wine vault and into a long, dimly lit chamber behind it. Our feet scraped loudly on the rough stone, the walls around us showed the stains of seepage, and warm as the night was outside, I could feel the chill of dampness turning my chest to gooseflesh. When the doctor shuddered and said hollowly, 'These are the very tombs of Atlantis,' I knew I wasn't alone in my feeling, and felt some relief at that.

We stopped at the very end of the chamber, before what I can best describe as a stone closet built from floor to ceiling in the farthest angle of the walls. It was about four feet wide and not quite twice that in length, and its open doorway showed impenetrable blackness inside. Hugh reached into the blackness and pulled a heavy door into place.

'That's it,' he said abruptly. 'Plain solid wood, four inches thick, fitted flush into the frame so that it's almost airtight. It's a beautiful piece of carpentry, too, the kind they practiced two hundred years ago. And no locks or bolts. Just a ring set into each side to use as a handle.' He pushed the door gently and it swung open noiselessly at his touch. 'See that? The whole thing is balanced so perfectly on the hinges that it moves like a feather.'

'But what's it for?' I asked. 'It must have been made for a reason.'

Hugh laughed shortly. 'It was. Back in the bad old days, when a servant committed a crime – and I don't suppose it had to be more of a crime than talking back to one of the ancient Loziers – he was put in here to repent. And since the air inside was good for only a few hours at the most, he either repented damn soon or not at all.'

'And that door?' the doctor said cautiously. 'That impressive door of yours which opens at a touch to provide all the air needed – what prevented the servant from opening it?'

'Look,' Hugh said. He flashed his light inside the cell and we crowded behind him to peer in. The circle of light reached across the cell to its far wall and picked out a short, heavy chain hanging a little above head level with a U-shaped collar dangling from its bottom link.

'I see,' Raymond said, and they were the first words I had heard him speak since we had left the dining room. 'It is truly ingenious. The man stands with his back against the wall, facing the door. The collar is placed around his neck, and then – since it is clearly not made for a lock – it is clamped there, hammered around his neck. The door is closed, and the man spends the next few hours like someone on an invisible rack, reaching out with his feet to catch the ring on the door which is just out of reach. If he is lucky he may not strangle himself in his iron collar, but may live until someone chooses to open the door for him.'

'My God,' the doctor said. 'You make me feel as if I were living through it.'

Raymond smiled faintly. 'I have lived through many such experiences, and, believe me, the reality is always a little worse than the worst imaginings. There is always the ultimate moment of terror, of panic, when the heart pounds so madly you think it will burst through your ribs, and the cold sweat soaks clear through you in the space of one breath. That is when you must take yourself in hand, must dispel all weaknesses, and remember all the lessons you have ever learned. If not—!' He whisked the edge of his hand across his lean throat. 'Unfortunately for the usual victim of such a device,' he concluded sadly, 'since he lacks the essential courage and knowledge to help himself, he succumbs.'

'But you wouldn't,' Hugh said.

'I have no reason to think so.'

'You mean,' and the eagerness was creeping back into Hugh's voice, stronger than ever, 'that under the very same conditions as someone chained in there two hundred years ago you could get this door open?'

The challenging note was too strong to be brushed aside lightly. Raymond stood silent for a long minute, face strained with concentration, before he answered.

'Yes,' he said. 'It would not be easy – the problem is made formidable by its very simplicity – but it could be solved.'

'How long do you think it would take you?'

'An hour at the most.'

Hugh had come a long way around to get to this point. He asked the question slowly, savoring it. 'Would you want to bet on that?'

'Now, wait a minute,' the doctor said. 'I don't like any part of this.'

'And I vote we adjourn for a drink,' I put in. 'Fun's fun, but we'll all wind up with pneumonia, playing games down here.'

Neither Hugh nor Raymond appeared to hear a word of this. They stood staring at each other – Hugh waiting on pins and needles, Raymond deliberating – until Raymond said, 'What is the bet you offer?'

'This. If you lose, you get out of the Dane house inside of a month, and sell it to me.'

'And if I win?'

It was not easy for Hugh to say it, but he finally got it out. 'Then I'll be the one to get out. And if you don't want to buy Hilltop I'll arrange to sell it to the first comer.'

For anyone who knew Hugh it was so fantastic, so staggering a statement to hear from him, that none of us could find words at first. It was the doctor who recovered most quickly.

'You're not speaking for yourself, Hugh,' he warned. 'You're a married man. Elizabeth's feelings have to be considered.'

'Is it a bet?' Hugh demanded of Raymond. 'Do you want to go through with it?'

'I think before I answer that, there is something to be explained.' Raymond paused, then went on slowly, 'I am afraid I gave the impression – out of false pride, perhaps – that when I retired from my work it was because of a boredom, a lack of interest in it. That was not altogether the truth. In reality, I was required to go to a doctor some years ago, the doctor listened to the heart, and suddenly my heart became the most important thing in the world. I tell you this because, while your challenge strikes me as being a most unusual and interesting way of settling differences between neighbors, I must reject it for reasons of health.'

'You were healthy enough a minute ago,' Hugh said in a hard voice.

'Perhaps not as much as you would want to think, my friend.'

'In other words,' Hugh said bitterly, 'there's no accomplice handy, no keys in your pocket to help out, and no way of tricking anyone into seeing what isn't there! So you have to admit you're beaten.'

Raymond stiffened. 'I admit no such thing. All the tools I would need even for such a test as this I have with me. Believe me, they would be enough.'

Hugh laughed aloud, and the sound of it broke into small echoes all down the corridors behind us. It was that sound, I am sure – the living contempt in it rebounding from wall to wall around us – which sent Raymond into the cell.

Hugh wielded the hammer, a short-handled but heavy sledge, which tightened the collar into a circlet around Raymond's neck, hitting with hard even strokes at the iron which was braced against the wall. When he was finished I saw the pale glow of the radium-painted numbers on a watch as Raymond studied it in his pitch darkness.

'It is now eleven,' he said calmly. 'The wager is that by midnight this door must be opened, and it does not matter what means are used. Those are the conditions. and you gentlemen the witnesses to them.'

Then the door was closed, and the walking began.

Back and forth we walked – the three of us – as if we were being compelled to trace every possible geometric figure on that stony floor, the doctor with his quick, impatient step, and I matching Hugh's long, nervous strides. A foolish, meaningless march, back and forth across our own shadows, each of us marking the time by counting off the passing seconds, and each ashamed to be the first to look at his watch.

For a while there was a counterpoint to this scraping of feet from inside the cell. It was a barely perceptible clinking of chain coming at brief, regular intervals. Then there would be a long silence, followed by a renewal of the sound. When it stopped again I could not restrain myself any longer. I held up my watch toward the dim yellowish light of the bulb overhead and saw with dismay that barely twenty minutes had passed.

After that there was no hesitancy in the others about looking at the time, and, if anything, this made it harder to bear than just wondering. I caught the doctor winding his watch with small, brisk turns, and then a few minutes later he would try to wind it again, and suddenly drop his hand with disgust as he realized he had already done it. Hugh walked with his watch held up near his eyes, as if by concentration on it he could drag that crawling minute hand faster around the dial.

Thirty minutes had passed.

Forty.

Forty-five.

I remember that when I looked at my watch and saw there were less than fifteen minutes to go I wondered if I could last out even that short time. The chill had sunk so deep into me that I ached with it. I was shocked when I saw that Hugh's face was dripping with sweat, and that beads of it gathered and ran off while I watched.

It was while I was looking at him in fascination that it happened. The sound broke through the walls of the cell like a wail of agony heard from far away, and shivered over us as if it were spelling out the words.

'*Doctor!*' it cried. '*The air!*'

It was Raymond's voice, but the thickness of the wall blocking it off turned it into a high, thin sound. What was clearest in it was the note of pure terror, the plea growing out of that terror.

'*Air!*' it screamed, the word bubbling and dissolving into a long-drawn sound which made no sense at all.

And then it was silent.

We leaped for the door together, but Hugh was there first, his back against it, barring the way. In his upraised hand was the hammer which had clinched Raymond's collar.

'Keep back!' he cried. 'Don't come any nearer, I warn you!'

The fury in him, brought home by the menace of the weapon, stopped us in our tracks.

'Hugh,' the doctor pleaded, 'I know what you're thinking, but you can forget that now. The bet's off, and I'm opening the door on my own responsibility. You have my word for that.'

'Do I? But do you remember the terms of the bet, Doctor? This door must be opened within an hour – *and it doesn't matter what means are used!* Do you understand now? He's fooling both of you. He's faking a death scene, so that you'll push open the door and win his bet for him. But it's my bet, not yours, and I have the last word on it!'

I saw from the way he talked, despite the shaking tension in his voice, that he was in perfect command of himself, and it made everything seem that much worse.

'How do you know he's faking?' I demanded. 'The man said he had a heart condition. He said there was always a time in a spot like this when he had to fight panic and could feel the strain of it. What right do you have to gamble with his life?'

'Damn it, don't you see he never mentioned any heart condition until he smelled a bet in the wind? Don't you see he set his trap that way, just as he locked the door behind him when he came into dinner! But this time nobody will spring it for him – nobody!'

'Listen to me,' the doctor said, and his voice cracked like a whip. 'Do you concede that there's one slim possibility of that man being dead in there, or dying?'

'Yes, it is possible – anything is possible.'

'I'm not trying to split hairs with you! I'm telling you that if that man is in trouble every second counts, and you're stealing that time from him. And if that's the case, by God, I'll sit in the witness chair at your trial and swear you murdered him! Is that what you want?'

Hugh's head sank forward on his chest, but his hand still tightly gripped the hammer. I could hear the breath drawing heavily in his throat, and when he raised his head, his face was gray and haggard. The torment of indecision was written in every pale sweating line of it.

And then I suddenly understood what Raymond had meant that day when he told Hugh about the revelation he might find in the face of a perfect dilemma. It was the revelation of what a man may learn about himself when he is forced to look into his own depths, and Hugh had found it at last.

In that shadowy cellar, while the relentless seconds thundered louder and louder in our ears, we waited to see what he would do.

# Broker's Special

I t was the first time in a good many years that Cornelius, a Wall Street broker, had made the homeward trip in any train other than the Broker's Special. The Special was his kind of train; the passengers on it were his kind of people. Executives, professionals, men of substance and dignity who could recognize each other without introductions, and understand each other without words.

*If it weren't for the Senator's dinner party*, Cornelius reflected. But the Senator had insisted, so there was no escape from that abomination of abominations, the midweek dinner party. And, of course, no escape from the necessity of taking an earlier train home to the tedium of dressing, and an evening of too much food, too much liquor, and all the resultant misery the next morning.

Filled with this depressing thought Cornelius stepped down heavily from the train to the familiar platform and walked over to his car. Since Claire preferred the station wagon, he used the sedan to get to and from the station. When they were first married two years ago she had wanted to chauffeur him back and forth, but the idea had somehow repelled him. He had always felt there was something vaguely obscene about the way other men publicly kissed their wives good-by in front of the station every morning, and the thought of being placed in their position filled him with a chilling embarrassment. He had not told this to Claire, however. He had simply told her he had not married her to obtain a housekeeper or chauffeur. She was to enjoy her life, not fill it with unnecessary duties.

Ordinarily, it was no more than a fifteen-minute drive through the countryside to the house. But now, in keeping with the already exasperating tenor of the day's events, he met an unexpected delay. A mile or so past where the road branched off from the highway it crossed the main line of the railroad. There was no guard or crossing gate here, but a red light, and a bell which was ringing an insistent warning as Cornelius drove up. He braked the car, and sat tapping his fingers restlessly on the steering wheel while the endless, clanking length of a freight went by. And then, before he could start the car again, he saw them.

It was Claire and a man. His wife and some man in the station wagon roaring past him into town. And the man was driving – seated big and blond and arrogant behind the wheel like a Viking – with one arm around Claire who, with eyes closed, rested her head on his shoulder. There was a look on her face, too, such as Cornelius had never seen there before, but which he had sometimes dreamed of seeing. They passed by in a flash, but the picture they made was burned as brilliant in his mind as a photograph on film.

He would not believe it, he told himself incredulously; he refused to believe it! But the picture was there before him, growing clearer each second, becoming more and more terribly alive as he watched it. The man's arm possessing her. Her look of acceptance. Of sensual acceptance.

He was shaking uncontrollably now, the blood pounding in his head, as he prepared to turn the car and follow them. Then he felt himself go limp. Follow them where? Back to town undoubtedly, where the man would be waiting for the next train to the city. And then what? A denunciation in the grand style? A scene? A public humiliation for himself as much as for them?

He could stand anything, but not such humiliation. It had been bad enough when he had first married Claire and realized his friends were laughing at him for it. A man in his position to marry his secretary, and a girl half his age at that! Now he knew what they had been laughing at, but he had been blind then. There had been such an air of cool formality about her when she carried on her duties in the office; she sat with such prim dignity when she took his notes; she had dressed so modestly – and when he had first invited her to dinner she had reddened with the flustered naiveté of a young girl being invited on her first date. Naiveté! And all the time, he thought furiously, she must have been laughing at me. She, along with the rest of them.

He drove to the house slowly, almost blindly. The house was empty, and he realized that, of course, it was Thursday, the servant's day off, which made it the perfect day for Claire's purpose. He went directly to the library, sat down at the desk there, and unlocked the top drawer. His gun was in that drawer, a short-barreled .38, and he picked it up slowly, hefting its cold weight in his hand, savoring the sense of power it gave him. Then abruptly his mind went back to something Judge Hilliker had once told him, something strangely interesting that the old man had said while sharing a seat with him on the Broker's Special.

'Guns?' Hilliker had said. 'Knives? Blunt instruments? You can throw them all out of the window. As far as I'm concerned there is just one perfect weapon – an automobile. Why? Because when an automobile is going fast enough it will kill anyone. And if the driver gets out and looks sorry he'll find that he's the one getting everybody's sympathy, and not that bothersome corpse on the ground who shouldn't have been in the way anyhow. As long as the driver isn't drunk or flagrantly reckless he can kill anybody in this country he wants to, and suffer no more than a momentary embarrassment and a penalty that isn't even worth worrying about.

'Think it over, man,' the Judge continued, 'to most people the automobile is some sort of god, and if God happens to strike you down it's your hard luck. As for me, when I cross a street I just say a little prayer.'

There was more of that in Judge Hilliker's mordant and long-winded style, but Cornelius had no need to remember it. What he needed he now had, and very carefully he put the gun back in the drawer, slid the drawer shut, and locked it.

Claire came in while he still sat brooding at the desk, and he forced himself to regard her with cold objectivity – this radiantly lovely woman who was playing him for a fool, and who now stood wide-eyed in the doorway with an incongruously large bag of groceries clutched to her.

'I saw the car in the garage,' she said breathlessly. 'I was afraid something was wrong. That you weren't feeling well . . .'

'I feel very well.'

'But you're home so early. You've never come this early before.'

'I've always managed to refuse invitations to midweek dinner parties before.'

'Oh, Lord!' she gasped. 'The dinner! It never even entered my mind. I've been so busy all day . . .'

'Yes?' he said. 'Doing what?'

'Well, everyone's off today, so I took care of the house from top to bottom, and then when I looked in the pantry and saw we needed some things I ran into town for them.' She gestured at the bulky paper bag with her chin. 'I'll have your bath ready, and your things laid out as soon as I put this stuff away.'

Watching her leave he felt an honest admiration for her. Another woman would have invented a visit to a friend who might, at some later time, accidentally let the cat out of the bag. Or another woman would not have thought to burden herself with a useless package to justify a trip into town. But not Claire, who was evidently as clever as she was beautiful.

And she *was* damnably attractive. His male friends may have laughed behind his back, but in their homes she was always eagerly surrounded by them. When he entered a roomful of strangers with her he saw how all men's eyes followed her with a frankly covetous interest. No, nothing must happen to her; nothing at all. It was the man who had to be destroyed, just as one would destroy any poacher on his preserves, any lunatic who with ax in hand ran amok through his home. Claire would have to be hurt a little, would have to be taught her lesson, but that would be done most effectively through what happened to the man.

Cornelius learned very quickly that his plans would have to take in a good deal more than the simple act of waylaying the man and running him down. There were details, innumerable details covering every step of the way before and after the event, which had to be jigsawed into place bit by bit in order to make it perfect.

In that respect, Cornelius thought gratefully, the Judge had been far more helpful than he had realized in his irony. Murder by automobile was the perfect murder, because, with certain details taken care of, it was not even murder at all! There was the victim, and there was the murderer standing over him, and the whole thing would be treated with perfunctory indifference. After all, what was one more victim among the thirty thousand each year? He was a statistic, to be regarded with some tongue-clicking and a shrug of helplessness.

Not by Claire, of course. Coincidence can be stretched far, but hardly far enough to cover the case of a husband's running down his wife's lover. And that was the best part of it. Claire would know, but would be helpless to say anything, since saying anything must expose her own wrongdoing. She would spend her life, day after day, knowing that she had been found out, knowing that a just vengeance had been exacted, and standing forewarned against any other such temptations that might come her way.

But what of the remote possibility that she might choose to speak out and expose herself? There, Cornelius reflected, fitting another little piece of the jigsaw into place, coincidence would instantly go to work for him. If there was no single shred of evidence that he had ever suspected her affair, or that he had ever seen the man before, the accident *must* be regarded by the law as coincidence. Either way his position was unassailable.

It was with this in mind that he patiently and single-mindedly went to work on his plans. He was tempted at the start to call in some professional investigator who could promptly and efficently bring him the information he wanted, but after careful consideration he put this idea aside. A smart investigator might easily put two and two together after the accident. If he were honest he might go to the authorities with his suspicions; if he were dishonest he might be tempted to try blackmail. Obviously, there was no way of calling in an outsider without risking one danger or the other. And nothing, nothing at all, was going to be risked here.

So it took Cornelius several precious weeks to glean the information he wanted, and, as he admitted to himself, it might have taken even longer had not Claire and the man maintained such an unfailing routine. Thursday was the one day of the week on which the man would pay his visits. Then, a little before the city-bound train arrived at the station, Claire would drive the station wagon into an almost deserted side-street a block from the Plaza. In the car the couple would kiss with an intensity that made Cornelius's flesh crawl.

As soon as the man left the car Claire would drive swiftly away, and the man would walk briskly to the Plaza, make his way through the cars parked at the curb there, cross the Plaza obviously sunk in his own thoughts and with only half an eye for passing traffic, and would enter the station. The third time Cornelius witnessed this performance he could have predicted the man's every step with deadly accuracy.

Occasionally, during this period, Claire mentioned that she was going to the city to do some shopping, and Cornelius took advantage of this as well. He was standing in a shadow of the terminal's waiting room when her train pulled in, he followed her at a safe distance to the street, his cab trailed hers almost to the door of the shabby apartment house where the man lived. The man was sitting on the grimy steps of the house, obviously waiting for her. When he led her into the house, as Cornelius bitterly observed, they held hands like a pair of school children, and then there was a long wait, a wait which took up most of the afternoon; but Cornelius gave up waiting before Claire reappeared.

The eruption of fury he knew after that scene gave him the idea of staging the accident there on the city streets the next day, but Cornelius quickly dismissed the thought. It would mean driving the car into the city, which was something he never did, and that would be a dangerous deviation from his own routine. Besides, city tabloids, unlike his staid local news-paper, sometimes publicized automobile accidents not only by printing the news of them, but also by displaying pictures of victim and culprit on their pages. He wanted none of that. This was a private affair. Strictly private.

No, there was no question that the only place to settle matters was right in the Plaza itself, and the more Cornelius reviewed his plans in preparation for the act the more he marveled at how flawless they were.

Nothing could conceivably go wrong. If by some mischance he struck down the man without killing him, his victim would be in the same position as Claire: unable to speak openly without exposing himself. If he missed the man entirely he was hardly in the dangerous position of an assassin who misses his victim and is caught with the gun or knife in his hand. An automobile wasn't a weapon; the affair would simply be another close call for a careless pedestrian.

However, he wanted no close calls, and to that end he took to parking the car somewhat farther from the station than he ordinarily did. The extra distance, he estimated, would allow him to swing the car across the Plaza in an arc which would meet the man as he emerged from between the parked cars across the street. That would just about make explanations uncalled-for. A man stepping out from between parked cars would be more in violation of the law than the driver who struck him!

Not only did he make sure to set the car at a proper distance from the station entrance, but Cornelius also took to backing it into place as some other drivers did. Now the front wheels were facing the Plaza, and he could quickly get up all the speed he wanted. More than that, he would be facing the man from the instant he came into sight.

The day before the one he had chosen for the final act, Cornelius waited until he was clear of traffic on his homeward drive, and then stopped the car on a deserted part of the road, letting the motor idle. Then he carefully gauged the distance to a tree some 30 yards ahead; this, he estimated, would be the distance across the Plaza. He started the car and then drove it as fast as he could past the tree, the big machine snarling as it picked up speed. Once past the tree he braced himself, stepped hard on the brake, and felt the pressure of the steering wheel against his chest as the car slewed to a shrieking stop.

That was it. That was all there was to it . . .

He left the office the next day at the exact minute he had set for himself. After his secretary had helped him on with his coat he turned to her as he had prepared himself to do and made a wry face.

'Just not feeling right,' he said. 'Don't know what's wrong with me, Miss Wynant.'

And, as he knew good secretaries were trained to do, she frowned worriedly at him and said, 'If you didn't work so hard, Mr Bolinger . . .'

He waved that aside brusquely. 'Nothing that getting home early to a good rest won't cure. Oh,' he slapped at the pockets of his coat, 'my pills, Miss Wynant. They're in the top drawer over there.'

They were only a few aspirins in an envelope, but it was the impression that counted. A man who was not feeling well had that much more justification for a mishap while he was driving.

The early train was familiar to him now; he had ridden on it several times during the past few weeks, but always circumspectly hidden behind a newspaper. Now it was to be different. When the conductor came through to check his commutation ticket, Cornelius was sitting limp in his seat, clearly a man in distress.

'Conductor,' he asked, 'if you don't mind, could you get me some water?'

The conductor glanced at him and hastily departed. When he returned with a dripping cup of water Cornelius slowly and carefully removed an aspirin from the envelope and washed it down gratefully.

'If there's anything else,' the conductor said; 'just you let me know.'

'No,' Cornelius said, 'no, I'm a little under the weather, that's all.'

But at the station the conductor was there to lend him a solicitous hand down, and dally briefly. 'You're not a regular, are you?' the conductor said. 'At least, not on this train.'

Cornelius felt a lift of gratification. 'No,' he said, 'I've only taken this train once before. I usually travel on the Broker's Special.'

'Oh.' The conductor looked him up and down, and grinned. 'Well, that figures,' he said. 'Hope you found our service as good as the Special's.'

In the small station Cornelius sat down on a bench, his head resting against the back of the bench, his eyes on the clock over the ticket agent's window. Once or twice he saw the agent glance worriedly through the window at him, and that was fine. What was not so fine was the rising feeling in him, a lurching nervousness in his stomach, a too-heavy thudding of his heart in his chest. He had allowed himself ten minutes here; each minute found the feeling getting more and more oppressive. It was an effort to contain himself, to prevent himself from getting to his feet and rushing out to the car before the minute hand of the clock had touched the small black spot that was his signal.

Then, on the second, he got up, surprised at the effort it required to do this, and slowly walked out of the station, the agent's eyes following him all the way, and down past the station to the car. He climbed behind the wheel, closed the door firmly after him, and started the motor. The soft purring of the motor under his feet sent a new strength up through him. He sat there soaking it up, his eyes fixed on the distance across the Plaza.

When the man first appeared, moving with rapid strides toward him, it struck Cornelius in some strange way that the tall, blond figure was like a puppet being drawn by an invisible wire to his destined place on the stage. Then, as he came closer, it was plain to see that he was smiling broadly, singing aloud in his exuberance of youth and strength – and triumph. That was the key which unlocked all paralysis, which sent the motor roaring into furious life.

For all the times he had lived the scene in his mind's eye, Cornelius was unprepared for the speed with which it happened. There was the man stepping out from between the cars, still blind to everything. There was Cornelius's hand on the horn, the ultimate inspiration, a warning that could not possibly be heeded, and more than anything else an insurance of success. The man swung toward the noise, his face all horror, his hands outthrust as if to fend off what was happening. There was the high-pitched scream abruptly cut off by the shock of impact, more violent than Cornelius had ever dreamed, and then everything dissolving into the screech of brakes.

The Plaza had been deserted before it had happened; now, people were running from all directions, and Cornelius had to push his way through them to catch a glimpse of the body.

'Better not look,' someone warned, but he did look, and saw the crumpled form, the legs scissored into an unnatural position, the face graying as he watched. He swayed, and a dozen helping hands reached out to support him, but it was not weakness which affected him now, but an overwhelming, giddy sense of victory, a sense of victory heightened by the voices around him.

'*Walked right into it with his eyes wide open.*'

'*I could hear that horn a block away.*'

'*Drunk, maybe. The way he stood right there . . .*'

The only danger now lay in overplaying his hand. He had to watch out for that, had to keep fitting piece after piece of the plan together, and then there would be no danger. He sat in the car while a policeman questioned him with official gravity, and he knew from the growing sympathy in the policeman's voice that he was making the right impression.

No, he was free to go home if he wished. Charges, of course, had to be automatically preferred against him, but the way things looked . . . Yes, they would be glad to phone Mrs Bolinger. They could drive him home, but if he preferred to have her do it . . .

He had allowed time enough for her to be at home when the call was made, and he spent the next fifteen minutes with the crowd staring at him through the window with a morbid and sympathetic curiosity. When the station wagon drew up nearby, a lane magically appeared through the crowd; when Claire was at his side the lane disappeared.

Even frightened and bewildered, she was a beautiful woman, Cornelius thought, and, he had to admit to himself, she knew how to put on a sterling show of wifely concern and devotion, false as it was. But perhaps that was because she didn't know yet, and it was time for her to know.

He waited until she had helped him into the station wagon, and when she sat down in the driver's seat he put an arm tight around her.

'Oh, by the way, officer,' he asked with grave anxiety through the open window. 'Did you find out who the man was? Did he have any identification on him?'

The policeman nodded. 'Young fellow from the city,' he said, 'so we'll have to check up on him down there. Name of Lundgren. Robert Lundgren, if his card means anything.'

Against his arm Cornelius felt, rather than heard, the choked gasp, felt the uncontrollable small shivering. Her face was as gray as that of the man's out there in the street. 'All right, Claire,' he said softly. 'Let's go home.'

She drove by instinct out through the streets of the town. Her face was vacuous, her eyes set and staring. He was almost grateful when they reached the highway, and she finally spoke in a quiet and wondering voice. 'You knew,' she said. 'You knew about it, and you killed him for it.'

'Yes,' Cornelius said, 'I knew about it.'

'Then you're crazy,' she said dispassionately, her eyes still fixed ahead of her. 'You must be crazy to kill someone like that.'

Her even, informative tone fired his anger as much as what she was saying.

'It was justice,' he said between his teeth. 'It was coming to him.'

She was still remote. 'You don't understand.'

'Don't understand what?'

She turned toward him, and he saw that her eyes were glistening wet. 'I knew him before I ever knew you, before I ever started working in the office. We always went together; it didn't seem as if there was any point living if we couldn't be together.' She paused only a fraction of a second. 'But things didn't go right. He had big ideas that didn't make any money, and I couldn't stand that. I was born poor, and I couldn't stand marrying poor and dying poor ... That's why I married you. And I tried to be a good wife – you'll never know how hard I tried! – but that wasn't what you wanted. You wanted a showpiece, not a wife; something to parade around in front of people so they could admire you for owning it, just like they admire you for everything else you own.'

'You're talking like a fool,' he said harshly. 'And watch the road. We turn off here.'

'Listen to me!' she said. 'I was going to tell you all about it. I was going to ask for a divorce. Not a penny to go with it, or anything like that – just the divorce so that I could marry him and make up for all the time I had thrown away! That's what I told him today, and if you had only asked – only talked to me—'

She would get over it, he thought. It had been even more

serious than he had realized, but, as the saying went, *all passes*. She had nothing to trade her marriage for any longer; when she understood that clearly they would make a new start. It was a miracle that he had thought of using the weapon he had, and that he had used it so effectively. *A perfect weapon*, the Judge had said. He'd never know how perfect.

It was the warning clangor of the bell at the grade crossing that jarred Cornelius from his reverie – that, and the alarming realization that the car's speed was not slackening at all. Then everything else was submerged by the angry bawling of a diesel horn, and when he looked up incredulously, it was to the raging mountain of steel that was the Broker's Special hurling itself over the crossing directly ahead.

'Watch out!' he cried out wildly. 'My God, what are you doing!'

In that last split second, when her foot went down hard on the accelerator, he knew.

# The Blessington
# Method

Mr Treadwell was a small, likeable man who worked for a prosperous company in New York City, and whose position with the company entitled him to an office of his own. Late one afternoon of a fine day in June a visitor entered this office. The visitor was stout, well-dressed, and imposing. His complexion was smooth and pink, his small, near-sighted eyes shone cheerfully behind heavy horn-rimmed eyeglasses.

'My name,' he said, after laying aside a bulky portfolio and shaking Mr Treadwell's hand with a crushing grip, 'is Bunce, and I am a representative of the Society for Gerontology. I am here to help you with your problem, Mr Treadwell.'

Mr Treadwell sighed. 'Since you are a total stranger to me, my friend,' he said, 'and since I have never heard of the outfit you claim to represent, and, above all, since I have no problem which could possibly concern you, I am sorry to say that I am not in the market for whatever you are peddling. Now, if you don't mind—'

'Mind?' said Bunce. 'Of course, I mind. The Society for Gerontology does not try to sell anything to anybody, Mr Treadwell. Its interests are purely philanthropic. It examines case histories, draws up reports, works toward the solution of one of the most tragic situations we face in modern society.'

'Which is?'

'That should have been made obvious by the title of the organization, Mr Treadwell. Gerontology is the study of old age and the problems concerning it. Do not confuse it with geriatrics, please. Geriatrics is concerned with the diseases of old age. Gerontology deals with old age as the problem itself.'

'I'll try to keep that in mind,' Mr Treadwell said impatiently. 'Meanwhile, I suppose, a small donation is in order? Five dollars, say?'

'No, no, Mr Treadwell, not a penny, not a red cent. I quite understand that this is the traditional way of dealing with various philanthropic organizations, but the Society for Gerontology works in a different way entirely. Our objective is to help you with your problem first. Only then would we feel we have the right to make any claim on you.'

'Fine,' said Mr Treadwell more amiably. 'That leaves us all even. I have no problem, so you get no donation. Unless you'd rather reconsider?'

'Reconsider?' said Bunce in a pained voice. 'It is you, Mr Treadwell, and not I who must reconsider. Some of the most pitiful cases the Society deals with are those of people who have long refused to recognize or admit their problem. I have worked months on your case, Mr Treadwell. I never dreamed you would fall in that category.'

Mr Treadwell took a deep breath. 'Would you mind telling me just what you mean by that nonsense about working on my case? I was never a case for any damned society or organization in the book!'

It was the work of a moment for Bunce to whip open his portfolio and extract several sheets of paper from it.

'If you will bear with me,' he said, 'I should like to sum up the gist of these reports. You are forty-seven years old and in excellent health. You own a home in East Sconsett, Long Island, on which there are nine years of mortgage payments still due, and you also own a late-model car on which eighteen monthly payments are yet to be made. However, due to an excellent salary you are in prosperous circumstances. Am I correct?'

'As correct as the credit agency which gave you that report,' said Mr Treadwell.

Bunce chose to overlook this. 'We will now come to the point. You have been happily married for twenty-three years, and have one daughter who was married last year and now lives with her husband in Chicago. Upon her departure from your home your father-in-law, a widower and somewhat crotchety gentleman, moved into the house and now resides with you and your wife.'

Bunce's voice dropped to a low, impressive note. 'He's seventy-two years old, and, outside of a touch of bursitis in his right shoulder, admits to exceptional health for his age. He has stated on several occasions that he hopes to live another twenty years, and according to actuarial statistics which my Society has on file *he has every chance of achieving this*. Now do you understand, Mr Treadwell?'

It took a long time for the answer to come. 'Yes,' said Mr Treadwell at last, almost in a whisper. 'Now I understand.'

'Good,' said Bunce sympathetically. 'Very good. The first step is always a hard one – the admission that there *is* a problem hovering over you, clouding every day that passes. Nor is there any need to ask why you make efforts to conceal it even from yourself. You wish to spare Mrs Treadwell your unhappiness, don't you?'

Mr Treadwell nodded.

'Would it make you feel better,' asked Bunce, 'if I told you that Mrs Treadwell shared your own feelings? That she, too, feels her father's presence in her home as a burden which grows heavier each day?'

'But she can't!' said Mr Treadwell in dismay. 'She was the one who wanted him to live with us in the first place, after Sylvia got married, and we had a spare room. She pointed out how much he had done for us when we first got started, and how easy he was to get along with, and how little expense it would be – it was she who sold me on the idea. I can't believe she didn't mean it!'

'Of course, she meant it. She knew all the traditional emotions at the thought of her old father living alone somewhere, and offered all the traditional arguments on his behalf, and was sincere every moment. The trap she led you both into was the pitfall that awaits anyone who indulges in murky, sentimental thinking. Yes, indeed, I'm sometimes inclined to believe that Eve ate the apple just to make the serpent happy,' said Bunce, and shook his head grimly at the thought.

'Poor Carol,' groaned Mr Treadwell. 'If I had only known that she felt as miserable about this as I did—'

'Yes?' said Bunce. 'What would you have done?'

Mr Treadwell frowned. 'I don't know. But there must have been something we could have figured out if we put our heads together.'

'What?' Bunce asked. 'Drive the man out of the house?'

'Oh, I don't mean exactly like that.'

'What then?' persisted Bunce. 'Send him to an institution? There are some extremely luxurious institutions for the purpose. You'd have to consider one of them, since he could not possibly be regarded as a charity case; nor, for that matter, could I imagine him taking kindly to the idea of going to a public institution.'

'Who would?' said Mr Treadwell. 'And as for the expensive kind, well, I did look into the idea once, but when I found out what they'd cost I knew it was out. It would take a fortune.'

'Perhaps,' suggested Bunce, 'he could be given an apartment of his own – a small, inexpensive place with someone to take care of him.'

'As it happens, that's what he moved out of to come live with us. And on that business of someone taking care of him – you'd never believe what it costs. That is, even allowing we could find someone to suit him.'

'Right!' Bunce said, and struck the desk sharply with his fist. 'Right in every respect, Mr Treadwell.'

Mr Treadwell looked at him angrily. 'What do you mean – right? I had the idea you wanted to help me with this business, but you haven't come up with a thing yet. On top of that you make it sound as if we're making great progress.'

'We are, Mr Treadwell, we are. Although you weren't aware of it we have just completed the second step to your solution. The first step was the admission that there was a problem; the second step was the realization that no matter which way you turn there seems to be no logical or practical solution to the problem. In this way you are not only witnessing, you are actually participating in, the marvelous operation of The Blessington Method which, in the end, places the one possible solution squarely in your hands.'

'The Blessington Method?'

'Forgive me,' said Bunce. 'In my enthusiasm I used a term

not yet in scientific vogue. I must explain, therefore, that The Blessington Method is the term my co-workers at the Society for Gerontology have given to its course of procedure. It is so titled in honor of J. G. Blessington, the Society's founder, and one of the great men of our era. He has not achieved his proper acclaim yet, but he will. Mark my words, Mr Treadwell, someday his name will resound louder than that of Malthus.'

'Funny I never heard of him,' reflected Mr Treadwell. 'Usually I keep up with the newspapers. And another thing,' he added, eyeing Bunce narrowly, 'we never did get around to clearing up just how you happened to list me as one of your cases, and how you managed to turn up so much about me.'

Bunce laughed delightedly. 'It does sound mysterious when you put it like that, doesn't it? Well, there's really no mystery to it at all. You see, Mr Treadwell, the Society has hundreds of investigators scouting this great land of ours from coast to coast, although the public at large is not aware of this. It is against the rules of the Society for any employee to reveal that he is a professional investigator – he would immediately lose effectiveness.

'Nor do these investigators start off with some specific person as their subject. Their interest lies in *any* aged person who is willing to talk about himself, and you would be astonished at how garrulous most aged people are about their most intimate affairs. That is, of course, as long as they are among strangers.

'These subjects are met at random on park benches, in saloons, in libraries – in any place conducive to comfort and conversation. The investigator befriends the subjects, draws them out – seeks, especially, to learn all he can about the younger people on whom they are dependent.'

'You mean,' said Mr Treadwell with growing interest, 'the people who support them.'

'No, no,' said Bunce. 'You are making the common error of equating *dependence* and *finances*. In many cases, of course, there is a financial dependence, but that is a minor part of the picture. The important factor is that there is always an *emotional* dependence. Even where a physical distance may separate the older person from the younger, that emotional dependence is always present. It is like a current passing between them. The younger person by the mere realization that the aged exist is burdened by guilt and anger. It was his personal experience with this tragic dilemma of our times that led J. G. Blessington to his great work.'

'In other words,' said Mr Treadwell, 'you mean that even if the old man were not living with us, things would be just as bad for Carol and me?'

'You seem to doubt that, Mr Treadwell. But tell me, what makes things bad for you now, to use your own phrase?'

Mr Treadwell thought this over. 'Well,' he said, 'I suppose it's just a case of having a third person around all the time. It gets on your nerves after a while.'

'But your daughter lived as a third person in your home for over twenty years,' pointed out Bunce. 'Yet, I am sure you didn't have the same reaction to her.'

'But that's different,' Mr Treadwell protested. 'You can have fun with a kid, play with her, watch her growing up—'

'Stop right there!' said Bunce. 'Now you are hitting the mark. All the years your daughter lived with you you could take pleasure in watching her grow, flower like an exciting plant, take form as an adult being. But the old man in your house can only wither and decline now, and watching that process casts a shadow on your life. Isn't that the case?'

'I suppose it is.'

'In that case, do you suppose it would make any difference if he lived elsewhere? Would you be any the less aware that he was withering and declining and looking wistfully in your direction from a distance?'

'Of course not. Carol probably wouldn't sleep half the night worrying about him, and I'd have him on my mind all the time because of her. That's perfectly natural, isn't it?'

'It is, indeed, and, I am pleased to say, your recognition of that completes the third step of The Blessington Method. You now realize that it is not the *presence* of the aged subject which creates the problem, but his *existence*.'

Mr Treadwell pursed his lips thoughtfully. 'I don't like the sound of that.'

'Why not? It merely states the fact, doesn't it?'

'Maybe it does. But there's something about it that leaves a bad taste in the mouth. It's like saying the only way Carol and I can have our troubles settled is by the old man's dying.'

'Yes,' Bunce said gravely, 'it is like saying that.'

'Well, I don't like it – not one bit. Thinking you'd like to see somebody dead can make you feel pretty mean, and as far as I know it's never killed anybody yet.'

Bunce smiled. 'Hasn't it?' he said gently.

He and Mr Treadwell studied each other in silence. Then Mr Treadwell pulled a handkerchief from his pocket with nerveless fingers and patted his forehead with it.

'You,' he said with deliberation, 'are either a lunatic or a practical joker. Either way, I'd like you to clear out of here. That's fair warning.'

Bunce's face was all sympathetic concern. 'Mr Treadwell,' he cried, 'don't you realize you were on the verge of the fourth step? Don't you see how close you were to your solution?'

Mr Treadwell pointed to the door. 'Out – before I call the police.'

The expression on Bunce's face changed from concern to disgust. 'Oh, come, Mr Treadwell, you don't believe anybody would pay attention to whatever garbled and incredible story you'd concoct out of this. Please think it over carefully before you do anything rash, now or later. If the exact nature of our talk were even mentioned, you would be the only one to suffer, believe me. Meanwhile, I'll leave you my card. Anytime you wish to call on me I will be ready to serve you.'

'And why should I ever want to call on you?' demanded the white-faced Mr Treadwell.

'There are various reasons,' said Bunce, 'but one above all.' He gathered his belongings and moved to the door. 'Consider, Mr Treadwell: anyone who has mounted the first three steps of The Blessington Method inevitably mounts the fourth. You have made remarkable progress in a short time, Mr Treadwell – you should be calling soon.'

'I'll see you in hell first,' said Mr Treadwell.

Despite this parting shot, the time that followed was a bad one for Mr Treadwell. The trouble was that having been introduced to The Blessington Method he couldn't seem to get it out of his mind. It incited thoughts that he had to keep thrusting away with an effort, and it certainly colored his relationship with his father-in-law in an unpleasant way.

Never before had the old man seemed so obtrusive, so much in the way, and so capable of always doing or saying the thing most calculated to stir annoyance. It especially outraged Mr Treadwell to think of this intruder in his home babbling his private affairs to perfect strangers, eagerly spilling out details of his family life to paid investigators who were only out to make trouble. And, to Mr Treadwell in his heated state of mind, the fact that the investigators could not be identified as such did not serve as any excuse.

Within a very few days Mr Treadwell, who prided himself on being a sane and level-headed businessman, had to admit he was in a bad way. He began to see evidences of a fantastic conspiracy on every hand. He could visualize hundreds – no, thousands – of Bunces swarming into offices just like his all over the country. He could feel cold sweat starting on his forehead at the thought.

But, he told himself, the whole thing was *too* fantastic. He could prove this to himself by merely reviewing his discussion with Bunce, and so he did, dozens of times. After all, it was no more than an objective look at a social problem. Had anything been said that a *really* intelligent man should shy away from? Not at all. If he had drawn some shocking inferences, it was because the ideas were already in his mind looking for an outlet.

On the other hand—

It was with a vast relief that Mr Treadwell finally decided to pay a visit to the Society for Gerontology. He knew what he would find there: a dingy room or two, a couple of underpaid clerical workers, the musty odor of a piddling charity operation – all of which would restore matters to their proper perspective again. He went so strongly imbued with this picture that he almost walked past the gigantic glass and aluminum tower which was the address of the Society, rode its softly humming elevator in confusion, and emerged in the anteroom of the Main Office in a daze.

And it was still in a daze that he was ushered through a vast and seemingly endless labyrinth of rooms by a sleek, long-legged young woman, no less sleek and long-legged multitudes of brisk, square-shouldered young men, rows of streamlined machinery clicking and chuckling in electronic glee, mountains of stainless-steel card indexes, and, over all, the bland reflection of modern indirect lighting on plastic and metal – until finally he was led into the presence of Bunce himself, and the door closed behind him.

'Impressive, isn't it?' said Bunce, obviously relishing the sight of Mr Treadwell's stupefaction.

'Impressive?' croaked Mr Treadwell hoarsely. 'Why, I've never seen anything like it. It's a ten-million-dollar outfit!'

'And why not? Science is working day and night like some Frankenstein, Mr Treadwell, to increase longevity past all sane limits. There are fourteen million people over sixty-five in this country right now. In twenty years their number will be increased to twenty-one million. Beyond that no one can even estimate what the figures will rise to!

'But the one bright note is that each of these aged people is surrounded by many young donors or potential donors to our Society. As the tide rises higher, we, too, flourish and go stronger to withstand it.'

Mr Treadwell felt a chill of horror penetrate him. 'Then it's true, isn't it?'

'I beg your pardon?'

'This Blessington Method you're always talking about,' said Mr Treadwell wildly. 'The whole idea is just to settle things by getting rid of old people!'

'Right!' said Bunce. 'That is the exact idea. And not even J. G. Blessington himself ever phrased it better. You have a way with words, Mr Treadwell. I always admire a man who can come to the point without sentimental twaddle.'

'But you can't get away with it!' said Mr Treadwell incredulously. 'You don't really believe you can get away with it, do you?'

Bunce gestured toward the expanses beyond the closed doors. 'Isn't that sufficient evidence of the Society's success?'

'But all those people out there! Do they realize what's going on?'

'Like all well-trained personnel, Mr Treadwell,' said Bunce reproachfully, 'they know only their own duties. What you and I are discussing here happens to be upper echelon.'

Mr Treadwell's shoulders drooped. 'It's impossible,' he said weakly. 'It can't work.'

'Come, come,' Bunce said not unkindly, 'you mustn't let yourself be overwhelmed. I imagine that what disturbs you most is what J. G. Blessington sometimes referred to as the Safety Factor. But look at it this way, Mr Treadwell: isn't it perfectly natural for old people to die? Well, our Society guarantees that the deaths will appear natural. Investigations are rare – not one has ever caused us any trouble.

'More than that, you would be impressed by many of the names on our list of donors. People powerful in the political world as well as the financial world have been flocking to us. One and all, they could give glowing testimonials as to our efficiency. And remember that such important people make the Society for Gerontology invulnerable, no matter at what point it may be attacked, Mr Treadwell. And such invulnerability extends to every single one of our sponsors, including you, should you choose to place your problem in our hands.'

'But I don't have the right,' Mr Treadwell protested despairingly. 'Even if I wanted to, who am I to settle things this way for anybody?'

'Aha.' Bunce leaned forward intently. 'But you do want to settle things?'

'Not this way.'

'Can you suggest any other way?'

Mr Treadwell was silent.

'You see,' Bunce said with satisfaction, 'the Society for Gerontology offers the one practical answer to the problem. Do you still reject it, Mr Treadwell?'

'I can't see it,' Mr Treadwell said stubbornly. 'It's just not right.'

'Are you sure of that?'

'Of course I am!' snapped Mr Treadwell. 'Are you going to tell me that it's right and proper to go around killing people just because they're old?'

'I am telling you that very thing, Mr Treadwell, and I ask you to look at it this way. We are living today in a world of progress, a world of producers and consumers, all doing their best to improve our common lot. The old are neither producers nor consumers, so they are only barriers to our continued progress.

'If we want to take a brief, sentimental look into the pastoral haze of yesterday we may find that once they did serve a function. While the young were out tilling the fields, the old could tend to the household. But even that function is gone today. We have a hundred better devices for tending the household, and they come far cheaper. Can you dispute that?'

'I don't know,' Mr Treadwell said doggedly. 'You're arguing that people are machines, and I don't go along with that at all.'

'Good heavens,' said Bunce, 'don't tell me that you see them as anything else! Of course, we are machines, Mr Treadwell, all of us. Unique and wonderful machines, I grant, but machines nevertheless. Why, look at the world around you. It is a vast organism made up of replaceable parts, all striving to produce and consume, produce and consume until worn out. Should one permit the worn-out part to remain where it is? Of course not! It must be cast aside so that the organism will not be made inefficient. It is the whole organism that counts, Mr Treadwell, not any of its individual parts. Can't you understand that?'

'I don't know,' said Mr Treadwell uncertainly. 'I've never thought of it that way. It's hard to take in all at once.'

'I realize that, Mr Treadwell, but it is part of The Blessington Method that the sponsor fully appreciate the great value of his contribution in all ways – not only as it benefits him, but also in the way it benefits the entire social organism. In signing a pledge to our Society a man is truly performing the most noble act of his life.'

'Pledge?' said Mr Treadwell. 'What kind of pledge?'

Bunce removed a printed form from a drawer of his desk and laid it out carefully for Mr Treadwell's inspection. Mr Treadwell read it and sat up sharply.

'Why, this says that I'm promising to pay you two thousand dollars in a month from now. You never said anything about that kind of money!'

'There has never been any occasion to raise the subject before this,' Bunce replied. 'But for some time now a committee of the Society has been examining your financial standing, and it reports that you can pay this sum without stress or strain.'

'What do you mean, stress or strain?' Mr Treadwell retorted. 'Two thousand dollars is a lot of money, no matter how you look at it.'

Bunce shrugged. 'Every pledge is arranged in terms of the sponsor's ability to pay, Mr Treadwell. Remember, what may seem expensive to you would certainly seem cheap to many other sponsors I have dealt with.'

'And what do I get for this?'

'Within one month after you sign the pledge, the affair of your father-in-law will be disposed of. Immediately after that you will be expected to pay the pledge in full. Your name is then enrolled on our list of sponsors, and that is all there is to it.'

'I don't like the idea of my name being enrolled on anything.'

'I can appreciate that,' said Bunce. 'But may I remind you that a donation to a charitable organization such as the Society for Gerontology is tax-deductible?'

Mr Treadwell's fingers rested lightly on the pledge. 'Now just for the sake of argument,' he said, 'suppose someone signs one of these things and then doesn't pay up. I guess you know that a pledge like this isn't collectible under the law, don't you?'

'Yes,' Bunce smiled, 'and I know that a great many organizations cannot redeem pledges made to them in apparently good faith. But the Society for Gerontology has never met that difficulty. We avoid it by reminding all sponsors that the young, if they are careless, may die as unexpectedly as the old . . . No, no,' he said, steadying the paper, 'just your signature at the bottom will do.'

When Mr Treadwell's father-in-law was found drowned off the foot of East Sconsett pier three weeks later (the old man fished from the pier regularly although he had often been told by various local authorities that the fishing was poor there), the event was duly entered into the East Sconsett records as Death by Accidental Submersion, and Mr Treadwell himself made the arrangements for an exceptionally elaborate funeral. And it was at the funeral that Mr Treadwell first had the Thought. It was a fleeting and unpleasant thought, just disturbing enough to make him miss a step as he entered the church. In all the confusion of the moment, however, it was not too difficult to put aside.

A few days later, when he was back at his familiar desk, the Thought suddenly returned. This time it was not to be put aside so easily. It grew steadily larger and larger in his mind, until his waking hours were terrifyingly full of it, and his sleep a series of shuddering nightmares.

There was only one man who could clear up the matter for him, he knew; so he appeared at the offices of the Society for Gerontology burning with anxiety to have Bunce do so. He was hardly aware of handing over his check to Bunce and pocketing the receipt.

'There's something that's been worrying me,' said Mr Tread-well, coming straight to the point.

'Yes?'

'Well, do you remember telling me how many old people there would be around in twenty years?'

'Of course.'

Mr Treadwell loosened his collar to ease the constriction around his throat. 'But don't you see? I'm going to be one of them!'

Bunce nodded. 'If you take reasonably good care of yourself there's no reason you shouldn't be,' he pointed out.

'You don't get the idea,' Mr Treadwell said urgently. 'I'll be in a spot then where I'll have to worry all the time about someone from this Society coming in and giving my daughter or my son-in-law ideas! That's a terrible thing to have to worry about all the rest of your life.'

Bunce shook his head slowly. 'You can't mean that, Mr Treadwell.'

'And why can't I?'

'Why? Well, think of your daughter. Mr Treadwell. Are you thinking of her?'

'Yes.'

'Do you see her as the lovely child who poured out her love to you in exchange for yours? The fine young woman who has just stepped over the threshold of marriage, but is always eager to visit you, eager to let you know the affection she feels for you?'

'I know that.'

'And can you see in your mind's eye that manly young fellow

who is her husband? Can you feel the warmth of his handclasp as he greets you? Do you know his gratitude for the financial help you give him regularly?'

'I suppose so.'

'Now, honestly, Mr Treadwell, can you imagine either of these affectionate and devoted youngsters doing a single thing – the slightest thing – to harm you?'

The constriction around Mr Treadwell's throat miraculously eased; the chill around his heart departed.

'No,' he said with conviction. 'I can't.'

'Splendid,' said Bunce. He leaned far back in his chair and smiled with a kindly wisdom. 'Hold on to that thought, Mr Treadwell. cherish it and keep it close at all times. It will be a solace and comfort to the very end.'

# The Faith of
# Aaron Menefee

When the big black car came limping into the gas station I could tell that it was hurting inside, the way I hurt whenever the old hot-spot jabbed into my belly. There was a chauffeur driving, and three people sitting in back: a discontented-looking girl and a weasel-like fellow, and in between them this man with the red face and the shock of gray hair. They all got out to look while I poked into the motor.

'It's the carburetor,' I told them. 'Seems like it was just worked on, but whoever did it made a mess of it.'

The red-faced man gave the chauffeur a look like a thundercloud coming up over old Turtleback Mountain.

'How long will it take to fix?' he said to me. 'And I mean a real good job on it. I've got to be in Cincinnati by early evening, and there's still forty miles to go. I don't aim to break down on the way again.'

'I'll fix it while you wait,' I said. 'As for the kind of job it'll be, you ask anyone around here, and they'll tell you that if it's a machine made by man and run by gas, Aaron Menefee'll fix it right.'

He looked around at the empty road. 'Don't seem to be many around here to ask,' he said, and then he laughed so that you had to like him on the spot. 'All right, Brother Menefee,' he said, 'it's my feeling that most folks are honest and willing. I'll put my trust in you.'

It took a little longer than I figured, but I finally had the motor tuned up and idling, sweet as a kitten purring. The red-faced man looked happy about that. When I told him the price he looked even happier. 'Brother Menefee,' he said, 'you've just boosted my high opinion of the human race one more notch.'

197

And then it happened. And it happened in a way that I know was *meant*. Just as he was handing me the money, the old hot-spot caught me a lick so fierce that I had to double over and hold my breath until the feeling eased up.

'What is it?' the man said. 'What's wrong?'

I felt ashamed at making such a fuss in front of people. 'Nothing,' I said. 'Leastways, nothing that can be helped. Doc Buckles says it's an ulcer, and I'm on milk, potatoes, and prayer to heal it, but it looks like it's here to stay.'

He was interested. Not the way most people are just glassy-eyed polite, but deep-down concerned. He looked at me from head to foot, and then he made a fist of one hand and beat it into the other a couple of times. Then he walked right around me as if he were measuring me for a suit of clothes, and the others just stood there and watched us.

'Brother Menefee,' he finally said, 'you don't know who I am, do you?'

'I guess I don't.'

'Well, brother, my name is Otis Jones. Healer Jones, they call me. Did you ever hear of that name?'

'I guess I never did.'

'You mean, you never followed my Faith Meetings on radio or TV? But I'm coast to coast, brother. Two hundred radio stations' and eighty TV stations' worth of coast to coast each and every Wednesday night of the year!'

'Maybe so,' I said, 'but I don't bear with radio and TV. From what I hear there's a load of sinful stuff on 'em. Stuff about women and drinking and killing and such. A man's got to work hard enough fighting down the old Adam in him without looking on such temptations.'

'There's no sin and temptation on my program, brother. All they show is the meetings where I carry on the work the Almighty empowered me to do. What work, you ask? Healing, brother – healing! In this right arm here is the power to lift the sick from their beds, take the crutches from the maimed so that they can walk again, and restore a man to all the good fortune he can ask for on this everlasting earth! Do you have faith, brother?'

'I have faith,' I said. 'I've mortified the flesh, I've prayed until my knees were skinned raw, and I've still got faith to spare.'

'Good. Because if you've got faith my power can take hold of you and cure you. If not, you're just fooling yourself. Here, take hold of my hand, and see if you don't feel the power just pouring into you. See if it don't happen.'

I took his hand, and, sure as I was standing there, old hot-spot started to settle down as if it felt a couple of Doc Buckles' pills working on it. That was when I knew it had all been *meant*. The way he picked that old highway to travel, the car breaking down, and my being right on the spot with old hot-spot set up to act up worse than usual.

He must have known it was meant, too. He said, 'You've got faith, brother. Tonight, you come to my Faith Meeting in Cincinnati, and I'll turn all my power on you, and heal you from this day henceforth. My daughter here'll give you a card with the address, and I'll expect to see you there, cleansed and ready. And pass the word along, brother. All are welcome, faithful and scoffers alike.'

I took the seven o'clock bus to Cincinnati – sixty cents' worth of riding each way – and got there just before meeting time. It was like nothing I had ever seen before – bigger than the circus and a lot more gratifying to the soul. A monstrous tent, white as snow, was pitched in the middle of the grounds with people swarming in from every direction. Ten big trailer trucks which, I figured, were used to carry the equipment for the meeting, stood in a line off to one side. Two other trucks were rigged up with power plants, and one of them had a spotlight on it which sent a beam straight up into the sky like a fiery sword.

I bought a hymn book for a dime on the way into the tent, and when I was sitting there in the middle of maybe ten thousand people, I looked into it and found a card which said to fill out your name and address and infirmity and turn it in to an usher, so you could be called for healing right at the meeting. I did that, and then I joined in with the rest, and we sang some hymns from the book, with the Healer's daughter leading us in a nice sweet soprano from the platform up front. They were all good hymns, too. The kind to twist old Satan's arm behind his back and bring him howling to his knees.

It was after this that lights came on so bright in the tent that you had to blink your eyes against them. That was for TV, sure enough. You could see the two big cameras, one aimed at the platform and one at us in the seats, with men waiting at them. And as soon as those lights came on, the Healer walked out on the platform, moving slow and easy, his hands out in greeting, a king among men, but a good, plain man himself for all that, you could tell.

He didn't waste any time; he exhorted us right from the beginning, and so hard that first he opened his necktie, then he pulled off his coat, and then you could see the honest sweat dripping off his face and coming out in big splotches on his shirt. It is good to see a man sweat like that; you know he means what he says, and he is working hard to get it across.

Mostly it was about how faith had led him to his power, and how faith would lead us to our cure, and when he came to the part where he told how right in a little back room of the Rocky Heights First National Bank where he was clerking for miserable pay, and sick and ailing at that, he had dropped to his knees and felt the power seize him, it was enough to make a lot of the folks around me shout and groan and carry on in their joy for him.

Then came the healing. The little weasel-like fellow who the Healer said to us was Charles M. Fish, his manager, stood on the platform and read off the names on the cards, while one by one we marched down to take our turn. When it came my turn, and I had to walk down that aisle with everyone craning to see, and that big glass eye of the TV camera staring at me, I felt my knees would buckle under me before I made it.

But I did make it, and there I stood at the foot of the platform with the Healer on his knees just above me, a microphone in his hand.

'Brother,' he said into it, and when I heard his voice booming out in the tent behind me I almost jumped, 'what is your affliction?'

He held the microphone at me, and I said, 'Ulcers.'

'Did you hear that?' the Healer yelled at the crowd. 'This big, good-looking young man in the prime of his life is being eaten alive by a sickness that defies man's medicine, cursed by a fiery torment licking at his vitals day and night – and yet he has faith to stand before me and seek deliverance! Do you think he can be healed?'

'Yes!' everyone yelled back at him. 'He can be healed!'

The Healer mopped the sweat from his face and looked down at me. 'Do *you* think you can be healed, brother?'

I could feel the power crackling out of him like electricity now. I couldn't wait for it to take hold of me and settle things once and for all.

'I can be healed,' I said.

'Then bend your head, brother. Bend your head, and make sure your faith is just as strong as my power. Because if it is, you're going to walk out of here a new man!'

He didn't wait for me to bend my head. He shoved it down with his big hand, and called out, 'Heal this man! Be merciful and heal him,' and then suddenly hit me on the back of my neck with his fist, so that the power in him ran right into me, clear down to the roots. There wasn't a flicker in old hot-spot. It was as if nothing had been wrong there in my whole life.

'I'm healed!' I said, hardly daring to believe it. 'I'm healed!'

He shoved the microphone at me. 'Say it again, brother. Cry it aloud in your jubilation!'

I grabbed my belly to make sure. I didn't feel a twinge. 'It's gone!' I said. 'It's a miracle.'

I didn't care what happened then. I jumped up and down. I waved at everyone in the crowd and shouted right along with them when they shouted hallelujah for me. Even with that TV camera aimed at me all the time I didn't care. I was never happier in my life.

When I came back to town to pack my bag and say goodbye, most folks just gave me a pat and a handshake and let it go at that. But Doc Buckles was terribly soured on me. Doc was short and fat, a good man in some ways, always willing to lend a hand where it was called for, and I had the kind of weakness for him that he had for strong drink and godless talk. He walked up and down his office, waving his arms the way he does, and talking to me on and on. Even though he knew my ears were closed against him he didn't stop. Once Doc gets started it takes a lot to stop him.

'What kind of life is that?' he said. 'Being an auto mechanic for a traveling tent show? Working day and night for less money than Ab Nolan pays you at the gas station, making a holy show of yourself at those meetings, living with a bunch of swindling strangers! You'll find out what it's like, boy.'

'Maybe,' I said, 'but I've been called. And I'm following the call.'

'Called!' He threw up his hands. 'You were called to get rid of lustful thoughts by rolling around naked in the snow one night, so that I had to pull you through pneumonia. You've been called to bust up Glenn Lyman's rabbit traps every time he sets them, so you've been to jail twice already for that. Every time you're called it means trouble for you, Aaron. Don't you have sense enough to see that? It always means trouble when a man's too good for his own good.'

'*My* body was healed,' I said, 'but there's many another got to be helped now. I'm just adding my mite to the work.'

'I don't tell you how to fix my car,' Doc said, 'so don't you go telling me about healing. The way you're acting you're being just as crazy as your old Dad was. From the time you quit sucking your thumb he filled you up with so much of his hellfire, and talking in strange tongues, and fear of the devil that he clean addled your wits. For all I know, anybody smells sulphur and brimstone, as much as you do is bound to get an ulcer from it.'

It scared me to hear him talk like that, but I know it was no use trying to argue back. I just don't have the gift of speech, and Doc, especially when he's got a load of Old Reliable in him, has more than his fair share.

'I've been called,' I said. 'If I pass this way again I'll drop in and say hello.'

And that's how we left it.

Most of what Doc had said was wicked nonsense, of course, but after a few months I found out that he was right about one thing: there could be plenty of swindling strangers even in the camp of righteousness. I worked with the crew of mechanics tending the Healer's limousine, and the trailers for sleeping in, and the twelve big trucks that carried the Faith Meetings from one town to another. And what I found among those mechanics was enough to curl your hair. Smoking and drinking. Gambling and loose talk. And loose women.

They gave me a rough time of it when they found out that I stood foursquare against the devil, and they made it even rougher when they saw I wouldn't play along and fake expenses for repairs, so that they could pocket the money. Many a time I was tempted to speak right up about it to the Healer, or to Charles M. Fish, or even to Miss Emily Jones, the Healer's daughter, who I got to know pretty well along the way. But I never did, because it seemed wrong to turn in my fellow-man to be fired when maybe he could learn salvation a better way. In the long run, I was glad I hadn't carried tales, because things took care of themselves without that.

What happened was that I finally had a run-in with Everett Kane himself, the foreman of the crew, and the chief cook of the sinful brew that was always boiling around me. He was a nag and a torment, always giving me more jobs than two men could handle and always complaining about them, even though he knew I was the best man they had, better than he was, for that matter. But I kept clear of him, because he was the one who had done that poor job on the carburetor of the Healer's car which led the Healer right to me that day. I figured that if it had all been *meant*, maybe Everett Kane was meant, too, and so I spared him as long as possible.

But one day I caught him signing my name on a requisition for parts I had never asked for, and I put it to him straight out. He was a strong man, vain about his strength, and he chose to let his fists talk for him. He knocked me down, and while I was praying for courage not to answer violence with violence, he knocked me down again. So having turned the other cheek, as you might say, I got up with a clear conscience and went to work on Everett until he was quite messy and had to be carried off for doctoring.

When word of this got to the Healer he called me in and talked to me like an angry father. So I finally explained matters to him, and then everything changed for the better. Everett and the sinners close to him were let out, and I was given his job with power to run things the way they should be run.

That was the beginning of a better time for me. I made the men under me do an honest job and render an honest accounting, and while there was a little grumbling now and then among the backsliders, there was never anything said or done that could mean real trouble. As for myself, I was so grateful for the way things turned out that I made sure to put the biggest part of my pay every week into the hand of the Healer himself as a Faith Offering.

That was how the Healer was rewarded – by Faith Offerings. He would never charge a red cent for using his power; he would just remind folks that all Faith Offerings were welcome and would go to carrying on the good work. And as we moved along, town by town, staying a week at each town, the offerings came pouring in like the waters of Stony Brook when the spring freshets are running.

It was wonderful to see how many people there were who wanted to carry on the good work. Even those stuck at home where they had to follow the meetings on radio or TV joined in. Charles M. Fish once told me that so many offerings came in every day to the post office near Paradise Point where the Healer's Faith Temple was being built, the post office set up a special department there to handle them. There was nothing surprising in that, he said. Many a poor sufferer had been practically brought back from the grave by just touching a hand to the Healer's picture on TV. He carried letters from them in his pocket to show scoffers and jeerers along the way, mostly men from newspapers that had nothing better to do than try and make a mockery of the Healer.

So we moved across the north part of the United States that summer, and then swung down and around through the south that winter. And it was on the southward swing that I knew there was trouble brewing in me because of Miss Emily Jones, the Healer's daughter.

She wasn't what you'd call a real pretty girl like some – she was usually too pale and peaked for that – but she had a nice trim figure, and big dark eyes, and the longest, blackest hair you ever did see. At first I didn't take much notice of her, but then she seemed to be around me a good deal wherever I was, so that I started looking at her, and then I started liking what I saw. That was the trouble, because along with it the devil would pop the most terrible thoughts into my head. It was enough to make me break into a sweat every time I saw them for what they were and had to put up a battle against them.

And I did battle them with all my might. I changed my diet from red meat to greenery; I immersed my body in ice-cold water until I was blue from neck to heels; I prayed with my arms held wide until it felt as if knives were sticking into them; but nothing helped. Worst of all was the way Miss Emily liked to take long walks with me at night after the meeting was over, without any idea of what those walks were doing to me. I figured that if I could get up courage to tell her my plight it would settle things, but I just couldn't do it.

I finally did, though, one night in a grove of trees right outside Tulsa, Oklahoma. We walked for a while, and then we sat down on a log to talk in the darkness with the insects chirping away around us and the breeze sighing in the leaves overhead like a lost soul.

I told her everything then, but it didn't work out as I expected. Because when I was done she sat quiet for a long time, and then she said, as if she were thinking it out loud: 'The Good Book says *Be fruitful and multiply*. And there's a legal and holy way of doing it, Aaron Menefee.'

It took me a second to see what she meant, and when I did it was quite a shocker. 'You mean, get married, Miss Emily?'

'I don't see why not. You don't have any objections to matrimony, do you, Aaron?'

I had trouble finding my tongue. 'I don't guess I have. But I never thought of it. I didn't figure I was ready for it yet.'

She leaned up against me, and when her shoulder rubbed against mine it was as if her father's power was in it. 'Don't you ever again call me Miss Emily,' she said. 'From now on my name is Emily to you, Aaron Menefee. And as for being ready for marriage, you're twenty-five years old and long overdue. If you had as much sense as you had good looks you'd know that's what those thoughts in your head were trying to tell you.'

I had never seen the matter like that, and when she spoke

those words it was like a stone being lifted off my back. Suddenly it seemed that her shoulder being tight against mine was *meant*, and that my arm going around her waist was the most natural thing in the world. But in the midst of the rejoicing I had a worrisome thought.

'What's the matter, Aaron?' said Miss Emily. 'You were doing fine.'

'Maybe so,' I said, 'but what's the Healer going to think about all this? Everything I am right now I owe to him. I can't see going one step further along with this without his knowledge and blessing.'

Miss Emily sighed like the night wind in the trees. 'I'm my pa's only child, Aaron,' she said, 'and he's inclined to keep me on a mighty short tether. Don't you think it would be better to slip off somewhere to get married, and tell him afterward?'

'No,' I said, 'that would be sharper than a serpent's tooth. We can't do it that way.'

'We can't?'

'No,' I said. 'It's got to be done right, or not at all.'

So we went to the Healer then and there, where he was sitting at a table in the back of the big tent along with Charles M. Fish and a couple of others, counting the Offerings and fixing them up to be banked the next day. When everyone else was gone I made a clean breast of everything to the Healer, Miss Emily sitting pale and quiet alongside of me, and I put the matter squarely into his hands.

'It's not for any man to judge himself,' I said, 'so I leave it up to you as to whether I'm worthy or not. Although I have hopes that you'll see it the way Miss Emily and I do.'

He wasn't happy about it, I could tell right away. He sat there a while, working his fingers together, and when he spoke it was with a sad voice.

'Believe me, Brother Menefee,' he said, 'it isn't a question of being worthy, because you are among the worthiest souls I know. There's more to it than that. Emily here is my only begotten child, and heir to all that has come my way. And I can tell you, Brother Menefee, that a lot of good has been coming my way these last few years.'

'Well,' said Miss Emily, 'if you're saying that Aaron wants to marry me for my money you can take my word for it he doesn't.'

'I'm not saying that,' the Healer told her. 'What I'm trying to say is that I've got a big proposition on my hands here. A mighty big proposition. What with Offerings coming in from the meetings, and the national hookups, and the book sales, and pretty soon from the Temple when we get it going, I've got a job on my hands. It's going to take a big man to step into my shoes, and I mean it to be someone who can do it right.'

'If you're talking about Charlie Fish,' said Miss Emily, 'I told you a hundred times over I wouldn't marry him if he was the last man on earth. He makes my skin crawl.'

The Healer reached out and patted her hand. 'All right,' he said, 'if not Charlie Fish somebody else with his talents, but maybe more to your taste. When the power was sent down to me it enabled me to reap a mighty harvest, most of it tax-free. Some day you're going to be trustee for all that, Emily, and your wedded mate has to be a fit partner. Worthy as Brother Menefee is I don't see him as the right one. I can't give my blessing to any such unlikely marriage, and, from this day thenceforth, I don't want to hear any more about it from either of you.'

My heart sank in me, heavy as a stone going down in deep waters. 'I've got faith in you, Healer,' I told him, 'but it's a hard row you've given me to hoe. No woman has ever made me feel like Miss Emily does, and I don't expect any ever will.'

'It is faith, after all, which can move mountains,' said the Healer, 'so you trust to it and let Miss Emily be. As long as I'm on earth I reign over her. When I'm gone to glory she'll be free to walk her own path, but that won't be for a long time, Brother Menefee, not with the way my health is and with the power in me. If I were you I'd hoe that long row and keep my eyes peeled for a woman more suitable.'

I went away from there feeling as low as I ever had, and in the time that passed nothing could seem to brighten up the days and weeks, although Miss Emily gave it a good try.

'I'll never marry anyone else, Aaron,' she said to me. 'I'll wait all my life for you, if I have to. Any time you just turn around and hold out your arms I'll be there.'

Knowing that only made it hurt the more, because somehow

it seemed to pile the whole thing on my back alone. It was like being speared at the end of the devil's pitchfork. As long as you fought to hang on, you couldn't be dumped into the blazing fires below, but you still couldn't ever wriggle off and be free.

It went along that way when we started moving up north with the coming of spring, and it was as bad as ever when we came to Cincinnati, right near the old home town. It was that feeling in me which led me to see Doc Buckles, I guess – that and the way I had promised him I'd drop in if I was nearby. Doc couldn't give me the kind of consolation I needed, of course, but he was always full of fizz and ginger, and a good man to brighten you up, if you kept him steered away from foul talk and quarrelsome arguments.

I borrowed the limousine to drive over to Doc's place after meeting was over that night, and the way I had worked on the motor it took no time at all. I wasn't surprised when I pulled up in front of the house to see that the lights were on and the shades pulled down, because Doc kept all hours and didn't like people peeking in on him when he wanted to sit alone with a bottle of Old Reliable. But I was mighty surprised when as soon as I walked into the hallway the door behind me seemed to slam shut by itself, and I felt something hard poking dead center into my back. I never in my life had a gun shoved into my back, so it's strange, when you think of it, how I knew it was a gun right off without even looking.

'Put your hands up,' said the man holding it – he had a hard city voice and an ugly way of using it – 'and keep walking.'

He pushed me along that way into the back office, and shut that door, too, and then I saw I was in the middle of quite a to-do. Doc sat behind his desk looking sick, and a man sat on the edge of the examining table, his legs dangling in a strange, loose sort of way, and his face dead-white and twisted with pain.

Doc looked at me as if he couldn't believe it, and then he shook his head. 'Aaron,' he said, 'you sure picked a fine time to come barging in here.'

The man on the table pointed at me. 'You know him?' he asked Doc. 'What's his business here?'

'Nothing,' said Doc. 'He's a friend of mine, and you let him be. There's no sense making trouble for everybody in town just because you got yourself in a mess. I examined you and I told you God's honest truth. Your legs are paralyzed, and there's nothing can be done about it. Not by me, nor by anybody else.'

The man slammed his hand down on the table. 'You talk too much!' he said, and then he looked at me, his eyes blinking and fluttering like a woman's when she's real scared. 'Is there any other doctor in this hole?'

I thought that over a spell, and then I said, 'No, I don't guess there is.'

He slammed the table again. 'You're lying! You're covering up for someone!'

'Mister,' I told him, 'I never yet told a lie to anybody on the face of this blessed earth. And I'm not going to risk my everlasting soul by telling you one now.'

'All right!' he said. 'All right! But who do you go to around here, if you're hurt real bad? You can't tell me everybody depends on this old quack to know what he's doing.'

And that was when it suddenly came to me, like the dawn coming up over old Turtleback, that all this was *meant*, too, just as everything had been meant from the day I first met the Healer a long year before. It was being made my bounden duty to snatch Doc back from damnation like a brand from the burning. Once he saw the power at work with his own eyes he'd be saved for sure.

I said, 'Doc Buckles is a good man, even if there are a lot of things outside his powers. But I can take you to somebody whose power has never failed. He healed me when Doc couldn't, and every night he heals all those who come to him, no matter what their affliction.'

The man on the table looked at me with his mouth open, his eyes half closed. 'What kind of story is that?' he said.

'It's the truth,' I cried out, 'and Doc Buckles here will bear witness to it. Go on and ask him.'

Doc leaned across his desk. 'Aaron Menefee,' he said to me, 'I want you to keep out of this, and to keep your healing friend out of this. You don't know who you're talking to here, so I'll tell you. His name's Vern Byers, and he's half crazy and all bad. He killed the cop that put the bullet into him, and then in cold blood he killed the doctor that bungled taking it out, probably because there was a gun at his head when he was doing it. You don't want to go playing spooky games with anybody like this, Aaron. You want to keep your mouth shut, and trust you'll see the sunrise tomorrow morning, if you're lucky!'

Vern Byers looked at Doc with eyes like burning coals in his white face. 'You old goat,' he said. 'So you were covering up for somebody all the time!'

'No,' I said, 'he wasn't. It's just that he doesn't know about the kind of healing that comes from the inside.'

'I don't care what kind of healing it is! You bring that guy to me right now!'

'You'll need faith, Brother Byers,' I told him. 'Do you think you can be healed?'

'I've *got* to be healed! You hear that? I've *got* to be healed! Here,' he said, and when he pulled open his coat I could see the nasty-looking gun strapped to his chest. He took out a wallet and shuffled money from it into a big wad. 'Here's a thousand dollars cash. That's right. Don't look so dumb about it; just stick it in your pocket. That's for this doctor of yours to come out here, and you can tell him there's another thousand waiting for him when he gets here. Is that a deal?'

'Brother Byers,' I said, 'the Healer won't take payment for his work. But if this is a Faith Offering it ought to do just fine.'

'Call it what you want, but get him here quick. I've got only a couple of hours before they block off every highway out of this state, and I'm not waiting around to see that happen. And here,' he said very slowly, his eyes half closed again, 'is what you *don't* tell the guy you're sending. This fat quack was right. I killed the one who put my legs wrong like this, and I'll kill any man who takes my money and can't put them right for me. I swear that on my mother's grave.'

He was done with me then, and the other man, the one with the gun at my back, pushed me along out of the house and into the car and then got into the seat alongside me. I was a little upset driving that way with a gun pointing at me, but I made good time in the camping grounds anyhow.

The man got out of my side of the car almost on top of me, the gun pushing into my ribs, and when I went into the tent he just stood outside, and I knew that gun was aimed my way every second of the time. The Healer was there at the table with Charles M. Fish and the others, and I walked straight up to him without flickering an eyelash.

'Healer,' I said, 'there's a man outside who needs your help for a friend of his.'

'At this hour?' said the Healer. 'It must be mighty serious, Brother Menefee.'

'It's all of that, Healer,' I told him, the others all gawking at me, 'and maybe you can judge of that from the Faith Offering that was made. And,' I said, laying the wad of bills in his hand, 'there's more waiting where that came from.'

The Healer looked at the roll, and you could see his eyes lighting up with gratitude for his power. Then he handed the money over to Charles M. Fish. 'Brother Fish,' he said, 'you add this to the tally, and if I don't miss my guess it'll make it just about one of the biggest nights we ever had.'

Then he got up from his chair and clapped me right on the shoulder. 'And you say there's another such Offering waiting for me, Brother Menefee?'

'There is. But there's sort of a worrisome thing about all this, Healer.'

'And what might that be?'

'Well, it might be that this Brother Byers who needs your power is short on faith. I put it to him straight, but the way he spoke up I couldn't figure whether it was yes or no. He's a sinner all the way, Healer, and aimed straight for perdition right now, but whether or not he's working up real faith in his time of trouble I can't say.'

The Healer laughed right out loud, so that I felt my face turning beet-red. 'You're young and willing, Brother Menefee,' he said to me, 'but you're real ignorant of these things. Otherwise you'd know that anyone who makes the kind of Faith Offering you just turned over to me is set and ready for my power to enter him. Now, where is this poor unfortunate?'

'Back in town,' I said, 'the other side of Cincinnati. But his friend's right outside waiting to take us to him.'

When we walked out of the tent the man was there, but with his hand in his pocket now, so that I knew the gun was in it and still aiming at me. I wished I could let the Healer know about this, but it seemed a mite risky right then. He and the man got into the front of the car, the Healer behind the wheel, but when I started to get into the back, the Healer held me off with his hand out of the window and slammed the door against me.

'It's kind of you, Brother Menefee,' he said, 'but I don't figure to need your company along on this mission.'

And before anybody could do anything about it he had gunned the big car into a fast start and was heading for the highway.

I stood there with my jaw slack in my head, watching the taillights going off down that road, knowing that when they dipped a little they had hit the highway and turned on to it, and seeing them get smaller and smaller until finally they blinked out like little stars in the first light at morning time. And all that while I was praying as hard as I could that Vern Byers's faith would bear up under the coming trial, the way the Healer figured it.

Not that I'd become a doubter, whatever happened. A man's got no right to question what is *meant*.

# You Can't Be a Little Girl
# All Your Life

It was the silence that woke her. Not suddenly – Tom had pointed out more than once with a sort of humorous envy that she slept like the dead – but slowly; drawing her up from a hundred fathoms of sleep so that she lay just on the surface of consciousness, eyes closed, listening to the familiar pattern of night sounds around her, wondering where it had been disarranged.

Then she heard the creak of a floorboard – the reassuring creak of a board under the step of a late-returning husband – and understood. Even while she was a hundred fathoms under, she must have known that Tom had come into the room, must have anticipated the click of the bed-light being switched on, the solid thump of footsteps from bed to closet, from closet to dresser – the unfailing routine which always culminated with his leaning over her and whispering, 'Asleep?' and her small groan which said yes, she was asleep but glad he was home, and would he please not stay up all the rest of the night working at those papers.

So he was in the room now, she knew, but for some reason he was not going through the accustomed routine, and that was what had awakened her. Like the time they had the cricket, poor thing; for a week it had relentlessly chirped away the dark hours from some hidden corner of the house until she'd got used to it. The night it died, or went off to make a cocoon or whatever crickets do, she'd lain awake for an hour waiting to hear it, and then slept badly after that until she'd got used to living without it.

Poor thing, she thought drowsily, not really caring very much but waiting for the light to go on, the footsteps to move comfortingly between bed and closet. Somehow the thought became a serpent crawling down her spine, winding tight around her chest. *Poor thing*, it said to her, *poor stupid thing – it isn't Tom at all.*

She opened her eyes at the moment the man's gloved hand brutally slammed over her mouth. In that moment she saw the towering shadow of him, heard the sob of breath in his throat, smelled the sour reek of liquor. Then she wildly bit down on the hand that gagged her, her teeth sinking into the glove, grinding at it. He smashed his other fist squarely into her face. She went limp, her head lolling half off the bed. He smashed his fist into her face again.

After that, blackness rushed in on her like a whirlwind.

She looked at the pale balloons hovering under the ceiling and saw with idle interest that they were turning into masks, but with features queerly reversed, mouths on top, eyes below. The masks moved and righted themselves. Became faces. Dr Vaughn. And Tom. And a woman. Someone with a small white dunce cap perched on her head. A nurse.

The doctor leaned over her, lifted her eyelid with his thumb, and she discovered that her face was one throbbing bruise. He withdrew the thumb and grunted. From long acquaintance she recognized it as a grunt of satisfaction.

He said, 'Know who I am, Julie?'

'Yes.'

'Know what happened?'

'Yes.'

'How do you feel?'

She considered that. 'Funny. I mean, far away. And there's a buzzing in my ears.'

'That was the needle. After we brought you around you went into a real sweet hysteria, and I gave you a needle. Remember that?'

'No.'

'Just as well. Don't let it bother you.'

It didn't bother her. What bothered her was not knowing the time. Things were so unreal when you didn't know the time.

She tried to turn her head toward the clock on the night table, and the doctor said, 'It's a little after six. Almost sunrise. Probably be the first time you've ever seen it, I'll bet.'

She smiled at him as much as her swollen mouth would permit. 'Saw it last New Year's,' she said.

Tom came around the other side of the bed. He sat down on it and took her hand tightly in his. 'Julie,' he said. 'Julie, Julie, Julie,' the words coming out in a rush as if they had been building up in him with explosive force.

She loved him and pitied him for that, and for the way he looked. He looked awful. Haggard, unshaven, his eyes sunk deep in his head, he looked as if he were running on nerve alone. Because of her, she thought unhappily, all because of her.

'I'm sorry,' she said.

'Sorry!' He gripped her hand so hard that she winced. 'Because some lunatic – some animal—!'

'Oh, please!'

'I know. I know you want to shut it out, darling, but you mustn't yet. Look, Julie, the police have been waiting all night to talk to you. They're sure they can find the man, but they need your help. You'll have to describe him, tell them whatever you can about him. Then you won't even have to think about it again. You understand, don't you?'

'Yes.'

'I knew you would.'

He started to get up but the doctor said, 'No, you stay here with her. I'll tell them on my way out. Have to get along, anyhow – these all-night shifts are hard on an old man.' He stood with his hand on the doorknob. 'When they find him,' he said in a hard voice, 'I'd like the pleasure—' and let it go at that, knowing they understood.

The big, white-haired man with the rumpled suit was Lieutenant Christensen of the police department. The small, dapper man with the mustache was Mr Dahl of the district attorney's office. Ordinarily, said Mr Dahl, he did not take a personal part in criminal investigations, but when it came to – that is, in a case of this kind special measures were called for. Everyone must cooperate fully. Mrs Barton must cooperate, too. Painful as it might be, she must answer Lieutenant Christensen's questions frankly and without embarrassment. Would she do that?

Julie saw Tom nodding encouragement to her. 'Yes,' she said.

She watched Lieutenant Christensen draw a notebook and pen from his pocket. His gesture, when he pressed the end of the pen to release its point, made him look as if he were stabbing an insect.

He said, 'First of all, I want you to tell me exactly what happened. Everything you can remember about it.'

She told him, and he scribbled away in the notebook, the pen clicking at each stroke.

'What time was that?' he asked.

'I don't know.'

'About what time? The closer we can pin it down, the better we can check on alibis. When did you go to bed?'

'At ten thirty.'

'And Mr Barton came home around twelve, so we know it happened between ten thirty and twelve.' The lieutenant addressed himself to the notebook, then pursed his lips thoughtfully. 'Now for something even more important.'

'Yes?'

'Just this. Would you recognize the man if you saw him again?'

She closed her eyes, trying to make form out of that monstrous shadow, but feeling only the nauseous terror of it. 'No,' she said.

'You don't sound so sure about it.'

'But I am.'

'How can you be? Yes, I know the room was kind of dark and all that, but you said you were awake after you first heard him come in. That means you had time to get adjusted to the dark. And some light from the street lamp outside hits your window shade here. You wouldn't see so well under the conditions, maybe, but you'd see something, wouldn't you? I mean, enough to point out the man if you had the chance. Isn't that right?'

She felt uneasily that he was right and she was wrong, but

there didn't seem to be anything she could do about it. 'Yes,' she said, 'but it wasn't like that.'

Dahl, the man from the district attorney's office, shifted on his feet. 'Mrs Barton,' he started to say, but Lieutenant Christensen silenced him with a curt gesture of the hand.

'Now look,' the lieutenant said. 'Let me put it this way. Suppose we had this man some place where you could see him close up, but he couldn't see you at all. Can you picture that? He'd be right up there in front of you, but he wouldn't even know you were looking at him. Don't you think it would be pretty easy to recognize him then?'

Julie found herself growing desperately anxious to give him the answer he wanted, to see what he wanted her to see; but no matter how hard she tried she could not. She shook her head hopelessly, and Lieutenant Christensen drew a long breath.

'All right,' he said, 'then is there anything you can tell me about him? How big was he? Tall, short, or medium?'

The shadow towered over her. 'Tall. No, I'm not sure. But I think he was.'

'White or colored?'

'I don't know.'

'About how old?'

'I don't know.'

'Anything distinctive about his clothes? Anything you might have taken notice of?'

She started to shake her head again, then suddenly remembered. 'Gloves,' she said, pleased with herself. 'He was wearing gloves.'

'Leather or wool?'

'Leather.' The sour taste of the leather was in her mouth now. It made her stomach turn over.

*Click-click* went the pen, and the lieutenant looked up from the notebook expectantly. 'Anything else?'

'No.'

The lieutenant frowned. 'It doesn't add up to very much, does it? I mean, the way you tell it.'

'I'm sorry,' Julie said, and wondered why she was so ready with that phrase now. What was it that *she* had done to feel sorry about? She felt the tears of self-pity start to rise, and she drew Tom's hand to her breast, turning to look at him for comfort. She was shocked to see that he was regarding her with the same expression that the lieutenant wore.

The other man – Dahl – was saying something to her.

'Mrs Barton,' he said, and again, 'Mrs Barton,' until she faced him. 'I know how you feel, Mrs Barton, but what I have to say is terribly important. Will you please listen to me?'

'Yes,' she said numbly.

'When I talked to you at one o'clock this morning, Mrs Barton, you were in a state – well, you do understand that I wasn't trying to badger you then. I was working on your behalf. On behalf of the whole community, in fact.'

'I don't remember. I don't remember anything about it.'

'I see. But you understand now, don't you? And you do know that there's been a series of these outrages in the community during recent years, and that the administration and the press have put a great deal of pressure – rightly, of course – on my office and on the police department to do something about it?'

Julie let her head fall back on the pillow, and closed her eyes. 'Yes,' she said. 'If you say so.'

'I do say so. I also say that we can't do very much unless the injured party – the victim – helps us in every way possible. And why won't she? Why does she so often refuse to identify the criminal or testify against him in cases like this? Because she might face some publicity? Because she might have started off by encouraging the man, and is afraid of what he'd say about her on the witness stand? I don't care what the reason is, that woman is guilty of turning a wild beast loose on her helpless neighbors!

'Look, Mrs Barton. I'll guarantee that the man who did this has a police record, and the kind of offences listed on it – well, I wouldn't even want to name them in front of you. There's a dozen people at headquarters right now looking through all such records and when they find the right one it'll lead us straight to him. But after that you're the only one who can help us get rid of him for keeps. I want you to tell me right now that you'll do that for us when the time comes. It's your duty. You can't turn away from it.'

'I know. But I didn't see him.'

'You saw more than you realize, Mrs Barton. Now, don't get me wrong, because I'm not saying that you're deliberately holding out, or anything like that. You've had a terrible shock. You want to forget it, get it out of your mind completely. And that's what'll happen, if you let yourself go this way. So, knowing that, and not letting yourself go, do you think you can describe the man more accurately now?'

Maybe she had been wrong about Tom, she thought, about the way he had looked at her. She opened her eyes hopefully and was bitterly sorry she had. His expression of angry bewilderment was unchanged, but now he was leaning forward, staring at her as if he could draw the right answer from her by force of will. And she knew he couldn't. The tears overflowed, and she cried weakly; then magically a tissue was pressed into her hand. She had forgotten the nurse. The upside down face bent over her from behind the bed, and she was strangely consoled by the sight of it. All these men in the room – even her husband – had been made aliens by what had happened to her. It was good to have a woman there.

'Mrs Barton?' Dahl's voice was unexpectedly sharp, and Tom turned abruptly toward him. Dahl must have caught the warning in that, Julie realized with gratitude; when he spoke again his voice was considerably softer. 'Mrs Barton, please let me put the matter before you bluntly. Let me show you what we're faced with here.

'A dangerous man is on the prowl. You seem to think he was drunk, but he wasn't too drunk to know exactly where he could find a victim who was alone and unprotected. He probably had this house staked out for weeks in advance, knowing your husband's been working late at his office. And he knew how to get into the house. He scraped this window sill here pretty badly, coming in over it.

'He wasn't here to rob the place – he had the opportunity but he wasn't interested in it. He was interested in one thing, and one thing only.' Surprisingly, Dahl walked over to the dresser and lifted the framed wedding picture from it. 'This is you, isn't it?'

'Yes,' Julie said in bewilderment.

'You're a very pretty young woman, you know.' Dahl put down the picture, lifted up her hand mirror, and approached her with it. 'Now I want to show you how a pretty young woman looks after she's tried to resist a man like that.' He suddenly flashed the mirror before her and she shrank in horror from its reflection.

'Oh, please!' she cried.

'You don't have to worry,' Dahl said harshly. 'According to the doctor you'll heal up fine in a while. But until then, won't you see that man as clear as day every time you look into this thing? Won't you be able to point him out, and lay your hand on the Bible, and swear he was the one?'

She wasn't sure any more. She looked at him wonderingly, and he threw wide his arms summing up his case. 'You'll know him when you see him again, won't you?' he demanded.

'Yes,' she said.


She thought she would be left alone after that, but she was wrong. The world had business with her, and there was no way of shutting it out. The doorbell chimed incessantly. The telephone in the hall rang, was silent while someone took the call, then rang again. Men with hard faces – police officials – would be ushered into the room by Tom. They would solemnly survey the room, then go off in a corner to whisper together. Tom would lead them out, and would return to her side. He had nothing to say. He would just sit there, taut with impatience, waiting for the doorbell or telephone to ring again.

He was seldom apart from her, and Julie, watching him, found herself increasingly troubled by that. She was keeping him from his work, distracting him from the thing that mattered most to him. She didn't know much about his business affairs, but she did know he had been working for months on some very big deal – the one that had been responsible for her solitary evenings at home – and what would happen to it while he was away from his office? She had only been married two years, but she was already well-versed in the creed of the businessman's wife. Troubles at home may come and go, it said, but Business abides. She used to find that idea repellent, but now it warmed her. Tom would go to the office, and she would lock the door against everybody, and there would be continuity.

But when she hesitantly broached the matter he shrugged it off. 'The deal's all washed up, anyhow. It was a waste of time. That's what I was going to tell you about when I walked in and found you like that. It was quite a sight.' He looked at her, his eyes glassy with fatigue. 'Quite a sight,' he said.

And sat there waiting for the doorbell or phone to ring again.

When he was not there, one of the nurses was. Miss Shepherd, the night nurse, was taciturn. Miss Waldemar, the day nurse, talked.

She said, 'Oh, it takes all kinds to make this little old world, I tell you. They slow their cars coming by the house, and they walk all over the lawn, and what they expect to see I'm sure I don't know. It's just evil minds, that's all it is, and wouldn't they be the first ones to call you a liar if you told them that to their faces? And children in the back seats! What is it, sweetie? You look as if you can't get comfy.'

'I'm all right, thank you,' Julie said. She quailed at the thought of telling Miss Waldemar to please keep quiet or go away. There were people who could do that, she knew, but evidently it didn't matter to them how anyone felt about you when you hurt their feelings. It mattered to Julie a great deal.

Miss Waldemar said, 'But if you ask me who's really to blame I'll tell you right out it's the newspapers. Just as well the doctor won't let you look at them, sweetie, because they're having a party, all right. You'd think what with Russia and all, there's more worthwhile things for them to worry about, but no, there it is all over the front pages as big as they can make it. Anything for a nickel, that's their feeling about it. Money, money, money, and who cares if children stand there gawking at headlines and getting ideas at their age!

'Oh, I told that right to one of those reporters, face to face. No sooner did I put foot outside the house yesterday when he steps up, bold as brass, and asks me to get him a picture of you. Steal one, if you please! They're all using that picture from your high school yearbook now; I suppose they want something like that big one on the dresser. And I'm not being asked to do him any favors, mind you; he'll pay fifty dollars cash for it! Well, that was my chance to tell him a thing or two, and don't think I didn't. You are sleeepy, aren't you, lamb? Would you like to take a little nap?'

'Yes,' said Julie.

Her parents arrived. She had been eager to see them, but when Tom brought them into her room the eagerness faded. Tom had always despised her father's air of futility – the quality of helplessness that marked his every gesture – and never tried to conceal his contempt. Her mother, who had started off with the one objection that Tom was much too old for Julie – he was thirty to her eighteen when they married – had ultimately worked up to the point of telling him he was an outrageous bully, a charge which he regarded as a declaration of war.

That foolish business, Julie knew guiltily, had been her fault. Tom, who could be as finicking as an old maid about some things, had raged at her for not emptying the pockets of his jackets before sending them to the tailor, and since she still was, at the time, more her mother's daughter than her husband's wife, she had weepingly confided the episode to her mother over the telephone. She had not made that mistake again, but the damage was done. After that her husband and her parents made up openly hostile camps, while she served as futile emissary between them.

When they all came into the room now, Julie could feel their mutual enmity charging the air. She had wistfully hoped that what had happened would change that, and knew with a sinking heart that it had not. What it came to, she thought resignedly, is that they hated each other more than they loved her. And immediately she was ashamed of the thought.

Her father weakly fluttered his fingers at her in greeting, and stood at the foot of the bed looking at her like a lost spaniel. It was a relief when the doorbell rang and he trailed out after Tom to see who it was. Her mother's eyes were red and swollen; she kept a small, damp handkerchief pressed to her nose. She sat down beside Julie and patted her hand.

'It's awful, darling,' she said. 'It's just awful. Now you know why I was so much against your buying the house out here, way at the end of nowhere. How are you?'

'All right.'

Her mother said, 'We would have been here sooner except for Grandma. We didn't want her to find out, but some busybody neighbor went and told her. And you know how she is. She was prostrated. Dr Vaughn was with her for an hour.'

'I'm sorry.'

Her mother patted her hand again. 'She'll be all right. You'll get a card from her when she's up and around.'

Her grandmother always sent greeting cards on every possible occasion. Julie wondered mirthlessly what kind of card she would find to fit this occasion.

'Julie,' her mother said, 'would you like me to comb out your hair?'

'No, thank you, Mother.'

'But it's all knots. Don't those nurses ever do anything for their money? And where are your dark glasses, darling? The ones you use at the beach. It wouldn't hurt to wear them until that discoloration is gone, would it?'

Julie felt clouds of trivia swarming over her, like gnats. 'Please, Mother.'

'It's all right, I'm not going to fuss about it. I'll make up a list for the nurses when I go. Anyhow, there's something much more serious I wanted to talk to you about, Julie. I mean, while Dad and Tom aren't here. Would it be all right if I did?'

'Yes.'

Her mother leaned forward tensely. 'It's about – well, it's about what happened. How it might make you feel about Tom now. Because, Julie, no matter how you might feel, he's your husband, and you've always got to remember that. I respect him for that, and you must, too, darling. There are certain things a wife owes a husband, and she still owes them to him even after something awful like this happens. She's duty bound. Why do you look like that, Julie? You do understand what I'm saying, don't you?'

'Yes,' Julie said. She had been chilled by a sudden insight into her parents' life together. 'But please don't talk about it. Everything will be all right.'

'I know it will. If we aren't afraid to look our troubles right in the eye they can never hurt us, can they? And, Julie, before

Tom gets back there's something else to clear up. It's about him.'

Julie braced herself. 'Yes?'

'It's something he said. When Dad and I came in we talked to him a while and when – well, you know what we were talking about, and right in the middle of it Tom said in the most casual way – I mean, just like he was talking about the weather or something – he said that when they caught that man he was going to kill him. Julie, he terrified me. You know his temper, but it wasn't temper or anything like that. It was just a calm statement of fact. He was going to kill the man, and that's all there was to it. But he meant it, Julie, and you've got to do something about it.'

'Do what?' Julie said dazedly. 'What can I do?'

'You can let him know he mustn't even talk like that. Everybody feels the way he does – we all want that monster dead and buried. But it isn't up to Tom to kill him. He could get into terrible trouble that way! Hasn't there been enough trouble for all of us already?'

Julie closed her eyes. 'Yes,' she said.

Dr Vaughn came and watched her walk around the room. He said, 'I'll have to admit you look mighty cute in those dark glasses, but what are they for? Eyes bother you any?'

'No,' Julie said. 'I just feel better wearing them.'

'I thought so. They make you look better to people, and they make people look better to you. Say, that's an idea. Maybe the whole human race ought to take up wearing them permanently. Be a lot better for their livers than alcohol, wouldn't it?'

'I don't know,' Julie said. She sat down on the edge of the bed, huddled in her robe, its sleeves covering her clasped hands, mandarin style. Her hands felt as if they would never be warm again. 'I want to ask you something.'

'All right, go ahead and ask.'

'I shouldn't, because you'll probably laugh at me, but I won't mind. It's about Tom. He told Mother that when they caught the man he was going to kill him. I suppose he was just – I mean, he wouldn't really try to do anything like that, would he?'

The doctor did not laugh. He said grimly, 'I think he might try to do something exactly like that.'

'To *kill* somebody?'

'Julie, I don't understand you. You've been married to Tom – how long is it now?'

'Two years.'

'And in those two years did you ever know him to say he would do something that he didn't sooner or later do?'

'No.'

'I would have bet on that. Not because I know Tom so well, mind you, but because I grew up with his father. Every time I look at Tom I see his father all over again. There was a man with Lucifer's own pride rammed into him like gunpowder, and a hair-trigger temper to set it off. And repressed. Definitely repressed. Tom is, too. It's hard not to be when you have to strain all the time, keeping the emotional finger off that trigger. I'll be blunt, Julie. None of the Bartons has ever impressed me as being exactly well-balanced. I have the feeling that if you gave any one of them enough motive for killing, he'd kill, all right. And Tom owns a gun, too, doesn't he?'

'Yes.'

'Well, you don't have to look that scared about it,' the doctor said. 'It would have been a lot worse if we hadn't been warned. This way I can tell Christensen and he'll keep an eye on your precious husband until they've got the man strapped into the electric chair. A bullet's too good for that kind of animal, anyhow.'

Julie turned her head away and the doctor placed his finger against her chin and gently turned it back. 'Look,' he said, 'I'll do everything possible to see Tom doesn't get into trouble. Will you take my word for that?'

'Yes.'

'Then what's bothering you? The way I talked about putting that man in the electric chair? Is that what it is?'

'Yes. I don't want to hear about it.'

'But why? You of all people, Julie! Haven't you been praying for them to find him? Don't you hate him enough to want to see him dead?'

It was like turning the key that unlocked all her misery.

'I do!' she said despairingly. 'Oh, yes, I do! But Tom doesn't believe it. That's what's wrong, don't you understand? He thinks it doesn't matter to me as much as it does to him. He thinks I just want to forget all about it, whether they catch the man or not. He doesn't say so, but I can tell. And that makes everything rotten; it makes me feel ashamed and guilty all the time. Nothing can change that. Even if they kill the man a hundred times over it'll always be that way!'

'It will not,' the doctor said sternly. 'Julie, why don't you use your head? Hasn't it dawned on you that Tom is suffering from an even deeper guilt than yours? That subconsciously he feels a sense of failure because he didn't protect you from what happened? Now he's reacting like any outraged male. He wants vengeance. He wants the account settled. And, Julie, it's his sense of guilt that's tearing you two apart.

'Do you know what that means, young lady? It means you've got a job to do for yourself. The dirtiest kind of job. When the police nail that man you'll have to identify him, testify against him, face cameras and newspapermen, walk through mobs of brainless people dying to get a close look at you. Yes, it's as bad as all that. You don't realize the excitement this mess has stirred up; you've been kept apart from it so far. But you'll have a chance to see it for yourself very soon. That's your test. If you flinch from it you can probably write off your marriage then and there. That's what you've got to keep in mind, not all that nonsense about things never changing!'

Julie sat there viewing herself from a distance, while the cold in her hands moved up along her arms turning them to gooseflesh. She said, 'When I was a little girl I cried if anybody even pointed at me.'

'You can't be a little girl all your life,' the doctor said.

When the time came, Julie fortified herself with that thought. Sitting in the official car between Tom and Lieutenant Christensen, shielded from the onlooking world by dark glasses and upturned coat collar, her eyes closed, her teeth set, she repeated it like a private *Hail Mary* over and over – until it became a soothing murmur circling endlessly through her mind.

Lieutenant Christensen said, 'The man's a janitor in one of

those old apartment houses a few blocks away from your place. A drunk and a degenerate. He's been up on morals charges before, but nothing like this. This time he put himself in a spot he'll never live to crawl away from. Not on grounds of insanity, or anything else. We've got him cold.'

*You can't be a little girl all your life*, Julie thought.

'We're here, Mrs Barton,' the lieutenant said.

The car had stopped before a side door of the headquarters building, and Tom pushed her through it just ahead of men with cameras who swarmed down on her, shouting her name, hammering at the door when it was closed against them. She clutched Tom's hand as the lieutenant led them through long institutional corridors, other men falling into step with them along the way, until they reached another door where Dahl was waiting.

He said, 'This whole thing takes just one minute, Mrs Barton, and we're over our big hurdle. All you have to do is look at the man and tell us yes or no. That's all there is to it. And it's arranged so that he can't possibly see you. You have nothing at all to fear from him. Do you understand that?'

'Yes,' Julie said.

Again she sat between Tom and Lieutenant Christensen. The platform before her was brilliantly lighted; everything else was in darkness. Men were all around her in the darkness. They moved restlessly; one of them coughed. The outline of Dahl's sharp profile and narrow shoulders was suddenly etched black against the platform; then it disappeared as he took the seat in front of Julie's. She found that her breathing was becoming increasingly shallow; it was impossible to draw enough air out of the darkness to fill her lungs. She forced herself to breathe deeply, counting as she used to do during gym exercises at school. *In-one-two-three. Out-one-two-three.*

A door slammed nearby. Three men walked onto the platform and stood there facing her. Two of them were uniformed policemen. The third man – the one they flanked – towered over them tall and cadaverous, dressed in a torn sweater and soiled trousers. His face was slack, his huge hand moved back and forth in a vacant gesture across his mouth. Julie tried to take her eyes off that hand and couldn't. Back and forth it went, mesmerizing her with its blind, groping motion.

One of the uniformed policemen held up a piece of paper.

'Charles Brunner,' he read loudly. 'Age forty-one. Arrests—' and on and on until there was sudden silence. But the hand still went back and forth, growing enormous before her, and Julie knew, quite without concern, that she was going to faint. She swayed forward, her head drooping, and something cold and hard was pressed under her nose. Ammonia fumes stung her nostrils and she twisted away, gasping. When the lieutenant thrust the bottle at her again, she weakly pushed it aside.

'I'm all right,' she said.

'But it was a jolt seeing him, wasn't it?'

'Yes.'

'Because you recognized him, didn't you?'

She wondered vaguely if that were why. 'I'm not sure.'

Dahl leaned over her. 'You can't mean that, Mrs Barton! You gave me your word you'd know him when you saw him again. Why are you backing out of it now? What are you afraid of?'

'I'm not afraid'

'Yes, you are. You almost passed out when you saw him, didn't you? Because no matter how much you wanted to get him out of your mind your emotions wouldn't let you. Those emotions wouldn't let you! Those emotions are telling you the truth, aren't they?'

'I don't know!'

'Then look at him again and see what happens. Go on, take a good look!'

Lieutenant Christensen said, 'Mrs Barton, if you let us down now, you'll go out and tell the newspapermen about it yourself. They've been on us like wolves about this thing, and for once in my life I want them to know what we're up against here!'

Tom's fingers gripped her shoulder. 'I don't understand, Julie,' he said. 'Why don't you come out with it? He is the man, isn't he?'

'Yes!' she said, and clapped her hands over her ears to shut out the angry, hateful voices clamoring at her out of the darkness. 'Yes! Yes!'

'Thank God,' said Lieutenant Christensen.

Then Tom moved. He stood up, something glinting metallically in his hand, and Julie screamed as the man behind her lunged at it. Light suddenly flooded the room. Other men leaped at Tom and chairs clattered over as the struggle eddied around and around him, flowing relentlessly toward the platform. There was no one on it when he was finally borne down to the floor by a crushing weight of bodies.

Two of the men, looking apologetic, pulled him to his feet, but kept their arms tightly locked around his. Another man handed the gun to Lieutenant Christensen, and Tom nodded at it. He was disheveled and breathing hard, but seemed strangely unruffled.

'I'd like that back, if you don't mind,' he said.

'I do mind,' said the lieutenant. He broke open the gun, tapped the bullets into his hand, and then, to Julie's quivering relief, dropped gun and bullets into his own pocket. 'Mr Barton, you're in a state right now where if I charged you with attempted murder you wouldn't even deny it, would you?'

'No.'

'You see what I mean? Now why don't you just cool off and let us handle this job? We've done all right so far, haven't we? And after Mrs Barton testifies at the trial Brunner is as good as dead, and you can forget all about him.' The lieutenant looked at Juliet 'That makes sense, doesn't it?' he asked her.

'Yes,' Julie whispered prayerfully.

Tom smiled. 'I'd like my gun, if you don't mind.'

The lieutenant stood there speechless for the moment, and then laid his hand over the pocket containing the gun as if to assure himself that it was still there. 'Some other time,' he said with finality.

The men holding Tom released him and he lurched forward and caught at them for support. His face was suddenly deathly pale, but the smile was still fixed on it as he addressed the lieutenant.

'You'd better call a doctor,' he said pleasantly. 'I think your damn gorillas have broken my leg.'

During the time he was in the hospital he was endlessly silent and withdrawn. The day he was brought home at his own insistence, his leg unwieldy in a cast from ankle to knee, Dr Vaughn had a long talk with him, the two of them alone behind the closed doors of the living room. The doctor must have expressed himself freely and forcefully. When he had gone, and Julie plucked up the courage to walk into the living room, she saw her husband regarding her with the look of a man who has had a bitter dose of medicine forced down his throat and hasn't quite decided whether or not it will do him any good.

Then he patted the couch seat beside him. 'There's just enough room for you and me and this leg,' he said.

She obediently sat down, clasping her hands in her lap.

'Vaughn's been getting some things off his chest,' Tom said abruptly. 'I'm glad he did. You've been through a rotten experience, Julie, and I haven't been any help at all, have I? All I've done is make it worse. I've been lying to myself about it, too. Telling myself that everything I did since it happened was for your sake, and all along the only thing that really concerned me was my own feelings. Isn't that so?'

'I don't know,' Julie said, 'and I don't care. It doesn't matter as long as you talk to me about it. That's the only thing I can't stand, not having you talk to me.'

'Has it been that bad?'

'Yes.'

'But you understand why, don't you? It was something eating away inside of me. But it's gone now, I swear it is. You believe that, don't you, Julie?'

She hesitated. 'Yes.'

'I can't tell whether you mean it or not behind those dark glasses. Lift them up, and let me see.'

Julie lifted the glasses and he gravely studied her face. 'I think you do mean it,' he said. 'A face as pretty as that couldn't possibly tell a lie. But why do you still wear those things? There aren't any marks left.'

She dropped the glasses into place and the world became its soothingly familiar, shaded self again. 'I just like them,' she said. 'I'm used to them.'

'Well, if the doctor doesn't mind, I don't. But if you're wearing them to make yourself look exotic and dangerous, you'll have to give up. You're too much like Sweet Alice. You can't escape it.'

She smiled. 'I don't tremble with fear at your frown. Not really.'

'Yes, you do, but I like it. You're exactly what Sweet Alice must have been. Demure, that's the word, demure. My wife is the only demure married woman in the world. Yielding, yet cool and remote. A lovely lady wrapped in cellophane. How is it you never became a nun?'

She knew she must be visibly glowing with happiness. It had been so long since she had seen him in this mood. 'I almost did. When I was in school I used to think about it a lot. There was this other girl – well, she was really a wonderful person, and she had already made up her mind about it. I guess that's where I got the idea.'

'And then what happened?'

'You know what happened.'

'Yes, it's all coming back now. You went to your first Country Club dance dressed in a beautiful white gown, with stardust in your hair—'

'It was sequins.'

'No, stardust. And I saw you. And the next thing I remember, we were in Mexico on a honeymoon.' He put his arm around her waist, and she relaxed in the hard circle of it. 'Julie, when this whole bad dream is over we're going there again. We'll pack the car and go south of the border and forget everything. You'd like that, wouldn't you?'

'Oh, very much.' She looked up at him hopefully, her head back against his shoulder. 'But no bullfights, please. Not this time.'

He laughed. 'All right, when I'm at the bullfights you'll be sightseeing. The rest of the time we'll be together. Any time I look around I want to see you there. No more than this far away. That means I can reach out my hand and you'll always be there. Is that clear?'

'I'll be there,' she said.

So she had found him again, she assured herself, and she used that knowledge to settle her qualms whenever she thought of Brunner and the impending trial. She never mentioned these occasional thoughts to Tom, and she came to see that there was a conspiracy among everyone who entered the house – her family and friends, the doctor, even strangers on business with Tom – which barred any reference to the subject of Brunner. Until one evening when, after she had coaxed Tom into a restless sleep, the doorbell rang again and again with maddening persistence.

Julie looked through the peephole and saw that the man standing outside was middle-aged and tired-looking and carried a worn leather portfolio under his arm. She opened the door with annoyance and said, 'Please, don't do that. My husband's not well, and he's asleep. And there's nothing we want.'

The man walked past her into the foyer before she could stop him. He took off his hat and faced her. 'I'm not a salesman, Mrs Barton. My name is Karlweiss. Dr Lewis Karlweiss. Is it familiar to you?'

'No.'

'It should be. Up to three o'clock this afternoon I was in charge of the City Hospital for Mental Disorders. Right now I'm a man without any job, and with a badly frayed reputation. And just angry enough and scared enough, Mrs Barton, to want to do something about it. That's why I'm here.'

'I don't see what it has to do with me.'

'You will. Two years ago Charles Brunner was institutional-ized in my care, and, after treatment, released on my say-so. Do you understand now? I am officially responsible for having turned him loose on you. I signed the document which certified that while he was not emotionally well, he was certainly not dangerous. And this afternoon I had that document shoved down my throat by a gang of ignorant politicians who are out to make hay of this case!'

Julie said incredulously, 'And you want me to go and tell them they were wrong? Is that it?'

'Only if you know they *are* wrong, Mrs Barton. I'm not asking you to perjure yourself for me. I don't even know what legal right I have to be here in the first place, and I certainly don't want to get into any more trouble than I'm already in.' Karlweiss looked over her shoulder toward the living room, and shifted his portfolio from one arm to the other. 'Can we go inside and sit down while we talk this over? There's a lot to say.'

'No.'

'All right, then I'll explain it here, and I'll make it short and to the point. Mrs Barton, I know more about Charles Brunner than anyone else in the world. I know more about him than he knows about himself. And that's what makes it so hard for me to believe that you identified the right man!'

Julie said, 'I don't want to hear about it. Will you please go away?'

'No, I will not,' Karlweiss said heatedly. 'I insist on being heard. You see, Mrs Barton, everything Brunner does fits a certain pattern. Every dirty little crime he has committed fits that pattern. It's a pattern of weakness, a constant manifestation of his failure to achieve full masculinity.

'But what he is now charged with is the absolute reverse of that pattern. It was a display of brute masculinity by an aggressive and sadistic personality. It was the act of someone who can only obtain emotional and physical release through violence. That's the secret of such a personality – the need for violence. Not lust, as the Victorians used to preach, but the need for release through violence. And that is a need totally alien to Brunner. It doesn't exist in him. It's a sickness, but it's not his sickness!

'Now do you see why your identification of him hit me and my co-workers at the hospital so hard? We don't know too much about various things in our science yet – I'm the first to admit it – but in a few cases we've been able to work out patterns of personality as accurately as mathematical equations. I thought we had done that successfully with Brunner. I would still think so, if you hadn't identified him. That's why I'm here. I wanted to meet you. I wanted to have you tell me directly if there was any doubt at all about Brunner being the man. Because if there is—'

'There isn't.'

'But if there is,' Karlweiss pleaded, 'I'd take my oath that Brunner isn't guilty. It makes sense that way. If there's the shadow of a doubt—'

'There isn't!'

'Julie!' called Tom from the bedroom. 'Who is that?'

Panic seized her. All she could envision then was Brunner as he would walk down the prison steps to the street, as he would stand there dazed in the sunlight while Tom, facing him, slowly drew the gun from his pocket. She clutched Karlweiss's sleeve and half-dragged him toward the door. 'Please, go away!' she whispered fiercely. 'There's nothing to talk about. Please, go away!'

She closed the door behind him and leaned back against it, her knees trembling.

'Julie, who is that?' Tom called. 'Who are you talking to?'

She steadied herself and went into the bedroom. 'It was a salesman,' she said. 'He was selling insurance. I told him we didn't want any.'

'You know I don't want you to open the door to any strangers,' Tom said. 'Why'd you go and do a thing like that?'

Julie forced herself to smile. 'He was perfectly harmless,' she said.

But the terror had taken root in her now – and it thrived. It was fed by many things. The subpoena from Dahl which Tom had her put into his dresser drawer for safekeeping and which was there in full view every time she opened the drawer to get him something. The red circle around the trial date on the calendar in the kitchen which a line of black crosses inched toward, a little closer each day. And the picture in her mind's eye which took many forms, but which was always the same picture with the same ending: Brunner descending the prison steps, or Brunner entering the courtroom, or Brunner in the dank cellar she saw as his natural habitat, and then in the end Brunner standing there, blinking stupidly, his hand moving back and forth over his mouth, and Tom facing him, slowly drawing the gun from his pocket, the gun barrel glinting as it moved into line with Brunner's chest—

The picture came into even sharper focus when Dr Vaughn brought the crutches for Tom. Julie loathed them at sight. She had never minded the heavy pressure of Tom's arm around her shoulders, his weight bearing her down as he lurched from one room to another, hobbled by the cast. The cast was a hobble, she knew, keeping him tied down to the house; he struggled with it and grumbled about it continually, as if the struggling and grumbling would somehow release him from it. But the crutches were a release. They would take him to wherever Brunner was.

She watched him as he practiced using the crutches that evening, not walking, but supporting himself on them to find his balance, and then she helped him sit down on the couch, the leg in its cast propped on a footstool before him.

He said, 'Julie, you have no idea how fed up a man can get, living in pajamas and a robe. But it won't be long now, will it?'

'No.'

'Which reminds me that you ought to give my stuff out to the tailor tomorrow. He's a slow man, and I'd like it all ready when I'm up and around.'

'All right,' Julie said. She went to the wardrobe in the hall and returned with an armful of clothing which she draped over the back of an armchair. She was mechanically going through the pockets of a jacket when Tom said, 'Come here, Julie.'

He caught her hand as she stood before him. 'There's something on your mind,' he said. 'What is it?'

'Nothing.'

'You were never any good at lying. What's wrong, Julie?'

'Still nothing.'

'Oh, all right, if that's the way you want it.' He released her hand and she went back to the pile of clothing on the armchair, sick with the feeling that he could see through her, that he knew exactly what she was thinking, and must hate her for it. She put aside the jacket and picked up the car coat he used only for driving. Which meant, she thought with a small shudder of realization, that he hadn't worn it since *that* night. She pulled the gloves from its pocket and tossed the coat on top of the jacket.

'These gloves,' she said, holding them out to show him. 'Where—?'

*These gloves*, an echo cried out to her. *These gloves*, said a smaller one behind it, and *these gloves, these gloves* ran away in a diminishing series of echoes until there was only deathly silence.

And a glove.

A grey suede glove clotted and crusted with dark-brown

stains. Its index finger gouged and torn. Its bitter taste in her mouth. Its owner, a stranger, sitting on the couch, holding out his hand, saying something.

'Give that to me, Julie,' Tom said.

She looked at him and knew there were no secrets between them any more. She watched the sweat starting from his forehead and trickling down the bloodless face. She saw his teeth show and his eyes stare as he tried to pull himself to his feet. He failed, and sank back panting.

'Listen to me, Julie,' he said. 'Now listen to me and take hold of yourself.'

'You,' she said drunkenly. 'It was you.'

'Julie, I love you!'

'But it was you. It's all crazy. I don't understand.'

'I know. Because it was crazy. That's what it was, I went crazy for a minute. It was overwork. It was that deal. I was killing myself to put it across, and that night when they turned me down I don't know what happened. I got drunk, and when I came home I couldn't find the key. So I came through the window. That's when it happened. I don't know what it was, but it was something exploding in me. Something in my head. I saw you there, and all I wanted to do– I tell you I don't even know why! Don't *ask* me why! It was overwork, that's what it was. It gets to everybody nowadays. You read about it all the time. You know you do, Julie. You've got to be reasonable about this!'

Julie whispered, 'If you had told me it was you. If you had only told me. But you didn't.'

'Because I love you!'

'No, but you knew how I felt, and you turned that against me. You made me say it was Brunner. Everything you've been doing to me – it was just so I'd say it and say it, until I killed him. You never tried to kill him, at all. You knew I would do it for you. And I would have!'

'Julie, Julie, what does Brunner matter to anybody? You've seen what he's like. He's a degenerate. He's no good. Everybody is better off without people like that around.'

She shook her head violently. 'But you knew he didn't do it! Why couldn't you just let it be one of those times where they never find out who did it?'

'Because I wasn't sure! Everybody kept saying it was only the shock that let you blank it out of your mind. They kept saying if you tried hard enough to remember, it might all come back. So if Brunner– I mean, this way the record was all straight! You wouldn't have to think about it again!'

She saw that if he leaned forward enough he could touch her, and she backed away a step, surprised she had the strength to do it.

'Where are you going?' Tom said. 'Don't be a fool, Julie. Nobody'll believe you. Think of everything that's been said and done, and you'll see nobody would even *want* to believe you. They'll say you're out of your mind!'

She wavered, then realized with horror that she was wavering. 'They will believe me!' she cried, and ran blindly out of the house, sobbing as she ran, stumbling when she reached the sidewalk so that she fell on her hands and knees, feeling the sting of the scraped knee as she rose and staggered farther down the dark and empty street. It was only when she was at a distance that she stopped, her heart hammering, her legs barely able to support her, to look at the house. Not hers any more. Just his.

He – all of them – had made her a liar and an accomplice. Each of them for his own reason had done that, and she, because of the weakness in her, had let them. It was a terrible weakness, she thought with anguish – the need to have them always approve, the willingness to always say yes to them. It was like hiding yourself behind the dark glasses all the time, not caring that the world you saw through them was never the world you would see through the naked eye.

She turned and fled toward lights and people. The glasses lay in the street where she had flung them, and the night wind swept dust through their shattered frames.

# Robert

The windows of the Sixth Grade classroom were wide open to the June afternoon, and through them came all the sounds of the departing school: the thunder of bus motors warming up, the hiss of gravel under running feet, the voices raised in cynical fervor.

> 'So we sing all hail to thee,
> District Schoo-wull Number Three . . .'

Miss Gildea flinched a little at the last high, shrill note, and pressed her fingers to her aching forehead. She was tired, more tired than she could ever recall being in her thirty-eight years of teaching, and, as she told herself, she had reason to be. It had not been a good term, not good at all, what with the size of the class, and the Principal's insistence on new methods, and then her mother's shocking death coming right in the middle of everything.

Perhaps she had been too close to her mother, Miss Gildea thought; perhaps she had been wrong, never taking into account that some day the old lady would have to pass on and leave her alone in the world. Well, thinking about it all the time didn't make it any easier. She should try to forget.

And, of course, to add to her troubles, there had been during the past few weeks this maddening business of Robert. He had been a perfectly nice boy, and then, out of a clear sky, had become impossible. Not bothersome or noisy really, but sunk into an endless daydream from which Miss Gildea had to sharply jar him a dozen times a day.

She turned her attention to Robert, who sat alone in the room at the desk immediately before her, a thin boy with neatly combed, colorless hair bracketed between large ears; mild blue eyes in a pale face fixed solemnly on hers.

'Robert.'

'Yes, Miss Gildea.'

'Do you know why I told you to remain after school, Robert?'

He frowned thoughtfully at this, as if it were some lesson he was being called on for, but had failed to memorize properly.

'I suppose for being bad,' he said, at last.

Miss Gildea sighed.

'No, Robert, that's not it at all. I know a bad boy when I see one, Robert, and you aren't like that. But I do know there's something troubling you, something on your mind, and I think I can help you.'

'There's nothing bothering me, Miss Gildea. Honest, there isn't.'

Miss Gildea found the silver pencil thrust into her hair and tapped it in a nervous rhythm on her desk.

'Oh, come, Robert. During the last month every time I looked at you your mind was a million miles away. Now, what is it? Just making plans for vacation, or, perhaps, some trouble with the boys?'

'I'm not having trouble with anybody, Miss Gildea.'

'You don't seem to understand, Robert, that I'm not trying to punish you for anything. Your homework is good. You've managed to keep up with the class, but I do think your inattentiveness should be explained. What, for example, were you thinking this afternoon when I spoke to you directly for five minutes, and you didn't hear a word I said?'

'Nothing, Miss Gildea.'

She brought the pencil down sharply on the desk. 'There must have been *something*, Robert. Now, I must insist that you think back, and try to explain yourself.'

Looking at his impassive face she knew that somehow she herself had been put on the defensive, that if any means of graceful retreat were offered now she would gladly take it. Thirty-eight years, she thought grimly, and I'm still trying to play mother hen to ducklings. Thirty-eight years passed meant only two more to go before retirement, the half-salary pension, the chance to putter around the house, tend to the garden properly. The pension wouldn't buy furs and diamonds, sure enough, but it could buy the right to enjoy your own home for the rest of your days instead of a dismal room in the County Home for Old Ladies. Miss Gildea had visited the County Home once, on an instructional visit, and preferred not to think about it.

'Well, Robert,' she said wearily, 'have you remembered what you were thinking?'

'Yes, Miss Gildea.'

'What was it?'

'I'd rather not tell, Miss Gildea.'

'I insist!'

'Well,' Robert said gently, 'I was thinking I wished you were dead, Miss Gildea. I was thinking I wished I could kill you.'

Her first reaction was simply blank incomprehension. She had been standing not ten feet away when that car had skidded up on the sidewalk and crushed her mother's life from her, and Miss Gildea had neither screamed nor fainted. She had stood there dumbly, because of the very unreality of the thing. Just the way she stood in court where they explained that the man got a year in jail, but didn't have a dime to pay for the tragedy he had brought about. And now the orderly ranks of desks before her, the expanse of blackboard around her, and Robert's face in the midst of it all were no more real. She found herself rising from her chair, walking toward Robert, who shrank back, his eyes wide and panicky, his elbow half lifted as if to ward off a blow.

'Do you understand what you've just said?' Miss Gildea demanded hoarsely.

'No, Miss Gildea! Honest, I didn't mean anything.'

She shook her head unbelievingly. 'Whatever made you say it? Whatever in the world could make a boy say a thing like that, such a wicked, terrible thing!'

'You wanted to know! You kept asking me!'

The sight of that protective elbow raised against her cut as deep as the incredible words had.

'Put that arm down!' Miss Gildea said shrilly, and then struggled to get her voice under control. 'In all my years I've never struck a child, and I don't intend to start now!'

Robert dropped his arm and clasped his hands together on his desk, and Miss Gildea, looking at the pinched white knuckles, realized with surprise that her own hands were shaking uncontrollably. 'But if you think this little matter ends here, young-feller-me-lad,' she said, 'you've got another thought coming. You get your things together, and we're marching right up to Mr Harkness. He'll be very much interested in all this.'

Mr Harkness was the Principal. He had arrived only the term before, and but for his taste in eyeglasses (the large, black-rimmed kind which, Miss Gildea privately thought, looked actorish) and his predilection for the phrase 'modern pedagogical methods' was, in her opinion, a rather engaging young man.

He looked at Robert's frightened face and then at Miss Gildea's pursed lips. 'Well,' he said pleasantly, 'what seems to be the trouble here?'

'That,' said Miss Gildea, 'is something I think Robert should tell you.'

She placed a hand on Robert's shoulder, but he pulled away and backed slowly toward Mr Harkness, his breath coming in loud, shuddering sobs, his eyes riveted on Miss Gildea as if she were the only thing in the room beside himself. Mr Harkness put an arm around Robert and frowned at Miss Gildea.

'Now, what's behind all this, Miss Gildea? The boy seems frightened to death.'

Miss Gildea found herself sick of it all, anxious to get out of the room, away from Robert. 'That's enough, Robert,' she commanded. 'Just tell Mr Harkness exactly what happened.'

'I said the boy was frightened to death, Miss Gildea,' Mr Harkness said brusquely. 'We'll talk about it as soon as he understands we're his friends. Won't we, Robert?'

Robert shook his head vehemently. 'I didn't do anything bad! Miss Gildea said I didn't do anything bad!'

'Well, then!' said Mr Harkness triumphantly. 'There's nothing to be afraid of, is there?'

Robert shook his head again. 'She said I had to stay after school.'

Mr Harkness glanced sharply at Miss Gildea. 'I suppose he missed the morning bus, is that it? And after I said in a directive that the staff was to make allowances—'

'Robert doesn't use a bus,' Miss Gildea protested. 'Perhaps I'd better explain all this, Mr Harkness. You see—'

'I think Robert's doing very well,' Mr Harkness said, and tightened his arm around Robert, who nodded shakily.

'She kept me in,' he said, 'and then when we were alone she came up close to me and she said, "I know what you're thinking. You're thinking you'd like to see me dead! You're thinking you'd like to kill me, aren't you?"'

Robert's voice had dropped to an eerie whisper that bound Miss Gildea like a spell. It was broken only when she saw the expression on Mr Harkness's face.

'Why, that's a lie!' she cried. 'That's the most dreadful lie I ever heard any boy dare—'

Mr Harkness cut in abruptly. 'Miss Gildea! I *insist* you let the boy finish what he has to say.'

Miss Gildea's voice fluttered. 'It seems to me, Mr Harkness, that he has been allowed to say quite enough already!'

'Has he?' Mr Harkness asked.

'Robert has been inattentive lately, especially so this afternoon. After class I asked him what he had been thinking about, and he dared to say he was thinking how he wished I were dead! How he wanted to kill me!'

'Robert said that?'

'In almost those exact words. And I can tell you, Mr Harkness, that I was shocked, terribly shocked, especially since Robert always seemed like such a nice boy.'

'His record—?'

'His record is quite good. It's just—'

'And his social conduct?' asked Mr Harkness in the same level voice.

'As far as I know, he gets along with the other children well enough.'

'But for some reason,' persisted Mr Harkness, 'you found him annoying you.'

Robert raised his voice. 'I didn't! Miss Gildea said I didn't do anything bad. And I always liked her. I like her better than *any* teacher!'

Miss Gildea fumbled blindly in her hair for the silver pencil, and failed to find it. She looked around the floor distractedly.

'Yes?' said Mr Harkness.

'My pencil,' said Miss Gildea on the verge of tears. 'It's gone.'

'Surely, Miss Gildea,' said Mr Harkness in a tone of mild exasperation, 'this is not quite the moment—'

'It was very valuable,' Miss Gildea tried to explain hopelessly. 'It was my mother's.' In the face of Mr Harkness's stony surveillance she knew she must look a complete mess. Hems crooked, nose red, hair all disheveled. 'I'm all upset, Mr Harkness. It's been a long term and now all this right at the end of it. I don't know what to say.'

Mr Harkness's face fell into sympathetic lines.

'That's quite all right, Miss Gildea. I know how you feel. Now, if you want to leave, I think Robert and I should have a long, friendly talk.'

'If you don't mind—'

'No, no,' Mr Harkness said heartily. 'As a matter of fact, I think that would be the best thing all round.'

After he had seen her out he closed the door abruptly behind her, and Miss Gildea walked heavily up the stairway and down the corridor to the Sixth Grade room. The silver pencil was there on the floor at Robert's desk, and she picked it up and carefully polished it with her handkerchief. Then she sat down at her desk with the handkerchief to her nose and wept soundlessly for ten minutes.

That night, when the bitter taste of humiliation had grown faint enough to permit it, Miss Gildea reviewed the episode with all the honesty at her command. Honesty with oneself had always been a major point in her credo, had, in fact, been passed on through succeeding classes during the required lesson on The Duties of an American Citizen, when Miss Gildea, to sum up the lesson, would recite: 'This above all, To thine ownself be true . . .' while thumping her fist on her desk as an accompaniment to each syllable.

*Hamlet*, of course, was not in the syllabus of the Sixth Grade, whose reactions over the years never deviated from a mixed bewilderment and indifference. But Miss Gildea, after some prodding of the better minds into a discussion of the lines, would rest content with the knowledge that she had sown good seed on what, she prayed, was fertile ground.

243

Reviewing the case of Robert now, with her emotions under control, she came to the unhappy conclusion that it was she who had committed the injustice. The child had been ordered to stay after school, something that to him could mean only a punishment. He had been ordered to disclose some shadowy, childlike thoughts that had drifted through his mind hours before, and, unable to do so, either had to make up something out of the whole cloth, or blurt out the immediate thought in his immature mind.

It was hardly unusual, reflected Miss Gildea sadly, for a child badgered by a teacher to think what Robert had; she could well remember her own feelings toward a certain pompadoured harridan who still haunted her dreams. And the only conclusion to be drawn, unpleasant though it was, was that Robert, and not she, had truly put into practice those beautiful words from Shakespeare.

It was this, as well as the sight of his pale accusing face before her while she led the class through the morning session next day, which prompted her to put Robert in charge of refilling the water pitcher during recess. The duties of the water pitcher monitor were to leave the playground a little before the rest of the class and clean and refill the pitcher on her desk, but since the task was regarded as an honor by the class, her gesture, Miss Gildea felt with some self-approval, carried exactly the right note of conciliation.

She was erasing the blackboard at the front of the room near the end of the recess when she heard Robert approaching her desk, but much as she wanted to she could not summon up courage to turn and face him. As if, she thought, he were the teacher, and I were afraid of him. And she could feel her cheeks grow warm at the thought.

He re-entered the room on the sound of the bell that marked end of recess, and this time Miss Gildea plopped the eraser firmly into its place beneath the blackboard and turned to look at him. 'Thank you very much, Robert,' she said as he set the pitcher down and neatly capped it with her drinking class.

'You're welcome, Miss Gildea,' Robert said politely. He drew a handkerchief from his pocket, wiped his hands with it, then smiled gently at Miss Gildea. 'I bet you think I put poison or something into that water,' he said gravely, 'but I wouldn't do anything like that, Miss Gildea. Honest, I wouldn't.'

Miss Gildea gasped, then reached out a hand toward Robert's shoulder. She withdrew it hastily when he shrank away with the familiar panicky look in his eyes.

'Why did you say that, Robert?' Miss Gildea demanded in a terrible voice. 'That was plain impudence, wasn't it? You thought you were being smart, didn't you?'

At that moment the rest of the class surged noisily into the room, but Miss Gildea froze them into silence with a commanding wave of the hand. Out of the corner of her eye she noted the cluster of shocked and righteous faces allied with her in condemnation, and she felt a quick little sense of triumph in her position.

'I was talking to you, Robert,' she said. 'What do you have to say for yourself?'

Robert took another step backward and almost tumbled over a schoolbag left carelessly in the aisle. He caught himself, then stood there helplessly, his eyes never leaving Miss Gildea's.

'Well, Robert?'

He shook his head wildly. 'I didn't do it!' he cried. 'I didn't put anything in your water, Miss Gildea! I told you I didn't!'

Without looking, Miss Gildea knew that the cluster of accusing faces had swung toward her now, felt her triumph turn to a sick bewilderment inside her. It was as if Robert, with his teary eyes and pale, frightened face and too-large ears, had turned into a strange jellylike creature that could not be pinned down and put in its place. As if he were retreating further and further down some dark, twisting path, and leading her on with him. And, she thought desperately, she had to pull herself free before she did something dreadful, something unforgivable.

She couldn't take the boy to Mr Harkness again. Not only did the memory of that scene in his office the day before make her shudder, but a repeated visit would be an admission that after thirty-eight years of teaching she was not up to the mark as a disciplinarian.

But for her sake, if for nothing else, Robert had to be put in his place. With a gesture, Miss Gildea ordered the rest of the class to their seats and turned to Robert, who remained standing.

245

'Robert,' said Miss Gildea, 'I want an apology for what has just happened.'

'I'm sorry, Miss Gildea,' Robert said, and it looked as if his eyes would be brimming with tears in another moment.

Miss Gildea hardened her heart to this. '*I apologize, Miss Gildea, and it will not happen again,*' she prompted.

Miraculously, Robert contained his tears. 'I apologize, Miss Gildea, and it will not happen again,' he muttered and dropped limply into his seat.

'Well!' said Miss Gildea, drawing a deep breath as she looked around at the hushed class. 'Perhaps that will be a lesson to us all.'

The classroom work did not go well after that, but, as Miss Gildea told herself, there were only a few days left to the end of the term, and after that, praise be, there was the garden, the comfortable front porch of the old house to share with neighbors in the summer evenings, and then next term a new set of faces in the classroom, with Robert's not among them.

Later, closing the windows of the room after the class had left, Miss Gildea was brought up short by the sight of a large group gathered on the sidewalk near the parked buses. It was Robert, she saw, surrounded by most of the Sixth Grade, and obviously the center of interest. He was nodding emphatically when she put her face to the window, and she drew back quickly at the sight, moved by some queer sense of guilt.

*Only a child*, she assured herself, *he's only a child*, but that thought did not in any way dissolve the anger against him that stuck like a lump in her throat.

That was on Thursday. By Tuesday of the next week, the final week of the term, Miss Gildea was acutely conscious of the oppressive atmosphere lying over the classroom. Ordinarily, the awareness of impending vacation acted on the class like a violent agent dropped into some inert liquid. There would be ferment and seething beneath the surface, manifested by uncontrollable giggling and whispering, and this would grow more and more turbulent until all restraint and discipline was swept away in the general upheaval of excitement and good spirits.

That, Miss Gildea thought, was the way it always had been,

but it was strangely different now. The Sixth Grade, down to the most irrepressible spirits in it, acted as if it had been turned to a set of robots before her startled eyes. Hands tightly clasped on desks, eyes turned toward her with an almost frightening intensity, the class responded to her mildest requests as if they were shouted commands. And when she walked down the aisles between them, one and all seemed to have adopted Robert's manner of shrinking away fearfully at her approach.

Miss Gildea did not like to think of what all this might mean, but valiantly forced herself to do so. Can it mean, she asked herself, that all think as Robert does, are choosing this way of showing it? And, if they knew how cruel it was, would they do it?

Other teachers, Miss Gildea knew, sometimes took problems such as this to the Teacher's Room where they could be studied and answered by those who saw them in an objective light. It might be that the curious state of the Sixth Grade was duplicated in other classes. Perhaps she herself was imagining the whole thing, or, frightening thought, looking back, as people will when they grow old, on the sort of past that never really did exist. Why, in that case – and Miss Gildea had to laugh at herself with a faint merriment – she would just find herself reminiscing about her thirty-eight years of teaching to some bored young woman who didn't have the fraction of experience she did.

But underneath the current of these thoughts, Miss Gildea knew there was one honest reason for not going to the Teacher's Room this last week of the term. She had received no gifts, not one. And the spoils from each grade heaped high in a series of pyramids against the wall, the boxes of fractured cookies, the clumsily wrapped jars of preserves, the scarves, the stockings, the handkerchiefs, infinite, endless boxes of handkerchiefs, all were there to mark the triumph of each teacher. And Miss Gildea, who in all her years at District School Number Three had been blushingly proud of the way her pyramid was highest at the end of each term, had not yet received a single gift from the Sixth Grade class.

After the class was dismissed that afternoon, however, the spell was broken. Only a few of her pupils still loitered in the hallway near the door, Miss Gildea noted, but Robert remained in his seat. Then, as she gathered together her belongings Robert approached her with a box outheld in his hand. It was, from its shape, a box of candy. Automatically, she reached a hand out, then stopped herself short. He'll never make up to me for what he's done, she told herself furiously; I'll never let him.

'Yes, Robert?' she said coolly.

'It's a present for you, Miss Gildea,' Robert said, and then as Miss Gildea watched in fascination he began to strip the wrappings from it. He laid the paper neatly on the desk and lifted the cover of the box to display the chocolates within. 'My mother said that's the biggest box they had,' he said wistfully. 'Don't you even want them, Miss Gildea?'

Miss Gildea weakened despite herself. 'Did you think I would, after what's happened, Robert?' she asked.

Robert reflected a moment. 'Well,' he said at last, 'if you want me to, I'll eat one right in front of you, Miss Gildea.'

Miss Gildea recoiled as if at a faraway warning. *Don't let him say any more*, something inside her cried; *he's only playing a trick, another horrible trick*, and then she was saying, 'Why would I want you to do that, Robert?'

'So you'll see they're not poison or anything, Miss Gildea,' Robert said. 'Then you'll believe it, won't you, Miss Gildea?'

She had been prepared. Even before he said the words, she had felt her body drawing itself tighter and tighter against what she knew was coming. But the sound of the words themselves only served to release her like a spring coiled too tightly.

'You little monster!' sobbed Miss Gildea and struck wildly at the proffered box, which flew almost to the far wall, while chocolates cascaded stickily around the room. 'How dare you!' she cried. 'How dare you!' and her small bony fists beat at Robert's cowering shoulders and back as he tried to retreat.

He half turned in the aisle, slipped on a piece of chocolate, and went down to his knees, but before he could recover himself Miss Gildea was on him again, her lips drawn back, her fists pummeling him as if they were a pair of tireless mallets. Robert had started to scream at the top of his lungs from the first blow, but it was no more than a remote buzzing in Miss Gildea's ears.

'Miss Gildea!'

That was Mr Harkness's voice, she knew, and those must be

Mr Harkness's hands which pulled her away so roughly that she had to keep herself from falling by clutching at her desk. She stood there weakly, feeling the wild fluttering of her heart, feeling the sick churning of shame and anguish in her while she tried to bring the room into focus again. There was the knot of small excited faces peering through the open doorway, they must have called Mr Harkness, and Mr Harkness himself listening to Robert who talked and wept alternately, and there was a mess everywhere. Of course, thought Miss Gildea dazedly, those must be chocolate stains. Chocolate stains all over my lovely clean room.

Then Robert was gone, the faces at the door were gone, and the door itself was closed behind them. Only Mr Harkness remained, and Miss Gildea watched him as he removed his glasses, cleaned them carefully, and then held them up at arm's length and studied them before settling them once more on his nose.

'Well, Miss Gildea,' said Mr Harkness as if he were speaking to the glasses rather than to her, 'this is a serious business.'

Miss Gildea nodded.

'I am sick,' Mr Harkness said quietly, 'really sick at the thought that somewhere in this school, where I tried to introduce decent pedagogical standards, corporal punishment is still being practiced.'

'That's not fair at all, Mr Harkness,' Miss Gildea said shakily. 'I hit the boy, that's true, and I know I was wrong to do it, but that is the first time in all my life I raised a finger against any child. And if you knew my feelings—'

'Ah,' said Mr Harkness, 'that's exactly what I would like to know, Miss Gildea.' He nodded to her chair, and she sat down weakly. 'Now, just go ahead and explain everything as you saw it.'

It was a difficult task, made even more difficult by the fact that Mr Harkness chose to stand facing the window. Forced to address his back this way, Miss Gildea found that she had the sensation of speaking in a vacuum, but she mustered the facts as well as she could, presented them with strong emotion, and then sank back in the chair quite exhausted.

Mr Harkness remained silent for a long while, then slowly

turned to face Miss Gildea. 'I am not a practicing psychiatrist,' he said at last, 'although as an educator I have, of course, taken a considerable interest in that field. But I do not think it needs a practitioner to tell what a clearcut and obvious case I am facing here. Nor,' he added sympathetically, 'what a tragic one.'

'It might simply be,' suggested Miss Gildea, 'that Robert—'

'I am not speaking about Robert,' said Mr Harkness soberly, quietly.

It took an instant for this to penetrate, and then Miss Gildea felt the blood run cold in her.

'Do you think I'm lying about all this?' she cried incredulously. 'Can you possibly—'

'I am sure,' Mr Harkness replied soothingly, 'that you were describing things exactly as you saw them, Miss Gildea. But – have you ever heard the phrase "persecution complex"? Do you think you could recognize the symptoms of that condition if they were presented objectively? I can, Miss Gildea. I assure you, I can.'

Miss Gildea struggled to speak, but the words seemed to choke her. 'No,' she managed to say, 'you couldn't! Because some mischievous boy chooses to make trouble—'

'Miss Gildea, no child of eleven, however mischievous, could draw the experiences Robert has described to me out of his imagination. He has discussed these experiences with me at length; now I have heard your side of the case. And the conclusions to be drawn, I must say, are practically forced on me.'

The room started to slip out of focus again, and Miss Gildea frantically tried to hold it steady.

'But that just means you're taking his word against mine!' she said fiercely.

'Unfortunately, Miss Gildea, not his word alone. Last weekend, a delegation of parents met the School Board and made it quite plain that they were worried because of what their children told them of your recent actions. A dozen children in your class described graphically at that meeting how you had accused them of trying to poison your drinking water, and how you had threatened them because of this. And Robert, it may interest you to know, was not even one of them.

'The School Board voted your dismissal then and there, Miss Gildea, but in view of your long years of service it was left for me to override that decision if I wished to on my sole responsibility. After this episode, however, I cannot see that I have any choice. I must do what is best.'

'Dismissal?' said Miss Gildea vaguely. 'But they can't. I only have two more years to go. They can't do that, Mr Harkness: all they're trying to do is trick me out of my pension!'

'Believe me,' said Mr Harkness gently, 'they're not trying to do anything of the sort, Miss Gildea. Nobody in the world is trying to hurt you. I give you my solemn word that the only thing which has entered into consideration of this case from first to last has been the welfare of the children.'

The room swam in sunlight, but under it Miss Gildea's face was gray and lifeless. She reached forward to fill her glass with water, stopped short, and seemed to gather herself together with a sudden brittle determination. 'I'll just have to speak to the Board myself,' she said in a high breathless voice. 'That's the only thing to do, go there and explain the whole thing to them!'

'That would not help,' said Mr Harkness pityingly. 'Believe me, Miss Gildea, it would not.'

Miss Gildea left her chair and came to him, her eyes wide and frightened. She laid a trembling hand on his arm and spoke eagerly, quickly, trying to make him understand. 'You see,' she said, 'that means I won't get my pension. I must have two more years for that, don't you see? There's the payment on the house, the garden – no, the garden is part of the house, really – but without the pension—'

She was pulling furiously at his arm with every phrase as if she could drag him bodily into a comprehension of her words, but he stood unyielding and only shook his head pityingly. 'You must control yourself, Miss Gildea,' he pleaded. 'You're not yourself, and it's impossible—'

'No!' she cried in a strange voice. 'No!'

When she pulled away he knew almost simultaneously what she intended to do, but the thought froze him to the spot, and when he moved it was too late. He burst into the corridor through the door she had flung open, and almost threw himself down the stairway to the main hall. The door to the street was just swinging shut and he ran toward it, one hand holding the rim of his glasses, a sharp little pain digging into his side, but before he could reach the door he heard the screech of brakes, the single agonized scream, and the horrified shout of a hundred shrill voices.

He put his hand on the door, but could not find the strength to open it. A few minutes later, a cleaning woman had to sidle around him to get outside and see what all the excitement was about.

Miss Reardon, the substitute, took the Sixth Grade the next day, and, everything considered, handled it very well. The single ripple in the even current of the session came at its very start when Miss Reardon explained her presence by referring to the 'sad accident that happened to dear Miss Gildea.' The mild hubbub which followed this contained several voices, notably in the back of the room, which protested plaintively, 'It was *not* an accident, Miss Reardon; she ran right in front of that bus,' but Miss Reardon quickly brought order to the room with a few sharp raps of her ruler and after that, classwork was carried on in a pleasant and orderly fashion.

Robert walked home slowly that afternoon, swinging his schoolbag placidly at his side, savoring the June warmth soaking into him, the fresh green smell in the air, the memory of Miss Reardon's understanding face so often turned toward his in eager and friendly interest. His home was identical with all the others on the block, square white boxes with small lawns before them, and its only distinction was that all its blinds were drawn down. After he had closed the front door very quietly behind him, he set his schoolbag down in the hallway, and went into the stuffy half-darkness of the living room.

Robert's father sat in the big armchair in his bathrobe, the way he always did, and Robert's mother was bent over him holding a glass of water.

'No!' Robert's father said. 'You just want to get rid of me, but I won't let you! I know what you put into it, and I won't drink it! I'll die before I drink it!'

'Please,' Robert's mother said, 'please take it. I swear it's only water. I'll drink some myself if you don't believe me.' But when she drank a little and then held the glass to his lips, Robert's father only tossed his head from side to side.

Robert stood there watching the scene with fascination, his lips moving in silent mimicry of the familiar words. Then he cleared his throat.

'I'm home, Mama,' Robert said softly. 'Can I have some milk and cookies, please?'

# Unreasonable Doubt

Mr Willoughby found a seat in the club car and gingerly settled into it. So far, he reflected with overwhelming gratitude, the vacation was a complete success. Not a hint of the headaches he had lived with the past year. Not a suggestion of the iron band drawing tight around the skull, the gimlet boring into it, the hammers tapping away at it.

'Tension,' the doctor had said. 'Physically you're sound as a nut, but you sit over your desk all day worrying over one problem after another until your mind is as tight as a mainspring. Then you take the problems home and worry them to death there. Don't get much sleep, do you?'

Mr Willoughby admitted that he did not.

'I thought so,' said the doctor. 'Well, there's only one answer. A vacation. And I do mean a real vacation where you get away from it all. Seal your mind up. Don't let anything get into it but idle talk. Don't think about any problems at all. Don't even try a crossword puzzle. Just close your eyes and listen to the world go round. That'll do it,' he assured him.

And it *had* done it, as Mr Willoughby realized even after only one day of the treatment. And there were weeks of blissful relaxation ahead. Of course, it wasn't always easy to push aside every problem that came to mind. For example, there was a newspaper on the smoking table next to his chair right now, its headline partly revealing the words *NEW CRISIS IN* – Mr Willoughby hastily averted his head and thrust the paper into the rack beneath the table. A small triumph, but a pleasant one.

He was watching the rise and fall of the landscape outside the window, dreamily counting mileposts as they flashed by, when he first became aware of the voice at his elbow. The corner of his chair was backed up near that of his neighbor, a stout, white-haired man who was deep in talk with a companion. The stout man's voice was not loud, but it was penetrating. The voice, one might say, of a trained actor whose every whisper can be distinctly heard by the gallery. Even if one did not choose to be an eavesdropper it was impossible not to follow every word spoken. Mr Willoughby, however, deliberately chose to eavesdrop. The talk was largely an erudite discourse on legal matters; the stout man was apparently a lawyer of vast experience and uncanny recollective powers; and, all in all, the combination had the effect on Mr Willoughby of chamber music being played softly by skilled hands.

Then suddenly his ears pricked like a terrier's. 'The most interesting case I ever worked on?' the stout man was saying in answer to his companion's query. 'Well, sir, there's one I regard not only as the most interesting I ever handled, but which would have staggered any lawyer in history, right up to Solomon himself. It was the strangest, most fantastic, damnedest thing that ever came my way. And the way it wound up – the real surprise after it was supposedly over and done with – is enough to knock a man out of his chair when he thinks of it. But let me tell it to you just as it took place.'

Mr Willoughby slid down in his chair, pressed his heels into the floor, and surreptitiously closed the gap between his chair and his neighbor's. With his legs extended, his eyes closed, and his arms folded peaceably on his chest he was a fair representation of a man sound asleep. Actually, he had never been more wide awake in his life.

Naturally [the stout man said], I won't use the right names of any of these people, even though all this took place a long time ago. That's understandable when you realize it involves a murder for profit, beautifully planned, flawlessly executed, and aimed at making a travesty of everything written in the law books.

The victim – let's call him Hosea Snow – was the richest man in our town. An old-fashioned sort of man – I remember him wearing a black derby and a stiff collar on the hottest days in summer – he owned the bank, the mill, and a couple of other local interests. There wasn't any secret among folks as to how much he was worth. On the day of his death it came to about two million dollars. Considering how low taxes were in those days, and how much a dollar could buy, you can see why he was held in such high esteem.

His only family consisted of two nephews, his brother's sons, Ben and Orville. They represented the poor side of the family, you might say. When their father and mother died all that was left to them was a rundown old house which they lived in together.

Ben and Orville were nice-looking boys in their middle twenties about that time. Smooth-faced, regular features, much of a size and shape, they could have been a lot more popular than they were, but they deliberately kept apart from people. It wasn't that they were unfriendly – any time they passed you on the street they'd smile and give you the time of day – but they were sufficient unto themselves. Nowadays you hear a lot of talk about sibling rivalry and fraternal complexes, but it would never fit those two boys.

They worked in their uncle's bank, but their hearts were never in it. Even though they knew that when Hosea died his money would be divided between them it didn't seem to cheer the boys any. Fact is, Hosea was one of those dried-out, leathery specimens who are likely to go on forever. Looking forward to an inheritance from somebody like that can be a trying experience, and there's no question that the boys had been looking forward to that inheritance from the time they first knew what a dollar was worth.

But what they seemed to be concerned with, meanwhile, was something altogether different from banking and money – something Hosea himself could never understand or sympathize with, as he told me on more than one occasion. They wanted to be songwriters, and, for all I know, they had some talent for it. Whenever there was any affair in town that called for entertainment, Ben and Orville would show up with some songs they had written all by themselves. Nobody ever knew which of them did the words and which the music, and that in itself was one of the small mysteries about them that used to amuse the town. You can pretty well judge the size and disposition of the place if something like that was a conversation piece.

But the situation was all shaken up the day Hosea Snow was found dead in his big house, a bullet hole right square in the middle of his forehead. The first I heard of it was when a phone call got me out of bed early in the morning. It was the County Prosecutor telling me that Ben Snow had murdered his uncle during the night, had just been arrested, and was asking me to come to the jail right quick.

I ran over to the jail half dressed, and was pulled up short by the sight of Ben locked in a cell, reading a newspaper, and seemingly indifferent to the fact that he was on his way to a trapdoor with a rope around his neck.

'Ben,' I said, 'you didn't do it, did you?'

'They tell me I did,' he said in a matter-of-fact voice.

I don't know which bewildered me more – what he said or the unconcerned way he said it.

'What do you mean?' I asked him. 'And you'd better have a good story to tell me, boy, because you're in serious trouble.'

'Well,' he said, 'in the middle of the night the police and the Country Prosecutor walked in on Orville and me, because Uncle Hosea was killed, and after some talking they said I did it. When I got tired of them nagging me about it I said, all right, I did do it.'

'You mean,' I said, 'they've got evidence against you?'

He smiled. 'That'll come out in court,' he said. 'All you've got to do is call Orville as my witness at the trial, and you won't have any trouble. I'm not going to testify for myself, so they can't cross-examine me. But don't you worry any. Orville'll take care of everything.'

I felt a terrible suspicion creeping into my mind, but I didn't let myself consider it. 'Ben,' I said, 'have you and Orville been reading law books?'

'We've been looking into them,' he admitted. 'They're mighty interesting' – and that was all I could get out of him. I got even less from Orville when I went over to the bank and tried to talk to him about his testimony.

Considering that, you can imagine my state of mind when we finally came to trial. The case was the biggest sensation the town had ever known, the courthouse was packed, and here I was in the middle of things with no idea of what I could do for Ben, and Ben himself totally indifferent. I felt sick every time I got a look at the prosecutor's smug and smiling face. Not that I could blame him for looking like the cat that ate the canary. The crime was a brutal one, he and the police had solved it in jig time, and here he was with an airtight case.

In his opening address to the jury he threw the works at them. The motive was obvious: Ben Snow stood to inherit a million dollars from his uncle's death. The method was right there on the clerk's desk where everyone could see it: an old pistol that Ben Snow's father had left among his effects years before, and which was found – one bullet freshly discharged from it – right in the kitchen where Ben and Orville were drinking coffee when the police broke in on them. And the confession signed by Ben before witnesses settled things beyond the shadow of a doubt.

The only thing I could do in the face of this was put blind faith in Ben and do what he wanted me to. I had Orville Snow called as my first witness – and my only witness, too, as far as I could see – and then, without any idea of what he was going to say, I put him on the stand. He took the oath, sat down, straightened the crease in his trousers, and looked at me with the calm unconcern his brother had shown throughout the whole terrible business.

You see, I knew so little about the affair that it was hard to think of even a good opening question for him. Finally, I took the bull by the horns and said, 'Would you please tell the jury where you were on the night of the crime?'

'Glad to,' said Orville. 'I was in Uncle Hosea's house with a gun in my hand. If the police had only gotten to me before they started pestering Ben about this, I could have told them so right off. Fact is, I was the one who killed uncle.'

Talk about sensations in court! And in the middle of the uproar I saw Ben eagerly signaling me over to him. 'Now, whatever you do,' he whispered to me, 'don't you ask this trial be stopped. It's got to go to the jury, do you understand?'

I understood, all right. I had had my suspicions all along, but for the sake of my own conscience I just didn't want to heed them. Now I knew for sure, and for all I hated Ben and Orville right then, I had to admire them just a little bit. And it was that little bit of admiration which led me to play it Ben's way. With the prosecutor waiting hang-dog for me to ask that the trial be stopped I went back to Orville on the witness stand and had him go ahead with his story as if nothing spectacular had happened.

He told it like a master. He started 'way back when the desire for his uncle's money had seeped into his veins like a drug, and went along in detail right up to the killing itself. He had the jury hypnotized, and just to make sure the job was complete I wound up my closing speech by reminding them that all they needed in finding a man innocent was a reasonable doubt of his guilt.

'That is the law of this state,' I told them. 'Reasonable doubt. It is exactly what you are feeling now in the light of Orville Snow's confession that he alone committed the crime his brother was charged with!'

The police grabbed Orville right after the verdict of 'Not Guilty' was brought in. I saw him that evening in the small cell Ben had been kept in, and I already knew what he was going to tell me.

'Ben's my witness,' he said. 'Just keep me off the witness stand and let him do the talking.'

I said to him, 'One of you two killed your uncle, Orville. Don't you think that as your lawyer I ought to know which of you it was?'

'No, I don't,' said Orville, pleasantly enough.

'You're putting a lot of faith in your brother,' I told him. 'Ben's free and clear now. If he doesn't want to testify for you the way you did for him, he gets two million dollars and you get the gallows. Doesn't that worry you any?'

'No,' said Orville. 'If it worried us any we wouldn't have done it in the first place.'

'All right,' I said, 'if that's the way you want it. But tell me one thing, Orville, just for curiosity's sake. How did you decide which one of you should kill Hosea?'

'We cut cards,' said Orville, and that was the end of it, as far as I was concerned.

If Ben's trial had stirred up the town, Orville's had people coming in from all over the county. It was the prosecutor's turn to look sick now when he faced that crowd. He knew in his bones what was coming, and he couldn't do a blessed thing about it. More than that, he was honestly outraged at what looked to be an obscene mockery of the law. Ben and Orville Snow had found a loophole in justice, so to speak, and were on their way to sneaking through it. A jury couldn't convict a man if it had a reasonable doubt of his guilt; a man couldn't be retried for a crime when a jury has acquitted him of it; it wasn't even possible to indict the two boys together for conspiracy to commit murder, because that was a lesser charge in the murder indictment and covered by it. It was enough to make any prosecutor wild with frustration.

But this one held himself in check until Ben had finished telling his story to the jury. Ben told that story every bit as well as Orville had told his at the previous trial. He made it so graphic you could almost see him there in the room with his uncle, the gun flashing out death, the old man crumpling to the floor. The jurymen sat there spellbound, and the prosecutor chewed his nails to the quick while he watched them. Then when he faced Ben he really cut loose.

'Isn't this all a monstrous lie?' he shouted. 'How can you be innocent of this crime one day, and guilty of it the next?'

Ben raised his eyebrows. 'I never told anybody I was inno-cent,' he said indignantly. 'I've been saying right along I was guilty.'

There was no denying that. There was nothing in the record to dispute it. And I never felt so sure of myself, and so unhappy, as when I summed up the case for the jury. It took me just one minute, the quickest summing-up in my record.

'If I were sitting among you good people in that jury box,' I said, 'I know just what I'd be thinking. A heinous crime has been committed, and one of two men in this very courtroom has committed it. But I can take my oath that I don't know which of them it was, any more than you do, and like it or not I'd know I had to bring in a verdict of "Not Guilty."'

That was all they needed, too. They brought in their verdict even quicker than the jury had in Ben's case. And I had the dubious pleasure of seeing two young men, one of them guilty of murder, smilingly walk out of that room. As I said, I hated them, but I felt a sort of infuriated admiration for them too. They had gambled everything on their loyalty to each other, and the loyalty had stood the test of fire . . .

The stout man was silent. From his direction came the sound of a match striking, and then an eddy of expensive cigar smoke drifted under Mr Willoughby's nostrils. It was the pungent scent of the present dissolving the fascinating web of the past.

'Yes, sir,' the stout man said, and there was a depth of nostalgia in his voice, 'you'd have to go a long way to find a case to match that.'

'You mean,' said his companion, 'that they actually got away with it? That they found a way of committing the perfect murder?'

The stout man snorted. 'Perfect murder, bosh! That's where the final, fantastic surprise comes in. They *didn't* get away with it!'

'They didn't?'

'Of course not. You see, when they – good heavens, isn't this our station?' the stout man suddenly cried, and the next instant he went flying past Mr Willoughby's outstretched feet, briefcase in hand, overcoat flapping over his arm, companion in tow.

Mr Willoughby sat there dazed for a moment, his eyes wide open, his mouth dry, his heart hammering. Then he leaped to his feet – but it was too late: the men had disappeared from the car. He took a few frantic steps in the direction they had gone, realized it was pointless, then ran to a window of the car overlooking the station.

The stout man stood on the platform almost below him, buttoning his coat, and saying something to his companion. Mr Willoughby made a mighty effort to raise the window, but failed to budge it. Then he rapped on the pane with his knuckles, and the stout man looked up at him.

'H-o-w?' Mr Willoughby mouthed through the closed window, and saw with horror that the stout man did not understand him at all. Inspiration seized him. He made a pistol of his hand, aimed the extended forefinger at the stout man, and let his thumb fall like a hammer on a cartridge. 'Bang!' he yelled, 'Bang, bang! H-o-w?'

The stout man looked at him in astonishment, glanced at his companion, and then putting his own forefinger to his temple, made a slow circling motion. That was how Mr Willoughby last saw him as the train slowly, and then with increasing speed, pulled away.

It was when he moved away from the window that Mr Willoughby became aware of two things. One was that every face in the car was turned toward him with rapt interest. The other was that an iron band was drawing tight around his skull, a gimlet was boring in, tiny hammers were tapping at it.

It was, he knew with utter despair, going to be a perfectly terrible vacation.

# The Day of
# the Bullet

I believe that in each lifetime there is one day of destiny. It may be a day chosen by the Fates who sit clucking and crooning over a spinning wheel, or, perhaps, by the gods whose mill grinds slow, but grinds exceedingly fine. It may be a day of sunshine or rain, of heat or cold. It is probably a day which none of us is aware of at the time, or can even recall through hindsight.

But for every one of us there is that day. And when it leads to a bad end it's better not to look back and search it out. What you discover may hurt, and it's a futile hurt because nothing can be done about it any longer. Nothing at all.

I realize that there is a certain illogic in believing this, something almost mystical. Certainly it would win the ready disfavor of those modern exorcists and dabblers with crystal balls, those psychologists and sociologists and caseworkers who – using their own peculiar language to express it – believe that there may be a way of controlling the fantastic conjunction of time, place, and event that we must all meet at some invisible crossroads on the Day. But they are wrong. Like the rest of us they can only be wise after the event.

In this case – and the word 'case' is particularly fitting here – the event was the murder of a man I had not seen for thirty-five years. Not since a summer day in 1923, or, to be even more exact, the evening of a summer day in 1923 when as boys we faced each other on a street in Brooklyn, and then went our ways, never to meet again.

We were only twelve years old then, he and I, but I remember the date because the next day my family moved to Manhattan, an earth-shaking event in itself. And with dreadful clarity I remember the scene when we parted, and the last thing said there. I understand it now, and know it was that boy's Day. The Day of the Bullet, it might be called – although the bullet itself was not to be fired until thirty-five years later.

I learned about the murder from the front page of the newspaper my wife was reading at the breakfast table. She held the paper upright and partly folded, but the fold could not conceal from me the unappetizing picture on the front page, the photograph of a man slumped behind the wheel of his car, head clotted with blood, eyes staring and mouth gaping in the throes of violent and horrifying death.

The picture meant nothing to me, any more than did its shouting headline – *RACKETS BOSS SHOT TO DEATH*. All I thought, in fact, was that there were pleasanter objects to stare at over one's coffee and toast.

Then my eye fell on the caption below the picture, and I almost dropped my cup of coffee. *The body of Ignace Kovac*, said the caption, *Brooklyn rackets boss who last night—*

I took the paper from my wife's hand while she looked at me in astonishment, and studied the picture closely. There was no question about it. I had not seen Ignace Kovac since we were kids together, but I could not mistake him, even in the guise of this dead and bloody hulk. And the most terrible part of it, perhaps, was that next to him, resting against the seat of the car, was a bag of golf clubs. Those golf clubs were all my memory needed to work on.

I was called back to the present by my wife's voice. 'Well,' she said with good-natured annoyance, 'considering that I'm right in the middle of Walter Winchell—'

I returned the paper to her. 'I'm sorry. I got a jolt when I saw that picture. I used to know him.'

Her eyes lit up with the interest of one who – even at secondhand – finds herself in the presence of the notorious. 'You did? When?'

'Oh, when the folks still lived in Brooklyn. We were kids together. He was my best friend.'

My wife was an inveterate tease. 'Isn't that something? I never knew you hung around with juvenile delinquents when you were a kid.'

'He wasn't a juvenile delinquent. Matter of fact—'

'If you aren't the serious one.' She smiled at me in a kindly dismissal and went back to Winchell, who clearly offered fresher and more exciting tidings than mine. 'Anyhow,' she said, 'I wouldn't let it bother me too much, dear. That was a long time ago.'

It was a long time ago. You could play ball in the middle of the street then; few automobiles were to be seen in the far reaches of Brooklyn in 1923. And Bath Beach, where I lived, was one of the farthest reaches. It fronted on Gravesend Bay with Coney Island to the east a few minutes away by trolley car, and Dyker Heights and its golf course to the west a few minutes away by foot. Each was an entity separated from Bath Beach by a wasteland of weedgrown lots which building contractors had not yet discovered.

So, as I said, you could play ball in the streets without fear of traffic. Or you could watch the gaslighter turning up the street lamps at dusk. Or you could wait around the firehouse on Eighteenth Avenue until, if you were lucky enough, an alarm would send three big horses there slewing the pump-engine out into the street in a spray of sparks from iron-shod wheels. Or, miracle of miracles, you could stand gaping up at the sky to follow the flight of a biplane proudly racketing along overhead.

Those were the things I did that summer, along with Iggy Kovac, who was my best friend, and who lived in the house next door. It was a two-story frame house painted in some sedate color, just as mine was. Most of the houses in Bath Beach were like that, each with a small garden in front and yard in back. The only example of ostentatious architecture on our block was the house on the corner owned by Mr Rose, a newcomer to the neighborhood. It was huge and stuccoed, almost a mansion, surrounded by an enormous lawn, and with a stuccoed two-car garage at the end of its driveway.

That driveway held a fascination for Iggy and me. On it, now and then, would be parked Mr Rose's automobile, a gray Packard, and it was the car that drew us like a magnet. It was not only beautiful to look at from the distance, but close up it loomed over us like a locomotive, giving off an aura of thunderous power even as it stood there quietly. And it had *two* running boards, one mounted over the other to make the climb into the tonneau easier. In fact, no one we knew had a car anywhere near as wonderful as that Packard.

So we would sneak down the driveway when it was parked there, hoping for a chance to mount those running boards without being caught. We never managed to do it. It seemed that an endless vigil was being kept over that car, either by Mr Rose himself or by someone who lived in the rooms over the garage. As soon as we were no more than a few yards down the driveway a window would open in the house or the garage, and a hoarse voice would bellow threats at us. Then we would turn tail and race down the driveway and out of sight.

We had not always done that. The first time we had seen the car we had sauntered up to it quite casually, all in the spirit of good neighbors, and had not even understood the nature of the threats. We only stood there and looked up in astonishment at Mr Rose, until he suddenly left the window and reappeared before us to grab Iggy's arm.

Iggy tried to pull away and couldn't. 'Leggo of me!' he said in a high-pitched, frightened voice. 'We weren't doing anything to your ole car! Leggo of me, or I'll tell my father on you. Then you'll see what'll happen!'

This did not seem to impress Mr Rose. He shook Iggy back and forth – not hard to do because Iggy was small and skinny even for his age – while I stood there, rooted to the spot in horror.

There were some cranky people in the neighborhood who would chase us away when we made any noise in front of their houses, but nobody had ever handled either of us the way Mr Rose was doing. I remember having some vague idea that it was because he was new around here, he didn't know yet how people around here were supposed to act, and when I look back now I think I may have been surprisingly close to the truth. But whatever the exact reasons for the storm he raised, it was enough of a storm to have Iggy blubbering out loud, and to make us approach the Packard warily after that. It was too much of a magnet to resist, but once we were on Mr Rose's territory we were like a pair of rabbits crossing open ground during the hunting season. And with just about as much luck.

I don't want to give the impression by all this that we were bad kids. For myself, I was acutely aware of the letter of the law, and had early discovered that the best course for anyone who was good-natured, pacific, and slow afoot – all of which I was in extra measure – was to try and stay within bounds. And Iggy's vices were plain high spirits and recklessness. He was like quicksilver and was always on the go and full of mischief.

And smart. Those were the days when at the end of each school week your marks were appraised and you would be reseated according to your class standing – best students in the first row, next best in the second row, and so on. And I think the thing that best explains Iggy was the way his position in class would fluctuate between the first and sixth rows. Most of us never moved more than one row either way at the end of the week; Iggy would suddenly be shoved from the first row to the ignominy of the sixth, and then the Friday after would just as suddenly ascend the heights back to the first row. That was the sure sign that Mr Kovac had got wind of the bad tidings and had taken measures.

Not physical measures, either. I once asked Iggy about that, and he said, 'Nah, he don't wallop me, but he kind of says don't be so dumb, and, well – you know—'

I did know, because I suspect that I shared a good deal of Iggy's feeling for Mr Kovac, a fervent hero worship. For one thing, most of the fathers in the neighborhood 'worked in the city' – to use the Bath Beach phrase – meaning that six days a week they ascended the Eighteenth Avenue station of the BMT and were borne off to desks in Manhattan. Mr Kovac, on the other hand, was a conductor on the Bath Avenue trolleycar line, a powerful and imposing figure in his official cap and blue uniform with the brass buttons on it. The cars on the Bath Avenue line were without side walls, closely lined with benches from front to back, and were manned by conductors who had to swing along narrow platforms on the outside to collect fares.

It was something to see Mr Kovac in action. The only thing comparable was the man who swung himself around a Coney Island merry-go-round to take your tickets.

And for another thing, most of the fathers – at least when they had reached the age mine had – were not much on athletics, while Mr Kovac was a terrific baseball player. Every fair Sunday afternoon down at the little park by the bay there was a pick-up ball game where the young fellows of the neighborhood played a regulation nine innings on a marked-off diamond, and Mr Kovac was always the star. As far as Iggy and I were concerned, he could pitch like Vance and hit like Zack Wheat, and no more than that could be desired. It was something to watch Iggy when his father was at bat. He'd sit chewing his nails right through every windup of the pitcher, and if Mr Kovac came through with a hit, Iggy would be up and screaming so loud you'd think your head was coming off.

Then after the game was over we'd hustle a case of pop over to the team, and they would sit around on the park benches and talk things over. Iggy was his father's shadow then; he'd be hanging around that close to him, taking it all in and eating it up. I wasn't so very far away myself, but since I couldn't claim possession as Iggy could, I amiably kept at a proper distance. And when I went home those afternoons it seemed to me that my father looked terribly stodgy, sitting there on the porch the way he did, with loose pages of the Sunday paper around him.

When I first learned that I was going to have to leave all this, that my family was going to move from Brooklyn to Manhattan, I was completely dazed. Manhattan was a place where on occasional Saturday afternoons you went, all dressed up in your best suit, to shop with your mother at Wanamakers or Macy's, or, with luck, went to the Hippodrome with your father, or maybe to the Museum of Natural History. It had never struck me as a place where people *lived*.

But as the days went by my feelings changed, became a sort of apprehensive excitement. After all, I was doing something pretty heroic, pushing off into the Unknown this way, and the glamor of it was brought home to me by the way the kids on the block talked to me about it.

However, none of that meant anything the day before we moved. The house looked strange with everything in it packed and crated and bundled together; my mother and father were in a harried state of mind; and the knowledge of impending change – it was the first time in my life I had ever moved from one house to another – now had me scared stiff.

That was the mood I was in when after an early supper I pushed through the opening in the hedge between our back yard and the Kovacs', and sat down on the steps before their kitchen door. Iggy came out and sat down beside me. He could see how I felt, and it must have made him uncomfortable.

'Jeez, don't be such a baby,' he said. 'It'll be great, living in the city. Look at all the things you'll have to see there.'

I told him I didn't want to see anything there.

'All right, then don't,' he said. 'You want to read something good? I got a new Tarzan, and I got *The Boy Allies at Jutland*. You can have your pick, and I'll take the other one.'

This was a more than generous offer, but I said I didn't feel like reading, either.

'Well, we can't just sit here being mopey,' Iggy said reasonably. 'Let's do something. What do you want to do?'

This was the opening of the ritual where by rejecting various possibilities – it was too late to go swimming, too hot to play ball, to early to go into the house – we would arrive at a choice. We dutifully went through this process of elimination, and it was Iggy as usual who came up with the choice.

'I know,' he said. 'Let's go over to Dyker Heights and fish for golf balls. It's pretty near the best time now, anyhow.'

He was right about that, because the best time to fish for balls that had been driven into the lone water hazard of the course and never recovered by their owners was at sunset when, chances were, the place would be deserted but there would still be enough light to see by. The way we did this kind of fishing was to pull off our sneakers and stockings, buckle our knickerbockers over our knees, then slowly and speculatively wade through the ooze of the pond, trying to feel out sunken golf balls with our bare feet. It was pleasant work, and occasionally profitable, because the next day any ball you found could be sold to a passing golfer for five cents. I don't remember how we came to fix on the price of five cents as a fair one, but there it was. The golfers seemed to be satisfied with it, and we certainly were.

In all our fishing that summer I don't believe we found more than a total of half a dozen balls, but thirty cents was largesse in those days. My share went fast enough for anything that struck my fancy: Iggy, however, had a great dream. What he wanted more than anything else in the world was a golf club, and every cent he could scrape together was deposited in a tin can with a hole punched in its top and its seam bound with bicycle tape.

He would never open the can, but would shake it now and then to estimate its contents. It was his theory that when the can was full to the top it would hold just about enough to pay for the putter he had picked out in the window of Leo's Sporting Goods Store on 86th Street. Two or three times a week he would have me walk with him down to Leo's, so that we could see the putter, and in between he would talk about it at length, and demonstrate the proper grip for holding it, and the way you have to line up a long putt on a rolling green. Iggy Kovac was the first person I knew – I have known many since – who was really golf crazy. But I think that his case was the most unique, considering that at the time he had never in his life even had his hands on a real club.

So that evening, knowing how he felt about it, I said all right, if he wanted to go fish for golf balls I would go with him. It wasn't much of a walk down Bath Avenue; the only hard part was when we entered the course at its far side where we had to climb over mountains of what was politely called 'fill.' It made hot and smoky going, then there was a swampy patch, and finally the course itself and the water hazard.

I've never been back there since that day, but not long ago I happened to read an article about the Dyker Heights golf course in some magazine or other. According to the article, it was now the busiest public golf course in the world. Its eighteen well-kept greens were packed with players from dawn to dusk, and on weekends you had to get in line at the clubhouse at three or four o'clock in the morning if you wanted a chance to play a round.

Well, each to his own taste, but it wasn't like that when Iggy and I used to fish for golf balls there. For one thing, I don't think it had eighteen holes; I seem to remember it as a nine-hole layout. For another thing, it was usually pretty empty, either because not many people in Brooklyn played golf in those days, or because it was not a very enticing spot at best.

The fact is, it smelled bad. They were reclaiming the swampy land all around it by filling it with refuse, and the smoldering fires in the refuse laid a black pall over the place. No matter when you went there, there was that dirty haze in the air around you, and in a few minutes you'd find your eyes smarting and your nose full of a curious acrid smell.

Not that we minded it, Iggy and I. We accepted it casually as part of the scenery, as much a part as the occasional Mack truck loaded with trash that would rumble along the dirt road to the swamp, its chain-drive chattering and whining as it went. The only thing we did mind sometimes was the heat of the refuse underfoot when we climbed over it. We never dared enter the course from the clubhouse side; the attendant there had once caught us in the pond trying to plunder his preserve, and we knew he had us marked. The back entrance may have been hotter, but it was the more practical way in.

When we reached the pond there was no one else in sight. It was a hot, still evening with a flaming red sun now dipping toward the horizon, and once we had our sneakers and stockings off – long, black cotton stockings they were – we wasted no time wading into the water. It felt good, too, as did the slick texture of the mud oozing up between my toes when I pressed down. I suspect that I had the spirit of the true fisherman in me then. The pleasure lay in the activity, not in the catch.

Still, the catch made a worthy objective, and the idea was to walk along with slow, probing steps, and to stop whenever you felt anything small and solid underfoot. I had just stopped short with the excited feeling that I had pinned down a golf ball in the muck when I heard the sound of a motor moving along the dirt track nearby. My first thought was that it was one of the dump trucks carrying another load to add to the mountain of fill, but then I knew that it didn't sound like a Mack truck.

I looked around to see what kind of car it was, still keeping my foot planted on my prize, but the row of bunkers between the pond and the road blocked my view. Then the sound of the motor suddenly stopped, and that was all I needed to send me splashing out of the water in a panic. All Iggy needed, too, for that matter. In one second we had grabbed up our shoes and stockings and headed around the corner of the nearest bunker where we would be out of sight. In about five more seconds we had our stockings and shoes on without even bothering to dry our legs, ready to take flight if anyone approached.

The reason we moved so fast was simply that we weren't too clear about our legal right to fish for golf balls. Iggy and I had talked it over a couple of times, and while he vehemently maintained that we had every right to – there were the balls, with nobody but the dopey caretaker doing anything about it – he admitted that the smart thing was not to put the theory to the test, but to work at our trade unobserved. And I am sure that when the car stopped nearby he had the same idea I did: somebody had reported us, and now the long hand of authority was reaching out for us.

So we waited, crouching in breathless silence against the grassy wall of the bunker, until Iggy could not contain himself any longer. He crawled on hands and knees to the corner of the bunker and peered around it toward the road. 'Holy smoke, look at that!' he whispered in an awed voice, and waggled his hand at me to come over.

I looked over his shoulder, and with shocked disbelief I saw a gray Packard, a car with double running boards, one mounted over the other, the only car of its kind I had ever seen. There was no mistaking it, and there was no mistaking Mr Rose who stood with two men near it, talking to the smaller one of them, and making angry chopping motions of his hands as he talked.

Looking back now, I think that what made the scene such a strange one was its setting. There was the deserted golf course all around us, and the piles of smoldering fill in the distance, everything seeming so raw and uncitylike and made crimson by the setting sun; and there in the middle of it was this sleek car and the three men with straw hats and jackets and neckties, all looking completely out of place.

Even more fascinating was the smell of danger around them, because while I couldn't hear what was being said I could see that Mr Rose was in the same mood he had been in when he caught Iggy and me in his driveway. The big man next to him said almost nothing, but the little man Mr Rose was talking to shook his head, tried to answer, and kept backing away slowly, so that Mr Rose had to follow him. Then suddenly the little man wheeled around and ran right toward the bunker where Iggy and I lay hidden. We ducked back, but he ran past the far side of it, and he was almost past the pond when the big man caught up with him and grabbed him, Mr Rose running up after them with his hat in his hand. That is when we could have got away without being seen, but we didn't. We crouched there spellbound, watching something we would never have dreamed of seeing – grownups having it out right in front of us the way it happens in the movies.

I was, as I have said, twelve years old that summer. I can now mark it as the time I learned that there was a difference between seeing things in the movies and seeing them in real life. Because never in watching the most bruising movie, with Tom Mix or Hoot Gibson or any of my heroes, did I feel what I felt there watching what happened to that little man. And I think that Iggy must have felt it even more acutely than I did, because he was so small and skinny himself, and while he was tough in a fight he was always being outweighed and overpowered. He must have felt that he was right there inside that little man, his arms pinned tight behind his back by the bully who had grabbed him, while Mr Rose hit him back and forth with an open hand across the face, snarling at him all the while.

'You dirty dog,' Mr Rose said. 'Do you know who I am? Do you think I'm one of those lousy small-time bootleggers you double-cross for the fun of it? *This* is who I am!' And with the little man screaming and kicking out at him he started punching away as hard as he could at the belly and face until the screaming and kicking suddenly stopped. Then he jerked his head toward the pond, and his pal heaved the little man right into it headfirst, the straw hat flying off and bobbing up and down in the water a few feet away.

They stood watching until the man in the water managed to get on his hands and knees, blowing out dirty water, shaking his head in a daze, and then without another word they walked off toward the car. I heard its doors slam, and the roar of the motor as it moved off, and then the sound faded away.

All I wanted to do then was get away from there. What I had just seen was too much to comprehend or even believe in; it was like waking up from a nightmare to find it real. Home was where I wanted to be.

I stood up cautiously, but before I could scramble off to home and safety, Iggy clutched the back of my shirt so hard that he almost pulled me down on top of him.

'What're you doing?' he whispered hotly. 'Where do you think you're going?'

I pulled myself free. 'Are you crazy?' I whispered back. 'You expect to hang around here all night? I'm going home, that's where I'm going.'

Iggy's face was ashy white, his nostrils flaring. 'But that guy's hurt. You just gonna let him stay there?'

'Sure I'm gonna let him stay there. What's it my business?'

'You saw what happened. You think it's right to beat up a guy like that?'

What he said and the way he said it in a tight, choked voice made me wonder if he really had gone crazy just then. I said weakly, 'It's none of my business, that's all. Anyhow, I have to go home. My folks'll be sore if I don't get home on time.'

Iggy pointed an accusing finger at me. 'All right, if that's the way you feel!' he said, and then before I could stop him he turned and dashed out of concealment toward the pond. Whether it was the sense of being left alone in a hostile world, or whether it was some wild streak of loyalty that acted on me, I don't know. But I hesitated only an instant and then ran after him.

He stood at the edge of the pond looking at the man in it who was still on his hands and knees and shaking his head vaguely from side to side. 'Hey, mister,' Iggy said, and there was none of the assurance in his voice that there had been before, 'are you hurt?'

The man looked slowly around at us, and his face was fearful to behold. It was bruised and swollen and glassy-eyed, and his dripping hair hung in long strings down his forehead. It was enough to make Iggy and me back up a step, the way he looked.

With a great effort he pushed himself to his feet and stood there swaying. Then he lurched forward, staring at us blindly, and we hastily backed up a few more steps. He stopped short and suddenly reached down and scooped up a handful of mud from under the water.

'Get out of here!' he cried like a woman screaming. 'Get out of here, you little sneaks!' – and without warning flung the mud at us.

It didn't hit me, but it didn't have to. I let out one yell of panic and ran wildly, my heart thudding, my legs pumping as fast as they could. Iggy was almost at my shoulder – I could hear him gasping as we climbed the smoldering hill of refuse that barred the way to the avenue, slid down the other side in a cloud of dirt and ashes, and raced toward the avenue without looking back. It was only when we reached the first street-light that we stopped and stood there trembling, our mouths wide open, trying to suck in air, our clothes fouled from top to bottom.

But the shock I had undergone was nothing compared to what I felt when Iggy finally got his wind back enough to speak up.

'Did you see that guy?' he said, still struggling for breath. 'Did you see what they did to him? Come on, I'm gonna tell the cops.'

I couldn't believe my ears. 'The cops? What do you want to get mixed up with the cops for? What do you care what they did to him, for Pete's sake?'

'Because they beat him up, didn't they? And the cops can stick them in jail for fifty years if somebody tells them, and I'm a witness. I saw what happened and so did you. So you're a witness too.'

I didn't like it. I certainly had no sympathy for the evil-looking apparition from which I had just fled, and, more than that, I balked at the idea of having anything to do with the police. It was just that, like most other kids I knew, I was nervous in the presence of a police uniform. It left me even more mystified by Iggy than ever. The idea of any kid voluntarily walking up to report something to a policeman was beyond comprehension.

275

I said bitterly, 'All right, so I'm a witness. But why can't the guy that got beat up go and tell the cops about it? Why do we have to go and do it?'

'Because he wouldn't tell anybody about it. Didn't you see the way he was scared of Mr Rose? You think it's all right for Mr Rose to go around like that, beating up anybody he wants to, and nobody does anything about it?'

Then I understood. Beneath all this weird talk, this sudden display of nobility, was solid logic, something I could get hold of. It was not the man in the water Iggy was concerned with, it was himself. Mr Rose had pushed *him* around, and now he had a perfect way of getting even.

I didn't reveal this thought to Iggy, though, because when your best friend has been shoved around and humiliated in front of you, you don't want to remind him of it. But at least it put everything into proper perspective. Somebody hurts you, so you hurt him back, and that's all there is to it.

It also made it much easier to go along with Iggy in his plan. I wasn't really being called on to ally myself with some stupid grownup who had got into trouble with Mr Rose; I was being a good pal to Iggy.

All of a sudden, the prospect of walking into the police station and telling my story to somebody seemed highly intriguing. And, the reassuring thought went, far in back of my head, none of this could mean trouble for me later on, because tomorrow I was moving to Manhattan anyhow; wasn't I?

So I was right there, a step behind Iggy, when we walked up between the two green globes which still seemed vaguely menacing to me, and into the police station. There was a tall desk there, like a judge's bench, at which a gray-haired man sat writing, and at its foot was another desk at which sat a very fat uniformed man reading a magazine. He put the magazine down when we approached and looked at us with raised eyebrows.

'Yeah?' he said. 'What's the trouble?'

I had been mentally rehearsing a description of what I had seen back there on the golf course, but I never had a chance to speak my piece. Iggy started off with a rush, and there was no way of getting a word in. The fat man listened with a puzzled expression, every now and then pinching his lower lip between his thumb and forefinger. Then he looked up at the one behind the tall desk and said, 'Hey, sergeant, here's a couple of kids say they saw an assault over at Dyker Heights. You want to listen to this?'

The sergeant didn't even look at us, but kept on writing. 'Why?' he said. 'What's wrong with your ears?'

The fat policeman leaned back in his chair and smiled. 'I don't know,' he said, 'only it seems to me some guy named Rose is mixed up in this.'

The sergeant suddenly stopped writing. 'What's that?' he said.

'Some guy named Rose,' the fat policeman said, and he appeared to be enjoying himself a good deal. 'You know anybody with that name who drives a big gray Packard?'

The sergeant motioned with his head for us to come right up to the platform his desk was on. 'All right, kid,' he said to Iggy, 'what's bothering you?'

So Iggy went through it again, and when he was finished the sergeant just sat there looking at him, tapping his pen on the desk. He looked at him so long and kept tapping that pen so steadily – tap, tap, tap – that my skin started to crawl. It didn't surprise me when he finally said to Iggy in a hard voice, 'You're a pretty wise kid.'

'What do you mean?' Iggy said. 'I saw it!' He pointed at me. 'He saw it, too. He'll tell you!'

I braced myself for the worst and then noted with relief that the sergeant was paying no attention to me. He shook his head at Iggy and said, 'I do the telling around here, kid. And I'm telling you you've got an awful big mouth for someone your size. Don't you have more sense than to go around trying to get people into trouble?'

This, I thought, was the time to get away from there, because if I ever needed proof that you don't mix into grownup business I had it now. But Iggy didn't budge. He was always pretty good at arguing himself out of spots where he was wrong; now that he knew he was right he was getting hot with outraged virtue.

'Don't you believe me?' he demanded. 'For Pete's sake, I was right there when it happened! I was this close!'

The sergeant looked like a thundercloud. 'All right, you were that close,' he said. 'Now beat it, kid, and keep that big mouth shut. I got no time to fool around any more. Go on, get out of here!'

Iggy was so enraged that not even the big gold badge a foot from his nose could intimidate him now. 'I don't care if you don't believe me. Wait'll I tell my father. You'll see!'

I could hear my ears ringing in the silence that followed. The sergeant sat staring at Iggy, and Iggy, a little scared by his own outburst, stared back. He must have had the same idea I did then. Yelling at a cop was probably as bad as hitting one, and we'd both end up in jail for the rest of our lives. Not for a second did I feel any of the righteous indignation Iggy did. As far as I was concerned, he had led me into this trap, and I was going to pay for his lunacy. I guess I hated him then even more than the sergeant did.

It didn't help any when the sergeant finally turned to the fat policeman with the air of a man who had made up his mind.

'Take the car and drive over to Rose's place,' he said. 'You can explain all this to him, and ask him to come along back with you. Oh yes, and get this kid's name and address, and bring his father along, too. Then we'll see.'

So I had my first and only experience of sitting on a bench in a police station watching the pendulum of the big clock on the wall swinging back and forth, and recounting all my past sins to myself. It couldn't have been more than a half hour before the fat policeman walked in with Mr Rose and Iggy's father, but it seemed like a year. And a long, miserable year at that.

The surprising thing was the way Mr Rose looked. I had half expected them to bring him in fighting and struggling, because while the sergeant may not have believed Iggy's story, Mr Rose would know it was so.

But far from struggling, Mr Rose looked as if he had dropped in for a friendly visit. He was dressed in a fine summer suit and sporty-looking black-and-white shoes and he was smoking a cigar. He was perfectly calm and pleasant, and, in some strange way, he almost gave the impression that he was in charge there.

It was different with Iggy's father. Mr Kovac must have been reading the paper out on the porch in his undershirt, because his regular shirt had been stuffed into his pants carelessly and part of it hung out. And from his manner you'd think that he was the one who had done something wrong. He kept swallowing hard, and twisting his neck in his collar, and now and then glancing nervously at Mr Rose. He didn't look at all impressive as he did at other times.

The sergeant pointed at Iggy. 'All right, kid,' he said, 'Now tell everybody here what you told me. Stand up so we can all hear it.'

Since Iggy had already told it twice he really had it down pat now, and he told it without a break from start to finish, no one interrupting him. And all the while Mr Rose stood there listening politely, and Mr Kovac kept twisting his neck in his collar.

When Iggy was finished the sergeant said, 'I'll put it to you straight out, Mr Rose. Were you near that golf course today?'

Mr Rose smiled. 'I was not.'

'Of course not,' said the sergeant. 'But you can see what we're up against.'

'Sure I can,' said Mr Rose. He went over to Iggy and put a hand on his shoulder. 'And you know what?' he said. 'I don't even blame the kid for trying this trick. He and I had a little trouble some time back about the way he was always climbing over my car, and I guess he's just trying to get square with me. I'd say he's got a lot of spirit in him. Don't you, sonny?' he asked, squeezing Iggy's shoulder in a friendly way.

I was stunned by the accuracy of this shot, but Iggy reacted like a firecracker going off. He pulled away from Mr Rose's hand and ran over to his father. 'I'm *not* lying!' he said desperately and grabbed Mr Kovac's shirt, tugging at it. 'Honest to God, pop, we both saw it. Honest to God, pop!'

Mr Kovac looked down at him and then looked around at all of us. When his eyes were on Mr Rose it seemed as if his collar were tighter than ever. Meanwhile, Iggy was pulling at his shirt, yelling that we saw it, we saw it, and he wasn't lying, until Mr Kovac shook him once, very hard, and that shut him up.

'Iggy,' said Mr Kovac, 'I don't want you to go around telling stories about people. Do you hear me?'

Iggy heard him, all right. He stepped back as if he had been walloped across the face, and then stood there looking at Mr Kovac in a funny way. He didn't say anything, didn't even move when Mr Rose came up and put a hand on his shoulder again.

'You heard your father, didn't you, kid?' Mr Rose said.

Iggy still didn't say anything.

'Sure you did,' Mr Rose said. 'And you and I understand each other a lot better now, kiddo, so there's no hard feelings. Matter of fact, any time you want to come over to the house you come on over, and I'll bet there's plenty of odd jobs you can do there. I pay good, too, so don't you worry about that.' He reached into his pocket and took out a bill. 'Here,' he said, stuffing it into Iggy's hand, 'this'll give you an idea. Now go on out and have yourself some fun.'

Iggy looked at the money like a sleepwalker. I was baffled by that. As far as I could see, this was a triumph, and here was Iggy in a daze, instead of openly rejoicing. It was only when the sergeant spoke to us that he seemed to wake up.

'All right, you kids,' the sergeant said, 'beat it home now. The rest of us got some things to talk over.'

I didn't need a second invitation. I got out of there in a hurry and went down the street fast, with Iggy tagging along behind me not saying a word. It was three blocks down and one block over, and I didn't slow down until I was in front of my house again. I had never appreciated those familiar outlines and lights in the windows any more than I did at that moment. But I didn't go right in. It suddenly struck me that this was the last time I'd be seeing Iggy, so I waited there awkwardly. I was never very good at goodbyes.

'That was all right,' I said finally. 'I mean Mr Rose giving you that dollar. That's as good as twenty golf balls.'

'Yeah?' said Iggy, and he was looking at me in the same funny way he had looked at his father. 'I'll bet it's as good as a whole new golf club. Come on down to Leo's with me, and I'll show you.'

I wanted to, but I wanted to get inside the house even more. 'Ahh, my folks'll be sore if I stay out too late tonight,' I said. 'Anyhow, you can't buy a club for a dollar. You'll need way more than that.'

'You think so?' Iggy said, and then held out his hand and

slowly opened it so that I could see what he was holding. It was not a one-dollar bill. It was, to my awe, a five-dollar bill.

That, as my wife said, was a long time ago. Thirty-five years before a photograph was taken of little Ignace Kovac, a man wise in the way of the rackets, slumped in a death agony over the wheel of his big car, a bullet hole in the middle of his forehead, a bag of golf clubs leaning against the seat next to him. Thirty-five years before I understood the meaning of the last things said and done when we faced each other on a street in Brooklyn, and then went off, each in his own direction.

I gaped at the money in Iggy's hand. It was the hoard of Croesus, and its very magnitude alarmed me.

'Hey,' I said. 'That's five bucks. That's a lot of money! You better give it to your old man, or he'll really jump on you.'

Then I saw to my surprise that the hand holding the money was shaking. Iggy was suddenly shuddering all over as if he had just plunged into icy water.

'My old man?' he yelled wildly at me, and his lips back showing his teeth clenched together hard, as if that could stop the shuddering. 'You know what I'll do if my old man tries anything? I'll tell Mr Rose on him, that's what! Then you'll see!'

And wheeled and ran blindly away from me down the street to his destiny.

# Beidenbauer's Flea

I was seated on a bench in Central Park, half drowsing in the autumn sunlight, when a strange figure approached – the cadaverous figure of a man who bore himself with the grandeur of an ancient matinee idol. As he walked, he swung a malacca stick with practiced ease. His hair was snowy-white and swept back almost to his collar, and on it was cocked with indescribable panache a battered homburg. His tight-waisted, velveteen-collared overcoat was long out of fashion and badly frayed at the cuffs. His narrow-toed, patent-leather shoes were scuffed and down at the heels. Yet, so noble was his demeanor and so profound the sorrow written on his lined face that I found myself pitying his curious garb, rather than being moved to scorn by it.

He sat down beside me, propped his stick between his legs, and said, 'It is a beautiful day, is it not?'

'Yes,' I said, 'it is.' Then I felt a sudden apprehension. I am too easy a mark for the wayfarer's sad story, his melting eyes, his extended palm. I have never learned to say no to the humble derelict who stops me with hat in hand and asks for carfare to places he never intends to visit. Now I had the feeling that I knew what was coming, and I drew a tight rein on my susceptibilities. This time, I silently resolved, I would escape before it was too late.

But there was no escape. As I started to rise, my companion placed a hand on my shoulder and gently pressed me back into my seat. 'It is a beautiful day,' he said, 'but what does that matter to one who is doomed to suffer and search, search and suffer through every day of his life, fair or foul?'

I was resigned to my fate, but in a bitter mood. He might tell his story to the end, but when he held out his hand for the expected offering he would get nothing more than a handshake. That much I took my oath on.

'Evidently,' I said, concealing my true emotions with an effort, 'you are spending your life in a search for something. What is that something?'

'A flea.'

'A flea?'

The aged curio nodded somberly. 'Yes, strange as it seems, that is the object of my search. But perhaps you will understand more readily if I reveal my name to you. It is Beidenbauer. Thaddeus Beidenbauer. There, does that enlighten you?'

He looked at me eagerly, but the light in his eyes faded when I shook my head. 'No,' I said, 'I'm sorry to say it doesn't.'

'It doesn't?'

'I'm afraid not.'

Beidenbauer sighed. 'Well, such is fame. A bubble – a glittering, weightless thing that one holds briefly in hand, and then – but let me tell you my story. There is pain and heartbreak in it, but I am inured to that now. I have lived my tragedy over and over so many times in my waking dreams that I can bear to talk about it freely when the occasion arises. I will tell it all to you just as it happened.'

'I am sure you will,' I said.


There was a time [Beidenbauer said] when my name was known in every mighty city of the world, when I was petted and sought after by the great, when I was drunk each day with my youth and wealth and the joy of my lot. Ah, I should have thought then how the gods destroy those who are too proud, but I did not. I lived only with the happy realization that I was the proprietor of Beidenbauer's Mighty Mites, the greatest flea circus on earth, the one that did more to honor the vast and unsung talents of the flea than any other before or since.

There have been flea circuses before mine and after mine, but always shabby affairs, dismal two-penny entertainments with none of the true glamor of the stage invested in them. But mine was different. It was superlative theater. Whether performed before the bumpkins who attend touring carnivals or before a soiree of society's bluest blue-bloods, it never failed to stir the audience to its depths, to bring it to its feet shouting for endless encores. And all because as a mere child I had learned the secret of the relationship between the flea and the trainer, and with infinite patience had put the secret to work.

I can see you are wondering what the secret is; you will be astonished to learn of its simplicity. There is a strange and wonderful symbiosis between flea and man. The flea feeds from its trainer's arm and thus strengthened goes into the arena to perform. The money earned this way is then used by the trainer to buy him his dinner, to enrich his blood, that the performer may feed and return to his performance. So we have a perfect cycle, flea and man feeding off each other, each contributing to their mutual existence.

That is all there is to it, but I was the one to discover that there must be more than mere food involved in this relationship. There must be a symbiosis of emotions as well. Respect, sympathy, understanding, and love – yes, love – must be there, for the flea, a quivering mass of sensitivity, needs them desperately. And unlike all other trainers, I provided them. Cruelty was the rule elsewhere. The harsh word, the heavy hand – these were all my confreres knew in trying to master and instruct the flea. But kindness was my rule, and for that reason I soared to success while all others remained mired in failure.

But enough of myself; after all, it was not I who entered the spotlighted ring every day to perform, to act the clown so that the crowd roared with laughter, to risk my neck in acrobatics so that it gasped, to woo it with grace so that it sighed in rapture. All this was done by the fleas, and it is they who must get the lion's share of admiration.

There were twenty-four members of the troupe, hand-picked, trained for weary hours on end, and it is impossible to imagine the range of their talents. But the unchallenged star of the show, and, sorrow of sorrows, the star of the tragedy I am unfolding, was a flea named Sebastian. Small, volatile, full of riotous wit and invention, he was our featured clown. And he was a true star in every respect. Tense and withdrawn before a performance, he was at ease the instant the spotlight fell on him and in absolute command of the audience.

I can see him now, waiting behind the scenes as the white silk handkerchief was laid on the table and tacks driven into each of its four corners to moor it securely. Then, as the darning hoop which was our main ring was set on it, Sebastian would fretfully start to pace up and down, his mouth drawn tight, his eyes faraway, fighting the fears reborn in him at every performance. I knew those signs, and I would give him a little nod – just one small nod – to make clear my confidence in him. And he would respond with a little nod of his own to show that he understood. It was our private ritual, those two almost imperceptible gestures, and it was all that was ever needed to assure another sterling performance from him. That, and the knowledge that the prima ballerina of our company, an enchanting, doe-eyed little flea named Selina, had eyes only for him and would stand worshipping from afar while he held the spotlight. For Selina, I think, was the only one on earth other than myself to whom he gave his unquestioning devotion.

But, alas, what he did not know at the time, and what I did not know – such is the cruel deviousness of the female heart – was that Selina worshipped only at the altar of his success. She loved him not for himself, but for the glory that was his: the laughter and applause of the crowd, the featured billing given him, and the favored place on my forearm at feeding time. She was a great dancer, but like so many of her kind she had no true warmth in her heart. Only a fanatic adoration of success.

Had I known that at the time I would have made a different turning somewhere along the road to disaster which lay ahead. But how could I know, how could anyone know, when Selina dissembled so brilliantly? When she looked at Sebastian with melting eyes she almost turned my head as well as his. She clung to him, comforted him in his times of doubt, let him know in a hundred different ways that he was her hero. And he, befuddled by her airs and grace, was completely her slave.

It was an apparently meaningless episode – meaningless at the time it occurred – that brought on the inexorable crisis. Hercules, our flea who performed feats of strength, had become old and stiff-legged, and one night while lifting a grape seed over his head before a hushed and awestruck audience he suddenly fell to the floor in a writhing agony. The veterinarian who diagnosed the case did not mince words. It was a serious rupture, and Hercules would perform no more.

It was shocking beyond measure to me, that news. Not only because of my warm regard for Hercules, but because it left me without one of my featured acts. I instantly gave orders to agents to scour the world, look high and low, pay any price for a flea who could duplicate Hercules's feats, but I did so with a heavy heart. I had already garnered the best there was in the entire world. What chance was there to find a replacement I had not previously considered and found unworthy?

But miracles can and do happen. I had rejected scores of applicants in despair when suddenly a cable arrived from an agent in Bulgaria. The length of the cable alone suggested his state of emotions, and what it said made them even more vivid. By pure chance he had entered a broken-down cafe in Sofia where the guests were being entertained by a flea circus. Not even a circus. A few acts badly performed by sullen, half-starved fleas. But one flea there—! Nothing would do, save that I come at once and see for myself.

I did not believe him, because I knew he was inordinately proud of his native fleas who are, at best, temperamental performers; but I went. When a man is desperate he will do anything, even to putting his faith in the potentialities of a Bulgarian flea. So I went. And to paraphrase the saying: I came, I saw, I was conquered.

The flea was named Casimir, and even the unspeakable surroundings in which he performed could not dim his luster. Barrel-chested, bull-necked, glowing with health, and with a frank, open face that gave clear evidence of an honest nature and willing heart, he dwarfed the fleas around him to insignificance. I saw at a glance that I might be looking at a born star. I waited for his performance in a fever of impatience.

At last the motley acts that preceded his were finished, and the cafe loungers crowded close around the table, I in the forefront. The trainer, a wizened wretch, placed two small wooden blocks on the table, one of which had a series of steps carved into it. Between the blocks I could see a single strand of dark hair – evidently from the trainer's head since it shone greasily in the dim light around me – which was stretched taut from block to block. The trainer then placed Casimir on the table, and before the flea he placed a gleaming pin two inches long which he drew from his lapel.

I could not believe my eyes. To a flea that pin was as a length of railroad track would be to me, yet Casimir stooped low, got a grip on it, and with bulging muscles suddenly lifted it overhead. I gasped, but I had not yet seen the full capabilities of this magnificent creature. Holding the pin overhead he made his way to the steps of the block, climbed them, and then slowly, cautiously, he stepped onto the hair itself. The hair sagged under the weight on it, and Casimir balanced himself with an effort. Then with precise steps, secure as if he were affixed to that hair, he walked its full length, the pin held high overhead throughout and never wavering in his grip. Only when the other block had been reached and the pin laid down could you detect in the convulsive tremors of his body and the heaving of his chest what the strain must have been.

I knew even before the applause started that my search was over. Six hours later, after passionate bargaining and endless rounds of slivovitz, I paid for Casimir's contract more money than anyone on earth would ever have dreamed of paying for a flea. And at that I felt I was fortunate.

I took my prize home with me. I allowed time for him to become accustomed to our Americans ways; I filled his starved soul with my affection and trust; and only when I was sure that he was accepted by the rest of the company and felt at ease with them did I put him on the stage. That night was his night. When the final curtain fell he was the unchallenged star of the show. Simple, honest, unassuming, it was clear that he would not permit this honor to inflate him; but there was no question about it, he was the star. And Sebastian, the great Punchinello, the unparalleled clown, was in second place.

What were Sebastian's feelings then? What could they have been but anguish at having to yield his place to another. But whatever the torments he suffered, he was a trouper through and through. To him the show was the thing, and if he were asked to sacrifice himself to it, he would do so like a stoic. The quality of his performances remained superb. If anything, they were better than ever. Each time he entered the spotlight he flung himself into his role with an abandon, a virtuosity, far beyond the powers of most fleas.

No, it was not the loss of his commanding place in the company that finally shattered him; it was the loss of his beloved. Selina had seen his glory transferred to Casimir. She watched with narrowed eyes as a new star rose on the horizon. And with cold-blooded deliberation, never heeding the consequences, she turned from the old to worship the new. She had eyes only for Casimir now, comfort only for him, flattery only for him, and he, poor, simple-minded male, accepted this at first incredulously, then eagerly, then with rapture.

That was what destroyed Sebastian. The sight of the couple together transfixed him like a needle. And there was no escaping the sight, no turning away from it. Selina was unabashed in her pursuit, and Casimir nakedly revered in it. The outsider might have seen this as a stirring romance; to Sebastian it would be an obscenity. Selina was his; what right did some burly stranger have to fondle her before his very eyes? He must have brooded himself into a state of madness over this.

The end came with shocking suddenness. It was during an evening performance, and the show had gone well until Casimir undertook his master feat. The audience leaned forward with bated breath as he lifted the pin over his head. It hummed with excitement as he climbed the block and set forth on his journey across the taut hair which stretched no less than a foot above the table. And it cried out in alarm when, as he reached the middle of the hair, it suddenly parted, and he plummeted to the table, the pin following him and crushing his chest.

I had leaped forward wildly when I saw the hair part, but I was too late. All I could do was remove the oppressive weight of the pin and turn my head away to conceal my tears from the expiring Casimir. He had his own pains to bear; I would spare him mine. But when my misted eyes fell on the broken strand of hair my grief turned to blazing rage. The hair had not worn through; it had been deliberately cut part of the way. I was looking, not at an accident, but at a murder!

I knew at once who the murderer was. And I could tell from the shock on Selina's face and the growing comprehension on the face of every flea huddled there that the story was clear to all of them. But before I could wreak vengeance on the criminal my glance fell on Casimir, lying there, breathing his last. He looked at me with lustrous eyes full of pain; he tried to smile – oh, pitiful sight – and with a great effort he shook his head at me. He understood, too, noble soul, and he was telling me that vengeance was not for him. Only pity for the malefactor, and forgiveness. It was his last gesture on earth, and the lesson struck me to my heart. It wiped the thirst for vengeance out of me on the spot. I felt only a great need to find Sebastian, to tell him that I alone was the cause of the sorrows that had befallen us. Obsessed by pride in the show, I had put another in his place, had deprived him of his beloved, had driven him at last to insanity and crime.

But when I looked for him I could not find him. Filled with horror at his deed he had fled into the night. And with his disappearance, with Casimir's death, with the company's morale destroyed, there was nothing left. I canceled my bookings, broke up the company, and set forth with only one thought in mind – to find Sebastian, to face him as a penitent, and to win forgiveness from him.

It has been a weary search. I have walked the lonely streets day and night, combed dog shows and zoological parks, looked every place where a wanderer like Sebastian might take refuge. But all to no avail. I am old and poor now. I must rely on alms from strangers to help me on my way, but I will never give up my search until I am successful in it. There is no other way for me. I am doomed to suffer and search, search and suffer until then.

Beidenbauer's voice ceased and his narrative ended on this plaintive note. We sat together in silence for a long while, contemplating the pigeons burbling on the grass beyond, and then I said, 'I have heard tell that the lifespan of the flea is extremely brief. Is it not likely that by now, in some unmarked grave—?'

'I do not allow myself to think of that,' said Beidenbauer with deep feeling. 'It would be the final blow.'

'Yes,' I said, 'I can see that it would be.'

We sat in silence again, and then with resignation I took a

coin from my pocket and offered it to him. He only looked at it reproachfully. I sighed, put the coin away, and offered him a dollar bill. This he took.

'You are kind,' he said, getting to his feet. 'I am only sorry that you never saw my circus in its glory. You would better understand then how far I have fallen.'

'Well,' I said, 'that's life.'

'No, my friend,' said Beidenbauer gravely, 'that's show business.'

# The Seven
# Deadly Virtues

As a mere stripling, Charles realized that he had been happily endowed with good breeding, keen intelligence, and overwhelming ambition. In fact, so heated and furious was this ambition that it had been a matter of grave concern to his father before the lad was out of knee-pants. But such concern did not move Charles. His father was a good man, a kindly and humble clergyman who had spent a lifetime of genteel poverty at his vocation, but who was hardly a fit model for an enterprising son. For himself Charles had chosen a far more worthy model – none other than that renowned magnate, P. O. D. Evergreen, Founder and President of Evergreen Enterprises.

Although late in the field, Evergreen Enterprises had swiftly become the most titanic of titanic corporations. It produced and sold every conceivable product from which profit could be extracted. It leveled forests, drilled oil wells, bored mines, erected factories, swept the land, sea and air with its carriers, and filled every avenue of public communication with its advertising. Banks kept its securities in the same portfolios as United States government bonds. Sprightly widows bought its shares with confidence that their declining years would be happy ones. Elder statesmen in Wall Street tipped their hats when they pronounced its name. To hold rank even as a Junior Executive in its councils was a distinction. And the future for an ambitious young man holding that distinction was a glowing one.

For these reasons, immediately after he graduated *summa cum laude* from the School of Commerce of New England University, Charles went to the New York office of Evergreen Enterprises, Inc., and applied for a position. He was placed in the hands of the Personnel Department, interviewed at length, confronted with batteries of tests, and reinterviewed. He was also informed that this process was only a method of appraising whether or not he would be allowed to face a final and fateful interview with P. O. D. Evergreen himself. So assiduous was this paragon among executives in seeking the right man for the right job that every deserving applicant for a place in his company's managerial staff had to be judged by him personally.

At last came the day when Charles was led into the office where behind a magnificent desk sat his idol, master of the greatest industrial empire on earth, boon companion to presidents and kings – yet, withal, a simple, unprepossessing figure, almost fatherly in the way he dismissed his secretary and waved Charles to a seat.

He said, 'Well, my boy, we are going to have a little talk, and I think you will find it a strange one. In fact, I think you will find it shocking in some ways. That is because we are going to talk without using any of the cant, any of the mealy-mouthed and sugar-coated language on which you have, no doubt, been raised. Don't misunderstand me. I have no objection to fine moralistic and sociological jargon as it is used outside the confines of this office. In fact, I publicly indulge in it myself with the consolation that it's good business to deliver what the customer wants. But within these four walls I will have no part of it. Do you understand that?'

Charles assured him that he did.

'Excellent. Now tell me in plain, unvarnished words why you wish to work for this company.'

Charles was prepared for that one. He said, 'I am looking for the biggest and best market for my talents. There I can perform a worthwhile public service which—'

The look in the President's eye stopped him short. P. O. D. Evergreen waited a moment and then said gently, 'My boy, you are being glib. I have not asked you to prepare a tract for the conversion of the benighted heathen – that is not our business here. Or are you under the impression that it is?'

Charles hung his head.

'Come, come,' said P. O. D. Evergreen, 'there is no need to look so downcast. You have started off badly, true, but so has every other applicant I ever interviewed. It is necessary to draw up this sanctimonious bilge before we can reach the crystal waters beneath it. And even then I find that some applicants persist in defining their motives in such terms as *security* and *status*. This would be fatal to your prospects, my boy. I want you to use the honest equivalents – *money* and *power* – in discussing this matter. Because, in a nutshell, these are your motives, aren't they?'

'I'm not sure,' Charles said, somewhat shaken. 'I don't believe I've ever thought of it like that.'

'Of course you have. You've simply been allowed to conceal the awareness of it from yourself by the vocabulary you've been instructed in. You want security, my boy, in terms of wealth that you can spend freely, and you want status based on a position of power. The greater the power you wield, the loftier the status. And I heartily approve of that – just as I approve of your coming to Evergreen Enterprises, where such ambitions can best be gratified. Evergreen Enterprises is, as you put it yourself, the biggest and the best. Do you have any idea why?'

'Well, for one thing, the many products—'

'No, no, don't go off on that track. We supply nothing to the consumer that many another company does not supply as conveniently. And sometimes even more cheaply, for that matter.'

Charles desperately grasped at a straw. 'Efficiency, then? It is widely believed that Evergreen Enterprises operates at a level of efficiency unknown to any of its competitors.'

'Right you are, my boy, and there's your answer. From the lowliest Junior Executive up to the Chairman of the Board, efficiency is the credo here. And the way we obtain it is the secret of our success. That secret enables us to find the most talented managerial team in the world, to hold that team together year in and year out with absolutely no turnover – an incredible feat in itself, you must admit – and to draw maximum effort from it at all times. What do you think of that?'

Charles said with deep feeling, 'I have always felt my place was here, sir. I am more certain of it than ever.'

'I am glad to hear you say so – it shows the kind of spirit we are looking for. But I wonder if you will feel the same after I fully explain what would be expected of you as a member of this team. In all fairness, my boy, I must warn you that this explanation will put you to your hardest test.'

He spoke with a kindliness that touched the youthful applicant. Charles was full of resolve to prove his mettle. He said quietly, 'I am ready to meet any test, sir.'

'I hope so. And I will get down to cases by saying that before I founded this organization I carefully studied the problems of others in this field. One weakness was quickly discernible in all of them: they simply could not get full value from their executives. Every high-salaried man of them had been so saturated by the moralistic nonsense he had been reared on that he could not release himself entirely to his job, where, of course, realistic attitudes must prevail. There was always a chasm between what he had been taught to be as a youth and what he had to practice on his company's behalf. Inevitably this made him guilt-ridden and subject to neuroses. It was a common condition. Still is, for that matter, but not here. Among the upper echelons of Evergreen Enterprises you will find only men who are well-balanced, well-adjusted, always ready and willing to give their best to the job.'

'But how was that achieved, sir?' Charles asked with eager interest.

'Very simply, my boy. Have you ever heard of the seven deadly sins?'

'I have. My father is a minister, and so I am well-informed on the subject.'

'That is all in your favor. Can you name them for me?'

'I can,' said Charles. 'They are pride, envy, anger, sloth, avarice, gluttony, and lust.'

'Quite right. And have you ever indulged in any of them?'

Charles remained speechless.

'Oh, come, come, my boy,' said P. O. D. Evergreen jovially. 'There is no need to blush, no need to dissemble. If it is any comfort to you, let me say that I don't regard these alleged sins as sins as all. Why, they are the very foundations on which morale is built here!'

Charles scented a trap. 'Are they?' he said warily.

'They are, indeed. Now force yourself to think of them, not

as sins, but as virtues, and see if you do not immediately feel a great sense of release. Of ease, of assurance, of well-being. Aha, I see from your expression that you do. It's a remarkable feeling, isn't it?'

He was right. But then doubts flooded in on Charles. He said, 'I don't see—'

'You will, my boy, you will.'

The doubts remained. Charles said, 'But let us take pride, for example. If I demonstrated it, wouldn't that stir up resentment against me?'

'Yes, but it would also advertise your worth to those who should know about it and otherwise might not. Imagine that you are working here in a lowly position. You come up with a good and profitable idea. In another company your immediate superior might steal that idea and claim credit for it. But here you are expected to express your pride in it so loudly that credit goes rightfully to you.'

'That is what I mean. This will undoubtedly make my immediate superior and many others bitterly envious of me.'

'It will, indeed. They will be eaten by naked envy until they come up with an idea to surpass yours. Then it will be your turn again. In this way we all prosper. Civilization is built on envy. The human race has always profited from it. Let us not disparage it.'

Charles pondered this. 'But,' he said challengingly, 'what about anger then? Surely, anger can't be made profitable in any case.'

'No? Then imagine your precious idea put into the hands of an underling for commission, and badly botched through his ineptitude or neglect. How are you to protect yourself against a repetition of such a disaster? Through anger, my boy – violent anger turned against the offender so that the lesson is well learned. When word gets out that you have a reservoir of anger always in store, you will find your instructions carried out with uncanny efficiency. There's a magic virtue in unrestrained bad temper, believe me.'

'Yes, I can see that,' Charles admitted. 'And I suppose that sloth, too – no, I'm afraid I can't see the businesslike virtue in sloth.'

'Because you are still young and unrealistic. But sloth in its many forms – the surreptitious coffee break, the added time at lunch, the napping at the desk, yes, and a dozen other variants – is the finest possible tool for sharpening the wits. Not to be caught, that is the trick. The executive role is not for the drudge; it is for the one who has best developed the immense skill needed to conceal his sloth.'

'That is hard to believe,' said Charles.

'But nonetheless true. Show me the man eternally drudging away at the details of his job and I'll show you a born clerk. Show me the man who seems to be drudging away and isn't, and I'll show you a future Chairman of the Board.'

Charles was glad to hear this. Despite his feverish ambition he was naturally slothful. That had worried him at times, but he could see that it need worry him no longer.

P. O. D. Evergreen said, 'Yes, and the rest of those so-called vices are the soundest of virtues, too, when you view them honestly and intelligently. Avarice I hardly need speak of: it is the driving force behind any man worth his salt. And gluttony and lust have very much come into their own today – speaking, of course, in practical terms. The Evergreen Enterprises man who attends conventions or travels on business is the representative of the company in every way. If he can out-eat, out-drink, and out-copulate all competition, the prestige he earns goes to the company, and with it more business. Of course, we provide him with an obvious advantage. He is expected to engage in these activities without guilt or inhibition. No one will ever ask him to answer for his expense account or his morals. He is truly a free man.

'You see, my boy, there is nothing mysterious about our success here. Our standards are the usual ones, but instead of feeling guilty when you exercise them, you must see how wise and sane they are, and must glory in them. That is all there is to it.'

The bright vista of the future swam before Charles' eyes in a golden haze. He said, 'How simple and logical it all seems. Yet, how inspired it is. To let a man always be himself, to have him act naturally at all times—'

'Yes, my boy, and to have this be the very means by which he advances himself – well, it was inspired, I'll admit that. But then, such inspirations are my job. If I couldn't come up with them now and then, I would have no right to occupy my high position.'

His friendly tone filled Charles with assurance. He said boldly, 'I envy you that high position, sir. I would like nothing better than a chance to oust you from it and take your place.'

P. O. D. Evergreen rose to his feet and thrust out a hand. 'And that chance you shall have, my boy. If I had any doubts about your good qualities, they are completely settled by what you have just said.' He shook Charles' hand with a powerful grip. 'There, that is all the contract we need. I am sure that you have a great deal to offer Evergreen Enterprises; in return, it offers you a limitless future. When do you wish to start?'

'At once,' said Charles.

'Good. Then I shall give you your final instructions now. For one thing, you will remember that our little talk here was entirely confidential. Our competitors will inevitably discover the solution to their problem, but there is no point in helping them do it. Moreover, if you were to confide what was said here to the world at large it would be misunderstood, and you would be the sufferer. You understand that, of course.'

'I do.'

'I am sure you do. Then tomorrow you will start as assistant to the head of a department. You will spend one year at that assignment, and it will be a year of probation, more or less. Everything depends on how you conduct yourself during that period. Then you will report to me and I will decide whether or not you are qualified to become a full executive.' He smiled engagingly at Charles. 'As you can see, my boy, I like to pull all the strings myself.'

There was a weariness in the way he said it that made Charles feel suddenly humble. It was easy to see why this man commanded the fierce loyalty that he did.

'You can count on me, sir,' Charles said. He rose from his chair, not wanting to overstay his leave. 'Is there anything else?'

'There is, my boy, but you must learn it for yourself through experience. Good luck in that.'

It was one year later to the day when Charles was again

summoned to the office of his President. He knew that he had done well during the year. Driven by ambition, guided by the good counsel given him, he had striven valiantly to make his mark. Yet, when he entered the presence of P. O. D. Evergreen he felt some apprehension. Were his efforts known? Would they be appreciated? He wondered about that.

P. O. D. Evergreen put his fears to rest at once. He said with affection, 'My boy, you have acquitted yourself nobly. I have received many reports on you, and all of them make clear not only your many talents but also the degree of hatred and respect you inspire in your department. That is your most gratifying testimonial. You will be put in charge of that department.'

Charles struggled for words. 'I owe it all to you, sir,' he said with an effort.

'No, no, my boy. It is your own spirit, your determination to succeed at all costs, that must get the credit. But tell me one thing. You have lived by my precepts for a year. During that time have you ever found yourself doubting their wisdom and merit?'

'Never,' Charles said, striking the desk before him with his fist. 'Not even when I considered that by following them to the letter I was irrevocably consigning my immortal soul to hell!'

'Hell?' P. O. D. Evergreen rose and stood there, a towering figure suddenly unearthly in his majesty. 'You dare use that word here?' Then his eyes grew warm with nostalgia; his words came gently, filling Charles with awful enlightenment. 'From here to eternity, my boy, you must think of it only as – The Home Office.'

# The Nine-to-Five
# Man

The alarm clock sounded, as it did every weekday morning, at exactly 7:20, and without opening his eyes Mr Keesler reached out a hand and turned it off. His wife was already preparing breakfast – it was her modest boast that she had a built-in alarm to get her up in the morning – and a smell of frying bacon permeated the bedroom. Mr Keesler savored it for a moment, lying there on his back with his eyes closed, and then wearily sat up and swung his feet out of bed. His eyeglasses were on the night table next to the alarm clock. He put them on and blinked in the morning light, yawned, scratched his head with pleasure, and fumbled for his slippers.

The pleasure turned to mild irritation. One slipper was not there. He kneeled down, swept his hand back and forth under the bed, and finally found it. He stood up, puffing a little, and went into the bathroom. After lathering his face he discovered that his razor was dull, and discovered immediately afterward that he had forgotten to buy new blades the day before. By taking a few minutes more than usual he managed to get a presentable, though painful, shave out of the old blade. Then he washed, brushed his teeth carefully, and combed his hair. He liked to say that he was in pretty good shape since he still had teeth and hair enough to need brushing.

In the bedroom again, he heard Mrs Keesler's voice rising from the foot of the stairway. 'Breakfast, dear,' she called. 'It's on the table now.'

It was not really on the table, Mr Keesler knew; his wife would first be setting the table when he walked into the kitchen. She was like that, always using little tricks to make the house run smoothly. But no matter how you looked at it, she was a sweetheart all right. He nodded soberly at his reflection in the dresser mirror while he knotted his tie. He was a lucky man to have a wife like that. A fine wife, a fine mother – maybe a little bit too much of an easy mark for her relatives – but a real sweetheart.

The small annoyance of the relatives came up at the breakfast table.

'Joe and Betty are expecting us over tonight, dear,' said Mrs Keesler. 'Betty called me about it yesterday. Is that all right with you?'

'All right,' said Mr Keesler amiably. He knew there was nothing good on television that evening anyhow.

'Then will you remember to pick up your other suit at the tailor's on the way home?'

'For Betty and Joe?' said Mr Keesler. 'What for? They're only in-laws.'

'Still and all, I like you to look nice when you go over there, so please don't forget.' Mrs Keesler hesitated. 'Albert's going to be there, too.'

'Naturally. He lives there.'

'I know, but you hardly ever get a chance to see him, and, after all, he's our nephew. He happens to be a very nice boy.'

'All right, he's a very nice boy,' said Mr Keesler. 'What does he want from me?'

Mrs Keesler blushed. 'Well, it so happens he's having a hard time getting a job where—'

'No,' said Mr Keesler. 'Absolutely not.' He put down his knife and fork and regarded his wife sternly. 'You know yourself that there's hardly enough money in the novelties line to make us a living. So for me to take in a lazy—'

'I'm sorry,' said Mrs Keesler. 'I didn't mean to get you upset about it.' She put a consoling hand on his. 'And what kind of thing is that to say, about not making a living? Maybe we don't have as much as some others, but we do all right. A nice house and two fine sons in college – what more could we ask for? So don't talk like that. And go to work, or you'll be late.'

Mr Keesler shook his head. 'What a softie,' he said. 'If you only wouldn't let Betty talk you into these things—'

'Now don't start with that. Just go to work.'

She helped him on with his coat in the hallway. 'Are you going to take the car today?' she asked.

'No.'

'All right, then I can use it for the shopping. But don't forget about the suit. It's the tailor right near the subway station.' Mrs Keesler plucked a piece of lint from his coat collar. 'And you make a very nice living, so stop talking like that. We do all right.'

Mr Keesler left the house by the side door. It was an unpretentious frame house in the Flatbush section of Brooklyn, and like most of the others on the block it had a small garage behind it. Mr Keesler unlocked the door of the garage and stepped inside. The car occupied nearly all the space there, but room had also been found for a clutter of tools, metal cans, paint brushes, and a couple of old kitchen chairs which had been partly painted.

The car itself was a four-year-old Chevrolet, a little the worse for wear, and it took an effort to open the lid of its trunk. Mr Keesler finally got it open and lifted out his big leather sample case, groaning at its weight. He did not lock the garage door when he left, since he had the only key to it, and he knew Mrs Keesler wanted to use the car.

It was a two-block walk to the Beverly Road station of the IRT subway. At a newsstand near the station Mr Keesler bought a *New York Times*, and when the train came in he arranged himself against the door at the end of the car. There was no chance of getting a seat during the rush hour, but from long experience Mr Keesler knew how to travel with the least inconvenience. By standing with his back braced against the door and his legs astride the sample case he was able to read his newspaper until, by the time the train reached 14th Street, the press of bodies against him made it impossible to turn the pages.

At 42nd Street he managed to push his way out of the car using the sample case as a battering ram. He crossed the platform and took a local two stations farther to Columbus Circle. When he walked up the stairs of the station he saw by his wristwatch that it was exactly five minutes to nine.

Mr Keesler's office was in the smallest and shabbiest building on Columbus Circle. It was made to look even smaller and shabbier by the new Coliseum which loomed over it on one side and by the apartment hotels which towered over it on the other. It had one creaky elevator to service its occupants, and an old man named Eddie to operate the elevator.

When Mr Keesler came into the building Eddie had his mail all ready for him. The mail consisted of a large bundle of letters tied with a string, and a half dozen small cardboard boxes. Mr Keesler managed to get all this under one arm with difficulty, and Eddie said, 'Well, that's a nice big load the same as ever. I hope you get some business out of it.'

'I hope so,' said Mr Keesler.

Another tenant picked up his mail and stepped into the elevator behind Mr Keesler. 'Well,' he said, looking at the load under Mr Keesler's arm, 'it's nice to see that somebody's making money around here.'

'Sure,' said Mr Keesler. 'They send you the orders all right, but when it comes to paying for them where are they?'

'That's how it goes,' said Eddie.

He took the elevator up to the third floor and Mr Keesler got out there. His office was in Room 301 at the end of the corridor, and on its door were painted the words *KEESLER NOVELTIES*. Underneath in quotation marks was the phrase 'Everything for the trade.'

The office was a room with a window that looked out over Central Park. Against one wall was a battered rolltop desk that Mr Keesler's father had bought when he himself had started in the novelties business long ago, and before it was a large, comfortable swivel chair with a foam-rubber cushion on its seat. Against the opposite wall was a table, and on it was an old L. C. Smith typewriter, a telephone, some telephone books, and a stack of magazines. There was another stack of magazines on top of a large filing cabinet in a corner of the room. Under the window was a chaise-longue which Mr Keesler had bought second-hand from Eddie for five dollars, and next to the rolltop desk were a wastepaper basket and a wooden coat-rack he had bought from Eddie for fifty cents. Tenants who moved from the building sometimes found it cheaper to abandon their shopworn furnishings than to pay cartage for them, and Eddie did a small business in selling these articles for whatever he was offered.

Mr Keesler closed the office door behind him. He gratefully set the heavy sample case down in a corner, pushed open the desk, and dropped his mail and the *New York Times* on it. Then he hung his hat and coat on the rack, checking the pockets of the coat to make sure he had forgotten nothing in them.

He sat down at the desk, opened the string around the mail, and looked at the return address on each letter. Two of the letters were from banks. He unlocked a drawer of the desk, drew out a notebook, and entered the figures into it. Then he tore the receipts into small shreds and dropped them into the wastepaper basket.

The rest of the mail was easily disposed of. Mr Keesler took each of the smaller envelopes and, without opening it, tore it in half and tossed it into the basket on top of the shredded deposit slips. He then opened the envelopes which were thick and unwieldy, extracted their contents – brochures and catalogues – and placed them on the desk. When he was finished he had a neat pile of catalogues and brochures before him. These he dumped into a drawer of the filing cabinet.

He now turned his attention to the cardboard boxes. He opened them and pulled out various odds and ends – good-luck charms, a souvenir coin, a plastic keyring, several packets of cancelled foreign stamps, and a small cellophane bag containing one chocolate cracker. Mr Keesler tossed the empty boxes into the wastepaper basket, ate the cracker, and pushed the rest of the stuff to the back of the desk. The cracker was a little bit too sweet for his taste, but not bad.

In the top drawer of the desk were a pair of scissors, a box of stationery, and a box of stamps. Mr Keesler removed these to the table and placed them next to the typewriter. He wheeled the swivel chair to the table, sat down, and opened the classified telephone directory to its listing of dentists. He ran his finger down a column of names. Then he picked up the phone and dialed a number.

'Dr Glover's office,' said a woman's voice.

'Look,' said Mr Keesler, 'this is an emergency. I'm in the neighborhood here, so can I come in during the afternoon? It hurts pretty bad.'

'Are you a regular patient of Dr Glover's?'

'No, but I thought—'

'I'm sorry, but the doctor's schedule is full. If you want to call again tomorrow—'

'No, never mind,' said Mr Keesler. 'I'll try someone else.'

He ran his finger down the column in the directory and dialed again.

'This is Dr Gordon's office,' said a woman's voice, but much more youthful and pleasant than the one Mr Keesler had just encountered. 'Who is it, please?'

'Look,' said Mr Keesler. 'I'm suffering a lot of pain, and I was wondering if the doctor couldn't give me a couple of minutes this afternoon. I'm right in the neighborhood here. I can be there any time that's convenient. Say around two o'clock?'

'Well, two o'clock is already filled, but I have a cancellation here for three. Would that be all right?'

'That would be fine. And the name is Keesler.' Mr Keesler spelled it out carefully. 'Thanks a lot, miss, and I'll be there right on the dot.'

He pressed the bar of the phone down, released it, and dialed again. 'Is Mr Hummel there?' he said. 'Good. Tell him it's about the big delivery he was expecting this afternoon.'

In a moment he heard Mr Hummel's voice. 'Yea?'

'You know who this is?' asked Mr Keesler.

'Sure I know who it is.'

'All right,' said Keesler, 'then meet me at four o'clock instead of three. You understand?'

'I get it,' said Mr Hummel.

Mr Keesler did not continue the conversation. He put down the phone, pushed aside the directory, and took a magazine from the pile on the table. The back pages of the magazine were full of advertisements for free gifts, free samples, and free catalogues. *Mail us this coupon, most of them said, and we will send you absolutely free—*

Mr Keesler studied these offers, finally selected ten of them, cut out the coupons with his scissors, and addressed them on the typewriter. He typed slowly but accurately, using only two fingers. Then he addressed ten envelopes, sealed the coupons into them, and stamped them. He snapped a rubber band around the envelopes for easier mailing and put everything else in the office back into its proper place. It was now 10:25, and the only thing left to attend to was the *New York Times*.

By twelve o'clock, Mr Keesler, stretched comfortably out on the chaise-longue, had finished reading the *Times*. He had, however, bypassed the stock market quotations as was his custom. In 1929 his father's entire capital had been wiped out overnight in the market crash, and since that day Mr Keesler had a cold and cynical antipathy to stocks and bonds and anything connected with them. When talking to people about it he would make it a little joke. 'I like to know that my money is all tied up in cash,' he would say. But inwardly he had been deeply scarred by what his father had gone through after the debacle. He had been very fond of his father, a gentle and hard-working man, well-liked by all who knew him, and had never forgiven the stock market for what it had done to him.

Twelve o'clock was lunchtime for Mr Keesler, as it was for almost everyone else in the building. Carrying his mail he walked downstairs along with many others who knew that it would take Eddie quite a while to pick them up in his overworked elevator at this hour. He dropped the letters into a mailbox on the corner, and banged the lid of the mailbox a couple of times for safety's sake.

Near 58th Street on Eighth Avenue was a cafeteria which served good food at reasonable prices, and Mr Keesler had a cheese sandwich, baked apple, and coffee there. Before he left he had a counterman wrap a cinnamon bun in waxed paper and place it in a brown paper bag for him to take along with him.

Swinging the bag in his hand as he walked, Mr Keesler went into a drugstore a block away and bought a roll of two-inch-wide surgical bandage. On his way out of the store he surreptitiously removed the bandage from its box and wrapper and dropped the box and wrapper into a litter basket on the street. The roll of bandage itself he put into the bag containing the cinnamon bun.

He repeated this process in a drugstore on the next block, and then six more times in various stores on his way down Eighth Avenue. Each time he would pay the exact amount in change, drop the box and wrappings into a litter basket, put the roll of bandage into his paper bag. When he had eight rolls of bandage in the bag on top of the cinnamon bun he turned around and walked back to the office building. It was exactly one o'clock when he got there.

Eddie was waiting in the elevator, and when he saw the paper bag he smiled toothlessly and said as he always did, 'What is it this time?'

'Cinnamon buns,' said Mr Keesler. 'Here, have one.' He pulled out the cinnamon bun wrapped in its waxed paper, and Eddie took it.

'Thanks,' he said.

'That's all right,' said Mr Keesler. 'There's plenty here for both of us. I shouldn't be eating so much of this stuff anyhow.'

At the third floor he asked Eddie to hold the elevator, he'd be out in a minute. 'I just have to pick up the sample case,' he said. 'Got to get to work on the customers.'

In the office he lifted the sample case to the desk, put the eight rolls of bandage in it, and threw away the now empty paper bag into the wastepaper basket. With the sample case weighing him down he made his way back to the elevator.

'This thing weighs more every time I pick it up,' he said to Eddie as the elevator went down, and Eddie said, 'Well, that's the way it goes. We're none of us as young as we used to be.'

A block away from Columbus Circle, Mr Keesler took an Independent Line subway train to East Broadway, not far from Manhattan Bridge. He ascended into the light of Straus Square, walked down to Water Street, and turned left there. His destination was near Montgomery Street, but he stopped before he came to it and looked around.

The neighborhood was an area of old warehouses, decaying tenements, and raw, new housing projects. The street Mr Keesler was interested in, however, contained only warehouses. Blackened with age, they stood in a row looking like ancient fortresses. There was a mixed smell of refuse and salt water around them that invited coveys of pigeons and seagulls to fly overhead.

Mr Keesler paid no attention to the birds, nor to the few waifs and strays on the street. Hefting his sample case, he turned into an alley which led between two warehouses and made his way to the vast and empty lot behind them. He walked along until he came to a metal door in the third warehouse down the row. Using a large, old-fashioned key he opened the door, stepped into the blackness beyond it, and closed it behind him, locking it from the inside and testing it to make sure it was locked.

There was a light switch on the wall near the door. Mr Keesler put down his sample case and wrapped a handkerchief loosely around his hand. He fumbled along the wall with that hand until he found the switch, and when he pressed it a dim light suffused the building. Since the windows of the building were sealed by metal shutters, the light could not be seen outside. Mr Keesler then put away the handkerchief and carried the sample case across the vast expanse of the warehouse to the huge door of the delivery entrance that faced on the street.

Near the door was a long plank table on which was a time-stamper, a few old receipt books, and some pencil stubs. Mr Keesler put down the sample case, took off his coat, neatly folded it and laid it on the table, and placed his hat on top of it. He bent over the sample case and opened it. From it he took the eight rolls of bandage, a large tube of fixative called Quick-Dry, a four-inch length of plumber's candle, two metal cans each containing two gallons of high octane gasoline, six paper drinking cups, a two-yard length of fishline, a handful of soiled linen rags, and a pair of rubber gloves much spattered with drops of dried paint. All this he arranged on the table.

Now donning the rubber gloves he picked up the length of fishline and made a series of loops in it. He fitted a roll of bandage into each loop and drew the string tight. When he held it up at arm's length it looked like a string of white fishing bobbers.

Each gasoline tin had a small spout and looked as if it were tightly sealed. But the lid of one could be removed entirely and Mr Keesler pried at it until it came off. He lowered the line of rolled bandages into the can, leaving the end of the string dangling over the edge for ready handling. A few bubbles broke at the surface of the can as the gauze bandages started to soak up gasoline. Mr Keesler observed this with satisfaction, and then, taking the tube of Quick-Dry with him, he made a thoughtful tour of inspection of the warehouse.

What he saw was a broad and high steel framework running

through the center of the building from end to end and supporting a great number of cardboard boxes, wooden cases, and paper-covered rolls of cloth. More boxes and cases were stacked nearly ceiling-high against two walls of the room.

He surveyed everything carefully, wrinkling his nose against the sour odor of mold that rose around him. He tested a few of the cardboard boxes by pulling away loose pieces, and found them all as dry as dust.

Then having studied everything to his satisfaction he kneeled down at a point midway between the steel framework and the angle of the two walls where the cases were stacked highest and squeezed some fixative on the wooden floor. He watched it spread and settle, and then went back to the table.

From the pocket of his jacket he drew out a finely whetted penknife and an octagon-shaped metal pencil which was also marked off as a ruler. He looked at his wristwatch, making some brief calculations, and measured off a length of the plumber's candle with the ruler. With the penknife he then sliced through the candle and trimmed away some wax to give the wick clearance. Before putting the knife back into his pocket he cleaned the blade with one of the pieces of cloth on the table.

When he looked into the can which contained the bandages soaking in gasoline he saw no more bubbles. He picked up the can and carried it to the place on the floor where the fixative was spread. Slowly reeling up the string so that none of the gasoline would spatter him he detached each roll of wet bandage from it. He loosened a few inches of gauze from six of the bandages and pressed the exposed gauze firmly into the fixative which was now gummy.

Unspooling the bandage as he walked he then drew each of the six lengths of gauze in turn to a designated point. Three went among the boxes of the framework and three went into the cases along the walls. They were nicely spaced so that they radiated like the main strands of a spiderweb to points high among the packed cases. To reach the farthest points in the warehouse Mr Keesler knotted the extra rolls of bandage to two of those which he had pulled out short of the mark. There was a sharp reek of gasoline in the warehouse now, added to its smell of mold.

Where the ends of the bandages were thrust between the boxes, Mr Keesler made sure that the upper box was set back a little to provide a narrow platform. He took the paper drinking cups from the table, filled each with gasoline, and set it on top of the end of the bandage, resting on this platform.

The fixative was now put to work again. Mr Keesler squeezed some of it over the juncture of the six bandages on the floor which were sealed there by the previous application. While it hardened he went to the table, took a handful of rags, and brought them to the open gasoline can. He lowered each rag in turn into the can, squeezed some of the excess gasoline back into the can after he pulled it out, and arranged all the rags around the fixative.

Then he took the stump of plumber's candle which he had prepared and pressed it down into the drying fixative. He tested it to make sure it was tightly set into place, looped the gasoline saturated fishline around and around its base, and pushed the rags close up against it. He made sure that a proper length of candle was exposed, and then stood up to view his handiwork. Everything, as far as he could see, was in order.

Humming a little tune under his breath, Mr Keesler took the two cans of gasoline and disposed of their contents among the boxes. He handled the cans expertly, splashing gasoline against the boxes where the bandages were attached, pouring it between the boxes wherever he detected a draft stirring in the dank air around him. When the cans were empty he wiped them thoroughly with a rag he had reserved for the purpose and added the rag to the pile around the candle.

Everything that needed to be done had now been done.

Mr Keesler went back to the table, tightly sealed the gasoline cans, and placed them in the sample case. He pulled off the rubber gloves and put them and the remnants of plumber's candle into the case, too. Then he locked the case and put on his hat and coat.

He carried the case to a point a few feet away from the candle on the floor, set it down, and took out a book of matches from his pocket. Cupping a hand around the matchbox he lit one, and walking with great care while shielding the flame, he approached the candle, bent over it, and lit it. The flame guttered and then took hold.

Mr Keesler stood up and put out the match, not by shaking it or blowing it, but by wetting his thumb and forefinger in his mouth and squeezing out the light between them. He dropped the used match into his pocket, went to the back door, switched off the electric light there with his handkerchiefed hand, and drew open the door a few inches.

After peering outside to make sure no one was observing him, Mr Keesler stepped through the door, locked it behind him, and departed.

He returned to his office by the same route he had come. In the elevator he said to Eddie, 'All of a sudden my tooth is killing me. I guess I'll have to run over to the dentist,' and Eddie said, 'Your teeth sure give you a lot of trouble, don't they?'

'They sure do,' said Mr Keesler.

He left the sample case in his room, washed his hands and face in the lavatory at the opposite end of the hallway, and took the elevator down. The dentist's office was on 56th Street near Seventh Avenue, a few minutes' walk away, and when Mr Keesler entered the reception room the clock on the wall there showed him that it was two minutes before three. He was pleased to see that the dentist's receptionist was young and pretty and that she had his name neatly entered in her appointment book.

'You're right on time,' she said as she filled out a record card for him. She handed him the card. 'Just give this to Dr Gordon when you go into the office.'

In the office Mr Keesler took off his glasses, put them in his pocket, and sat back in the dentist's chair. His feet hurt, and it felt good to be sitting down.

'Where does it hurt?' said Dr Gordon, and Mr Keesler indicated the back of his lower right jaw. 'Right there,' he said.

He closed his eyes and crossed his hands restfully on his belly while the doctor peered into his open mouth and poked at his teeth with a sharp instrument.

'Nothing wrong on the surface,' Dr Gordon said. 'Matter of fact, your teeth seem to be in excellent shape. How old are you?'

'Fifty,' said Mr Keesler with pride. 'Fifty-one next week.'

'Wish my teeth were as good,' said the dentist. 'Well, it might possibly be that wisdom tooth under the gum that's giving the trouble. But all I can do now is put something soothing on it and take X-rays. Then we'll know.'

'Fine,' said Mr Keesler.

He came out of the office at 3:30 with a sweet, minty taste in his mouth and with his feet well rested. Walking briskly he headed for the BMT subway station at 57th Street and took a train down to Herald Square. He climbed to the street there and took a position among the crowd moving slowly past the windows of R. H. Macy's Department Store, keeping his eyes fixed on the windows as he moved.

At four o'clock he looked at his watch.

At five minutes after four he looked at it with concern.

Then in the window of the store he saw a car coming up to the curb. He walked across the street and entered it, and the car immediately drew away from the curb and fell in with the rest of the traffic on the street.

'You're late, Hummel,' said Mr Keesler to the driver. 'Nothing went wrong, did it?'

'Nothing,' said Mr Hummel tensely. 'It must have started just about 3:30. The cops called me ten minutes ago to tell me about it. The whole building's going, they said. They wanted me to rush over right away.'

'Well, all right,' said Keesler. 'So what are you so upset about? Everything is fine. In no time at all you'll have sixty thousand dollars of insurance money in your pocket, you'll be rid of that whole load of stuff you were stuck with – you ought to be a happy man.'

Mr Hummel awkwardly manipulated the car into a turn that led downtown. 'But if they find out,' he said. 'How can you be so sure they won't? At my age to go to jail—!'

Mr Keesler had dealt with overwrought clients many times before. 'Look, Hummel,' he said patiently, 'the first job I ever did was thirty years ago for my own father, God rest his soul, when the market cleaned him out. To his dying day he thought it was an accident, he never knew it was me. My wife don't know what I do. Nobody knows. Why? Because I'm an expert. I'm the best in the business. When I do a job I'm covered up every possible way – right down to the least little thing. So quit worrying. Nobody will ever find out.

'But in the daytime,' said Mr Hummel. 'With people around. I still say it would have been better at night.'

Mr Keesler shook his head. 'If it happened at night, the Fire Marshal and the insurance people would be twice as suspicious. And what do I look like, anyhow, Hummel, some kind of bum who goes sneaking around at night? I'm a nine-to-five man. I go to the office and I come home from the office like anybody else. Believe me, that's the best protection there is.'

'It could be,' said Mr Hummel, nodding thoughtfully. 'It could be.'

A dozen blocks away from the warehouse, thick black smoke could be seen billowing into the air above it. On Water Street, three blocks away, Mr Keesler put a hand on Mr Hummel's arm.

'Stop here,' he said. 'There's always marshals and insurance people around the building looking at people, so this is close enough. You can see all you have to from here.'

Mr Hummel looked at the smoke pouring from the building, at the tongues of flame now and then shooting up from it, at the fire engines and tangles of hose in the street, and at the firemen playing water against the walls of the building. He shook his head in awe. 'Look at that,' he said, marveling. 'Look at that.'

'I did,' said Mr Keesler. 'So how about the money?'

Mr Hummel stirred himself from his daze, reached into his trouser pocket, and handed Mr Keesler a tightly folded roll of bills. 'It's all there,' he said. 'I had it made up the way you said.'

There were fourteen hundred-dollar bills and five twenties in the roll. Bending low and keeping the money out of sight Mr Keesler counted it twice. He had two bank deposit envelopes all filled out and ready in his pocket. Into one which credited the money to the account of K. E. Esler he put thirteen of the hundred-dollar bills. Into the other which was made out in the name of *Keesler Novelties* he put a single hundred-dollar bill. The five twenties he slipped into his wallet, and from the wallet took out the key to the warehouse.

'Don't forget this,' he said, handing it to Mr Hummel. 'Now I have to run along.'

'Wait a second,' said Mr Hummel. 'I wanted to ask you about something, and since I don't know where to get in touch with you—'

'Yes.'

'I have got a friend who's in a very bad spot. He's stuck with a big inventory of fur pieces that he can't get rid of, and he needs cash bad. Do you understand?'

'Sure,' said Mr Keesler. 'Give me his name and phone number, and I'll call him up in a couple of weeks.'

'Couldn't you make it any sooner?'

'I'm a busy man,' said Mr Keesler. 'I'll call him in two weeks.' He took out the book of matches and inside it wrote the name and number Mr Hummel gave him. He put away the matches and opened the door of the car. 'So long, Hummel.'

'So long, Esler,' said Mr Hummel.

For the second time that day Mr Keesler traveled in the subway from East Broadway to Columbus Circle. But instead of going directly to his office this time, he turned down Eighth Avenue and dropped the sealed envelope which contained the $1300 into the night-deposit box of the Merchant's National Bank. Across the street was the Columbus National Bank, and into its night-deposit box he placed the envelope containing the hundred dollars. When he arrived at his office it was ten minutes before five.

Mr Keesler opened his sample case, threw in the odds and ends that had come in the mail that morning, shut the sample case, and closed the rolltop desk, after throwing the *New York Times* into the wastebasket. He took a magazine from the pile on the filing cabinet and sat down in the swivel chair while he looked at it.

At exactly five o'clock he left the office, carrying the sample case.

The elevator was crowded, but Mr Keesler managed to wedge himself into it. 'Well,' said Eddie on the way down, 'another day, another dollar.'

In the subway station Mr Keesler bought a *World-Telegram*, but was unable to read it in the crowded train. He held it under his arm, standing astride the sample case, half dozing as he stood there. When he got out of the station at Beverly Road he stopped at the stationery store on the corner to buy a package of razor blades. Then he walked home slowly, turned into the driveway, and entered the garage.

Mrs Keesler always had trouble getting the car into the garage. It stood there now at a slight angle to the wall so that Mr Keesler had to squeeze past it to get to the back of the garage. He opened the sample case, took out the piece of plumber's candle and the tube of Quick-Dry, and put them into a drawer of the workbench there. The drawer was already full of other bits of hardware and small household supplies.

Then he took the two gasoline cans from the sample case and a piece of rubber tubing from the wall and siphoned gasoline from the tank of the car into the cans until they were full. He put them on the floor among other cans which were full of paint and solvent.

Finally he took out the rubber gloves and tossed them on the floor under one of the partly painted chairs. The spatters of paint on the gloves were the exact color of the paint on the chairs.

Mr Keesler went into the house by the side door, and Mrs Keesler, who had been setting the kitchen table, heard him. She came into the living room and watched as Mr Keesler turned the sample case upside down over the table. Trinkets rolled all over the table, and Mrs Keesler caught the souvenir charm before it could fall to the floor.

'More junk,' she said good-naturedly.

'Same as always,' said Mr Keesler, 'just stuff from the office. I'll given them to Sally's kids.' His niece Sally had two pretty little daughters of whom he was very fond.

Mrs Keesler put her hand over her mouth and looked around. 'And what about the suit?' she said. 'Don't tell me you forgot about the suit at the tailor's!'

Mr Keesler already had one arm out of his coat. He stood there helplessly.

'Oh, no,' he said.

His wife sighed resignedly.

'Oh, yes,' she said. 'And you'll go right down there now before he closes.'

Mr Keesler thrust an arm out behind him, groping for the sleeve of his coat, and located it with his wife's help. She brushed away a speck on the shoulder of the coat, and then patted her husband's cheek affectionately.

'If you could only learn to be a little methodical, dear,' said Mrs Keesler.

# The Question

I am an electrocutioner . . . I prefer this word to executioner; I think words make a difference. When I was a boy, people who buried the dead were undertakers, and then somewhere along the way they became morticians and are better off for it.

Take the one who used to be the undertaker in my town. He was a decent, respectable man, very friendly if you'd let him be, but hardly anybody would let him be. Today, his son – who now runs the business – is not an undertaker but a mortician, and is welcome everywhere. As a matter of fact, he's an officer in my Lodge and is one of the most popular members we have. And all it took to do that was changing one word to another. The job's the same but the word is different, and people somehow will always go by words rather than meaning.

So, as I said, I am an electrocutioner – which is the proper professional word for it in my state where the electric chair is the means of execution.

Not that this is my profession. Actually, it's a sideline, as it is for most of us who perform executions. My real business is running an electrical supply and repair shop just as my father did before me. When he died I inherited not only the business from him, but also the position of state's electrocutioner.

We established a tradition, my father and I. He was running the shop profitably even before the turn of the century when electricity was a comparatively new thing, and he was the first man to perform a successful electrocution for the state. It was not the state's first electrocution, however. That one was an experiment and was badly bungled by the engineer who installed the chair in the state prison. My father, who had helped install the chair, was the assistant at the electrocution, and he told me that everything that could go wrong that day did go wrong. The current was eccentric, his boss froze on the switch, and the man in the chair was alive and kicking at the same time he was being burned to a crisp. The next time, my father offered to do the job himself, rewired the chair, and handled the switch so well that he was offered the job of official electrocutioner.

I followed in his footsteps, which is how a tradition is made, but I am afraid this one ends with me. I have a son, and what I said to him and what he said to me is the crux of the matter. He asked me a question – well, in my opinion, it was the kind of question that's at the bottom of most of the world's troubles today. There are some sleeping dogs that should be left to lie; there are some questions that should not be asked.

To understand all this, I think you have to understand me, and nothing could be easier. I'm sixty, just beginning to look my age, a little overweight, suffer sometimes from arthritis when the weather is damp. I'm a good citizen, complain about my taxes but pay them on schedule, vote for the right party, and run my business well enough to make a comfortable living from it.

I've been married thirty-five years and never looked at another woman in all that time. Well, looked maybe, but no more than that. I have a married daughter and a granddaughter about a year old, and the prettiest, smilingest baby in town. I spoil her and don't apologize for it, because in my opinion that is what grandfathers were made for – to spoil their grandchildren. Let mama and papa attend to the business; grandpa is there for the fun.

And beyond all that I have a son who asks questions. The kind that shouldn't be asked.

Put the picture together, and what you get is someone like yourself. I might be your next-door neighbor, I might be your old friend, I might be the uncle you meet whenever the family gets together at a wedding or a funeral. I'm like you.

Naturally, we all look different on the outside but we can still recognize each other on sight as the same kind of people. Deep down inside where it matters we have the same feelings, and we know that without any questions being asked about them.

'But,' you might say, 'there is a difference between us. You're the one who performs the executions, and I'm the one who reads about them in the papers, and that's a big difference, no matter how you look at it.'

Is it? Well, look at it without prejudice, look at it with absolute honesty, and you'll have to admit that you're being unfair.

Let's face the facts, we're all in this together. If an old friend of yours happens to serve on a jury that finds a murderer guilty, you don't lock the door against him, do you? More than that: if you could get an introduction to the judge who sentences that murderer to the electric chair, you'd be proud of it, wouldn't you? You'd be honored to have him sit at your table, and you'd be quick enough to let the world know about it.

And since you're so willing to be friendly with the jury that convicts and the judge that sentences, what about the man who has to pull the switch? He's finished the job you wanted done, he's made the world a better place for it. Why must he go hide away in a dark corner until the next time he's needed?

There's no use denying that nearly everybody feels he should, and there's less use denying that it's a cruel thing for anyone in my position to face. If you don't mind some strong language, it's a damned outrage to hire a man for an unpleasant job, and then despise him for it. Sometimes it's hard to abide such righteousness.

How do I get along in the face of it? The only way possible – by keeping my secret locked up tight and never being tempted to give it away. I don't like it that way, but I'm no fool about it.

The trouble is that I'm naturally easygoing and friendly. I'm the sociable kind. I like people, and I want them to like me. At Lodge meetings or in the clubhouse down at the golf course I'm always the center of the crowd. And I know what would happen if at any such time I ever opened my mouth and let that secret out. A five-minute sensation, and after that the slow chill setting in. It would mean the end of my whole life then and there, the kind of life I want to live, and no man in his right mind throws away sixty years of his life for a five-minute sensation.

You can see I've given the matter a lot of thought. More than that, it hasn't been idle thought. I don't pretend to be an educated man, but I'm willing to read books on any subject that interests me, and execution has been one of my main interests ever since I got into the line. I have the books sent to the shop, where nobody takes notice of another piece of mail, and I keep them locked in a bin in my office so that I can read them in private.

There's a nasty smell about having to do it this way – at my age you hate to feel like a kid hiding himself away to read a dirty magazine – but I have no choice. There isn't a soul on earth outside of the warden at state's prison and a couple of picked guards there who know I'm the one pulling the switch at an execution, and I intend it to remain that way.

Oh, yes, my son knows now. Well, he's difficult in some ways, but he's no fool. If I wasn't sure he would keep his mouth shut about what I told him, I wouldn't have told it to him in the first place.

Have I learned anything from those books? At least enough to take a pride in what I'm doing for the state and the way I do it. As far back in history as you want to go there have always been executioners. The day that men first made laws to help keep peace among themselves was the day the first executioner was born. There have always been lawbreakers; there must always be a way of punishing them. It's as simple as that.

The trouble is that nowadays there are too many people who don't want it to be as simple as that. I'm no hypocrite, I'm not one of those narrow-minded fools who thinks that every time a man comes up with a generous impulse he's some kind of crackpot. But he can be mistaken. I'd put most of the people who are against capital punishment in that class. They are fine, high-minded citizens who've never in their lives been close enough to a murderer or rapist to smell the evil in him. In fact, they're so fine and high-minded that they can't imagine anyone in the world not being like themselves. In that case, they say anybody who commits murder or rape is just a plain, ordinary human being who's had a bad spell. He's no criminal, they say, he's just sick. He doesn't need the electric chair; all he needs is a kindly old doctor to examine his head and straighten out the kinks in his brain.

In fact, they say there is no such thing as a criminal at all.

There are only well people and sick people, and the ones who deserve all your worry and consideration are the sick ones. If they happen to murder or rape a few of the well ones now and then, why, just run for the doctor.

This is the argument from beginning to end, and I'd be the last one to deny that it's built on honest charity and good intentions. But it's a mistaken argument. It omits the one fact that matters. When anyone commits murder or rape he is no longer in the human race. A man has a human brain and a God-given soul to control his animal nature. When the animal in him takes control he's not a human being any more. Then he has to be exterminated the way any animal must be if it goes wild in the middle of helpless people. And my duty is to be the exterminator.

It could be that people just don't understand the meaning of the word *duty* any more. I don't want to sound old-fashioned, God forbid, but when I was a boy things were more straightforward and clear-cut. You learned to tell right from wrong, you learned to do what had to be done, and you didn't ask questions every step of the way. Or if you had to ask any questions, the ones that mattered were *how* and *when*.

Then along came psychology, along came the professors, and the main question was always *why*. Ask yourself *why, why, why* about everything you do, and you'll end up doing nothing. Let a couple of generations go along that way, and you'll finally have a breed of people who sit around in trees like monkeys, scratching their heads.

Does this sound far-fetched? Well, it isn't. Life is a complicated thing to live. All his life a man finds himself facing one situation after another, and the way to handle them is to live by the rules. Ask yourself *why* once too often, and you can find yourself so tangled up that you go under. The show must go on. Why? Women and children first. Why? My country, right or wrong. Why? Never mind your duty. Just keep asking *why* until it's too late to do anything about it.

Around the time I first started going to school my father gave me a dog, a collie pup named Rex. A few years later Rex suddenly became unfriendly, the way a dog will sometimes, and then vicious, and then one day he bit my mother when she reached down to pat him.

The day after that I saw my father leaving the house with his hunting gun and with Rex on a leash. It wasn't the hunting season, so I knew what was going to happen to Rex and I knew why. But it's forgivable in a boy to ask things that a man should be smart enough not to ask.

'Where are you taking Rex?' I asked my father. 'What are you going to do with him?'

'I'm taking him out back of town,' my father said. 'I'm going to shoot him.'

'But why?' I said, and that was when my father let me see that there is only one answer to such a question.

'Because it has to be done,' he said.

I never forgot that lesson. It came hard; for a while I hated my father for it, but as I grew up I came to see how right he was. We both knew why the dog had to be killed. Beyond that, all questions would lead nowhere. Why the dog had become vicious, why God had put a dog on earth to be killed this way – these are the questions that you can talk out to the end of time, and while you're talking about them you still have a vicious dog on your hands.

It is strange to look back and realize now that when the business of the dog happened, and long before it and long after it, my father was an electrocutioner, and I never knew it. Nobody knew it, not even my mother. A few times a year my father would pack his bag and a few tools and go away for a couple of days, but that was all any of us knew. If you asked him where he was going he would simply say he had a job to do out of town. He was not a man you'd ever suspect of philandering or going off on a solitary drunk, so nobody gave it a second thought.

It worked the same way in my case. I found out how well it worked when I finally told my son what I had been doing on those jobs out of town, and that I had gotten the warden's permission to take him on as an assistant and train him to handle the chair himself when I retired. I could tell from the way he took it that he was as thunderstruck at this as I had been thirty years before when my father had taken me into his confidence.

'Electrocutioner?' said my son. 'An *electrocutioner*?'

'Well, there's no disgrace to it,' I said. 'And since it's got to be done, and somebody has to do it, why not keep it in the family? If you knew anything about it, you'd know it's a profession that's often passed down in a family from generation to generation. What's wrong with a good, sound tradition? If more people believed in tradition you wouldn't have so many troubles in the world today.'

It was the kind of argument that would have been more than enough to convince me when I was his age. What I hadn't taken into account was that my son wasn't like me, much as I wanted him to be. He was a grown man in his own right, but a grown man who had never settled down to his responsibilities. I had always kept closing my eyes to that, I had always seen him the way I wanted to and not the way he was.

When he left college after a year, I said, all right, there are some people who aren't made for college, I never went there, so what difference does it make. When he went out with one girl after another and could never make up his mind to marrying any of them, I said, well, he's young, he's sowing his wild oats, the time will come soon enough when he's ready to take care of a home and family. When he sat daydreaming in the shop instead of tending to business I never made a fuss about it. I knew when he put his mind to it he was as good an electrician as you could ask for, and in these soft times people are allowed to do a lot more dreaming and a lot less working than they used to.

The truth was that the only thing that mattered to me was being his friend. For all his faults he was a fine-looking boy with a good mind. He wasn't much for mixing with people, but if he wanted to he could win anyone over. And in the back of my mind all the while he was growing up was the thought that he was the only one who would learn my secret some day, and would share it with me, and make it easier to bear. I'm not secretive by nature. A man like me needs a thought like that to sustain him.

So when the time came to tell him he shook his head and

said no. I felt that my legs had been kicked out from under me. I argued with him and he still said no, and I lost my temper.

'Are you against capital punishment?' I asked him. 'You don't have to apologize if you are. I'd think all the more of you, if that's your only reason.'

'I don't know if it is,' he said.

'Well, you ought to make up your mind one way or the other,' I told him. 'I'd hate to think you were like every other hypocrite around here who says it's all right to condemn a man to the electric chair and all wrong to pull the switch.'

'Do I have to be the one to pull it?' he said. 'Do you?'

'Somebody has to do it. Somebody always has to do the dirty work for the rest of us. It's not like the Old Testament days when everybody did it for himself. Do you know how they executed a man in those days? They laid him on the ground tied hand and foot, and everybody around had to heave rocks on him until he was crushed to death. They didn't invite anybody to stand around and watch. You wouldn't have had much choice then, would you?'

'I don't know,' he said. And then because he was as smart as they come and knew how to turn your words against you, he said, 'After all, I'm not without sin.'

'Don't talk like a child,' I said. 'You're without the sin of murder on you or any kind of sin that calls for execution. And if you're so sure the Bible has all the answers, you might remember that you're supposed to render unto Caesar the things that are Caesar's.'

'Well,' he said, 'in this case I'll let you do the rendering.'

I knew then and there from the way he said it and the way he looked at me that it was no use trying to argue with him. The worst of it was knowing that we had somehow moved far apart from each other and would never really be close again. I should have had sense enough to let it go at that. I should have just told him to forget the whole thing and keep his mouth shut about it.

Maybe if I had ever considered the possibility of his saying no, I would have done it. But because I hadn't considered any such possibility I was caught off balance, I was too much upset to think straight. I will admit it now. It was my own fault that I made an issue of things and led him to ask the one question he should never have asked.

'I see,' I told him. 'It's the same old story, isn't it? Let somebody else do it. But if they pull your number out of a hat and you have to serve on a jury and send a man to the chair, that's all right with you. At least, it's all right as long as there's somebody else to do the job that you and the judge and every decent citizen wants done. The shop is where you belong. You can be nice and cozy there, wiring up fixtures and ringing the cash register. I can handle my duties without your help.'

It hurt me to say it. I had never talked like that to him before, and it hurt. The strange thing was that he didn't seem angry about it; he only looked at me, puzzled.

'Is that all it is to you?' he said. 'A duty?'

'Yes.'

'But you get paid for it, don't you?'

'I get paid little enough for it.'

He kept looking at me that way. 'Only a duty?' he said, and never took his eyes off me. 'But you enjoy it, don't you?'

That was the question he asked.

*You enjoy it, don't you?* You stand there looking through a peephole in the wall at the chair. In thirty years I have stood there more than a hundred times looking at that chair. The guards bring somebody in. Usually he is in a daze; sometimes he screams, throws himself around and fights. Sometimes it is a woman, and a woman can be as hard to handle as a man when she is led to the chair. Sooner or later, whoever it is is strapped down and the black hood is dropped over his head. Now your hand is on the switch.

The warden signals, and you pull the switch. The current hits the body like a tremendous rush of air suddenly filling it. The body leaps out of the chair with only the straps holding it back. The head jerks, and a curl of smoke comes from it. You release the switch and the body falls back again.

You do it once more, do it a third time to make sure. And whenever your hand presses the switch you can see in your mind what the current is doing to that body and what the face under the hood must look like.

Enjoy it?

That was the question my son asked me. That was what he said to me, as if I didn't have the same feelings deep down in me that we all have.

Enjoy it?

But, my God, how could anyone *not* enjoy it?

# The Crime of
# Ezechiele Coen

Before the disenchantment set in, Noah Freeman lived in a whirl of impressions. The chaotic traffic. The muddy Tiber. The Via Veneto out of Italian movies about *la dolce vita*. The Fountain of Trevi out of Hollywood. Castel Sant'-Angelo out of *Tosca*. Rome.

'Rome?' Pop had said. 'But why Rome? Such a foreign place. And so far away.'

True. But to old Pop Freeman, even Rockland County, an hour from New York, was far away, and his two weeks of vacation there every summer an adventure. And, in fact, it was likely that Pop had not been too much surprised at his son's decision to go journeying afar. After all, this was the son who was going to be a doctor – at the very least a teacher – and who had become, of all things, a policeman.

'A policeman in the family,' Pop would muse aloud now and then. 'A detective with a gun in the family like on TV. My own son. What would Mama say if she ever knew, may she rest in peace?'

But, Noah had to admit, the old man had been right about one thing. Rome was far, far away, not only from New York, but also from the blood-quickening image of it instilled in young Noah Freeman when he was a schoolboy soaking himself in gaudy literature about Spartacus and Caesar and Nero. And the Pensione Alfiara, hidden away in an alley off Via Arenula, was hardly a place to quicken anyone's blood. It took an ill wind to blow an occasional American tourist there. In Noah's case, the ill wind was the cab driver who had picked him up at Fiumicino Airport and who happened to be Signora Alfiara's brother-in-law.

It was made to order for disenchantment, the Pensione Alfiara. Granting that it offered bargain rates, its cuisine was monotonous, its service indifferent, its plumbing capricious, and its clientele, at least in early March, seemed to consist entirely of elderly, sad-eyed Italian villagers come to Rome to attend the deathbed of a dear friend. Aside from Signora Alfiara herself and the girl at the portiere's desk, no one on the scene spoke English, so communication between Noah and his fellow boarders was restricted to nods and shrugs, well meant, but useless in relieving loneliness.

Its one marked asset was the girl at the portiere's desk. She was tall and exquisite, one of the few really beautiful women Noah had yet encountered in Rome, because among other disillusionments was the discovery that Roman women are not the women one sees in Italian movies. And she lived behind her desk from early morning to late at night as if in a sad, self-contained world of her own, skillful at her accounts, polite, but remote and disinterested.

She intrigued him for more than the obvious reasons. The English she spoke was almost unaccented. If anything, it was of the clipped British variety which led him to wonder whether she might not be a Briton somehow washed up on this Roman shore. And at her throat on a fine gold chain was a Mogen David, a Star of David, announcing plainly enough that she was Jewish. The sight of that small, familiar ornament had startled him at first, then had emboldened him to make a friendly overture.

'As a fellow Jew,' he had said smilingly, 'I was wondering if you—' and she had cut in with chilling politeness, 'Yes, you'll find the synagogue on Lungotevere dei Cenci, a few blocks south. One of the landmarks of this part of Rome. Most interesting, of course' – which was enough to send him off defeated.

After that, he regretfully put aside hopes of making her acquaintance and dutifully went his tourist way alone, the guidebook to Rome in his hand, the Italian phrase book in his pocket, trying to work up a sense of excitement at what he saw, and failing dismally at it. Partly, the weather was to blame – the damp, gray March weather which promised no break in the clouds overhead. And partly, he knew, it was loneliness – the kind of feeling that made him painfully envious of the few groups of tourists he saw here and there, shepherded by an officious guide, but, at least, chattering happily to each other.

But most of all – and this was something he had to force himself to acknowledge – he was not a tourist, but a fugitive. And what he was trying to flee was Detective Noah Freeman, who, unfortunately, was always with him and always would be. To be one of those plump, self-satisfied, retired businessmen gaping at the dome of St Peter's, that was one thing; to be Noah Freeman was quite another.

It was possible that Signora Alfiara, who had a pair of bright, knowing eyes buried in her pudding face, comprehended his state of mind and decided with maternal spirit to do something about it. Or it was possible that having learned his occupation she was honestly curious about him. Whatever the reason, Noah was deeply grateful the morning she sat down at the table where he was having the usual breakfast of hard roll, acid coffee, and watery marmalade, and explained that she had seen at the cinema stories about American detectives, but that he was the first she had ever met. Very interesting. And was life in America as the cinema showed it? So much shooting and beating and danger? Had he ever been shot at? Wounded, perhaps? What a way of life! It made her blood run cold to think of it.

The Signora was unprepossessing enough in her bloated shapelessness, her shabby dress and worn bedroom slippers; but, at least, she was someone to talk to, and they were a long time at breakfast settling the question of life in America. Before they left the table Noah asked about the girl at the portiere's desk. Was she Italian? She didn't sound like it when she spoke English.

'Rosanna?' said the Signora. 'Oh, yes, yes, Italian. But when she was a little one – you know, when the Germans were here – she was sent to people in England. She was there many years. Oh, Italian, but *una Ebrea*, a Jew, poor sad little thing.'

The note of pity rankled. 'So am I,' Noah said.

'Yes, she has told me,' the Signora remarked, and he saw that her pity was not at all for the girl's being *una Ebrea*. More than that, he was warmed by the knowledge that the beautiful and unapproachable Rosanna had taken note of him after all.

'What makes her sad?' he asked. 'The war's been over a long time.'

'For some, yes. But her people will not let her forget what her father did when the Germans were here. There was the Resistance here, the partisans, you know, and her father sold them to the Germans. So they believe. Now they hate her and her brother because they are the children of a Judas.'

'What do you mean, so they believe? Are they wrong about her father?'

'She says they are. To her, you understand, the father was like a saint. A man of honor and very brave. That might be. But when the Germans were here, even brave men were not so brave sometimes. Yet, who am I to say this about him? He was the doctor who saved my life and the life of my first son when I gave birth to him. That is why when the girl needed work I paid back a little of my debt by helping her this way. A good bargain, too. She's honest, she works hard, she speaks other languages, so I lose nothing by a little kindness.'

'And what about her brother? Is he still around?'

'You see him every day. Giorgio. You know Giorgio?'

'The cleaning man?'

'He cleans, he carries, he gets drunk whenever he can, that's Giorgio. Useless, really, but what can I do? For the girl's sake I make as much use of him as I can. You see the trouble with kindness? I wish to repay a debt, so now the windows are forever dirty. When you need that one he is always drunk somewhere. And always with a bad temper. His father had a bad temper, too, but at least he had great skill. As for the girl, she is an angel. But sad. That loneliness, you know, it can kill you.' The Signora leaned forward inquiringly, her bosom overflowing the table. 'Maybe if you would talk to her—'

'I tried to,' said Noah. 'She didn't seem very much interested.'

'Because you are a stranger. But I have seen her watch you when you pass by. If you were a friend, perhaps. If the three of us dined together tonight—'

Signora Alfiara was someone who had her own way when she wanted to. The three of them dined together that night, but in an atmosphere of constraint, the conversation moving only under the impetus of questions the Signora aimed at Noah, Rosanna sitting silent and withdrawn as he answered.

When, while they were at their fruit and cheese, the Signora took abrupt and smiling leave of them with transparent motive, Noah said with some resentment to the girl, 'I'm sorry about all this. I hope you know I wasn't the one to suggest this little party. It was the lady's idea.'

'I do know that.'

'Then why take out your mood on me?'

Rosanna's lips parted in surprise. 'Mood? But I had no intention – believe me, it has nothing to do with you.'

'What does it have to do with? Your father?' And seeing from her reaction that he had hit the mark, he said, 'Yes, I heard about that.'

'Heard what?'

'A little. Now you can tell me the rest. Or do you enjoy having it stuck in your throat where you can't swallow it and can't bring it up, one way or the other?'

'You must have a strange idea of enjoyment. And if you want the story, go to the synagogue, go to the ghetto or Via Catalena. You'll hear it there quick enough. Everyone knows it.'

'I might do that. First I'd like to hear your side of it.'

'As a policeman? You're too late, Mr Freeman. The case against Ezechiele Coen was decided long ago without policeman or judges.'

'What case?'

'He was said to have betrayed leaders of the Resistance. That was a lie, but partisans killed him for it. They shot him and left him lying with a sign on him saying *Betrayer*. Yes, Mr Freeman, Ezechiele Coen who preached honor to his children as the one meaningful thing in life died in dishonor. He lay there in the dirt of the Teatro Marcello a long time that day, because his own people – our people – would not give him burial. When they remember him now, they spit on the ground. I know,' the girl said in a brittle voice, 'because when I walk past them, they remember him.'

'Then why do you stay here?'

'Because he is here. Because here is where his blackened

memory – his spirit – remains, waiting for the truth to be known.'

'Twenty years after the event?'

'Twenty or a hundred or a thousand. Does time change the truth, Mr Freeman? Isn't it as important for the dead to get justice as the living?'

'Maybe it is. But how do you know that justice wasn't done in this case? What evidence is there to disprove the verdict? You were a child when all this happened, weren't you?'

'And not even in Rome. I was in England then, living with a doctor who knew my father since their school days. Yes, England is far away and I was a child then, but I knew my father.'

If faith could really move mountains, Noah thought. 'And what about your brother. Does he feel the way you do?'

'Giorgio tries to feel as little as he can about it. When he was a boy everyone said that some day he would be as fine a man and a doctor as his father. Now he's a drunkard. A bottle of wine makes it easy not to feel pain.'

'Would he mind if I talked to him about this?'

'Why would you want to? What could Ezechiele Coen mean to you anyhow? Is Rome so boring that you must play detective here to pass the time? I don't understand you, Mr Freeman.'

'No, you don't,' Noah said harshly. 'But you might if you listen to what I'm going to tell you. Do you know where I got the time and money to come on a trip like this, a plain, ordinary, underpaid cop like me? Well, last year there was quite a scandal about some policemen in New York who were charged with taking graft from a gambler. I was one of them under charges. I had no part of that mess, but I was suspended from my job and when they got around to it, I was put on trial. The verdict was not guilty, I got all my back pay in one lump, and I was told to return to duty. Things must have looked fine for me, wouldn't you think?'

'Because you did get justice,' Rosanna said.

'From the court. Only from the court. Afterward, I found that no one else really believed I was innocent. No one. Even my own father sometimes wonders about it. And if I went back on the Force, the grafters there would count me as one of them, and the honest men wouldn't trust me. That's why I'm here. Because I don't know whether to go back or not, and I need time to think, I need to get away from them all. So I did get justice, and now you tell me what good it did.'

The girl shook her head somberly. 'Then my father isn't the only one, is he? But you see, Mr Freeman, you can defend your own good name. Tell me, how is he to defend his?'

That was the question which remained in his mind afterward, angry and challenging. He tried to put it aside, to fix on his own immediate problem, but there it was. It led him the next morning away from proper destinations, the ruins and remains italicized in his guidebook, and on a walk southward along the Tiber.

Despite gray skies overhead and the dismally brown, turbid river sullenly locked between the stone embankments below, Noah felt a quickening pleasure in the scene. In a few days he had his fill of sightseeing. Brick and marble and Latin inscriptions were not really the stuff of life, and pictures and statuary only dim representations of it. It was people he was hungry to meet, and now that he had an objective in meeting them he felt more alive than he had since his first day in Rome. More alive, in fact, than in all those past months in New York, working alongside his father in the old man's tailor shop. Not that this small effort to investigate the case of Ezechiele Coen would amount to anything, he knew. A matter of dredging up old and bitter memories, that was about what it came to. But the important thing was that he was Noah Freeman again, alive and functioning.

Along Lungotevere dei Cenci construction work was going on. The shells of new buildings towered over slums battered by centuries of hard wear. Midstream in the Tiber was a long, narrow island with several institutional buildings on it. Then, facing it from the embankment, the synagogue came into view, a huge, Romanesque, marble pile.

There was a railing before the synagogue. A young man leaned at his ease against the railing. Despite the chill in the air he was in shirtsleeves, his tanned, muscular arms folded on his chest, his penetrating eyes watching Noah's approach with the light of interest in them. As Noah passed, the man came to attention.

'*Shalom.*'

'*Shalom,*' Noah said, and the young man's face brightened. In his hand magically appeared a deck of picture postcards.

'Postcards, hey? See, all different of Rome. Also, the synagogue, showing the inside and the outside. You an *Americano Ebreo*, no? A *landsman?*'

'Yes,' said Noah, wondering if only *Americano Ebreos* came this way. 'But you can put away the pictures. I don't want any.'

'Maybe a guidebook? The best. Or you want a guide? The ghetto, Isola Tiberina, Teatro Marcello? Anywhere you want to go, I can show you. Two thousand lire. Ask anybody. For two thousand lire nobody is a better guide than Carlo Piperno. That's me.'

'Noah Freeman, that's me. And the only place I want to go to is the rabbi's. Can I find him in the synagogue?'

'No, but I will take you to his house. Afterwards we see the ghetto, Tiberina—'

The rabbi proved to be a man of good will, of understanding, but, he explained in precise English, perhaps he could afford to be objective about the case of Ezechiele Coen because he himself was not a Roman. He had come to this congregation from Milan, an outsider. Yet, even as an outsider he could appreciate the depth of his congregation's hatred for their betrayer. A sad situation, but could they be blamed for that? Could it not be the sternest warning to all such betrayers if evil times ever came again?

'He's been dead a long time,' said Noah.

'So are those whose lives he sold. Worse than that.' The rabbi gestured at the shuttered window beyond which lay the Tiber. 'He sold the lives of friends who were not of our faith. Those who lived in Trastevere across the river, working people, priests, who gave some of us hiding places when we needed them. Did the daughter of Ezechiele Coen tell you how, when she was a child, they helped remove her from the city at night in a cart of wine barrels, risking their lives to do it? Does she think it is easy to forget how her father rewarded them for that?'

'But why her?' Noah protested. 'Why should your congregation make her an outcast? She and her brother aren't the guilty ones. Do you really believe that the sins of the fathers must be visited on the children?'

The rabbi shook his head. 'There are sins, Signor Freeman, which make a horror that takes generations to wipe away. I welcome the girl and her brother to the synagogue, but I cannot wipe away the horror in the people they would meet here. If I wished to, I could not work such a miracle.

'Only a little while ago there was a great and flourishing congregation here, signore, a congregation almost as ancient as Rome itself. Do you know what is left of it now? A handful. A handful who cannot forget. The Jews of Rome do not forget easily. To this day they curse the name of Titus who destroyed the Temple in Jerusalem as they remember kindly the name of Julius Caesar who was their friend, and for whose body they mourned seven days in the Forum. And the day they forgive Titus will be the same day they forgive Ezechiele Coen and his children and their children to come. Do you know what I mean, Signor Freeman?'

'Yes,' said Noah. 'I know what you mean.'

He went out into the bleak, cobblestoned street, oppressed by a sense of antiquity weighing him down, of two thousand years of unrelenting history heavy on his shoulders, and not even the racketing of motor traffic along the river embankment, the spectacle of the living present, could dispel it. Carlo Piperno, the postcard vender, was waiting there.'

'You have seen the rabbi? Good. Now I show you Isola Tiberina.'

'Forget Isola Tiberina. There's something else I want you to show me.'

'For two thousand lire, anything.'

'All right.' Noah extracted the banknotes from his wallet. 'Does the name Ezechiele Coen mean anything to you?'

Carlo Piperno had the hard, capable look of a man impervious to surprise. Nevertheless, he was visibly surprised. Then he recovered himself. 'That one? *Mi dispiace, signore.* Sorry, but he is dead, that one.' He pointed to the ground at his feet. 'You want him, you have to look there for him.'

334

'I don't want him. I want someone who knew him well. Someone who can tell me what he did and what happened to him.'

'Everybody knows that. I can tell you.'

'No, it must be someone who wasn't a child when it happened. *Capisce?*'

'*Capisco.* But why?'

'If I answer that, it will cost you these two thousand lire. Shall I answer?'

'No, no.' Carlo reached out and dexterously took possession of the money. He shrugged. 'But first the rabbi, now Ezechiele Coen who is in hell long ago. Well, I am a guide, no? So now I am your guide.'

He led the way through a labyrinth of narrow streets to an area not far from the synagogue, a paved area with the remains of a stone wall girdling it. Beyond the wall were tenements worn by time to the color of the clay that had gone into their brick. Yet their tenants seemed to have pride of possession. In almost every window were boxes of flowers and greenery. On steps and in stony courtyards, housewives with brushes and buckets scrubbed the stone and brick. In surrounding alleys were small stores, buzzing with activity.

With shock Noah suddenly realized that here was the ghetto, that he was standing before a vestige of the past which thus far in his life had been only an ugly word to him. It was the presence of the wall that provided the shock, he knew. It had no gate, there was no one to prevent you from departing through it, but if it were up to him he would have had it torn down on the spot.

A strange place, Rome. Wherever you turned were the reminders of the cruel past. Memorials to man, the persecuted. This wall, the catacombs, the churches built to martyrs, the Colosseum. There was no escaping their insistent presence.

Carlo's destination turned out to be a butcher shop – the shop of Vito Levi, according to the sign over it. The butcher, a burly, gray-haired man, stood behind his chest-high marble counter hacking at a piece of meat, exchanging loud repartee with a shriveled old woman, a shawl over her head, a string bag in her hand, waiting for her order. While Carlo was addressing him he continued to chop away with the cleaver, then suddenly placed it on the counter, and came around to meet Noah in the street, wiping his hands on his apron as he came. The old woman followed, peering at Noah with beady-eyed interest, and in another minute others from the street were gathering around, getting the news from her. Ezechiele Coen may have been dead twenty years, Noah thought, but his name was still very much alive in these quarters.

He was not sorry that the matter was going to be discussed in public this way. As a young patrolman on the beat he had learned not to be too quick to break up a crowd around an accident or crime; there might be someone in the crowd who had something to say worth hearing. Now he gathered from the heat of discussion around him that everyone here had something to say about Ezechiele Coen.

With Carlo serving as interpreter, he put his questions first to Levi the butcher, and then to anyone else who volunteered information. Slowly, piece by piece, the picture of Ezechiele Coen and his crime took shape. It was Levi who supplied most of the information – the time, the place, the event.

The butcher had known Ezechiele Coen well. Like all others he had trusted him, because no man had a greater reputation for honesty than the doctor. He was a great doctor, a man of science; yet he was a man of God, too, devout, each morning binding on his phylacteries and saying his prayers, each sabbath attending the synagogue. Not that there was any gentleness in him. He was a proud man, an arrogant man, a man who would insult you to your face for the least offense. After all, it was one thing to be honest, but it was something else again to behave as if you were the only honest man in the world. The only one on earth who would never compromise with truth. That was Ezechiele Coen. You might trust him, but you could not like him. He was too good for that.

Then the trust was betrayed. Over the years one had learned to live with Il Duce, but when the Germans came to Rome, the Resistance of a generation ago reawoke. Sabotage, spying, a hidden press turning out leaflets which told the truth about Il Duce and his ally. Many said it was useless, but Vito Levi, the butcher, and a few others continued their secret efforts, knowing they had nothing to lose. Jews were being deported now, were being shipped to the Nazi slaughter pens in carloads. What else to do then but join some of their Gentile neighbors in the Resistance?

'Ask him,' said Noah to Carlo, 'if Ezechiele Coen was one of the Resistance,' and when Carlo translated this, the butcher shook his head.

Only once was the doctor called on to help. Three leaders of the Resistance had managed to get into Rome from the mountains – to help organize the movement here, to give it leadership. They were hidden in a cellar in Trastevere, across the river, one of them badly wounded. The doctor's son, only a boy then, no more than fifteen years of age, was a courier for the partisans. He had brought his father to attend the wounded man, and then, soon after, the three men together were captured in their hiding place by the Germans. They had been betrayed by the honest, the noble, the righteous Ezechiele Coen.

'Ask him how he knows this,' Noah demanded of Carlo. 'Was there a confession?'

There was no need for one, as it happened. There was no need for any more evidence than the money case of Major von Grubbner.

Noah silently cursed the tedious process of translation. Carlo Piperno was the kind of interpreter who richly enjoys and intends to get the maximum effect from his role. It took him a long time to make clear who and what Major von Grubbner was.

The Major was one of the men assigned to the Panzer division quartered along the Tiber. But unlike the German officers around him, Major von Grubbner was cunning as a fox, smooth in his manner, ingratiating in his approach. Others came with a gun in their hands. He came with an attache case, a black leather case with a handsome gold ornament on it, a double-headed eagle which was a reminder of the greater name of his family. And in the case was money. Bundles of money. Packages of lire, fresh and crisp, a fortune by any estimate.

Give the devil his due. This von Grubbner was a brave man

as well as a cunning one. He walked alone, contemptuous of those who needed guards to attend them, the money case in his hand, a smile on his lips, and he invited confidences.

'After all,' he would say, 'we are businessmen, you and I. We are practical people who dislike trouble. Remove the trouble-makers and all is peaceful, no? Well, here I am to do business. Look at this money. Beautiful, isn't it? And all you have to do is name your own price, expose the troublemakers, and we are all happy. Name your own price, that's all you have to do.'

And he would open the case under your nose, showing you the money, fondling it, offering it to you. It was more than money. It was life itself. It could buy the few scraps of food remaining to be bought, it could buy you a refuge for your wife and children, it could buy your safety for another day. Life itself. Everyone wants life, and there it was in that little black leather case with the doubleheaded eagle in gold marking it.

Only one man was tempted. The day after the three partisans were taken, Ezechiele Coen was seen fleeing with that case through the alleys, running like a rabbit before the hounds of vengeance he knew would soon be on him. Only Ezechiele Coen, the devout, the honorable, the arrogant, fell, and died soon for his treachery.

Vito Levi's words needed translation, but not the emotion behind them. And the crowd around Noah, now staring at him in silence, did not need its feelings explained. Yet, the story seemed incomplete to him, to Detective Noah Freeman, who had learned at his job not to live by generalities. The evidence, that was what had meaning.

'Ask them,' he said to Carlo, 'who saw Ezechiele Coen with that case in his possession,' and when Carlo translated this, Levi drove a thumb hard into his own chest. Then he looked around the crowd and pointed, and a man on its outskirts raised his hand, and a woman nearby raised hers, someone else raised a hand.

Three witnesses, four, five. Enough, Noah thought to hang any man. With difficulty, prompting Carlo question by question, he drew their story from them. They lived in houses along Via del Portico. It was hot that night, a suffocating heat that made sleep impossible. One and all, they were at their windows.

One and all, they saw the doctor running down the street toward the Teatro Marcello, the leather case under his arm. His medical bag? No, no. Not with the golden eagle on it. It was the doctor with his blood money. This they swore on the lives of their children.

During siesta time that afternoon, Noah, with the connivance of Signora Alfiara, drew Rosanna out of doors for a walk to a cafe in the Piazza Navona. Over glasses of Campari he told her the results of his investigation.

'Witnesses,' she said scathingly. 'Have you found that witnesses always tell the truth?'

'These people do. But sometimes there can be a difference between what you imagine is the truth and the truth itself.'

'And how do you discover that difference?'

'By asking more questions. For example, did your father live in the ghetto?'

'During the war, yes.'

'And according to my street map the Teatro Marcello is outside it. Why would he be running there with the money instead of keeping it safe at home? Even more curious, why would he carry the money in the case, instead of transferring it to something that couldn't be identified? And why would he be given that case, a personal possession, along with the money? You can see how many unanswered questions come up, if you look at all this without prejudice.'

'Then you think—'

'I don't think anything yet. First, I want to try to get answers to those questions. I want to establish a rational pattern for what seems to be a whole irrational set of events. And there is one person who can help me.'

'Who?'

'Major von Grubbner himself.'

'But how would you ever find him? It was so long ago. He may be dead.'

'Or he may not be. If he is not, there are ways of finding him.'

'But it would mean so much trouble. So much time and effort.'

The way she was looking at him then, Noah thought, was more than sufficient payment for the time and effort. And the way she flushed when he returned her look told him that she knew his thought.

'I'm used to this kind of effort,' he said. 'Anyhow, it may be the last chance I'll have to practice my profession.'

'Then you're not going back to your work with the police? But you're a very good detective. You are, aren't you?'

'Oh, very good. And,' he said, 'honest, too, despite the popular opinion.'

'Don't say it like that,' she flashed angrily. 'You are honest. I know you are.'

'Do you? Well, that makes two of us at least. Anyhow, the vital thing is for me to locate von Grubbner if he's still somewhere to be found. After that, we'll see. By the way, do you know the date when all this happened? When your father was seen with that case?'

'Yes. It was the fifth of July in 1943. I couldn't very well forget that date, Mr Freeman.'

'Noah.'

'Of course,' said Rosanna. 'Noah.'

After returning her to her desk at the pensione, Noah went directly to police headquarters. There he found his credentials an open sesame. In the end he was closeted with Commissioner Ponziani, a handsome urbane man, who listened to the story of Ezechiele Coen with fascination. At its conclusion he raised quizzical eyebrows at Noah.

'And your interest in this affair?'

'Purely unofficial. I don't even know if I have the right to bother you with it at all.' Noah shrugged. 'But when I thought of all the red tape to cut if I went to the military or consular authorities—'

The Commissioner made a gesture which dismissed as beneath contempt the clumsy workings of the military and consular authorities. 'No, no, you did right to come here. We are partners in our profession, are we not, signore? We are of a brotherhood, you and I. So now if you give me all possible information about this Major von Grubbner, I will communicate with the German police. We shall soon learn if there is anything they can tell us about him.'

Soon meant days of waiting, and, Noah saw, they were bad days for Rosanna. Each one that passed left her more tense, more dependent on him for reassurance. How could anyone ever find this German, one man in millions, a man who might have his own reasons for not wanting to be found? And if by some miracle they could confront him, what would he have to say? Was it possible that he would say her father had been guilty?

'It is,' said Noah. He reached out and took her hand comfortingly. 'You have to be prepared for that.'

'I will not be! No, I will not be,' she said fiercely. Then her assurance crumpled. 'He would be lying, wouldn't he? You know he would.' The passage left Noah shaken. Rosanna's intensity, the way she had clutched his hand like a lost child – these left him wondering if he had not dangerously overreached himself in trying to exorcise the ghost of Ezechiele Coen. If he failed, it would leave things worse than ever. Worse for himself, too, because now he realized with delight and misery that he was falling hopelessly in love with the girl. And so much seemed to depend on clearing her father's reputation. Could it be, as Rosanna felt, that Ezechiele Coen's spirit really waited here on the banks of the Tiber to be set at rest? And what if there were no way of doing that?

When Signora Alfiara called him to the phone to take a message from the police, Noah picked up the receiver almost prayerfully.

'*Pronto*,' he said, and Commissioner Ponziani said without preliminary, 'Ah, Signor Freeman. This affair of Major von Grubbner becomes stranger and stranger. Will you meet with me in my office so that we may discuss it?'

At the office the Commissioner came directly to the point.

'The date of the unhappy event we are concerned with,' he said, 'was the fifth of July in 1943. Is that correct?'

'It is,' said Noah.

'And here,' said the Commissioner, tapping a finger on the sheet of paper before him, 'is the report of the German authorities on a Major Alois von Grubbner, attached to the Panzer division stationed in Rome at that time. According to the report, he deserted the army, absconding with a large amount of military funds, on the sixth of July in 1943. No trace of him has been discovered since.'

The Commissioner leaned back in his chair and smiled at Noah. 'Interesting, no? Very interesting. What do you make of it?'

'He didn't desert,' said Noah. 'He didn't abscond. That was the money seen in Ezechiele Coen's possession.'

'So I believe, too. I strongly suspect that this officer was murdered – assassinated may be a more judicious word, considering the circumstances – and the money taken from him.'

'But his body,' Noah said. 'Wouldn't the authorities have allowed for possible murder and made a search for it?'

'A search was made. But Major von Grubbner, it seems, had a somewhat—' the Commissioner twirled a finger in the air, seeking the right word '—a somewhat shady record in his civilian life. A little embezzling here, a little forgery there – enough to make his superiors quickly suspect his integrity when he disappeared. I imagine their search was a brief one. But I say that if they had been able to peer beneath the Tiber—'

'Is that where you think he ended up?'

'There, or beneath some cellar, or in a hole dug in a dark corner. Yes, I know what you are thinking, Signor Freeman. A man like this Doctor Ezechiele Coen hardly seems capable of assassination, robbery, the disposal of a body. Still, that is not much of an argument to present to people violently antagonistic to his memory. It is, at best, a supposition. Fevered emotions are not cooled by suppositions. I very much fear that your investigation has come to an abrupt and unhappy ending.'

Noah shook his head. 'That attaché case and the money in it,' he said. 'It was never found. I was told that when Ezechiele Coen was found shot by partisans and left lying in the Teatro Marcello, the case was nowhere to be seen. What happened to it?'

The Commissioner shrugged. 'Removed by those who did the shooting, of course.'

'If it was there to be removed. But no one ever reported seeing it then or afterward. No one ever made a remark – even after the war when it would be safe to – that money intended to be used against the Resistance was used by it. But don't you think that this is the sort of thing that would be a standing joke – a folk story – among these people?'

'Perhaps. Again it is no more than a supposition.'

'And since it's all I have to go on, I'll continue from there.'

'You are a stubborn man, Signor Freeman.' The Commissioner shook his head with grudging admiration. 'Well, if you need further assistance, come to me directly. Very stubborn. I wish some of my associates had your persistence.'

When Rosanna had been told what occurred in the Commissioner's office she was prepared that instant to make the story public.

'It is proof, isn't it?' she demanded. 'Whatever did happen, we know my father had no part in it. Isn't that true?'

'You and I know. But remember one thing: your father was seen with that attache case. Until that can be explained, nothing else will stand as proof of his innocence.'

'He may have found the case. That's possible, isn't it?'

'Hardly possible,' Noah said. 'And why would he be carrying it toward the Teatro Marcello? What is this Teatro Marcello anyhow?'

'Haven't you seen it yet? It's one of the ruins like the Colosseum, but smaller.'

'Can you take me there now?'

'Not now. I can't leave the desk until Signora Alfiara returns. But it's not far from here. A little distance past the synagogue on the Via del Portico. Look for number 39. You'll find it easily.'

Outside the pensione Noah saw Giorgio Coen unloading a delivery of food from a truck. He was, at a guess, ten years older than his sister, a big, shambling man with good features that had gone slack with dissipation, and a perpetual stubble of beard on his jowls. Despite the flabby look of him, he hoisted a side of meat to his shoulder and bore it into the building with ease. In passing, he looked at Noah with a hangdog, beaten expression, and Noah could feel for him. Rosanna had been cruelly wounded by the hatred vented against her father, but Giorgio had been destroyed by it. However this affair turned out, there was small hope of salvaging anything from these remains.

Noah walked past the synagogue, found the Via del Portico readily enough, and then before the building marked 39 he stood looking around in bewilderment. There was no vestige of any ruin resembling the Colosseum here – no ruin at all, in fact. Number 39 itself was only an old apartment house, the kind of apartment house so familiar to rundown sections of Manhattan back home.

He studied the names under the doorbells outside as if expecting to find the answer to the mystery there, then peered into its tiled hallway. A buxom girl, a baby over her shoulder, came along the hallway, and Noah smiled at her.

'Teatro Marcello?' he said doubtfully. '*Dove?*'

She smiled back and said something incomprehensible to him, and when he shook his head she made a circling gesture with her hand.

'Oh, in back,' Noah said. 'Thank you. *Grazie.*'

It was in back. And it was, Noah decided, one of the more incredible spectacles of this whole incredible city. The Teatro Marcello fitted Rosanna's description: it was the grim gray ruin of a lesser Colosseum. But into it had been built the apartment house, so that only the semicircle of ruins visible from the rear remained in their original form.

The tiers of stone blocks, of columns, of arches towering overhead were Roman remains, and the apartment house was a facade for them, concealing them from anyone standing before the house. Even the top tier of this ancient structure had been put to use, Noah saw. It had been bricked and windowed, and behind some of the windows shone electric lights. People lived there. They walked through the tiled hallway leading from the street, climbed flights of stairs, and entered kitchens and bedrooms whose walls had been built by Imperial slaves two thousand years before. Incredible, but there it was before him.

An immense barren field encircled the building, a wasteland of pebbly earth and weeds. Boys were playing football there, deftly booting the ball back and forth. On the trunks of marble columns half sunk into the ground, women sat and tended baby carriages. Nearby, a withered crone spread out scraps of meat on a piece of newspaper, and cats – the tough-looking, pampered cats of Rome – circled the paper hungrily, waiting for the signal to begin lunch.

Noah tried to visualize the scene twenty years before when Ezechiele Coen had fled here in the darkness bearing an attache case marked with a doubleheaded eagle. He must have had business here, for here was where he lingered until an avenging partisan had searched him out and killed him. But what business? Business with whom? No one in the apartment house; there seemed to be no entrance to it from this side.

At its ground level, the Teatro Marcello was a series of archways, the original entrances to the arena within. Noah walked slowly among them. Each archway was barred by a massive iron gate beyond which was a small cavern solidly bricked, impenetrable at any point. Behind each gate could be seen fragments of columns, broken statuary of heads and arms and robed bodies, a litter of filthy paper blown in by the winds of time. Only in one of those musty caverns could be seen signs of life going on. Piled on a slab of marble were schoolbooks, coats, and sweaters, evidently the property of the boys playing football, placed here for safety's sake.

For safety's sake. With a sense of mounting excitement, Noah studied the gate closely. It extended from the floor almost to the top of the archway. Its iron bars were too close together to allow even a boy to slip between them, its lock massive and solidly caked with rust, the chain holding it as heavy as a small anchor chain. Impossible to get under, over, or through it – yet the boys had. Magic. Could someone else have used that magic on a July night twenty years ago?

When Noah called to them, the boys took their time about stopping their game, and then came over to the gate warily. By dint of elaborate gestures, Noah managed to make his questions clear, but it took a package of cigarettes and a handful of coins to get the required demonstration.

One of the boys, grinning, locked his hands around a bar of the gate and with an effort raised it clear of its socket in the horizontal rod supporting it near the ground. Now it was held only by the cross rod overhead. The boy drew it aside at an

345

angle and slipped through the space left. He returned, dropped the bar back into place, and held out a hand for another cigarette.

With the help of the Italian phrase book, Noah questioned the group around him. How long had these locked gates been here? The boys scratched their heads and looked at each other. A long time. Before they could remember. Before their fathers could remember. A very long time.

And how long had that one bar been loose, so that you could go in and out if you knew the secret? The same. All the *ragazzi* around here knew about it as their fathers had before them.

Could any other of these gates be entered this way? No, this was the only one. The good one.

When he had dismissed them by showing empty hands – no more cigarettes, no more coins – Noah sat down on one of the sunken marble columns near the women and their baby carriages, and waited. It took a while for the boys to finish their game and depart, taking their gear with them, but finally they were gone. Then Noah entered the gate, using his newfound secret, and started a slow, methodical investigation of what lay in the shadowy reaches beyond it.

He gave no thought to the condition of his hands or clothes, but carefully pushed aside the litter of paper, probed under and between the chunks of marble, all the broken statuary around him. At the far end of the cavern he found that once he had swept the litter aside there was a clear space underfoot. Starting at the wall, he inched forward on his knees, sweeping his fingers lightly back and forth over the ground. Then his fingertips hit a slight depression in the flinty earth, an almost imperceptible concavity. Despite the chill in the air, he was sweating now, and had to pull out a handkerchief to mop his brow.

He traced the depression, his fingertips moving along it, following it to its length, turning where it turned, marking a rectangle the length and width of a man's body. Once before, in the course of his official duties, Detective Noah Freeman had marked a rectangle like this in the weed-grown yard of a Bronx shanty, and had found beneath it what he had expected to find. He knew he would not be disappointed in what would be dug up from this hole beneath the Teatro Marcello. He was tempted to get a tool and do the digging himself, but that, of course, must be the job of the police. And before they would be notified, the pieces of the puzzle, all at hand now, must be placed together before a proper witness . . .

When Noah returned to the Pensione Alfiara, he brought with him as witness the rabbi, bewildered by the unexplained urgency of this mission, out of breath at the quick pace Noah had set through the streets. Rosanna was at her desk. She looked with alarm at Noah's grimy hands, at the streaks of dirt and sweat on his face. For the rabbi she had no greeting. This was the enemy, an unbeliever in the cause of Ezechiele Coen. She had eyes only for Noah.

'What happened?' she said. 'What's wrong? Are you hurt?'

'No. Listen, Rosanna, have you told Giorgio anything about von Grubbner? About my meeting with the police commissioner?'

'No.'

'Good. Where is he now?'

'Giorgio? In the kitchen, I think. But why? Why—?'

'If you come along, you'll see why. But you're not to say anything. Not a word, do you understand? Let me do all the talking.'

Giorgio was in the kitchen listlessly moving a mop back and forth over the floor. He stopped when he saw his visitors, and regarded them with bleary bewilderment. Now is the time, Noah thought. It must be done quickly and surely now, or it will never be done at all.

'Giorgio,' he said, 'I have news for you. Good news. Your father did not betray anyone.'

Resentment flickered in the bleary eyes. 'I have always known that, signore. But why is it your concern?'

'He never betrayed anyone, Giorgio. But you did.'

Rosanna gasped. Giorgio shook his head pityingly. 'Listen to him! *Basta, signore. Basta.* I have work to do.'

'You did your work a long time ago,' Noah said relentlessly. 'And when your father took away the money paid to you for it, you followed him and killed him to get it back.'

He was pleased to see that Giorgio did not reel under this

wholly false accusation. Instead, he seemed to draw strength from it. This is the way, Noah thought, that the unsuspecting animal is lured closer and closer to the trap. What hurt was that Rosanna, looking back and forth from inquisitor to accused, seemed ready to collapse. The rabbi watched with the same numb horror.

Giorgio turned to them. 'Do you hear this?' he demanded, and there was a distinct mockery in his voice. 'Now I am a murderer. Now I killed my own father.'

'Before a witness,' Noah said softly.

'Oh, of course, before a witness. And who was that witness, signore?'

'Someone who has just told the police everything. They'll bring him here very soon, so that he can point you out to them. A Major von Grubbner.'

'And that is the worst lie of all!' said Giorgio triumphantly. 'He's dead, that one! Dead and buried, do you hear? So all your talk—!'

There are animals which, when trapped, will fight to the death for their freedom, will gnaw away one of their own legs to loose themselves. There are others which go to pieces the instant the jaws of the trap have snapped on them, become quivering lumps of flesh waiting only for the end. Giorgio, Noah saw, was one of the latter breed. His voice choked off, his jaw went slack, his face ashen. The mop, released from his nerveless grip, fell with a clatter. Rosanna took a step toward him, but Noah caught her wrist, holding her back.

'How do you know he's dead, Giorgio?' he demanded. 'Yes, he's dead and buried – but how did you know that? No one else knew. How do you happen to be the only one?'

The man swayed, fell back against the wall.

'You killed von Grubbner and took that money,' Noah said. 'When your father tried to get rid of it, the partisans held him guilty of informing and shot him while you stood by, refusing to tell them the truth. In a way, you did help kill him, didn't you? That's what you've been carrying around in you since the day he died, isn't it?'

'Giorgio!' Rosanna cried out. 'But why didn't you tell them? Why? Why?'

'Because,' said Noah, 'then they would have known the real informer. That money was a price paid to you for information, wasn't it, Giorgio?'

The word emerged like a groan. 'Yes.'

'You?' Rosanna said wonderingly, her eyes fixed on her brother. 'It was you?'

'But what could I do? What could I do? He came to me, the German. He said he knew I was of the Resistance. He said if I did not tell him where the men were hidden I would be put to death. If I told, I would be saved. I would be rewarded.'

The broken hulk lurched toward Rosanna, arms held wide in appeal, but Noah barred the way. 'Why did you kill von Grubbner?'

'Because he cheated me. After the men were taken, I went to him for the money, and he laughed at me. He said I must tell him about others, too. I must tell everything, and then he would pay. So I killed him. When he turned away, I picked up a stone and struck him on the head and then again and again until he was dead. And I buried him behind the gate there because only the *ragazzi* knew how to get through it, and no one would find him there.'

'But you took that case full of money with you.'

'Yes, but only to give to my father. And I told him everything. Everything. I swear it. I wanted him to beat me. I wanted him to kill me if that would make it all right. But he would not. All he knew was that the money must be returned. He had too much honor! That was what he died for. He was mad with honor! Who else on this earth would try to return money to a dead man?'

Giorgio's legs gave way. He fell to his knees and remained there, striking the floor blow after blow with his fist. 'Who else?' he moaned. 'Who else?'

The rabbi looked helplessly at Noah. 'He was a boy then,' he said in a voice of anguish 'Only a boy. Can we hold children guilty of the crimes we inflict on them?' And then he said with bewilderment, 'But what of the blood money? What did Eze-chiele Coen do with it? What became of it?'

'I think we'll soon find out,' said Noah.

*

349

They were all there at the gates of the Teatro Marcello when Commissioner Ponziani arrived with his men. All of them and more. The rabbi and Carlo Piperno, the postcard vender, and Vito Levi, the butcher, and a host of others whose names were inscribed on the rolls of the synagogue. And tenants of the Teatro Marcello, curious as to what was going on below them, and schoolboys and passersby with time to spare.

The Commissioner knew his job, Noah saw. Not only had he brought a couple of strong young *carabinieri* to perform the exhumation, but other men as well to hold back the excited crowd.

Only Giorgio was not there. Giorgio was in a bed of the hospital on Isola Tiberina, his face turned to the wall. He was willing himself to die, the doctor had said, but he would not die. He would live, and, with help, make use of the years ahead. It was possible that employment in the hospital itself, work which helped the unfortunate, might restore to him a sense of his own worth. The doctor would see to that when the time came.

Noah watched as the police shattered the lock on the gates and drew them apart, their hinges groaning rustily. He put an arm around Rosanna's waist and drew her to him as the crowd pressed close behind them. This was all her doing, he thought. Her faith had moved mountains, and with someone like this at his side, someone whose faith in him would never waver, it would not be hard to return home and face the cynics there. It didn't take a majority vote of confidence to sustain you; it needed only one person's granite faith.

The police strung up lights in the vaulted area behind the gate. They studied the ground, then carefully plied shovels as the Commissioner hovered around them.

'*Faccia attenzione,*' he said. '*Adagio. Adagio.*'

The mound of dirt against the wall grew larger. The men put aside their shovels. Kneeling, they carefully scooped earth from the hole, handful by handful. Then the form of a body showed fleshless bones, a grinning shattered skull. A body clad in the moldering tatters of a military uniform.

And, as Noah saw under the glare of droplights, this was not the first time these remains had been uncovered. On the chest of the skeletal form rested a small leather case fallen to rot, marked by the blackened image of a doubleheaded eagle. The case had come apart at all its seams, the money in it seemed to have melted together in lumps, more like clay than money, yet it was clearly recognizable for what it was. Twenty years ago Ezechiele Coen had scraped aside the earth over the freshly buried Major Alois von Grubbner and returned his money to him. There it was and there he was, together as they had been since that time.

Noah became aware of the rabbi's voice behind him. Then another voice and another, all merging into a litany recited in deep-toned chorus. A litany, Noah thought, older than the oldest ruins of Rome. It was the *kaddish*, the Hebrew prayer for the dead, raised to heaven for Ezechiele Coen, now at rest.

# The Great Persuader

On the morning of her seventy-fifth birthday Mrs Meeker dallied over her usual breakfast of coffee and a cigarette while reading through the pile of congratulatory messages on the table before her. Telegrams, notes, and cards. Messages from the governor of Florida himself, from dignitaries of the city of Miami Beach, from old, old friends who nested as far north as Palm Beach and Hobe Sound.

There was even an editorial in the Miami Beach *Journal* swimming in adjectives and dedicated to her. A half century ago, it pointed out (and the choice of phrase made Mrs Meeker feel incredibly ancient), Marcus Meeker had brought his fair young bride from the chilly north (tourists take note, thought Mrs Meeker) to help him shape a glittering wonderland out of the sun-kissed isle of Miami Beach. Honored be his memory. Happy the birthday of the partner who had shared his triumphs, the First Lady of the city.

There was, of course, no mention of Marcus junior, who in his time had provided the *Journal* with even more spectacular copy than his father. The painful memory of her long-dead son rose in Mrs Meeker. What a charmer he had been. How gay and clever and handsome. But with one fatal weakness. Where the horses were run or the cards dealt or the dice thrown, there he was simply a helpless, useless hulk, sick with the gambling madness. A lamb for the slaughter, easy pickings for the wolves. Because of them he had squandered the Meeker fortune – first his inheritance and then his mother's – had neglected his ailing wife until it was too late to do anything but mourn her death, and had made himself a stranger to his infant daughter. And finally had gone to a bloody and scandalous death, murdered in a dark alley as a lesson to others who might fail in the payment of their gambling debts.

Yes, what an enchanting boy he had been, Mrs Meeker thought. What a pitiful figure of a man.

She closed her mind to harrowing memories. There was other mail before her to attend to. A solemn warning from the tax commission, a heartfelt plea from the electric company, urgent reminders from various local merchants. Mrs Meeker dutifully read them all, then contemplated her barren dining room, wondering what was left in the house to sell and what price she could get for it.

Really, she told herself, it was like being captain of a luxurious ship whose fuel reserve was gone and whose precious furnishings had to be fed to the hungry boilers. It became a way of life after a while. Painful at first to see the jewelry go, and then the silver and china and curios and books and pictures and, at last, the furniture, piece by piece; but that was nothing to what her misery would be if she were forced to sell the estate and live out her remaining life elsewhere.

She smiled at the portrait of her husband on the wall. Dear brawling, arrogant Marcus, who had come out of a Boston slum to carry off a Beacon Street princess. He had brought her south with the assurance that he would make his fortune here, and he had kept his word. And once the fortune was made he had built this hacienda, building by building, to her design.

Casuarina, it was named, from the grove of trees around it; and the day she saw it complete, set among casuarinas and royal palms against the pale green waters of the Gulf Stream beyond, she knew that this was where she intended to live out her life. The buildings might be shabby with decay now, but they still stood defiantly against tropical sun and wind; and this was home – this was where the heart was, and life anywhere else would be unendurable. She was lost in these musings when her grandaughter Polly came down to breakfast, a song on her pretty lips, a birthday gift in her hand. It was a silver brooch, a profligate gift considering Polly's earnings, and Mrs Meeker swiftly calculated that it might placate the electric company for a month or so without Polly's knowing where it had gone.

Polly was an adorable child, as her grandmother readily

acknowledged; she was, along with Casuarina and a passion for cribbage, foremost among the things that still gave life meaning. But she had a head full of confetti, no doubt about it. She had failed out of the University at the end of one semester; she held her receptionist's job at the law offices of Peabody and Son only because young Duff Peabody was hopelessly infatuated with her; and at the age of twenty she had an ingenuousness about life that could be frightening at times.

But, Mrs Meeker wondered, how does one cope with a breathtakingly beautiful young woman who stubbornly insisted on taking everyone in the world at face value?

Before breakfast was over, a car horn sounded, and Polly leaped to her feet.

'Which one is that?' Mrs Meeker asked.

To her, the young louts from the University who danced attendance on Polly were indistinguishable from each other. All football players, apparently, and all astonishingly muscular, they had fallen under Polly's spell during her brief tenure at the University and now took turns driving her to her office.

'It's Frank,' said Polly, 'or Billy. I don't know which.' She flung her arms around her grandmother and kissed her loudly. 'Happy birthday again, darling, and whoever it is I'll have him pick you up later for your shopping.'

After she was gone, Mrs Meeker had Frazier, the houseman, clear the table and bring her the worn notebook containing the inventory of household belongings. As a young man, Frazier had been majordomo of Casuarina's numerous staff. Now white-haired, he was the sole remaining servant of the house – chef, butler, handyman, and sales manager all in one.

With him Mrs Meeker combed through the inventory book deciding which of the remaining pieces of furniture must be sacrificed to demanding creditors. There were twenty rooms in the house, most of them picked clean long ago, and her heart sank at the way page after page of the inventory showed how little was left for the market. The only thing of real value remaining was the property itself, and that, it went without saying, was sacrosanct.

With this dismal business at last settled, Mrs Meeker removed her shoes, donned a broadbrimmed straw hat and sunglasses, and walked down to the shore for solace. She was squatting at the water's edge feeding the gulls their daily ration of bread crumbs when she saw a man leave the house and make his way through the grove of casuarinas toward her.

She stood up as he approached. He was in his middle thirties, good-looking, deeply tanned, dressed in an expensive suit. Not a bill collector, she decided warily; more the expensive lawyer type.

'Mrs Meeker?'

'Yes.'

'My name is Yaeger. Edward Yaeger. I want to offer good wishes on your birthday and to tell you what a privilege it is to meet you.'

'Is it? And what's your business with me?'

Yaeger laughed. 'Not my business. I represent a Mr Leo August of Detroit. And since you evidently like to come right to the point, I'll do that. Mr August believes you may be considering the sale of this estate; and he wants to make an offer for it. I'm authorized to meet any fair price you set.'

'Indeed.' Mrs Meeker pointed her sharp little chin at the row of pastel and glass skyscrapers, the surprising outlines of gleaming new hotels, stretching southward into the distance. 'Aren't there enough of these things around here as it is?'

'Mr August doesn't intend adding to them. He wants this place as his residence. It won't be changed at all. It will only be restored.'

'Restored? Does he know what that would cost?'

'To the penny, Mrs Meeker.'

'But why Casuarina? I'm sure he could find a dozen places as suitable.'

'Because,' said Yaeger, 'he's looking for prestige. He's a man who made it to the top the hard way. I'd say that owning the Meeker estate would mean to him what a knighthood means to some successful junk dealer in England.'

Mrs Meeker decided that she did not like Edward Yaeger. Not only was he being impertinent to her, he was being downright disloyal to his client.

'I'm sorry,' she said, 'but Casuarina is not for sale. I don't know where you got the idea it was.'

'Oh, come, come, Mrs Meeker,' said Yaeger playfully. 'Your circumstances aren't any secret. Why not take a handsome profit while you have the chance?'

'Because this happens to be my home. So if you don't mind—'

She saw him to the driveway where his car was parked, and after he was gone she stood there surveying her domain. Everywhere were shattered windows sealed with cardboard, roofs denuded of their tiles, stuccoed walls scabrous and cracked, and rank vegetation forcing its way through broken roads and walks. The roof of the building containing the indoor swimming pool had long ago collapsed. The doors of the garage which had once held half a dozen cars hung awry on their rollers, revealing bleak emptiness within.

To anyone passing on Collins Avenue, thought Mrs Meeker resentfully, the place must look abandoned. But it was not. It was her home, and it would remain her home.

However, she soon learned that Edward Yaeger was not one to be readily discouraged. He appeared at the house a week later while she and Polly were at an after-dinner game of cribbage, and he brought with him gaudy temptation.

'I've been in touch with Mr August,' he said, 'and when he heard that you won't set a price on the estate, he decided to offer one you can't afford to turn down. A hundred thousand dollars.' Yaeger was carrying a leather portfolio under his arm. Now he placed it on the table, opened it with smiling assurance. 'In cash.'

Polly gasped at the display of packaged banknotes before her. Mrs Meeker felt somewhat unsettled by the spectacle.

'Your client does have a dramatic way of doing things, doesn't he?' she finally managed to say.

Yaeger shrugged. 'He believes that cash is the great persuader. If it is, all you have to do is sign this letter of agreement for the sale of the estate.'

'Isn't it risky carrying all that money around?' asked Polly with wide-eyed admiration.

'Hardly. If you look through that window at my car you'll see an unpleasant-looking gentleman whose job is to provide an ounce of prevention. He's one of Mr August's most loyal employees, and not only is he armed with a gun, but he would have no objection to using it.'

'Horrible,' said Mrs Meeker. 'Incredible. All this money, an armed bodyguard – really, your Mr August is too much for me. If I ever did sell Casuarina, it wouldn't be to someone like that. But, as I've already made plain, I don't intend selling.'

It was hard to convince Yaeger that she really meant it – in fact, it was hard to convince herself in the face of the offering before her – and that was bad enough. What was worse was Polly's naive regard of Yaeger, the unabashed interest she was taking in him. He was, Mrs Meeker realized with concern, something new to the girl – an older man, attractive, urbane, overwhelmingly sure of himself. For his part, it was evident that he had taken close note of Polly with a coolly appraising eye and liked what he saw. Liked it a great deal.

When he finally accepted temporary defeat, he turned his attention to the playing cards and pegboard on the table, obviously looking for an excuse to dally.

'It's cribbage,' said Mrs Meeker shortly. 'I gather you don't play.'

'No, but I'm a quick learner at cards. Show me the game, and I'll prove it.'

'Isn't there someone waiting for you in your car?'

'He'll wait,' Yaeger said. 'Waiting is his business.'

So, short of flagrant bad manners, there was nothing to do but show him the game. In truth, as Mrs Meeker explained the rules she found herself softening a little toward him. He listened intently, asked shrewd questions, and what more could any devotee of cribbage want than a willing convert? When the time came for a demonstration she shuffled the deck and started to deal.

'Don't we get a chance to cut the cards in this game?' Yaeger asked smilingly.

'Oh, I'm sorry,' said Mrs Meeker. 'As a matter of fact, I should be penalized two points just for not offering you the chance to cut. That's the rule that's used for very strict play. But I've been playing so long only with dear friends—'

'That you're inclined to skip the formality,' said Yaeger. 'Well, I'd much rather have the compliment of being thought a friend than the penalty,' and, Mrs Meeker observed, when it was his turn to deal, he didn't offer her the deck to cut either. After that, it was always a case of dealer cut for himself, as if they were the dearest of dear friends.

As he had remarked, he was a quick learner. At the start, unsure of the best discards, he made several blunders. then he gave Mrs Meeker an honest run for her money, losing the first game by a wide margin, but very nearly winning the second. And all this, Mrs Meeker observed, while he kept up a half-flirtatious dialogue with Polly. It was dismaying to watch the nonchalant skill with which he simultaneously handled both his cards and her moonstruck granddaughter. Somehow it seemed to deprecate cribbage and Polly together, just as the cash thrust under her nose had deprecated the true value of Casuarina to her.

All in all, it was a most disturbing evening.

Others followed. Yaeger came again and again to renew his client's offer, to play cribbage, to court Polly. It led Mrs Meeker to wonder if she should not bar him from the house. But on what grounds? As for appealing to Polly, that would be useless. All you had to do was look at Polly while in the man's company to see how useless.

So there was only one satisfaction to be gained from Edward Yaeger's intrusion on the scene. He became a superb cribbage player and, as Mrs Meeker guiltily knew, a good game of cribbage was as heady for her as fine old wine. Other card games had never interested her. Cribbage, she would point out, was the only true test of guile and nerve. The trouble had always been in finding an opponent of proper mettle, but now in Edward Yaeger she had one. Although he lost more often than he won, he made every game a challenge.

She began to relish those nightly duels with him. Nothing had tasted as sweet in a long time as the movement of pegging another victory over this formidable adversary. And to give up this pleasure because she was vaguely repelled by his cocksure manner, his disdainfully smiling self-assurance – well, she couldn't. Simply couldn't.

But she was not unprepared for dire revelation when it came. It was young Duff Peabody who brought it. His father had handled Marcus senior's legal affairs, and Duff had inherited not only the law office but a vested interest in the Meeker family. Especially Polly. As he had once frankly admitted to Mrs Meeker, having Polly working for him was a perpetual torment. For one thing, she was gaily and totally incompetent at her work; for another, her presence addled him completely. As far as he could see, the only solution was marriage to her, but, alas, Polly remained deaf to all his pleas.

Now he suddenly arrived at Casuarina in a lowering, gusty afternoon when Mrs Meeker was at the water's edge attending to the gulls who flocked around her. He was in a really bad state, Mrs Meeker saw, and she let the gulls fend for themselves while she heard him out. It was a damned mess, he said. Luckily, Polly was innocently pleased to reveal her intention of marrying this thug—

'Thug?' said Mrs Meeker in alarm. 'Marry?'

'Yes,' said Duff, 'that's the word she used – marry. And now that I've taken the trouble to look him up, I can tell you that your friend Yaeger is no better than a thug. The man he works for, Leo August, is a racketeer who runs a gambling syndicate behind a big-business facade. Yaeger is his front man in these parts. Not that he's faking a good background and education. He has all of that, and that's exactly what he sold to August. From what I was told, August yearns to get into the social swim. People like Yaeger impress him.'

Mrs Meeker found herself both angry and frightened. 'But it's all so obvious now. That large amount of cash. That ugly little man who's always waiting in the car—'

'Yes, that's August's pet gunman, Joe Michalik. He's got a few murders to his credit, if not on his record.'

'Does Polly know all this? Have you told her?'

'Of course. And when she put it to Yaeger he laughed it off. Made it look as if I was the jealous suitor trying to get rid of him.'

'But she knows what men like that did to her father. I've never kept it a secret from her.'

'And she refuses to draw any connection. As far as she's concerned, Yaeger is the most glamorous thing that's ever come her way, and that's it. It's impossible to talk to her.'

'How awful. Duff, we must do something. What can we do?'

'You mean, what can you do. Well, all this may be Yaeger's way of pressuring you into selling the estate. What if you make a deal with him? You sell him Casuarina, and he says goodbye to Polly.'

'Would someone like that keep any such bargain? And suppose he tells Polly I tried to buy him off? Can you imagine how she'd react? No, there must be some other way.'

But, Mrs Meeker knew, easier said than done. She stood there in despair while the gulls wheeled overhead screeching for their dinner, while lacy edges of the tide lapped at her bare feet. On an incoming wavelet rode the pale, blue-fringed bladder of a Portuguese man-of-war, and Mrs Meeker shudderingly backed away as the garish scarlet and purple of the creature's pulpy body, the slender black threads of its deadly tentacles washed ashore. These men-of-war were old enemies. She had once been stung by one while swimming, and it had felt like a white-hot iron playing over her arm. It had been an agonizing two days before the pain receded, and ever since then she had waged unremitting war on any of the pulps that came into her ken.

Now she looked with disgust at this one helpless on the sand, its bladder inflated and swaying back and forth in the warm breeze.

'Do fetch me that stick of driftwood, Duff,' she ordered, and when she had, she thrust it hard into the bladder, which collapsed with a pop.

'The object,' she said, 'is to deflate and then destroy.'

She carried the slimy residue of pulp inshore on the stick and buried it deep in the sand, leaving the stick as a grave marker. 'Deflate and destroy,' she said thoughtfully, staring at the upright stick while Duff watched her in puzzlement.

She suddenly turned to him. 'Duff, I'm going to have a party.'

'A party?'

'Yes, this coming Saturday. And you're to be there with a bill of sale for the estate. Can you prepare one on such short notice?'

'I suppose so. But what made you—?'

'Oh, do stop asking questions.' Mrs Meeker knit her brow in

concentration. 'And I'll have Polly invite her football-playing friends and some pretty girls. And, of course, Mr Yaeger and that nasty little associate of his—'

'Michalik?'

'Yes. And as for a collation – well, Frazier will have to persuade our shopkeeper friends to extend their credit just a bit further. That means we can have a buffet, then dancing after- wards, and perhaps games.'

'With Yaeger and Michalik running them, of course,' Duff said grimly. 'You sound as if you've gone completely out of your mind.'

'Do I?' said Mrs Meeker. 'Well, perhaps I do' – which to Duff's bafflement and concern were her last words on the subject.

She was not minded to offer further enlightenment when Duff arrived at the party Saturday evening. The patio and rooms fronting it were brightly lit and filled with young people alternating between dance floor and buffet. Yaeger and Polly were intent on each other; Michalik, gray-faced, stony-eyed, and dour, leaned against a wall and surveyed the proceedings with contempt; and Mrs Meeker was being royalty in a light mood, apparently delighted to find Casuarina once again alive with company and music.

She drew Duff aside. 'Do you have the bill of sale ready?'

'Yes, but I still don't know why. You said yourself that selling won't really settle matters.'

'So I did, but you must have faith in me, dear boy.' Mrs Meeker patted his hand. 'Remember that man-of-war on the beach? I handled it quite competently, didn't I?'

'It's hardly the same thing.'

'Perhaps you're wrong. Meanwhile, Duff, your job this eve- ning is to stand by me. What I intend to do may seem foolhardy, but you're not to put any obstacles in my way.'

'If I only knew what you intended—'

'You'll know soon enough.'

Mrs Meeker left him glowering and went about her business of playing hostess. She bided her time. The cool night breeze rose, couples abandoned the patio and crowded indoors. The hour grew late. And so, Mrs Meeker told herself, it is now or never. She took a deep breath and moved, serenely smiling, toward Yaeger, who had a possessive arm around Polly's waist.

'Enjoying yourselves?' Mrs Meeker asked, and Yaeger said, 'Very much. But as for our business—'

'I have the papers ready. And I suppose you have the money here?'

'I have. If you don't mind leaving the festivities for a few minutes, we can close the deal right now.'

Mrs Meeker sighed. 'I can't say I do mind. I'm afraid I am not up to parties like this any more. My idea of a good time is a little game of cribbage. Dear me, how angry Polly's grandfather would get when I lured someone into a game during a party. He always felt it was the worst of bad manners, but I could never resist the temptation.'

'No reason why you should,' said Yaeger with heavy gallantry. 'If you want a game right now, I'm your man.'

'How kind of you. That table is all arranged. The noise in the room won't bother you, will it?'

Yaeger laughed. 'Yes, I noticed that table before. I had a feeling we'd come to this before the night was over.'

'You're an old conspirator,' Polly told her grandmother fondly. 'You really are, darling.'

'Oh, sticks and stones,' said Mrs Meeker. As she sat down and opened the deck of cards, she was pleased to see that interested onlookers were gathering around the table – among them Duff Peabody and the dour Michalik. 'When it comes to cribbage I don't at all mind being humored. How far would you go in humoring me, Mr Yaeger?'

'I don't know what you mean.'

'I mean, would you mind playing for stakes? I've never done it in all my life, and the idea seems quite exciting.'

'All right, I leave the stakes to you. A dime, a dollar—'

'Oh, more than that.'

'How much more?'

Mrs Meeker riffled the cards. She set them neatly on the table before her. 'I should like to play you one game,' she said smilingly, 'for a hundred thousand dollars.'

Even at this, she saw, Yaeger did not lose his poise. In the midst of the surprised clamor that rose around the table he sat observing her with an amused curl to his lips.

'Are you serious?' he said.

'Entirely. Your Mr August is eager to get possession of this estate, isn't he?'

'He is.'

'And I am just as eager to lay my hands on some money. A large amount of money. I think it would be entertaining to settle the matter over the cribbage board. Therefore, I'll wager the signed bill of sale for Casuarina against your hundred thousand dollars. If I lose, Mr August gets the estate, and you, of course, would have the money for yourself.'

'And suppose he loses?' Michalik interposed in a hard voice. He turned to Yaeger. 'Forget it, bigshot. You don't play games with August's money. Understand?'

The smile vanished from Yaeger's face. 'Michalik, remember that you're hired help. When I want your advice, I'll ask for it.'

'But he's right,' said Duff Peabody. 'Mrs Meeker, this is out of the question.' He appealed to Polly. 'Don't you agree? Don't you have something to say about this?'

'I don't know,' Polly said unhappily. She stood with a hand on Yaeger's shoulder as if drawing strength from him. 'After all, Casuarina isn't mine.'

'And the money isn't yours,' Michalik told Yaeger contemptuously. 'So don't take any chances with it.'

It was, Mrs Meeker knew, the worst way to handle any male as arrogant as Edward Yaeger. And, as she could see, Leo August had been right. Cash was the great persuader. In Yaeger's eyes was a visible hunger for that money.

Still he hesitated. But he was wavering. Mrs Meeker said, 'Do you know, in all our games I've had the feeling you were humoring an old woman, that you weren't really playing to beat her at any cost. Now I wonder. Do you admit that I'm the better player? Is that it?'

Yaeger set his jaw. 'Do you know what you're letting yourself in for? This isn't like playing for matchsticks.'

'Of course.'

'And if I win, August gets this bill of sale and I get the money. If you win—'

'Winner take all,' said Mrs Meeker. 'Those are the terms.'

'One game?'

'One game, and that settles it.'

'All right,' said Yaeger. 'High card deals.'

It was only when she picked up her first hand that Mrs Meeker realized the full enormity of what she was doing.

Up to now she had not allowed herself to think of losing, to think of giving up Casuarina lock, stock, and barrel, and of making herself dependent on someone's charity for survival. Whose, she had no idea, but someone's it would obviously have to be. The thought was so unnerving that she discarded too cautiously, fell squarely into the trap Yaeger had set for her, and at the end of the first deal was already behind in score.

Watching his imperturbable expression, his deft handling of the cards, made it worse. She had meant what she told him. In their previous matches he had never seemed to extend himself. He had always been paying as much attention to Polly as to the game, and even then he had been a tough opponent. Now, relaxed in his chair, his eyes fixed with absolute concentration on his cards, he took on frightening dimensions.

Mrs Meeker found herself suddenly weak with apprehension. Her fingers, when she dealt, were clumsy. He was a professional – that was it. He would never have accepted the challenge unless he knew the odds favored him. So she had baited her trap perfectly – and now had a tiger by the tail.

By this time everyone in the room had gathered around the table, silently watching. Not many understood the game, Mrs Meeker knew, but all could follow the progress of the pegs moving along the scoreboard – Yaeger's red peg now far ahead, her white peg pursuing it feebly.

They played out the deal swiftly, the tension rising around them. Yaeger turned over his cards. 'Fifteen two, four, six, and a pair makes eight.' The pegboard clicked merrily as he measured off his eight points.

Mrs Meeker matched his score and sighed with relief that at least she had held her own for that deal. Now for the crib, the two discards from each player, which was tallied to the dealer's score. It took only a glance for her to see that there wasn't a point in it. It was as if Yaeger had read her mind. Perhaps he had. He knew she would be discarding recklessly to make up lost ground, and he was prepared for that.

She changed her tactics. At the halfway mark she made a little headway; then a lucky deal came her way, a twenty-point hand, and now the white peg was only a short distance behind the red one.

But no sign of concern showed on Yaeger's face.

'Fifteen two,' he said, 'and a pair makes four.'

It was not his face she should have been watching as he pegged his score. It was Polly who said to him with surprise, 'Oh, no, you've only made four points. You've given yourself five,' and reached for the red peg.

Yaeger's hand caught Polly's wrist in a sudden hard grip – how hard was easy to tell from her look of alarm. Then the grip was immediately relaxed. Yaeger showed his teeth in a smile. 'I'm sorry, dear. I thought it was your mistake, but you were right. Go ahead, put the peg where it belongs.'

'Thank you,' said Polly in a strange voice. 'I will.' And after she had done so, Mrs Meeker saw with gratitude, Polly no longer leaned tenderly close to the man, her hand on his shoulder.

There was not much else to be grateful for. Yaeger, his face growing taut with strain, his eyes narrowed, discarded flawlessly and played his cards brilliantly. Mrs Meeker, knowing that she must look as drawn with strain, drew even with him, and that was all. One point from victory, the two pegs stood side by side.

One point, thought Mrs Meeker as she watched him gather the cards together and prepare to shuffle them. One point, and winner take all. Then realization suddenly burst on her. One point was needed, and there were two points waiting for her if—

She tried to turn her eyes away from those supple, beautifully manicured fingers riffling the cards, riffling them again, but they held her spellbound. Yaeger dealt the first cards across the table, and Mrs Meeker barely had strength to place a hand protectively over them.

'Two points' penalty for not offering me a chance to cut the deck,' she said, feeling as if she were about to faint. 'And that means game to me.'

365

It took Yaeger a moment to comprehend what had happened. Then he rose from his chair. 'You old biddy,' he whispered, 'you tricked me into that.'

'Did I?'

'You tricked me into it. That means the bet is off. Nobody wins and nobody loses.'

'You're wrong, Mr Yaeger. You lost and must pay. I learned long ago by bitter experience that one must always pay his gambling debts.'

'All right, if that's the way you want it, consider yourself paid. And since Polly and I are getting married, consider this money your wedding present to us. Now Mr Michalik will take care of it. He'll be very unhappy otherwise.'

'Who cares about that?' said Polly furiously. 'As for marrying you—'

Her voice failed. In his hand Michalik was holding a gun. It was not very large and it was not flourished with menace, but it was clearly and indisputably a gun ready for use. And it was, Mrs Meeker saw, one of Polly's huge football players who almost indifferently knocked the gun out of Michalik's hand. Others, even bigger and brawnier than the first, surrounded Michalik and took ungentle charge of him.

'Little man,' said the biggest and brawniest, Frank or Billy or whoever he was, 'the party's over. It's time for you to go.'

Michalik struggled wildly and futilely as he was borne to the door; but he managed to point a quivering finger at Yaeger.

'Not without him!' he cried. 'You hear me? Not without him. Just give him to me. That's all I want.'

The news of Edward Yaeger's murder broke in the Miami Beach *Journal* a few days later. Mrs Meeker read it with equanimity; Polly seemed badly shaken by it. No matter, thought Mrs Meeker comfortably, she's young and healthy, and with Duff Peabody on hand for solace, she'll soon recover. For herself, she went down to the shore to enjoy the familiar scene with new zest.

She was there when Duff came scrambling down the sandy slope to the beach, bringing with him a tall, shy young man who seemed uncomfortably conscious of being in the presence of royalty.

'This is Detective Morissey,' Duff said. 'After I saw the paper this morning I had a long talk with him. He's working on the Yaeger case and wants to hear your story about what happened the other night. He just booked Michalik for the killing, and he thinks he can land Leo August as the one who gave the orders for it, if Michalik can be made to talk.'

'Indeed?' said Mrs Meeker. 'And what about the money?'

'Oh, it's all yours, ma'am,' said Detective Morissey earnestly. 'I mean, unofficially speaking, there sure won't be anybody else to claim it. You can take my word it's all yours.' Then he said with concern, 'Ma'am, hadn't you better come away from there? You don't have any shoes on and those things can sting like fury.'

Mrs Meeker raised her eyebrows at the man-of-war drifting toward her on the ripples of the placid sea.

'Not at all,' she said graciously. 'Really, these creatures are no trouble at all when you know how to handle them.'

# The Day the
# Thaw Came to 127

Every winter the tenants of Number 127 would develop an almost maniacal desire for heat, for the sound of steam pipes clanking and radiators singing, for the delicious feeling of warmth enfolding them, penetrating the very bone. It was bad enough other times of the year what with the paint peeling, the plaster falling, the electricity failing, the woodwork rotting, and the water leaking; but these were troubles which, taken one by one, could be lived with. The absence of heat in the winter, however, was regarded by the tenants of 127 as no mere trouble. It was a disaster.

In all fairness to the landlord it must be said that he did permit a few pieces of coal to be thrown into the furnace each day. Not quite enough to keep the blood from congealing, perhaps, but at least enough to keep the water pipes from freezing. One could detect these periods by placing an ungloved hand on the radiator and finding the metal a little less frigid than usual, but that was all.

'In my opinion,' said C-1 who was old and bearded and thus inclined to be philosophical, 'no heat at all is better. That way we face reality. This way we are not encouraged to dream, to imagine a fantastic way of life where it is not necessary to wear an overcoat in the living room.'

'But why not dream?' demanded C-4 fiercely. He was a young man whose wife had a persistent cold in the head. 'I tell you that some day you will hear these radiators sing like birds. Some day—!'

'Enthusiast,' said C-1, shaking his head pityingly. 'Fanatic. Tell that to the landlord and see what it gets you.'

But despite his pessimism, the tenants sustained themselves with the dream.

'Some day,' they said.

'Even one day,' said the more practical ones. 'Just one little day when the fire roars in the furnace.'

'Maybe Christmas Day.'

'Maybe New Year's.'

'Dreamers,' said C-1 sadly, combing his fingers through his long beard. 'See what it gets you.'

It was hard to dispute him. Uselessly, they all descended together on the office of the Department of Buildings. Together they stood in court to plead their cause. Together they banged on the radiators and went downstairs to demand their rights of the janitor.

The janitor was a small, unshaven man who drank heavily and hated the tenants as much as he feared the landlord. In return for his meager services he was given free tenancy of a cubbyhole in the cellar next to the coal bin which he guarded like Cerberus.

When the tenants knocked at his door, he would throw it open, then dance drunkenly around his little room, skipping from side to side, his fists flailing the air like a prizefighter's.

'Come on,' he would shout, 'I'm ready. One at a time or all together. I'm ready!' he would cry, shadow-boxing furiously, and swinging his fists he would sometimes throw himself off balance and fall to the floor. Then he would crawl unsteadily to his feet and start the make-believe battle again.

'Hit but not hurt,' he would gasp. 'Down but not out. Come on!' until the tenants would leave in a rage.

So nothing helped. And A-3 who had six children and worked as a busboy in an expensive restaurant said that he had it on good authority – the brother-in-law of the salad chef was a court clerk – that the landlord must be bribing city officials to close their eyes to his shortcomings.

'From what I was told,' said A-3 hopelessly, 'this is not unusual for either landlords or city officials.'

'Especially such a landlord as ours,' said D-4 who was a stout widow with a mustache and a remarkably beautiful daughter.

In truth, it was possible to believe anything about the

landlord. On the first day of each month he came to collect rents, because one thing the law had impressed on the tenants of 127 was that rents must be paid, no matter their complaints. Tenants' complaints were one thing, landlord's rents another, and there must be no confusion between the two. So the landlord collected rents door by door, stirring up fury as he went by his arrogance, his duplicity, his very appearance.

He was a short, fat man, so fat that when he sat down to write a receipt for the rent he had to lower his belly into his lap with his hands. His eyes were small and menacing. His mouth was pursed with disapproval. Worst of all, he had a tongue like a whiplash.

'You're cold?' he told C-1. 'Do you know why you're cold? Because you're an old man, that's why. You think your beard will keep you warm? You think all the coal I burn will keep you warm? Never. What you should do, old man, is save your pennies and move to a fine house in the tropics. A beautiful hacienda with a heated swimming pool – that's what you need at your age.'

And to B-2 who worked as a butcher's apprentice he said, 'You're cold even with all the heat I give you? Naturally. After working like a donkey in a refrigerator all day, how can you ever warm up?'

B-1 especially angered him. 'More heat?' the landlord roared. 'More painting, more everything? But you're on relief, in case you forget. Relief. Taxpayer's money – that's what you're living on. And I am a taxpayer. You ought to thank me for my money instead of making trouble. Try sleeping on a park bench tonight and see how warm you'll be.'

So each tenant in turn had his complaint used against him, although a few escaped more lightly. These the landlord would deal with humorously.

'More heat?' he would say, and look around the room with stupefaction. 'But it's unbearable here as it is. Look at me,' he would say, tearing open his collar, 'I can hardly breathe. I'm stifling. Please open the window before I faint.'

Only with D-4 was he circumspect. There, sometimes the beautiful daughter of the stout widow would open the door to him, and when he saw her his eyes would glitter appreciatively. Not even the loudest complaints of D-4 disturbed him then, not even the slap in the face he once got from the beautiful daughter when he went so far as to pat her enticing behind.

So the tenants of Number 127 lived with their dream.

'Some day.'

'One day – just one day when the furnace roars and the radiators sing.'

'Christmas perhaps. Or do you think it will be New Year's?'

But again Christmas passed, and then New Year's.

'Dreamers,' said C-1 who spent many daylight hours dozing in the public library over pictures of tropical islands. 'You will be warm again when summer comes.'

Even the visionary C-4, whose wife always had a cold in the head, found the dream growing dim. One day he brought home an electric heater, and for three minutes he and his wife stood before it, rejoicing in its radiance. Then the radiance suddenly vanished. The lights in the room went out. All the lights in the building went out.

'Idiot,' snarled the janitor as he replaced the fuse in the cellar. 'Do you think the wiring here was made for fancy electric heaters? Do you know what a fuse costs? Wait until I tell the landlord about this.'

But it was not the landlord who came to collect rents the next month. In his place came a young man as tall as the landlord was short, as thin as the landlord was fat, as gentle in manner as the landlord was ferocious. Behind his thick eyeglasses shone large, kindly, nearsighted eyes. Yet, to the astonishment of the tenants, he said that he was the landlord's son.

'Incredible,' said C-1. 'For a wolf to produce a lamb is altogether against nature. I suppose you resemble your mother?'

The landlord's son smiled sadly. 'That would be hard to tell, since she died a long time ago. However, I must admit that my father and I seem to have very little in common.'

'And how is he?' C-1 asked hopefully. 'Has something bad happened to him?'

'No, he sent me in his place to learn the business. Since I will inherit it some day, he feels I should know how to manage it properly when the time comes.'

'Would you like to start by hearing a few complaints?' said C-1.

'Certainly.'

'Do you mean that?' said C-1, clutching the young man's arm.

'Of course. I will write all your complaints in this notebook.'

'Then what?'

'Then I will give the notebook to my father.'

'Thank you,' said C-1. 'Here is your rent and goodbye.'

So it went from one tenant to the next, with the landlord's son growing more pitiable and apologetic with each rebuff.

'But what else can I do?' he pleaded, holding out his notebook and pencil.

'Tell the janitor to give us heat.'

'I'm not allowed to tell the janitor anything.'

'Then put some coal in the furnace yourself.'

'I'm not allowed to.'

'Well, thank you,' said the tenants scornfully. 'Here is your rent and goodbye.'

At last the landlord's son came to the door of D-4, the apartment of the stout widow with the mustache and the beautiful daughter. He knocked on the door, and the daughter opened it. He looked at her and turned pale with emotion. His knees buckled. He tried to speak but his voice failed him.

'You are beautiful,' he finally managed to whisper.

She blushed and hung her head.

'A vision,' he said fervently. 'From my childhood days I have been writing poetry. Now I know it was being written only for you.'

She regarded him with wondering eyes. 'But I don't even know who you are.'

'True, true. How stupid of me. I am the landlord's son, come to collect the rent.'

'And you write poetry?'

'Yes, whenever I am inspired I write poetry. Here, look at the last page in my notebook. This was written only yesterday.'

She read it. 'It's a real poem,' she said with awe. 'I never knew anybody who could write a real poem.'

'It's nothing. It needs a lot of work yet. But when it's finished I'll give it to you.'

'To me?'

'Yes.'

They swayed toward each other.

'Would you like some coffee?' whispered the beautiful daughter of D-4. 'It's cold here.'

'Yes, I know,' said the young man. 'The front of the notebook is for complaints.'

Before long, all the tenants of Number 127 were buzzing with gossip about the landlord's son and the beautiful daughter of D-4.

'Every morning he sends her a poem in the mail.'

'Every Saturday night he visits her.'

'He's madly in love with her.'

'Why not?' sighed B-2, the butcher's apprentice, who was secretly in love with her himself.

'And she returns his love.'

'She is making a mistake,' said B-2 gloomily. 'He is a weakling without muscle. Now here is what I call muscle,' he said, flexing his mighty biceps.

'But,' pointed out the elderly C-1, 'with all of that, can you write one little poem?'

They plied the widow of D-4 with questions.

'It is true,' she said. 'Every Saturday night they sit on the couch in their overcoats and look at each other.'

'Is that all?'

'No. He talks and she listens.'

'You are to be commended,' said C-1, nodding his beard. 'Very few young girls have been brought up nowadays to listen.'

'Never mind that,' said the others. 'Will they be married soon?'

D-4 shook her head sadly. 'I am afraid not. His father has told him he will be disinherited if he ever dares to marry a poor girl.'

'What a monster!'

'You have no idea,' said D-4, her upper lip curled in a sneer which almost hid her mustache. 'His father gives him nothing but threats and curses. The unfortunate boy doesn't have money enough in his pocket to take my daughter to the movies.'

'He should do something about it!' cried the fiery C-4, the one whose wife always had a cold in the head, and whose electric heater stood useless in the corner of the closet.

'But what?' said D-4. 'All he knows how to do is write poetry and collect rents. What can he do but wait for the day when he will inherit this house and the twelve others his father also owns?'

'It shows you,' said C-1 philosophically, 'that being a landlord's son is not all milk and honey.'

'What difference does it make?' said B-2, the butcher's apprentice. 'Whenever the day comes, he will be no better than his father.'

'Aha,' said D-4 triumphantly, 'and there you are wrong. He has told my daughter that when he is landlord, everything will be different. There will be heat day and night. There will be painting—'

'Two coats?'

'Two coats of the very best paint. Or wallpaper for those who want it.'

'Wallpaper!'

'And,' said D-4, 'repairs to the plumbing when it leaks.'

They were all silent, awed.

'May heaven speed the day,' murmured C-1 at last, stroking his beard with trembling fingers.

The eyes of the fiery C-4 narrowed. He looked from one to the other. 'Heaven?' he said softly. 'But why must it be left to heaven?'

For a moment his words puzzled them. Then understanding dawned. With it came a growing excitement. They knew that they all shared the same thought, and this gave them courage.

Yet some wavered.

'It's illegal.'

'What if it is? Let's not split hairs.'

'It's unkind.'

'But to whom?'

'It's dangerous.'

'No,' said the fiery C-4 commandingly, 'it is not dangerous.'

His tone swept all doubts away.

'Listen,' he said, as they gathered around him, 'and I will explain what must be done.'

By the next day every tenant of Number 127 understood his role. By Saturday he was letter-perfect in it. All that day the wind howled and the snow piled high.

'Good,' said the tenants. 'Tonight will be the night.'

Darkness came early. The children were fed their suppers and allowed to watch television. They liked especially to watch shows where cowboys and Indians fought in the desert under a blazing sun which made heat waves shimmer on the sand. Over the noise of television could be heard the sound of the front door opening and closing. Then footsteps ascending flight after flight of stairs.

'He's here,' whispered the tenants to each other. 'It's the landlord's son.'

'Even weather like this couldn't keep him away from her.'

'What a monster his father is to treat him so cruelly,' they whispered, hardening their hearts.

When the cowboy and Indian shows were over, the children turned to their mothers and fathers and said they didn't want to go to bed, they wanted to watch more television.

'All right,' said the mothers and fathers, smiling. 'Watch more television.'

'What!' said the children suspiciously.

'Don't argue,' said the fathers sternly. 'And turn up the sound so that we can all hear it a little better.'

The children put aside their suspicions and sat down again to watch a show about gangsters in Miami Beach where the sun beat down fiercely on palm trees.

A-3 was keeping his eyes fixed on the clock in his kitchen. At the appointed moment he took a bottle of whiskey he had brought from the restaurant where he was a busboy, and went down to the cellar. He knocked on the janitor's door, and the janitor flung it open.

'Come on!' he shouted threateningly, putting up his fists. 'One at a time or all together!'

'No, no,' said A-3. 'I'm your friend. See what I brought you?'

He held out the bottle, and the janitor greedily snatched it from his hand. While A-3 watched in amazement, the janitor put the bottle to his lips, and throwing his head back he drained it to the bottom. With a wild cry he threw the bottle against the wall where it smashed to bits.

'Come on!' he said drunkenly, trying to raise his fists again, and then his eyes turned up in his head and he fell flat on his back to the floor. A-3 bent over him and poked him in the shoulder, but the janitor only lay still and snored so loud that it made the room shake.

A-3 left the room, closing the door tight behind him. Then he climbed to the top floor of the house and tapped on the door of D-4. The stout widow opened it.

'Now?' she said.

'Now,' said A-3.

As she followed him downstairs to the street hallway where a telephone hung on the wall, the other tenants joined them.

'What about the landlord's son?' asked B-2, the butcher's apprentice, with a touch of jealousy.

'He and my daughter are sitting on the couch in their overcoats,' answered D-4. 'They are holding hands and looking at each other.'

'Good,' said the tenants.

'Yes,' said D-4, 'they're living in a dreamland. Nothing can distract them from each other.'

She picked up the telephone and called the landlord's number.

'Hello,' she said. 'This is your tenant D-4 in Number 127.'

'Who?' said the landlord, and then one could almost hear him licking his lips. 'Yes, yes, you're the one with the daughter.'

'Right. That's what I want to talk to you about.'

'What do you mean?'

'I mean my daughter,' said D-4 loudly, 'and your son.'

'What? What was that?'

'You heard me.'

'I must have heard wrong,' said the landlord. 'My son has no time for girls. He's in his room every night of the week studying books on real estate. He is there at this very minute.'

'Is he?' said D-4. 'Well, I will wait while you see for yourself that he is not.'

In two minutes the landlord was back at the telephone.

'He is gone!' he said in a fury. 'Where is he?'

'Here with my daughter.'

'What are they doing?'

'Do you have to ask?' said D-4 in a suggestive voice.

'Then it's your daughter's fault. I knew the first time I saw her the kind of girl she was!'

'Ha ha.'

'She wants the money he'll inherit!'

'Ha ha.'

'Don't laugh,' the landlord said, beside himself. 'I'm coming there to put a stop to this myself.' Then he groaned. 'But how can I? With this snowstorm I can't even get my car out of the garage. I can't even take a bus, because the buses have stopped running.'

'Walk.'

'Walk?'

'Why not?' said D-4 mockingly. 'Your son did.'

That was all the landlord needed. 'Wait!' he cried. 'I'll be there as soon as I can. Then you'll see what'll happen.'

'You'd better hurry,' said D-4. 'Otherwise you may be too late.'

All the tenants waited in the hallway. At last the landlord came through the front door, stamping his feet and beating the snow from his shoulders. He looked astonished at the sight of the tenants gathered there.

'What is this?' he demanded of D-4. 'Do you want the whole world to know our business?'

'Believe me,' she told him, 'not a word of it will ever be heard outside Number 127.'

'Not a word,' said all the tenants.

'Well, I'm grateful for that much,' said the landlord sarcastically. He looked around. 'What is that noise? I never heard such a racket.'

'The children are watching television.'

'Are they all deaf? I can hardly hear myself think. And where is my son? Lead me to him at once.'

'Down there.'

'In the cellar?' said the landlord. 'I don't believe you.'

The tenants surrounded him and pushed him down the cellar steps.

'What are you doing?' he shouted. 'Stop pushing me! Where is my son?'

'Never mind your precious son,' the tenants said.

They gathered around him before the furnace. Some held him tightly. Others neatly spread newspapers on the floor. B-2, the butcher's apprentice, unrolled a long cloth which contained shining knives and cleavers.

'Please be careful with these,' B-2 warned the tenants. 'They must be back in the shop tomorrow morning.'

The landlord watched all this with mounting horror.

'What are you going to do?' he asked in a frightened voice.

'You'll soon find out. Now please take off your coat.'

'Never.'

They removed his coat.

'But it's cold here,' the landlord pleaded. 'I can't stand such cold.'

'You'll soon be warm.'

'Help!' the landlord shouted. 'Help!' But all that could be heard in answer was the snoring of the janitor asleep in his room.

After a while the mothers went upstairs.

'That's enough television,' they told the children. 'Go to bed.'

'But we want to watch more television.'

'That's enough for now,' the mothers said affectionately. 'Tomorrow is another day.'

Later the men came upstairs rolling down their sleeves. There was not a sound to be heard in Number 127 as they all waited.

Then they looked at each other.

'Listen, do you hear it?'

'This radiator is growing hot.'

'This one, too.'

'Be careful not to burn yourself on that pipe,' C-4 warned his wife who always had a cold in the head.

The elderly C-1 sniffed through his beard. 'There seems to be a slightly unpleasant odor in the hallway.'

'I'll put more coal on the fire,' said A-3. 'The smell will soon go away.'

'Yes,' said C-1. 'And while you're at it, stir the fire with the poker. Give it a good stirring. It must need it by now.'

In D-4 the beautiful daughter looked at the landlord's son with wide eyes.

'I must be dreaming,' she said in wondering tones. 'It seems to be getting so warm here.'

'You are not dreaming,' he assured her. 'I suppose the janitor became so drunk that he built up an extraordinarily big fire. How lucky for us on such a bitter night.'

'But it's not bitter any more,' she said, putting her arms around him. 'It's like springtime now.'

And all through Number 127 the radiators sang like birds.

# Death of an
# Old-Fashioned Girl

The knife was an old carving knife pressed into service as an artist's tool, used for trimming canvas, for shaping wedges for stretchers, for a dozen other duties. Its blade, honed to a razor edge, had been driven up to the handle into the woman's body, the impact of the blow so unexpected and violent that she had not even had time to scream under it. She had simply doubled over and fallen, her face a mask of horror, and then she had lain still, her blood puddling on the floor.

She must have died almost at once. I had never seen death by violence before, but I needed no past experience to tell me that the abrupt relaxation of those limbs and the graying of that horror-stricken face meant death.

So, as the police knew at a glance, the knife had been the weapon. In view of that, one could hardly blame them for their skeptical manner toward us. And note as well that this was Greenwich Village, home of the emotional and irrational, that there was every evidence in the studio of a liberal consumption of alcohol, that the walls around were hung with paintings capable of baffling the canniest policeman – and there you have all the grounds you need for official hostility.

The one painting I would except was the huge nude on its slab of masonite hanging almost directly over the lifeless body on the floor, a fleshy, voluptuous nude which even a policeman could appreciate, as all these so evidently did.

There was – although they did not know it yet – a relationship between that nude and the body on the floor. The model for the picture had been Nicole Arnaud, first wife of Paul Zachary, the man who had painted it. The blood-soaked body on the floor had been Elizabeth Ann Moore, second wife of Paul

Zachary. I have known cases where a man's first and second wives managed a sort of amiable regard for each other, but they were the rare exceptions to the rule. The case of Nicole and Elizabeth Ann was not among the exceptions. Fearing each other desperately, they had naturally hated each other virulently. It was their misfortune that Paul Zachary was as talented and attractive as he was. One or another of those endowments should be enough for any man. Put them together so that you have a superb painter with an immediate and magnetic appeal for any woman in his ken, and you have the makings of a tragedy.

There were five of us to be questioned by the police: my wife Janet and myself, Sidney and Elinor Goldsmith who ran the Goldsmith Galleries, and Paul Zachary. Five of us, any of whom might be regarded as capable of murder. We had motive, we had means, and we had certainly drunk enough to enter the necessary mood.

The officer in charge was a lieutenant of detectives, a sharp-featured man with cold grey eyes, who surveyed us with a sort of dour satisfaction. There on the floor was a dead woman. Nearby lay the knife that had butchered her, still stained with her blood. And here were the five of us, birds in a coop, one of whom was certainly due to be plucked and roasted very soon. The victim's husband, dazed and incoherent, sweating and blood-spattered, was the prime suspect, which made it that much easier. It was now four in the morning. Before sunrise our stories would be out, and the case would be closed.

Therefore, the lieutenant made it clear, the immediate objective was to separate us, to prevent any collusion, any conspiracy against the truth. There was a stenographer present to take our statements, but until they were dictated and signed we were not to communicate with each other. And, he added, with a bilious look at the litter of empty bottles and glasses on the scene, if we needed sobering up before the questioning, he would see to it that we were supplied with sufficient black coffee to do the job.

The studio was on the upper floor of Paul's duplex. Of the host of men in it, fingerprinting, photographing, and examining, two were delegated to accompany us to the apartment below. In the living room there they dispersed us well apart from each other and then stood at opposite ends of the room, eyeing us like suspicious proctors.

The coffee was brought, steaming hot and acid strong, and because it was offered to us we drank it, the clink of cup against saucer sounding loud in the deathly silence of that room. Then a uniformed man appeared at the kitchen door, and Paul was removed.

Now there were four of us left to sit and look at each other numbly and wonder how Paul was describing what had happened. I had a part in that explanation. One hour ago Elizabeth Ann had been standing here before me, very much alive, and I had been the one to speak the words which started the clock ticking away her last minutes.

Not that I was entirely to blame for what had happened. There was in Elizabeth Ann a fatal quality. She was, as she herself chose to put it, an old-fashioned girl. This is a phrase which may have many meanings, but there was never a doubt about the exact meaning it held for her. During her brief lifetime she must have ingested enough romantic literature and technicolored movies to addle a much larger brain than hers, and in the end she came to believe that human beings actually behaved the way the heroine of a melodrama would. Perhaps — because whenever she looked into a mirror she saw how golden-haired and blue-eyed and beautiful she was — identification with her wish-fulfillment heroine came that much easier.

So Elizabeth Ann became that heroine and played her role, although neither she nor the times were quite suited to it. She should have given thought to that before the murderous knife-blade plunged into her — should have considered that times change, that poets no longer need to scratch their verses on parchment, nor painters smear their paints on canvas. Times change, and it may be dangerous to act out your little role as if they don't.

Across the room Sidney Goldsmith looked at his watch, and, involuntarily, I looked at mine. It had only been five minutes since Paul was closeted with his inquisitors. How much longer would it take? Sooner or later it would be my turn, and I could feel my stomach churn at the prospect.

From the room overhead came sounds of heavy-footed activity; from the dark street below, a radio in one of the police cars parked there squawked something unintelligible. Later, I knew, there would be newspapermen and photographers, avid curiosity seekers and inquisitive friends. Afterward, all our lives would be changed and redirected – as if Elizabeth Ann had the power to manipulate us even from the grave.

Would a policeman be interested in that? Not likely. Yet, if I were to tell the story my own way, that would be part of it – a closing note, perhaps. As for the beginning, it would have to be the day, long, long ago, when I first met Paul Zachary.

We met that chill, damp Parisian day twelve years ago in Michelette's, the cafe on the corner of Rue Soufflot near the University where art students, especially homesick American art students, congregated. Possibly because we were so dissimilar, Paul and I took to each other at once. He was a big, handsome, easy-going North Carolina boy, soft-voiced, slow-speaking, someone who, I suspected, would rather have cut out his tongue than to say anything unkind to you, no matter how justified unkindness might be on occasion. I learned that, watching him under provocation. He had a temper which was slow to heat, but when heated it would roar up in a blaze of physical rage, an overturning of a table, a smashing of a glass against the wall, but never the spoken insult.

As for me, I was small and aggressive, a born New Yorker with, I suppose, the New Yorker's sharp tongue and touchy ways. To Paul this was as intriguing as his country ways were to me. More important, we honestly admired each other's talents, and that is not as usual among artists as you might think. Making pictures may be art, but it is also a brutally competitive business for those engaged in it. There are just so many patrons and fellowships to support an artist, just so much space on gallery walls to display his work, and until a painter's reputation is assured beyond a doubt he is the rival of every other painter, including masters long dead and gone.

The meeting in Michelette's led very soon to our sharing a combined bedroom-studio on Rue Raspail, since such sharing is a natural way of life for students with little money. But there was one thing I could not share with Paul, no matter what I would have offered for it in those days. That was Nicole.

He had met her at Au Printemps, the big department store on Boulevard Haussmann, where she was a salesgirl. How to describe her? The best way, I think, is to say that she was a true Parisienne. And there is in every Parisian woman I have known a special quality. Beautiful or plain, she is always fully alive, always mercurial. Opinionated, too, for that matter, but what she does succeed in communicating to her man is that he is the one who has quickened her spirit this way.

All this vivacity, this spirit, this tenderness Nicole brought to Paul with single-minded devotion. And more. Much more. She was no fool about art and no coward about expressing her opinions on it. Every artist worth his salt must have an ego-maniac confidence in himself. But underneath this confidence will always be one small lump of uncertainty, of self-doubt, which is waiting to flare up cancerously and destroy him. Why can't I sell, he wonders. Am I on the wrong track? If I fell in line with the vogue, wouldn't I do better for myself? And then he is lost, sunk in guilt if he does sell out, full of misery if he doesn't.

It was Nicole who, by acting as Paul's conscience, barred the way to retreat from the course he had set himself. Whenever he would throw up his hands in despair for the future, they would have furious quarrels which she always won, because, I think, he wanted her to win, wanted the constant evidence of her faith in him to keep him on his chosen course.

Like a good little bourgeoise, Nicole lived at home with her papa and mama, and, since they took a dim view of threadbare young American artists, she had a hard time of it with them after Paul entered her life. But she stubbornly held her own, until at last there was a wedding service at the Mairie of the XVIII Arrondisement followed by a banquet at which papa and mama, between mouthfuls, loudly discussed their daughter's cheerless prospects. That same evening, out of money but with the promise of a job in New York, I said goodbye to the newlyweds at Orly airport and went my way homeward to America. As a wedding present – the only one I could afford – I left them my share of the room that Paul and I inhabited on Rue Raspail.

I didn't see them again for two years, but during that time we corresponded regularly. Nicole did the writing for them, and somehow, despite her schoolbook English, she managed to express all her warmth and wit in those letters. She was still working at Au Printemps and had wonderful stories to tell about tourists. And stories about her family, and about old friends at the University. But no stories about Paul. Only occasional phrases about her happiness with him, her concern with his working so hard, her certainty that he would very soon be recognized as a great artist. Apparently, one does not write stories about God. He is there to be worshipped, and that is all.

Then came the momentous news of Mrs Goldsmith in six crowded pages of dashing script. Nicole had fallen into conversation with this American woman at the store, the subject of Paul had come up – it never took Nicole long to introduce that subject into any conversation – and it seemed that this woman and her husband had recently opened a gallery in New York and were seeking works of art by newcomers. Naturally, she had introduced them to Paul, had shown them his work, and they were much impressed. When they left for New York they would be taking several of his pictures with them. They would also be calling on me as soon as they were home.

So they did, which was how I came to meet Sid and Elinor Goldsmith, and how I finally came into my own. At the time I had few pictures to show them – I was doing art layouts for a Madison Avenue agency at the time – but what they saw they liked.

They were not new at the game. They had worked for a big uptown gallery for years, but now had obtained financial backing sufficient to open their own place. With their wide acquaintance among people who bought art they had a head start over most, but they needed some new and exciting work to put on the market. Paul and I were not their first discoveries, but we were, within a few years, their most important. I sometimes think of what might have become of me if Nicole and Elinor had not met that day in Au Printemps, and it is not a pleasant thought.

As it was, not long after meeting the Goldsmiths I had made

my first worthwhile sales and had left the agency to try my hand at painting full-time again. Also, I had got myself married to one of the agency's loveliest secretaries. Very soon after meeting Janet in the office, I had visions of exchanging wedding rings with her some day in the remote future. When I had told her that, explaining we would have to wait because no wife of mine was going to work to help pay my rent, she smiled a Mona Lisa smile, and, somewhat to my surprise, I found myself married immediately afterward.

So there were the four of us to meet Paul and Nicole when they arrived at Kennedy one rainy night. Their appearance in New York was not unexpected. Nicole had mentioned the possibility to me in one of her letters, trying to sound lightsome about it but not quite succeeding, and Paul had written the Goldsmiths at length, saying that he was fed up with living abroad, and asking if they could not arrange some kind of part-time work for him, teaching art classes, perhaps. It would not be harder, Paul observed, than trying to get along on what Nicole earned at the store and on the few sales he had made.

As it turned out, there was no demand for art instructors, but there was a large demand among various chic Fifth Avenue stores for salesgirls just like Nicole. So at one of the most chic she took up where she had left off at Au Printemps, while Paul continued his eight hours a day at the easel. I found them a cheap flat in the Greenwich Village walk-up where Janet and I lived, and, as in my case, one room was set up as Paul's studio.

A man will work harder out of the compulsion to create art than for any other reason. That was true of me during that period, and it applied to Paul in double measure. Because of that, because the time became ripe for us, and because the Goldsmiths were more apostles for us than agents, we made it.

There is a great divide between being an artist and being a successful artist. On one side is only hard work. On the other side is still hard work, but now there are collectors attending your shows, reviews in the press, places on the panels of Sunday television shows. And suddenly there is money, more and more of it, the feel of it in your hand assuring you that all this is real. A great divide. And crossing it can sometimes change a man greatly.

Up to the time Paul and I made the crossing, he had been submerged in his work with fanatical dedication. And he had leaned heavily on Nicole, sustained by her encouragement, grateful for the paycheck she brought home each week, for the housekeeping she did, for the role of wife, mother, and mistress she played so devotedly. She had also been a convenient model for him, and it used to enrage Janet that Nicole, after a hard day at the store, would pose for Paul until all hours of the night, holding some bone-racking position until she must have been ready to collapse.

From Nicole, however, there were few complaints, and those few always delivered with wry self-mockery. Having art as a rival for your husband's affections was not so bad, she would point out. There were more dangerous rivals. The unscrupulous two-legged kind with an eye for a handsome man.

Did she have a foreboding of the future when she said that? Or was it only the expression of the fear in every wife as her youth fades, especially a wife whose husband has removed her so far from homeland and family and who is that much more dependent on him? Whichever it was, when Paul's success brought about the great change, it was clear that she had spoken prophetically.

At first, the change was superficial. Nicole left her job, as Janet had already done, to become the complete housewife. Paul leased the duplex off Sheridan Square. There was a glossy new car parked in front of it. Then there were parties every weekend, and very good and plentiful liquor to ignite the social spirit.

And there were women. There were always women at those parties, and where they came from and where they went to when the party was over was often a mystery to me. I do not mean the usual wives and mistresses. I mean those unescorted young charmers who appeared from nowhere to sit at your feet, a drink in their hands, and look up at you meltingly. There were so many of them, all strangely resembling each other in their vacuous prettiness, all apparently available to any man who cared to stake a claim. Certainly they were available to Paul. The fact that his wife was on the premises eyeing them with loathing only seemed to amuse them.

More than once I saw Paul make a fool of himself with them.

On his behalf I can only say that it would have been hard for him not to. For all his years in Paris and New York, he was still the country boy, and this alluring breed of female drawn his way by the smell of money and success was new to him. And its rapt, odalisque adoration of him, so unlike Nicole's strong-minded partnership, was unsettling. Why not? Give any healthy man a few drinks and face him with a lovely young creature who, eyes limpid with emotion and lips parted, strains toward him, offering him the luscious fullness of her decolletage, and he is likely to make the same kind of fool of himself. Face him with Elizabeth Ann Moore, and he is in real danger.

In the kaleidoscope of those weekend gatherings, Elizabeth Ann remained a constant. Others came and went, finally disappearing for good, but she remained. I believe that from the time she first met Paul she had decided that he was to be hers, and slowly, inexorably, like an amoeba flowing around its prey and ingesting it, she devoured him.

She had the means for it. As an artist I can say that she was almost too flawlessly beautiful to make a good model, but, of course, she was not offering herself to Paul as a model. And she conveyed an air of childlike innocence, of wide-eyed, breathless rapture with life. That was the role she must have set herself long before; by now she played it to perfection. She was not one for furs and jewels either. A shrewd child, she dressed, as Janet once remarked, like a sweet little milkmaid who had $200 to spend on a dress.

In matters of the intellect she was totally ignorant. And here there was no pretence about her. She evidently lived on a diet of sickly romantic novels, lush movies, and popular music played in a slow, dreamy tempo, and when she was charged with that she would say, smiling at her own naivete, 'Well, I guess I'm sort of old-fashioned, aren't I?'

But she said that – she uttered all her banalities – in a soft little voice, a honeyed, insinuating whisper, which suggested that you weren't really annoyed with her, were you? How could you be, when you were such a great big strong man, and she was such a helpless little girl?

She was as helpless as Catherine de Medici. And she had a skin thick enough to withstand any blow. That, of course, is essential equipment for the woman invading another woman's territory. Not only Nicole, but Janet and Elinor detested her and let her know it. For all the effect their remarks had on her, Elizabeth Ann might have been getting compliments on her new hairdo. To the intent of the remarks she was deaf, dumb, and blind, sweetly smiling, more childlike than ever.

Then one night we were shocked witnesses to a scene in which Nicole could no longer restrain herself. Paul and Elizabeth Ann had left the room together, and had been gone so long that their absence became embarrassing. When they returned, absorbed in each other, slightly disheveled, Nicole burst out and told them in the idiom of Rue Pigalle what they were. Then she fled to her room while Paul stood there, ashamed and angry, hesitating about following her, finally taking the first step after her.

That was the deciding moment for Elizabeth Ann. Another woman told off in public this way would have left. She might have done it with bravado, but she would have left. Elizabeth Ann remained. And wept. It was not the ugly, helpless weeping that Nicole had given way to as she fled the scene; it was a pathetic teariness, a whispered sobbing. Face buried in her hands in the approved melodramatic style, she whimpered like a stricken child. And when Paul stopped in his tracks, when he turned to take her in his arms and soothe her anguish, we knew it was all over for Nicole.

It was Janet who went with her to Juarez a month later to arrange the divorce. The night before they left for Mexico, Nicole stayed with us at our new apartment uptown, and we were up till dawn while she talked in a nerveless, exhausted way of what was happening to her. She seemed past the point of tears now, suddenly much older and stouter, her face bloated, her eyes sunk in her head. Only when she described the great confrontation scene that Elizabeth Ann had finally contrived, the performance Elizabeth Ann had given in it, did a spark of the old animation show.

'They were together,' Nicole said, 'but he did not speak a word. What a coward he is. How contemptible to let her be the one to tell me. And she? I swear she was like a diva in an opera performance. She was like Tosca preparing to die for her lover. She stood like this—' Nicole pressed a fist between her breasts and raised her head with jaw proudly outthrust '—and told me about their love, their undying passion for each other, as if someone had written the lines for her. And he never spoke a word. Not one. I don't understand, I cannot understand what she has done to him.'

What Elizabeth Ann had done to Paul might be bewildering. What she did to Nicole was very simple. After the divorce Nicole settled down in a hotel room near us. She had intended to return to Paris, she said, but the thought of facing her family after what had happened was too much. So she lived in her hotel room, visiting us sometimes at Janet's insistence, growing a little stouter, a little blowsier, a little more apathetic at each visit. And then one night she put an end to her misery with an overdose of sleeping pills.

The scene at the cemetery was one I will never forget. It was bad enough that Paul should appear at the services, although meanly rewarding to see from his drawn and haggard look how hard he had been hit. Much worse was the sight of Elizabeth Ann at his side. There may be more obscene demonstrations of bad taste on record, but her presence in genteel mourning, a handkerchief pressed to her lips, a pitiful moaning forcing Paul's attention her way while Nicole's body was being lowered into the grave, will stand me well enough the rest of my life.

It was the last I was to see of Paul and Elizabeth Ann for a long time. But since they were topics of conversation when Janet and I were with the Goldsmiths, we were kept very much in touch with their affairs.

As Elinor put it, it seemed that Elizabeth Ann had a job cut out for her. Paul was obviously morbid about Nicole's death, so Elizabeth Ann now lived with the ghost of the first wife always beside her. To exorcise it, she was, said Elinor, giving her cute little all to Paul's career. Of his work she knew nothing and cared less, but in the art of career making she had set herself up as an expert. There were no more unattached and alluring females at the parties; not for Elizabeth Ann the mistake her predecessor had made. Now in attendance were only those who could add luster to an artist's reputation. Museum curators and rich collectors, critics and celebrities – these were the grist for Elizabeth Ann's mill.

When I asked how Paul took to this, Sid said, 'With bile. His manner, if you know what I mean. He drinks too much for one thing, and then there's this ugly way he has of baiting Elizabeth Ann into talking about things she's completely blank on. After which he apologizes for her with elaborate sarcasm while she blushes and looks prettily confused.'

'Darling little bitch,' said Elinor 'She has what to blush for. My guess is that she and Paul hate each other like poison now, and nothing is going to be done about it. He wouldn't know how to get rid of her, and she won't get rid of him because he's a winning horse. So there they are.'

How much a winning horse became painfully clear to me not long after that, because, as it happened, I was the other horse in a race he and I were to run.

It was Sid who broke the news to me. As part of its cultural exchange program, the State Department was going to pick an artist to represent America in a one-man show in Russia. The artist would be in attendance for interviews, and, Sid pointed out, his eyes alight, he would be accompanied not only by State Department bigwigs, but by reporters from every important newspaper and by a photographer and writer from *Life*. Back in America the show would be taken across the country for a year, starting at San Francisco and winding up at the Museum of Modern Art in New York.

He didn't have to explain what this prize could mean to the one who drew it. But when he confided that I was a leading contender for it – the leading contender, in fact – I was actually left weak-kneed and sick with a sense of anticipation

It was Paul Zachary who won the race. I am not decrying his talent when I say that with a jockey like Elizabeth Ann handling him he could not lose. Among those she entertained and charmed were State Department people very much concerned with making the final choice. They must have been keenly interested when she repeated to them some scathing remarks about our national leaders and their handling of international affairs I had incautiously made before her in the dim past. She gave me due credit as the author of the remarks, of course. More than enough to settle matters for me then and there.

When the Goldsmiths reported this, I could have killed

Elizabeth Ann on the spot, while Janet, I think, would have preferred to slowly torture her to death, which was the only difference between our reactions. As for Sid and Elinor, they could hardly be expected to take it too hard since Paul was as much their client as I was, and they were winners either way. Which was why they could be insensitive enough to invite us to the celebration party the Zacharys would be giving.

'You're out of your mind,' Janet said. 'Do you really think we'd go after all this?'

Sid shrugged. 'I know. But everybody who is anybody will be there. If you don't go, you'll look like the worst kind of bad losers.'

'And under the circumstances,' Elinor said shrewdly, 'aren't you the least bit anxious to look Elizabeth Ann right in the eye and tell her what you think of her?'

So we went. Angrily and vengefully, which is hardly the right approach to a celebration – but we went. And throughout the evening, while Janet and I drank to get up courage for the showdown with Elizabeth Ann, Sid and Elinor drank for conviviality. And Paul drank for his own dark reasons.

Only Elizabeth Ann remained sober. She never drank much, because, I am sure, she never, not even for a moment, wanted to risk losing control of herself in any situation. And she knew that there was a situation brewing here. It was obvious from our manner that something unpleasant was going to happen before the party ended.

Elizabeth Ann did everything possible to forestall it. Even in the small hours when all the rest of the company had gone and Paul had disappeared somewhere so that we four were left alone with her, she maintained a sprightly poise, an air of amused patience. She wanted us out of there, but she wasn't going to say so. Instead, she darted about, bright and quick as a hummingbird, intent on straightening a table cover, arranging a chair, placing empty glasses on a tray.

'Oh, sit down,' I told her at last. 'Stop playing parlormaid and sit down. I want to talk to you.'

She didn't sit down. She stood before me regarding me with pretty bewilderment, fingertips pressed to her cheek. 'Talk? About what?'

So I told her. Loudly, angrily, and not too coherently, I let her know my feelings about the peculiar tactics she had used to get her husband his prize. As I spoke, her bewilderment deepened to incredulity. Then she pressed the back of her hand to her forehead in a gesture meant to express mortal suffering.

'How can you say such things?' she whispered. 'Someone like you jealous of Paul's success? I can't believe it.'

Sid hooted raucously. 'Marvelous,' he said. 'Three sentences, three cliches. A perfect score.'

'And you,' said Elizabeth Ann, wheeling on him, 'posing as Paul's friend and telling stories behind his back. Well, if that's the kind of friend you are, I'm glad he's decided—'

She stopped short in simulated panic, but she had both the Goldsmiths frozen to attention now. The silence grew until it started to ring in my ears.

'Go on, dear,' Elinor said in a hard voice. 'He's decided what?'

'To change dealers,' Elizabeth Ann said in a rush. 'To let the Wedeking Galleries represent him from now on. It's all settled. After we get back from Russia, Wedeking is handling all his work.'

Wedeking was the biggest and the best. It had few modern artists on its list, but if you were a millionaire in a buying mood, its marble showroom on 57th Street was the place to buy a Rembrandt or a Cezanne. And now an original Paul Zachary. It must have been hard for the Goldsmiths to comprehend that. Paul was their boy. They were the ones who had discovered him, who had beat the drums for him, who had helped carry him through the hard times, and who should now share his triumphs with him. They and Nicole. Now they were getting the same medicine she had got, and it stuck in their throats.

Sid lurched from his chair. 'I don't believe it.' He looked around the room. 'Where's Paul? Where is he, damn it? We're going to settle this before I get out of here.'

'It is settled,' said Elizabeth Ann. 'Anyhow, he's in the studio. He doesn't like people going up there.'

'Since when?' Sid demanded.

'For a long time,' Elizabeth Ann said with hauteur. 'I've never been in the studio at all. Not ever. I don't see why you should have special privileges.'

I thought Sid was going to hit her. He took a step forward, his hand upraised, then managed to restrain himself. His hand, when he lowered it, was trembling; all color had drained from his face. 'I want to see Paul,' he said thickly. 'Now.'

Elizabeth Ann knew the voice of authority when she heard it. Nose in the air, she led the way disdainfully up the staircase to the studio, tried its door, flung it open.

It was brilliantly lighted, and Paul in shirtsleeves, dinner jacket flung on the table beside him, was touching up what seemed to be a completed nude on the wall. When he turned to us, I saw that he was very drunk, his eyes glassy, his brow furrowed by frowning incomprehension. From the accumulation of empty bottles and glasses on the premises, it was obvious that for quite a while the studio had been not only a workroom but a private saloon.

He swayed on his feet. 'My dear friends,' he said, enunciating each word with painstaking effort. 'My – dear – wife.'

Like Elizabeth Ann, I had never been in that studio. It was a large room, and on display in it were a number of Paul's experimental works. But more than that, and startling to behold, the room was a shrine to Nicole.

One whole wall was covered with the early portraits of her, the life studies, the charcoal sketches. On a stand in the middle of the floor was a bust of her done long ago in our room on Rue Raspail. And the nude Paul had been working on was of Nicole. A splendid picture I had not seen before, where the image of Nicole, vibrant and warm and fleshy as the living woman had been, sat poised on the edge of a chair, looking into the eyes of the viewer as if he were a mirror, loving him because he was her husband.

Before he had entered the room, Sid Goldsmith had been fuming aloud with rage. Now, taking in the scene with wondering eyes, he seemed struck dumb. So were we all. And drawn magnetically by that inspired nude, the fresh streaks of oil glistening on its surface, we gathered before it in silence. There was nothing to be said about it that would not sound fatuous. It was that good.

It was Elizabeth Ann who broke the silence.

'I don't like it,' she suddenly said in a tight voice, and I saw that for once the mask had slipped, and what showed beneath it was the face of the Medusa. 'I don't like it. It's ugly.'

Paul focused on her blearily. 'Is it?'

Elizabeth Ann pointed around the room. 'Can't you see what she looked like? She was just a plain, sloppy woman, that's all she was!' Her voice rose shrilly. 'And she's dead. Don't you understand? She's dead, and there's nothing you can do about it!'

'Nothing?' Paul said.

The siren of a police car sounded outside the living-room windows. I had been so deep in my thoughts that I had forgotten where I was and why I was there. Now as the sound faded and the car raced off down the street, I looked up with a start, realizing where I was, realizing that the policeman standing at the kitchen door was beckoning to me that it was my turn for quesioning. The Goldsmiths were watching me with concern. Janet tried to smile at me.

I got to my feet with an effort. How much of this, I wondered, would the lieutenant want to hear. Very little, perhaps. Only the final scene in that room upstairs, because that was all that was needed for the records.

'Nothing?' said Paul, and Elizabeth Ann said venomously, 'That's right – nothing. So stop thinking about her and talking about her and living with her. Get rid of her!' The long-bladed knife was close at hand on the table, invitingly close, and she snatched it up. 'Like this!'

She was, as I have said, addicted to playing the heroine out of melodrama, so I knew what was in her mind then. It was that similiar scene in which the outraged heroine slashes apart the canvas on which the image of her hated rival is painted. And she was ignorant. Tragically ignorant. How could she know that this picture was not on canvas, but on masonite which is as smooth and resistant as a polished sheet of steel?

She raised the knife high as we stood watching in stupefaction, then with all her strength she drove it downward into the painted flesh of her rival. And in that last stroke of folly and ignorance, the blade, clutched tight in her hand, slid in a flashing arc over the impenetrable surface of the painting and plunged full into her own body.

# The Twelfth Statue

One fine midsummer evening, in the environs of the ancient city of Rome, an American motion picture producer named Alexander File walked out of the door of his office and vanished from the face of the earth as utterly and completely as if the devil had snatched him down to hell by the heels.

However, when it comes to the mysterious disappearance of American citizens, the Italian police are inclined to shrug off the devil and his works and look elsewhere for clues. There had been four people remaining in the office after File had slammed its door behind him and apparently stepped off into limbo. One of the people had been Mel Gordon. So Mel was not surprised to find the note in his letter box at the hotel politely requesting him to meet with *Commissario* Odoardo Ucci at Police Head-quarters to discuss *l'affaire* File.

He handed the note to his wife at the breakfast table.

'A Commissioner, no less,' Betty said gloomily after she had skimmed through it. 'What are you going to tell him?'

'I guess the best policy is to answer everything with a simple yes or no and keep my private thoughts private.' The mere sight of the coffee and roll before him made Mel's stomach churn. 'You'd better drive me over there. I don't think I'm up to handling the car in this swinging Roman traffic, the way I feel right now.'

His first look at Commissioner Ucci's office didn't make him feel any better. It was as bleak and uninviting as the operating room of a rundown hospital, its walls faced with grimy white tile from floor to ceiling, and, in a corner, among a tangle of steam and water pipes, there was a faucet which dripped with a slow, hesitant tinkle into the wash basin below it.

The Commissioner seemed to fit these surroundings. Bald, fat, sleepy-eyed, his clothing rumpled, his tie askew, he asked his questions in precise, almost uninflected English, and painstakingly recorded the answers with a pencil scarred by toothmarks. Sublimation, thought Mel. He can't chew up witnesses, so he chews up pencils. But don't let those sleepy-looking eyes fool you, son. There might be a shrewd brain behind them. So stay close to the facts and try to keep the little white lies to a minimum.

'Signor File was a cinema producer exclusively? He had no other business interests?'

'That's right, Commissioner.'

And so it was. File might have manufactured only the cheapest quickies of them all, the sleaziest kind of gladiator-and-slave-girl junk, but he was nonetheless a movie producer. And his other interests had nothing to do with business, but with dewy and nubile maidens, unripe lovelies all the more enticing to him because they were unripe. He loved them, did File, with a mouth-watering, hard-breathing, popeyed love. Loved them, in fact, almost as much as he loved his money.

'There were two other people besides yourself and your wife who were the last to see the missing man, Signor Gordon. One of them, Cyrus Goldsmith, was the director of the picture you were making?'

'Yes, he was.'

And a sad case, too, was Cy Goldsmith. Started as a stunt man in horse operas, got to be a Second Unit Director for DeMille – one of those guys who handled chariot races and cavalry charges for the Maestro – and by the time he became a full director of his own, of low-budget quickies, he had absorbed too much of DeMille into his system for his own good.

The trouble was that, whatever else DeMille's pictures might be, as spectacles they are the best. They are demonstrations of tender loving care for technical perfection, of craftsmanship exercised on every detail, and hang the expense. Quickies, on the other hand, have to be belted out fast and cheap. So Cy made them fast and cheap, but each time he did it he was putting an overdeveloped conscience on the rack, he was betraying all those standards of careful movie-making that had become ingrained in him. And, as the psychology experts would have it, a compulsive perfectionist forced to do sloppy work is like someone with claustrophobia trapped in an elevator between floors. And to be trapped the rest of your lifetime this way—!

That's what happened to Cy, that's why he hit the bottle harder and harder until he was marked unreliable, on the skids, all washed up, so that finally the only producer who would give him work was good old Alexander File who paid him as little as possible to turn out those awful five-and-dime spectaculars of his. This is no reflection on others who might have been as charitable to Cy. The sad truth is that Signor File was the only producer on record who, as time went on, could keep Cy sober enough for a few weeks at a stretch to get a picture out of him, although, unless you like watching a sadistic animal trainer put a weary old lion through its paces, it wasn't nice to watch the way he did it. A razor-edged tongue can be a cruel instrument when wielded by a character like File.

And, of course, since he was as small and skinny as Cy was big and brawny it must have given him a rich satisfaction to abuse a defenseless victim who towered over him. It might have been as much the reason for his taking a chance on Cy, picture after picture, as the fact that Cy always delivered the best that could be made of the picture, and at the lowest possible price.

'Regarding this Cyrus Goldsmith, Signor Gordon—'

'Yes?'

'Was he on bad terms with the missing man?'

'Well – no.'

Commissioner Ucci rubbed a stubby forefinger up and down his nose. A drop of water tinkled into the wash basin approximately every five seconds. Very significant, that nose rubbing. Or was it simply that the Commissioner's nose itched?

'And this other man who was with you that evening, this Henry MacAaron. What was his function?'

'He was director of photography for the picture, in charge of all the cameramen. Is, I should say. We still intend to finish the picture.'

'Even without Signor File?'

'Yes.'

'*Ah. And this MacAaron and Goldsmith are longtime associates of each other, are they not?*'

'*Yes.*'

Very longtime, Commissioner. From as far back as the DeMille days, in fact, when Cy gave MacAaron his first chance behind a camera. Since then, like Mary and her lamb, where Cy is, there is MacAaron, although he's a pretty morose and hardbitten lamb. And, incidentally, one hell of a good cameraman. He could have done just fine for himself if he hadn't made it his life's work to worshipfully tag after Cy and nurse him through his binges.

'*And you yourself, Signor Gordon, are the author who wrote this cinema work for Signor File?*'

'*Yes.*'

Yes, because it's not worth explaining to this dough-faced cop the difference between an author and a rewrite man. When it comes to that, who's to say which is the real creator of any script – the author of the inept original or the long-suffering expert who has to make a mountain out of its molehill of inspiration?

Commissioner Ucci rubbed his nose again, slowly and thoughtfully.

'*When all of you were with Signore File in the office that evening, was there a quarrel? A violent disagreement?*'

'*No.*'

'*No. Then is it possible that immediately after he left he had a quarrel with someone else working on the picture?*'

'Well, as to that, Commissioner—'

An hour later, Mel escaped at last to the blessed sunlight of the courtyard where Betty was waiting in the rented Fiat.

'Head for the hills,' he said as he climbed in beside her. 'They're after us.'

'Very funny. How did it go?'

'All right, I guess.' He was dripping with sweat, and when he lit a cigarette he found that his hands were trembling uncontrollably. 'He wasn't very friendly though.'

Betty maneuvered the car through the traffic jamming the entrance to the bridge across the Tiber. When they were on the other side of the river she said, 'You know, I can understand how the police feel about it because it's driving me crazy, too. A man can't just disappear the way Alex did. He just can't, Mel. It's impossible.'

'Sure it is. All the same he *has* disappeared.'

'But where? Where is he? What happened to him?'

'I don't know. That's the truth, baby. You can believe every word of it.'

'I do,' Betty sighed. 'But, my God, if Alex had only not mailed you that script—'

That was when it had all started, of course, when File air-mailed that script the long distance from Rome to Los Angeles. It had been a surprise, getting the script, because a few years before, Mel had thought he was done with File forever and had told him so right there on the job. And File had shrugged it off to indicate he couldn't care less.

The decision that day to kiss off File and the deals he sometimes offered hadn't been an act of bravado. A TV series Mel had been doctoring was, according to the latest ratings, showing a vast improvement in health, and with a successful series to his credit he envisioned a nice secure future for a long time to come. It worked out that way, too. The series had a good run, and when it folded, the reruns started paying off, which meant there was no reason for ever working for File again or even of thinking of working for him.

Now File suddenly wanted him again, although it was hard to tell why since it was obvious that a Mel Gordon with those residuals rolling in would be higher-priced than the old Mel Gordon who took what he could get. In the end they compromised, with File, as usual, getting the better of the deal. The trouble was that he knew Mel's weakness for tinkering with defective scripts, knew that once Mel had gone through the unbelievably defective script of *Emperor of Lust* he might be hooked by the problems it presented, and if hooked he could be reeled in without too much trouble.

That was how it worked out. File's Hollywood lawyer – a Big Name who openly despised File and so, inevitably, was the one man in the world File trusted – saw to the signing of the contract, and before the ink was dry on it, Mel, his wife at his side, and the script of *Emperor of Lust* under his arm, was on his way to a reunion with File.

They held the reunion at a sidewalk cafe on the Via Veneto, the tables around crowded by characters out of Fellini gracefully displaying their ennui in the June sunlight and by tourists ungracefully gaping at the Fellini characters.

There were four at their table besides Mel and Betty. File, of course, as small and pale and hard-featured as ever, his hair, iron-gray when Mel had last seen it, now completely white; and Cy Goldsmith, gaunt and craggy and bleary-eyed with hangover; and the dour MacAaron with that perpetual squint as if he were always sizing up camera angles; and a newcomer on the scene, a big, breasty, road-company version of Loren named Wanda Pericola who, it turned out, was going to get a leading role in the picture and who really had the tourists all agape.

Six of them at the table altogether. Four Camparis, a double Scotch for Cy, a cup of tea for File. File, although living most of each year abroad, distrusted all foreign food and drink.

The reunion was short and to the point. File impatiently allowed the necessary time to renew old acquaintance and for an introduction to Wanda who spoke just enough English to say hello, and then he said abruptly to Mel, 'How much have you done on the script?'

'On the script? Alex, we just got in this morning.'

'What's that got to do with it? You used to take one look at a script and start popping with ideas like a real old-fashioned corn popper. You mean making out big on the idiot box has gone and ruined all that gorgeous talent?'

Once, when payments on house, car, and grocer's bills depended on the inflections of File's voice, Mel had been meek as a lamb. Now, braced by the thought of those residuals pouring out of the TV cornucopia, he found he could be brave as a lion.

'You want to know something, Alex?' he said. 'If my gorgeous talent is ruined you're in real bad trouble, because the script is a disaster.'

'So you say. All it needs is a couple of touches here and there.'

'It needs a whole new script, that's what it needs, before we make sense out of all that crummy wordage. After I read it I looked up the life of the emperor Tiberius in the history books—'

'Well, thanks for that much anyhow.'

'—and I can tell you everything has to build up the way he's corrupted by power and suspicion and lust until he goes mad, holed up in that palace on Capri where they have the daily orgies. And the key scene is where he goes off his rocker.'

'So what? That's in the script right now, isn't it?'

'It's all wrong right now, with this Jekyll into Hyde treatment. All that raving and rug chewing makes the whole thing low comedy. But suppose no one around him can see that Tiberius has gone mad – if only the audience realizes it—'

'Yeah?' File was warily interested now. 'And how do you show that?'

'This way. In that corridor outside Tiberius' bedroom in the palace we want a row of life-sized marble statues. Let's say six of them, a round half dozen. Statues of some great Romans, all their traditions. We establish in advance his respect for those marble images, the way he squares his shoulders with dignity when he passes them. Then the big moment arrives when he cracks wide open.

'How do we punch it across? We leave the bedroom with him, track with him past those statues, see them as *he* sees them – and what we see is all his madness engraved on *their* faces! Get it, Alex? The faces of those statues Tiberius is staring at are now distorted, terrifying reflections of the madman he himself has finally become. That's it. A few feet of film and we're home free.'

'Home free,' echoed Cy Goldsmith. He gingerly pivoted his head toward MacAaron. 'What do you think, Mac?' and Mac-Aaron grunted, 'It'll do' – which from him was a great deal of conversation, as well as the stamp of high approval.

'Do?' Wanda said anxiously. '*Che succede?*' – because, as Mel knew sympathetically, what she wanted to hear was her name being bandied about by these people in charge of her destiny; so it was only natural when Betty explained to her in her San

Francisco Italian what had been said that Wanda should look disappointed.

But it was File's reaction that mattered, and Mel was braced for it.

'Statues,' File finally said with open distaste.

'Twelve of them, Alex,' Mel said flatly. 'Six sanes and six mads. Six befores and six afters. This is the key scene, the big scene. Don't shortchange it.'

'You know what artwork like that costs, sonny boy? You look at our budget—'

'Ah, the hell with the budget on this shot,' Cy protested. 'This scene can make all the difference, Alex. The way I see it—'

'You?' File turned to him open-mouthed, as if thunderstruck by this interruption. And File's voice was penetrating enough to be heard over all the racket of the traffic behind him. 'Why, you're so loaded right now you can't see your hand in front of your face, you miserable lush. And with the picture almost ready to shoot, too. Now go on and try to sober up before next week. You heard me. Get going.'

The others at the table – and this, Mel saw, included even Wanda who must have got the music if not the words – sat rigid with embarrassment while Cy clenched his empty glass in his fist as if to crush it into splinters, then lurched to his feet and set off down the street full-tilt, ricocheting into bypassers as he went. When MacAaron promptly rose to follow him File said, 'Where are you going? I didn't say I was done with you yet, did I?'

'Didn't you?' said MacAaron, and then was gone, too.

File shrugged off this act of mutiny.

'A great team,' he observed. 'A rummy has-been and his nursemaid. A fine thing to be stuck with.' He picked up his cup of tea and sipped it, studying Mel through drooping eyelids. 'Anyhow, the statues are out.'

'They're in, Alex. All twelve of them. Otherwise, it might take me a long, long time to get going on the script.'

This was the point where, in the past, File would slap his hand down on the table to end all argument. But now, Mel saw as File digested his tea, there was no slapping of the table.

'If I say okay,' said File, 'you should be able to give me a synopsis of the whole story tomorrow, shouldn't you?'

You give me my synopsis and I'll give you your statues. It was File's way of bargaining, because File never gave something for nothing. And even though it meant a long night's work ahead, Mel said, with a sharp sense of triumph, 'I'll have it for you tomorrow.' For once – for the first time in all his dealings with File – he hadn't knuckled under at the mention of that sacred word Budget.

When he and Betty departed, not even the thought of the ugly scene with Cy could dim his pleasure in knowing he had browbeaten File into allotting the picture a few thousand dollars more than his precious budget provided. After all, Mel told himself, Cy hardly needed others to comfort him in his sad plight when he had MacAaron to do that for him on a full-time basis.

Back in the hotel room, Mel stretched out on the bed with the script of *Emperor of Lust* – a title, he was sure, that had to be File's inspiration – while Betty readied herself at her portable typewriter, waiting for her husband to uncork the creative flow. Fifteen years before, she had been the secretary assigned him on his first movie job; they were married the second week on the job, and ever since then she had admirably combined the dual careers of amanuensis and wife. Married this long and completely, it was hard for them to surprise each other with anything said or done, but still Mel was surprised when Betty, who had been sitting in abstracted silence, said out of a clear sky, 'She isn't the one.'

'What?'

'Wanda. I mean, she's not Alex's playmate-of-the-month. She's not the one he's going to bed with.'

'I'd say that's their problem. Anyhow, what makes you so sure about it?'

'For one thing, she's too old.'

'She must be a fast twenty or twenty-one.'

'That's still past the schoolgirl age. And she's just too much woman for him, no matter how you look at it. I think Alex is afraid of real women, the way he always goes for the Alice in Wonderland type.'

'So?'

'So you know what I'm getting at. We've been through it before with him. Sooner or later he'll turn up with some wide-eyed little Alice, and it makes me sick if it does sound terribly quaint, but I think a man of sixty parading down the Via Veneto with a kid in her first high heels is really obscene. And sitting at the table with us, playing footsie with her. And showing her what a big man he is by putting down someone like Cy—'

'Oh?' said Mel. 'And which one is really on your mind? The Alice type or Cy?'

'I pity both of them. Mel, you said last time you'd never work for Alex again. Why did you take this job anyhow?'

'So that I could put him down, the way I did about those statues. I needed that for the good of my soul, sweetheart; it was long overdue. Also because *The New York Times* said that the last one I did for Alex was surprisingly literate, and maybe I can get them to say it again.'

'Still and all—'

'Still and all, it'll be a hectic enough summer without worrying about Cy and Alice in Movieland and all the rest of it. Right now we've got to put together some kind of story synopsis, so tomorrow we'll run over to Cinecitta to see what sets we'll have to work with, and after that we'll be so busy manufacturing stirring dialogue that there won't be time to think of other people's troubles.'

'Unless they're shoved down your throat,' said Betty. 'Poor Cy. The day he kills Alex, I want to be there to see it.'

Cinecitta is the Italian-style Hollywood outside Rome where most of File's pictures were shot. But when Mel phoned him about meeting him there, he was told to forget it; this one would be made in a lot a few miles south of the city right past Forte Appia on the Via Appia Antica, the Old Appian Way.

This arrangement, as File described it, was typical of his manipulations. Pan-Italia Productions had built its sets on that lot for an elaborate picture about Saint Paul, and when the picture was completed File had rented the lot, sets and all, dirt-cheap, on condition that he clear away everything when he left. The fact that the sets might be useless in terms of the script File had bought – also dirt-cheap – didn't bother him any. They were out of Roman history and that was good enough for him.

In a way, it was this kind of thing which often made working for File as intriguing to Mel as it was infuriating. The script he was handed and the sets and properties File provided usually had as much relationship to each other as the traditional square peg and round hole, and there was a fascination in trying to fit them together. When it came to an Alexander File Production, Mel sometimes reflected, necessity was without doubt the mother of improvisation.

The next day he and Betty rented a car and drove out to the lot to see what Pan-Italia had left him to improvise with. They went by way of the Porta San Sebastiano, past the catacombs, and along the narrow ancient Roman road through green countryside until they arrived at what looked like a restoration of Caesar's forum rising out of a meadow half a mile off the road. Beyond it was the production's working quarters, a huddle of buildings surrounding a structure the size of a small airplane hangar which was undoubtedly the sound stage.

There was a ten-foot-high wire fence running around the entire lot, and the guard at its gate, a tough-looking character with a pistol strapped to his hip, made a big project out of checking them through. Once inside, it wasn't hard to find File's headquarters, which was the building nearest the gate and had a few cars parked before it, among them File's big Cadillac convertible. The only sign of activity in the area was a hollow sound of hammering from inside the sound stage nearby.

File was waiting in his office along with Cy, MacAaron, and a couple of Italian technicians whom Mel remembered from the last picture, a Second Unit Director and a lighting man. Neither of them was much good at his job, Cy had once told him – DeMille wouldn't have let them sweep up for him – but they came cheap and understood English, which was all File wanted of them.

Mel found that the procedure of starting work for File hadn't varied over the years.

'All right, all right, let's see it,' File said to him without preliminary, and when the story synopsis was handed across the desk to him he read it through laboriously, then said, 'I guess it'll have to do. When can you have some stuff to start shooting?'

'In about a week.'

'That's what you think. This is Friday. Monday morning, Wanda and the other leads are showing up bright and early along with a flock of extras for mob scenes. So eight o'clock Monday morning you'll be here with enough for Goldsmith to work on for a couple of days. And you'll have some interior scenes ready, too, in case it rains, then everybody won't be sitting around on the payroll doing nothing.'

'Look, Alex, let's get one thing straight right now—'

'Let's, sonny boy. And what we'll get straight is that it don't matter how big you made it on TV, when you work for me you produce like you always did. You are not Ernie Hemingway, understand? You are a hack, a shoemaker, and all you want to do is get some nails into the shoes before the customer gets sore. And no use looking daggers about it, because if you got any ideas of making trouble or walking out on this contract, I'll tie you up so tight in court you'll never write another script for anybody for the next fifty years. What do you think of that?'

Mel felt his collar grow chokingly tight, knew his face must be scarlet with helpless, apoplectic rage. The worst of it, as far as he was concerned, was that everyone else in the room was embarrassedly trying to avoid his eye the way those at the table the day before had tried to avoid Cy's when File had put him in his place. Only Betty aimed an outraged forefinger at File and said, 'Listen, Alex—!'

'Stay out of this,' File said evenly. 'You're married to him, so maybe you like it when he makes like a genius. I don't.'

Before Betty could fire back, Mel shook his head warningly at her. After all, the contract had been signed, sealed, and delivered. There was no way out of it now.

'All right, Alex,' he said, hating to say it, 'Monday, I'll have some nails in your shoes.'

'I figured you would. Now let's go take a look at the layout.'

They all trooped out into the blazing sunshine, File leading the way, Mel lagging behind with Betty's hand clutching his in consolation. As insurance against mud and dust, Pan-Italia had laid down a tarmac, a hard-surfaced shell, on this section of the lot, and although it was hardly noon Mel could feel it already softening underfoot in the heat. Most of Rome closed up shop and took a siesta during the worst of the midday heat in summer, but there were no siestas on an Alexander File Production.

Cy Goldsmith fell in step beside Mel. The heat seemed to weigh heavily on Cy; yesterday's ruddiness was gone from his face, leaving it jaundiced and mottled, and his lips with an unhealthy bluish tinge. But his eyes were bright and sharp, the bleariness cleared from them, which meant that he was, temporarily at least, off the bottle.

'What the hell,' he said. 'It figured Alex would want to slip the knife into you because of those statues, didn't it?'

'Did it? Well, if it wasn't for the contract I'm stuck with he could shove his whole picture. And if he thinks I'm going to really put out for him—'

'Don't talk like that, Mel. Look, for once we've got everything going for us – a good story, first-class sets, even some actors who know what it's all about. I signed them on myself.'

'Like Wanda, our great big beautiful leading lady? Who are you kidding, Cy? What kind of performance can you get out of someone whose lines have to be written in phonetic English?'

'I'll get a good performance out of her. Just don't let Alex sour you on this job, Mel. You never dogged it on the job yet. This is no time to start doing it.'

The pleading note in his voice sickened Mel. Bad enough this big hulk should have taken what File dished out over the years. Now, God help him, he seemed to be gratefully licking File's hand for it.

The tarmac came to an end beyond the huge structure housing the sound stage, and another high wire fence here bisected the property and barred the way to the backlot and the replica of the forum on it. The guard at the backlot gate, like his counterpart at the front gate, wore a pistol on his hip.

When they had passed through the fence and caught up to File he jerked a thumb in the direction of the guard.

'That's how the money goes,' he said. 'You need a guy like that on duty twenty-four hours a day around here. Otherwise, these ginzos would pick the place clean.'

'Well, thanks,' said Betty, whose maiden name happened to be Capoletta. '*Mille grazie, padrone.*'

'Don't be so touchy,' File said. 'I'm not talking about any Italians from Fisherman's Wharf, I'm talking strictly about the local talent'; and Mel observed that the pair of technicians who must have understood every word of this looked as politely expressionless as if they didn't. After all, a job was a job.

The tour of the sets on the backlot indicated that File had got himself a real bargain. Pan-Italia had built not only the replica of the forum for its Saint Paul picture, but also a beautifully detailed full-scale model of an ancient Roman street complete with shops and houses, and a magnificent porticoed villa which stood on a height overlooking the rest.

This last, said File, would serve as Tiberius' palace in Capri, although its interiors would be done on the sound stage. MacAaron and a couple of the camera crew had already been to Capri the week before and taken some footage of the scenery there to make establishing shots look authentic. A Cy Goldsmith brainstorm, that Capri footage, he added irritably, because what difference could it make to the slobs in the audience—

To get away from File, Mel climbed alone to the portico of the villa. Standing there, looking out over the forum and the umbrella pines and cypresses lining the Appian Way, he could see the timeworn curves of the Alban Hills on the horizon and had the feeling that all this might well be ancient Rome come to life again. Only a dazzle of sunlight reflected from a passing car in the distance intruded on that feeling, but even that flash of light might have come from the burnished armor of some Roman warrior heading south to Ostia in his chariot.

Then Cy was there beside him, looking at him quizzically.

'How do you like it?'

'I like it.'

'And everything fits in with the Tiberius period. Now do you get what I meant about making an honest-to-God picture this time out? I mean, with everything done right. It's all here waiting to be made.'

'Not by us. Why don't you quit pushing so hard, Cy? It takes rewrites and retakes and rehearsals to make the kind of picture you're talking about. The three R's. And you know how Alex feels about them.'

'I know. But we can fight it out with Alex right down the line.'

'Sure we can.'

'Mel, I'm on the level. Would you believe me if I told you this was the last picture I'll ever work on?'

'You're kidding.'

Cy smiled crookedly. 'Not from what the doctors had to say. This is strictly between you and me and Mac – Betty, too, if you want to let her know – but I'm all gone inside.' He patted his sagging belly. 'It'll be a big deal if the machinery in here holds out for this picture, let alone another year.'

So that was it, Mel thought wonderingly, and just how corny can a man wind up being after a long hard lifetime? That explained everything. Cy Goldsmith was a dying man close to the end of his string, and this picture was to be his swan song. A good one, the best he was capable of, no matter how Alexander File felt about it.

'Look, Cy, doctors can make mistakes. If you went back to the States right now and saw a specialist there – maybe tried the Mayo Clinic—'

'That's where they gave me the word, Mel, at Mayo. Straight from the shoulder. You want to know how straight? Well, the first thing I did before flying out here on this job was to hop back to LA and make all the arrangements to be put away in Elysian Park when the time came. A big mausoleum, a nice box, everything. The funny part was that I felt a hell of a lot better when I signed those papers. It gave me a good idea why those old Romans and Egyptians wanted to make sure everything was all set for the big day. It makes you look the facts in the face. After that, you can live with them.'

At least, Mel thought, until this picture was made the way you wanted it made. And, in the light of that, Cy had paid him the handsomest tribute he could. Everything depended on the script, and it was Mel Gordon who had been called a long way to work on it.

'Tell me one thing, Cy,' he said. 'It was your idea to get me out here on this script, wasn't it? Not Alex's.'

'That's right. Doesn't that prove I can win a battle with Alex when I have to?'

'I guess it does,' said Mel. 'Now all we have to do is win the war.'

And it was war, even without shot and shell being fired. Once File had the first draft of the complete script in his hands and had drawn up a shooting schedule from it, he quickly caught onto the fact that something strange was going on. After that, life became merry hell for everyone involved in the making of *Emperor of Lust*.

Including, as Mel pointed out to Betty with satisfaction, File himself. For the first time in File's career one of his pictures lagged steadily behind its schedule as Cy grimly ordered retake after retake until he got what he wanted of a scene, doubled in brass as his own Second Unit Director, drilling Roman legions and barbarian hordes in the fields outside the lot until they threatened open rebellion, bullied Mel into endlessly rewriting one scene after another until the dialogue suited the limited capabilities of the cast without losing any of its color or sense.

For that matter, all the conspirators doubled in brass. Mel found himself directing two-shots between his writing chores. MacAaron took over lighting and sound mixing despite roars of protest from outraged union delegates. Even Betty, toiling without pay, spent hours drilling Wanda Pericola in the pronunciation of her lines until the two of them hated the sight of each other.

Long days, long nights for all of them, culminated usually in the projection room where they wearily gathered to see the latest rushes while File sat apart from them in a cold fury delivering scathing comment on what he viewed on the screen and what it was costing him. The most grotesque part of it, Mel saw, was that File never understood what they were trying to do and flatly refused to believe the explanation of it that Betty gave him in a loud and frustrating private conference. As far as File was concerned, they were deliberately and maliciously goldbricking on the job, sabotaging him, driving him to ruin, and he let them know it at every turn.

In the long run it was his own cheapness that kept him from doing more than that. As Cy noted, he could have fired them all, but contracts cut ice both ways. Firing them would mean paying them off in full for having done only part of the picture, and replacing them would mean paying others in full for doing the other part, and this for File was unthinkable.

'I know,' Mel said. 'All the same, I wish there was some way of keeping him off our backs for five minutes at a time. Now if he'd only find himself some nice little distraction—'

It wasn't the wish that made it so, of course. But for better or worse, early next morning along came the distraction.

She arrived riding pillion on a noisy motorbike – a small slender girl with one arm around the waist of the bearded young man who drove the motorbike and the other arm clutching to her a bulky parcel done up in wrapping paper. A northerner, Mel surmised, taking in the fair skin, the honey-colored hair, the neatly chiseled, slightly upturned Tuscan nose. A skinny, underfed kid, really, but pretty as they come.

They were standing in front of File's headquarters when the bike pulled up – Mel and Betty, Cy, MacAaron, and File – having the usual morning squabble about the day's shooting schedule. As the girl dismounted, now gingerly holding the parcel in both hands as if it were made of fine glass, her skirt rode up over her thighs, and Mel saw File do almost a comic double-take, the man's eyes fixing on the whiteness of exposed thigh, then narrowing with interest as they moved up to take in the whole girl.

What made it worse, Mel thought, was the quality of flagrant innocence about her, of country freshness. He glanced at Betty. From her expression he knew the same word must have flashed through her mind as his at that instant. *Alice*.

The bearded driver of the motorbike came up to them, the girl following in his shadow as if trying to keep out of sight. Close up, Mel saw that the driver's straggling reddish beard was a hopeless attempt to add years and dignity to a guileless and youthful face.

'Signor File, I am here as you requested.'

'Yeah,' File grunted. He turned sourly to Mel. 'You wanted statues? He's the guy who'll take care of them for you.'

'Paolo Varese,' said the youth. 'And this is my sister, Claudia.' He reached a hand behind him to draw her forward. 'What are you afraid of, you stupid girl?' he asked her teasingly. 'You must forgive her,' he said to the others. 'She is only a month from Campofriddo, and all this is new to her. It impresses her very much.'

'Where's Campofriddo?' asked Betty.

'Near Lucca, in the hills there.' Paolo laughed deprecatingly. 'You know. Twenty people, forty goats. That kind of place. So Papa and Mama let Claudia come to live with me in Rome where she could get good schooling, because she did well in school at home.'

He put an arm around the girl's narrow shoulders and gave her a brotherly hug which made her blush bright red. 'But you know how girls are about the cinema. When she heard I was to work here where you are photographing one—'

'Sure,' Cy said impatiently, 'but about those statues—'

'Yes, yes, of course.' Paolo took the parcel from his sister, tore open its wrappings, and held up before them a statuette of a robed figure. It was beautifully carved out of what looked like polished white marble, and, Mel saw with foreboding, it was not quite two feet tall.

'The statues were supposed to be lifesized,' he said, bracing himself for another bout with File. 'This one—'

'But this is only the – the—' Paolo struck his knuckles to his forehead, groping for the word '—the sample. They will be lifesized. Twelve of them, all lifesized.' He held out the sample at arm's length and regarded it with admiration. 'This is Augustus. The others will be Sulla, Marius, Pompey, Caesar, and Tiberius himself, all copies of the pieces in the Museo Capitoline, all lifesized.'

Mel took the figurine and found it surprisingly light. 'It's not marble?'

'How could it be?' Paolo said. 'Marble would take months to work, perhaps more. No, no, this is a trick. A device of my own. If you will show me where I am to work, I can demonstrate it for you.'

413

His sister anxiously tugged at his arm. '*Che cosa devo fare, Paolo?*' she asked, then whispered to him in more rapid Italian.

'Oh, yes.' Paolo nodded apologetically at File. 'Claudia has a little time before she must go along to school, and she would like to look around here and see how a cinema is made. She would be very careful.'

'Look around, hey?' File considered this frowningly, his eyes on the girl. 'Well, why not? I'll even show her around myself,' and from the way Claudia's face lit up, Mel saw she knew at least enough English to understand this. 'And I have to go back to town in a little while,' said File, 'so I can drop her off at her school on the way.'

Paolo seemed simultaneously alarmed and delighted by this kindness. 'But, Signor File, to take such trouble—'

'It's all right, it's all right.' File curtly waved aside the stammered gratitude. 'You just get on the job and do what you're being paid for. Goldsmith here'll show you the shop.'

Watching File motion the girl to follow him and then briskly stride off with her in his wake, Mel felt an angry admiration for the way the man handled these little situations. You had to know him to know the score. Otherwise, what you were seeing was a small white-haired grandfatherly type, concealing a heart of gold beneath a crusty exterior.

A sculptor's studio had been partitioned off in the carpenters' shop near the entrance to the sound stage, and it was already crowded with the materials and equipment for the making of the statues. The sculpturing process itself, as Paolo described it in rapt detail, was intriguing. A pipework armature, the size of the subject, was set up, its crosspiece at shoulder height. From the crosspiece, wire screening was then unspooled around and around down to the base where it was firmly attached, the whole thing making a cylinder of screening in roughly human proportions. To this was applied a thin layer of clay which was etched into the flowing lines of a Roman toga. As for the head—

Paolo took the statuette, and, despite Betty's wail of protest, ruthlessly chipped away its features with a knifeblade.

'It would take a long time to model the head in clay,' he said, 'but this way it can be done very quickly.'

He brushed away marble-colored flakes, revealing beneath

them what appeared to be a skull, although its eyes and nose sockets were filled in. He tapped it with a fingernail. 'Hollow, you see. *Papier mache*, such as masks are made of. One merely soaks it in this stuff – *colla* – you know?'

'Glue,' said Betty.

'Yes, yes. Then it can be quickly shaped into a whole head. It dries almost at once. Then clay goes over it for the fine work, and here is our Roman.'

'How do you get it to look like marble?' Cy asked.

'Enamel paint is sprayed on, white and ivory mixed. That, too, dries while you wait.'

'But the clay under it is still wet, isn't it?'

'Oh, no. Before the paint goes on, one uses the torch – the blowtorch, that is – up and down and back and forth for a few hours. But with all this it takes only one day. So there will be twelve statues in twelve days, as I have promised Signor File.'

'Do you have the designs for the other statues with you?' Cy asked, and when they were produced, much crumpled and stained, from Paolo's pocket, it was clear that File had once again made himself an excellent deal.

Standing at the open door of the shop ready to take their departure, they saw File heave into sight with Claudia, direct her into the Cadillac, and climb behind the wheel.

'Beautiful,' breathed Paolo, his eyes on the car rather than his sister. Then as the car headed for the garage, he reminded himself of something. '*La bicicletta! La bicicletta!*' he shouted after the girl, waving toward the motorbike propped on the ground before File's office, but she only made a small gesture of helplessness, and then the car was out of range.

Paolo shrugged in resignation.

'The autobus out here is very irregular, so she is supposed to bring me here on the bicycle each morning and then use it herself to go to school. That means I must take the autobus home at night, but today it looks as if I will be able to drive myself home without any trouble.'

'There's a piece of luck,' Betty said drily. 'You know, Paolo, Claudia is a very pretty girl.'

'But how well I know.' Paolo raised his eyes to heaven in despair. 'That was one reason I had so much trouble with Mama and Papa about permitting her to live with me here, where she could improve herself, become educated, perhaps become a teacher at school, not the wife of some stupid peasant. They are good people, Mama and Papa, but they hear stories, you know? So they think all the men in Rome want to do is eat the pretty little girls. They forget Claudia is with me, and that I—'

'Paolo,' Betty cut in, 'sometimes she is not with you. And while I don't know about all the other men in Rome, I know about Signor File. Signor File likes to eat pretty little girls.'

The boy looked taken aback.

'He? Really, signora, he does not seem like someone who—'

'*Faccia attenzione, signore,*' said Betty in a hard voice. '*Il padrone e un libertino. Capisce?*'

Paolo nodded gravely.

'*Capisco, signora.* Thank you. I will tell Claudia. She is already sixteen, not a child. She will understand.'

But, Mel observed, there were days after that when File, contrary to his custom, left the lot in midafternoon and returned only late in the evening, if at all.

Betty observed this as well.

'And you know where he goes, don't you?' she said to her husband.

'I don't know. I suspect. That's different from knowing.'

'Look, dear, let's not split hairs. He's with that child, and you darn well know it.'

'So what? For one thing, Mother of the Gracchi, sixteen, going on seventeen, is not a child in these parts, as her brother himself remarked. For another thing, you've done all you could about it – angels could do no more. As far as I'm concerned—'

'Oh, sure. As far as you're concerned – and Cy and Mac, too – you're just as glad Alex isn't around all the time, no matter what.'

There was no denying that. It was a godsend not having File always underfoot, and they weren't going to question whatever reason he had for staying away from them. Their nerves were ragged with overwork and tension, but the picture was near completion, and all they needed was enough stamina to finish it in style. Considering the drain that File was on their stamina –

complaining, threatening, countermanding orders – the sight of that Cadillac convertible pulling out of the gate in the afternoon was like a shot in the arm.

For that matter, Mel wasn't sure that even if Paolo suspected what might be going on he would be so anxious to rock the boat himself. The commission to do the statues, he had confided to Mel, meant enough money to see him through a difficult time. It was lucky Signor File had asked the Art Institute to recommend someone who would handle the commission at the lowest possible rate, because as one of their prize graduates the year before, he, Paolo, had got the recommendation. Very lucky. Money was hard to come by for a young sculptor without a patron; the family at home had no money to spare, so it was a case of always scratching for a few lire, taking odd jobs, doing anything to get up enough for the next rent day. But now—!

So from early morning to late at night, stripped to the waist and pouring sweat, Paolo toiled happily at the statues, and one by one they were carted away to the sound stage and mounted in place on the set there. The first six, faces in stern repose, looked good in the establishing shots; the ones that followed, faces distorted with madness, looked even better. The last to be done, and, Mel thought, the most effective of all according to the sketches of those agonized features, would be Tiberius in his madness.

When this was in its place along with the other five in the corridor of the palace, and MacAaron had made his tracking shots and closeups, the picture was all but finished. Finished, that is, except for Cy's editing – the delicate job of cutting, rearranging, finding the proper rhythm for each scene, and finally resplicing the whole thing into what would be shown on the screen. In the last analysis, everything depended on the editing, but this would be Cy's baby alone.

With the end in sight none of them wanted to rock the boat. And then, one stormy night, it came close to capsizing.

The storm had begun in the late afternoon, one of those drought-breaking Roman downpours that went on hour after hour, turning the meadows around them into a quagmire and covering even the tarmac with an inch of water. At midnight, when Mel and Betty splashed their way to the car, they saw Paolo standing hopelessly in the doorway of the carpenter's shop looking out into the deluge, and so they stopped to pick him up.

He was profusely grateful as he scrambled past Betty into the back seat. He lived in Trastevere, but if they dropped him anywhere in the city he could easily find his way home from there.

'No, it won't be any trouble taking you right to the door,' Mel lied. 'You just show me the way.'

The way, as Paolo pointed it out, lay across the Ponte Sublicio and to the Piazza Matrai, in the heart of a shabby, working-class district. The apartment he and his sister occupied was in a tenement that looked centuries old and stood in an alleyway leading off from the piazza. And parked in solitary grandeur at the head of the alley was a big Cadillac convertible.

Mel's foot came down involuntarily on the brake when he saw it, and the little Fiat lurched to a stop halfway across the piazza. At the same moment he heard Paolo make a hissing sound between his teeth, felt the pressure of the boy's body against the back of the driver's seat as he leaned forward and stared through the rain-spattered windshield.

And then, as if timing his approach to settle all doubts, File came into view down the alley, heading for the Cadillac at a fast trot, head down and shoulders hunched against the rain. He had almost reached it before Paolo suddenly roused himself from his paralysis of horror.

He pushed frantically at the back of Betty's seat. '*Signora*, let me out!'

Betty stubbornly remained unmoving. 'Why? So you can commit murder and wind up in jail for the rest of your life? What good will that do Claudia now?'

'That is my affair. Let me out. I insist!'

From his tone Mel had the feeling there would be murder committed if Betty yielded. Then File was out of reach. The Cadillac's taillights blinked on, started to move away, then disappeared down the Via della Luce. Paolo hammered his fist on his knee.

'You had no right!' he gasped. 'Why should you protect him?'

Mel thought of the next morning when this half-hysterical boy would have a chance to catch up to File on the lot.

'Now look,' he said reasonably, although it struck him that under the circumstances reason was the height of futility. 'Nobody knows exactly wht happened up in that apartment, so if you keep your head and talk to Claudia—'

'Yes,' Paolo said savagely, 'and when I do—!'

'But I'll talk to her first,' Betty announced. 'I know,' she said as Paolo started to blurt out an angry protest. 'It's not my affair, I have no right to interfere, but I'm going to do it just the same. And you'll wait here with Signor Gordon until I'm back.'

It was a tedious, nerve-racking wait, and the ceaseless drumming of the rain on the roof of the car made it that much more nerve-racking. The trouble was, Mel glumly reflected, that not having children of her own, Betty was always ready to adopt any waif or stray in sight and recklessly try to solve his problems for him. Only in this case, nothing she could say or do would mean anything. The boy sitting in deadly silence behind him had too much of a score to settle. The one practical way of forestalling serious trouble was to warn File about it and hope he had sense enough to take the warning to heart. If he didn't—

At last Betty emerged from the building and ducked into the car.

'Well,' said Paolo coldly, 'you have talked to her?'

'Yes.'

'And she told you how much she was paid to – to—?'

'Yes.'

Paolo had not expected this. 'She would never tell you that,' he said incredulously. 'She would lie, try to deceive you the way she did with me. She—'

'First let me tell you what she said. She said your agreement with Signor File was that you would get a small payment for the statues in advance and the rest of the money when the work was done. Is that the truth?'

'Yes. But what does that have to do with it?'

'A great deal. Everything, in fact. Because Signor File told her that if she wasn't nice to him, you would never get the rest of the money. He would say your work was no good, and, more than that, he would let everyone know this so that you'd never

419

get a chance at such commissions again. So what your sister thought she was sacrificing herself for, *signore*, was the money and the reputation she was sure you would otherwise be cheated of.'

Paolo clapped a hand to his forehead.

'But how could she think this?' he said wildly. 'She knows there was a paper signed before the lawyers. How could she believe such lies?'

'Because she is only a child, no matter what your opinion is of that, and she had no one to tell her better. Now when you go upstairs, you must let her know you understand that. Will you?'

'*Signora*—'

'Will you?'

'Yes, yes, I will. But as for that man—?'

'Paolo, listen to me. I know how you feel about it, but anything you do to him can only mean a scandal that will hurt Claudia. Whatever happens will be in all the newspapers. After that, can the girl go back to school? Can she ever go back home to Compofriddo without everyone staring at her and whispering about her? Even if you take him to court—'

'Even that,' Paolo said bitterly. He placed a hand on the latch of the door. 'But I must not keep you any longer with my affairs.' And when Betty reluctantly leaned forward so that he could climb past her out of the car, he added, 'You do not understand these things, *signora*, but I will think over what you have said. *Ciao*.'

Mel watched him disappear into the tenement, and then started the car.

'It doesn't sound very promising,' he said. 'I guess I'll have to slip Alex a word of warning tomorrow, much as I'd like to see him get what's coming to him.'

'I know.' Betty shook her head despairingly. 'My God, you ought to see the way those kids are living. A room like a rathole with a curtain across the middle so they can each have a little privacy. And rain seeping right through the walls. And the furniture all orange crates. And a stinking, leaky toilet out in the hall. You wouldn't believe that in this day and age—'

'Oh, sure, but *la vie Boheme* is hardly ever as fancy as *la dolce vita*. Anyhow, whatever Alex is paying for this commission means some improvement in those living standards when he settles up.'

'Does it? Mel, how much do you think Alex is paying?'

'How would I know? Why? Did Claudia tell you how much?'

'She did. Now take a guess. Please.'

Mel did some swift mental arithmetic.

'Well,' he said, 'since the statues are all Paolo's work from the original designs up to the finished product, they ought to be worth between five and ten thousand bucks. But I'll bet the kid never got more than two thousand from Alex.'

'Mel, he got five hundred. One hundred down, and the rest on completion. Five hundred dollars altogether!'

You couldn't beat File, Mel thought almost with awe as they recrossed the bridge over the swollen and murky Tiber. A lousy $500 for all twelve statues. And with Claudia Varese thrown in for good measure.

Mel had it out with File the next morning, glad that Cy and MacAaron were there in the office with them to get an earful about what had been going on.

Physically, File was not the bravest man in the world. He was plainly alarmed by the outlook.

'What the hell,' he blustered, 'you know these girls around here. If it wasn't me yesterday, it would be somebody else today. But if this brother of hers got any ideas about sticking a shiv in my back, maybe I can—'

'I didn't say that,' Mel pointed out. 'All I said was you'd be smart to steer clear of him. He'll be done with his job tomorrow. You might find something to do in town until he's gone.'

'You mean, let this ginzo kid run me off my own property?'

'You started the whole thing, didn't you? Your bad luck you just happened to pick the wrong kind of girl this time.'

'All right, all right! But I'll be back in the evening to see that last set of rushes, and we've got an important meeting in the office here right afterward. All of us, you understand? So you all be here.'

That had an ominous sound, they agreed after File left, but it didn't bother them. There were only a couple of scenes left to be shot, about a week's work editing the picture, and that was it. File had done his worst, but it hadn't stopped them from doing their best. Whatever card he now had up his sleeve – and File could always produce some kind of nasty surprise at those meetings – it was too late for him to play it. That was all that mattered.

They were wrong. File returned late in the evening to view the rushes with them, and when they gathered in his office afterward, he pulled from his sleeve, not a card, but a bombshell.

'I want to clear up one little point,' he said, 'and then the meeting's over. One little point is all. Goldsmith, I got an idea you're finally supposed to be done with the photography this week. Is that a fact?'

'By Friday,' Cy said.

'Then it's settled. So Friday night when you all walk out of here it'll be for the last time. Get the point? Once you're on the other side of that gate you're staying there. And don't try to con the guard into anything, because he'll have special instructions about keeping you there.'

'Sure,' said Cy, 'except that you overlooked one little detail, Alex. The picture has to be edited. You'll have to wait another week before you tell the guard to pull his gun on me.'

'Oh?' said File with elaborate interest. 'Another week?' His face hardened. 'No, thanks, Goldsmith. We're already carrying a guy on the payroll as film editor, so you just wave goodbye Friday and forget you ever knew me.'

'Alex, you're not serious about Gariglia doing the editing. But he's completely useless. If I'm not there to tell him what to do—'

'So from now on I'll tell him what to do.'

'You?'

'That's right. Me.' File angrily jabbed a forefinger into his chest. 'Me. Alex File who was making pictures when you were still jumping ponies over a cliff for Monogram at ten bucks a jump.'

'You never made a picture like this in your life.'

'You bet I didn't.' File's voice started to rise. 'A month over schedule. Twenty per cent over budget. Twenty per cent, you hear?'

Cy's face was bloodless now, his breath coming hard.

'Alex, I won't let you or anybody else butcher this picture. If you try to bar me from the lot before the editing is done—'

'If I try to?' File smashed his fist down on the desk. 'I'm not trying to, Goldsmith, I'm doing it! And this meeting is finished, do you hear? It's all over. And there won't be any more meetings, because I'm staying away from here until Saturday. All I got from this picture so far is ulcers, but Saturday the cure begins!'

This was no feigned fury, Mel saw. The man was blind with rage, literally shaking with it. The gods he worshipped were Budget and Schedule, and he had seen them spat on and overthrown. Now, like a high priest fleeing a place of sacrilege, he strode to the door bristling with outrage.

Cy's pleading voice stopped him there, hand on the knob.

'Look, Alex, we've known each other too long for this kind of nonsense. If we—'

'If we what?' File wheeled around, hand still on the knob. 'If we sit and talk about it all night, maybe I'll change my mind? After what's been going on here all summer? Well, get this straight, you lousy double-crosser, I wouldn't!'

The door was flung open. It slammed shut. File was gone.

The four of them stood there staring at each other. It was so silent in the room that Mel heard every sound from outside as if it were being amplified – the high-pitched piping of a train whistle in the distance, the creaking of the light globe outside the building swinging back and forth on its chain in the warm nighttime breeze, the sharp rapping of File's footsteps as he walked toward his car.

It was Betty who broke the silence in the room.

'Dear God,' she whispered, and it sounded as if she didn't know whether to laugh or cry, 'he meant it. He'll ruin the picture and not even know he's ruining it.'

'Wait a second,' Mel said. 'If Cy's contract provides him with the right to edit the picture—'

'Only it don't,' said MacAaron. He was watching Cy closely. 'How do you feel?' he asked.

Cy grimaced.

'Great. It only hurts when I laugh.'

'You look lousy. If I thought you'd settle for one little drink—'

'I'll settle for it. Let's just get the hell out of here, that's all.'

They went outside. The moon, low on the horizon, was only a wafer-thin crescent, but the stars were so thickly clustered overhead that they seemed to light the way to the parked cars with a pale phosphorescence.

Then Mel noticed that File's Cadillac was still standing there, headlights not on, but the door to the driver's seat swung open. And File was not in the car.

Mel looked around at the dark expanse of the lot. Strange, he thought. File was a creature of rigid habit who got into his car when the day's work was done and headed right out of the gate. He had never before been known to go wandering around the deserted lot after working hours, and what reason he might have for doing it now—

Cy and MacAaron had been walking ahead, and Mel saw Cy suddenly pull up short. He walked back to Mel with MacAaron at his heels.

'I could have sworn I heard that little punk going this way when we were inside,' he said. 'He doesn't have another car stashed around here, does he?'

Mel shook his head. 'Just the Caddie. The door is open, too, so it looks as if he was getting in when he changed his mind about it. Where do you figure he went?'

'I don't know,' said Cy. 'All I know is that it's not like him to make any tour of inspection this time of night.'

They all stood and looked vaguely around the emptiness of the lot. There was a dim light suspended over the office door, another light over the gate, half revealing the gatekeeper's house which was the size of a telephone booth, and that was all there was to be seen by way of illumination. The rest was the uncertain shadowy forms of buildings against pitch blackness, the outline of the sound stage towering over all the others.

'Well, what are we waiting for?' MacAaron said at last. 'If something happened to him, we can always send poison ivy to the funeral. Come on, let's get going.'

It would have been better if he hadn't said it, Mel thought resentfully. Then they could have shrugged off the mystery and left. Now the spoken suggestion that something might be wrong seemed to impose on them the burden of doing something about it, no matter how they felt about File.

It appeared that Cy shared this thought.

'You know,' he said to Mel, 'Mac is right. There's no need for you and Betty to hang around.'

'What about you?'

'I'll wait it out a while. He'll probably show up in a few minutes.'

'Then we can wait with you,' Mel said, closing his ears to Betty's muttered comment on File.

The minutes dragged by. Then, at the sound of approaching footsteps, they all came to attention. But it wasn't File who showed up out of the darkness, it was the projectionist who had screened the rushes for them. He had been rewinding the film, he explained in answer to Cy's questions, and no, he had not seen Signore File since the screening. *Buona sera, signora, signori* – and off he went on his scooter amid a noisome belching of gasoline fumes.

They watched the guard emerge from his booth to open the gate for him, the scooter disappeared through the gate, and then all was silence again.

'Hell,' Cy said abruptly, 'we should have thought of it right off. That guard might have seen Alex.' And he shambled off to engage the guard in brisk conversation.

When he returned, shaking his head, he said, 'No dice. The guard heard the office door slam, but he was reading his paper in the booth so he didn't see anything. And he says the only ones he hasn't signed out yet are Alex and us – and Paolo Varese.'

That was it, Mel thought. If they all felt about it the way he did, that was the ominous possibility they had all been trying to close their eyes to. It was the real reason for this sense of disaster in the air. File and Paolo Varese. The boy hidden out of sight in back of the car, File opening the door, seating himself behind the wheel, the knife or gun suddenly menacing him, the two figures, one prodding the other out of the car, moving off into the darkness so that the job could be finished in some safe corner.

Or there was a skull-crushing blow delivered right there on the spot with one of those iron bars used in assembling the armature for the statues, then the body hoisted to a muscular shoulder and borne away into that all-enveloping darkness? But the evidence would remain. Spatters of blood. Worse, perhaps.

The temptation to look into the car, see what there was to be seen on its leather upholstery, rose in Mel along with a violent nausea. He weakly gestured toward the car.

'Maybe we ought to—'

'It's all right,' Cy said, clearly taking pity on him, 'I'll do it.'

Mel gratefully watched him walk to the car and lean inside it. Then the small glow of the light on the instrument panel could be seen behind the windshield.

'The keys are in the lock,' Cy called in a muffled voice, 'but there's no sign of any trouble here.'

The dashboard light went off, and he withdrew from the car. Keys in hand, he went around behind it, opened the trunk lid, and peered inside. He closed the lid and returned to them.

'Nothing,' he said. 'All we know is that Alex got into the car and then got out again.'

'So?' Betty said.

'So I'm going to look in at the carpenters' shop and see if Varese is there in that studio of his. Meanwhile, Mac can take a look through the sound stage. But there's no need for you and Mel—'

'Don't worry about that,' Betty said. 'It's still the shank of the evening.'

'All right, then you two take your car and run over to the backlot gate and check with the guard there. On the way back here cruise around and look over as much of the grounds as you can. Take your time and keep the headlights on full.'

They followed instructions to the letter, and when they rejoined Cy and MacAaron in front of the office twenty minutes later, Mel was relieved to see that both still reflected only puzzlement.

'Mac tells me the sound stage is all clear,' Cy said. 'As for the kid, he's in the shop working on that last statue, and he swears on his mother's life he hasn't been out of there since dinner. I believe him, too, not that he made any secret about how happy he'd be if Alex broke his neck. The fact is, if he really intended to jump Alex, he'd never do it out here in the open with that guard only fifty feet away and with us likely to walk out of the office any minute. So unless you can picture a chickenheart like Alex walking into that studio all by himself and looking for trouble—'

'Not a chance,' said Mel.

'That's how I feel about it. What did the guard at the backlot have to say?'

'Nothing, except that he locked up the gate at quitting time and hasn't seen a soul around here since then. We covered the lot, too, and all we turned up was a couple of stray cats. Now where does that leave us?'

Cy shook his head. 'With a ten-foot fence all around and no way out for Alex unless he learned how to fly with his hands and feet. He's sure as hell around here somewhere, but I can't think where. The only thing left to do is comb through every building and see what turns up. Mac will help me with that. You get Betty back to the hotel. She looks dead on her feet.'

She did, Mel saw. And he could well imagine what she was thinking. As long as Paolo was in the clear—

'Well, if you can get along without us,' he said.

'We'll manage. Oh, yeah, on your way out, find some excuse to have the guard look into your car trunk. Make sure he gets a good look. And don't worry about what he'll find there, because I already checked it. You don't mind, do you?'

'No,' said Mel, 'not as long as Alex wasn't in it.'

He was wakened early the next morning by a phone call from Cy at the lot reporting that he and MacAaron – and Paolo Varese, too, when he had finished the twelfth statue – had searched every inch of the lot and turned up no trace of File.

'He's gone all right,' Cy said tiredly. 'I even called his hotel just now on the wild chance he somehow got out of here, but they told me he didn't show up all night and isn't there now. So I figured the best thing to do was call in the police. They'll be here in a little while.'

'I'll get out there right away. But wasn't this calling in the police pretty fast, Cy? It's only been a few hours altogether.'

'I know, but later on someone might ask why we didn't get the cops in as soon as we smelled something wrong. Anyhow, it's done now, and the only question is what we tell them about that little fracas in the office just before Alex walked out. I'll be honest with you, Mel. I think it would be a mistake to say anything about the film editing or about being barred from the lot after Friday. Betty was there, too, so if they want to start pinning things on us—'

Mel glanced at Betty who was sitting up in bed and regarding him with alarm. 'What is it?' she whispered. 'What's wrong?'

'Nothing. No,' he said in answer to Cy's query, 'I was talking to Betty. I'll explain everything to her. She'll understand. I suppose you already talked it over with Mac?'

'Yes. He sees it the way we do.'

'And how much do we tell about Paolo?'

'Anything we're asked to tell. Why not?'

'Don't play dumb, Cy. If the cops find out what happened when I drove the kid home in the rain the other night—'

'Let them. As long as he had nothing to do with Alex disappearing, there's nothing they can pin on him. And maybe you didn't notice, but Wanda Pericola was standing right outside that office window when you were giving Alex hell about him and Varese's sister. What'll you bet Wanda spills the beans first chance she gets?'

It was not a fair bet, Mel knew. It was too much of a sure thing.

The police, two men in plainclothes, were already at the lot when he and Betty arrived there, and, as the day passed, Mel saw that in terms of the official attitude it was divided into three distinct periods.

First, there was the cynical period when the two plainclothes-men smilingly indicated that this whole affair was obviously a publicity stunt arranged by File Productions.

Then, persuaded otherwise, they became the sober investiga-tors, ordering everyone to report to the sound stage for a brisk questioning and a show of identification papers.

And finally, now thoroughly baffled and angry, they called headquarters for help and led a squad of uniformed men through a painstaking search of the entire lot.

Close behind the squad of police came reporters and a gang of *paparazzi* – free-lance photographers, most of them mounted on battered scooters – and the sight of them gathered before the front gate, aiming their cameras through the wiring, shouting questions at anyone who passed within hailing distance, seemed to annoy Inspector Conti, the senior of the two plainclothesmen, almost as much as his failure to locate the missing Alexander File.

'Nuisances,' he said when Cy asked about holding some sort of press conference in the office. 'They will stay on the other side of that fence where they belong. There can be no doubt that Signor File, alive or dead, is here inside the perimeter of that fence, and until we find him no one is permitted to enter or leave. It will not take long. Assuming the worst, that a crime has been committed, it is impossible to dispose of the victim beneath the pavement which covers the entire area. And thanks to your foresight, *signore*—' he nodded at Cy who wearily shrugged off the compliment '—this place has been hermetically sealed since immediately after the disappearance. There can be no question about it. Signore File is here. It is only a matter of hours at the most before we find him.'

The Inspector was a stubborn man. Not until sunset, after his squad had, to no avail, moved across the lot like a swarm of locusts, not until File's records and correspondence had futilely been examined page by page, did he acknowledge temporary defeat.

'You may leave now,' he announced to the company assembled in the sound stage, 'but you will make yourselves available for further questioning when called on. Until permission is granted by the authorities, no one will enter here.'

By now Cy was groggy with exhaustion, but this brought him angrily to his feet. 'Look, we've got a movie to finish, and if you—'

'All in good time, *signore*.' The Inspector's voice was flat with finality. 'Those of you who are not citizens will now surrender their passports to me, please. They will be held for you at headquarters.'

Outside in the parking space, Mel saw that the door of File's Cadillac had been closed but was discolored by a greyish powder. It took him a moment to realize that this must have been the work of a fingerprint expert, and that realization, more than anything else that had happened during the day, made File's disappearance real and menacing. The questions asked by the police had only scratched the surface so far – there had been no need to mention either Claudia Varese or the editing of the picture, but there was further questioning to come, and next time it was likely to do much more than scratch the surface.

Cy was pursuing a different line of thought.

'First thing,' he said, 'is to make sure everybody we need for those last scenes stays on call.'

'For what?' Mel said. 'Without Alex, who takes care of the payroll, the release, the promotion? We can't sign anything for him.'

'We won't have to. Look,' Cy said urgently, 'that big Hollywood lawyer of Alex's is empowered to act for him in his absence. He also happens to have a lot of dough tied up in this picture, and he's damn near as tight as Alex about money. When I get in touch with him and tell him what's going on here he'll see to it we finish the job. I guarantee that.'

'Only if Alex is absent,' Mel said. 'But what if he's dead?'

'Then we're licked. The footage we shot so far is part of his estate, and by the time the Surrogates Court settles the estate we'll all be dead and gone ourselves. But we don't know Alex is dead, do we? Nobody knows if he is or not. So what we do is get his lawyer's okay to finish the picture in return for an agreement to deliver it to him for release.'

'Without being allowed back on the lot?' said Betty. 'And who knows how long it'll be before we are allowed back? Further questioning, the detective said. It might take weeks before they get around to it. Or months.'

'It might,' said Cy, 'but I have a hunch it won't.'

He was right. The very next morning Mel was called to his interview with Commissioner Odoardo Ucci at Police Headquarters and had as unpleasant a time of it as he had anticipated.

The worst of it was when the Commissioner, after much deliberate nose scratching, suddenly introduced the subject of Paolo Varese's hostility toward his employer, and when Mel hedged in his answers, Ucci revealed an astonishing familiarity with the scene played that rainy night on the Piazza Matrai.

Which meant, Mel thought hopelessly, that Wanda had indeed spilled the beans at the first opportunity.

Under such conditions, Mel knew, there was no use being evasive about it. So he described the scene in detail and took what consolation he could from the memory of Cy's reminder that since Paolo had nothing to do with File's disappearance, there was nothing that could be pinned on him.

Ucci's reaction jolted him.

'If you had given this vital information to Inspector Conti at once—' he said.

'Vital?' Mel said. 'Listen, Commissioner, we walked out of that office a minute or two after Mr File. If Varese had tried to do anything to him out there—'

'But the possibility did enter your mind, *signore*, that he might have tried?'

'Yes, and I found out very quickly that I was wrong about it.'

'I think I will soon prove otherwise, *signore*. Before the day is over, in fact. So you and Signora Gordon will please remain *incommunicado* in your hotel until then. As a favor to yourself, no telephone calls and no visitors, please.'

It was Ucci himself who picked them up in a chauffeured car late in the afternoon.

'Where are we going?' Betty asked him as the car swung away from the curb.

'To the location of your cinema company, *signora*, to demonstrate that the mystery of Signor File's disappearance was never a mystery at all.'

'Then you found him? But where? What happened to him?'

'Patience, *signora*, patience.' The Commissioner's manner was almost playful. 'You will shortly see the answer for yourself. If,' he added grimly, 'you have the stomach for it.'

A *carabiniere* bearing a Tommy gun admitted them through the gate of the lot; another came to attention at the door of the carpenter's shop as they entered it. In the sculptor's studio behind the partition at the rear of the shop was a small gathering waiting for them.

Cy and MacAaron stood at one side of the room and Paolo Varese, tight-lipped and smoldering, stood at the other side between Inspector Conti and the subordinate plainclothesmen. And in the center of the room, towering over them all on its pedestal, was a life-sized statue.

Tiberius mad, Mel thought, and then recoiled as understanding exploded in him. There was a distinct resemblance between this statue and the one of Tiberius sane which had already been photographed and stored away in the prop room; but there was an even greater resemblance between these distorted features and the face of Alexander File in a paroxysm of rage.

'Oh, no,' Betty whispered in anguish, 'it looks like—'

'Yes?' prompted Ucci, and when Betty mutely shook her head he said, 'I am sorry, *signora*, but I wanted you to observe for yourself why the mystery never was a mystery. Once I had compared this statue with photographs of Signore File, the solution was clear. Wet *papier mache* molded to the face seems to reproduce it so that even a layer of clay over the mask, skillfully worked as it may be, does not conceal the true image underneath.

'However—' he nodded toward Inspector Conti '—it was my assistant who unearthed the most important clue. A series of these statues had been made before the disappearance. Only one – this one – was completed *after* the disappearance, and the use it was put to is obvious. Also, *signora*, highly unpleasant. So if you wish to leave the room now while we produce the evidence of the crime—'

When she left, moving as if she were sleepwalking through a nightmare, Mel knew guiltily that he should have gone with her; but he found himself helplessly rooted to the spot, transfixed by the sight of the Commissioner picking up a mallet and chisel and approaching the statue.

The sight stirred Paolo Varese to violent action. He suddenly flung himself at Ucci, almost overthrowing him in the effort to wrest the tools from his hands. When the two plainclothesmen locked their arms through his and dragged him back he struggled furiously to free himself from their grasp, then subsided, gasping.

'You can't!' he shouted at Ucci. 'That is a work of art!'

'And a clever one,' said Ucci coldly. 'Almost brilliant, in fact. A work of art that can be removed from here at your leisure and sent anywhere in the world without a single person knowing its contents. A fine business, young man, to use such a talent as yours for the purpose of concealing a murder. Do you at least confess to that murder now?'

'No! Whatever you find in my statue, I will never confess to any murder!'

'Ah? Then perhaps this will change your mind?'

The Commissioner placed the edge of the chisel into a fold of the toga draping the figure and struck it a careful blow. Then another and another.

As shards of white-enameled clay fell to the floor Mel closed his eyes, but that couldn't keep him from hearing the sound of those remorseless blows, the thudding on the floor of chunks of clay.

Then there was a different sound – the striking of metal against metal.

And finally a wrathful exclamation by Ucci.

Mel opened his eyes. What he saw at first glance was Ucci's broad face, almost ludicrous in its open-mouthed incredulity. Cy, MacAaron, the two plainclothesmen, all wore the same expression; all stared unbelievingly at the exposed interior of the statue which revealed the rods of an armature, a cylinder of wire screening – and nothing more.

'Impossible,' Ucci muttered. 'But this is impossible.'

As if venting his frustration on the statue, he swung the mallet flush against its head. The head bounded to the floor and lay there, an empty mask of *papier mache*, patches of whitened clay still adhering to it.

Paolo pulled himself free of the plainclothesmen's grasp. He picked up the mask and tenderly ran his fingers over the damage in it made by the mallet.

'Barbarian,' he said to Ucci. 'Vandal. Did you really think I was a murderer? Did you have to destroy my work to learn better?'

Ucci shook his head dazedly.

'Young man, I tell you that everything, all the evidence—'

'What evidence? Do I look like some peasant from the south who lives by the vendetta?' The boy thrust out the mask toward Ucci who recoiled as if afraid it would bite him. 'This was my revenge – to shape this so that the whole world would know what an animal that man was. And it was all the revenge I asked, because I am an artist, you understand, not a butcher. Now you can try to put the pieces of my statue together, because I am finished here.' He looked at Cy. 'As soon as I have packed my tools, *signore*, I will go.'

'But we'll be back tomorrow,' Cy pleaded. He turned to Ucci. 'You can't have any objections to that now, can you?'

'Objections?' The Commissioner still seemed lost in a daze. 'No, no, *signore*. The premises have been fully investigated, so you are free to use them. But it is impossible. I cannot understand—'

'You see?' Cy said to Paolo. 'And all I ask is one more day's work. Just one more day.'

'No, *signore*. I have done the work I agreed to do. I am finished here.'

As Mel started out of the studio, Cy followed him with lagging steps.

'Damn,' he said. 'I hate to do that scene one statue short.'

'You can shoot around it. Hell, I'm glad it turned out like this, statue or not. For a minute, that cop had me convinced—'

'You? He had us all convinced. When Betty walked out of here she looked like she was ready to cave in. You want my advice, Mel, you'll book the first flight home tomorrow and get her away from here as quick as you can. The picture's just about done anyhow, and Betty's the one you have to worry about, not Alex.'

The *carabiniere* on guard at the door motioned around the building, and they found Betty waiting for them there, her eyes red and swollen, the traces of tears shiny on her cheeks.

'What happened?' she asked, as if dreading to ask it. 'Did they—'

'No,' said Mel, 'they didn't. Paolo is out of it.' And then as she stood there, helplessly shaking her head from side to side – looking, in fact, as if she were ready to cave in – Mel put his arms tight around her.

'It's all right, baby,' he said, 'it's all right. We're going home tomorrow.'

*

Cy Goldsmith died the first day of winter that year, a few weeks after the picture was released; so at least, as Betty put it, he knew before he went that the critics thought the picture was good. Not an Oscar winner, of course, but plausible, dramatic, beautifully directed. It wasn't a bad send-off for a man on his deathbed.

The mystery of File's disappearance didn't hurt at the box office either. The press had a field day when the story first broke, and even when interest had died down somewhat it didn't take much to revive it. Every week or so Alexander File would be reported seen in some other corner of the world, a victim of amnesia, of drug addiction, of a Red plot, and the tabloids would once more heat up the embers of public interest. Then there was the release of the picture and Cy's death soon afterward to keep the embers burning.

Mel and Betty were in San Francisco getting ready to spend the Christmas week with her family when they saw the news in the paper – Cyrus Goldsmith died in Cedars of Lebanon Hospital after a long illness and would be buried at Elysian Park Cemetery – and it was the unpleasant thought of the reporters and photographers flocking around again that made Mel decide not to attend the funeral, but to settle instead for an extravagant wreath.

Reading that mention of Elysian Park reminded him also of the time when he and Cy had stood on the portico of the make-believe palace in the backlot, looking down on the Appian Way, and Cy had confided to him how comforting it had been to arrange for the mausoleum he would soon be occupying. He had been like a relic of antiquity, had Cyrus Goldsmith. A devout believer in the idea that a chamber of granite with one's name on it somehow meant a happier afterlife than a six-foot hole in the ground.

Mel shook his head at the thought. Cy had no family to mourn him, the only person in the world close to him had been MacAaron, so MacAaron must have been in charge of the funeral arrangements. Too bad Mac wasn't the kind of man to do things up in real imaginative style. Seen to it, perhaps, that, just as the Pharoahs had been buried with the full equipage for a happy existence in heaven, Cy should have been provided with his idea of the necessities for a pleasant eternity – a supply of Scotch, a print of *Emperor of Lust*, even a handsomely mounted picture of a futilely snarling Alexander File on the mausoleum wall to keep fresh that taste of the final victory.

A few days later – the day after Christmas when the household was still trying to recover from the festivities – Mel and Betty slipped away and drove downtown to see the picture for the first time. Mel had long ago given up attending public showings of anything he had worked on because watching the audience around him fail to appreciate his lines was too much like sitting in a dentist's chair and having a tooth needlessly drilled; but this time Betty insisted.

'After all, we didn't go to the funeral,' she argued with a woman's logic, 'so this is the least we can do for Cy.'

'Darling, no disrespect intended, but where Cy is now, he couldn't care less what we do for him."

'Then I'll go see it by myself. Don't be like that, Mel. You know this one is different.'

And so it was, he saw. Different and shocking in a way that no one else in the audience would appreciate. At his suggestion, and to Betty's pleased bewilderment, they sat through it a second time. Then, while Betty was in the theater lounge, he raced to a phone in the lobby and put through a call to MacAaron's home in North Hollywood.

'Mac, this is Mel Gordon.'

'Sure. Say, I'm sorry you couldn't make it to the funeral, but those flowers you sent—'

'Never mind that. Mac, I just saw the picture, and there's one shot in it – well, I have to get together with you about it as soon as possible.'

There was a long silence at the other end of the line.

'Then you know,' MacAaron said at last.

'That's right. I see you do, too.'

'For a long time. And Betty?'

'I'm sure she doesn't.'

'Good,' said MacAaron with obvious relief. 'Look, where are you right now?'

'With my in-laws, in San Francisco. But I can be at your place first thing tomorrow.'

'Well, first thing tomorrow I have to go over to Elysian Park and settle Cy's account for him. He put me in charge of it. You ever see the way he's fixed up?'

'No.'

'Then this'll give you a chance to. You can meet me there at ten. The man at the gate will show you where Cy is.'

Punctuality was a fetish with MacAaron. When Mel arrived for the meeting a few minutes after ten, Mac was already there, seated on a bench close by a mausoleum with the name GOLDSMITH inscribed over its massive bronze door. The structure was made of roughhewn granite blocks without ornamentation or windows, and it stood on a grassy mount overlooking a somewhat unkempt greensward thickly strewn with grave markers. Unlike the fashionable new cemeteries around Los Angeles, Elysian Park looked distinctly like a burial ground.

MacAaron moved to make room for Mel on the bench.

'How many times did you see the picture?' he asked without preliminary,

'Twice around.'

'That all? You caught on quick.'

'It was simple arithmetic,' Mel said, wondering why he felt impelled to make it almost an apology. 'Six statues already used and locked up in the prop room, six more in that long shot of the corridor – and the one in the studio that the police smashed up. Thirteen statues. Not twelve. Thirteen.'

'I know, I caught wise the day we shot the last scenes with those statues, and I counted six of them standing there, not five. That's when I backed Cy into a corner and made him tell me everything, much as he didn't want to. After he did, I had sense enough to cut away from that sixth statue before the camera could get it; but I never did notice that one long shot of the whole corridor showing all six of those damn things until the night of the big premiere, and then it was too late to do anything about it. So there they were, just waiting for you to turn up and start counting them.' He shook his head dolefully.

'As long as the police didn't start counting them,' Mel said.

'Anyhow, all it proves is that Paolo Varese was a lot smarter than we gave him credit for. The statue in his studio was just a dummy, a red herring. All that time we were watching the Commissioner chop it apart, Alex was sealed up in the sixth one in the corridor. Right there on that set in the sound stage, with everyone walking back and forth past him.'

'He was. But do you really think it was Varese who had the brains to handle the deal? He was as green as he looked, that kid. Him and his little sister both. A real pair of babes in the woods.'

'You mean it was Cy who killed Alex?'

'Hell, no. The last thing Cy wanted was Alex dead, because then the picture would be tied up in Surrogates Court. No, the kid did it, all right, but it was Cy – look, maybe the best way to tell it is right from the beginning.'

'Maybe it is,' said Mel.

'Then first of all, you remember what Cy had us do after we saw the Caddie standing there that night with the door open and Alex nowhere around?'

'Yes. He had you go through the sound stage hunting for Alex, and Betty and me look around the grounds.'

'Because he wanted all three of us out of the way for the time being. He had an idea Alex had gone to see the kid and that something might have happened. So he—'

'Hold on,' Mel said. 'We all agreed right there that Alex would never have the guts to face the kid.'

'That's the track Cy put us on, but in the back of his mind he figured Alex might have one good reason for getting together with Varese. Just one. Alex was yellow right down to the bottom of the backbone, right? But he also had to do business in Rome every year, and that's where the kid lived. Who knew when they'd bump into each other, or when the kid would get all steamed up after a few drinks and come looking for him?

'So what does a guy like Alex do about it? He goes to the kid waving a white flag and tries to buy him off. Cheap, of course, but the way things are with Varese and the sister he feels a few hundred bucks should settle the case very nicely. About three hundred bucks, in fact. Twenty thousand lire. Cy knew how much it was because when he walked into the studio there was the money all over the floor, and Alex lying there dead with his face all black, and the kid standing there not knowing what had happened. Cy says it took him five minutes just to bring him out of shock.

'Anyhow, he finally got the kid to making sense, and it turned out that Alex had walked into the studio, waving the money in his hand, a big smile on that mean little face of his, and he let the kid know that, what the hell, the girl wasn't really hurt in any way, but if it would make her feel better to buy something nice for herself—'

'But how stupid could he be? To misjudge anyone that way!'

'Yeah, that's about the size of it.' MacAaron nodded somberly. 'Anyhow, it sure lit the kid's fuse. He didn't even know what happened next. All he knew was that he got his hands around that skinny throat, and when he let go it was too late.'

'Even so,' Mel said unhappily, 'it was still murder.'

'It was,' agreed MacAaron. 'And a long stretch in jail, and the papers full of how the little sister had gone wrong. It sure looked hopeless, all right. And you know the weirdest part of it?'

'What?'

'That the only thing on Varese's mind was the way he'd let his folks down, his Mama and his Papa. Going to jail didn't seem to bother him one bit as much as that he had argued his people into letting the girl go to Rome and then he had let her become a pigeon for Alex. It never struck him anything could be done about Alex being dead. As far as he was concerned, it was just a case of calling in the cops now and getting it over with.

'But, naturally, the last thing Cy wanted was for anyone to know Alex was dead, because then the picture was really washed up. And looking at that Tiberius statue which was almost finished, he got the idea that maybe something *could* be done. The hitch was that you and me and Betty were right there on the spot, but once he got you two off the lot and then had me hunting for Alex like a fool through all those buildings and shops, he had room to move in.

'First off, he had the kid rush through a whole new Tiberius statue. That was the thirteenth statue, the one they stuck Alex inside of, and Cy said it was all he and the kid could do to keep their dinner down while they were at it. It took almost all night, too, and when it was done they trucked it over to the sound stage and set it up there and brought the other one back to the studio.'

'But he told me he had Paolo helping you and him look for Alex most of the night. If I had asked you about it—'

'Oh, that.' The ghost of a smile showed on MacAaron's hardbitten face. 'He wasn't taking any chance with that story, because he had the kid go by me a couple of times looking around the lot with a flashlight in his hand. If I had any doubts about him up to then, that settled them. When Inspector Conti questioned me next day I didn't even mention the kid, I was so sure he was in the clear about Alex.'

'You didn't have to mention him. Wanda was only waiting to.'

'Wanda?' MacAaron said with genuine surprise. 'What would she know? Hell, it was Cy who told the Inspector about what happened when you took the kid home that night. But the right way, you understand, sort of letting it be dragged out of him. And sort of steered him around to the studio so he could get a good look at that statue after seeing some photos of Alex.

'It was Cy all the way. Once he made sure the Inspector and the Commissioner knew those other statues in the prop room and on the sound stage had absolutely been there before Alex disappeared, Cy wanted that showdown in the studio. He wanted everything pinned on the kid and then cleared up once and for all. The only question was whether the kid could hold up under pressure in the big scene, and you saw for yourself how he did.

'Now do you get the whole setup? Make the lot look like it was sealed up airtight, make it look like the kid was the only possible suspect, and then clear him completely. If I could swear on the Bible that the kid was helping us hunt for Alex that night, and if Alex isn't in that statue – what's left?'

'A statue with a body in it,' Mel said. 'A murder.'

'Yeah, I understand,' MacAaron said sympathetically. 'Now you're sorry you know the whole thing. But I'm not, Mel. And I don't mean because it's been so hard keeping it to myself. What's been eating me is that up to now nobody else in the world knew how Cy proved the kind of man he was.'

'Proved what?' Mel said harshly. 'It wasn't hard for him to be that kind of man, feeling the way he did about the picture and knowing he had only a little while to live. How much was he really risking under those conditions? If things went wrong, he'd be dead before they could bring him to trial, and the kid would take the whole rap.'

'You still don't get it. You don't get it at all. How could you if you weren't even there at the finish? Well, I was.'

To Mel's horror, MacAaron, the imperturbable, the stoic, looked as if he were fighting back tears, his face wrinkling monkey-like in his effort to restrain them. 'Mel, it went on forever in that hospital. Week after week, and every day of it the pain got worse. It was like knives being run into him. But all that time he would never let them give him a needle to kill the pain. They wanted to, but he wouldn't let them. He told them it was all right, he wouldn't make any fuss about how it hurt, and he didn't. Just lay there twisting around in that bed, chewing on a handkerchief he kept stuffed in his mouth, and sweat, the size of marbles, dripping down his face. But no needles. Not until right near the end after he didn't know what was going on any more.'

'So what? If he was afraid of a lousy needle—'

'But don't you see why?' MacAaron said despairingly. 'Don't you get it? He was scared that if he had any dope in him he might talk about Alex and the kid without even knowing it. He might give the whole thing away and send the kid to jail after all. That was the one big thing on his mind. That was the kind of man he was. So however you want to fault him—'

He stared at Mel, searching for a response, and was evidently satisfied with what he saw.

'It'll be tough keeping this to ourselves,' he said. 'I know that, Mel. But we have to. If we didn't, it would mean wasting everything Cy went through.'

'And how long do you think we'll get away with it? There's still the statue with Alex rotting away inside of it, wherever it is. Sooner or later—'

'Not sooner,' MacAaron said. 'Maybe a long time later. A couple of lifetimes later.' He got up stiffly, walked over to the mausoleum and inserted a key into the lock of the bronze door.

'Take a look,' he said. 'This is the only key, so now's your chance.'

An unseen force lifted Mel to his feet and propelled him toward that open door. He knew he didn't want to go, didn't want to see what was to be seen, but there was no resisting that force.

Sunlight through the doorway flooded the chill depths of the granite chamber and spilled over an immense casket on a shelf against its far wall. And standing at its foot, facing it with features twisted into an eternal, impotent fury, was the statue of Tiberius mad.

# The Last Bottle
## in the World

It was a bad moment. This cafe on the rue de Rivoli near the Meurice had looked tempting, I had taken a chair at one of its sidewalk tables, and then, glancing casually across at the next table, had found myself staring into the eyes of a young woman who was looking at me with startled recognition. It was Madame Sophia Kassoulas. Suddenly, the past towered over me like a monstrous genie released from a bottle. The shock was so great that I could actually feel the blood draining from my face.

Madame Kassoulas was instantly at my side.

'Monsieur Drummond what is it? You look so ill. Is there anything I can do?'

'No, no. A drink, that's all. Cognac, please.'

She ordered me one, then sat down to solicitously undo the buttons of my jacket. 'Oh, you men. The way you dress in this summer heat.'

This might have been pleasant under other conditions, but I realized with embarrassment that the picture we offered the other patrons of the cafe must certainly be that of a pitiful, white-haired old grandpa being attended to by his soft-hearted granddaughter.

'Madame, I assure you—'

She pressed a finger firmly against my lips. 'Please. Not another word until you've had your cognac and feel like yourself again. Not one little word.'

I yielded the point. Besides, turnabout was fair play. During that nightmarish scene six months before when we were last in each other's company she had been the one to show weakness and I had been the one to apply the restoratives. Meeting me now, the woman must have been as hard hit by cruel memory

443

as I was. I had to admire her for bearing up so well under the blow.

My cognac was brought to me, and even *in extremis*, so to speak, I automatically held it up to the sunlight to see its color. Madame Kassoulas' lips quirked in a faint smile.

'Dear Monsieur Drummond,' she murmured. 'Always the connoisseur.'

Which, indeed, I was. And which, I saw on grim reflection, was how the whole thing had started on a sunny Parisian day like this the year before . . .

That was the day a man named Max de Marechal sought me out in the offices of my company, Broulet and Drummond, wine merchants, on the rue de Berri. I vaguely knew of de Marechal as the editor of a glossy little magazine, *La Cave*, published solely for the enlightenment of wine connoisseurs. Not a trade publication, but a sort of house organ for *La Societe de la Cave*, a select little circle of amateur wine fanciers. Since I generally approved the magazine's judgments, I was pleased to meet its editor.

Face to face with him, however, I found myself disliking him intensely. In his middle forties, he was one of those dapper, florid types who resemble superannuated leading men. And there was a feverish volatility about him which put me on edge. I tend to be low-geared and phlegmatic myself. People who are always bouncing about on top of their emotions like a Ping-Pong ball on a jet of water make me acutely uncomfortable.

The purpose of his visit, he said, was to obtain an interview from me. In preparation for a series of articles to be run in his magazine, he was asking various authorities on wine to express their opinions about the greatest vintage they had ever sampled. This way, perhaps, a consensus could be made and placed on record. If—

'If,' I cut in, 'you ever get agreement on the greatest vintage. Ask a dozen experts about it and you'll get a dozen different opinions.'

'It did look like that at the start. By now, however, I have found some small agreement on the supremacy of two vintages.'

'Which two?'

'Both are Burgundies. One is the Richebourg 1923. The other is the Romanee-Conti 1934. And both, of course, indisputably rank among the noblest wines.'

'Indisputably.'

'Would one of these be your own choice as the vintage without peer?'

'I refuse to make any choice, Monsieur de Marechal. When it comes to wines like these, comparisons are not merely odious, they are impossible.'

'Then you do not believe any one vintage stands by itself beyond comparison?'

'No, it's possible there is one. I've never tasted it, but the descriptions written of it praise it without restraint. A Burgundy, of course, from an estate which never again produced anything like it. A very small estate. Have you any idea which vintage I'm referring to?'

'I believe I do.' De Marechal's eyes gleamed with fervor. 'The glorious Nuits Saint-Oen 1929. Am I right?'

'You are.'

He shrugged helplessly. 'But what good is knowing about it when I've never met anyone who has actually tasted it? I want my series of articles to be backed by living authorities. Those I've questioned all know about this legendary Saint-Oen, but not one has even seen a bottle of it. What a disaster when all that remains of such a vintage – possibly the greatest of all – should only be a legend. If there were only one wretched bottle left on the face of the earth—'

'Why are you so sure there isn't?' I said.

'Why?' De Marcehal gave me a pitying smile. 'Because, my dear Drummond, there can't be. I was at the Saint-Oen estate myself not long ago. The *vigneron*'s records there attest that only forty dozen cases of the 1929 were produced altogether. Consider. A scant forty dozen cases spread over all the years from then to now, and with thousands of connoisseurs thirsting for them. I assure you, the last bottle was emptied a generation ago.'

I had not intended to come out with it, but that superior smile of his got under my skin.

'I'm afraid your calculations are a bit off, my dear de Marechal.' It was going to be a pleasure setting him back on his heels. 'You see, a bottle of Nuits Saint-Oen 1929 is, at this very moment, resting in my company's cellars.'

The revelation jarred him as hard as I thought it would. His jaw fell. He gaped at me in speechless wonderment. Then his face darkened with suspicion.

'You're joking,' he said. 'You must be. You just told me you've never tasted the vintage. Now you tell me—'

'Only the truth. After my partner's death last year I found the bottle among his private stock.'

'And you haven't been tempted to open it?'

'I resist the temptation. The wine is dangerously old. It would be extremely painful to open it and find it has already died.'

'Ah, no!' De Marechal clapped a hand to his brow. 'You're an American, monsieur, that's your trouble. Only an American could talk this way, someone who's inherited the obscene Puritan pleasure in self-denial. And for the last existing bottle of Nuits Saint-Oen 1929 to have such an owner! It won't do. It absolutely will not do. Monsieur Drummond, we must come to terms. What price do you ask for this Saint-Oen?'

'None. It is not for sale.'

'It must be for sale!' de Marechal said explosively. With an effort he got himself under control. 'Look, I'll be frank with you. I am not a rich man. You could get at least a thousand francs – possibly as much as two thousand – for that bottle of wine, and I'm in no position to lay out that kind of money. But I am close to someone who can meet any terms you set. Monsieur Kyros Kassoulas. Perhaps you know of him?'

Since Kyros Kassoulas was one of the richest men on the Continent, someone other magnates approached with their hats off, it would be hard not to know of him despite his well-publicized efforts to live in close seclusion.

'Of course,' I said.

'And do you know of the one great interest in his life?'

'I can't say I do. According to the newspapers, he seems to be quite the man of mystery.'

'A phrase concocted by journalists to describe anyone of such wealth who chooses to be reticent about his private affairs. Not that there is anything scandalous about them. You see, Monsieur Kassoulas is a fanatic connoisseur of wines.' De Marechal gave me a meaningful wink. 'That's how I interested him in founding our *Societe de la Cave* and in establishing its magazine.'

'And in making you its editor.'

'So he did,' said de Marechal calmly. 'Naturally, I'm grateful to him for that. He, in turn, is grateful to me for giving him sound instruction on the great vintages. Strictly between us, he was a sad case when I first met him. A man without any appetite for vice, without any capacity to enjoy literature or music or art, he was being driven to distraction by the emptiness of his life. I filled that emptiness the day I pointed out to him that he must cultivate his extraordinarily true palate for fine wine. The exploration of the worthier vintages since then has been for him a journey through a wonderland. By now, as I have said, he is a fanatic connoisseur. He would know without being told that your bottle of Nuits Saint-Oen is to other wines what the Mona Lisa is to other paintings. Do you see what that means to you in a business way? He's a tough man to bargain with, but in the end he'll pay two thousand francs for that bottle. You have my word on it.'

I shook my head. 'I can only repeat, Monsieur de Marechal, the wine is not for sale. There is no price on it.'

'And I insist you set a price on it.'

That was too much.

'All right,' I said, 'then the price is one hundred thousand francs. And without any guarantee the wine isn't dead. One hundred thousand francs exactly.'

'Ah,' de Marechal said furiously, 'so you really don't intend to sell it! But to play dog in the manger—'

Suddenly he went rigid. His features contorted, his hands clutched convulsively at his chest. As crimson with passion as his face had been the moment before, it was now ghastly pale and bloodless. He lowered himself heavily into a chair.

'My heart,' he gasped in agonized explanation. 'It's all right. I have pills—'

The pill he slipped under his tongue was nitroglycerine, I was sure. I had once seen my late partner Broulet undergo a seizure like this.

'I'll call a doctor,' I said, but when I went to the phone de Mareschal made a violent gesture of protest.

'No, don't bother. I'm used to this. It's an old story with me.'

He was, in fact, looking better now.

'If it's an old story you should know better,' I told him. 'For a man with a heart condition you allow yourself to become much too emotional.'

'Do I? And how would you feel, my friend, if you saw a legendary vintage suddenly appear before you and then found it remained just out of reach? No, forgive me for that. It's your privilege not to sell your goods if you don't choose to.'

'It is.'

'But one small favor. Would you, at least, allow me to see the bottle of Saint-Oen? I'm not questioning its existence. It's only that the pleasure of viewing it, of holding it in my hands—'

It was a small enough favor to grant him. The cellars of Broulet and Drummond were near the Halles au Vin, a short trip by car from the office. There I conducted him through the cool, stony labyrinth bordering the Seine, led him to the Nuits Saint-Oen racks where, apart from all the lesser vintages of later years, the one remaining bottle of 1929 rested in solitary grandeur. I carefully took it down and handed it to de Marechal, who received it with reverence.

He examined the label with an expert eye, delicately ran a fingertip over the cork. 'The cork is in good condition.'

'What of it? That can't save the wine if its time has already come.'

'Naturally. But it's an encouraging sign.' He held the bottle up to peer through it. 'And there seems to be only a normal sediment. Bear in mind, Monsieur Drummond, that some great Burgundies have lived for fifty years. Some even longer.'

He surrendered the bottle to me with reluctance. His eyes remained fixed on it so intensely as I replaced it in the rack that he looked like a man under hypnosis. I had to nudge him out of the spell before I could lead him upstairs to the sunlit outer world.

We parted there.

'I'll keep in touch with you,' he said as we shook hands. 'Perhaps we can get together for lunch later this week.'

'I'm sorry,' I said without regret, 'but later this week I'm leaving for New York to look in on my office there.'

448

'Too bad. But of course you'll let me know as soon as you return to Paris.'

'Of course,' I lied.

However, there was no putting off Max de Marechal now that he had that vision of the Nuits Saint-Oen 1929 before his eyes. He must have bribed one of the help in my Paris office to tell him when I was back from the States, because no sooner was I again at my desk on the rue de Berri than he was on the phone. He greeted me with fervor. What luck he had timed his call so perfectly! My luck, as well as his. Why? Because *La Societe de la Cave* was to have a dinner the coming weekend, a positive orgy of wine sampling, and its presiding officer, Kyros Kassoulas himself, had requested my presence at it!

My first impulse was to refuse the invitation. For one thing, I knew its motive. Kassoulas had been told about the Nuits Saint-Oen 1929 and wanted to get me where he could personally bargain for it without losing face. For another thing, these wine-tasting sessions held by various societies of connoisseurs were not for me. Sampling a rare and excellent vintage is certainly among life's most rewarding experiences, but, for some reason I could never fathom, doing it in the company of one's fellow *aficionados* seems to bring out all the fakery hidden away in the soul of even the most honest citizen. And to sit there, watching ordinarily sensible men vie with each other in their portrayals of ecstasy over a glass of wine, rolling their eyes, flaring their nostrils, straining to find the most incongruous adjectives with which to describe it, has always been a trial to me.

Weighed against all this was simple curiosity. Kyros Kassoulas was a remote and awesome figure, and here I was being handed the chance to actually meet him. In the end, curiosity won. I attended the dinner, I met Kassoulas there, and quickly realized, with gratification, that we were striking it off perfectly.

It was easy to understand why. As de Marechal had put it, Kyros Kassoulas was a fanatic on wines, a man with a single-minded interest in their qualities, their history, and their lore, and I could offer him more information on the subject than anyone else he knew. More, he pointed out to me, than even the knowledgeable Max de Marechal.

As the dinner progressed, it intrigued me to observe that where everyone else in the room deferred to Kassoulas – especially de Marechal, a shameless sycophant – Kassoulas himself deferred to me. I enjoyed that. Before long I found myself really liking the man instead of merely being impressed by him.

He was impressive, of course. About fifty, short and barrel-chested, with a swarthy, deeply lined face and almost simian ears, he was ugly in a way that some clever women would find fascinating. Somehow, he suggested an ancient idol roughhewn out of a block of mahogany. His habitual expression was a granite impassivity, relieved at times by a light of interest in those veiled, ever-watchful eyes. That light became intense when he finally touched on the matter of my bottle of Saint-Oen.

He had been told its price, he remarked with wry humor, and felt that a hundred thousand francs – twenty thousand hard American dollars – was, perhaps, a little excessive. Now if I would settle for two thousand francs—

I smilingly shook my head.

'It's a handsome offer,' Kassoulas said. 'It happens to be more than I've paid for any half dozen bottles of wine in my cellar.'

'I won't dispute that, Monsieur Kassoulas.'

'But you won't sell, either. What are the chances of the wine's being fit to drink?'

'Who can tell? The 1929 vintage at Saint-Oen was late to mature, so it may live longer than most. Or it may already be dead. That's why I won't open the bottle myself or sell anyone else the privilege of opening it. This way, it's a unique and magnificent treasure. Once its secret is out, it may simply be another bottle of wine gone bad.'

To his credit, he understood that. And, when he invited me to be a guest at his estate near Saint-Cloud the next weekend, it was with the blunt assurance that it was only my company he sought, not the opportunity to further dicker for the bottle of Saint-Oen. In fact, said he, he would never again broach the matter. All he wanted was my word that if I ever decided to sell the bottle, he would be given first chance to make an offer for it. And to that I cheerfully agreed.

The weekend at his estate was a pleasant time for me, the first of many I spent there. It was an enormous place, but smoothly run by a host of efficient help under the authority of a burly, grizzled majordomo named Joseph. Joseph was evidently Kassoulas' devoted slave. It came as no surprise to learn he had been a sergeant in the Foreign Legion. He responded to orders as if his master was the colonel of his regiment.

What did come as a surprise was the lady of the house, Sophia Kassoulas. I don't know exactly what I expected Kassoulas' wife to be like, but certainly not a girl young enough to be his daughter, a gentle, timid creature whose voice was hardly more than a whisper. By today's standards which require a young woman to be a lank-haired rack of bones she was, perhaps, a little too voluptuous, a little too ripely curved, but I am an old-fashioned sort of man who believes women should be ripely curved. And if, like Sophia Kassoulas, they are pale, dark-eyed, blushing beauties, so much the better.

As time passed and I became more and more a friend of the family, I was able to draw from her the story of her marriage, now approaching its fifth anniversary. Sophia Kassoulas was a distant cousin of her husband. Born to poor parents in a mountain village of Greece, convent bred, she had met Kassoulas for the first time at a gathering of the family in Athens, and, hardly out of her girlhood, had married him soon afterward. She was, she assured me in that soft little voice, the most fortunate of women. Yes, to have been chosen by a man like Kyros to be his wife, surely the most fortunate of women—

But she said it as if she were desperately trying to convince herself of it. In fact, she seemed frightened to death of Kassoulas. When he addressed the most commonplace remark to her she shrank away from him. It became a familiar scene, watching this happen, and watching him respond to it by then treating her with an icily polite disregard that only intimidated her the more.

It made an unhealthy situation in that household because, as I saw from the corner of my eye, the engaging Max de Marechal was always right there to soothe Madame's fears away. It struck me after a while how very often an evening at Saint-Cloud wound up with Kassoulas and myself holding a discussion over our brandy at one end of the room while Madame Kassoulas and Max de Marechal were head to head in conversation at the other end. There was nothing indecorous about those *tete-a-*

*tetes*, but still I didn't like the look of them. The girl appeared to be as wide-eyed and ingenuous as a doe, and de Marechal bore all the earmarks of the trained predator.

Kassoulas himself was either unaware of this or remarkably indifferent to it. Certainly, his regard for de Marechal was genuine. He mentioned it to me several times, and once, when de Marechal got himself dangerously heated up in an argument with me over the merits of some vintage or other, Kassoulas said to him with real concern, 'Gently, Max, gently. Remember your heart. How many times has the doctor warned you against becoming overexcited?' – which, for Kassoulas, was an unusual show of feeling. Generally, like so many men of his type, he seemed wholly incapable of expressing any depth of emotion.

Indeed, the only time he ever let slip any show of his feelings about his troublesome marriage was once when I was inspecting his wine cellar with him and pointed out that a dozen Volnay-Caillerets 1955 he had just laid in were likely to prove extremely uneven. It had been a mistake to buy it. One never knew, in uncorking a bottle, whether or not he would find it sound.

Kassoulas shook his head.

'It was a calculated risk, Monsieur Drummond, not a mistake. I don't make mistakes.' Then he gave an almost imperceptible little shrug. 'Well, one perhaps. When a man marries a mere child—'

He cut it short at that. It was the first and last time he ever touched on the subject. What he wanted to talk about was wine, although sometimes under my prodding and because I was a good listener, he would recount stories about his past. My own life has been humdrum. It fascinated me to learn, in bits and pieces, about the life of Kyros Kassoulas, a Piraeus wharf rat who was a thief in his childhood, a smuggler in his youth, and a multimillionare before he was thirty. It gave me the same sense of drama Kassoulas appeared to feel when I would recount to him stories about some of the great vintages which, like the Nuits Saint-Oen 1929, had been cranky and uncertain in the barrel until, by some miracle of nature, they had suddenly blossomed into their full greatness.

It was at such times that Max de Marechal himself was at his best. Watching him grow emotional in such discussions, I had to smile inwardly at the way he had once condescendingly described Kassoulas as a fanatic about wines. It was a description which fitted him even better. Whatever else might be false about Max de Marechal, his feelings about any great vintage were genuine.

During the months that passed, Kassoulas proved to be as good as his word. He had said he wouldn't again bargain with me for the precious bottle of Saint-Oen, and he didn't. We discussed the Saint-Oen often enough – it was an obsession with de Marechal – but no matter how much Kassoulas was tempted to renew the effort to buy it, he kept his word.

Then, one dismally cold and rainy day in early December, my secretary opened my office door to announce in awestruck tones that Monsieur Kyros Kassoulas was outside waiting to see me. This was a surprise. Although Sophia Kassoulas, who seemed to have no friends in the world apart from de Marechal and myself, had several times been persuaded to have lunch with me when she was in town to do shopping, her husband had never before deigned to visit me in my domain, and I was not expecting him now.

He came in accompanied by the ever dapper de Marechal who, I saw with increased mystification, was in a state of feverish excitement.

We had barely exchanged greetings when de Marechal leaped directly to the point.

'The bottle of Nuits Saint-Oen 1929, Monsieur Drummond,' he said. 'You'll remember you once set a price on it. One hundred thousand francs.'

'Only because it won't be bought at any such price.'

'Would you sell it for less?'

'I've already made clear I wouldn't.'

'You drive a hard bargain, Monsieur Drummond. But you'll be pleased to know that Monsieur Kassoulas is now prepared to pay your price.'

I turned incredulously to Kassoulas. Before I could recover my voice, he drew a check from his pocket and, impassive as ever, handed it to me. Involuntarily, I glanced at it. It was for one hundred thousand francs. It was worth, by the going rate of exchange, twenty thousand dollars.

'This is ridiculous,' I finally managed to say. 'I can't take it.'

'But you must!' de Marechal said in alarm.

'I'm sorry. No wine is worth a fraction of this. Especially a wine that may be dead in the bottle.'

'Ah,' said Kassoulas lightly, 'then perhaps that's what I'm paying for – the chance to see whether it is or not.'

'If that's your reason—' I protested, and Kassoulas shook his head.

'It isn't. The truth is, my friend, this wine solves a difficult problem for me. A great occasion is coming soon, the fifth anniversary of my marriage, and I've been wondering how Madame and I could properly celebrate it. Then inspiration struck me. What better way of celebrating it than to open the Saint-Oen and discover it is still in the flush of perfect health, still in its flawless maturity? What could be more deeply moving and significant on such an occasion?'

'That makes it all the worse if the wine is dead,' I pointed out. The check was growing warm in my hand. I wanted to tear it up but couldn't bring myself to do it.

'No matter. The risk is all mine,' said Kassoulas. 'Of course, you'll be there to judge the wine for yourself. I insist on that. It will be a memorable experience, no matter how it goes. A small dinner with just the four of us at the table, and the Saint-Oen as climax to the occasion.'

'The *piece de resistance* must be an *entrecote*,' breathed de Marechal. 'Beef, of course. It will suit the wine perfectly.'

I had somehow been pushed past the point of no return. Slowly I folded the check for the hundred thousand francs and placed it in my wallet. After all, I was in the business of selling wine for a profit.

'When is this dinner to be held?' I asked. 'Remember that the wine must stand a few days before it's decanted.'

'Naturally, I'm allowing for that,' said Kassoulas. 'Today is Monday; the dinner will be held Saturday. That means more than enough time to prepare every detail perfectly. On Wednesday I'll see that the temperature of the dining room is properly adjusted, the table set, and the bottle of Saint-Oen placed upright on it for the sediment to clear properly. The room will then be locked to avoid any mishap. By Saturday the last of the sediment should have settled completely. But I don't plan to decant the wine. I intend to serve it directly from the bottle.'

'Risky,' I said.

'Not if it's poured with a steady hand. One like this.' Kassoulas held out a stubby-fingered, powerful-looking hand which showed not a sign of tremor. 'Yes, this supreme vintage deserves the honor of being poured from its own bottle, risky as that may be. Surely you now have evidence, Monsieur Drummond, that I'm a man to take any risk if it's worthwhile to me.'

I had good cause to remember those concluding words at a meeting I had with Sophia Kassoulas later in the week. That day she phoned early in the morning to ask if I could meet her for lunch at an hour when we might have privacy in the restaurant, and, thinking this had something to do with her own plans for the anniversary dinner, I cheerfully accepted the invitation. All the cheerfulness was washed out of me as soon as I joined her at our table in a far corner of the dimly lit, almost deserted room. She was obviously terrified.

'Something is very wrong,' I said to her. 'What is it?'

'Everything,' she said piteously. 'And you're the only one I can turn to for help, Monsieur Drummond. You've always been so kind to me. Will you help me now?'

'Gladly. If you tell me what's wrong and what I can do about it.'

'Yes, there's no way around that. You must be told everything.' Madame Kassoulas drew a shuddering breath. 'It can be told very simply. I had an affair with Max de Marechal. Now Kyros has found out about it.'

My heart sank. The last thing in the world I wanted was to get involved in anything like this.

'Madame,' I said unhappily, 'this is a matter to be settled between you and your husband. You must see that it's not my business at all.'

'Oh, please! If you only understood—'

'I don't see what there is to understand.'

455

'A great deal. About Kyros, about me, about my marriage. I didn't want to marry Kyros, I didn't want to marry anybody. But my family arranged it, so what could I do? And it's been dreadful from the start. All I am to Kyros is a pretty little decoration for his house. He has no feeling for me. He cares more about that bottle of wine he bought from you than he does for me. Where I'm concerned, he's like stone. But Max—'

'I know,' I said wearily. 'You found that Max was different. Max cared very much for you. Or, at least, he told you he did.'

'Yes, he told me he did,' Madame Kassoulas said with defiance. 'And whether he meant it or not, I needed that. A woman must have some man to tell her he cares for her or she has nothing. But it was wicked of me to put Max in danger. And now that Kyros knows about us Max is in terrible danger.'

'What makes you think so? Has your husband made any threats?'

'No, he hasn't even said he knows about the affair. But he does. I can swear he does. It's in the way he's been behaving toward me these past few days, in the remarks he makes to me, as if he were enjoying a joke that only he understood. And it all seems to have something to do with that bottle of Saint-Oen locked up in the dining room. That's why I came to you for help. You know about these things.'

'Madame, all I know is that the Saint-Oen is being made ready for your dinner party Saturday.'

'Yes, that's what Kyros said. But the way he said it—' Madame Kassoulas leaned toward me intently. 'Tell me one thing. Is it possible for a bottle of wine to be poisoned without the cork being drawn? Is there any way of doing that?'

'Oh, come now. Do you seriously believe for a moment that your husband intends to poison Max?'

'You don't know Kyros the way I do. You don't know what he's capable of.'

'Even murder?'

'Even murder, if he was sure he could get away with it. They tell a story in my family about how, when he was very young, he killed a man who had cheated him out of a little money. Only it was done so cleverly that the police never found out who the murderer was.'

That was when I suddenly recalled Kassoulas' words about taking any risk if it were worthwhile to him and felt a chill go through me. All too vividly, I had a mental picture of a hypodermic needle sliding through the cork in that bottle of Saint-Oen, of drops of deadly poison trickling into the wine. Then it struck me how wildly preposterous the picture was.

'Madame,' I said, 'I'll answer your question this way. Your husband does not intend to poison anyone at your dinner party unless he intends to poison us all, which I am sure he does not. Remember that I've also been invited to enjoy my share of the Saint-Oen.'

'What if something were put into Max's glass alone?'

'It won't be. Your husband has too much respect for Max's palate for any such clumsy trick. If the wine is dead, Max will know it at once and won't drink it. If it's still good, he'd detect anything foreign in it with the first sip and not touch the rest. Anyhow, why not discuss it with Max? He's the one most concerned.'

'I did try to talk to him about it, but he only laughed at me. He said it was all in my imagination. I know why. He's so insanely eager to try that wine that he won't let anything stop him from doing it.'

'I can appreciate his feelings about that.' Even with my equanimity restored I was anxious to get away from this unpleasant topic. 'And he's right about your imagination. If you really want my advice, the best thing you can do is to behave with your husband as if nothing has happened and to steer clear of Monsieur de Marechal after this.'

It was the only advice I could give her under the circumstances. I only hoped she wasn't too panic-stricken to follow it. Or too infatuated with Max de Marechal.

Knowing too much for my own comfort, I was ill at ease the evening of the party, so when I joined the company it was a relief to see that Madame Kassoulas had herself well in hand. As for Kassoulas, I could detect no change at all in his manner toward her or de Marechal. It was convincing evidence that Madame's guilty conscience had indeed been working overtime on her imagination and that Kassoulas knew nothing at all about her *affaire*. He was hardly the man to take being cuckolded with composure, and he was wholly composed. As we sat down to dinner, it was plain that his only concern was about its menu, and, above all, about the bottle of Nuits Saint-Oen 1929 standing before him.

The bottle had been standing there three days, and everything that could be done to insure the condition of its contents had been done. The temperature of the room was moderate; it had not been allowed to vary once the bottle was brought into the room, and, as Max de Marechal assured me, he had checked this at regular intervals every day. And, I was sure, had taken time to stare rapturously at the bottle, marking off the hours until it would be opened.

Furthermore, since the table at which our little company sat down was of a size to seat eighteen or twenty, it meant long distances between our places, but it provided room for the bottle to stand in lonely splendor clear of any careless hand that might upset it. It was noticeable that the servants waiting on us all gave it a wide berth. Joseph, the burly, hardbitten majordomo who was supervising them with a dangerous look in his eye, must have put them in fear of death if they laid a hand near it.

Now Kassoulas had to undertake two dangerous procedures as preludes to the wine-tasting ritual. Ordinarily, a great vintage like the Nuits Saint-Oen 1929 stands until all its sediment has collected in the base of the bottle, and is then decanted. This business of transferring it from bottle to decanter not only insures that sediment and cork crumbs are left behind, but it also means that the wine is being properly aired. The older a wine, the more it needs to breathe the open air to rid itself of mustiness accumulated in the bottle.

But Kassoulas, in his determination to honor the Saint-Oen by serving it directly from its original bottle, had imposed on himself the delicate task of uncorking it at the table so skillfully that no bits of cork would filter into the liquid. Then, after the wine had stood open until the entree was served, he would have to pour it with such control that none of the sediment in its base would roll up. It had taken three days for that sediment to settle. The least slip in uncorking the bottle or pouring from it, and it would be another three days before it was again fit to drink.

As soon as we were at the table, Kassoulas set to work on the first task. We all watched with bated breath as he grasped the neck of the bottle firmly and centered the point of the corkscrew in the cork. Then, with the concentration of a demolitions expert defusing a live bomb, he slowly, very slowly, turned the corkscrew, bearing down so lightly that the corkscrew almost had to take hold by itself. His object was to penetrate deep enough to get a grip on the cork so that it could be drawn, yet not to pierce the cork through; it was the one sure way of keeping specks of cork from filtering into the wine.

It takes enormous strength to draw a cork which has not been pierced through from a bottle of wine which it has sealed for decades. The bottle must be kept upright and immobile, the pull must be straight up and steady without any of the twisting and turning that will tear a cork apart. The old-fashioned corkscrew which exerts no artificial leverage is the instrument for this because it allows one to feel the exact working of the cork in the bottleneck.

The hand Kassoulas had around the bottle clamped it so hard that his knuckles gleamed white. His shoulders hunched, the muscles of his neck grew taut. Strong as he appeared to be, it seemed impossible for him to start the cork. But he would not give way, and in the end it was the cork that gave way. Slowly and smoothly it was pulled clear of the bottle-mouth, and for the first time since the wine had been drawn from its barrel long years before, it was now free to breathe the open air.

Kassoulas waved the cork back and forth under his nose, sampling its bouquet. He shrugged as he handed it to me.

'Impossible to tell anything this way,' he said, and of course he was right. The fumes of fine Burgundy emanating from the cork meant nothing, since even dead wine may have a good bouquet.

De Marechal would not even bother to look at the cork. 'Only the wine. And in an hour we'll know its secret for better or worse. It will seem like a long hour, I'm afraid.'

I didn't agree with that at first. The dinner we were served was more than sufficient distraction for me. Its menu, in tribute to the Nuits Saint-Oen 1929, had been arranged the way a symphony conductor might arrange a short program of lighter composers in preparation for the playing of a Beethoven masterwork. Artichoke hearts in a butter sauce, *langouste* in mushrooms, and, to clear the palate, a lemon ice unusually tart. Simple dishes flawlessly prepared.

And the wines Kassoulas had selected to go with them were, I was intrigued to note, obviously chosen as settings for his diamond. A sound Chablis, a respectable Muscadet. Both were good, neither was calculated to do more than draw a small nod of approval from the connoisseur. It was Kassoulas' way of telling us that nothing would be allowed to dim the glorious promise of that open bottle of Nuits Saint-Oen standing before us.

Then my nerves began to get the better of me. Old as I was at the game, I found myself more and more filled with tension and as the dinner progressed I found the bottle of Saint-Oen a magnet for my eyes. It soon became an agony, waiting until the entree would be served, and the Saint-Oen poured.

Who, I wondered, would be given the honor of testing the first few drops? Kassoulas, the host, was entitled to that honor, but as a mark of respect he could assign it to anyone he chose. I wasn't sure whether or not I wanted to be chosen. I was braced for the worst, but I knew that being the first at the table to discover the wine was dead would be like stepping from an airplane above the clouds without a parachute. Yet, to be the first to discover that this greatest of vintages had survived the years—! Watching Max de Marechal, crimson with mounting excitement, sweating so that he had to constantly mop his brow, I suspected he was sharing my every thought.

The entree was brought in at last, the *entrecote* of beef that de Marechal had suggested. Only a salver of *petite pois* accompanied it. The *entrecote* and peas were served. Then Kassoulas gestured at Joseph, and the majordomo cleared the room of the help. There must be no chance of disturbance while the wine was being poured, no possible distraction.

When the servants were gone and the massive doors of the dining room were closed behind them, Joseph returned to the table and took up his position near Kassoulas, ready for anything that might be required of him.

The time had come.

Kassoulas took hold of the bottle of Nuits Saint-Oen 1929. He lifted it slowly, with infinite care, making sure not to disturb the treacherous sediment. A ruby light flickered from it as he held it at arm's length, staring at it with brooding eyes.

'Monsieur Drummond, you were right,' he said abruptly.

'I was?' I said, taken aback. 'About what?'

'About your refusal to unlock the secret of this bottle. You once said that as long as the bottle kept its secret it was an extraordinary treasure, but that once it was opened it might prove to be nothing but another bottle of bad wine. A disaster. Worse than a disaster, a joke. That was the truth. And in the face of it I now find I haven't the courage to learn whether or not what I am holding here is a treasure or a joke.'

De Marechal almost writhed with impatience.

'It's too late for that!' he protested violently. 'The bottle is already open!'

'But there's a solution to my dilemma,' Kassoulas said to him. 'Now watch it. Watch it very closely.'

His arm moved, carrying the bottle clear of the table. The bottle slowly tilted. Stupefied, I saw the wine spurt from it, pour over the polished boards of the floor. Drops of wine splattered Kassoulas' shoes, stained the cuffs of his trousers. The puddle on the floor grew larger. Trickles of it crept out in thin red strings between the boards.

It was an unearthly choking sound from de Marechal which tore me free of the spell I was in. A wild cry of anguish from Sophia Kassoulas.

'Max!' she screamed. 'Kyros, stop! For God's sake, stop! Don't you see what you're doing to him?'

She had reason to be terrified. I was terrified myself when I saw de Marechal's condition. His face was ashen, his mouth gaped wide open, his eyes, fixed on the stream of wine relentlessly gushing out of the bottle in Kassoulas' unwavering hand, were starting out of his head with horror.

Sophia Kassoulas ran to his side but he feebly thrust her away and tried to struggle to his feet. His hands reached out in supplication to the fast emptying bottle of Nuits Saint-Oen 1929.

'Joseph,' Kassoulas said dispassionately, 'see to Monsieur de Marechal. The doctor warned that he must not move during these attacks.'

The iron grasp Joseph clamped on de Marechal's shoulder prevented him from moving, but I saw his pallid hand fumbling into a pocket, and at last regained my wits.

'In his pocket!' I pleaded. 'He has pills!'

It was too late. De Marechal suddenly clutched at his chest in that familiar gesture of unbearable pain, then his entire body went limp, his head lolling back against the chair, his eyes turning up in his head to glare sightlessly at the ceiling. The last thing they must have seen was the stream of Nuits Saint-Oen 1929 become a trickle, the trickle become an ooze of sediment clotting on the floor in the middle of the vast puddle there.

Too late to do anything for de Marechal, but Sophia Kassoulas stood swaying on her feet ready to faint. Weak-kneed myself, I helped her to her chair, saw to it that she downed the remains of the Chablis in her glass.

The wine penetrated her stupor. She sat there breathing hard, staring at her husband until she found the strength to utter words.

'You knew it would kill him,' she whispered. 'That's why you bought the wine. That's why you wasted it all.'

'Enough, madame,' Kassoulas said frigidly. 'You don't know what you're saying. And you're embarrassing our guest with this emotionalism.' He turned to me. 'It's sad that our little party had to end this way, monsieur, but these things do happen. Poor Max. He invited disaster with his temperament. Now I think you had better go. The doctor must be called in to make an examination and fill out the necessary papers, and these medical matters can be distressing to witness. There's no need for you to be put out by them. I'll see you to the door.'

I got away from there without knowing how. All I knew was that I had seen a murder committed and there was nothing I could do about it. Absolutely nothing. Merely to say aloud that what I had seen take place was murder would be enough to convict me of slander in any court. Kyros Kassoulas had planned and executed his revenge flawlessly, and all it would cost him, by my bitter calculations, were one hundred thousand francs and the loss of a faithless wife. It was unlikely that Sophia Kassoulas would spend another night in his house even if she had to leave it with only the clothes on her back.

I never heard from Kassoulas again after that night. For that much, at least, I was grateful . . .

Now, six months later, here I was at a cafe table on the rue de Rivoli with Sophia Kassoulas, a second witness to the murder and as helplessly bound to silence about it as I was. Considering the shock given me by our meeting, I had to admire her own composure as she hovered over me solicitously, saw to it that I took down a cognac and then another, chattered brightly about inconsequential things as if that could blot the recollection of the past from our minds.

She had changed since I had last seen her. Changed all for the better. The timid girl had become a lovely woman who glowed with self-assurance. The signs were easy to read. Somewhere, I was sure, she had found the right man for her and this time not a brute like Kassoulas or a shoddy Casanova like Max de Marechal.

The second cognac made me feel almost myself again, and when I saw my Samaritan glance at the small, brilliantly jeweled watch on her wrist I apologized for keeping her and thanked her for her kindness.

'Small kindness for such a friend,' she said reproachfully. She rose and gathered up her gloves and purse. 'But I did tell Kyros I would meet him at—'

'Kyros!'

'But of course. Kyros. My husband.' Madame Kassoulas looked at me with puzzlement.

'Then you're still living with him?'

'Very happily.' Then her face cleared. 'You must forgive me for being so slow-witted. It took a moment to realize why you should ask such a question.'

'Madame, I'm the one who should apologize. After all—'

'No, no, you had every right to ask it.' Madame Kassoulas smiled at me. 'But it's sometimes hard to remember I was ever unhappy with Kyros, the way everything changed so completely for me that night—

'But you were there, Monsieur Drummond. You saw for yourself how Kyros emptied the bottle of Saint-Oen on the floor, all because of me. What a revelation that was! What an awakening! And when it dawned on me that I really did mean more to him than even the last bottle of Nuits Saint-Oen 1929 in the whole world, when I found the courage to go to his room that night and tell him how this made me feel – oh, my dear Monsieur Drummond, it's been heaven for us ever since!'

# Coin of the Realm

A mong other things, he had learned over the years to wait patiently while his wife made herself ready to go out with him, and under no conditions to distract her from the job being done before the dressing-table mirror. So now he waited patiently at the open window of the hotel room, abstractedly looking down at what seemed to be most of the motor traffic of Paris jammed into the narrow rue Cambon below.

'Walt,' Millie said, 'I'm ready. Walt, did you hear me? I said I was ready.'

He turned to face her and saw she was indeed gleamingly, faultlessly ready, wearing that simple little black number which, to his surprise, had cost him $200. She looked fine in it. Just fine. At 46, Millie was as trim and slim as she had been on her wedding day, and a lot more chic.

'You look like a million,' he said, soberly nodding his approval.

Her own expression, as she eyed him from head to foot, was anything but approving.

'I wish I could say the same for you. Is that how you expect to go out? That ridiculous Hawaiian shirt and not even a jacket?'

'It's too hot for a jacket. And we're only going to the Flea Market, for Pete's sake, not the opera.'

'Even so. And that camera and that great big camera bag slung around your neck. And that awful cigar shoved into your mouth. Do you know what you look like?'

'What?'

'An American tourist, that's what. A real corny American tourist.'

Walt glanced at the beefy, red-faced, bald-headed image of himself in the full-length mirror on the closet door and unsuccessfully tried to suck in the roll of fat overhanging his belt buckle. No question about it, Millie had spoken the truth, but that was all right with him. Even better than all right.

'I am an American tourist,' he protested mildly. 'Nothing wrong with letting people know it, is there?'

'Oh, yes, there is. You don't go around like this back home, so there's no reason to go around here like some good-natured hick from the sticks. You can look very impressive when you want to.'

'Sure, I can. That's how I get the girls.' He gave her a broad, comic wink and was disconcerted when she refused to smile in return. In fact, she was looking downright sullen. She was building up to a real storm, Walt thought uneasily, she had been since breakfast.

'Come on, hon,' he said placatingly, 'something's eating you, isn't it? What is it?'

'Nothing's eating me.'

'Don't hand me that. I'll bet you're still bushed from the plane ride yesterday, aren't you? You know what? If you want to stay here and rest while I tend to this Flea Market expedition by myself—'

'I will not!' Millie's nostrils flared. 'And it's some expedition, all right. Hunting up old coins for Ed Lynch's precious collection. We've got three little days in Paris for our whole vacation, and he has the gall—'

So that was it.

'Now, let's leave old Ed out of this,' Walt said.

'I wish we could.' Millie shook her head ruefully. 'Walt, you don't know how much I wish you'd remember you're Ed Lynch's partner, not his errand boy. You hardly ever get away with me like this – a few days in Paris two years ago, a few days in Naples the year before that – but any time you do, there's good old Ed handing you that shopping list for his stupid coin collection.'

'Millie, if the man asks me to do him a little favor, I can't turn him down, can I?'

'Why not? And I'm sure he didn't ask any favor, he told you

to do it. He just has no manners at all. The way he is, he should have been some kind of gangster, not a businessman.'

'Now, Millie—'

'I don't care. All I know is I wish you were partners with anybody else in the whole world but good old Ed.'

'Well, I'm not!'

It burst out of him so explosively that Millie gaped at him in astonishment. Then her face crumpled woefully. Quickly Walt crossed the room to her, drew her down to sit beside him on the edge of the bed.

'Ah, come on, hon,' he said. 'I'm sorry. You know I am, don't you?'

She sniffled a couple of times but managed to hold back the tears. 'Maybe.'

'No maybes about it. But please be reasonable, Millie. Face the facts. You know everything we've got – and we've got plenty – is only because Ed took me into the plant twenty years ago and taught me the engraving and printing business from A to Z. It doesn't matter how much of a roughneck he is, just look at our balance sheet. A fine home in Scarsdale, a big summer place on the Cape, two cars, a new mink whenever you feel like it. As far as that goes, do you know how much your daughter's wedding cost us?'

'She's your daughter, too. And what difference does it make how much it cost? That doesn't make Ed Lynch any easier to tolerate.'

'Twenty thousand dollars, Millie. Twenty thousand in cash. And because of Ed I could sign checks for a dozen weddings like that and never feel it. That's what you have to keep in mind.'

She shook her head stubbornly. 'You've got a lot of ability. You always did. You could have done just as well with somebody else.'

'Done what?' Walt demanded. 'I hate to bring up ancient history, but what the hell was I fitted for when I got done winning World War Number Two for the OSS? Superspy, that was me. Some qualifications to offer the boys running the rat-race. A thirty-year-old superspy who could get along in a few foreign languages nobody wanted to hear him talk anyhow. But with enough sense to know that when everyone else in the world

467

is swimming in money he's not going to be any ragpicker. That's where Ed came into the picture, Millie, and one thing you have to admit about him. He didn't just talk big money, he delivered it.'

'All right, but please don't get so excited. You know it's bad for you.'

'I am not excited. I am only trying to settle this between us once and for all. Maybe I'm old-fashioned, but I say it's not a wife's place to mix into her husband's business. I hate to tell you how many times I've seen trouble between partners just because of that. Ed and I are partners, that's how it is, and there's no use talking about it any more. Is that all right with you?'

Millie shrugged ungraciously.

'Nothing to say?' Walt asked.

'No. Except sometimes I wonder if you aren't more married to Ed Lynch than to me.'

'Hardly. But come to think of it—' Walt playfully nudged his wife with his elbow '—it might be tougher getting a divorce from him than from you.'

'Well, you're not getting any from me, if that's what you've got on your mind,' Millie retorted, and Walt saw with relief that she had decided to forgive him.

He wasted no more time – he got up and helped her to her feet.

'Ready to do some shopping then?' he asked.

'You know I always am,' said Millie pertly.

Outside the hotel the doorman asked if he should call a cab for them, but Walt said no, and led the way to the Metro station on the Place de la Concorde.

'The subway?' Millie said in surprise at the head of the stairway.

'Why not? I thought you might like to see how the other half lives for a change.'

She gave him a look for that but went along amiably, and, it was plain, thoroughly enjoyed the ride. Her tantrum over, the storm clouds quickly blown away, she was the old Millie again, taking pleasure in something simply because she was sharing it with him, just glad to be with him, her arm tight through his.

Married almost 25 years, he thought, but when it came to him she was still like a school kid on her first date. That was all right with him – highly gratifying, in fact – but it did raise problems now and then. For instance, it made it just about impossible to tell her that sometimes when they were on these trips abroad he would have preferred to be by himself, away from her company.

Ed Lynch had disagreed with his feeling about it, and insisted that having Millie tagging along with him almost every step of the way was the perfect final touch. The complete American tourist with the cute little wife on his arm chattering to him. But that was Ed for you. A cold-blooded specimen, divorced three times and now on the verge of the fourth, he didn't know what marriage to someone like Millie could mean. For Ed it was always some pinup girl, as hard-bitten as he was. No wonder Millie hated him and his succession of wives like poison.

At Marcadet-Poissionniers station Walt steered the way through the iron-fenced maze of the transfer point to the train going to Clignancourt at the end of the line. There he and Millie ascended the stairs into the golden, summertime sunlight of Paris and crossed the boulevard to the Flea Market.

They were caught up in a crowd as they entered the market grounds. Tourists with Americans predominating, French family parties, young couples dreamily strolling, arms around each other's waist, as if taking a moonlight walk beside the Seine, but all with an eye out for a bargain. And from what Walt could see as he and Millie were carried along by the throng, there was certainly the stuff here to suit the weirdest tastes.

The market was an endless congeries of roadways and alleyways lined with rickety shacks and stands which displayed every conceivable kind of second-hand goods from rusty paper clips to the stripped-down chassis of a once magnificent limousine. There was an almost insane quality to the variety of merchandise, Walt discovered. At one point, while Millie stopped to admire a shabby Tiffany lamp hanging over the doorway of one of the shacks, he found himself looking through a shoebox full of browned, waterstained, beautifully engraved party invitations issued by various members of the nineteenth century French nobility to each other. It was the engraving that caught his professional eye, it was the kind of meticulous craftsmanship devoted to lettering that was so hard to duplicate today; and it was only on second thought that he wondered who would possibly be interested in buying a collection of decaying party invitations.

Offhand, it would have seemed impossible to find the way to any particular location in that bewildering complex, but Ed Lynch had provided careful directions to the one dealer he had assured Millie she should do business with, and they located the place without too much trouble. Millie had been on the verge of buying the Louis Quatorze escritoire she had long yearned for at the antique shop she frequented on Third Avenue in Manhattan, and it had been Ed who had talked her out of the idea. Bullied her out of it, really. If she and Walt were hopping to Paris for a long weekend, he pointed out, they must make the trip pay off by going to this antique furniture dealer in the Flea Market who, so Ed had heard, gave real value for your money. And, of course, while they were at the Flea Market it would be no trouble for Walt to hunt up some rare coins that Ed wanted for his collection. Trust Ed to plan everything so neatly, like a chess master looking six moves ahead.

But the resentful mood that Millie had been plunged into when she saw through Ed's game was gone now as she wandered among the collection of furniture in the shop, her eyes bright with greed. The proprietor of the shop was a brisk, helpful young woman, as quick and hungry as a piranha. She was so insistently helpful, in fact, that Millie had to draw her husband out of doors to have a private word with him.

'What's our limit?' she asked.

'I guess it depends. Did you see what you want?'

'Yes, there's a couple of stunning pieces to pick from. But I have a feeling she'll ask a fortune for either one of them. I'd like to know how much bargaining I have to do.'

'From what Ed said, all you can. Remember he told you to go over every inch of the piece and make sure you're not getting stuck. And not to look like you're interested in buying, whatever you do.'

'Can I go as high as five hundred dollars?'

'If you think it's worth it. Just take your time before you sign anything.'

'But what about you?' Millie said as he had been sure she would. 'You know how itchy you get standing around while I shop.'

'I don't have to. I can look around for Ed's coins meanwhile. You can wait for me here. I won't be gone long anyhow.'

He left, thankful that she always preferred having him out from underfoot while she was at her haggling, and drifted along the rutted, stony, dirt-surfaced roadway, taking no heed of the crowd of bargain-hunters going their way around him, his eyes fixed on the signs marking the owners of the stands he passed. Brument, Fermanter, Duras, Puel, Schmitt, Bayle, Mazel, Piron. Battered furniture, from rusty cafe chairs to gigantic chests of drawers, seemed to be the stock in trade of all these tradesmen except the last one. While a few articles of furniture could be glimpsed through the open door of C. Piron's ramshackle premises, outside his shanty, instead of a display of the best he had to offer, were only some cartons containing broken bottles. Wine and beer bottles, Walt saw when he went over to take a closer look at them, not one of them undamaged. It made as unappetizing a display as he had seen anywhere in the market.

A man emerged from the shanty and leaned against its doorway to watch Walt make his inspection. Cadaverously thin, hard-featured, cold-eyed, he folded his arms on his chest and stood there in indifferent silence.

Walt turned to him and pointed at the tattered cardboard sign tacked to the wall of the shanty. 'Piron?' he asked.

The man admitted to this by an almost imperceptible nod.

'I'm looking for a place to buy some coins,' Walt said. 'Rare coins. I wondered if you could help me.'

'*Je ne comprends pas,*' the man said. 'Don't understand. Don't speak English.'

'Oh, in that case,' Walt said amiably, and repeated the words in fluent French.

The man's eyes widened in surprise, then were veiled again.

'Coins,' he said. 'What kind?'

'American pennies. Old ones. The ones with the Indian head on them.'

'What years?'

'1903 and 1904.'

'And?'

'And 1906.'

'Three, four, six – that's the magic numbers, all right,' Piron said. 'So you're the one.'

'Yes.'

'And Mercier got my message through to you, I see. But I thought he'd be bringing back the answer himself.'

'No, he's only in charge of distribution around here. I handle the complaints.'

'So you had to come all the way from America just to handle mine.' The man looked Walt over and smiled broadly, showing a mouthful of gold fillings. 'Beautiful,' he said. 'Just beautiful. Who'd ever suspect it? The way you're made up you look like the biggest innocent to ever hit town. You could walk off with the Louvre under your arms, and the cops wouldn't even give you a second look.'

Walt motioned at the throng eddying by. 'Do we have to talk about it out here?'

'You're right.' Piron gestured him into the shanty, closed the door behind them, and slid its bolt into place. With no window to admit the light, the room was bleakly lit by a single flickering kerosene lamp. Its furnishings, Walt saw, consisted of an old kitchen table and chair; its stock was a few monstrously oversized cabinets, highboys, and armoires ranged around the walls.

'We've got all the privacy we need here,' Piron assured him. 'Hardly anybody seems to be in the market for broken bottles.'

'Very smart.'

'It is, if I say so myself. And those pieces of junk you're looking at are all so damn big you'd have to buy a cathedral to put them in. No, you don't have to worry about any customers popping in here while we settle our business. All you have to worry about is making me happy. And you can start by sitting down at that table there and keeping your hands on it.'

The man was standing behind him. Walt gingerly turned his head and saw the malevolent-looking little automatic levered at his back.

'What's that for?' he asked.

'What do you think?' retorted Piron. 'After what happened a couple of years ago to the guy who operated over in the Belleville district, I take no chances. I also heard something unpleasant happened to that poor stiff in Naples who got out of line before that. So you sit quiet and don't do anything to make me nervous. If you even want to blow your nose, ask me first.'

Walt sat down at the table and rested his hands on it, palms down. He leaned back to give the camera and its accessory case clearance. 'You seem to know a lot of things that aren't strictly your business,' he said. 'I suppose that's what it comes to. We pay, or you sing to the cops.'

Piron stood a few feet away from the table, the gun steady in his hand. 'That's what it comes to.'

'And what do you sing about?' Walt inquired placidly. 'A couple of crooks being bumped off? Who would you finger for those jobs? Mercier? I guarantee he's got an alibi for both of them that would make you look silly.'

'Sure he has. But maybe I know a lot more about your whole operation than just what happened to those two stiffs. Do I look like the kind of idiot who'd try to put the squeeze on you unless I did?'

'You're bluffing. It's a nice try, but it's only a bluff.'

'The hell it is. You want to hear how much I know?'

'If you put that gun away. It's hard to concentrate with a gun shoved in your face.'

'That's too bad,' Piron said with venom, 'but it took me a lot of trouble to get this story together, and I'd hate to be interrupted while I'm telling it. After it's over you can judge just what you're up against and what kind of deal you'll have to make.'

'I still say you're bluffing.'

'Am I? Then listen to this. For one thing, your stuff is being turned out in some plant in America. A big classy print shop. And you've got a first-class engraver stashed away there doing the plates, a real genius who used to turn out counterfeit for the military during the war that they dumped in Germany and Italy. The records say he's been dead for twenty years, but you and I know better, don't we? We know that fancy print shop is just a front for the jobs he's still turning out in the back room, don't we?'

Walt shrugged. 'It's your story,' he said.

'And a good one, too, isn't it? Maybe worth plenty more than you figured on paying when you walked in here. Because I also happen to know you're too smart to turn out American counterfeit and stir up trouble at home. No, all these years it's strictly franc notes, and lire, and deutsche marks, and maybe pesetas and pounds, too, all shipped inside those pretty bookbinding jobs to dealers like Mercier here, and the one in Naples, and another one in Berlin, and so on all over the place. And they turn over the stuff to small-timers like me to get rid of at thirty percent of the face value of which I can keep a lousy five percent. Five percent,' Piron said with scathing contempt, 'and for taking all the risks. Well, it's not enough. That's what I told Mercier and what I'm telling you now. When you know as much as I do you don't rate as a small-timer any more, and you don't have to settle for small-time pay!'

'What kind of pay did you have in mind?' Walt said.

'Oho!' Piron leered at him in golden-toothed triumph. 'So you're singing a different tune now. That's a good joke, all right. You sing sweet or I sing sour.'

'You're wasting time. Get to the point.'

'I will. I don't like these commission deals where I only get my cut from the stuff I peddle. That means when things are slow I could starve to death here. I want some cash, too. Whenever Mercier hands me a bundle of the stuff I want him to stick a wad of real money in my fist. A big wad.'

'How big?'

'Let's do it this way,' Piron said coldly. 'You name me a figure, and I'll tell you if it makes me happy.'

Walt shrugged. 'I'll do better than that. I'll make the first payment myself right now. But you have to put that gun away. You ought to know you're not scaring me with it. You're not really so stupid you'd want to kill the goose that lays the golden eggs.'

'And you can't be sure of that until you've tried me out,' jeered Piron, the gun remaining fixed on its target. 'Now let's see your money. And it better be government issue, too, none of your pretty art works.'

'If that's the way you want to do it,' said Walt. He slowly stood up, apparently oblivious of the menacing gun, and pressed the catch of the bulky leather case resting against the roundness of his belly.

'Hold it!' snarled Piron. 'What the hell do you think you're doing?'

'The money's in here.'

'I'll see for myself. Just stick that thing on the table.'

Walt unslung the case from around his neck and placed it on the table. Piron approached it as warily as if it might blow up in his face. He prodded its cover back, his eyes never leaving Walt, and lifted out a sizeable roll of franc notes bound with a heavy rubber band. He hefted the roll.

'Not bad,' he said. 'Not bad at all. How much is it?'

'You'll find out when you count it,' Walt said. 'But one thing has to be understood. This is what you're on the payroll for from now on, and it's what Mercier will have ready for you when you report to him. But try to put the bite on us for more, and you'll be in real trouble.'

'And you know what real trouble is, don't you?' gibed Piron.

'Don't strain yourself being funny. Is it a deal?'

'If this is real money. You can pay off some pigeon in counterfeit, not me.'

'All right,' Walt said impatiently, 'take a look at it. Hold it up to the light and see for yourself.'

Piron thrust his gun into his pocket, unsnapped the rubber band from the roll of banknotes, and selected one from the middle of the roll. He held it up to the uncertain light of the kerosene lamp, stretching it tight between his fingers, examining it with the eye of experience.

He had time for only one choked cry when the leather strap of the carrying case was snapped around his neck in a garrotte. His hands flailed the air wildly as Walt, leaning back against the edge of the table, a knee planted solidly in the small of the man's back, drew the garrotte steadily tighter.

Piron's body arched against the restraining knee until it seemed his spine must crack. The only sound in the room was a strangled wheezing in his chest which finally dwindled into total silence. When Walt released his grip on the garrotte, the lifeless body sagged to the floor and lay face up, features distorted and sightless eyes glaring at the ceiling.

Any of the armoires in the place had room in it to store a body with twice Piron's heft. With unhurried efficiency Walt unlocked one, placed Piron's remains in it, and locked it. Carefully he polished its massive key with his handkerchief; then, using the handkerchief as a sling, he tossed the key on top of a highboy in a far corner of the shanty where it landed with a metallic clatter.

That chore attended to, he polished the tabletop with the handkerchief, reclaimed the banknote from the floor where it had fluttered from Piron's hand, replaced it in the roll of banknotes which he thrust into his pocket. He slung the camera case around his neck and looked the room over to make sure everything was in order. Satisfied it was, he doused the kerosene lamp, slid back the bolt on the door with his elbow, casually walked out of the shanty, and swung the door shut behind him with another thrust of the elbow. Then he joined the crowd in the teeming, sunlit roadway and moved along at its tempo, taking in the sights around him with bland interest.

Millie was still at her haggling in the furniture mart when he got back to it. He could see her inside, volubly addressing its proprietor, and he patiently waited outside the place until she appeared before him, her face glowing.

'It's stunning,' she told him eagerly. 'It's rosewood and only six hundred dollars and that includes shipping. Walt, you don't mind if it costs a little more than we figured, do you?'

'Not if it's what you want,' Walt said.

'You're an angel,' Millie said. 'You really are.' Then she remembered. 'What about you? Did you find those coins Ed wanted? Those old pennies?'

'I did. Took care of the deal just the way I was supposed to.'

'Old faithful,' Millie said teasingly. She squeezed his hand. 'But oh, Walt, you really should have seen me take care of that biddy inside. Believe it or not, she started off by asking a thousand!'

'A thousand? Say, that's pretty steep.'

'Well, it was your fault,' Millie said accusingly. 'I'll guarantee she took one good look at you and decided, well, here's some more of those stupid tourists who'll fall for anybody's hard-luck story.'

'I guess she did,' said Walt, apologetically.

# Kindly Dig
# Your Grave

The story of Madame Lagrue, the most infamously successful dealer in bad art on Butte-Montmartre, and of O'Toole, the undernourished painter, and of Fatima, the vengeful model who loved O'Toole, and of what happened to them, properly begins in Madame Lagrue's gallery on rue Hyacinthe.

It is possible that the worst art in the whole world was displayed on the walls of the Galerie Lagrue.

Madame, of course, did not know this, nor, one must surmise, did her customers. To Madame, every picture on her walls from the leaden landscapes to the cunning kittens peeping out of boots – every one of these was beautiful.

That was the first reason for her fantastic success as a dealer in low-priced art – her abominable taste.

The second reason was that long before any of her competitors, Madame Lagrue had smelled out the renaissance in faraway America. After the war, all over that golden land, it seemed, the middle-aged middle class had developed a furious appetite for, as Madame's brochure so neatly described it, *genuine works of art, hand-painted on high quality canvas by great French artists for reasonable prices.*

So, when the trickle of American interior decorators and department-store buyers became a tide regularly lapping at the summit of Butte-Montmartre, Madame was ready for it. Before her competitors around the Place du Tertre in the shadow of Sacre-Coeur knew what was happening, she had cornered the fattest part of the market, and where others occasionally sold a picture to a passing tourist, she sold pictures by the dozen and by the gross to a wholesale clientele.

Then, having created a sellers' market among those who produced the kittens and clowns, Madame saw to it that she was not made the victim of any economic law dictating that she pay higher prices for this merchandise.

Here, her true talent as an art dealer emerged most brilliantly.

Most of the artists she dealt with were a shabby, spiritless lot of hacks, and, as Madame contentedly observed, their only pressing need was for a little cash in hand every day. Not enough to corrupt them, of course, but barely enough for rent, food, and drink and the materials necessary for creating their pictures.

So where Madame's competitors, lacking her wealth, offered only dreams of glory – they would price your picture at 100 francs and give you half of that if it sold – Madame offered the reality of 20 or 30 francs cash in hand. Or, perhaps, only ten francs. But it was cash paid on the spot, and it readily bought her first claim on the services of the painters who supplied her stock in trade.

The danger was that since Madame needed the painters as much as the painters needed Madame, it put them in a good bargaining position. It was to solve this problem that she invented a method of dealing with her stable which would have made Torquemada shake his head in admiration.

The painter, work in hand, was required to present himself at her office, a dank and frigid cubbyhole behind the showroom with barely enough room in it for an ancient rolltop desk and swivel chair and an easel on which the painting was placed for Madame's inspection. Madame, hat firmly planted on her head as if to assert her femininity – that hat was like a large black flower-pot worn upside down with a spray of dusty flowers projecting from its crown – would sit like an empress in the swivel chair and study the painting with an expression of distaste, her eyes narrowing and lips compressing as she examined its details. Then on a piece of scrap paper, carefully shielding the paper with her other hand to conceal it, she would jot down a figure.

That was the price the artist had to meet. If he asked a single franc more than the figure on that scrap of paper, he would be turned away on the spot. There was no second chance offered, no opportunity to bargain. He might have started out from his hutch on rue Norvins confident that the property under his arm was worth at least 50 francs this time. Before he was halfway to rue Hyacinthe, the confidence would have dwindled, the asking price fallen to 40 francs or even 30 as the image of Madame Lagrue's craggy features rose before him. By the time he had propped his picture on the easel he was willing to settle for 20 and praying that the figure she was mysteriously noting on her scrap paper wasn't ten.

'*A vous la balle,*' Madame would say, meaning it was his turn to get into the game. 'How much?'

Thirty, the painter would think desperately. Every leaf on those trees is painted to perfection. You can almost hear the water of that brook gurgling. This one is worth at least 30. But that sour look on the old miser's face. Maybe she's in no mood for brooks and trees this morning—

'Twenty?' he would say faintly, the sweat cold on his brow.

Madame would hold up the scrap of paper before him to read for himself, and whatever he read there would fill him with helpless rage. If he had asked too little, he could only curse his lack of courage. If too much, it meant no sale, and there was no use raising a hubbub about it. Madame did not tolerate hubbubs, and since she had the massive frame and short temper of a Norman farmhand, one respected her sensibilities in such matters.

No, all one could do was take a rejected picture to Florelle, the dealer down the block, and offer it to him for sale at commission, which meant waiting a long time or forever for any return on it. Or, if Madame bought the picture, take the pittance she offered and head directly to the Cafe Hyacinthe next door for a few quick ones calculated to settle the nerves. Next to Madame Lagrue herself, it was the Cafe Hyacinthe that profited most from her method of dealing with her painters.

*A vous la balle.* It was a bitter jest among the painters in Madame's stable, a greeting they sometimes used acidly on one another, the croaking of a bird of ill omen which nightmarishly entered their dreams and could only be muted by the happy thought of some day landing a fist on Madame's bulbous nose.

Of them all, the one who was worst treated by Madame and

yet seemed to suffer least under her oppression was O'Toole, the American painter who had drifted to Butte-Montmartre long ago in pursuit of his art. He was at least as shabby and unkempt and undernourished as the others, but he lived with a perpetual, gentle smile of intoxication on his lips, sustained by his love of painting and by the cheapest *marc* the Cafe Hyacinthe could provide.

*Marc* is distilled from the grape pulp left in the barrel after the wine is pressed, and when the wine happens to be a Romanee-Conti of a good year its *marc* makes an excellent drink. The Cafe Hyacinthe's *marc*, on the other hand, was carelessly, sometimes surreptitiously, distilled from the pulp of unripe grapes going to make the cheapest *vin du pays*, and it had the taste and impact of grape-flavored gasoline.

As far as anyone could tell, it provided all the sustenance O'Toole required, all the vision he needed to paint an endless succession of pastoral scenes in the mode of the Barbizon School. The ingredients of each scene were the same – a pond, a flowery glen, a small stand of birch trees – but O'Toole varied their arrangement, sometimes putting the trees on one side of the pond, sometimes on the other. The warmth of a bottle of *marc* in his belly, the feel of the brush in his hand, this was all the bliss O'Toole asked for.

He had had a hard time of it before entering Madame's stable. During the tourist season each year he had worked at a stand near the Place du Tertre doing quick portraits in charcoal – *Likeness Guaranteed Or Your Money Back* – but business was never good since, although the likenesses were indisputable, naive and kindly mirror images, the portraits were wholly uninspired. His heart just wasn't in them. Trees and flowery glens and ponds, that was where his heart lay. The discovery that Madame Lagrue was willing to put money in his hand for them was the great discovery of his life. He was her happiest discovery, too. Those pastorals, she soon learned, were much in demand by the Americans. They sold as fast as she could put them on display.

O'Toole was early broken in to Madame's method of doing business. That first terrible experience when he was taught there was no retreat from his overestimate of a picture's value, no chance to quote a second price, so that he had to trudge away, pastoral under his arm unsold, had been enough to break his spirit completely. After that, all he asked was 20 francs for a large picture and ten for a small one and so established almost a happy relationship with Madame.

The one break in the relationship had been where Florelle, who owned the shop on the other side of the Cafe Hyacinthe and who was not a bad sort for an art dealer, had finally persuaded him to hand over one of his paintings for sale at commission. The next time O'Toole went to do business with Madame Lagrue he was dismayed to find her regarding him with outright loathing.

'No sale,' she said shortly. 'No business. I'm not interested.'

O'Toole foggily stared at his picture on the easel, trying to understand what was wrong with it.

'But it's beautiful,' he said. 'Look at it. Look at those flowers. It took me three days just to do those flowers.'

'You're breaking my heart,' said Madame. 'Ingrate. Traitor. You have another dealer now. Let him buy your obscene flowers.'

In the end, O'Toole had to reclaim his picture from Florelle and beg Madame's forgiveness, almost with tears in his eyes. And Madame, contemplating the flow of landscapes which would be coming her way until O'Toole drank himself to death, almost had tears of emotion in her own eyes. The landscapes were bringing her at least 100 francs each, and the thought of 500 to 1000 percent profit on a picture can make any art dealer emotional.

Then Fatima entered the scene.

Fatima was not her name, of course; it was what some wag at the Cafe Hyacinthe had christened her when she had started to hang around there between sessions of modeling for life classes. She was a small swarthy Algerian, very plain of feature, but with magnificent, dark, velvety eyes, coal-black hair which hung in a tangle to her waist, and a lush figure. She was also known to have the worst disposition of anyone who frequented the cafe and, with a few drinks in her, the foulest mouth.

'She's not even eighteen yet,' the bartender once observed, listening awestruck as she told off a hapless painter who had sat down uninvited at her table. 'Think how she'll sound when she's a full-grown woman!'

She also had her sentimental side, blubbering unashamedly at sad scenes in the movies, especially those in which lovers were parted or children abused, and had a way of carting stray kittens back to her room on the rue des Saulles until her concierge, no sentimentalist at all, raised a howl about it.

So although it was unexpected, it was not totally mystifying to the patrons of the Cafe Hyacinthe that Fatima should suddenly demonstrate an interest in O'Toole one rainy day when he stumbled into the cafe and stood in the doorway dripping cold rainwater on the floor, sneezing his head off, and, no question about it, looking even more forlorn than any of the stray kittens Fatima's concierge objected to.

Fatima was alone at her usual table, sullenly nursing her second Pernod. Her eyes fell on O'Toole, taking him in from head to foot, and a light of interest dawned in them. She crooked a finger.

'Hey, you. Come over here.'

It was the first time she had ever invited anyone to her table. O'Toole glanced over his shoulder to see whom she was delivering the invitation to and then pointed to himself.

'Me?'

'Yes, you, stupid. Come here and sit down.'

He did. And it was Fatima who not only stood him a bottle of wine but ordered a towel from the bartender so that she could dry his sodden hair. The patrons at the other tables gaped as she toweled away, O'Toole's head bobbing back and forth helplessly under her ministrations.

'You're a real case, aren't you?' she told O'Toole. 'Don't you have brains enough to wear a hat in the rain so you don't go around trying to kill yourself in this stinking weather?'

'A hat?' O'Toole said vaguely.

'Yes, imbecile. That thing one uses to keep his head dry in the rain.'

'Oh,' said O'Toole. Then he said in timid apology, 'I don't have one.'

Everyone in the cafe watched with stupefaction as Fatima tenderly patted his cheek.

'It's all right, baby,' she said. 'Someone left one in my room last week. When we get out of here you'll walk me back there and I'll give it to you.'

The whole thing came about as abruptly as that. And it was soon clear to the most cynical beholder that Fatima had fallen hopelessly in love with this particular stray cat. She began to bathe regularly, she combed out the tangles in her splendid hair, she showed up at the cafe wearing dresses recently laundered. And, surest sign of all, the little red welts and the bite marks once bestowed on her neck and shoulders by various overnight acquaintances all faded away.

As for O'Toole, Fatima mothered him passionately. She moved him into her room, lock, stock, and easel; saw to it that he was decently fed and clothed; threatened to slit the throat of the bartender of the Cafe Hyacinthe if he dared serve her man any more of that poisonous *marc* instead of a drinkable wine; and promised to gut anyone in the cafe who made the slightest remark about her *grand amour*.

No one there or elsewhere on Butte-Montmartre made any remarks. In fact, with only one exception among them, they found the situation rather touching. The one exception was Madame Lagrue.

It was not merely that paintings of nudes outraged Madame – in her loudly expressed opinion, the Louvre itself would do well to burn its filthy exhibitions of nakedness – but the knowledge that the degraded models for such paintings should be allowed to walk the very streets she walked was enough to turn her stomach. And that one of these degraded, venal types should somehow take possession of a cherished property like O'Toole—!

Madame recognized that the corruption had set in the day O'Toole appeared before her almost unrecognizably dandified. The shabby old suit was the same, but it had been cleaned and patched. The shoes were still scuffed and torn, but the knotted pieces of string in them had been replaced by shoelaces. The cheeks were shaven for the first time in memory, and, to Madame's narrowed eyes, they did not appear quite so hollow as they used to be. All in all, here was the sad spectacle of a once dedicated artist being prettified and fattened up like a shoat for the market, and, no doubt, having the poison of avarice injected into him by the slut who was doing all this prettifying and fattening. It was easy to visualize the way Fatima must be demanding of him that he ask some preposterous price for this landscape on the easel. Well, Madame grimly decided, if a showdown had to come, it might as well come right now.

Madame glanced at the landscape and at O'Toole who stood there beaming with admiration at it, then wrote down on her scrap of paper the usual price of 20 francs.

'Come on,' she said tartly, '*a vous la balle*. Name your price. I'm a busy woman. I don't have all day for this nonsense.'

O'Toole stopped beaming. Just before departing for the gallery he had been admonished by Fatima to demand 100 francs for this painting.

'Simpleton,' she had said kindly, 'you've put a week's work into this thing. Florelle told me a painting like this was worth at least a hundred francs to the old witch. You have to stop letting her bleed you to death. This time if she offers only twenty or thirty, just spit in her ugly face.'

'Yes, this time,' O'Toole had said bravely.

Now, with Madame's flinty eyes on him, he smiled not so bravely. He opened his mouth to speak, closed it, opened it again.

'Well?' said Madame in a voice of doom.

'Would twenty francs be all right?' said O'Toole.

'Yes,' said Madame triumphantly.

It was the first of her many triumphs over Fatima's baleful influence. The greatest triumph, one Madame herself never even knew of, came the time Fatima announced to O'Toole that she would accompany him on his next sales meeting. If he didn't have the guts of a decayed flounder in dealing with his exploiter, at least she, thank God, did. She watched as O'Toole, after giving her a long troubled look, started to pack his paints together.

'What are you doing, numskull?' she demanded.

'I'm leaving,' O'Toole said with a dignity that astonished and alarmed her. 'This is no good. A woman shouldn't mix in her husband's business.'

'What husband? We're not married, imbecile.'

'We're not?'

'No, we're not.'

'I'm leaving anyhow,' said O'Toole, somewhat confusingly. 'I don't want anyone to help me sell my paintings.'

It took Fatima a flood of tears and two bottles of *vin rouge* to wheedle him out of his decision, and she never made the same mistake again. It was a lost cause, she saw. All O'Toole wanted besides the pleasure of painting was the pleasure of having a ready cash market for his paintings, and Madame Lagrue, by offering him one, had bought his soul like the devil.

Until she had to face this realization Fatima had merely detested Madame Lagrue. Now she hated her with a devouring hatred. Oh, to have revenge on the evil old woman, some lovely revenge that would make her scream her head off. Many a night after that Fatima happily put herself to sleep with thoughts of revenge circling through her head, most of them having to do with hot irons. And would wake up in the morning knowing despondently how futile those happy thoughts were.

Then Nature decided to play a card.

O'Toole was, as is so often the case, one of the last to learn the news. He received it with honest bewilderment.

'You're going to have a baby?' he said, trying to understand this.

'We are going to have a baby,' Fatima corrected. 'Both of us. It's already on the way. Is that clear?'

'Yes, of course,' said O'Toole with becoming sobriety. 'A baby.'

'That's right. And it means some big changes around here. For one thing, it means we really are getting married now, because my kid's not going to be any miserable, fatherless alley rat. It's going to have a nice little mama and papa, and a nice little house to grow up in. You're not already married, are you?'

'No.'

'Well, I'll take my chances on that. And for another thing, we're getting out of Paris. I've had my bellyful of this horrible place, and so have you. We're packing up and going to my home town in Algeria. To Bougie where the kid will get some sunshine. My aunt and uncle own a cafe there, a nice little place, and they've got no kids of their own, so they'd give anything to have me help them run the joint. You can paint meanwhile.'

'A baby,' said O'Toole. To Fatima's immense relief he seemed to be rather pleased with the idea. Then his face darkened. 'Bougie,' he said. 'But how will I sell my paintings?'

'You can ship them to your old witch. You think she'll turn down such bargains because they come in the mail?'

O'Toole considered this unhappily. 'I'll have to talk to her about it.'

'No, I will, whether you like it or not,' said Fatima, risking everything on this throw of the dice. 'I've got another piece of business to settle with her anyhow.'

'What business?'

'Money. We'll need plenty of it to get to Bougie and set up in a house there. And it wouldn't hurt to have a few francs extra put away for the bad times so the kid can always have a pair of shoes when he needs them.'

'He?'

'Or she. It's even more expensive with a girl, if it comes to that. Or would you rather have your daughter selling her innocent little body as soon as she's able to walk?'

O'Toole shook his head vigorously at the suggestion. Then he looked wonderingly at the mother-to-be.

'But this money—' he said. 'You think Madame Lagrue will give it to us?'

'Yes.'

Finally, he had found something on which he could express a firm opinion. 'You're crazy,' he said.

'Am I?' Fatima retorted. 'Well, simpleton, you leave it to me and I'll show you how crazy I am. And get this straight. If you don't let me handle that miserable old hyena my own way, I'll turn you over to the cops for giving me a baby without marrying me, and they'll throw you in jail for twenty years. Nobody does any painting in jail either. He just sits there and rots until he's an old man. Do you understand?'

For the first time O'Toole found himself face to face with a presence even more overwhelming than Madame Lagrue's.

'Yes,' he said.

486

'All right then,' said Fatima. 'Now get a nice big canvas ready. You're going to paint me a picture.'

So it was that a week later, Fatima appeared in the Galerie Lagrue bearing a large painting clumsily wrapped in newspaper. Madame's assistant, a pale, timid girl, tried to bar her from the office and was shoved aside.

Madame was at her desk in the office. At the sight of her visitor who came bearing what must be an original O'Toole, she quivered with indignation. She aimed a commanding forefinger at the door.

'Out!' she said. 'Out! I don't do business with your kind!'

Fatima summed up her answer to this in a single unprintable word. She slammed the office door shut with a backward kick of the foot, hoisted the painting to the easel and stripped its wrapping from it.

'Is it your business to refuse masterpieces, harpy?'' she demanded. 'Look at this.'

Madame Lagrue looked. Then she looked again, her eyes opening wide in horror.

The painting was larger than any O'Toole had ever offered her before, and it was not the usual landscape. No, this time it was a nude. A ripely curved, full-blown nude with not an inch of her fleshy body left to the imagination. And with Fatima in a tight, highly revealing blouse and skirt standing side by side with the painting, there was no doubt in Madame's shocked mind as to who its model had been. The nude was an uninspired pink and white, not swarthy as Fatima was, but it was without question Fatima's body so painstakingly delineated on the canvas.

But that was only the beginning of the horror, because while it was Fatima from the neck down, it was, abomination of abominations, Madame Lagrue herself from the neck up. Photographically exact, glassy-eyed, the black flower pot upside down on the head with the dusty flowers sprouting from its crown, the stern face staring at Madame was Madame's own face.

'A masterpiece, eh?' said Fatima sweetly.

Madame made a strangled noise in her throat, then found her voice. 'What an insult! What an outrage!'

She came to her feet prepared to rend the outrage to shreds, and suddenly there was a wicked little paring knife gleaming in Fatima's hand. Madame hastily sat down again.

'That's better,' Fatima advised her. 'Lay one little finger on this picture before you buy it, you old sow, and I'll slice your nose off.'

'Buy it?' Madame refused to believe her ears. 'Do you really believe I'd buy an obscenity like that?'

'Yes. Because if you don't, Florelle will take it on commission. And he'll be glad to put it right in the middle of his window where everyone on Butte-Montmartre can see it. Then everyone in Paris. Those fancy Americans you do business with will see it, too. They'll all have a chance to see it, bloodsucker, because I'll tell Florelle not to sell it at any price for at least a year. It'll be worth it to him to keep it in his window just to draw trade. Think that over. Think it over very carefully. I'm in no rush.'

Madame thought it over very carefully for a long time.

'It's blackmail,' she said at last in bitter resignation. 'Plain blackmail. A shakedown, nothing more or less.'

'You've hit the nail right on the head,' Fatima said cheerfully.

'What if I submit to this blackmail?' Madame asked warily. 'Can I do whatever I wish with this disgusting object?'

'Anything. If you pay its price.'

'And what is its price?'

Fatima reached into a pocket and came up with a folded slip of paper which she waved tantalizingly just out of Madame's reach.

'The price is written down here, old lady. Now all you have to do is meet it, and the picture is yours. But remember this. Offer me one solitary franc less than what's written down on this paper, and the deal is off. There's no second chance. You get one turn in this game, that's all. Prove yourself one franc too thrifty, and the picture goes straight to Florelle.'

'What kind of talk is that?' Madame demanded angrily. 'A game, she says. I'm willing to do business with this creature, and she talks about games.'

'Vulture,' retorted Fatima. 'Destroyer of helpless artists. Don't you think everyone knows this is the way you do business? *A vous la balle*, eh? Kindly dig your grave, artist, and bury yourself. Isn't that the way it goes? Well, now it's your turn to learn how it feels.'

Madame opened her arms wide in piteous appeal. 'But how can I possibly know what you intend to rob me of? How can I even guess what it would cost to buy you off?'

'True,' admitted Fatima. 'Well, I'm soft-hearted so I'll give a hint. My man and I are moving to Bougie in Algeria, and we'll need travel money for that. And some decent clothes and a trunk to put them in. And we want to buy a little house there—'

'A house!' said Madame, the blood draining from her face.

'A little house. Nothing much, but it must have electricity. And a motor bicycle to get around on.'

Madame Lagrue clasped her hands tightly against her stout bosom and rocked back and forth in the chair. She looked at the nude on the easel and hastily averted her eyes from it.

'Dear God,' she whimpered, 'what have I done to deserve such treatment?'

'And,' said Fatima relentlessly, 'a little *pourboire*, a little money extra to put in the bank like respectable people should. That's what I see in my future, old lady. You've got a good head on your shoulders, so you shouldn't have much trouble adding it all up.' She held up the slip of paper. 'But make sure your arithemetic is right. Remember, you only get one chance to guess what's written here.'

In her rage and frustration Madame found herself groping wildly for elusive figures. Travel money to Algeria, 300 francs. No, 400. No, better make it 500, because rather safe than sorry. Another 500 should certainly buy all the clothes needed for such a pair of ragamuffins. Throw in 100 for a trunk. But a house, even a mud hut, with electricity! Madame groaned aloud. What, in the devil's name, would that cost? Possibly 7000 or 8000 francs. And *pourboire*, the slut had said, and a motor bicycle. There was no use trying to work it all out to the exact franc. The best thing to do was call it a round 10,000.

Ten thousand francs! Madame Lagrue felt as if a cold wind were howling around her, as if she were being buried alive beneath a snowdrift of misery.

'Well?' said Fatima cruelly. 'Let's have it. *A vous la balle, madame.*'

'I'll have the law on you,' croaked Madame Lagrue. 'Ill have the police destroy that scandalous object.'

'Save your breath, miser. This is a work of art, and you know as well as I do that nobody destroys a work of art because it might bother someone. Now enough of such nonsense. What's your offer?'

Madame stared at the slip of paper in her tormentor's hand. Oh, for one little look at the figure written on it—

'Ten thousand,' she gasped.

The look of contempt on Fatima's face, the curl of that lip, told Madame she had miscalculated after all, she had cut it too fine. She thought of the crowds gathered before Florelle's window staring with obscene delight at the picture; she thought of them gathering before her own window, leering and nudging each other, hoping to get a glimpse of her in her disgrace. She'd never be able to go out on the street again. She'd be driven out of business in a month, a week—

'No, wait!' she cried. 'I meant fifteen thousand! Of course, fifteen thousand. I don't know what got into me. It was a slip of the tongue!'

'You said ten thousand.'

'I swear it was a mistake! Take fifteen. I insist you take it.'

Fatima glanced at her slip of paper. She gnawed her lip, weighing the case in her mind. 'All right, I'll be merciful. But I want my money right now.'

'I don't have that much in cash here. I'll send the girl to the bank.'

'And I want a paper to show that the deal is strictly on the level.'

'Yes, of course. I'll make it out for you while we're waiting.'

The pale, timid assistant must have run like a rabbit. She was back in almost no time with an envelope stuffed full of banknotes which she handed to Madame Lagrue through the partly opened door of the office. Tears trickled down Madame's cheeks as she gave the money to Fatima.

'This is my life's blood,' Madame said. 'You've drained me dry, criminal.'

'Liar, you've made a million from your poor painters,' Fatima retorted. 'It's time at least one of them was paid what you owe him.'

As she left, she crumpled the slip of paper in her hand and carelessly tossed it to the floor.

'You don't have to see us off at the plane,' she said in farewell. 'Just stay here and enjoy your picture.'

No sooner had the office door slammed behind her than Madame snatched up the crumpled paper from the floor and opened it with trembling fingers. Her eyes, as she saw the figure written on it in a large childish hand, almost bulged from her head.

*Twenty francs!*

Madame Lagrue wildly pounded her fists on the desk and screamed and screamed until the frightened assistant had to throw water in her face to quiet her.

# The Payoff

The four men aboard *Belinda II* watched the Coast Guard helicopter racketing its way southward on patrol along the Miami Beach shoreline.

'Handy little gadget,' Broderick said, and Yates, echoing the boss man as usual, said, 'Very handy.'

'Depends,' Del said sourly. He glanced at Chappie, who said nothing.

Broderick and Yates were in their middle forties, both of them big and hefty, with paunches showing under their yachting jackets. Chappie and Del were in their early twenties, flat-bellied in swim trunks.

Broderick, glassy-eyed with bourbon, squinted at his watch. 'Thirty-five minutes. Last time was thirty-three. Let's call it an even half hour to be on the safe side.' He looked Chappie up and down. 'You sure that's enough time for you?'

Chappie said, 'It's enough,' and went back to whetting the blade of his clasp knife on the stone Broderick had turned up in the galley. The blade was four inches long, Bowie-shaped.

Broderick, one hand on the wheel, steadied *Belinda II*, keeping her bow toward the swells riding inshore, her motor almost idling. 'You absolutely sure?'

Del said angrily, 'You heard him, didn't you? What the hell you want to keep picking on him about it?'

'Because we are cutting down on the excuse quotient,' Yates said. He was as stoned as Broderick, his face even more flaming red with windburn and Jim Beam. 'Because we do not want to hear afterward how you couldn't do it because that chopper didn't allow enough time. Or any other excuse.'

'Well, you won't be hearing no excuses,' Del said, and

Chappie snapped the knife shut and said to him, 'Cool it, man. Just get that baby boat over here.'

As Del hauled the dinghy alongside *Belinda II* by its line, Chappie shoved the knife into a plastic sandwich-bag, rolled up the bag, and thrust it into the waistband of his trunks. The outboard motor had already been clamped to the sternboard of the dinghy. Del stepped down into the dinghy, took his place at the motor. Chappie dropped down into the bow of the dinghy, untied its line, pushed off from *Belinda II*. Broderick joined Yates at the rail of the cabin cruiser, both of them watching with the same tight little smiles. Broderick cupped his hands to his mouth and yelled over the noise of the outboard. 'Twenty-eight minutes left.'

They were about two miles away from the towering line of hotels and high-rises along the shore. The sunlight was scorching but a cool gusting breeze made it bearable. Del centered the bow of the dinghy on the big hotel dead ahead, the Royal Oceanic, tried to keep the boat from yawing and chopping too badly as it moved landward. He eyed Chappie who squatted there on the bow seat, rocking with the motion, his face empty.

'Suppose the layout's changed over there from the way Broderick told it,' Del said. He pointed his chin at the hotel.

'Changed how?'

'Rooms, halls, you know what I mean. That was a couple of years ago he stayed there. They could have tore down things, built up things, so it's all changed around now.'

'You worry too much,' Chappie said.

'Because I just don't like this kind of a deal, man. We wouldn't even be in it if that big-mouth Broderick wasn't a mess of bad vibrations. Now ain't that the truth?'

'Nothing but,' Chappie said.

'You see.' Del solemnly shook his head. 'Man, it sure is different from yesterday. I mean like up Palm Beach way when they said come on along and they'd give us a hitch right to Freeport. Fact is, I kind of took to them first look.'

'Only way to find out about people is move in with them,' Chappie said.

They were getting close to shore now. The swells the dinghy had been riding were taking shape as combers that crested and broke on the narrow, dirty-looking strip of sand fronting the hotel. Some people were standing in the surf. One of them shaded his eyes to look at the dinghy. Del swung it around, bow pointing seaward, and cut the motor. He stood up to gauge the distance to the beach.

'Maybe a hundred yards,' he said. 'Just remember the low profile, man.'

'You, too,' Chappie said. He slid overboard, ducked underwater, came up shaking the hair out of his eyes. He rested a hand on the edge of the dinghy. 'Don't let it look like you're waiting here. Take a ride for yourself. Then when you're back here, fool around with the motor.'

He went deep under the boat, swam hard, and when he bobbed to the surface on the crest of a wave he turned and saw the dinghy wheeling away northward. He let the next wave carry him half the remaining distance to the beach. When he got to his feet he found the water only up to his waist. Off-balance, he was thrown forward on his hands and knees by a following wave. As he pitched forward, he felt the plastic bag with the knife in it slither down his thigh. He clutched at it, missed it, and came up with a handful of slimy, oil-soaked seaweed instead. He flung the seaweed aside. Then he saw the bag, open now, the knife showing through it, come to roost on the tide line up ahead. None of the bathers around him seemed to take any special notice as he got to the bag fast, poured the water out of it, wrapped it tight around the knife again, and shoved it back into his waistband.

He stood for a few seconds looking seaward. *Belinda II*, a small white patch on the horizon, got even smaller as it ran out into the Gulf Stream. Overhead there was no helicopter in sight. Nobody to take in the scene and connect the cabin cruiser with its dinghy or the dinghy with the passenger it had just landed.

He turned, crossed the strip of beach to the walled-in sun deck of the hotel. A broad flight of concrete steps led to the still deck. A lifeguard type in white ducks and a T-shirt marked *Royal Oceanic* stood at the head of the steps, his arms folded on his chest, his eyes on the beach. As Chappie passed by, the eyes swiveled toward him, flicked over him, then went back to surveying the beach.

Lounges in long neat rows took up most of the sun deck. The rest was taken up by a big swimming pool, its deep end toward the beach, its shallow end not far from the rear entrance to the hotel. A lot of the lounges were occupied; the pool was almost empty. Chappie strolled toward the pool, stepped up on the edge of it.

'Hey, you!'

Chappie froze there. He glanced over his shoulder and saw the lifeguard type walking toward him, aiming a finger at him. 'You,' the man said. 'What goes on?' The finger aimed downward now at Chappie's feet. 'Bring all that sand up from the beach, mister, you ought to know enough to take a shower before you get in the pool.' He nodded toward what looked like a phone booth with canvas walls. 'Shower's right over there.'

Chappie slowly released his breath. Thumb in the waistband of his trunks, hand covering the bulge of the knife in the waistband, he went over to the shower booth, stepped inside, braced himself against the shock of cold water jetting down on him.

When he walked out of the booth the lifeguard type gave him a nod and a smile, and he nodded and smiled in return. Then he went into the pool feet first, keeping a grip on the knife in his belt until he picked up his swimming stroke. He covered almost the whole length of the pool under water, hoisted himself out at the shallow end. It was only a few steps from there to the hotel entrance. Inside the entrance he was in an arcade, a coffee shop on one side, a souvenir shop on the other. After the searing glare of the sunlight outside, the arcade seemed like a cool, damp, unlit cave, but by the time he had walked past the coffee shop he was used to the lighting. A door behind the shop was marked *Men's Sauna*, and there was a steady traffic coming and going through it.

Chappie went in and entered a long and wide corridor, narrower corridors branching off from it on both sides. It was hot and close here, the air growing steadily hotter and more humid as he walked along counting, and when he turned into the fourth corridor on the left a smell of sweat became unpleasantly noticeable. The walls in this section were all white tile, and each door along the way had a lettered plate on it: *Steam Room,*

*Dry Heat, Showers, Personnel, Service.* The door to the service room was wide open, kept in place by a rubber doorstop. As he passed it, Chappie took quick notice of the shelves of towels and sheets there. Almost out of sight in a corner of the room, someone was hauling towels from a shelf.

When he reached the end of the corridor, Chappie leaned against the wall, bent down as if to examine an ankle, his eyes sidelong on the open door of the service room. Then a boy in sandals and swim trunks emerged from the room with a bundle of towels under his arm. As soon as he was out of sight around a corner, Chappie went into the service room and helped himself to an armful of towels. He carried them back to the end of the corridor which ran into a short hallway that crossed it like the head of a capital T.

The doors in this hallway were numbered. Chappie carefully pushed open Number One an inch and looked inside. The room was small and windowless, its only furnishings a rubbing table and a shelf on the wall with a row of bottles and jars on it. On the table a big man with the build of a football linebacker was getting a rubdown from a masseur.

Chappie left the door as it was and tried the next room. It was empty. The third room, however, was occupied. A man wearing dark goggles lay stretched out on his back on the rubbing table, a cigar clamped between his teeth and pointing up at the ceiling, a sunlamp brilliantly lighting his naked body. A white-haired man, skinny and wrinkled, his face and body tanned a leathery brown. Clearly visible in the glare of the sunlamp was a tattoo on one scrawny forearm, done in garish colors. A coiled rattlesnake, and circling it in bold print the words *Don't Tread On Me*.

Chappie looked over his shoulder. There was no hotel staff man in sight, only some customers walking around in sandals and bathsheets. He got a good grip on the bundle of towels under his arm and went into the room. It reeked of cigar smoke and was hot enough to make him break into a sweat as he stood there closing the door softly behind him. He could feel the beads of sweat starting to trickle down his forehead and chest.

The click of the door lock roused the man. Without turning his head he said, 'Benny?'

'No, sir,' Chappie said. He moved toward the table. 'But he sent me in to check up.'

'Check up?' the man said. 'What the hell's he trying to do, fix up everybody in the place with a handout?'

'No, sir. But he said you're not to get too much of that lamp on your front and more on your back.'

As Chappie walked over to the table, his toes struck something on the floor beside it. A plastic ashtray with cigar ash in it. More cigar ash was scattered on the floor around it. Chappie stacked his armful of towels on the foot of the rubbing table and picked up the ashtray, the clasp knife digging into his groin as he did so. He said, 'If you don't mind, sir,' and took the cigar from between the man's teeth and deposited it in the ashtray. He put the ashtray back on the floor, pushing it far under the table.

The lenses in the goggles were so dark that Chappie couldn't see the man's eyes through them as he leaned forward over him. The man's head was resting on a folded towel. Chappie lifted the head barely enough to slide the towel out, and found the towel soaked through with sweat. He dropped it on the floor and gently set the man's head down again. 'Want me to help you turn over, sir?'

The goggles fixed on him. 'You new around here, boy?'

'Yes, sir.'

'I thought so. Well, if you know what's good for you you'll help me turn over so nice and easy I don't feel a twinge. Damn bursitis is killing me. So very nice and easy, you hear?'

'Yes, sir.'

The man grunted and groaned as he was arranged on his belly. Then he raised his head a little. 'What the hell are you saving those towels for? This thing is like an ironing board.'

'Yes, sir,' said Chappie.

He took a towel from the pile, folded it and slid it under the man's head. The man rested his head on it. 'All right,' he said, 'now beat it.'

Chappie glanced at the closed door. Then he came up on his toes like a bullfighter preparing to plant his *pics*, both arms raised, left elbow out as if warding off an attack. His right hand flashed down expertly, all his strength behind it, and the edge of the palm drove into the nape of the man's neck like an ax blade. The leathery old body jerked violently, the legs snapping backward from the knees, then falling to the table again, one leg shivering. Chappie came up on his toes again, struck again. The leg stopped shivering. The body settled down into the table like a tub of fresh dough poured on it. One stringy arm slipped off the table and dangled there, its fingers half curled.

Chappie pulled the plastic bag from his waistband, took the knife out of it, opened the blade. He pulled the goggles high up on the man's forehead to give himself room, then slashed off the man's ear with one stroke of the knife. There was no welling of blood, just an ooze of it along the line of the wound. He cleaned the knife blade hastily with a fresh towel from the pile, snapped it shut, and put the knife and ear into the plastic bag.

Coming out of the arcade into glaring daylight he was blinded by the sun and almost bumped into a couple of people as he made his way to the pool. He swam fast to the deep end, giving the diving boards there a wide berth, but as he neared the ladder at the deep end there was a sudden loud splash in his face, a blow on the side of the head that pulled him up short.

It was a girl who had jumped off the side of the pool and was now treading water face to face with him. She was about 16 or 17, her long straight hair in strings down her face. She pulled some of the strings aside and said worriedly, 'Honest, I didn't mean that. Are you all right?'

'Sure,' Chappie said. He rested his hands on her shoulders and she let them stay there. She seemed to like it.

Chappie saw that some of the people standing on the edge of the pool were looking down at them. He released the girl and went up the ladder. 'Hey,' the girl called after him, 'are you staying here at the hotel?' but he didn't answer or look back.

The lifeguard type was still at the head of the stairway to the beach. Chappie slowed down to a casual walk going past the man and down the steps. He took his time crossing the narrow strip of beach and looked out over the pale green water. The dinghy was rocking up and down beyond the line of breakers, its motor pulled up horizontal, Del pretending to fiddle with it. *Belinda II* was barely in sight on the horizon. She seemed to be stationary now, but it was hard to judge from that distance. Chappie looked up. No helicopter showing anywhere.

He waded into the surf, went under a couple of lines of breakers, and swam to the dinghy. As he hauled himself into the bow, Del dropped the motor back into the water, got it snarling into life with a quick flick of the cord. The dinghy aimed for *Belinda II*, bouncing hard, and Chappie said, 'Don't make it look like a getaway, man. Cut it down.'

Del eased up on the throttle. He looked at Chappie. 'You do it?'

'I did it.'

'No sweat?'

'No. He looked about ready to go anyhow. And you can swim right up to that door there. You don't even have to walk in front of people.' Chappie spat overboard to get the taste of salt water out of his mouth. 'There's some massage artist name of Benny who is in for a big surprise pretty soon. Maybe even got it already.' He had to smile at the thought.

Del said, 'All the same, man, you ain't getting near enough bread for this kind of a deal. And that Broderick is loaded. I mean loaded.'

'All I want is what's coming to me. If I wanted more I would have told him so.'

'Sure enough. But you know how much that Yates said that Belinda boat cost? Forty thousand. And that Caddie of theirs up in Palm Beach. Man, that heap had everything in it but a Coke machine.'

'What about it? All they are is a couple of fat old men with a lot of money. You want to trade around with them, just remember that the fat and the old goes along with the money.'

Del shook his head. 'Then it's no trade, man. What happens after Freeport? You don't figure to come back with them two, do you?'

'Hell, no. I figure we do some of those islands around there. Then maybe Mexico. Acapulco. How does that grab you?'

'Any place as long as it ain't Danang or like that grabs me just fine.' Del looked up over his shoulder. 'And talking about that—' The Coast Guard helicopter was in sight again, loudly making its northward run along the coast. 'Man, it makes me sick to even hear the sound of them things now,' Del said. 'I can feel that pack breaking my back all over again.'

'Full field pack,' Chappie said. 'Stuffed full of those delicious C-rations.'

When they pulled alongside *Belinda II*, Broderick was at the wheel of the cruiser, Yates was at the rail watching them. Yates took the line Chappie handed up to him and made it fast to *Belinda II*. 'Well, well,' he said, 'look who's home again. And with a tale to tell, I'm sure, about what went wrong and why.'

Chappie disregarded him. He went aboard the cruiser, and Del, after tilting the outboard motor out of the water, followed him. Broderick looked them over.

'Not even breathing hard,' he said. 'A couple of real tough ones.'

Chappie went over to the card table where Broderick and Yates played gin when someone else was at the wheel. He pulled the plastic bag from under his waistband, turned it upside down, and let the knife and the ear fall out on the table. The ear was putty-colored now, its severed edge a gummy red and brown where the ooze of blood had clotted.

The little smile on Broderick's face disappeared. He released the wheel and walked over to the table, eyes fixed on it. Del immediately grabbed the wheel and steadied it. He said to Broderick, 'What the hell you looking so surprised at, man? He told you he could do it, didn't he? And bring back all the proof you wanted, didn't he?'

Broderick stood staring at the table. Then he stared at Chappie the same intent way, wiping a hand slowly back and forth over his mouth. Finally he said in a thick voice, 'You really killed somebody? I mean, killed him?'

Chappie nodded at the table. 'You think he just lay there and asked me to cut that off him?'

'But who was he? My God, you couldn't even know who he was!'

'I'm in no rush,' Chappie said. 'I can wait to find out when we see the papers over in Freeport tomorrow. But I'm not waiting until then for the payoff.' He held out his hand and wiggled the fingers invitingly. 'Right now's the time.'

'Payoff?'

'Man, you said it was your ten dollars to my dime I couldn't do it. So I did it. Now it's payoff time.'

Broderick said in anguish, 'But I swear to God I never meant you to go through with it. I never expected you to. It was just talk, that's all. You knew it was just talk. You must have known it.'

'You told him the layout there,' Del said. 'You told him where to look for somebody he could waste. You were the one scared about that chopper spotting us coming back here. Man, don't you start crawfishing now.'

'Now look,' Broderick said, then stopped short, shaking his head at his own thoughts.

Yates walked over to him fast, caught hold of his wrist. 'Listen to me, Brod. I'm talking to you as your lawyer. You give him any money now, you are really in this up to your neck. And you're not taking them to the Bahamas or anywhere else out of the country. We can make it to Key Largo before dark and they'll haul out right there.'

Chappie shrugged. 'Freeport, Key Largo, whatever makes you happy.' He picked up the knife from the table, opened its blade, held it up, admiring the way the sunlight ran up and down the blade. Then he levered the knife at Broderick's belly. 'But first I collect everything that's coming to me.'

Broderick looked down at the knife, looked up at Chappie's face. Behind him at the wheel, Del said, 'There's two of us, man,' and Broderick pulled his wrist free of Yates' grip on it, shoved his hand into his hip pocket. He came up with a wad of bills in a big gold clip. He drew a ten-dollar bill from the clip and held it out to Chappie. 'For ten lousy dollars,' he said unbelievingly.

Chappie took the bill, studied it front and back as if making sure it was honest money. Then he slowly tore it in half, held the two halves high and released them to the breeze. They fluttered over the jackstaff at the stern of *Belinda II* and landed in her wake not far behind the trailing dinghy.

'That was the nothing part of the deal,' Chappie said. 'Now how about the real payoff?'

'The real payoff?' Broderick asked.

'Mister, you told me that if I pulled it off you'd come right out and say you didn't know what it was all about. You told me you'd look me straight in the eye and say there's just as good men in Nam right now as that chicken company you were with in Korea. Just as good and maybe a lot better. Now say it.'

Broderick said between his teeth, 'If your idea of a good man—'

Chappie reached out, and lightly prodded Broderick's yachting jacket with the point of the knife. 'Say it.'

Broderick said it. Then he suddenly wheeled and lurched into the cabin, Yates close on his heels. Through the open door Chappie watched them pour out oversized drinks.

'Key Largo's the place,' he said to Del at the wheel, and as *Belinda II* swung southward, picking up speed as she went, Chappie stood there, his lip curled, watching the two men in the cabin gulping down their Jim Beam until Yates took notice of him and slammed the cabin door shut as hard as he could.

# The Other Side
## of the Wall

S o,' Dr Schwimmer said. 'So. It comes to this at last. The inevitable. Confrontation, penetration, decision-making, action. Wait.'

The office door was partly open. Through it could be heard the sound of a typewriter being pecked at slowly and uncertainly. The doctor rose from behind his desk, crossed the room, and closed and locked the door. He returned to the swivel chair behind the desk. The desk was long and wide, a polished slab of walnut mounted on stainless steel legs and without drawers. Arranged on it were a crystal ashtray; a cardboard box of straw-tipped Turkish cigarettes – ('I don't even enjoy smoking,' the doctor remarked, squaring the edge of the box with the edge of the ashtray, 'but these help the image, you understand. The exotic, somewhat mysterious image I cultivate to impress the impressionable females in my clientele.'); a razor-edged, needle-pointed letter-opener of Turkish design – ('Also part of the image, naturally. Again the exoticism of the Near East, with its suggestion of the menacingly virile.'); a cigarette lighter; a small brass tube like a lipstick container, which did not contain lipstick but a breath deodorant that left the mouth reeking of pepper-mint; and a neat little tape recorder, an XJE-IV Memocord, not much larger than the box of Turkish cigarettes.

'So.' The doctor leaned toward the tape recorder. He hesitated, then sat back in his chair. 'No. No need to put any of this on tape, Albert.'

'Why, Doctor? Is it too intensely personal to be recorded for posterity?'

'I am a psychotherapist, Albert. All the business transacted in this room is intensely personal.'

'Never to this extent though, is it? And that name Albert. Must you continually address me by it? You know how I detest it.'

'Too bad. But I will address you as Albert. This is necessary. It is a way of establishing identities and relationships. And consider the distinguished men who bore that name. Einstein. Schweitzer. They seemed to survive it reasonably well, didn't they?'

'I still detest it. There wasn't even a sensible reason for being saddled with it. No one in the family ever had it. Mother was enamored of the figure on the tins of tobacco Father smoked, that's all. An incredible woman. Imagine naming one's first-born after a pipe tobacco. Or was she so viciously foresighted that she knew this was the perfect name for a child who was doomed to become a bald, potbellied, blobby-nosed little man with weak vision and a perpetually nagging sinus condition?'

'So. Suddenly we are faced with the ghost of the mother?'

'Why not, Doctor? I didn't manufacture my own ugliness, did I?'

'Albert, if I were a Freudian, we could have such a good time with this mother image. We could make it your sacrificial goat, stuff all your problems into it, and slaughter it. So. But luckily for us, I am not a Freudian. Your dead mother deserves better than to be declared guilty of your misfortunes. Consider how she made it her duty to bolster your shaky ego every day of her life. Your academic brilliance, your professional success, your devotion to her – it was like a catechism to her, the recitation of her admiration for you day after day.'

'It was a trap. It was a pit I lived in like a captured tiger, feeding on those greasy chunks of admiration she flung to me.'

'So. Very dramatic. Very colorful. But an evasion, Albert. Only an evasion.'

'Is it? Then what about the father image? The big, handsome, loud-mouthed father. And the two handsome, muscular brothers. The overwhelming males in my home. And me the runt of the litter.'

'You were, Albert. But never overwhelmed. Consider the facts. Your father died when you were a child. His absence may have affected you, but never his presence. And that pair of clods,

Albert, those two handsome, muscular brothers, stood in awe of your intellect, were wary of your cold self-restraint, terrified of your unpredictable explosions of temper. They quickly learned not to step over the lines you drew. Do you remember how one earned a broken leg when he was tripped up by you at the head of the staircase for trying a little bullying? How the other found himself playing a game where he was locked in a trunk and almost smothered in payment for a small insult? Yes, yes, a few such episodes and they soon came to understand that one did not carelessly tread on the toes of this small, fat, pale older brother with the thick eyeglasses and the sniffle. They are still afraid of you, Albert. They are two of your very few triumphs. But it is your failure alone that concerns us. Let us get on with it.'

'My failure? Am I the only one in this room stamped with failure? My dear Doctor, what about the way you've managed to destroy a splendid practice in a few short months? Eccentricity is one thing, Doctor. Patients like a little eccentricity in their therapists. But they also draw lines. A therapist who lives in a daze, who sits lost to the world when patients are trying to communicate with him, who angrily sends them packing when they resent this – what did you think was bound to happen to this practice in short order? And what course did you think your fellow professionals would take when they observed your grotesque behavior? Did you really expect them to continue to refer patients to you? No, Doctor, there is no need to rush through this consultation. No need to look at clocks and measure out your time in expensive little spoonfuls any longer. The clocks have stopped. We have all the time to ourselves now we can possibly use.'

'Albert, listen to me. This room is not meant to be an arena where we turn our cruelty on each other. We are not antagonists. We will achieve nothing through antagonism.'

'You're a coward, Doctor.'

'We are both cowards about some things, Albert. Do you think I disparage you when I say you are essentially a creature of emotion? Believe me, I do not.'

'I don't believe you. You're much too clever with words, Doctor, to be believed in that regard. Creature of emotion.

What you mean is incorrigible romantic, don't you? An ugly little wretch stuffed to the bursting point with romantic visions. Made self-destructive by them. A fifty-year-old man flung back into adolescence and unable to claw his way out of it. Why shouldn't you disparage him?'

'Because, Albert, you are not play-acting your condition. You are not pretending you face a crisis. The condition is real. The crisis is real. One does not disparage a reality.'

'A reality based on dreams? On sexual fantasies dredged up from my unconscious while I lie snoring in bed?'

'All these are realities, too. Are scientific laws and material objects the only reality? No, no, Albert. Your mistake from the start was in not recognizing the validity of those dreams. Of the situation they depicted.'

'But the situation was all in my own mind.'

'In your emotions. Your emotions, Albert. If tests were made while you were asleep and dreaming of this woman, they would clearly indicate physiological reactions. A quickened breathing, an increase in blood pressure, sexual excitation.'

'Just as I told you. All the symptoms of delayed adolescence. The pimply high school boy's nightly dreams of his nubile girl friend. The only difference is that in the daylight he joins her in some noisy roost where they happily share a nauseous concoction of ice cream and syrup and hold hands under the table. While all I could do was turn night dreams into day dreams.'

'Slowly, Albert. Confrontation, penetration, decision-making, action. Each in its turn. So far we have barely begun the penetration. We have merely put aside the cliches of the possessive mother and bullying siblings and turned to the image of the dream woman herself. We have a distance to go before the decision-making.'

'Girl, Doctor. Maiden, if you will. Not woman.'

'So? Is it important that she has not reached full womanhood?'

'Yes. I don't like women. Something happens to a girl the instant she becomes one. In that instant she becomes too knowing, too wise, too self-sufficient to provide happiness for any man.'

'Not any man. Perhaps only men who are afraid they don't measure up. Tell me, Albert. What kind of man were you in your first dreams of this girl? Still the small, fat, fifty-year-old lump of self-hatred? Or heroic in dimensions?'

'I don't know. It's hard to remember.'

'Think. Penetrate.'

'I'm trying to. Not heroic. That much I'm sure of. Beyond that, I still don't know. I wasn't aware of my body, my appearance, my deficiencies. Only of my sensations when I saw her there. Ecstatic recognition. Passionate desire for her. And I remember my own astonishment that I should feel this. I hadn't even known I was capable of such feelings. All my life I've paid for my female companionship. Paid to satisfy my physical needs. There was never a suggestion of emotional involvement in the transactions. Now here I was, being drowned in emotionalism. I woke up suffocating with it.'

'So. And you knew on waking that this dream girl was based on an actuality? That she had a flesh-and-blood counterpart?'

'Not then. Not the first time. Only later when I realized the dream was recurrent. And then only when in one of the later dreams I realized that I knew her name. Sophia. When I woke that morning it struck me that of course she was the counterpart of a real Sophia. The inept child I had recently hired as my receptionist.'

'She resembled her?'

'More and more, once I knew her name. At first she was shadowy. She was only the suggestion of a beautiful Greek maiden. After I knew her name she took on clearer and clearer definition. Still shadowy, because we always met at night in dim lighting, but now as if a veil had been removed from her face. No more chiaroscuro, but every delicate curve of feature revealed. Sophia. I can even remember the idiotic imagery, the coinage of every bad poet, that crossed my mind in that dream when I stood there looking at her in full recognition for the first time. Doe-eyed, raven-haired, swan-necked. My God, I didn't even blush at my own puerile poeticizing of her. I rejoiced in it.'

'You think this girl in the dream was aware of your feelings?'

'She must have been. How could she help it? I tell you, Doctor, I yearned toward her with such intensity that she must have felt the current surging from me. This was before I even recognized her identity. I walked into this room, a bedroom lit by a small lamp somewhere, and she stood silent and unmoving in the middle of the room dressed in a white gown – the classically simple Greek gown – and with what seemed like an almost transparent veil covering her hair and face. A tender, living goddess. I was stricken by the sight of her. The emptiness in me, my lifetime of emptiness, was suddenly filled with a white-hot lava of emotion. You see? Again I am poeticizing like a fool, but what other way is there to describe it? In psychologic jargon? In those deadly words: *I fell in love*? Although, believe me, Doctor, coming from me, those words mean infinitely more than they would coming from the ordinary man.'

'I do believe you, Albert. But are you sure you never knew such an emotion before?'

'Never.'

'Think, Albert. You were not born middle-aged. In your youth there must have been some woman – girl – who excited this emotion in you.'

'Never. I never permitted myself to feel anything like this. I knew the response my size, my ugliness, my sweaty, tongue-tied ineptitude in conversation would draw from any girl I thought desirable. Why invite disaster? Better to freeze the heart into a block of ice than have it torn to pieces.'

'And you did not experience any of this when you confronted the dream Sophia? When you let her feel the current of emotion surging from you?'

'No. I seemed to have no room in me for anything but that aching desire.'

'Sexual desire?'

'That would have been later. In the early dream, all I wanted to do was touch her. Just touch her shoulder gently with my fingertips. To reassure her, perhaps. Or myself. I moved toward her with my hand outstretched, and she moved away a little, barely out of my reach. Then suddenly we were someplace else. I recognized where at once. The hallway outside the room. The hallway of my brownstone house.'

'Yes?'

'The old brownstone. My living tomb. My office downstairs, the bedrooms on the second floor where we stood. All those empty bedrooms. I was jubilant. This lovely, veiled creature was with me in my domain. I was not trespassing on hers. I looked and saw her standing now in the middle of that long gloomy hallway. While I watched she held out a hand as if inviting me to clasp it in mine. She pressed her other hand against the wall there, the blank, wallpapered expanse between two doors, and an opening showed in it. She moved through the opening, it closed behind her, and she was gone. I was frantic. Wild with despair. I ran to the wall and searched for some clue to the opening, but there was none. I struck my fist against the wall, but my fist had no substantiality, no strength. It moved in slow motion against the wall, it met it with hardly the impact of a feather brushing against it. That was all. I woke up drenched with sweat, weak with a sense of futility.

'I knew at once it had been a dream. I knew that the logical thing to do was either lie there and dispassionately analyze it or to clear it completely from my mind. But I knew that neither way would purge me of the glorious new emotions I had discovered in the girl's presence. I was in love. For the first time in my life – at the age of fifty, mind you – I was willingly and hopelessly in love. I had the sense of it in my every nerve.

'It was dawn now. Incredibly, I got out of bed in that gray light and went out into the hallway, searching along its wall for the mysterious opening in it, desperately running my hands over its smooth surface. I went into the room on the other side of the wall there, my younger brother's room, empty of all its furniture since his marriage, and it was as empty as ever, a fine dust on its floor and that was all. I knew then that the only thing left to me was the recurrence of the dream, a reentry into the shadowy world where the girl might be waiting for me. Would surely be waiting for me.'

'So.' Dr Schwimmer rested his head against the back of his swivel chair and closed his eyes. 'Then from the very start, Albert, you surrendered to this girl completely.'

'Completely.'

'You asked nothing in return. You expected nothing in return.'

'At the start, nothing. Only her presence.'

'And later?'

'Later, as the dream recurred again and again, I wanted her response. Her acknowledgement that she felt for me at least a part – a little – of what I felt for her. I wanted her not to retreat from me every time I reached toward her. But I forgave her for it each time she did. I knew it was because this experience was as strange and novel for her as it was for me. She was very young. Untouched. Timid. She was to be wooed gently, not taken by force. And I was willing to be patient, because my fingertips came infinitesimally closer to her each time. I settled for that.'

'So. And when you realized that this girl of the dreams was, in reality, the pretty little receptionist who sat in your outer office every working day of the week it did not break the spell?'

'No, because it didn't end the dreams. At night I had the Sophia of the dreams; in daylight I had the Sophia of reality nearby where, whenever I chose, I could look at her, speak to her.

'And the living reality, as it turned out, made the dreams that much more exciting. Every detail of the flesh-and-blood Sophia was transmitted to the dream image I loved. Now that image removed its veil and showed me the glowing eyes and parted lips and curve of cheek of the enchanting child I employed in my office. The length of leg, swell of breast, everything became substantial in the dreams.'

'But you did not transfer your emotions to this flesh-and-blood girl? Then or ever?'

'No.'

'Are you sure of that, Albert? Consider this very carefully. It is important.'

'I still say no. I didn't want to risk it. I didn't have to. It was more than enough that I had the dream Sophia to woo and win. In the daylight there were mirrors in the house where I would catch sight of myself at unexpected moments. A self that invited rejection. In the dimly lit room and hallway of the dreams there were no mirrors. I had no view of myself then. I never gave thought to what I looked like. Above all, somehow I knew that the brownstone house stood all alone in the dream world and that there was no one else in it besides the girl and me. I was the only man in her existence, she had no freedom of choice. Ultimately she would have to give herself to me.'

'A quaint way to phrase it, Albert. Almost Victorian. And what does it connote? She allows you to touch her at last? To press your lips to her blushing cheek? Or more?'

'More. Much more.'

'Yes?'

'She would be my slave. My willing slave. Grateful that she could be possessed by me. She would not so much love me as worship me.'

'So. And all this, Albert, in the light of your futile pursuit of her through dream after dream? The nightly confrontation in the bedroom, the scene in the shadowy hallway where, at the crucial moment, she disappears through a blank wall? Now tell me. Did you never wonder what lay on the other side of that wall?'

'I didn't have to. I was sure I knew what was there. Her room. The small room with carpeted walls and floor where she lay on a bed under some diaphanous covering breathlessly waiting for me to find my way to her. Afraid of the moment when I would, but eagerly anticipating it. Her room. Her solitary, sweetly scented refuge.'

'So there it is, Albert. That preconception was your great mistake. Your tragic misjudgment.'

'The room was there. I entered it. I found it exactly as I had imagined it.'

'No, you did not. Otherwise, would there be this crisis? This anguish? You should have been prepared, Albert, for more than you bargained for. You should have known yesterday when you first saw your real Sophia's young man in her office, when she proudly introduced him to you, that there was a crisis brewing. Admit it. Didn't your hackles rise when you met that young man? When you took his measure?'

'All right, yes. Yes. But I didn't make anything of it then. Why should I? All my life I've hated these hulking Adonises, these huge, handsome, brute images of masculinity. My hatred for this specimen was innate. Why should I think it had anything to do with the adoration my infatuated, flesh-and-blood Sophia aimed at him?'

'Hard words, Albert. But the dream Sophia is cast in the image of the flesh-and-blood Sophia. There was one danger signal. The other was at the instant in your dream last night when you pressed a hand against that wall, that barrier to her hidden room, and at last it opened to you. Didn't you wonder why, at long last, it should suddenly open? Didn't it enter your mind that it might be a means of providing you, not with the ultimate experience, but with the ultimate truth?'

'No. And you yourself know this only through hindsight. When I entered that room I felt jubilation. Utter ecstasy. Nothing else. I had no premonition I would find them on that bed together, she and that hulk. I had no idea until that incredible moment that this room was their refuge, not hers alone. Or, worst of all, that when caught shamelessly sprawled beside him in their love-making, she would only smile pityingly at me.

'How could I be prepared for any of that? After all, those dreams were mine. How could I ever imagine they would be invaded by any gross stranger? And now—'

'Yes?'

'Now that I know the truth I can't turn my mind away from it. Awake or asleep, all I can think of is that she was taken from me. Violated. And with her eager consent. God almighty, since I found my way into that room I've lived only with the picture of them in my mind. I can't live with it any longer.'

'So. Then it must be exorcised, Albert, must it not?'

'Yes.'

'At last we come to the decision-making. And is it to be my decision to make, Albert? Mine alone?'

'Yes.'

'You will accept it without question?'

'Completely.'

'Good. Then I will state the case directly. It is obvious that someone must pay the penalty for your betrayal, Albert. As a sane and intelligent man you must know that a blood sacrifice offers the only possible solution in a case like this. The only one. Under any conditions it would be impossible for you to be released from your agony while your betrayers maintain their obscene relationship. Yes. One or the other must be eliminated. But which? The intruder?'

'And then what, Doctor? Another such intruder to take his place in that room? Another crisis? Now that I know what the girl really is – what she's capable of – can I expect more than that?'

'True. Then you plainly see she herself must be sacrificed.'

'Yes.'

'So. And you also understand how it must be done?'

'Yes. With a blade, naturally.'

'Naturally. A blade of the finest steel. That is traditional, and there are times when one sees the wisdom behind these time-worn traditions.' The doctor picked up the letter opener from his desk and regarded it with admiration. He turned it slowly back and forth so that sunlight from the window flowed up and down the blade. 'The finest steel, a tradition in itself. More than eight inches of it, Albert. More than enough for its purpose.

'And you realize, of course, that the first killing blow deep between the lower ribs does not mean the completion of the ritual. There must be total release of the emotions immediately afterward. A frenzied hacking until the lovely image is made a horror. A full measure of blood must flow to wash away betrayal. Remember, Albert, the therapeutic value of the act lies in that.'

'Yes. Of course.'

'Then,' said the doctor, 'all that is left is action.'

He unlocked the door and opened it slightly on the drafty ground-floor corridor of the old brownstone. And, when in answer to his call, Miss Sophia Kaloosdian, doe-eyed, raven-haired, swan-necked, a large wad of chewing gum working rhythmically in her jaws, left her desk in the outer office and came to see what he wanted, he was waiting for her with smiling confidence, the hilt of the letter opener gripped tight in his fist and hidden behind his back.

The confidence was not misplaced. Dr Albert Schwimmer may have been short, fat, nearsighted, and with a perpetual sniffle, but he was very strong.

# The Corruption of Officer Avakadian

In regard to this heated issue of police corruption, I take the position—

No.

What with one thing and another, I believe it would be best to simply describe the curious event which led me to the position I take. And to start with the call received by Officer Schultz and me in our patrol car that night some time ago – I can measure the time by reflecting that two cherubic daughters have since been added to my roster of four sturdy sons, the Avakadians always having been a precocious and prolific breed – because that dispatcher's message was, I now see, the opening curtain on the event.

The call came at one A.M., abruptly breaking the bleak silence in the car. That silence, as we cruised along, was entirely Schultz's doing. I had been expostulating on various aspects of our profession – informatively, I knew; brightly, I hoped – until Schultz said, 'Will you kindly shut up, Avakadian?' after which I kept my thoughts entirely to myself.

I suppose that the kindest way to put it was that Schultz was not dedicated to his job. I had graduated with highest honors from Police School, having spent my months there among highly motivated and dedicated men. I had served my probationary period as foot patrolman among several young officers who also demonstrated this spirit. Now, for the first time, I was encountering an entirely different kind of police officer. Indeed, after only three days as Schultz's partner in police patrol car Number 8, I had begun to wonder whether I had been placed in his company to glean the lessons an experienced old hand could provide or whether he had been placed in my company so that a bit of my own keen spit-and-polish attitude, my devotion to the departmental rule book, might rub off on him.

In that latter case, it was time wasted. Schultz was only a few months from retirement, a bloated old time-server who seemed to make up his own rules as he went along. He was slovenly of person – his uniform jacket always appeared to be buttoned at the wrong buttons – and, worse than that, he was slovenly in manner and attitude, always more willing to expend his scant energies in crawling through loopholes in the rule book than in carrying them out to the letter.

Despite his uncongenial manner toward me, I believe he did have a grudging respect for what I represented. This surfaced briefly when, during our first tour of duty together, he suddenly asked me – and there was genuine wonderment in his tone – 'Were you always like this, Avakadian?' To which, in honest response, I explained that in my youth I had been the youngest Eagle Scout in the history of my troop and that before I set my course by the departmental rule book, I had steered it by nothing else than the Boy Scout Handbook. I even recited for him from memory the Scout Laws on being trustworthy, loyal, helpful, friendly, courteous, kind, obedient, cheerful, thrifty, brave, clean and reverent, to which he only said in quick retreat to his curmudgeon role, 'And how did friendly get in there?'

That stung me a little, though I well understood the reasons for it. As for example, any snacks we had during our tour of duty Schultz apparently regarded as gifts from the proprietors of the hamburger stands we stopped at, but I had insisted we pay in full for them, even though this procedure seemed to bewilder and alarm those proprietors. And twice, when we had caught up with traffic violators who were as transparently eager to buy their way out of trouble as Schultz was to take their money, my stern insistence on writing out the ticket made any such transaction impossible.

So in answer to his gibe, all I said was, 'Remember, Schultz, friendliness does not mean condoning moral laxity.' He had no answer to that, of course.

But, not to digress, that night in question we were cruising along sharing a bleak silence when the dispatcher's voice was heard. 'Car eight. Householder at 77 Pineview, northwest,' to which Schultz responded, as was his wont, 'Yeah, sure,' so that I, as I was invariably forced to do, had to take the speaker from Schultz's hand before he could hang it up and crisply reply to the dispatcher, 'Ten-four,' the only proper response.

I then remarked to Schultz – and it was not the first time I had been forced to do so – that since we were now on call, both the flasher and the siren had to be put into operation.

'Why?' Schultz said. 'Why, Avakadian? Take a look. There isn't any traffic. Why do we have to make a circus of every call?'

'Because, Schultz, the rules prescribe it. And if you want the number of the exact rule—'

'Forget it,' Schultz snarled, but willy-nilly he did turn on flasher and siren.

The northwest district was and is an area of luxurious homes, each surrounded by beautifully tended lawns. The door of Number 77 was already ajar as Schultz and I approached it along a flagstoned path, and when we reached the door I saw on the wall beside it a brass plaque inscribed *Cyrus Cahoon, MD*. No surprise, that, since many of the finest properties in these parts were owned by members of the medical profession.

The tall aristocratic woman in robe and slippers who stood in the doorway motioned us inside the house. There, on one side of the foyer we entered, open doors revealed a waiting room and medical examining room. On the other side was a living room where a man dressed in a rather rumpled suit stood regarding us from beneath lowering brows. The woman pointed at him and said, 'This is my husband, Dr Cyrus Cahoon. He wishes to report an atrocious crime.'

'I wish to report nothing, Florence,' said Dr Cahoon. 'You were the one who invited these men here. Now do me the favor of inviting them out.'

'Yeah, sure,' Schultz said, and was already preparing to depart when Mrs Cahoon grasped his arm firmly. 'Officer,' she said, 'my husband may choose to stand mute, but if kidnapping is a crime, I cannot.'

'It's a crime,' Schultz said uncomfortably, and I must admit I felt an excitement at what I was hearing. My third day on this detail, and here I was confronted by one of the most heinous and dramatic of all felonies. I could only regret that I was not yet in detective grade where the task of handling the case would be mine. It was incredible that Schultz should manage to remain so stolid as he put the question, 'Who's been kidnaped?'

Mrs Cahoon again levered a forefinger at her husband. 'He was.'

'He looks all right to me,' Schultz said.

'I am all right,' Dr Cahoon said.

Schultz tried to detach his arm from Mrs Cahoon's grip. He said, 'Lady, if you and your husband would settle it between yourselves and then let us know how it came out—'

Mrs Cahoon hung onto his arm. 'It has been settled. My husband was kidnaped by a gang of criminals, do you hear? And he cannot deny it.'

Plainly, Schultz wanted nothing more than to make a quick exit. Even more plainly, leaving now would be gross neglect of duty. At the very least, information on the crime had to be entered into our notebooks; the detective squad would have to be informed. So, although I had been advised by the department to follow Schultz's lead in all calls, I saw that, so to speak, I must now take the bit between my teeth.

I pulled out my notebook and pencil. I said to Dr Cahoon, 'Sir, what is the problem here? Are you afraid of reprisals if you take proper action against your alleged kidnapers?'

Dr Cahoon regarded me steadily for a few moments. Then he looked at Schultz. 'Is he for real?' he asked.

Happily, Mrs Cahoon recognized the authority in my tone. She released Schultz's arm and turned to me. 'I want you to write all this down,' she said.

I held up my notebook and pencil to indicate that I was more than ready to do my duty.

'Oh, hell,' Dr Cahoon said.

'Officer,' Mrs Cahoon said, 'an hour ago, I woke from a sound sleep wondering why it was suddenly so light in the bedroom. Then I saw this woman standing there with a gun pointed at me. Then I saw another woman on the other side of the bed pointing a gun at my husband, and a man getting some of my husband's clothing from the closet. It was horrible. It was like a bad dream.'

'I have survived the experience,' Dr Cahoon said.

Mrs Cahoon disregarded this. 'The man told my husband to put on his suit over his pajamas. My husband will not admit it but he was very much shaken. He offered the man all the money we had in the house, and the man said, "No. We want you."'

'Three of them,' I said. 'Can you describe them?'

'Yes,' said Mrs Cahoon. 'The women wore house dresses. The one pointing the gun at me was short and stout. At least a size eighteen. She had curlers in her hair. Large pink plastic rollers. The other woman could have been a size twelve. She had gray hair done in a very unattractive permanent. The man was gray-haired, too. Medium height, medium weight, totally undistinguished in appearance. Then two of them removed my husband from the room—'

'I removed myself from the room,' Dr Cahoon said. 'I left under my own power, putting one foot ahead of the other in the customary fashion.'

'With a gun at your head,' Mrs Cahoon pointed out.

'That I cannot deny.'

'And where were you taken?' I asked.

'Downstairs to my examining room.'

'And then?' I said encouragingly.

'Then I was asked to produce my medical bag, which I did, and to submit to having my eyes blindfolded by a length of bandage. And since there seems to be no way of turning off your tape, officer, I will tell you that I was then conducted to a car and driven for about ten or fifteen minutes to some location where I was led indoors. When the blindfold was removed I saw that I was in a rather poorly furnished bedroom. A young man was in bed there apparently suffering acute pain, and a young woman whom I took to be his wife was also there, hysterically sympathizing with him.'

Inspiration struck me. I said, 'That young man was suffering a gunshot or knife wound, wasn't he? And you were expected to treat him without informing the authorities.'

'The young man,' Dr Cahoon said, 'was suffering what in layman's language is called a sprained ankle, although it was his impression, and his wife's, that the ankle was broken. After diagnosing the condition, I gave him a sedative, bound the ankle properly, advised bed rest. By now I imagine he is sound asleep, his pain eased.'

'Well, mine isn't,' Mrs Cahoon said sharply. 'After what I went through when they hauled you away—'

'Yes?' I prompted.

'That horrible little fat woman stayed right here with me all that time. She plonked herself down on the chair next to my bed and kept that gun pointed at me. She said to me, "Just keep cool, sister," and in the most threatening way.'

'That's all she said?' I asked. 'Nothing about what her accomplices were up to?'

'Nothing,' said Mrs Cahoon. 'Later on she did ask me about my bedroom drapes.'

'Your bedroom drapes?'

'Yes. She asked how much they cost, and when I told her she said in a very sneering manner, "They really took you, didn't they?" But every time I asked about my husband she just stared at me with those beady little eyes and wouldn't say a word.'

Schultz stirred himself. He said to Dr Cahoon, 'But they brought you back okay, didn't they?'

'Yes,' Dr Cahoon said. 'They also paid me.' He dug into a pocket and held up a twenty-dollar bill to our view. 'The wife, or whoever she was, gave it to me before I was blindfolded again and led away. She said, "That should take care of it, Doc," and since I was in no position to negotiate at length, I said yes, it did.'

Schultz drew a long slow breath as if to fill his lungs for an ordeal ahead. He pointed at a chair. 'Can I sit down?' he said.

'My home is your home,' Dr Cahoon said.

Schultz sat down and stretched out his legs. I was dismayed to see that this glaringly exposed to all his scuffed shoes and bedraggled socks. He said to Dr Cahoon, 'You don't make house calls, do you?'

'I used to,' the doctor said. 'But you understand that my practice now—'

'Yeah, sure,' Schultz said, and then remarked complainingly, 'When I was a kid, doctors made house calls. Even this time of night.'

'And what,' demanded Mrs Cahoon, justifiably angry, 'does that have to do with the crime committed against us?'

Schultz made no effort to answer this unanswerable question. Instead, he said to Dr Cahoon, 'You know there's been other cases like this lately? Other doctors being snatched?'

From Mrs Cahoon's expression I saw that she was as astonished by this as I was. I was even more astonished to hear Dr Cahoon say, 'Yes. So some of my colleagues have been saying.'

'What!' Mrs Cahoon said explosively. 'And not a word of it getting out? I don't believe it.'

'Lady, you can believe it,' Schultz advised. 'As for no word getting out, I guess all those other doctors who got hit this way feel like your husband does about it. They'd kind of like to keep it strictly in the family.'

'Do you hear that, Florence?' Dr Cahoon said. He said to Schultz, 'I tried to explain this to her. Maybe you'll have better luck at it than I did.'

'Yeah, sure,' Schultz said. He shook his head reproachfully at Mrs Cahoon. 'You see, lady, if we turn in a report on this, tomorrow you won't be able to walk out of your door what with all the reporters and TV guys there. And all of them looking to play it for comedy.'

'Comedy?' Mrs Cahoon said. 'A crime like this?'

'Well, nobody got hurt, did they? And doc here got paid for the job, just like all the others did. Now what do you make of a kidnaping where it's the victim that gets paid off? And let's face it, lady, the public will not be with you. Same goes for any jury that gets this case. Push the wrong button right now, and next thing you'll be a coast-to-coast joke.'

Plainly, Mrs Cahoon was hard hit by this. She stared at Schultz, her mouth opening and closing in a rather fishlike way. At last she found her voice. 'Incredible,' she said weakly.

'A coast-to-coast joke, Florence,' Dr Cahoon said. 'Yes, indeed, the whole medical profession will have much to thank you for.'

'Incredible,' Mrs Cahoon said again. She grasped the back of a chair and managed to seat herself. Her eyes remained glassily fixed on a far wall of the room. 'Incredible.'

Dr Cahoon said to Schultz, 'I think you have made your point, officer. Thank you for that. Now if you gentlemen would like a drink before you leave—'

'Well—' Schultz said, hauling himself out of his chair, then he glanced my way. 'No, not while we're on duty.'

One does not enter into a confrontation with a fellow officer before the public. I maintained a tight-lipped silence until we were seated in the patrol car. I made an effort to keep my voice level. 'Schultz,' I said, 'are you aware that a felony must be placed on record, however the complainant may feel about it?'

'Yeah, sure. So we'll put this down as a prowler who took off when we came around.'

'You may do that, Schultz. I, however, am going to enter a detailed report on everything I have just seen and heard, including the unpleasant fact that a kidnap ring is being allowed to operate with impunity right under the department's nose.'

'Yeah,' Schultz said. 'Well, you're way off base, Avakadian.'

'If you are suggesting that the exposure of a crime wave—'

'I already exposed it, Avakadian. Unofficial like. On my own, see? I figured out after the first few snatches that it had to be that phone-answering service all these doctors use that was behind it. It was the one thing tied in with all of them. And that's what it was. Some nice old lady on the night switchboard there got so upset by doctors turning down house calls that she got some friends of hers to do something about it. That way, at least, they can take care of anybody they know personally and can count on not to spill the beans. And the guns are toy guns.'

'Schultz, hasn't it entered your mind that your nice old lady is guilty of at least a dozen felonies?'

'I know. But if everybody wants it hushed up, why make trouble? And I'll let you in on something good, Avakadian, if you forget the book for once. I got a deal with that old lady, so any time me or the family needs a doctor she sees to it one shows up quick. Say the word, and she'll sign you on with the rest of the department.'

'Do you mean that the whole department is in on this?'

'Sure. They're practically all family men, ain't they? Look at you, Avakadian, with a wife and four kids. How many times did you get turned down so far when you wanted a doctor to come fix one of them up?'

My mind was whirling, part of it doing painful arithmetic in answer to that question, part of it recoiling in horror from the proposition being coldbloodedly offered me. But the arithmetic seemed to be submerging all other thoughts.

'Schultz,' I said at last, 'do you absolutely guarantee that those were only toy guns?'

'Absolutely,' said Schultz.

And now, looking back, I must say that things have worked out very well, especially during influenza seasons.

Which is why I take the position in regard to police corruption that one must not be too inflexible. Let us face one indisputable fact. The rule book serves well in most cases, but it does not bring healing.

# A Corner
## of Paradise

B ut it's a jungle,' well-intentioned suburban acquaintances
would tell him with horror. 'You know it's a jungle.'

Meaning that it was idiotic of Mr Hotchkiss – retired
on a comfortable pension, two years into his Social Security, and
with a few dollars in the bank – it was absolutely idiotic of him
to continue living in the heart of the jungle that was New York
City. Crime in the streets, in the subways, the parks, disorder,
virtual anarchy. New York City.

And here was this small, bespectacled, elderly citizen, almost
shoutingly vulnerable to assault by any thug who hungered for a
ready-made victim, here he was voluntarily occupying an apartment in the upper East Side of Manhattan. Definitely the heart
of the jungle.

Mr Hotchkiss would take it with a shrug. Futile, he knew, to
explain that he was a born and bred New Yorker who found
himself at the mere thought of life in the suburbs aching with
boredom. And it would be even more futile to try convincing
these fearful outlanders that the apartment he had occupied for
the past 20 years and the street it was situated on provided him
with a small neat corner of paradise.

The street was a solid rank of brownstones and graystones
shaded by trees which seemed to thrive on polluted air. If
anything at all marred its comfortable, old-fashioned look, it was
the gigantic towers of two newly built highrises, one at each end
of the block. On the other hand, as Mr Hotchkiss had appraised
it, luxury highrises also meant the kind of tenantry able to meet
the fantastically steep rents in those shiny glass cracker boxes.
Not bad at all having people like that settle down on the borders
of your peaceable little kingdom.

Mr Hotchkiss was not insensitive to the plight of the down-trodden, but he was one to look facts in the face. As far as he was concerned, those towers might be stuffed from top to bottom with embezzlers, corrupt politicians, and dishonest corporation officers, but such were not likely to go out on the streets for exercise at purse-snatching, mugging, and assault. So, simply as a matter of self-preservation in the jungle, it was better to live among the prosperous than the poor.

And that was the best part of it, because one did not have to be overly prosperous to occupy Mr Hotchkiss' own apartment in that brownstone midway along the block. The building was rent-controlled by city law, and the apartment, thought not all that cheap, was just within Mr Hotchkiss' carefully budgeted means. By any standards, especially the prevailing inflationary ones, it was the wildest of bargains. Three large, high-ceilinged rooms – bedroom, living room, and kitchen – more than ample closet space, and in a midtown building provided with excellent service by a dour, hard-working Teutonic couple named Braun who occupied the first floor rear. Not only was Mr Braun an artist at unsticking windows, splicing wires, and sealing leaky plumbing, but for a comparatively small gratuity he would descend to his basement workshop and knock up sturdy wooden shelving or put together elaborate lighting arrangements which would have drawn admiration from any master electrician.

Shelving and lighting arrangements. The shelving, three broad tiers of it, extended halfway along the walls on either side of the huge bay windows which overlooked the street. The lighting arrangements were fluorescent tubes skillfully fixed over and behind the shelves to provide on sunless days a rather macabre, but effective, artificial sunlight for the treasures on those shelves. The coleus.

There were, by exact count, 72 of these treasures filling the table in the bay windows and lining the shelves. Six dozen small potted plants whose leaves were each an enchanting pattern of green and red in all their various shades, and of black and white providing balance with the greens and reds. And, Mr Hotchkiss had discovered with amazement and delight, no two leaves ever reproduced the precisely same pattern. One had to look closely to realize that here was infinite variety, no end to it.

Coleus, Mr Hotchkiss would whisper now and then, the word delectable in his mouth. Coleus. Certainly not painted nettle, the flat and ugly name tacked onto them in parentheses in all those gardening books.

Coleus.

He had been introduced to coleus by chance not long after his retirement when he had been asked by the Ostroffs, the ancient, long-retired pharmacist and his wife who inhabited the rear apartment on his floor, to do some plant-sitting for them while they were away visiting children and grandchildren. Having learned from Mrs Braun, they had said hopefully, that Mr Hotchkiss was now retired himself and possibly with time on his hands, would he kindly keep an eye on these few potted plants for a week or two? The sad fact was that Mr and Mrs Braun who ordinarily took this responsibility had no talent for it. The plants, more often than not, suffered from their ministrations.

Well, Mr Hotchkiss had not been all that enthusiastic about saying yes. For one thing, he felt no great warmth for potted plants, especially this odd variety which appeared to be just a bunch of leaves and no flowers. For another thing, he suspected that if, when the Ostroffs returned home, there were anything wrong with even one of those multicolored leaves, he would be held responsible.

However, there was really no way out of it, so there he had been each day, watering and feeding according to instructions, and, most unpleasant duty of all, carefully examining each plant for the insidious mealybug.

This, according to Mrs Ostroff, loathing in her voice as she described it, was kind of a very tiny fuzzy white thing which destroyed any plant it could get its teeth into. And if, God forbid, found, it must be instantly exterminated by a solution of alcohol delicately applied with a swab. Otherwise—!

Grimly determined that there be no otherwise, Mr Hotchkiss each day did insect inspection, using a reading glass for the purpose. And it was with this particular duty that he found himself first mildly interested, then fascinated, then enamored of the plants. Really obsessed by those delicately formed leaves, their varieties of color, their infinite variations of pattern, and, as he finally admitted to himself, the fact that these small ornamental objects were actually living things wholly dependent on his good will and attention.

By the time the Ostroffs returned and relieved him of his duties, he had already started his own window garden of coleus. Then, as new varieties caught his eye in florist shops, he expanded the garden and kept expanding it until finally Mr Braun had to be called in for the construction of shelving and lighting the better to cosset the collection and keep order among it. There was indeed mealybug along the way, obscene little gray-white ovals which, when Mr Hotchkiss studied them with revulsion through the reading glass, seemed to stare back at him menacingly.

One or two precious plants were lost to them, but the alcohol solution did the trick for the rest. After that, along with their watering and feeding, there was also a rigorous mealybug inspection of each plant, and so mornings, from after breakfast to lunch, were pretty well taken up with this gardening.

The results, as the Ostroffs themselves enviously admitted, were worth it. The coleus thrived in all their glory, a southern exposure and added fluorescence making them considerably more impressive than the Ostroffs' rather meager specimens, the intense devotion they got certainly contributing to their magnificence. Mr and Mrs Ostroff could never, as they guiltily admitted, talk to their plants, although this was so highly recommended by some devotees.

'I'd feel like a fool,' said Mrs Ostroff. 'They don't have ears, do they? If something's got ears, then I'll talk to it.'

Mr Hotchkiss talked to his plants. At first he did it uneasily, whispering his praise of them, his encouragement of them almost inaudibly, glancing over his shoulder as he did so, as if some cynic might be standing there behind him sneering at this eccentricity. Then he became bolder. He crooned lovingly to the coleus, singled out some of the more dazzling plants for special attention, made sure the others would not be miffed by this favoritism by addressing kind remarks to them, and would bid them all an equally affectionate good night when the time came in the early evening to draw the shades of the bay windows and douse the fluorescent lighting.

Did they appreciate this? If the glowing velvety perfection of each leaf was the evidence, they appreciated it with all their flowery hearts.

Yes, Mr Hotchkiss would gratefully reflect as he entered the living room each new morning, this lovingly tended, orderly profusion of beauty was all that had been needed to make even more paradisiacal this neat little corner of paradise.

Not that the coleus made up his entire life. After all, here at his doorstep was glamorous Manhattan itself in its infinite, and often admission-free, variety. And at the Golden Age Club there were kinspirits, gentlemen and ladies both, eager to share visits to the park, concerts, museums, and, sometimes, movies, although movies calculated to entertain rather than shock were getting harder and harder to find. Safe in the streets as they wended their way around town? As Mr Hotchkiss put it, 'There's safety in numbers,' and so they always moved safely in a group. The wolves prowling the city were out for stragglers. With Mr Hotchkiss in charge of the outings, there never were any Golden Age stragglers.

Best of all were those afternoons when he entertained a select gathering in his own apartment, serving coffee and cake and getting as a reward the company's unstinted admiration of his coleus. He had, as one and all agreed, the greenest of all green thumbs.

So there it was. The coleus, the apartment, the city, the comparative good health except for a tendency to nervous stomach and occasional insomnia, neither of which, as he cheerfully recognized, was fatal. A good, contented retirement. Everything he had dreamed of during those long years grinding away at his bookkeeping.

The trouble started – though who could predict it at the time – when Mr Ostroff died, and a few weeks later Mrs Ostroff, forlorn in her widowhood, was induced to give up the apartment and move in with a daughter and son-in-law who had a room to spare in their fine Long Island home. The day before the removal, Mrs Ostroff called Mr Hotchkiss in and weepily presented him with some gifts of remembrance which he would just as soon have done without but could ill refuse. Her few coleus, all of them now in such wretched condition from neglect that they were plainly beyond salvation, and, in remembrance of her late husband and his pharmaceutical career, the heavy brass mortar and pestle which had once ornamented the window of his store and which had then become a centerpiece on the mantel over the Ostroff fireplace.

Mr Hotchkiss took the gifts, and when the donor was safely gone he disposed of the plants in his garbage can and, after lugging the mortar and pestle through the apartment searching for a place to store it until he could decently dispose of it, he decided to follow its donor's example and so set it on the mantelpiece over his fireplace. He felt it struck rather an odd note there, but when one of the ladies from the Golden Age Club who knew about such esoterica commented admiringly on it, he left it there, and in a very short while it seemed as familiar and properly in place as the multitude of coleus did on their tables and shelves.

Meanwhile, as could be seen through its frequently open door, the Ostroff apartment was undergoing a complete painting and polishing until one day a truckload of furniture was carted up the stairs to it. Mr Hotchkiss who up until now had not greatly concerned himself about the nature of his new neighbors took note that the furniture appeared to be brand-new, extremely ornate and expensive, and not in very good taste.

On his way out he stopped on the ground floor where Mr Braun was supervising the carting in of the furniture. Mr Braun's ordinarily sour expression now seemed almost amiable as he steered moving men and their loads through the foyer. On the other hand, Mrs Braun looked even grimmer than usual.

'I see the new tenants are here,' Mr Hotchkiss remarked.

Mrs Braun sniffed. 'Not them. Just one.'

'One?'

'By herself. An actress. She says.'

'If she says, then it's so, mama,' Mr Braun said reprovingly. 'You don't call people a liar for no reason.'

'Ho,' Mrs Braun said. She turned to Mr Hotchkiss. 'You know what is her name, she says? Choo Choo. That is a name? Choo Choo?'

'If the owner says she will be a good tenant,' said Mr Braun majestically, 'she will be a good tenant. Enough now.'

'What the owner says,' Mrs Braun declared, 'is only because now the apartment is no more rent controlled, he gets plenty more for it.'

According to city law, Mr Hotchkiss knew, when leasehold was given up on a rent-controlled apartment, the apartment did become subject to a stiff increase in rental. The thought made him that much more aware of his own pleasantly rent-controlled apartment.

He stopped at the mailboxes in the outer foyer before going out to the street. Sure enough, there was a new nameplate in the box of 2B – second floor rear – and it read C. C. Guilfoyle. C. C. for Choo Choo? Choo Choo Guilfoyle. Had the senior Guilfoyles really attached this curious name to their offspring? Unlikely, Mr Hotchkiss decided.

He went out to the street. There, giving sharp instructions to the moving men in their coming and going, was a young woman who must be C. C. Guilfoyle. A tall, slender, red-haired young woman, extremely long-legged and full-breasted, the tightness of sweater and shortness of skirt accentuating what Mr Hotchkiss had to admit was a really remarkable figure. A pretty girl too. Strikingly pretty. Well, well, Mr Hotchkiss thought, it wouldn't hurt the old building to have someone like this brightening it up. Indeed, from the reactions of male passersby, it was plain that he was not alone in appreciating the picture she made.

He walked over to her. 'Miss Guilfoyle?'

She warily took his measure. 'Uh huh.'

'Well, in that case, 'said Mr Hotchkiss brightly, 'I am your hallway neighbor. Upstairs. I just wanted to wish you welcome to your new home.'

'Yeah,' Miss Guilfoyle said chillingly. 'Well, thanks.' Evidently, she was not keen on neighborliness. She turned away and addressed herself to the moving men again, and Mr Hotchkiss left it at that. After all, the Ostroffs had occupied the second floor rear for ten years before they and Mr Hotchkiss had even visited each other's apartments. It was the New York style, the only way really to assure one's privacy in an overcrowded city.

So Miss Guilfoyle settled in, and, like the other tenants of the building, became largely invisible. And life in the building again moved on its placid course.

Until at a few minutes after four one morning – the darkest of the dark hours – when Mr Hotchkiss' sleep was blasted apart by a roaring and snarling which suggested nothing so much as a cageful of angry lions loosed into the bedroom and sounding off in furious temper. Two seconds later Mr Hotchkiss, sitting up in bed, his heart racing, realized that the lions were not there surrounding the bed but were outside in the street. Were not lions at all, but a car motor being raced as if the driver were warming it up for a recordbreaking run down the Indianapolis Speedway.

Actually, the uproar below was not all that unusual. Early every weekday morning, at about the time Mr Hotchkiss was breakfasting, there would be an intermittent racket up and down the block as cars, locked bumper to bumper against the curb where they had been parked overnight, would strain to pull free of each other and be on the move. But during daylight hours one accepted such noises as part of life in the big city.

Between midnight and dawn, however, noisy as the block might be during the day it now fell into a blessed silence. The occasional wail of a siren on an emergency vehicle rushing by, yes. The occasional loud voice of unsober revelers making their way to one of the buildings on the block, yes. But one was so accustomed to such as this that it never broke through the shell of a deep refreshing sleep.

But this roaring and snarling below was distinctly an aberration. Ear-shattering and nerve-shattering, it went on and on until Mr Hotchkiss crawled out of bed and made his way to the window. Sure enough the car was directly below. A monstrous object, one of those oversized, overpowered sports cars with such an exaggerated sweep and curve of chassis that it resembled a gleaming, low-slung snowplow. One of those noxious contrivances so streamlined that even when at rest it appeared to be lunging full speed ahead.

It was jockeying back and forth between the two vehicles which hemmed it in fore and aft, sometimes stopping between its small frustrated motions to crouch there and snarl savagely in resentment of its plight.

Back and forth it went, back and forth, until at last it maneuvered free, and with a long triumphant blast on its horn by the driver it was gone.

And, as far as Mr Hotchkiss was concerned, so was the rest of his night's sleep. No use even getting into bed again with this blazing sense of outrage in him. Good Lord, even granting that a car like that was constructed to be extraordinarily noisy, who, for heaven's sake, would want to own any such loud, wasteful toy unless he had no regard for his neighbors to start with? And that final blast of the horn was the most brutal stroke. The ultimate outrage.

Oh, well, Mr Hotchkiss told himself before he finally fell asleep long after dawn, no use dwelling on it forever. It was over and done with.

It was not.

It happened the next morning a few minutes before five o'clock.

It happened the morning after that at half-past three.

It did not happen the following morning, although it might as well have since Mr Hotchkiss came bolt awake at three o'clock, anticipating it.

Then, a day later, just as Mr Hotchkiss had taken desperate hope that perhaps this blight was permanently removed from his life, it happened once more.

He phoned the police and got sympathy. He got sympathy from his circle at the Golden Age Club, that and a recounting of similar blights afflicting them. He spoke to the tenant in the first floor front, elderly Mrs Gordon, and even as he put the question to her of how she bore this violent interruption to her slumbers before dawn almost every morning, he realized from her politely smiling expression of inquiry, her hand cupped to her ear, that of course it would take nothing less than an earthquake to interrupt her slumbers; she was deaf as a post.

He spoke to the Clearys on the top floor, third floor front, and discovered that they were happily addicted to sleeping pills which their kindly doctor had long ago prescribed. If he wanted the name of the doctor—?

As the blight continued through the second week and the third – loud mornings followed unpredictably by an occasional silent morning – Mr Hotchkiss found that his every waking moment was filled with black and vengeful thoughts of that unholy machine. There was a vampirish aspect to it, too, since the car was never in evidence during daylight hours.

Finally, much as he detested putting himself in the same category as those old ladies on the block who spent their time seated at their windows behind flimsy curtains, keeping an eye on their neighbors, Mr Hotchkiss planted himself at the open window of his bedroom after dinner one evening and kept tedious watch until the car made its appearance a little before midnight. There was no space for it directly in front of the house that night, but there was one a short distance away. He watched it enter the space and could foresee exactly what would happen when it strove to leave it in a few hours.

Then the driver pulled himself out of the car – a large bulky man, he needed an effort to do it – and moved down the street toward the house itself. Mr Hotchkiss heard the door below him open and close. He went quickly to his foyer door, opened it an inch, and peered out. The bulky figure tiptoed heavily up the stairway into his vision, a complete stranger, no one at all who belonged to the building, and stopped before Miss Guilfoyle's door. He thrust a key into the door, swung it open, and disappeared within.

Miss Guilfoyle's apartment.

So that was it.

Choo Choo Guilfoyle. An actress, indeed.

How shrewd Mrs Braun had been in her sour estimate of this new tenant.

But that was really not the issue. Mr Hotchkiss was no prude. Since it was always the same car, Miss Guilfoyle could hardly be charged with operating on a public basis. Indeed, if her – whatever you wanted to call him – her admirer would only exit the scene quietly after each visit, one could ask little more of the young lady as a neighbor. But to have her attended to by someone who kept blasting off before dawn like an astronaut headed for the moon – well, it made life absolutely intolerable.

And, face it, not only intolerable for him but for the coleus. Sensitive life forms that they were, responsive to every emotional current around them, they were no longer thriving. It took an eye like Mr Hotchkiss' to detect it, but to that eye it was plain that the glow was fading, the vigor departing from those leaves. What use to put on a falsely smiling face while watering and tending these plants, what use to heap encouragement and endearments on them, when, right down to their newest, barely formed leaves they saw through the mask? As long as their beloved caretaker knew only vengeful and bitter thoughts, all the sunshine and fluorescent lighting in the world would not suffice to brighten their days.

No, they would not long survive under these conditions.

The time had come for action.

But what action?

To knock on that door this moment, have it out politely but firmly with the gentleman caller, that was the ticket.

No, not this moment. It would be, Mr Hotchkiss suspected, the most awkward possible time for any such confrontation. But within a very few hours, the caller would be departing. He would be, to put it delicately, fulfilled. In a pleasant mood. Receptive to well-justified complaint.

Leaving the foyer door open the merest bit, Mr Hotchkiss settled himself behind it in a straightbacked chair – no chance of dozing off that way – and waited. It was a long aching wait, but a little before four o'clock he heard the sound of the door in the rear opening and stepped out into the hallway just as the gentleman caller emerged from Miss Guilfoyle's apartment.

Miss Guilfoyle, standing in her doorway in negligee, made an extremely attractive appearance. The man, Mr Hotchkiss took note, certainly did not. He was very large and bulky indeed, with a moonlike face somewhat too large for its snub nose, pursy lips, and piggish eyes. The only thing on that unpleasant face in proportion to it was a sweeping mustache. The mustache was gray, as was the elaborate hairdo. This was no young buck, Mr Hotchkiss saw at a glance, not at all the sort of man one would attribute that car to, but someone who was distinctly on the downhill side of middle age.

Gray. And so was the outfit he wore, matching jacket and trousers in pale gray suede. Modish it may have been on some young cavalier, but it made this boorish hulk resemble nothing so much as a gigantic mealybug. Exactly that. A veritable two-legged mountain of a mealybug.

The man stared as Mr Hotchkiss in robe and slippers approached him. 'Sir,' said Mr Hotchkiss, his voice discreetly lowered in view of the time and the place, 'there is something I would like to settle with you. When you—'

'What?' the man said in a loud whisper. 'Who the hell are you?'

'I happen to live in that apartment there which overlooks the street. And every time you visit here—'

'Every time you visit here?' The piggish eyes glared. 'What's that to you, mister?'

There seemed to be no way of delivering an uninterrupted sentence to this fellow. 'Sir,' Mr Hotchkiss said patiently, 'please understand that I am not meddling in your affairs.' Too late it struck him that this might not be the most politic way to put it. 'All I ask of you—'

This time the interruption came from a different direction. 'Oh, for God's sake, knock it off,' Miss Guilfoyle told the mealybug. 'It's getting late.'

The man wheeled on her. 'Is it? You know, baby, I'm getting the idea you do a lot of talking to the neighbors, don't you?'

'Me?' Miss Guilfoyle motioned at Mr Hotchkiss. 'To this little creep?' Then her lip curled scornfully. 'You've got that in your mind a lot, don't you?' she said to the man. 'My even saying one little word to anybody in the whole world.'

'That I do,' the man said. 'So keep it in mind, big mouth.' He put a hand against her overwhelming chest and thrust her back through the doorway. He turned to Mr Hotchkiss. 'As for you—' he said.

Mr Hotchkiss firmly held his ground. 'Sir, if you will hear me out—'

'As for you,' the man said, 'you just keep that pointy nose out of other people's business. My business especially.' He accompanied this with a violent shove against Mr Hotchkiss' distinctly unimpressive chest which sent Mr Hotchkiss staggering backward. 'Look here—' Mr Hotchkiss said in protest, but another shove sent him right through his own doorway, and then his door was pulled shut against him.

Mr Hotchkiss stood there in his foyer shaking with impotent outrage. Literally shaking, he realized. He couldn't even get his feet to move him off this spot.

The Urge to Kill.

His widowed mother, with whom he had lived and to whom he had devoted himself until her death – yes, his mother, that gentle soul, on rare occasions when she had been pushed to the point of ultimate exasperation by someone, would use that phrase, capitals and all. *I tell you, son, after what she did, I felt the Urge to Kill.*

He felt it now in every wildly vibrating nerve. If he had gun in hand this moment, he would gladly use it against that monstrous mealybug and his female and never mind the consequences. Fire every bullet into both of them until they fell down and lay writhing in their final agony. A prolonged agony.

Mr Hotchkiss stood there, his fist around the imaginary gun, and even from where he stood he suddenly heard the car snarl into action. Snarl and roar on and on endlessly until, at last, there was that familiar blast of the horn, a sound of departure, and silence.

That did it.

With an effort Mr Hotchkiss made his way into the living room. Wrong of him, he knew, to even enter the presence of the coleus with such waves of fury emanating from him, bewildering and terrifying them, shattering their nerves. Looking around at the row on row of plants, he had the feeling that, indiscernible as the motion might be, they were actually shrinking away from him. He, the caretaker, the fount of security and tenderness for them, was now providing what? Only catastrophe.

Simple choice. Either he and the coleus would be driven forever from their rent-controlled Eden, or he must strike an overwhelming blow in its defence.

But how could any effective blow be struck against a mustached and ruthless bravo who was twice one's size and strength?

A bullet from the bedroom window? A bomb tossed into that automobile? Ridiculous. Sheer fantasy.

The mortar and pestle on the mantelpiece caught Mr Hotchkiss' eye. He lifted out the pestle. Eight inches of solid metal, capped with a small knob at one end, a large one at the other. And heavy. Mr Hotchkiss hefted it, considered it, his thoughts racing frantically, until little by little they took on craftily logical form.

Yes. Oh, yes.

He slipped the pestle into the pocket of his robe, keeping a concealing hand over its smaller knob. He want out into the hallway and pressed the bell on Miss Guilfoyle's door. Her expression, when she appeared, all raised eyebrows and knowing smile, suggested that she was prepared to welcome the apologetic return of her angry cavalier. Her face hardened at the sight of her caller. 'Oh, it's you, is it?'

'Yes,' said Mr Hotchkiss. 'Miss Guilfoyle, I'm aware that I've made some difficulties for you. I must speak to you about that right now.'

'All you have to do, mister—'

'Right now,' Mr Hotchkiss said firmly. He aimed a commanding finger at the interior of her apartment. 'Inside, please. In private.'

'Look, mister—'

'Oh, I realize that you are, so to speak, under orders, Miss Guilfoyle,' said Mr Hotchkiss, 'but even so—'

'Me?' said Miss Guilfoyle incredulously. 'Under orders?'

'Well, I did have the impression—'

Miss Guilfoyle motioned him into her living room. 'Now let's get something straight,' she said.

Mr Hotchkiss aimed the finger again, this time at the couch occupying the center of the room. 'Please sit down. All I ask is that you bear with me for one minute. After that—'

'One minute?'

'Less.'

Miss Guilfoyle seated herself firmly, her face stony. She raised her arm and fixed her eyes on a jeweled wristwatch. 'Exactly one minute,' she said, 'and then it's my turn.'

'Of course,' said Mr Hotchkiss as he withdrew the pestle from his pocket and brought it down on her skull as hard as he could. Her arm dropped into her lap, but she remained in the same sitting position. He struck again and again until she fell forward on the floor. He gingerly sounded her pulse to make sure there was no beat at all, and then returned to his apartment, leaving her door wide open.

There had been no blood spilled, as far as he saw, but when he examined the pestle closely he saw that, yes, there were telltale stains on it. He washed them off carefully under the kitchen faucet, then brought to the table the mortar and three of the most leafy coleus. He transplanted them, good moist earth and all, into the mortar, arranging the pestle as a center-piece sunk deep into the earth, only its small end showing a bit above the surface and the coleus leaves luxuriantly surrounding it.

He placed the mortar back on the mantelpiece and put a few plants from the shelves on either side of it. A little readjustment of the pots on the shelves closed the gaps among them, and all that remained to do was wash out and store away the pots from which the transplanted coleus had been removed

Done.

He was wakened from the most satisfying sleep he had known for weeks by a ringing of the doorbell along with a lusty banging on the door. Ten o'clock. When he opened the door two men were standing there, and there was a uniformed policeman standing at rest in front of Miss Guilfoyle's door. One of the men held out a wallet toward him to display the badge pinned to it.

'Police,' the man informed Mr Hotchkiss succinctly. 'Lieuten-ant Noble.' He motioned at his companion. 'Detective Gomez. I take it you're Mr Hotchkiss?'

'Yes.'

'We'd like to ask you some questions. Mind if we come in?'

'Not at all.' As Mr Hotchkiss led them into the living room, he saw that he had not yet drawn up the shades of the bay windows, thus depriving the coleus of several precious hours of daylight. He drew them up, and Lieutenant Noble surveyed the array of plant life with interest. 'Well now, looks like the Botanic Gardens, don't it?'

'Yes,' said Mr Hotchkiss. 'But questions, you said. Questions about what? Is something wrong?'

'You might call it that. Lady across the hall there. Guilfoyle. You know her?'

'We exchanged a few words once or twice. She only moved in recently.'

'So the super tells me. Well, she was killed last night. Beat to death.'

'Good heavens!' said Mr Hotchkiss.

'Yeah. People upstairs saw her door wide open on their way down to work, and there she was. Now I'd like you to take a look at this' – the lieutenant held out a large photograph toward Mr Hotchkiss – 'and tell me if you know this guy. Ever seen him around?'

There was no mistaking that face decorated by that grotesque mustache. 'But that was the man—' Mr Hotchkiss said.

'Yeah?'

'Well, he was right out there in the hall last night. Actually, this morning. About four o'clock.'

'And you saw him? How did that happen?'

'I don't sleep well sometimes – I suffer from insomnia – and last night was one of my bad nights. I was up and doing when I heard a noise in the hallway. That's very unusual here at that hour.'

'And then?'

'Then I opened my door and saw this man facing Miss Guilfoyle at her open door.'

'In a bad mood maybe? Angry? Threatening?'

'Well, that didn't become evident until I approached them. When he saw me he became enraged. He said something to Miss Guilfoyle about talking too freely to people. Then he pushed her right through the doorway. Hard.'

'And?'

'When I tried to intercede he did the same to me. He was really very powerful. He pushed me right down the hall through my door and slammed it on me. But since Miss Guilfoyle hadn't asked for my help—'

'She didn't seem scared?'

'No, angry rather. So I let it go at that. If I had known—'

'Well,' said Lieutenant Noble, 'you did what you could. More than most, matter of fact. Anyhow, we already nailed the guy. Wasn't hard. She had only a couple of addresses in her book and this picture on her dresser. But so far he's denying everything. He'd be a tough nut to crack too. Big businessman, high society wife, that kind of stuff. Now it looks like you wrapped him up for us. You understand you'll have to testify about all this, don't you? And it happened exactly the way you said?'

'Exactly,' Mr Hotchkiss said.

'Good. I have to run along now, but Gomez here'll stand by. You get yourself dressed, have your coffee, whatever, and then he'll drive you down to the DA.' Lieutenant Noble turned his attention to the plant life around him, openly admiring it. 'My wife had one like that,' he said, 'then some damn bugs moved in on it and she had to get rid of it.'

'Sometimes it's the only thing you can do,' said Mr Hotchkiss.

# Generation Gap

She had been named Elizabeth, but it very soon became Bitsy, and Bitsy it stayed even after she got her growth. Which was a drag, but not so much of a drag that you couldn't live with it. Matter of fact, this was how just about everything in the whole world shaped up: a drag, but not so much of a drag that you couldn't live with it. And when you really started to go down, down, down, there was always The Sound – the delicious blast of it on transistor or stereo – to help pick you up again. Life, let's face it, was at its best when it was strictly audio.

At sixteen, Bitsy just about had her growth. An Aquarius, tall, skinny, and, from the front at least, straight up and down. From the back – well, a few of the boys in school had already let her know that, walking away from them in those jeans, man, she really turned them on. Also, she had that straight blonde hair coming almost down to the handworked leather belt, and those big pale blue eyes – made all the bigger when she laid on the eyeliner and eyelash darkener – and a cute nose, and what with one thing and another she was, as she admitted to herself, definitely on the up side. That is, allowing for some minor skin trouble now and then.

Of course, it still didn't put her in a class with Sis, a ripe twenty, front and back. And, add to the injustice of it, Sis was born with brains enough for two which, as Pa kept pointing out, was a lucky thing because Bitsy herself didn't have brains enough for one. Big joke. But one had to face the facts. There was Sis, out of high school and right into that filing and typing job at the Fort Myers Citizens Bank, and here was Bitsy who could just about make it through roll call in school before the fog set in.

What made Sis bearable at all, really, was that she still had one foot on the right side of the generation gap. There were signs she was already starting to go uptight like Ma and Pa, but she sometimes did remember how it had been for her four years ago and sometimes even acted like a True Friend. Take hitchhiking. Ma and Pa were death on hitchhiking. Somehow they had got it into their pointy little heads that the world was full of evil men just itching to hand lollipops to little girls and then rip them off. But until she had put together enough money to get her own car, Sis had hitchhiked, and while Ma and Pa had never known about it, Bitsy had. And now Bitsy hitchhiked, and Sis knew about it, and, True Friend, kept her mouth shut about it.

Well, except for one time.

That was the time Bitsy had hitched all the way back home alone from that Disneyland weekend with some girl friends and had carelessly let herself be dropped off at the shopping plaza just when Sis was parking in the plaza one jump away. Sis had ordered her in the car and cut loose then and there. 'Was that messy stud with the pickup the one who got you back to town?'

'Mmm,' said Bitsy.

'Then you listen to me. Are you listening?'

'Mmm.'

'There's plenty of family folks on the road to ride with, and from now on that's who you ride with, stupid. No more studs like that, you hear?'

'Mmm,' said Bitsy. She reached out to switch on the radio, but Sis pushed her hand away from it. Bitsy leaned back in her seat and closed her eyes. It wasn't all that hard to get The Sound in your head without even switching on the radio.

'Are you still listening?' Sis said slowly and loudly.

'Mmm.'

'Then no more studs, you hear? And another thing. If somebody stops, and you see a six-pack right there on the seat, you stay clear, because it could mean trouble. From now on, family folks only, you hear?'

'The way you talk,' Bitsy said tiredly, 'how can I help hearing?'

Sis often spoke like that to her, a little too slow, a little too loud, the way you'd talk to somebody who was deaf. Or, let's face it, somebody who was so fuzzy in the brain that she had to have things said to her the way they said it in the Dick and Jane schoolbooks when she was a kid. Run, Dick, run. Careful, Bitsy, careful.

Except you weren't supposed to show Sis you resented it. If you did, Sis resented your resenting it.

'You mind your manners when I talk to you,' Sis now told her.

'All right, all right,' said Bitsy. 'From now on, only family folks.'

Meaning, naturally, uptight old men like Pa. It couldn't possibly mean getting hitches from cars where there was a family team up front. Nothing on the road went by faster than that kind of a car. Maybe the man at the wheel would like to slow down and lend a hand to a sixteen-year-old Aquarius in tight jeans, but sure as God made little green apples, the lady next to him was not going to buy that package.

Family folks. Like Pa.

She lived up to it too. On trips home from school where she would ask to be dropped off a couple of blocks from the house so Ma wouldn't catch on, and on jumps out of town to kinfolk in Sarasota and Manatee. Truth to tell, although she had no intention of letting Sis in on it, that messy stud in the pickup had scared her a little, what with all the handwork he was trying out on her thigh and meanwhile whooping it down the highway at seventy an hour. And, as if to show that Sis knew what she was talking about, there had been a six-pack on the seat, all of it gone by the time they pulled into Fort Myers. So it really wasn't that much of a drag letting the studs go by and keeping an eye out for something in Pa's class.

She even lived up to it all the way across Florida on the big Thanksgiving trip to Cousin Sheralyn's in South Miami. Big was the word for that trip, because from the way Pa carried on counting out the bus fare, you'd have to believe he was paying for a trip twice around the world. It gave you something to think about, all right, how he would carry on if he knew that almost all the bus fares he had been laying out for quite a while were going, not to the bus company, but for the essentials of life. Records, hair stuff, face stuff, clothes, fast food. Put it all together it didn't really add up to all that much, but it was the difference between life and death. Death came when you ran out of your week's allowance two days after you got it and Sis said no, she wouldn't lend you even a raggedy dollar bill because you were just as knotheaded about money as about everything else.

So, Ma's old valise in hand and all that beautiful bus money tucked away in her shoulder bag, Bitsy made it down to Naples as guest of an exterminator-service salesman, a sad case who talked about termite control the whole trip, and then, by way of that straight, wide-open, hundred-mile run along the Tamiami Trail through the Everglades, she was fetched right into the middle of Miami by a bank-president type driving a gilt-edged Cadillac. Not too bad, except that this one kept the radio tuned to news broadcasts all the way, even when, after a while, it was the same news broadcasts all over again.

Anyhow, news broadcasts or not, there she was in the middle of Miami, which turned out to be a lot bigger city than Fort Myers, so that she had to ask directions a few times and haul that suitcase a lot of distance before she wound up at the bus depot and phoned Cousin Sheralyn to come pick her up. Cousin Sheralyn was seventeen and drove the family car sometimes. She was also the one who, the Thanksgiving before when she had been Bitsy's guest at Fort Myers, had said that once you did the Thomas Edison house and some hunting for shells on Sanibel Island you just about had Fort Myers, and you really had to see Miami to know where the action was, and that was why this whole trip. Now she turned up at the bus depot in the car, and the first thing she said to Bitsy was, 'Did you really hitchhike it all the way, like you said you would?'

'Mmm,' said Bitsy. She showed Cousin Sheralyn all those five-dollar bills in the shoulder bag. 'Supposed to be bus money. Only now it's fun money.'

'Man,' said Cousin Sheralyn, her eyes opening wide, 'you really do have something going, don't you? I wish I had the nerve.'

Then she drove Bitsy to her house, keeping the car radio at full volume so that the two of them would not only hear The Sound but feel it, the way it was meant to be felt, and there was

Aunt Willa Mae and Uncle Frank and the two older boy cousins, a couple of clowns really, all of them waiting to dig into the turkey and trimmings.

'My,' said Aunt Willa Mae, 'you get taller every time I see you, Bitsy. I bet you're taller than Sis now.'

'Mmm,' said Bitsy.

'And how's your ma?'

'All right,' said Bitsy.

'And your pa?'

'All right,' said Bitsy, and that, all formalities attended to nicely, took care of the old folks.

From then on it was one of those holiday times to remember the rest of your life. Miami was where the action was, no argument about it. Mornings, trying to surfboard off the end of Miami Beach with everybody the right age and all high on sun, salt water, and some grass now and then. Afternoons, a lot of driving around, seeing outside and inside those Gold Coast hotels you'd only see in the movies otherwise, and a lot of souvenir hunting, and along Flagler Street into the record shops, all mixed up with a lot of eating any time you felt like it.

Nighttimes, out to one place after another for the dancing and fooling around and more eating. The fooling around, which Sis had also warned Bitsy about in that Dick and Jane style, turned out to be strictly nothing, since both boy cousins were always nearby and both of them linebacker types. Bitsy agreed with Cousin Sheralyn that it was a drag being supervised like this, but actually she didn't mind it all that much. As far as she could see, it certainly saved her the trouble of making some decisions she'd just as soon not make.

Anyhow, as Aunt Willa Mae said, all good things had to come to an end sometime, so Sunday, right after lunch, Bitsy got her stuff together for Cousin Sheralyn to take her to the bus depot. It turned out that what with all the souvenirs and the new-bought decorated T-shirts and beach hats and the pile of new records, Bitsy found that she needed an extra piece of luggage, whereupon Uncle Frank dug up a good strong carton, and into it went all the extras and around it went a strong piece of cord. So, as if to show what kind of wild weekend it had been, when Bitsy went out to the car where Cousin Sheralyn was waiting to take her to the bus depot she was carrying not only the valise but that carton.

Cousin Sheralyn took a look at the carton. 'You got any money left at all?' she asked.

Bitsy opened the shoulder bag and showed her what was left. One dollar and two nickels.

'I thought so,' said Cousin Sheralyn. 'Well, I'll drop you off Eighth Street downtown. That's the Trail. You can start hitching right there.'

'Mmm,' said Bitsy.

'But don't you ever let your folks know I didn't put you on that bus. It'll get right back to my folks, and I hate to tell you what would happen to me then.'

'A real drag,' said Bitsy.

She got off at Eighth Street which didn't look at all like the Tamiami Trail there, just a busy corner full of Latins walking all around and Spanish signs on all the stores, and as soon as Cousin Sheralyn drove off, she arranged the valise and the carton at her feet near the curb, and when a likely-looking car went by, pointed her finger westward. Plenty went by, and for those on the lookout for family-type folks there seemed to be an assortment in almost every car, and none with any idea of stopping.

A couple of one-man cars did pull up and stop, but in both cases this was stud stuff – Latin stud at that – so Bitsy gave them a head-shake, and then, when they persisted in being friendly out of the car window, she just turned her back on them until they took off.

Finally a small truck pulled over, one of those emergency trucks with a hoist in back. The man driving it, strictly family-type except he needed a shave, leaned out and said to Bitsy, 'How far?'

'Fort Myers,' said Bitsy.

'Nope. Just going back to the shop little past Forty Mile Bend on the Trail. But if it'll help any, hop right in.'

So she planted the valise and carton in back of the truck and hopped right in, and that way got as far as a gas station and garage right out in the middle of nowhere, halfway along the Trail. Like every other business along the Trail here, this was on the eastbound side of the road heading back to Miami, so she lugged the valise and the carton across to the westbound side and took up her station there. Trouble was, not much went by, and what did go by looked like it was out to break all speed records. Even the bus she was supposed to have been on went by so fast that it was almost out of sight down the road when she suddenly realized that the sign over its front window had said *Fort Myers* and she felt depressed about that. And, of course, the cars that did pull in at the gas station across the road were mostly heading in the wrong direction.

After a while one of the men from the gas station walked across to her and said, 'You figure to stand out here like a sore thumb with a red, white, and blue bandage on it, girlie, you are sure going to buy yourself a lot of trouble in about ten minutes when the police patrol goes by. They are real hardnosed about this kind of hitchhike stuff right now. Had a bad time account of it couple of months ago. And not so far down the road from here, neither.'

'I have to get a hitch,' Bitsy said.

'All the same, girlie, if you don't want cop trouble, you will hang around for a spell in that ladies room over there. I'll let you know when the patrol goes by.'

Maybe it was a put-on, but it didn't seem to be. So Bitsy took the valise and carton with her into the ladies room and hung around there looking through the screened window at the swamp country out in back until the man knocked on the door and said, 'Okay now, girlie. They just went by.'

So it was back across the road with the valise and carton, and, from the way it looked, nothing to do but stand there and watch the cars whoosh by and feel more and more down about it. Then when she was right near bottom, a car slowed down passing her and came to a stop about fifty feet up ahead. She grabbed up the valise and carton, but the car slowly started off again, and all she could do was stand there feeling like a fool. The car only went about ten feet more though, and stopped again. It was an old black sedan, looked like something out of the museum, but without a dent in it and with a high shine. A weirdo car all right. And with a weirdo driver, too, what with this stop and start business. As if to prove that, he now stuck his jug-eared head out of the window and called back, 'You looking for a ride, girl?'

Mister Weirdo himself, because what did he think she was looking for?

She didn't even bother to answer, just headed down the road as fast as she could with the valise and carton banging her legs, hoping he wouldn't change his mind again before she got there. The one good part of it was that she was still playing by the rules Sis had laid down. The car was sure family-style – it looked like the kind of thing you lay away all week and drive only to church – and when she got up to it she could see that the driver might have been the deacon of the church. A redneck with gray hair chopped short in a real redneck haircut, but still he was all dressed up in a black suit and white shirt and necktie.

But old Mister Weirdo himself all right. Anybody picked you up on the road was likely to have a friendly way about him. This one, when she came up to him out of breath, looked anything but friendly. Then, when she tried to open the back door to shove her things in, she found it was locked. 'Hey,' she said, but he made no move to open the door, just looked at her through the open window, taking her in.

'Your folks know you travel around like this?' he asked.

'Mmm,' Bitsy said.

'What's that mean?'

'It means they know.'

'You sure of it?'

'Yes. Anyhow, what's the difference?'

He appeared to think this over, his lips pulled into a thin line, his eyes squinting at her. 'That's the truth,' he finally said. 'It don't make any difference, does it?' He reached over to unlock both doors, and Bitsy got the valise and carton on the back seat, then got into the front seat with him.

He started the car off. 'Where you supposed to be headed for?'

'Fort Myers,' Bitsy said. 'You going all the way there?'

'No.'

All right, but at least she was heading in the right direction. She looked over the dashboard to find the radio dial and found there was no radio dial. No radio, believe it or not. She dug into her shoulder bag and came up with the baby transistor. She put it to her ear, tuning it in to get The Sound, and after a while she did. Mister Weirdo didn't seem to mind. He just kept the car moving along at a speed where anything else going their way easily passed them by.

He seemed to be keeping his eyes straight ahead on the road, but Bitsy could tell that every now and then he was giving her a slantwise look, taking her in from top to bottom. It made her realize that there was no bra under her T-shirt with the *Miami Beach* written across it and the palm trees painted on. On the other hand, there was nothing so special under the shirt – as there would be, say, with Sis – to make him pop his cork. So here you had one of those times where what was almost always a drag could be a kind of a comfort.

Then she caught him looking square at her. He didn't seem flustered by this. Only came on more squinty-eyed and thin-lipped than ever. 'Kind of pretty ain't you?' he said.

Bitsy shifted over in her seat a little, but she was up against the door as it was. She pressed the transistor hard against her ear to cut out that redneck voice, but it wasn't all that easy.

'I had a daughter about like you,' said Mister Weirdo. 'Used to travel around the same way, and I never knew about it. So your folks don't really know the way you go hitchhiking, do they?'

'Mmm,' said Bitsy.

'What's that mean? You got a mouth, don't you? Why don't you open it up and talk like people?'

Bitsy showed him the transistor. 'I'm listening to this,' she pointed out. 'I can't listen to everything at the same time.'

'Then you listen to me!' He suddenly snatched the transistor right out of her hand and jammed it down on the seat. The way he did it, he probably wrecked it. She reached for it and he slapped her hand away. 'I said you listen to me. I was telling you about my girl. Same age as you. Just as pretty. Same kind of long blondie hair too.'

So it wasn't lollipops they came on with when you got to this age. It was talk about their pretty girl just like you. And with blondie hair just like yours, so next thing there would be that big old hand stroking your hair to show you. And working its way right down your back. And that would just be the start of it. No lollipops for grownup girls. Just that slow, roundabout come-on easing things along to big, big trouble.

But even if you could somehow get clear of the car, what do you do about Ma's valise and that carton?

And for sure this was Mister Weirdo's kind of country they were now traveling through. Empty wherever you looked with not even a gas station or hamburger stand showing up any more. Just a lot of swamp greenery and sickly looking trees. Bitsy pushed so tight up against the door that the handle of it hurt her side.

He was watching her like a hawk now. 'You scared?' he asked.

Bitsy shook her head to show she wasn't.

'Yes, you are.' He seemed to like the idea. 'And that's all right. That's like it should be when you climb in a car with some man you don't even know. That's what you should have in your head before you start climbing in. Afterward is maybe a little too late, ain't it?'

Bitsy started to answer, but it stuck in her throat. She cleared her throat to get it out. 'Nothing to be scared about,' she said.

'You mean you don't care what a man can do to you? Kind of free and easy with men, is that it?'

'No,' Bitsy said. 'Look, you can let me out here. It's all right. I can get a hitch from somebody else.'

'You sit right where you are. And no tricks, hear?'

'You let me out.'

'Like I already told you, girl, it's too late for that. I didn't pull no gun on you and make you get in here, did I? You did it all on your own.'

While he was saying this he was slowing down the car, squinting up the road on the other side like he was looking for something there. Then when the car was really slowed down he grabbed her wrist and held it tight so that for the few seconds when she could have just walked out of that door she had no chance to.

With his other hand he turned the wheel hard and pulled the car right across the road and into a clearing among the trees. Dried twigs cracked under the wheels and the car rocked from

549

side to side on the bumpy ground, but it kept crawling further and further away from the road.

'You let me out!' Bitsy said. 'I am scared.'

'Maybe not enough yet.'

There was a freaked-out answer for you. The worst of it was she had heard about crazies like this. They got some of their kicks from what they did to you. But they got even more from watching you be scared because of it. So here she was, acting up just the way he liked. And not able to keep herself from doing it, either.

The road was well out of sight when he stopped the car among some scraggly trees. He reached across her to shove open the door and then pushed her right through it, still holding her wrist and following almost on top of her. He snatched the shoulder bag loose and tossed it on the seat next to the transistor. 'Come on,' he said. 'I want to show you something.'

'There's cops on that road,' Bitsy said. 'The gas-station man told me so. They go right up and down all the time. They could be coming right now.'

'No,' the man said. 'They ain't coming now. They only come after it's all over. A couple of months after it's all over. Now look there.' He pointed. 'Right there.'

Bitsy looked. Nothing but a patch of beat-up dead grass. He dragged her toward it, and for all she dug in her heels and tried to hold back it was no use.

'Right here,' the man said. He gripped the nape of her neck between his fingers and pushed her head down as if making sure she got a good look. 'This is where the cops show up after it's all over. Then you know what they do? They come knock on the door and they say, "Mister, you remember that little girl of yours that never got back home again couple of months ago? Well, it seems like she was always hitchhiking around, and she finally got picked up by a real bad one. We think we just found what's left of her, so you come along with us and see if it's really her."'

Those fingers digging into her neck had Bitsy bent almost double now. Her eyes were all filled up so that everything looked watery. 'Let go!' she said. 'You're hurting me.'

He didn't let go. 'You ain't hurting,' he said. 'You don't know what hurting is. Not till a man does what he wants with you until he's tired of it, and then beats you to death. That's when you'll find out, won't you?'

'Yes,' Bitsy sobbed.

Now he took his hand from her neck and let her straighten up and wipe her runny nose with the back of her hand. He turned her by the arm so that she faced him. 'Girl,' he said, 'you understand what I'm trying to get into that dumb babyface head of yours?'

'Yes,' Bitsy said, her eyes brimming over. 'Look, mister, there's that valise in the car and it's a real good valise. And that other box has a lot of good things in it. I swear it has. You can have both of them if you let me go. And the transistor.'

He dropped her arm and stood there facing her like that. All of a sudden he looked beat-up and tired. All washed out. 'God Almighty,' he said, and turned and started walking back to the car. Bitsy watched him go, not believing it. At the car he motioned to her. 'Come on. I'll get you far as Naples.'

Bitsy still wasn't moving.

'You better come on,' said Mister Weirdo. 'You stand around there any longer, you are going to have swamp snakes crawling right over your feet.'

This time Bitsy did move.

And he did drive her right to the bus depot in Naples, the old car really putting out all the way. Bitsy sat as far from him as she could, tight up against the door again, and after a while she got her mirror out of the shoulder bag and did a job on her face, which was a mess. Then she tried out the transistor and found that even with the banging around it had taken it was still working fine.

Too bad in a way, because when she was let out at Naples she'd have to give it up along with the valise and carton. No sense trying to back out of the deal and stirring up old Mister Weirdo again. The smart thing was to let him go drive away with his loot and then tell Ma and Pa it was stolen from her in the Miami bus depot. They'd believe her all right, because why shouldn't they? Better that than ever let them find out about all the hitchhiking.

But right there at the bus depot in Naples, Mister Weirdo

showed he was as freaked-out as ever. He pulled up the car and said to Bitsy, 'Tell me the truth, girl. You got money on you for that bus ride?'

'No,' said Bitsy.

'I figured not.'

And then what did he do but get out of the car with her and haul out the valise and carton and go right along with her to the ticket window and buy her a ticket for Fort Myers. So he hadn't let her go because of him settling for the valise and carton and transistor, and that was just about the weirdest part of it. It was really something to think about. Then Bitsy stood there, ticket in one hand, transistor in the other, valise and carton at her feet, and watched him walk out into the street, that redneck haircut of his finally getting lost among the people there, and that was the last she saw of him.

She waited to make sure he was really gone, then went to the door and peeked out to see if the car was gone too, and it was. So she went back to the ticket window and told the girl there she had changed her mind and wanted to get the money back for her ticket, and, no trouble at all, it was taken care of.

So that was that, and she even had some money to show for it.

Getting up to Fort Myers went the way everything should have gone from the start. Bitsy carried her things out to the street some distance from the depot and made it plain she was looking for a hitch until along came this stripped-down job with kind of a nice-looking stud at the wheel, big beard and a big gold earring, tape deck blasting away so you could hear it right across the Gulf, and he got her to Fort Myers in no time. And except for some pushing and pulling she had to do with that wandering hand of his, with no trouble at all. In fact, he made the run up the coast so fast that she walked into the Fort Myers depot only about an hour after the bus she might have been on checked in.

She phoned the house, hoping it would be Sis, not Ma or Pa, and her luck, it was Sis. Fifteen minutes later Sis showed up at the back end of the depot in her car and helped get Bitsy's stuff into it. By this time Bitsy was really loaded up for Sis. During that fifteen minutes she had wondered if maybe she shouldn't keep it all to herself, but the more she thought of it the more she knew she'd never be able to hold it in. She had too much to settle with Sis.

As soon as they were in the car she said to Sis, 'You and your family folks.'

'What?' said Sis.

'You know what. You said I should only look to ride with family folks. And that's what I've been doing. And you know what happened on account of it?'

'Suppose you tell me,' said Sis, jockeying the car out into the street.

'All right, I will. I got picked up by real family folks on the Trail coming back just now. I mean *real* family folks,' Bitsy said, making it slow and loud the way Sis always did. 'Like, you know, a shiny old black car and somebody driving it dressed up maybe for a funeral. Real family folks,' she said even slower and louder.

'And?' said Sis.

'And first place he could find that was all empty, this nice old man drove off into the swamp there and pulled me out of his nice old car.'

'Bitsy!' Sis said. She stepped on the brake, not evening noticing they were right in the middle of traffic, cars all going by and honking at them. Then she got her wits halfway together and pulled over to the curb and parked there. 'Bitsy, what happened? You tell me straight out what happened, you hear?'

'I *am* telling you. He pulled me out of the car and he showed me where it was going to happen when he was good and ready and he talked wild trying to scare me and he choked me too. Because maybe you don't know about it, but some of those nice old family folks you're so high on are crazies. And this one sure was.'

'But what else did he do? Did he—?'

'No,' Bitsy said, 'he didn't. All of a sudden he just turned off. Just like that. Like he wasn't interested in the whole thing any more. Then he drove me the rest of the way to Naples, and I got another hitch there.'

Sis took a deep breath. 'You're lying,' she said. 'You're making up the whole thing.'

'I am not lying,' Bitsy said very slowly and loudly.

Sis didn't seem convinced. 'You mean some man practically kidnapped you? And got you all alone? And got himself all worked up about it? And then when it came time for the big finish he just turned off? Look, Bitsy—'

'But I told you what he was like, didn't I?' Bitsy said. It almost made up for that whole bad scene in the swamp, because for the first time she could ever remember, she was on the telling end, and Sis, like it or not, was on the listening end. 'Don't you see? No matter how much he got himself worked up for a big finish, he couldn't do anything about it because he was just too old. Honest to God, Sis, he was at least as old as Pa!'

# The Family Circle

That day – it happened to be the very same day President Truman scored his upset victory at the polls over Thomas E. Dewey – Howard, then in his senior year at college, walked into his dormitory room, and his roommate said, 'Oh, there, Wicks, there's something you ought to know.'

'Yes?' said Howard, a little surprised to find his roommate in such a loquacious mood. From first acquaintance the two of them had got along nicely by almost never addressing each other. This was not out of animosity. The roommate was a cadaverous, unkempt genius at science, sweating it out on a full scholarship, forever deep in his books, who had made it plain from the outset that he had no time whatsoever for idle conversation. Howard, plump, neat as a pin, and not a genius at anything, had been tongue-tied from childhood in the presence of any member of the human race, including his immediate family. For as long as he could remember, he had suffered from the deep-rooted conviction that as soon as he opened his mouth and let a word out he was being weighed and found wanting.

Now, on being addressed at this unusual length by his roommate, he said a little warily, 'What ought I to know?' and the roommate said, 'Your father just died. Some kind of car crash. Your sister phoned and wants you to get home right away.'

So Howard took the plane home to Midlandsville, Minnesota, that night and never came back to college again. He intended to – or, more precisely, he didn't intend not to – but, as it turned out, he never did. Not even to pack and ship home his belongings. At the close of term when he was planning to go

555

east and attend to this chore, his mother firmly pointed out that the college authorities could very well attend to it for him, and that was how it was attended to.

As it turned out, it never did matter that Howard failed to earn a diploma. He had reluctantly entered college only because it was the thing to do and because money was certainly no problem. And it happened to be a faraway and very Ivy League college because his mother's father had been a distinguished alumnus of it – captain of the football team in his time, president of the senior class – and his mother had maintained a sentimental regard for the place.

What Howard himself had found there were three years of unalloyed loneliness. Lonely even in the bosom of the family, he was at least identifiable to those around him. At college he sometimes had the feeling that he had simply become invisible. A competent if not shining student, he was the one least likely to be called on in class, and on those rare occasions when he was called on, it was noticeable that the instructor, whichever it was, had to do some awkward brow-wrinkling and finger-snapping before he could attach the name to the body. It was also noticeable, at least to Howard, that at any social gathering on or off campus, no matter how crowded it might be, he always had plenty of elbow room. Not rejected, really. Simply, so to speak, not present.

His only pleasure during school terms was, inevitably, a solitary pleasure. One can play golf solo, and so Howard did. A neat, consistent game of straight short drives, careful iron play, and sound putting. Very sound putting. Watching the ball find its way over a rolling green into the cup ten feet away, Howard felt he was as close to being blissfully happy as he ever could be.

Back home in Midlandsville, however, the college life now only a vaguely unpleasant memory, it seemed there wasn't much opportunity for the playing of games. The late Mr Wicks had been his wife's zealously devoted attendant from the day he first laid eyes on her until his untimely death. It was Howard's obligation, his widowed mother soon let him know, to fill the gap made by his father's departure. No hypocrite, she didn't whine or wheedle or play forlorn in passing along this information. Mrs Wicks was a strikingly handsome woman, strong-willed, sharp-tongued, and with a penchant for stating the facts as she saw them.

She was also a woman who had suffered two gross betrayals, a condition which did nothing to sweeten her prevailing mood. Howard's older sisters, Regina and Ada, as handsome and imperious as their mother, had each made what Mrs Wicks regarded as an impossible marriage. The Wickses were by far the richest family in the area, their home on the ridge overlooking town a well-kept monument to the most extravagant late Victorian architecture and landscaping. Inevitably, as the sisters blossomed into maidenhood, the Wicks' place became a magnet for a number of highly eligible suitors. Then, abruptly, all were rejected for a pair of ruggedly virile and good-looking ineligibles who, catching the girls during the brief romantic phase of their lives, swept them off to the most commonplace of commonplace existences.

For Regina it was Vernon Birkenshaw, physical training instructor at Midlandsville High School. For Ada, only three months later, it was Thomas Dove, well-regarded by the townsfolk as the best mechanic in the Midlandsville Garage. Mr Wicks, who had worked his way up from the bottom to make a cool million and wed into the town's most aristocratic family, rather liked his new sons-in-law. But for Mrs Wicks one disaster following hard on another made the ultimate nightmare, the one you know you'll never wake up from.

Consequently, the wedding portion in each case was the bare minimum needed to keep face in the community: a trim little house right there in the newly developed tract at the foot of the ridge. Certainly this was not what the brides had anticipated, not from their adoring and wealthy father, but it was their mother who had the last word, and so Regina and Ada had to settle for what they loudly and clearly regarded as an outright insult.

Mr Wicks had borne up under this a little while, and then, an uneasy eye on his wife, had started to weaken. Perhaps, he suggested, a partnership for Vernon in distinguished Midlandsville Boys Academy might be in order. And considering that the Midlandsville Garage would be a sound investment, there was no good reason why Thomas should be a grease-monkey there when full ownership could be obtained for a fair price. As it happened, Mrs Wicks could come up with several good reasons, all having to do with heedless and ungrateful children, and that was the way things stood when a drunken driver plowed into Mr Wicks' car at 80 miles an hour.

It was no great surprise for Regina and Ada to learn at the reading of the will that their father's entire estate was the inheritance of their unsympathetic mother. And it was small comfort to them to learn soon afterward that Mrs Wicks, in drafting her own will, was not carrying her resentment of her daughters' unfortunate marriages to the limit and depriving them forever of what they felt was due them. Not forever, because the will divided her estate, when the time came, equally among her three children. When the time came. Meanwhile, as she put it, her daughters, having made their beds to their willful satisfaction, had better learn to lie in them. If they were so anxious to find out what life was like on a schoolteacher's salary and a garage mechanic's pay, they'd have plenty of time to do it.

Howard, retired from college life, soon came to see that if only the contending parties would keep their distance, things would not be too bad. Unfortunately, the contending parties had good reason not to keep their distance. Every Friday evening without fail there was a family dinner at the Wicks' place where Mother would serve in a style best calculated to make her guests realize their own insufficient means. There was small point to a triumph, her attitude seemed to be, if the victims couldn't be on hand to share it.

As for Regina and Ada, they were simply not taking any chances. They were allied in the same cause, but like all allies they had their suspicions of each other. Mrs Wicks never made any secret of it that her three children were going to share alike in the loot someday. But what if one of them stepped on Mother's toes too hard before that day? What was there to prevent Mother from calling in the family lawyer and having him draft a new will cutting out the offender entirely? Not a thing. In fact, there were moments during those Friday night dinners when it seemed that Mother was looking for just such an excuse.

So there it was. And there was Howard in the middle of it. He didn't fully appreciate just how deep the middle of it was and how hot the water there until one day when his sisters chose to offer him enlightenment.

'Waiting on Mother hand and foot,' Regina said to him scornfully that day. 'Jumping whenever she snaps her fingers. Taking all her abuse with that sweet smile.'

'For good reason,' said Ada, looking wise.

'Oh, for very good reason,' said Regina. 'But mark my words, Howard, it won't work. It will absolutely not work.'

'Absolutely not,' said Ada. 'If you think for one moment, Howard, that you are going to have us cut out of that will—'

Nor did Howard's stammering denial of any such intentions move his sisters in the least. As far as they were concerned, the endless little services he rendered his mother couldn't possibly be motivated by anything but greedy calculation. And as he could see with dejection, the logic was all on their side. Even outsiders getting a glimpse of his home life might well agree with them.

The sad irony of it – and although he had no bent for irony he could appreciate it in this case – was that he was more than content with the role he played in his mother's household. Finally, he had, if not a friend, a close companion. With his father and the girls at home in bygone years he had been almost invisible. The same at school, whatever school it was. But here, alone in the inescapable and overwhelming presence of his mother, he had an identity and a function. It struck him with wonder one day to realize that the aching loneliness was gone for good. No drifting along, trying to win a pleased look of recognition from some bypasser. No more solitary hours. In fact, very few solitary minutes.

To be absolutely accurate, he was not all alone with his mother. From the time Mr and Mrs Wicks had returned from their honeymoon there had been a housekeeping couple to tend the premises, Lorenzo for the chauffeuring, gardening, and heavy work, Mattie for the cooking and other domestic service. A morose team inclined to much *sotto voce* grumbling as they went about their duties, they had a pleasant apartment on the attic floor and seemed to find each other's company sufficient for their needs.

As time passed it came to Howard that with the exception of the cooking and housecleaning, he was absorbing their duties, one by one. He was now making all those trips to market that Mattie once made. He was now in charge of the building's maintenance, overseeing the hired hands who came in to make repairs and improvements. He was doing all his mother's chauffeuring, although, unlike Lorenzo, he had the doubtful privilege of joining the company she visited. And under her instruction, although up to now he had never demonstrated any interest in gardening or any talent for it, he even became something of a gardener, down on his knees among the flora while Mrs Wicks, her broad-brimmed straw hat shielding her fine complexion from the sun, stood at his shoulder and tartly supervised.

Going far beyond Lorenzo and Mattie, he also came to serve as social partner every evening. Then Mrs Wicks, who had a preferred list of television entertainments marking each day of the week, would have him tune in her favored programs – usually the most lachrymose of dramas – and join with her in witnessing them to the bitter end.

In the broad area of economics Howard attended to the household accounts, making out the checks for his mother to sign; supervised the supervisors of the brokerage house in town who handled Mrs Wicks' investments; put together the tax materials for the family accountant; and served as liaison to the family lawyer. What with one thing and another, starting in the late morning when Howard carted up the breakfast tray to his mother in bed and ending after the nightly late newscast on television when, with Mrs Wicks again settled in bed, Howard provided her with the gentle massage that helped relieve those aching back and shoulder muscles, it made for quite a full day, seven days a week.

Yet, serving faithfully and well for small thanks, he had no complaints to make. It was Regina and Ada who, starting with that confrontation where they first opened fire on him, gave vent to the complaints. At every opportunity they let him know how they viewed the services he rendered their mother, playing the same tune over and over with only small variations.

'I don't see why she keeps on Lorenzo and Mattie,' Regina told him. 'Not with your waiting on her hand and foot every live-long minute of the day.'

'And night,' Ada put in. 'Bedtime massages indeed. Anything to let poor dear Mother know how devoted her son is. Not at all like her neglectful daughters. Really, it's almost obscene, Howard, the efforts you're making to get her under your influence.'

The most painful part of it for Howard was that neither of his sisters seemed to have the least idea how desperately he yearned for their affection. He had a hazy recollection of a golden period in his early childhood: little Howard being convoyed by his big sisters, each with one of his hands in a tight grip, as they merrily made their way down the main street of town on a shopping trip. And their comic, if sometimes painful, teasing of him when they were at their games in the playroom or in the tree house their father had built for them. A very hazy and faraway recollection, and a heartwarming one. And the way things were going, more and more a hopeless one.

Hopeless. Because while he would have been glad to prove his feelings for the sisters he cherished by handing over to them whatever they wanted of his mother's fortune he had no control over that fortune. He made out the checks, but it was Mrs Wicks who signed them, keeping a sharp eye on every digit. Actually, in terms of cash flow, he was the poorest one of them all, wholly dependent on the few dollars his mother grudgingly allotted him now and then. He couldn't find it in himself to honestly resent this – after all, he was only a boarder in her home – but it was a nagging misery to know that he had no means of ever proving his regard for his sisters and thus winning theirs in return.

So, in this fashion, time went on as time will, 30 years of it no less, the last few of them more and more seeming to confirm Regina and Ada's grim foreboding – they openly expressed it to Howard – that their mother obviously intended to outlive them all. Approaching 75, Mrs Wicks had withered a little, had suffered a couple of minor heart episodes which Dr Gottschalk, leading practitioner of Midlandsville, had smilingly shrugged off as meaningless, and had developed some sharper pains in neck and shoulders which the doctor, a rough-hewn and blunt-spoken fellow, had dismissed, much to her annoyance, as the natural consequences of old age. Howard's fine hand at massage, he said, was all the prescription required.

Beyond this Mrs Wicks certainly did appear to be in excellent condition for her years, and, without question, as active, demanding, and testy as ever. Lorenzo and Mattie who were about her age, Howard took note, now looked considerably older and more fragile than she did. They still remained on, however, wispy inefficient shades of their old selves, and Howard once found himself wondering if his mother refused to pension them off only because they provided her with a cheering contrast to her own condition.

As for Regina and Ada, things had slightly improved for them in their middle age, but only slightly. Regina's Vernon had become head of his department at the high school, but the economic advantages of this were canceled out by the twins who had come along – a pair of strikingly handsome, sturdy boys – and so, as Regina put it, it was still uphill all the way. Still uphill for Ada too, even though her Thomas was now manager of the Midlandsville Garage, because, as she took pains to inform her sister in Howard's presence, one properly brought-up, extremely sensitive and talented girl – her sole issue – could mean at least the expense of two crude boys.

It had very soon become clear after the arrival of her grandchildren that Mrs Wicks was not one of your doting grandmothers. She took occasional notice of these little people but not much more. Her gifts to them – and there was no change in this policy with the passing years – were always moderately priced and, from Howard's point of view, depressingly practical. Much worse, as he saw it, was the reception the children received in his mother's home during their formative years. Mrs Wicks objected to noise, active play, and dirtied clothing, thus making it a painful experience, it was plain, for any of the children to enter her presence. Their parents, making sure that an errant offspring didn't cost them an inheritance, firmly reinforced this code, so that Howard, who would have been the willing slave of his nephews and niece, was steadfastly denied the opportunity for it. Like it or not, he could see that he was regarded by these small stony-faced creatures as an adjunct of their formidable grandmother. When on rare occasion he worked up enough courage to offer them some token of friendship, they backed away in open alarm as if he were setting a trap for them.

This cut so deep that Howard at last presented his case to his mother. He did it during one of her pre-slumber massages when she was, if not in an amiable mood, at least in a neutral one.

'I think you're much too strict with the children, Mother, that's the trouble. They just don't enjoy being with us here.'

'Nonsense,' said Mrs Wicks, stretched out prone in her terry-cloth robe, her eyes closed, luxuriating in the gentle kneading of neck and shoulders. 'If their own parents don't know how to bring up those children, someone had better instruct them in their manners right now.'

'Mother, there's a difference between—'

'You're digging your thumbs into me, Howard. And the matter is closed. I don't want to hear any more about it.'

But the matter wasn't quite closed, although the children had sprouted into their early teens before it did come up again and this time led to an unpredictable and astonishing explosion in the Wicks' household.

That day – a fine springtime Friday – Howard had carted up the winter blankets to the cedar chest in the attic storeroom across the hallway from Lorenzo and Mattie's apartment. There in the storeroom he had come upon his set of long-forgotten golf clubs, the complete set, along with one stained and battered ball. Wistfully he had slid the putter out of the bag and tapped the ball back and forth across the floor a few times. Then, in the very act of replacing the clubs in the bag, he had been filled by a sudden excitement.

Golf club and ball in hand, he had explored the kitchen until he turned up a can of fruit really a little too large for his purpose but all the better for that reason. He had emptied the syrupy fruit into a bowl, placed it in the refrigerator, and carefully washed out the empty can. Then, using a trowel, he had dug a proper hole in the center of the spacious lawn behind the house, had sunk the can into it, neatly replaced the turf around it, and had discovered, after a few tries, that he hadn't lost too much of his putting touch.

When Regina and Ada and their families arrived in the late afternoon Howard was ready for them. Ordinarily, during the tedious couple of hours before dinner, the children, maintaining a glum silence, kept their elders company in the living room. Now Howard, with a nod and a wink – it took several nods and winks, in fact – lured them out of the room, much to the mystification of their parents and grandmother, and led them to his one-hole golf course. When he held up the club and ball before them he saw with joy that they looked interested.

'Do you play golf, Uncle Howard?' asked one of the twins doubtfully.

'I used to,' said Howard. 'A long time ago.'

'Let's see,' said the other twin, even more doubtfully.

Howard placed the ball about six feet from the hole – it had to be a respectable distance, he knew, to make it properly impressive – and hands shaking a little on the club, stomach churning at the magnitude of this test, he sank the putt.

'Hey, there,' said both nephews, and his niece said with honest admiration, 'Hey, wow.'

'We'll take turns,' Howard said, 'starting close and getting farther back.'

They were raptly taking turns when the kitchen window was thrust up and Mattie's head appeared. 'Your mother says what's going on here,' she called to Howard. 'And you better get inside right away.'

'Is dinner ready?' Howard said.

'Not for a while, but she says come in right away. She's in a real snit, Howard.'

It was decision-making time, Howard saw. He drew a deep breath and made the decision. 'Whenever dinner's ready,' he called to Mattie.

Two minutes later the screen door of the kitchen squealed on its hinges and Mrs Wicks appeared there, freezing the golfers in their tracks. 'Howard, what do you think you're doing? And look at that lawn, all trampled apart. Get in here at once, all of you.'

Howard took another deep breath. 'The lawn isn't being trampled apart, Mother. And there's plenty of time before dinner.'

Howard looked at his companions. A minute before, they had been having a merry time of it, evidently as happy in their company as he was in theirs. Now all three faces were stony again, taking his measure. Howard turned back to the menacing figure in the doorway. 'Mother, there's no need for us to . . .'

The rest of it trailed off to inaudibility as Mrs Wicks marched down the steps and across the lawn. It had been Howard's turn at the game; the ball rested near his feet. Mrs Wicks reached down, picked up the ball, and marched back the way she had come. It was the slamming of the screen door after her that brought Howard slowly out of his daze. Then, unaware that he was still gripping the golf club, he headed for the house in such a turmoil of emotion that he tripped going up the porch steps and nearly fell headlong.

He righted himself, pulled open the door hard enough to almost tear it from its hinges, and found his mother already reseated in her favorite armchair in the living room at the head of the family semicircle. Her cheeks were flushed, her lips compressed. The absconded golf ball was nowhere in sight.

'Mother,' said Howard without ceremony, 'I'd like my golf ball back.'

'Indeed?' said Mrs Wicks coolly.

'Mother—'

'Don't raise your voice, Howard. I've given that thing to Vernon.' Mrs Wicks motioned with her chin at Vernon who looked thoroughly uncomfortable. 'He plays golf. He'll have much more use for it than you will.'

'All the same, Howard,' said Vernon, embarrassedly digging into his pocket, 'I don't really need—'

'No,' Mrs Wicks said sharply. 'You will keep that thing, Vernon. I will not have my lawn destroyed by any foolish games.'

All question about this in Vernon's mind was promptly put to rest by his wife. 'Vernon,' said Regina in a deadly voice, 'you heard Mother, didn't you?'

He had, Howard knew. So had they all, including the children who from the doorway were taking this in. Howard stared at his mother through a red mist, feeling the blood pounding in his head so hard that it was like a series of painful blows against his skull.

Not far from Mrs Wicks' chair, purely decorative, was a handsome little table, a square of polished marble on ebony legs. Howard raised his golf club high over his head with both hands and brought it down with savage impact on the table. Regina and Ada gave small screams. Vernon and Thomas sprang to their feet. Mrs Wicks sat there rigid, her nostrils flaring.

Howard looked with incredulity at the crack running the width of the marble, looked at the bent shaft of the golf club, and felt all the strength drain out of him. His stomach heaved, his legs felt like rubber under him. 'I'm terribly sorry, Mother,' he said breathlessly.

'You should be,' said Mrs Wicks. She appeared in complete control of herself. 'That table was one of your grandfather's treasures.'

'It can be repaired,' Howard pleaded. 'I'm sure it can be repaired.'

'It had better be,' said Mrs Wicks.

'Tomorrow,' said Howard. 'The first thing tomorrow. Meanwhile, if you'll all excuse me—'

So for the first time in all those years Howard was not at his place during a Friday dinner, but, of course, in all the years that followed, this dereliction was never repeated. As he came to see with the passing of time, it was as if the episode had never taken place. His mother never mentioned it, and no other witness to it ever brought it up. The table was repaired, and that's all there was to it. Naturally, as a sad aftermath, there was no getting close to the children again as he had that magical hour. Too bad really. It had, up to its shocking denouement, really been a magical hour.

The children grew up, entered the State University, dropped out of it, and went their way, the boys to share chronic unemployment in Chicago, the girl to share unwedded bliss with a dubious young man in New York. Regina and Ada aged perceptibly under these trials but lost none of their spirit in dealing with Howard. Nor was the relationship made any easier for Howard by the fact that since Mr Wicks' death the original million bequeathed to his widow had become, under wise management, three million.

'Three million?' said Regina. 'Really three million?'

'Really,' said Howard apologetically. 'It's been very soundly invested.'

'A million dollars each,' said Regina bitterly.

'And there it is,' said Ada even more bitterly.

And there it was, every dollar of it tight in their mother's unyielding grasp. Even a fraction of it, Howard thought miserably, would bring smiles to those two aging faces confronting him. He didn't share their feelings, true, but he could understand them. And how good it would be to finally see those smiles turned his way. At the same time, the thought of his mother's remains being laid away under the ground, of the house empty of her presence, filled him with a cold sense of the old loneliness lying in wait for him. It was not a thought he liked to dwell on.

'I've said it once,' Regina stated, 'and I'll say it again. Mother is bound and determined to outlive us all.'

'That includes you, Howard,' said Ada.

They were wrong. At least, whatever Mrs Wicks was bound and determined to do she didn't succeed in doing.

That night Howard was waiting for her to come out of the tub he had prepared for her – moderately hot water fortified by a cup of scented crystals – so that he could apply the usual massage. Fifteen minutes was the time she always allotted for the tub, so he waited as ever on her bedside chair, an eye on the clock. The 15 minutes went by, then 20, and Howard began to get a little uneasy. He waited a few more minutes, then knocked tentatively on the bathroom door and got no response. With nerves on edge he knocked harder. Still no response.

This, he finally told himself, was no time for modesty. He pushed open the door and saw at a glance all there was to be seen.

The bathtub was the old-fashioned kind that stood on claw feet, and it was long and deep enough for anyone to stretch out in at full length. Mrs Wicks' body was stretched out in it at full length, face just under the surface of the water, wide-open eyes staring sightlessly at the ceiling.

For the life of him Howard couldn't bring himself to enter the bathroom. Instead, he pulled the door shut and stood there trying to get his wits together. Then, holding himself in tight control, he phoned Dr Gottschalk to come at once.

'Dead?' said the doctor. 'You're sure of that?'

'Yes,' said Howard, the dreadful old loneliness now with a suffocating grip on him. 'Please hurry, doctor.'

He managed to maintain an outward composure when he went upstairs to rouse Lorenzo and Mattie with the news. Lorenzo took it well – there was even a hint of triumph in him, Howard suspected, at this information that he had outlived the lady of the house – but Mattie proved a highly emotional case. It gratified Howard, as he comforted her, to find his own composure standing up so well to this flood of tears and lamentations. Finally, almost as an afterthought once Mattie was under control, he phoned Regina and Ada.

The doctor showed up almost at once. He went quickly about his business, then said to Howard, 'Of course you realize the police must be called in. I'll attend to it right now.'

'The police?' Howard said.

'Legal fol-de-rol, Howard. A death under these conditions is a police matter, willy-nilly. And there must be an autopsy, too. Sorry, but that's the way it goes.'

So when Regina and Ada and their husbands arrived, the police were very much present, several of them, led by an unpleasantly large and officious man who had identified himself as Lieutenant Steele. The family party looked taken aback at this display of officialdom and, seating itself in the living room, had very little to say. Still, Howard felt, it would have been comforting to have them all present when Lieutenant Steele, at his overbearing worst, said that he now wanted Howard to describe in detail the events leading up to the death. This comfort was not granted Howard, however, because the lieutenant led him away for a private interview in the sitting room across the hall where Howard told all there was to tell and the lieutenant laboriously recorded it all in a small notebook.

But at last it was all over, and when the body was removed to a waiting ambulance the family was first to depart, offering the briefest of farewells on its way out, then the police took their leave, and Dr Gottschalk alone remained for a parting word.

'Think you can use a sedative?' the doctor asked.

'No, thank you,' said Howard, thinking he probably could.

'If you say so. Anyhow, stay by the phone tomorrow. I'll try to have the medical examiner get the autopsy report to me by noon.'

The call came at precisely noon. 'No unusual marks on the body,' said Dr Gottschalk bluntly. 'No signs of drugs. Looks like she blacked out in the bath and just went under. I warned her more than once about those hot baths.'

'She never told me that,' said Howard.

'No, she wouldn't, I suppose. It might have meant your tattling to me about it, and your mama always did know how to have things her way, didn't she? Well, any time you want to claim the body, Howard—'

The funeral was elaborate and well-attended, and Howard, watching the shovelfuls of earth fall with thuds on the coffin, manfully managed to restrain tears that were very near the surface. Just as he had anticipated, the chilling loneliness was always with him now, spelling out his bleak future. So when the ceremony was over he was gratified that Regina, as if to demonstrate an unexpected sensitivity to his feelings, should propose that the family members gather together in the old house, where Mattie and Lorenzo could easily enough whip up a lunch. He was even more gratified at the way the others instantly nodded agreement.

Back in the house they gathered in the living room, all taking their familiar seats, with Mrs Wicks' empty chair a powerful presence among them, while Regina gave Mattie her instructions and sent her off to the kitchen. As soon as Mattie was out of the room Regina drew its heavy double doors tight shut. The shining brass key in the lock had, within Howard's memory, never been used, but now it was. Regina twisted it firmly, locking the doors and testing them to make sure they were locked. When Howard looked surprised at this she said tersely, 'Mattie can be an awful busybody, you know. This is no time for her to come barging in here.'

'It isn't?' said Howard.

'No,' said Regina. She seated herself and fixed her eyes on Howard. At last she said, 'I guess this shouldn't be brought out into the open at all, Howard, even behind locked doors. But if I didn't come out with it, it would stick in my throat the rest of my life.'

'We all feel that way, Howard,' said Ada.

'So,' said Regina, 'I'll speak my piece, Howard, and then never again will any of us even touch on the subject.' She pointed to the small marble-topped table which had been so perfectly repaired that the damage once done to it was impossible to detect. 'All those years ago, Howard, when you smashed that thing right in front of us all – well, we had the idea that someday you might – just possibly might – have the nerve to do what had to be done in this house.'

'And you did,' said Ada. 'It took a long, long time, but you did, didn't you, Howard?'

Howard stared at them with disbelief and then with mounting horror. His mouth opened, but he couldn't seem to find words that would properly express the horror.

'And the way you handled it,' said Regina's Vernon. 'Putting it over on a tough old coot like Dr Gottschalk.'

'And,' said Ada's Thomas with a broad wink, 'not to mention whatever song and dance you gave that mean-looking cop.'

Howard finally found his voice, although it was hard for him to recognize it as his voice. 'Now look here. If any of you believes for one minute—'

'Oh, come on, Howard,' said Regina with amusement. 'You know we'll keep this in the family. Really, you don't have to play games with us.'

And she was, Howard saw, smiling at him. She was bright-eyed with admiration, smiling with affection. And so was Ada. And Vernon. And Thomas. All of them were actually smiling at him with open and honest and long-overdue affection.

Howard allowed himself a few seconds to consider the future. Then he smiled back at them. 'Well,' he said, 'as long as it's kept in the family—'

# Reasons Unknown

This is what happened, starting that Saturday in October.

That morning Morrison's wife needed the station wagon for the kids, so Morrison took the interstate bus into downtown Manhattan. At the terminal there, hating to travel by subway, he got into a cab. When the cabbie turned around and asked, 'Where to, Mister?' Morrison did a double take. 'Slade?' he said. 'Bill Slade?'

'You better believe it,' said the cabbie. 'So it's Larry Morrison. Well, what do you know.'

Now, what Morrison knew was that up to two or three years ago, Slade had been – as he himself still was – one of the several thousand comfortably fixed bees hiving in the glass-and-aluminum Majestico complex in Greenbush, New Jersey. There were 80,000 Majestico employees around the world, but the Greenbush complex was the flagship of the works, the executive division. And Slade had been there a long, long time, moving up to an assistant managership on the departmental level.

Then the department was wiped out in a reorganizational crunch, and Slade, along with some others in it, had been handed his severance money and his hat. No word had come back from him after he finally sold his house and pulled out of town with his wife and kid to line up, as he put it, something good elsewhere. It was a shock to Morrison to find that the something good elsewhere meant tooling a cab around Manhattan.

He said in distress, 'Jeez, I didn't know, Bill – none of the Hillcrest Road bunch had any idea—'

'That's what I was hoping for,' said Slade. 'It's all right, man.

I always had a feeling I'd sooner or later meet up with one of the old bunch. Now that it happened, I'm just as glad it's you.' A horn sounding behind the cab prompted Slade to get it moving. 'Where to, Larry?'

'Columbus Circle. The Coliseum.'

'Don't tell me, let me guess. The Majestico Trade Exposition. It's that time of the year, right?'

'Right.'

'And it's good politics to show up, right? Maybe one of the brass'll take notice.'

'You know how it is, Bill.'

'I sure do.' Slade pulled up at a red light and looked around at Morrison. 'Say, you're not in any tearing hurry, are you? You could have time for a cup of coffee?'

There was a day-old stubble on Slade's face. The cap perched on the back of his graying hair was grimy and sweat-stained. Morrison felt unsettled by the sight. Besides, Slade hadn't been any real friend, just a casual acquaintance living a few blocks farther up Hillcrest Road. One of the crowd on those occasional weekend hunting trips of the Hillcrest Maybe Gun and Rod Club. The 'Maybe' had been inserted in jest to cover those bad hunting and fishing weekends when it temporarily became a poker club.

'Well,' Morrison said, 'this happens to be one of those heavy Saturdays when—'

'Look, I'll treat you to the best Danish in town. Believe me, Larry, there's some things I'd like to get off my chest.'

'Oh, in that case,' said Morrison.

There was a line of driverless cabs in front of a cafeteria on Eighth Avenue. Slade pulled up behind them and led the way into the cafeteria which was obviously a cabbies' hangout. They had a little wrestling match about the check at the counter, a match Slade won, and, carrying the tray with the coffee and Danish, he picked out a corner table for them.

The coffee was pretty bad, the Danish, as advertised, pretty good. Slade said through a mouthful of it, 'And how is Amy?' Amy was Morrison's wife.

'Fine, fine,' Morrison said heartily. 'And how is Gertrude?'

'Gretchen.'

'That's right. Gretchen. Stupid of me. But it's been so long, Bill—'

'It has. Almost three years. Anyhow, last I heard of her, Gretchen's doing all right.'

'Last you heard of her?'

'We separated a few months ago. She just couldn't hack it any more.' Slade shrugged. 'My fault mostly. Getting turned down for one worthwhile job after another didn't sweeten the disposition. And jockeying a cab ten, twelve hours a day doesn't add sugar to it. So she and the kid have their own little flat out in Queens, and she got herself some kind of cockamamie receptionist job with a doctor there. Helps eke out what I can give her. How's your pair, by the way? Scott and Morgan, isn't it? Big fellows now, I'll bet.'

'Thirteen and ten,' Morrison said. 'They're fine. Fine.'

'Glad to hear it. And the old neighborhood? Any changes?'

'Not really. Well, we did lose a couple of the old-timers. Mike Costanzo and Gordie McKechnie. Remember them?'

'Who could forget Mike, the world's worst poker player? But McKechnie?'

'That split-level, corner of Hillcrest and Maple. He's the one got himself so smashed that time in the duck blind that he went overboard.'

'Now I remember. And that fancy shotgun of his, six feet underwater in the mud. Man, that sobered him up fast. What happened to him and Costanzo?'

'Well,' Morrison said uncomfortably, 'they were both in Regional Customer Services. Then somebody on the top floor got the idea that Regional and National should be tied together, and some people in both offices had to be let go. I think Mike's in Frisco now, he's got a lot of family there. Nobody's heard from Gordie. I mean—' Morrison cut it short in embarrassment.

'I know what you mean. No reason to get red in the face about it, Larry.' Slade eyed Morrison steadily over his coffee cup. 'Wondering what happened to me?'

'Well, to be frank—'

'Nothing like being frank. I put in two years making the rounds, lining up employment agencies, sending out enough resumes to make a ten-foot pile of paper. No dice. Ran out of unemployment insurance, cash, and credit. There it is, short and sweet.'

'But why? With the record you piled up at Majestico—'

'Middle level. Not top echelon. Not decision-making stuff. Middle level, now and forever. Just like everybody else on Hillcrest Road. That's why we're on Hillcrest Road. Notice how the ones who make it to the top echelon always wind up on Greenbush Heights? And always after only three or four years? But after you're middle level fifteen years the way I was—'

Up to now Morrison had been content with his twelve years in Sales Analysis. Admittedly no ball of fire, he had put in some rough years after graduation from college – mostly as salesman on commission for some product or other – until he had landed the job at Majestico. Now he felt disoriented by what Slade was saying. And he wondered irritably why Slade had to wear that cap while he was eating. Trying to prove he was just another one of these cabbies here? He wasn't. He was a college man, had owned one of the handsomest small properties on Hillcrest Road, had been a respected member of the Majestico executive team.

Morrison said, 'I still don't understand. Are you telling me there's no company around needs highly qualified people outside decision-making level? Ninety percent of what goes on anyplace is our kind of job, Bill. You know that.'

'I do. But I'm forty-five years old, Larry. And you want to know what I found out? By corporation standards I died five years ago on my fortieth birthday. Died, and didn't even know it. Believe me, it wasn't easy to realize that at first. It got a lot easier after a couple of years' useless job-hunting.'

Morrison was 46 and was liking this less and less. 'But the spot you're in is only temporary, Bill. There's still—'

'No, no. Don't do that, Larry. None of that somewhere-over-the-rainbow line. I finally looked my situation square in the eye, I accepted it, I made the adjustment. With luck, what's in the cards for me is maybe someday owning my own cab. I buy lottery tickets, too, because after all somebody's got to win that million, right? And the odds there are just as good as my chances of ever getting behind a desk again at the kind of money Majestico was paying me.' Again he was looking steadily at

Morrison over his coffee cup. 'That was the catch, Larry. That money they were paying me.'

'They pay well, Bill. Say, is that what happened? You didn't think you were getting your price and made a fuss about it? So when the department went under you were one of the—'

'Hell, no,' Slade cut in sharply. 'You've got it backwards, man. They do pay well. But did it ever strike you that maybe they pay too well?'

'Too well?'

'For the kind of nine-to-five paperwork I was doing? The donkey work?'

'You were an assistant head of department, Bill.'

'One of the smarter donkeys, that's all. Look, what I was delivering to the company had to be worth just so much to them. But when every year – every first week in January – there's an automatic cost-of-living increase handed me I am slowly and steadily becoming a luxury item. Consider that after fourteen-fifteen years of those jumps every year, I am making more than some of those young hotshot executives in the International Division. I am a very expensive proposition for Majestico, Larry. And replaceable by somebody fifteen years younger who'll start for a hell of a lot less.'

'Now hold it. Just hold it. With the inflation the way it is, you can't really object to those cost-of-living raises.'

Slade smiled thinly. 'Not while I was getting them, pal. It would have meant a real scramble without them. But suppose I wanted to turn them down just to protect my job? You know that can't be done. Those raises are right there in the computer for every outfit like Majestico. But nobody in management has to like living with it. And what came to me after I was canned was that they were actually doing something about it.'

'Ah, look,' Morrison said heatedly. 'You weren't terminated because you weren't earning your keep. There was a departmental reorganization. You were just a victim of it.'

'I was. The way those Incas or Aztecs or whatever used to lay out the living sacrifice and stick the knife into him. Don't keep shaking your head, Larry. I have thought this out long and hard. There's always a reorganization going on in one of the divisions. Stick a couple of departments together, change their names, dump a few personnel who don't fit into the new table of organization.

'But the funny thing, Larry, is that the ones who usually seem to get dumped are the middle-aged, middle-level characters with a lot of seniority. The ones whose take-home pay put them right up there in the high-income brackets. Like me. My secretary lost out in that reorganization too, after eighteen years on the job. No complaints about her work. But she ran into what I did when I told them I'd be glad to take a transfer to any other department. No dice. After all, they could hire two fresh young secretaries for what they were now paying her.'

'And you think this is company policy?' Morrison demanded.

'I think so. I mean, what the hell are they going to do? Come to me and say, "Well, Slade, after fifteen years on the job you've priced yourself right out of the market, so goodbye, baby?" But those reorganizations? Beautiful. "Too bad, Slade, but under the new structure we're going to have to lose some good men." That's the way it was told to me, Larry. And that's what I believed until I woke up to the facts of life.'

The piece of Danish in Morrison's mouth was suddenly dry and tasteless. He managed to get it down with an effort. 'Bill, I don't want to say it – I hate to say it – but that whole line sounds paranoid.'

'Does it? Then think it over, Larry. You still in Sales Analysis?'

'Yes.'

'I figured. Now just close your eyes and make a head count of your department. Then tell me how many guys forty-five or over are in it.'

Morrison did some unpalatable calculation. 'Well, there's six of us. Including me.'

'Out of how many?'

'Twenty-four.'

'Uh-huh. Funny how the grass manages to stay so green, isn't it?'

It was funny, come to think of it. No, funny wasn't the word. Morrison said weakly, 'Well, a couple of the guys wanted to move out to the Coast, and you know there's departmental transfers in and out—'

'Sure there are. But the real weeding comes when there's one of those little reorganizations. You've seen it yourself in your own department more than once. Juggle around some of those room dividers. Move some desks here and there. Change a few descriptions in the company directory. The smokescreen. But behind that smoke there's some high-priced old faithfuls getting called upstairs to be told that, well, somebody's got to go, Jack, now that things are all different, and guess whose turn it is.'

Slade's voice had got loud enough to be an embarrassment. Morrison pleaded: 'Can't we keep it down, Bill? Anyhow, to make villains out of everybody on the top floor—'

Slade lowered his voice, but the intensity was still there. 'Who said they were villains? Hell, in their place I'd be doing the same thing. For that matter, if I was head of personnel for any big outfit, I wouldn't take anybody my age on the payroll either. Not if I wanted to keep my cushy job in personnel, I wouldn't.' The wind suddenly seemed to go out of him. 'Sorry, Larry. I thought I had everything under control, but when I saw you – when I saw it was one of the old Hillcrest bunch – it was too much to keep corked up. But one thing—'

'Yes?'

'I don't want anybody else back there in on this. Know what I mean?'

'Oh, sure.'

'Don't just toss off the oh, sure like that. This is the biggest favor you could do me – not to let anybody else in the old crowd hear about me, not even Amy. No post-mortems up and down Hillcrest for good old Bill Slade. One reason I let myself cut loose right now was because you always were a guy who liked to keep his mouth tight shut. I'm counting on you to do that for me, Larry. I want your solemn word on it.'

'You've got it, Bill. You know that.'

'I do. And what the hell' – Slade reached across the table and punched Morrison on the upper arm – 'any time they call you in to tell you there's a reorganization of Sales Analysis coming up, it could turn out you're the guy elected to be department head of the new layout. Right?'

Morrison tried to smile. 'No chance of that, Bill.'

'Well, always look on the bright side, Larry. As long as there is one.'

Outside the Coliseum there was another of those little wrestling matches about paying the tab – Slade refusing to take anything at all for the ride, Morrison wondering, as he eyed the meter, whether sensitivity here called for a standard tip, a huge tip, or none at all – and again Slade won.

Morrison was relieved to get away from him, but, as he soon found, the relief was only temporary. It was a fine Indian summer day, but somehow the weather now seemed bleak and threatening. And doing the Majestico show, looking over the displays, passing the time of day with recognizable co-workers turned out to be a strain. It struck him that it hadn't been that atrocious cap on Slade's head that had thrown him, it had been the gray hair showing under the cap. And there was very little gray hair to be seen on those recognizable ones here at the Majestico show.

Morrison took a long time at the full-length mirror in the men's room, trying to get an objective view of himself against the background of the others thronging the place. The view he got was depressing. As far as he could see, in this company he looked every minute of his 46 years.

Back home he stuck to his word and told Amy nothing about his encounter with Slade. Any temptation to was readily suppressed by his feeling that once he told her that much he'd also find himself exposing his morbid reaction to Slade's line of thinking. And that would only lead to her being terribly understanding and sympathetic while, at the same time, she'd be moved to some heavy humor about his being such a born worrier. He was a born worrier, he was the first to acknowledge it, but he always chafed under that combination of sympathy and teasing she offered when he confided his worries to her. They really made quite a list, renewable each morning on rising. The family's health, the condition of the house, the car, the lawn, the bank balance – the list started there and seemed to extend to infinity.

Yet, as he was also the first to acknowledge, this was largely a quirk of personality – he was, as his father had been, somewhat sobersided and humorless – and, quirks aside, life was a generally all-right proposition. As it should be when a man can lay claim to a pretty and affectionate wife, and a couple of healthy young sons, and a sound home in a well-tended neighborhood. And a good steady job to provide the wherewithal.

At least, up to now.

Morrison took a long time falling asleep that night, and at three in the morning came bolt awake with a sense of foreboding. The more he lay there trying to get back to sleep, the more oppressive grew the foreboding. At four o'clock he padded into his den and sat down at his desk to work out a precise statement of the family's balance sheet.

No surprises there, just confirmation of the foreboding. For a long time now, he and Amy had been living about one month ahead of income which, he suspected, was true of most families along Hillcrest Drive. The few it wasn't true of were most likely at least a year ahead of income and sweating out the kind of indebtedness he had always carefully avoided.

But considering that his assets consisted of a home with ten years of mortgage payments yet due on it and a car with two years of payments still due, everything depended on income. The family savings account was, of course, a joke. And the other two savings accounts – one in trust for each boy to cover the necessary college educations – had become a joke as college tuition skyrocketed. And, unfortunately, neither boy showed any signs of being scholarship material.

In a nutshell, everything depended on income. This month's income. Going by Slade's experience in the job market – and Slade had been the kind of competent, hardworking nine-to-five man any company should have been glad to take on – this meant that everything depended on the job with Majestico. Everything. Morrison had always felt that landing the job in the first place was the best break of his life. Whatever vague ambitions he had in his youth were dissolved very soon after he finished college and learned that out here in the real world he rated just about average in all departments, and that his self-effacing, dogged application to his daily work was not going to have him climbing any ladders to glory.

Sitting there with those pages of arithmetic scattered around the desk, Morrison, his stomach churning, struggled with the idea that the job with Majestico was suddenly no longer a comfortable, predictable way of life but for someone his age, and with his makeup and qualifications, a dire necessity. At five o'clock, exhausted but more wide-awake than ever, he went down to the kitchen for a bottle of beer. Pills were not for him. He had always refused to take even an aspirin tablet except under extreme duress, but beer did make him sleepy, and a bottle of it on an empty stomach, he estimated, was the prescription called for in this case. It turned out that he was right about it.

In the days and weeks that followed, this became a ritual: the abrupt waking in the darkest hours of the morning, the time at his desk auditing his accounts and coming up with the same dismal results, and the bottle of beer which, more often than not, allowed for another couple of hours of troubled sleep before the alarm clock went off.

Amy, the soundest of sleepers, took no notice of this, so that was all right. And by exercising a rigid self-control he managed to keep her unaware of those ragged nerves through the daylight hours as well, although it was sometimes unbearably hard not to confide in her. Out of a strange sense of pity, he found himself more sensitive and affectionate to her than ever. High-spirited, a little scatterbrained, leading a full life of her own what with the boys, the Parent-Teachers Club, and half a dozen community activities, she took this as no less than her due.

Along the way, as an added problem, Morrison developed some physical tics which would show up when least expected. A sudden tremor of the hands, a fluttering of one eyelid which he had to learn to quickly cover up. The most grotesque tic of all, however – it really unnerved him the few times he experienced it – was a violent, uncontrollable chattering of the teeth when he had sunk to a certain point of absolute depression. This only struck him when he was at his desk during the sleepless times considering the future. At such times he had a feeling that those teeth were diabolically possessed by a will of their own, chattering away furiously as if he had just been plunged into icy water.

In the office he took refuge in the lowest of low profiles. Here the temptation was to check on what had become of various colleagues who had over the years departed from the company, but this, Morrison knew, might raise the question of why he had, out of a clear blue sky, brought up the subject. The subject was not a usual part of the day's conversational currency in the department. The trouble was that Greenbush was, of course, a company town, although in the most modern and pleasant way. Majestico had moved there from New York 20 years before; the town had grown around the company complex. And isolated as it was in the green heartland of New Jersey, it had only Majestico to offer. Anyone leaving the company would therefore have to sell his home, like it or not, and relocate far away. Too far, at least, to maintain old ties. It might have been a comfort, Morrison thought, to drop in on someone in his category who had been terminated by Majestico and who could give him a line on what had followed. Someone other than Slade. But there was no one like this in his book.

The one time he came near bringing his desperation to the surface was at the Thanksgiving entertainment given by the student body of the school his sons attended. The entertainment was a well-deserved success, and after it, at the buffet in the school gym, Morrison was driven to corner Frank Lassman, assistant principal of the school and master of ceremonies at the entertainment, and to come out with a thought that had been encouragingly flickering through his mind during the last few insomniac sessions.

'Great show,' he told Lassman. 'Fine school altogether. It showed tonight. It must be gratifying doing your kind of work.'

'At times like this it is,' Lassman said cheerfully. 'But there are times—'

'Even so. You know, I once had ideas about going into teaching.'

'Financially,' said Lassman, 'I suspect you did better by not going into it. It has its rewards, but the big money isn't one of them.'

'Well,' Morrison said very carefully, 'suppose I was prepared to settle for the rewards it did offer? A man my age, say. Would there be any possibilities of getting into the school system?'

'What's your particular line? Your subject?'

'Oh, numbers. Call it arithmetic and math.'

Lassman shook his head in mock reproach. 'And where were you when we really needed you? Four or five years ago we were sending out search parties for anyone who could get math across to these kids. The last couple of years, what with the falling school population, we're firing, not hiring. It's the same everywhere, not that I ever thought I'd live to see the day. Empty school buildings all over the country.'

'I see,' said Morrison.

So the insomnia, tensions, and tics continued to worsen until suddenly one day – as if having hit bottom, there was no place for him to go but up – Morrison realized that he was coming back to normal. He began to sleep through the night, was increasingly at ease during the day, found himself cautiously looking on the bright side. He still had his job and all that went with it, that was the objective fact. He could only marvel that he had been thrown so far off balance by that chance meeting with Slade.

He had been giving himself his own bad time, letting his imagination take over as it had. The one thing he could be proud of was that where someone else might have broken down under the strain, he had battled it out all by himself and had won. He was not a man to hand himself trophies, but in this case he felt he had certainly earned one.

A few minutes before five on the first Monday in December, just when he was getting ready to pack it in for the day, Pettengill, departmental head of Sales Analysis, stopped at his desk. Pettengill, a transfer from the Cleveland office a couple of years before, was rated as a comer, slated sooner or later for the top floor. A pleasant-mannered, somewhat humorless man, he and Morrison had always got along well.

'Just had a session with the brass upstairs,' he confided. 'A round table with Cobb presiding.' Cobb was the executive vice president in charge of Planning and Structure for the Greenbush complex. 'Looks like our department faces a little reorganization. We tie in with Service Analysis and that'll make it Sales and Service Evaluation. What's the matter? Don't you feel well?'

'No, I'm all right,' said Morrison.

'Looks like you could stand some fresh air. Anyhow, probably because you're senior man here, Cobb wants to see you in his office first thing tomorrow morning. Nine sharp. You know how he is about punctuality, Larry. Make sure you're on time.'

'Yes,' said Morrison.

He didn't sleep at all that night. The next morning, a few minutes before nine, still wearing his overcoat and with dark glasses concealing his reddened and swollen eyes, he took the elevator directly to the top floor, There, out of sight on the landing of the emergency staircase, he drew the barrel and stock of his shotgun from beneath the overcoat and assembled the gun. His pockets bulged with 12-gauge shells. He loaded one into each of the gun's twin barrels. Then concealing the assembled gun beneath the coat as well as he could, he walked across the hall into Cobb's office.

Miss Bernstein, Cobb's private secretary, acted out of sheer blind, unthinking instinct when she caught sight of the gun. She half rose from her desk as if to bar the way to the inner office. She took the first charge square in the chest. Cobb, at his desk, caught the next in the face. Reloading, Morrison exited through the door to the executive suite where Cobb's assistants had been getting ready for the morning's work and were now in a panic at the sound of the shots.

Morrison fired both barrels one after another, hitting one man in the throat and jaw, grazing another. Reloading again, he moved like an automaton out into the corridor where a couple of security men, pistols at the ready, were coming from the staircase on the run. Morrison cut down the first one, but the other, firing wildly, managed to plant one bullet in his forehead. Morrison must have been dead, the medical examiner later reported, before he even hit the floor.

The police, faced with five dead and one wounded, put in two months on the case and could come up with absolutely no answers, no explanations at all. The best they could do in their final report was record that 'the perpetrator, for reasons unknown, etc, etc.'

Management, however, could and did take action. They learned that the Personnel Department psychologist who had put Morrison through the battery of personality-evaluation tests given every applicant for a job was still there with the company. Since he had transparently failed in those tests to sound out the potentially aberrant behavior of the subject, he was, despite sixteen years of otherwise acceptable service, terminated immediately.

Two weeks later, his place in Personnel was filled by a young fellow named McIntyre who, although the starting pay was a bit low, liked the looks of Greenbush and, with his wife in complete agreement, saw it as just the kind of quiet, pleasant community in which to settle down permanently.